# FORTUNATE SON

A William Langdon Novel

By
Stephen Fredrick

## Copyright Page

Published by Stephen Fredrick, Author

First Printing, August 2012

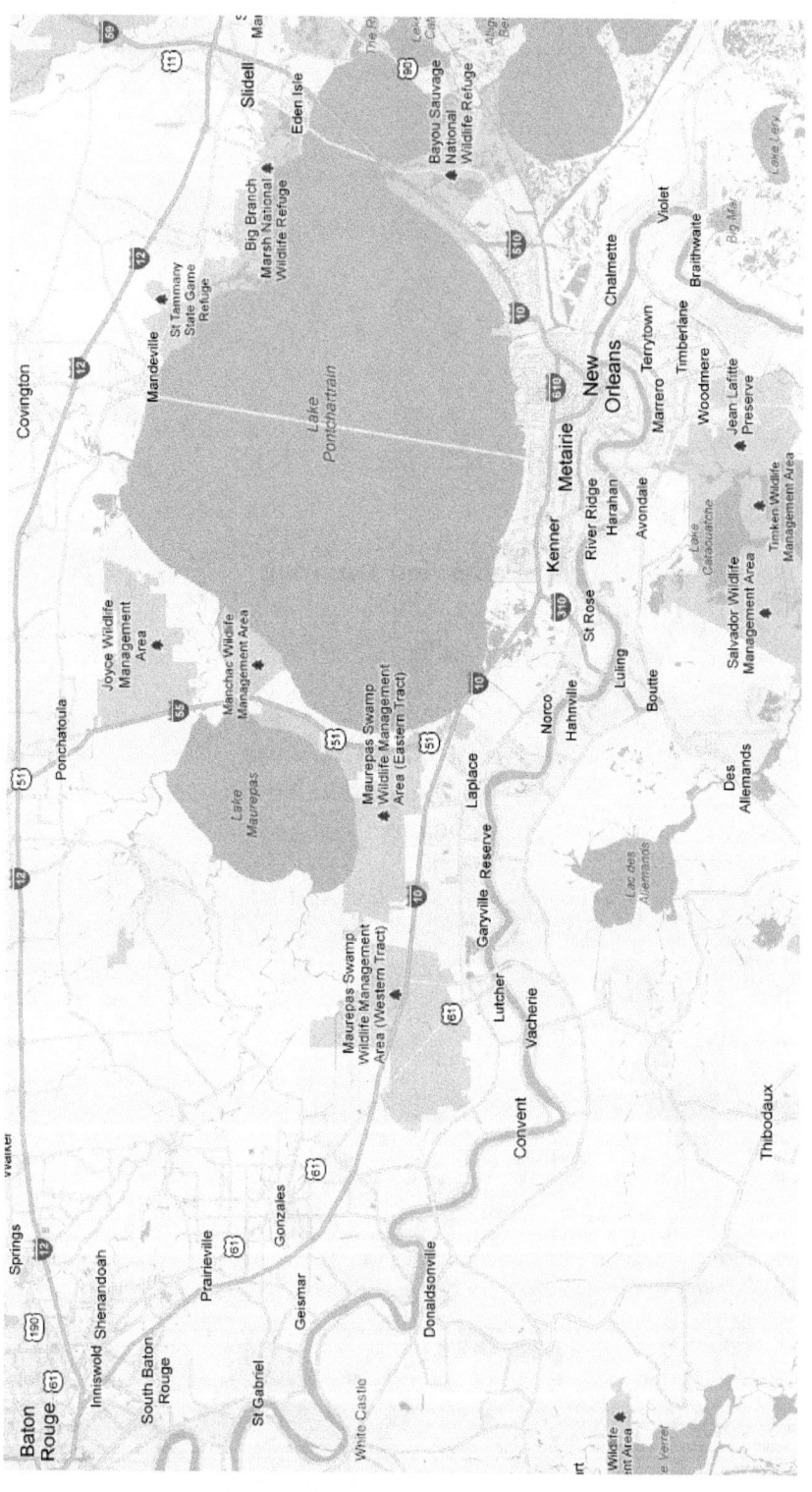

**For my wife, Shelly**
**My real life Sandy Langdon**

# Fortunate Son

Some folks are born made to wave the flag,
Ooh, they're red, white and blue.
And when the band plays "Hail to the chief",
Ooh, they point the cannon at you, Lord,

It ain't me, it ain't me, I ain't no senator's son, son.
It ain't me, it ain't me; I ain't no fortunate one, no,

Yeah!
Some folks are born silver spoon in hand,
Lord, don't they help themselves, oh.
But when the taxman comes to the door,
Lord, the house looks like a rummage sale, yes,

It ain't me, it ain't me, I ain't no millionaire's son, no.
It ain't me, it ain't me; I ain't no fortunate one, no.

Some folks inherit star spangled eyes,
Ooh, they send you down to war, Lord,
And when you ask them, "How much should we give?"
Ooh, they only answer More! more! more! yo,

It ain't me, it ain't me, I ain't no military son, son.
It ain't me, it ain't me; I ain't no fortunate one, one.

It ain't me, it ain't me, I ain't no fortunate one, no no no,
It ain't me, it ain't me, I ain't no fortunate son, no no no,

Credence Clearwater Revival
Copyright 1969
Lyrics by Bob Fogerty

# PART I

February 1998

# Chapter One

Dace Lamoureux turned twenty-one years of age on Valentine's Day, the fourteenth of February in 1998. God had designed the day to be wet, cold, and painted in shades of misty grey; and that's exactly how it dawned. Dace's father, the Honorable Senator Allard Lamoureux, however, had envisioned something more fitting to mark the day his only son became a man, and by midmorning, the skies were deep blue and cloudless. At noon, a record temperature had been set for the date in Connecticut; and that's before it climbed a few more points in the early afternoon to seventy-four degrees in New London, which became a record that still stands.

From his familiar location at the second-floor office window in the family home perched along the southern shore of the Thames River (pronounced 'thames' sounding like James, not 'temz' like its Great Britain namesake) and inland of the seaside twin cities of Groton and New London, The Senator watched Dace jog down the driveway in his running shorts and T-shirt and marveled at the tall, handsome, smart, and muscular miracle who was his son. The Senator tossed a glance over his shoulder at his wife, Libby, seated at the couch in front of the hearth containing the dying embers of a fire started early that morning. The fire had been left to burn out as the day cleared and warmed. He winked, she smiled; then he returned his attention outside.

Libby had given The Senator four beautiful daughters over the first twenty-five years of their marriage, but it wasn't until she was fifty that the union finally produced a male heir.

Medical professionals had warned them both of the dangers associated with a later-life pregnancy. It was a warning neither had needed, however, for the point was reinforced every day in the problems with which their fourth daughter contended. Mary Rose had been born with Down Syndrome three years before Dace Lamoureux came into the world. As he had watched the images of his son on the sonogram's screen, The Senator had confidently informed the doctors in the room that this child would be born healthy and whole, and nobody had dared argue with Connecticut's senior delegate to the United States Senate.

Libby had spent the majority of the pregnancy in bed rest, monitored by around-the-clock nurses, pampered by a household staff, and overseen by a team of the country's best obstetricians. The Senator had decided he would use every dollar of his family's wealth to ensure his unborn son's health should his Will not directly correspond with God's Plan.

As The Senator stood at the window twenty-one years later, his back to the room and his wife, he recalled the words she had spoken to him on the day Dace had been born: 'Your daughters are the sparkle in your eyes, my dear husband, but today I can see in those very same eyes that it is Dace who holds your heart.'

"He still does," The Senator said aloud to the memory, then took a draw from the glass of single malt Scotch in his left hand. His right hand was in its ubiquitous position lodged against the small of his back. Those who did not know The Senator felt the posture emoted an aloof air, however, those who were his familiars understood it was his longtime method for controlling and hiding his emotions. Holding his right hand behind his back was a habit which began when he was a small boy, and it was often whispered that if you wanted a true reading of The Senator's mood and thoughts, it was best to stand behind him since his eyes and face were rarely decipherable to anyone beyond Libby; and she still didn't always get it right, even after forty-six years of marriage.

"What was that dear?" Libby asked, again turning her gaze from the fireplace. She noted her husband's right palm was facing out and his thumb was massaging over the palm pads at the base of the fingers. She knew that meant he was genuinely emotional.

The Senator turned to face her, there now being nothing left he wanted to see out the window with Dace having just turned the corner at the end of the driveway and passing from his view.

"Our son," he said, motioning over his shoulder with his glass out toward the driveway. "I was just thinking of the words you said to me on the day he was born."

Libby said nothing, but merely smiled warmly across the room at her husband, then reached out her hand in a familiar gesture which bid he come and sit by her. He glanced over his shoulder out the window again, then reluctantly relinquished the perch and walked over to sit on the tufted leather sofa next to his wife. He put his right arm around her and she leaned into his large chest.

As couples of that longevity are often able to do, they sat in comfortable silence linked like that while each considered Dace within their own thoughts. The cool white ash forming over the fading heat of orange embers in the fireplace captured their attention and fed their independent memories of the years which led them to this point in their lives.    As the day had grown warmer and drier, Caroline, their housekeeper and cook, had opened windows to let the fresh air move through the three levels of the family home. Just as Libby's mind lit upon thoughts of Mary Rose and the events which had led to her disability three years before Dace's birth, a chilled gust rushed through the house as if on cue.  The Senator rubbed his hand over her lightly clad arm in response to her sudden shiver and took another draw from his glass.  He squeezed his wife a little closer and revisited the memory he spoke to moments ago.

"Do you remember the words you said to me exactly twenty-one years ago today?" he asked to remind her she had made no comment on his earlier expressed memory.

"Of course I do," she said and then repeated the words she had spoken that day as she had watched The Senator pacing in the room holding their newborn son, a look of incredible awe in his eyes.  When she had finished repeating it, she separated from him, sat upright, and gazed warmly into his face.    "Is that what you were speaking to a moment ago?"

He returned her look and smiled, but said nothing.  She took note that his eyes were filled with pride, just as they had been in her hospital room as he held Dace for the first time; then Libby cocked her head in consideration of something new which she detected there.  What had changed was his fire, the spark of ambition, and somehow she understood in that moment the glow was not for himself anymore, but that today the torch had been passed to Dace.  From father to son.  She could tell he was proud in that moment, but also apprehensive.  Her husband's eyes had always held a fire within them, a drive, and a confidence which had been some of what had initially attracted her to him.  Until that moment, however, Libby could not recall a time when that fire hadn't been reflective of his own ambitions and accomplishments; or when his confidence of self had before wavered.

He broke their gaze suddenly, and sat forward on the couch, placed both elbows on his knees.  He cradled the nearly empty tumbler in both hands and slowly rolled the last of the amber liquid over the remaining ice.    He also sensed something changing inside of him and he felt suddenly impotent; and he hated that feeling and all that it portended.

Libby understood she needed to allow him to adjust to this change at his own pace.  She watched as he breathed out the emotion, refilled his lungs with determination and she saw his renowned confidence flow back into his body.  She placed her hand on his back and gently soothed him.  Even at seventy-five, the man recovered quickly.

"Dace still holds my heart, Libby," he said, his back to her still. He drained the remaining Scotch, set the empty glass on the end table and stood and moved several steps away from her. She followed his gaze which had returned to passing through the window, then he turned to face her again from a distance. "You know the girls are my pride and joy, Libby; the sparkle in my eyes as you said to me that day, but that boy is truly something special. Mark my words, he is going to change the world. Dace Lamoureux is going to leave his mark upon history."

He walked over to the window again and searched the view outside even though he knew Dace would not be back for an hour or more. Libby watched him move. The Senator was seventy-five that year, yet to her he maintained the same aura of strength and virility of the man he was over half a century earlier when he had first captured her attention. He still moved with a confident and steady gait, and while his hair had long ago gone from jet black to fully white, he still wore it brushed back like a lion's mane just as he always had.

The first time she had noticed the man who would become her husband was the day she had accompanied her father to Harvard Stadium for the annual gridiron showdown with rival Yale, known to both campuses simply as 'The Game'. Then quarterback and team captain Allard Lamoureux was running to the sideline while removing his leather helmet after scoring a touchdown which put Harvard on top again in the seesaw battle.

After accepting the congratulations of his coaches and teammates, he moved to the bench and before sitting had acknowledged with a wave of his hand the cheers of the crowd. She had been mesmerized as she watched him shake his head and brush his fingers through his hair as every strand seemed to know just where to fall. How many times since then had she seen him use the same movement at rallies and political events? Hundreds? Thousands?

Then, in a single, magical movement, the memory of which could still gooseflesh her skin, he had stopped his turn back toward the field and she swore he had looked directly into her eyes. Her eighteen-year-old heart had flip-flopped for the first time at that instant, and more than half a century later as she watched him move across the room, she marveled that just his presence still could make her heart flip-flop. Whatever they had been through over the years, she still loved him more than life itself.

"How I wish I had the opportunities his life is going to make available to him," he said to her finally. "The future he will have. I truly believe he will be the President of the United States one day, Libby. I just hope I am here to see it happen."

So that was what was weighing so heavily upon his mind and ginning his emotions, she thought. She had believed his pensiveness was as simple as he was feeling his age today with Dace turning twenty-one, but now realized it was more than that.    The man who could control everything he set to his mind, was suddenly aware of his lack of control over his own mortality.    At the same time that he was attempting to continue the beguiling of himself into believing that he was more than human, he was cursing the realization the great Allard Lamoureux was, like everyone else, merely a temporary, flickering prescience in the unrelenting and largely anonymous expanse of time, and there was no trade or barter or bargain - no back room deal - he could craft which would change that fact or add a single tick to his clock of life.

"I'm certain you already have it all arranged, dear," she said with hint of playfulness.    She offered the intonation to hide from him her genuine understanding of the man's undercurrent of pain.    "I cannot imagine the Good Lord would deprive Senator Allard Lamoureux the joy of witnessing his dream."    She delivered the last thought with a loving smile to reveal both her wish and true belief.

He glanced over his shoulder at her and reflected her gentle smile before returning his gaze to the still empty driveway.    The hills of the seemingly endless countryside were visible at that time of year through the leafless trees.    He walked across the room to look out at the river and the granite bluffs which were again being exposed by the melting snow cover.    He didn't need to say anything more about his apprehensions. After fifty-three years of being together, forty-six as husband and wife, time had gifted each of them with a comfort and familiarity for the silences of the other.    He understood all Libby was considering in the moment from the bits of conversation and shared glances, and he waited for her to conclude her thoughts before he responded.    He understood there was much running through her head, and her heart, as well on that day.

He realized she was serious about her belief in how the Good Lord would handle things, and accepted as harmless her gentle jibe in the delivery.    In the reflection of her in the glass, he could still envision Libby as that shy and uncertain Radcliffe freshman he had met after Harvard defeated Yale during his senior year.    He had undertaken dating her a month later, during the short respite between football and basketball seasons; and after his father had approved of her pedigree.    They had been together ever since.

Her hair was still silky and auburn, although now by means of a treatment applied every couple of weeks at the hairdresser, but worn in a more mature length and styling than the ponytail and bangs she had sported in the beginning.    Her eyes remained clear and that deep and intoxicating emerald green.    Her features were seemingly ageless and she could pass for a woman twenty-five years her junior.    To him, she was still the most beautiful woman he had ever seen; and he had seen, and bedded, all manner of women all over the world.    He felt no regret over his dalliances over the years. He had never rubbed them in her face, but he was certain she understood, and knew, although she never mentioned them save one time. It was what powerful men do, he knew she realized. His acts contained absolutely no intention of malice, and even less emotion; and because she possessed a woman's heart, he knew for certain she was incapable of the double-dealing required by that particular betrayal. He crossed the room again to watch the driveway.

"My concern, Allard, is that your dream may not be Dace's," she said moments later in a soft-toned challenge which barely crossed into his distracted consciousness. "How did your talk go with him this morning, by the way? He seemed more than a bit distracted at lunch, and even the girls mentioned he seemed rather out of sorts earlier this afternoon before he went on his run."

The Senator waved over his shoulder without turning, as if he were shooing away a pesky gnat. It was a brutally dismissive gesture in itself, and had Libby not known him so well she may have taken it as a slight, but she understood he used the gesture to merely dismiss the essence of Dace's distractions and not challenge or belittle the validity of her comment. He continued to stare after his long-gone son, and when he spoke, it was directed to the entirety of the universe, not just to its only inhabitant within earshot.

"Ah, he's just distracted because today's a big day for the boy, nothing more and nothing less," he said in his tone of self-assurance which he used with wavering colleagues who were not quite as certain as he that what they were about to do was ordained by God Himself, and relayed to their ears by no less than His servant, the Honorable Senator Allard Lamoureux. He turned to face her and leaned against the bottom of the window frame. "Becoming a man in this family is an historic event, Libby. Burdensome perhaps, but also brimming with power and honor. Dace is staring into the face of the nearly overwhelming combination of history and destiny today. Even though he's known this day has been coming for years and has been conditioned for the mantle, its arrival is still a great deal for any Lamoureux male to take in." He paused for a beat and Libby noted his right hand had moved again to the small of his back. "I know facing the responsibility of the Lamoureux legacy passing to me when my father brought me into his study on the day I turned twenty-one had been a difficult day; and that was before I had added six years in the House and forty-two in the Senate to the weight of the legacy which now falls to Dace. It's been fifty-four years since I looked into the heart of the Lamoureux heritage, yet, I can still recall every word my father spoke to me that day. Just as Dace will always recall each of mine as he gains the clarity of age and the wisdom of experience. He will speak words to thank me one day, just as I did to my father before he died. Whether I am still walking this realm or not, I will know when that day comes and my heart will be warmed." He looked deeply into his wife's eyes. "No matter where in God's universe I may be then, I will know."

"Times are different, now, Allard," she reminded in a tone blended of gentleness and firmness. "Fifty-four years is a long time to the generations." She broke eye contact and shifted her gaze past him outside through the leafless trees and the deepening sky beyond. "I know Dace honors the Lamoureux family history and will do his utmost to uphold those *foundational* expectations placed upon him as the next bearer of its legacy, but perhaps he has his own opinions for the design and construction of *his* future built upon that foundation."

"He'll do all of what's expected of him, when the time comes." The Senator again turned his back to his wife, his right hand tightly clenched in the small of his back. "He's a Lamoureux man, no matter what may come. He has a role to play in the history of this world."

Libby paused for an extended time before responding. She watched the repeated clenching and flexing of his right hand which finally settled into a loose fist. The movement reminded her of a computer processing information and then settling upon an answer. She understood the looser the fist, the more room there would be for compromise and while it was never wise to argue with The Senator, one could sometimes gently move his perspective if he was approached correctly; and, who better to know how to approach him than a wife of forty-six years?

"Of that I have no doubt, dear," she said, and then paused for several beats before continuing. Libby understood the next few steps could be dangerous ones, but she had assured Dace shortly after lunch they would be taken. The Senator may be her husband, but Dace was *her* son, and while marriages forged in the sight of God may be placed asunder by mere men, the relationship between son and mother was inviolable, even to God Himself. She drew a nervous breath and then took the next step. "My question still stands, Allard, about what Dace may prefer for the unfolding of his life. Has your obedience to your father's wishes made you happy all these years, or have you been happiest when you could exercise some control over *your* destiny?" Then she waited, knowing the seed had been planted in the properest of soil.

Though his back remained toward her, The Senator felt her final words strike him in the center of the chest; Libby had crafted their import to strike at the heart, not the brain. He smiled out the window. Over the years, his wife had learned well. It was several long moments before he again turned to look at her. Libby's gaze was unflinching, he saw, and he admired her as much for her strength of conviction as for the words she had put to them. He crossed his arms over his chest and looked into her eyes from across the room. He smiled in her direction; and Libby released her held breath.

The basis of her query concerning his happiness was true. There were many moments he had regretted so obediently following his father's hand and timetable; times when the pressures of forging a new layer upon the family legacy had been nearly overwhelming for him. However, he had realized it had been his duty whether he liked it or not. His birthright had cleared the path, and his destiny was to walk it. His father had made that quite clear to him. Over the expansion of time, he had realized his father had been correct in his insistences. The Senator then recalled his childhood dream to be a flyer, perhaps to even enter the military and pilot airplanes in the post-World War II era, which emerged as the golden age of flight in the twentieth century.

His father had encouraged his boyhood interest in the field. He had even allowed Allard to hang all types of models from fishing line on hooks from the ceiling in his room, and fill shelves with magazines and more models. He was allowed to hang barnstorming posters on his walls with thumbtacks pressed into the plaster and wood panels. Many childhood days had been spent staring at those models and posters, often squinting to remove the background while imagining all sorts of air adventures and battles in the days before the second world war. It had been a wonderful time for a carefree boy, one he recalled now with tenderness as opposed to regret, because it was a the period of his life which had been filled with the boundless dreams and fantasies of boyhood.

However, on the day he had turned twenty-one, all those childish things, as his father had referred to them, were to be put away. So during the time his father talked to him in the office of his boyhood home near Hartford, the staff had packed away the models and books and magazines and posters and had transformed his room into one more representative of a man. The Senator, as would Dace eventually, had henceforth accepted the mantle of manhood, bowed himself to family tradition, and assumed his role in the adult world as envisioned by his father. It was to this adult world The Senator's focus then returned.

"In the end, Libby, I find there to be no difference between my father's plans for me and the way my life has unfolded under my own direction," he said with a strength of conviction he rarely used outside the political arena. "Dace will find it the same once he accepts his role in the family legacy. How he conforms to the twists and turns of the road may *at times* be his choice, but the destination is out of his hands." He returned to his watch, again turning from his wife, but that time as an indication the matter was now closed. Libby noted his right hand had become an unchanging, tight fist, the knuckles white with strain.

She observed him for a moment longer and then silently rose to go check on the party preparations underway throughout the house. She knew there would be no more discussion now. The Senator had closed the matter. She accepted that fact, for now. As she paused at the portal to the hallway, she glanced back one more time at the man who currently stood as guardian of the family's gates. She applied a smile to her face, one composed of equal parts of pride and sadness, then closed the door.

He heard her go, but did not turn to watch. Destiny, he thought. My son, President of the United States. The Senator smiled to himself; it was a smile created from the same constituents as was Libby's, but in different proportions, reflecting tremendous pride with only a touch of sadness. He walked to the desk and sat behind it, opened the center drawer and removed a book which laid out the Lamoureux family history in America. The Senator had seen to it that nearly every library in the United States carried at least one copy. Senator Allard Lamoureux was shown as the author and researcher, even though he had commissioned the work.

The same ghost genealogist had also researched and written a second volume on spec which traced the clan back to France in the mid-1100s when the first linked Lamoureux turned up in the Court of the House of Capet which ruled the kingdom from 987 until 1328. The Senator had rejected it, telling the woman after he had reviewed the work and discovered more than several extremely negative stories from history that the 'Lamoureux story was a distinctly American family heritage' and he did not wish to 'clutter the public's image of them with unfounded tales of prehistoric European trash'. He had demanded the woman hand over every copy of the unordered work along with all of her research without compensation before he would pay her for the commissioned volume. He had burned her research and every copy of the second volume, save one which he kept in a wall safe. He leaned back in his chair, put his feet on his desk and leafed through the pages of the American volume.

This particular Senator Lamoureux was the fifth Lamoureux male in the powerful political family to rise to hold the title of United States Senator. His was a lineage, which some would call a dynasty, that also included four governors and seven congressmen, one of whom ironically became both infamous in Lamoureux lore as the Black Sheep of the family and the man whose demise established the foundation of the family's 'selfless sacrifice for the public good' mythology.

The year was 1834 when Congressman Lennard Lamoureux was ignobly felled by a lead ball fired from the pistol of an Englishman of some historic note during a duel over an undisclosed matter of honor. While dueling was at the time illegal in most states, to many highbred gentlemen of the era that fact was considered only a technicality if the cause was honorable; and in such fashion the art of the duel continued to be discretely practiced throughout the 1800s in the United States.

Following the congressman's untimely death, rather than admit the truth of the undisclosed matter of honor which within the closely held family lore had something or other to do with the Englishman's wife, the family released a statement to the newspapers that the death was the tragic culmination of an assassination plot carried out by 'a group of foreign revolutionaries hostile to the interests of the United States', the identity of whom the family would not disclose due to 'greater national concerns'.  The ruse worked with the general public, and even in the face of back room whisperings which no person would dare carry beyond those smoke-filled confines, served to galvanize the dead congressman's reputation in, if not gold, then silver which may have occasionally needed some polishing to remove any hint of tarnish.  Over the decades, however, the family had been able to gild the story's heroic themes which grew in the retelling and eventually became the foundation of the now unassailable 24-karat Lamoureux Family Legend.

'Selfless sacrifice and service for the good of the country and its citizens' became the family's public mantra.  Privately, however, the truth of the Lennard Lamoureux affair had been kept alive over the generations to serve notice upon the family's members that neither scandal nor failure would be tolerated within their ranks.  Lamoureux men did not get caught, regardless of their indiscretion, and they never lost, at anything.  It was the overarching Code which the family enforced upon itself since that fateful day in 1834.  Of course, as the Lamoureux clan in America grew in political power and wealth, it had become easier to enforce the myth with the media and destroy anyone who would dare attempt to shine any light into the skeleton-laden closets of the family.

Necessarily, along with the political powers the family amassed, through the years there had been a number of industrial titans whose labors had supplied the financial fuel for the ravenous engine which had been required over the last two-and-one-half centuries to pull the Lamoureux clan from the relative obscurity as French Courtiers and hangers-on to the rarified status as one of America's wealthiest and most powerful families.

Lamoureux women lived a life filled with privilege and societal perks. For the Lamoureux men, however, wealth and power did not translate into a life of idleness or frivolous pursuit, and those few who sought that route out were quickly dispatched from inheritances and ironclad trusts. Thus, nearly all had readily accepted the mantle and publicly adhered to the familial credo of selfless public service.  Legacy was an edifice to which they would sacrifice anything, or anyone who dared stand in their way or challenged their motives.

Protecting the family name was a duty of honor which the Lamoureux men held higher than the vast worldly treasure which had been accumulated over the generations.  Money could always be made, they said, but a reputation, once *publicly* tarnished, can never be repolished.   They were a family of wealthy servants; at least, that's how they interpreted the worldview of themselves.

Dace ran at a steady, measured pace along the asphalt roadway alongside the Thames River toward New London.   The sound of his footfalls provided a disciplined cadence within his mind, which churned with everything his father had said to him that morning.   He had just crossed the earth-bridge spanning Smith Cove and continued toward the grounds of the Coast Guard Academy.   At the gate, he would wave to the guards without breaking stride, then turn around and head back toward the estate.   This was the longer of his two routine running routes when he was home and took him just over an hour to complete.   Had he made the right turn out the driveway toward the power plant across from Gales Ferry instead of going left as he did, the route would take him only about forty-five minutes to complete.

During high school, and now when he was home from college, he would run the route to the CGA three times a week.   On the other days that he would run, Dace would head toward the power plant.   Today, he had already decided to combine the routes knowing a couple of hours of running was just what he needed to clear the maelstrom of his thoughts.

Running normally allowed Dace to close his mind to everything but the sound of each step along the roadway.   It was his escape to solitude from a lifetime crowded by family pressure to perform at a superior level in every endeavor.   He was expected to be the captain of every team, the student body president, the quarterback, the basketball team's star player, and all while maintaining perfect grades and achieving the top spot, or very near it, on every academic ranking.   Every other minute of every day he was The Senator's son, but when he ran he could put aside that pressure and just be Dace for an hour or two; and in that there was no need to compete with himself, so he'd simply listen to the rhythm of his steps and for that time, nothing else would matter.

Stride, pace, stride.

Today, however, his mind refused to clear and remained cluttered with the words his father had said to him.   According to The Senator, that day was an 'auspicious date in history', but Dace wanted it to be just another birthday.   He didn't feel any different now that he was a man; yet The Senator had told him he had somehow changed at the stroke of midnight last.   The calculus was simple: yesterday he had been a boy; today he was a man.   Dace just didn't quite get it.   He had known his whole life this day would come, he was just surprised it had arrived so quickly.

Stride, pace, stride.

Dace wasn't certain he was ready for all the responsibilities of some ethereal legacy which apparently now fell upon him simply because a page had been torn from the desk calendar. His father had reminded him that no longer could he fall back on the excuses of youth for any shortcoming or failure. Everything he did from that day forward would be judged against an entirely new and yet unfamiliar scale: the measure of manhood. Boyhood, and its easy forgivenesses were gone forever. Some of it he could accept, but his father had also spoken to him about the plans for the unfolding of *his* future, and that he was not ready to embrace.

Stride, pace, stride. Breathe.

He still had the rest of the last semester of his undergraduate studies to complete, and then next year he would begin law school. As could be expected, he had been accepted into both Harvard and Yale, as well as Stanford Law, to which he had applied on a rebellious whim. Sarah was headed for Stanford Medical School next fall and he had applied to the school as an option to eliminate the tearing stresses of being a bi-coastal couple. Of course, he hadn't shared that little tidbit about applying to Stanford Law with his father. His mother knew he had been toying with the idea of following Sarah to California, but he was certain she would not tell The Senator. Dace wondered if her promise to protect his secret had simply been her shielding him from another lecture in his father's study or if she had known Dace would never take that step outside of family tradition and thus there would be no need to burden The Senator with the possibility.

Stride, pace, stride. Breathe.

As his father had reminded him that morning, the men of the Lamoureux family had attended either Harvard or Yale for the last two centuries, so it really didn't matter which school he selected as his alma mater for undergraduate or law school studies; just so long as it was one of those two. Through the generations, the family had provided substantial endowments to both schools, so admission of any Lamoureux male, or female in recent years, by either college was certain. The Senator had been a Harvard man, but Dace's grandfather had attended Yale. Dace had often wondered if his father had selected the rival school as his last act of defiance, although The Senator never let on that it had been against grandfather's wishes. Dace already had decided on Harvard Law because he simply preferred the professors currently teaching there over the lineup at Yale. Stanford had been just a fantasy, after all; something to consider late at night when he could still smell Sarah's perfume on himself.

Stride, pace, stride. Breathe. Thoughts of Sarah.

He hadn't told his father of his decision yet. Dace smiled at the thought of keeping a secret from The Senator, but that smile quickly faded when he remembered something else his father had said to him that morning which could only have meant that he already knew. As his next steps hit pavement in a faster rhythm now driven by aggravation, Dace shook his head vigorously in another effort to clear his mind.

Stride, pace, stride.

All through his life, it had seemed to Dace that his father possessed some type of omniscience, especially when it came to *his* existence. There had been times during high school when Dace had thought his father had either bugged his room or had people following him to have known so much in advance of the telling.   Once, when he was a freshman, he and his best friend Dave Saunders had liberated a canoe from the Yale rowing camp across the river and had gone exploring the Thames River while smoking a couple of cheap, flavored cigars.   They had returned the canoe no worse for wear a few hours later and no one had seen them, yet as he walked into the house, his father was on the phone from Washington wanting to speak to him regarding some 'mischief perpetrated across the river'.

Stride, pace, stride. Breathe.

Dace had only told his mother when he arrived home for this weekend visit that he was going to accept the offer to Harvard Law in the fall and she had seemed pleased with the decision; even though that meant three more years of living away from home.  He knew his mother missed him around the house over the past four years, and part of the reason, he knew, was she wasn't getting any younger.  Yale, after all, was the hometown school in New Haven, Connecticut less than an hour's drive away, while Harvard was in Cambridge, Massachusetts, more than twice that drive.  She had told him his father would be proud, and she had seemed genuinely relieved by the rendering moot of the potential burden of telling The Senator Dace would be headed to California to follow a girl.

Stride, pace, stride. Breathe. Sarah.

His heart was beating strongly now and as he made the turn at the Coast Guard Academy, physically, he was feeling good.  The sun was warm and the unseasonable temperatures had helped him work up a good sweat.  He glanced off to his right after waving to the guards and making the turn back toward home.  The hardworking Thames was millpond flat that day with not one breath of wind to stir the surface, and the current flowed strongly with the added water from the melting snow further inland.   He watched the swirling eddies, visible today in the glassine surface, which hinted at the turbulence below.   On the bluffs along the other side, he could see the small waterfalls which had formed with the runoff of melting snow and ice.  The roadway he ran along was wet and he splashed through the scattered rivulets headed to join the river, while he deftly avoided the larger and deeper puddles and flows. The sun had begun moving lower in the afternoon sky and he could already sense the night's threatening return to winter in the air.

His thoughts turned to Sarah.

Sarah. Stride, pace, stride. Breathe.

She would be at his party that night; he had made certain of her invitation, and her acceptance. The Senator didn't fully approve of Sarah, he knew, although his father had always been kind to the girl when Dace brought her around. While The Senator would never betray his public face as a paternal populist, reading between the lines of conversations they had concerning Sarah led Dace to conclude the reason his father didn't approve of his relationship with her was because he felt her family just wasn't of the proper social heritage and caliber for where Dace was destined. Predictably, Sarah's future with Dace had been a key ancillary topic of The Senator's lecture that morning, and it was perhaps the part of the conversation which Dace felt most disconcerting.

Sarah.

Sarah Avidago was perfectly acceptable in the role of transient sweetheart to a boy, his father had said, but now that he was a man his choices in women would be more closely scrutinized. Dace had asked his father just who would be doing the scrutinizing and The Senator had shot back with a list which included the media, political opponents, and the American people. The 'unwashed masses', The Senator postulated, were longing for a return to the gloried days of Camelot, meaning the reemergence under a new ascendancy of the optimistic times of the early 1960s when JFK was the young president who had brought new vitality and purpose along with his beautiful, society-approved wife and their children to the White House and the nation. Camelot had been the literary metaphor which the media had applied for the burgeoning epoch which had transformed a bored, complacent, and stagnating world into an era of new spirit, vitality, and vision; a time which The Senator said could be reborn through Dace when the time was right. His father had made it quite clear that morning that this vision would not include Sarah.

Political opponents, the media, the public, Dace thought.

What political opponents? He had just turned twenty-one, had not even decided on a career in politics yet, so why should he worry about the phantasms of future political opponents at this point in his life? He wouldn't be eligible to become a United States Senator until he reached the age of thirty, and the presidency was precluded to him until he was thirty-five. Those milestones were near lifetimes away to a newly minted twenty-one year old man. His father had spoken to him that morning as if those two targets were weeks, not years in the distance; adding: 'Because today you are a man, and as of this moment you will put away childish things.' What exactly did that mean?

Stride, stride, stride. Breathe, stride.

Dace increased his pace. He desperately wanted the sound of his footfalls to chase all these thoughts from his mind.

The first thing Dace noticed as he returned from his run was that The Senator was still watching out his office window. As he turned up the driveway, Dace could see his father silhouetted in the center of the expanse of segmented glass, standing there, constantly watching, omnipotent and confident, and peering down in judgment of mere mortals like God Himself. As Dace moved closer to the house, he could better make out the features of the man in the window. Tanned, even in the middle of winter, his mane of thick white hair brushed back and every strand perfectly in place. He wore his ubiquitous deep navy blue, double-breasted suit, pinstriped or not depending upon mood, white shirt, and red tie - striped that season - worn even on a weekend at home just in case a camera crew showed up unexpectedly to obtain a quote from one of the most highly regarded members of the United States Senate. The only time The Senator would dress down would be when he went golfing or played poker with his friends, and while he could be cajoled into wearing upscale yachting clothes on vacation, 'The Suit', as the kids had teasingly called it, was never far away.

Dace slowed halfway up the drive to a cool-down, walking pace. When he glanced up again, he could see his father smiling, his perfectly straightened and artificially whitened teeth in strong contrast to his tan. He could see his father's eyes. They reflected the pride they held for his son, and for an instant Dace felt a strong connection to the man. Then the look was gone, and he was The Senator again, and his emotions became indecipherable behind impenetrable, deep blue orbs. Dace's did not allow his face to reflect the disconnect his heart felt at that instant.

He noticed his father turn slightly and then his mother arrived in frame and stood beside her husband. Dace watched as she moved close, placed her right hand upon her husband's chest, saw his father's right arm moving around her shoulder. Now, she smiled down at him. What was it he saw in her eyes that next moment? Empathy? Sadness? Then those things, too, were gone, and her eyes became unreadable. Decades under public scrutiny had honed his mother's abilities to mask her emotions almost as well as could his father. They had become complimentary to each other, like bookends, each doing an independent job of holding the family upright and together, and each reliant upon the other to share the burden.

Yet while his father's strength had seemed unchangeable and his mother was physically still a dynamo, Dace had noticed over recent months she had begun to show small signs of intellectually succumbing to the clutches of age. Perhaps, it wasn't just the aging process, he thought, but rather weariness resultant of a lifetime of pressures and expectations of being married to Senator Allard Lamoureux. His mother had been the epitome of the image of a Lamoureux woman, and that was one of the hardest jobs in the world, Dace knew.

Not that his mother had not all her life led one of the most privileged lives outside of the realm of true royalty. She had. Elizabeth 'Libby' McIntire Lamoureux was the youngest daughter of Governor George and Margaret McIntire and raised in the proper style of the rich and politically connected in the state of Connecticut: private day schools leading to boarding schools, elite social inclusions and all the required extracurricular lessons required to transform a girl of proper breeding into a young woman of acceptability. Forging a trail before the days of modern feminism, Libby had even obtained a degree from Radcliffe, although in typical fashion of her married position never really used it. Regardless of the preparations brought on by the combination of breeding and polish, she was now a Lamoureux woman and with that status came an almost endless list of responsibilities and expectations, both public and private.

The scrutiny which would now be settling upon Dace, according to his father, had been for decades relentless in pursuit of any hint of a crack in the facade of his mother as well as The Senator himself. When every move you made was photographed, every look on your face was analyzed, every event you attended and every person with whom you were publicly seen was vetted, it would be easy to falter in the course of fifty-plus years. Yet, to his knowledge, his mother never had. After forty-six years of marriage, and six years of courtship before that, Dace's mother had performed flawlessly, but it was becoming increasingly apparent to her son, that the woman's spirit had begun to slowly ebb away.

Dace turned his gaze toward the ground at the sobering thought of his mother giving in to the relentless march of time. He silently counted each of his steps as he walked slow circles around the drive's roundabout at the front of the house so his muscles wouldn't cramp during the cool down from the day's extra distance run. He resisted the urge to look up again because he didn't wish to see her gone from his father's side. That was a mental image he did not want, especially on that day. His mother had always been there for him. She was that one person who could, and would, stand up for him to his father. What would he do were she not there to run the occasional interference for him? Dace pondered that thought repeatedly as the crushed granite crunched under each step. His father may be the family's Ship of State, but his mother had always been the lighthouse by whom the entire family found home.

Dace passed under the portico and entered the main level of the house, walked through the foyer and made his way back to the kitchen. He checked the clock on the wall. It was just over two hours before the guests would begin arriving for the party and the kitchen was already overflowing with catering and wait staff. Throughout the home, other workers moved quietly and efficiently in their jobs of cleaning, decorating, and preparing for the event. Originally, The Senator had wanted the celebration to be held at their house outside of Washington, D.C., but had eventually relented to the combined wishes of Libby and Dace that the party be held at their Connecticut estate. New London was, after all, the family's home, regardless of how much time The Senator spent in the nation's capital, Libby had reminded him.

Dace wove his way through the people working along every inch of counter space to the refrigerator, opened it and looked around inside. He grabbed a plastic bottle of low-calorie Gatorade from off the top shelf, then turned, surveyed the countertops, reached between two catering employees and stole a chocolate cupcake from a perfectly arranged tray. Caroline let out an exasperated sigh, so he winked at her and then headed to the front stairs and began bounding the steps two at a time up to his third-floor room to shower and dress.

On the landing between the second and third floors, he came upon Mary Rose sitting on one of the steps. When Dace had been born, his three oldest sisters had been in their late teens to early twenties. Miriam, the eldest, had been twenty-four, married and already the mother of two-year-old twins. So, as a result of the time-separated sibling groups, two of his nephews were older than their uncle and Mary Rose and Dace had grown up extremely close in a world all their own. In the very early years, the sister had watched over the brother, and when he was six, the roles had reversed.

Mary Rose was wearing her party dress. She had insisted on wearing it all day since that day was her only baby brother's birthday and Mary Rose so enjoyed parties. While his three other sisters were often less than patient with Mary Rose, which Dace generously attributed to the difference in their ages rather than Mary Rose's condition, Dace always took whatever time with her that she needed, whether it was to help with a task she found difficult or merely taking the time to listen to her.

Mary Rose's Down Syndrome had been one of the reasons the doctors had warned against their mother carrying to term the pregnancy which resulted in Dace's birth. Down Syndrome was a genetic malady found in the general population, but which more often afflicted the children of older parentage. While Mary Rose had escaped many of the associated physical problems, she did suffer from a more severe inhibition of cognitive development which meant she would forever have the mental functioning of a four-year-old. Regardless, she had been the most loving of sisters while Dace grew up with her. Mary Rose was his heart; and Dace was her hero.

Their other siblings seemed more like aunts than sisters to him. Dace and Mary Rose were something akin to the children of a second marriage, often disconnected in time by decades from the first set of kids. During their early childhood, they had been inseparable. When Dace was in the first grade, he had once asked his mother if he could take Mary Rose to school for Show and Tell. Their mother was at first appalled by the thought, but when she had asked him why he wanted to take his sister to school, he had replied because Mary Rose had never been able to go to school and he wanted her to see what it was like.

Dace sat down on the step next to his sister.

"Hey, Kiddo," he said. "You certainly do look beautiful today."

Mary Rose looked at him and it was then he saw she had been crying. She half-smiled at him and tried to hide something behind her back. As he had approached, Dace had seen she was trying to put one of her drawings into an envelope but it had been folded too large to fit. He decided to first tease and cajole her into forgetting the troubles she had been having and then solve her problem.

"What are you all dressed up for, Mary Rose? Got a big date or something?" He gave her one of his trademark toothy smiles.

She laughed and smoothed out her dress a bit.

"No," she said, shaking her head.

"That's good," he replied. "Because you're *my* best girl, Mary Rose." He made a show of looking around her back. "What are you hiding?"

"Nothing," she said. "It's for the party."

"Party?" Dace teased. "What party?" He changed his voice to mimic her favorite cartoon character, Foghorn Leghorn, and delivered the next line: "Why, I say, why, don't people tell me about these things?"

Mary Rose giggled. She loved it when Dace would do the voice of the big, potbellied, white cartoon rooster whom since childhood, she and Dace called Foghorn Egghead.

"You know about the party," Mary Rose said. "It's not a surprise. Mama said it's not a surprise."

"Oh, *that* party," Dace said with another smile. He dropped his head so his forehead touched Mary Rose's head above her ear. "Do you need my help with anything, Mary Rose?" he whispered.

He held his head there, seeing her face move as her mind worked the problem of whether she could show him the homemade card. He enjoyed watching her think, because sometimes she came up with the most brilliant ideas. Then her face stopped moving about.

"Close your eyes," she said to him.

He shut them and then felt her place the items into his lap.

"Keep them shut," she instructed. "Put that together for me, Dace, please? But don't look."

"How can I do it if I don't look, Mary Rose?"

When she whispered the next words, his soul Dace heard them as if they were spoken by a healthy, twenty-four-year-old sister.

"Because you can do anything, Dace," she said.

He assembled the card into the envelope with just a little bit of peeking, found the flap and licked it to seal the package. He handed it back to Mary Rose and then asked if he could now open his eyes. She took the card back and placed it between herself and the railing.

"Yeah," she said. "Now you can."

"You're sweaty, Dace," she said, and then sniffed. "And stinky."

"I was out running along the river," he responded. "You remember how I like to go running."

"Yeah," she said. "Go take a shower. It's party day. You have to be clean and happy on party day."

He watched her as she got up, made efforts to keep the envelope hidden from him, and started to walk down the stairs. Dace picked up the cupcake and Gatorade and as he turned at the landing to the final section of stairs, he saw his mother had been watching them through the rails from the second floor hallway. She took hold of Mary Rose's hand and just before she walked off, she kissed her fingertips and placed them to her heart. It was a gesture which had long been a secret expression of love only he and his mother shared.

Dace bounded up the remaining flight of stairs and then walked down the hall to his room. After he closed the door and placed the cupcake and the Gatorade onto the dresser, he looked into the mirror and smiled because his mind had finally cleared, not with the run but because of Mary Rose's simple reminder: 'It's party day.'

"Indeed it is, Mary Rose," he said as he stripped down and went to the shower. "And it's a day to be happy, even if it's only for a day."

# Chapter Two

Ashley Monreale was five-foot-six and one-hundred-twenty pounds. She had inherited her mother's curves and her father's height. Her thick, dark-brown hair which hung nearly halfway down her back and bewitching green eyes had come from neither parent. Her best friend, Veronica 'Ronnie' Broussard, on the other hand, had inherited her mother's height and her father's curves. She stood five-foot-seven and weighed one-hundred-fifteen pounds soaking wet; she had thin, light brown hair worn long and big brown puppy dog eyes. They were each sixteen, soon to turn seventeen and they each ached for adulthood.

Ashley and Ronnie were also celebrating that day in February of 1998, but for a very different reason. They had been planning their attendance at that year's Mardi Gras celebrations in New Orleans ever since last year's party plans had been discovered and quashed by their parents. Ronnie had blabbed to her then-roommate and the girl had squealed to Sister Regina, their school's principal. This year, they had pledged to each other, things would be different. Standing there now with the laminated cards in their hands and the having kept their pledge to say nothing to anyone, they knew things would be different.

That February the fourteenth, the pair - those who knew them would say set - of girls were over halfway through their junior year at Immaculate Conception Catholic Girls Preparatory School near Convent, Louisiana, where they had been boarding and attending classes for the last two-and-one-half years. They had met on the first day of freshman orientation and had hit it off immediately. Their junior year they had finally been able to arrange to be roommates, thanks mainly to staying in the good graces of the Head Mother and nearly incessant lobbying.

The school was located north of the Mississippi River and more than thirty miles from each of their family homes. Ashley had come from outside Thibodaux further south, and Ronnie's parents lived in White

Castle, further west and nearer Baton Rouge than New Orleans, but both on the south side of the river which provided a certain degree of privacy for the girls. Six months ago, Ronnie obtained her driver's license, and shortly thereafter her own car. Even though she kept her burgundy, two-door, 1997 Chevrolet Cavalier at her boyfriend Bobby's house, having it meant they also enjoyed a degree of freedom and mobility.

Ashley had just returned to their dormitory room following a short visit from one of her many 'uncles' and pulled from her purse the two fake IDs he had obtained for them. The man wasn't really an uncle, wasn't even related by blood, but rather an associate of her father who had a reputation for having certain connections within state government. A month ago Ashley had asked him for a favor. Today, the man had come through. The favor normally cost five hundred dollars, a high price to match the fact the documents were neither forgeries nor cheap street reproductions, but genuine State of Louisiana Department of Motor Vehicles driver's licenses, just with some *creative* information. According to the state of Louisiana, the pair of best friends were now twenty-one.

"You know, Ronnie," Ashley said with a coy giggle. "I really don't feel any older. Do you?" She batted her eyes dramatically and fanned herself mockingly with the small card.

"Why, no, Ash, not really."

They both fell onto Ashley's bed and rolled together and laughed. Suddenly Ashley stopped and sat up. She brushed her long hair from her face and looked into Ronnie's eyes with an adult seriousness.

"We tell *nobody*, Ronnie," she warned and pointed a finger down at the girl. "Not this year. Not about anything. You understand? About *anything*."

Ronnie lay there and stared back through the mussed, light brown strands which still covered much of her face.

"Of course, Ash," she said and sat up and brushed away the hair. "This is way too cool, though. We'll be getting into bars and having a ball. We'll be like legends after. Why would I tell anyone about it before?"

"Ah, because, last year you told that bitch Brittany and she told her mother on us that very day." She paused. "We have to be very careful before, and there will be no legends after, either. We can't risk telling anyone anything. Ever."

Ronnie was a bit embarrassed by the reprised memory of confiding in her ex-roommate, but last year she had been only fifteen and in truth a little afraid to go with Ashley into New Orleans for Mardi Gras on their own. This year, though, she was nearly seventeen, no, twenty-one. Now.

"Yeah, I know," she said sheepishly. "That was then, and this is now, though, Ash. You can trust me."

"I better be able to, because this year it's not just for me and you." She leaned closer to Ronnie and whispered the next sentence as she waved the fake ID in her friend's face. "Do you have any idea what my dad would do to the guy who got us these things?" She dramatically drew a finger across her neck.

"Seriously?" Ronnie said, her already big brown eyes appearing to grow to the size of silver dollars. She had heard rumors about Ashley's dad from her parents, but they were only that, and she and Ash never spoke of her businessman father's other 'career'. It was one of their unspoken rules.

Ashley took both of her friends hands in hers and looked deeply into her eyes.

"Yeah, seriously."

Dace trotted downstairs to his father's office in response to his mother's summoning knock at his bedroom door about ninety minutes after he went up to shower. He arrived dressed in the new black Armani tuxedo Caroline had laid out for him earlier and walked into the center of the room to light applause from the gathered older sisters, their husbands, and Mary Rose. He noticed that Miriam's twins, who were now twenty-three, and Patricia's three kids who were in their mid-teens, weren't included in the little gathering. Dace felt a small grin come to his face as he considered the irony and misogynistic undercurrent of the gathering after concluding the invitations were obviously handed out by his father to include only full-blooded Lamoureux clan members. Dace had no doubt, had he older children, they would have been invited because they would have been sired by a Lamoureux man. Husbands of the older sisters were present as a courtesy, however, offspring of the girls were never going to be considered full *family*.

Everyone in attendance held a freshly topped drink, including Mary Rose who had her Kiddie Cocktail consisting of 7-Up and maraschino cherry juice. Dace watched as his father came over to him holding two glasses of Scotch on the rocks in cut crystal tumblers. He handed one to Dace, then took a couple of steps back and began to speak a birthday toast as everyone except Dace and Mary Rose held out their glass at the proper elevation.

"I'd like to take the occasion of this private family time before the public celebration begins downstairs to offer a few words in honor of my son, Dace. Happy birthday, son."

Dace noted Miriam's eyebrow raise with a glance cast toward sister Patricia across the room when the words 'private family time' were spoken, yet when The Senator concluded, everyone raised their glasses high to the toast and held them there while offering muted echoes of the happy birthday wishes. Mary Rose, who sat on the floor off toward the corner, the card which Dace had put into the envelope on her lap, did the same. Dace raised his glass in acknowledgement around the room, but lingered toward Mary Rose, whose echo and sentiment seemed the most genuine. Everyone drank, except for Dace, who never had touched alcohol, or drugs for that matter, and didn't intend to begin today just because the date made him now legal to do so.

The Senator restarted his speech after sipping from his glass of single malt and half the attendees silently prayed he wouldn't be embarking on one of his famous filibuster speeches. The other half took another, deeper draw from their glasses in anticipation he would. The quality of the alcohol and the brevity of what came next made everyone happy.

"Twenty-one years ago today, God blessed Libby and myself with a son, after already having blessed us with four wonderful and beautiful daughters," he began, acknowledging them all.

Standing husbands dutifully placed free hands onto the shoulder of their seated wives.

"I love you all very much, and you all know I'd never play favorites between my children," The Senator continued.

A look bounced between the three older girls. The husbands did the same between each other.

"However, this is Dace's day, and I would like you to join with me as family to wish him every good thing life has in store for him. You are the future of this family, Dace, and I pray God gives you the strength, wisdom, and courage to accomplish what the world will be expecting of you. I know you'll always make us proud, my son." The Senator glanced about the room, and satisfied with the returned smiles, concluded, and extended his glass higher. "To Dace."

"To Dace," they all chimed this time as one, except Mary Rose who again echoed the 'happy birthday' a second later.

They all drank again, except Dace, who accepted the toast and then set the untouched glass of Scotch onto a nearby end table. He assumed, correctly, that he was now expected to give a bit of a speech. Again, half the room hoped for the short and sweet version. What they all received was short and anything but sweet.

"Thank you, dad," he began, wiping the residual moisture on his fingers from the glass between both hands.

Only his mother took proper note of the nervous gesture and felt herself cringe at what may be coming next.

"I would like to thank all of you for coming to this celebration on the twenty-first anniversary of the day of my birth, which we all understand is an auspicious occasion for a *male* member of the Lamoureux family."

He caught a bit of disapproval in his father's eyes at the thinly veiled sarcasm, but also noted the understanding smirks which came over his sisters' faces in unison.

"Seriously, though, I truly appreciate the well wishes from each of you. It has already been quite the day to remember for me. As some of you may know, father had me in for 'the discussion' today." In reality, it had been more lecture than discussion. "And I wish to share a couple of the decisions which I have made following consideration of his words and much soul searching on my part."

His mother silently inhaled and then held her breath. She alone properly noted something in Dace's tone and continued self-soothing mannerisms; while an anticipatory glint came to Miriam's eyes. The Senator confidently relaxed further into his large, tufted, burgundy leather wingback chair and crossed his legs. He was in his element, seated upon the patriarch's throne and presiding over his family, and clearly anticipated nothing outside of his Will to flow from his only son.

"First, I wish to say that I will be honoring family tradition and will be entering Harvard Law School in the fall, just as my father did fifty-three years ago."

Dace glanced to his father and received in return a nod and concurring smile. He took a deep breath before continuing and almost wished at that moment that he had taken a healthy draw from the tumbler of whiskey now sitting on the end table. He noted the glass was beginning to sweat more than he was and took some comfort in that irony. Finally, he let out part of the breath and then just said it.

"Second, and which is more important, to me anyway..." He paused, licked his lips and looked directly at his father, but quickly fell into a well-known speaker's anxiety-salving trick and focused his gaze not into his father's eyes, but rather at a spot in the center of The Senator's forehead. "I have decided to ask Sarah Avidago to marry me."

The collective reaction to his second announcement was like the oxygen being sucked out of the room. Nobody dared move. His mother and sisters, except for Mary Rose, all sat in stunned silence. Miriam's expression remained fixed by sheer will, but the gleeful glint in her eyes belied her true feelings. For a moment, Dace wondered if Miriam was salivating more at the thought of yet more opportunity to practice her 'I'm better than you are, and don't you forget it' charms on a future sister-in-law, or the explosion which she anticipated would come from their father.

The husbands fired silent glances to each other, only their eyes darting back and forth. When Dace finally found the courage to focus his gaze lower and directly into his father's eyes, he saw not what he expected, but rather a calm resolve which efficiently moved from his eyes through his face and then his entire body. Frankly, Dace would have preferred to have seen any other mask upon his father's face than the one which now stared back at him. It was the man's impenetrable mask he would affect, Dace knew, during times where he had to move another vote to his side and was employing a poker player's bluff with the other colleague. The Senator rarely invoked a *true* bluff. Those who really knew the man understood he would push the nuclear release button were he cornered, rendering moot any thought the man may be actually employing a bluff. Dace shuddered at that realization, for what he now saw on his father's face was an inviolable resolve which meant whatever it took to forge *his* Will into realty, The Senator would now do.

It was Mary Rose who shattered the tension as only she could.

"Happy Birthday, Dace," Mary Rose hollered, bouncing over to him and holding her homemade card in her outstretched hand. She reached up with both arms and rose onto tiptoes to hug him and he bent down slightly to accept her kiss on his cheek.

"Thank you, Mary Rose," he said when she released him.

"Did I surprise you, Dace?" she said, her face brightly expectant.

"You certainly did," he said. "The biggest surprise of the day."

"Not quite," The Senator said toward his son, his eyes boring right through Dace.

Dace turned to look at his father and then noticed that during his momentary interplay with Mary Rose the study had silently cleared, leaving him, The Senator and Mary Rose alone in the room. Even his mother was gone.

"Honey, why don't you go find your mother," The Senator said to Mary Rose as he approached to shepherd her out. "Daddy needs to speak with Dace. Alone."

"Okay, daddy," she said, then kissed him on the cheek and bounded out of the room. "Mommy!" she called down the hallway.

The Senator followed behind and slowly closed the door. He calmly walked across the room to the bar area, poured himself another glass of single malt and then returned to his chair.

"Sit down, son," he said in the tone of an unmistakable command and gestured toward one of the now vacant couches. "I think we're needing to talk."


The guests began arriving at seven that evening. Libby and the girls greeted them and Libby apologized for The Senator and Dace being absent, citing, with a smile, an overrun in the father and son talk, but assured everyone that they'd both be along shortly. They all nodded in some sort of acceptance or understanding. What else were they to do? These were members of polite society; the people who would smile and nod and say nothing confrontational regarding the unconventionality of their reception directly to their hostess, but would undoubtedly later weave snippets of speculation into truth-be-told stories.

About a dozen of Dace's acquaintances from high school, people whom he had insisted be invited, arrived together and piled out of four cars. They arrived inside noisily, dressed in jeans and leather or denim jackets and dragging along local girls in every manner of the early twenty-something female's idea of formal dress. Libby shot a warning look down the line of her daughters, who all got the message and greeted the people cordially and without sharp-tongued commentary, and then Libby informed the incoming group that ice-cold beers could be found in a galvanized tub next to the roaring fire pit out back.

Dave Saunders, who had been Dace's best friend since the age of eight and was his roommate at Harvard, arrived moments later in an obviously rented tuxedo draping his large frame as Libby was explaining the route to take through the kitchen to the back yard area. Dave took over with a wink and a hug and told Libby he'd show them the way. She thanked him and watched in relief as he corralled the group and then indeed led them to the left, out through the kitchen and away from the great room to the right where most of the formal guests were gathering. A few minutes later, he alone was back inside, standing at the hosted bar.

Sarah Avidago arrived closer to seven-thirty wearing a full-length, draped, black satin halter gown with fishtail hem and sable shrug, all of which Dace had bought for her the previous week in Boston. Though only Libby and Mary Rose were there to greet Sarah, they did so with genuine warmth and affection; the other sisters having abandoned their posts to get a jump on the speculative conversation about what exactly was taking place on the floor above and incessantly chatter away amongst themselves like teenagers. The juiciness of Dace's surprise announcement had been just too much for any of them to contain themselves in the welcoming line any longer. The husbands closed ranks near the bar, content to talk about anything but family politics, so long as they remained close to the alcohol. The sisters gathered on the periphery and barely out of earshot of the growing throng, near the hearth where the cauldron would have hung in centuries past.

"My, Sarah, what a lovely dress," Libby said genuinely, offering the girl a hug and peck on the cheek. "Welcome."

"Thank you, Mrs. Lamoureux," Sarah replied, breathing in a sigh of silent relief as she glanced around the inside assemblage to see her dress, as stunning as it was, was nothing more or less than appropriate. When she had modeled the gown and shrug for Dace the day they went out to shop, she had felt very uncomfortable with what she viewed as the ostentatiousness of the getup. Although the dress was indeed flattering to her figure, and as the warmth of the day had given way to a frosty evening making the fur shrug a welcome protection to her bare shoulders, it all just wasn't what she was comfortable wearing. "Dace bought it for me. Last week, in Boston. I thought it was ridiculously extravagant, I mean, Russian Sable? Dace had been insistent, though, and from looking around now that I'm here, and considering the other choices I had in my closet, I am now relieved he was." She again glanced about the room, noted the tuxedoed men of every age, and the women drowning in jewels and then let out the next breath as nervous little sigh.

The engraved invitation Dace had handed her at school had said, 'black tie' and she had no idea what that would entail until she researched it in the library. Dace had at first told her he didn't care what she wore, so long as she was there, but then later had insisted they go shopping.

"I'm afraid I'm a bit out of my element," Sarah admitted to Libby a moment later.

"Why, nonsense, Sarah," Libby said. "Consider yourself part of the family, so just relax and enjoy tonight."

Sarah smiled and saw in the older woman's eyes the invitation was genuinely offered. She had not spent much time with the Lamoureux family, but when she had, Sarah had found Libby to be nothing less than gracious and welcoming.

"Thank you again, Mrs. Lamoureux," Sarah said and then the random thought of how the woman had not ever invited Sarah to call her by the universal Libby quickly passed through her mind. Then, to Mary Rose, while taking the girl's two hands in hers: "Why Mary Rose, you look absolutely wonderful this evening in your party dress."

Mary Rose smiled broadly and turned around so Sarah could see her dress from all sides.

"This is my nighttime party dress," Mary Rose said. "My daytime party dress got all scrunchy." She wrinkled her nose.

"Wrinkled, dear," Libby corrected lovingly.

"Yeah, wrinkled, like a prune," Mary Rose laughed, "and, Caroline said nobody wears prunes to a party. I told her, even I know that."

The three of them laughed and Sarah felt the apprehensions of the previous few moments fade away. Mary Rose alone, in her continued innocence, possessed that magic. Mary Rose then wandered off into the crowd, leaving Libby and Sarah to watch her go. Libby wondered if Sarah had any idea of what Dace had announced earlier, and if so, how long the two of them had been talking so seriously about the future. Sarah started to feel a bit uneasy and began to sense the eyes of some of the other guests moving upon her now. She glanced around the room, but didn't see Dace or The Senator anywhere.

"Are Dace and Senator Lamoureux not here yet?" Sarah asked, a bit uncomfortable without Dace at her side.

Sarah had interacted with the family several times, during a visit once to Cambridge and a couple of less formal family gatherings down in New London, but Dace had always been with her. She never liked being alone, even in a crowd, something which had followed her from her earliest memories. After the death of her parents when she was five,

Sarah had been raised by her grandmother in a working-class, Portuguese neighborhood in Providence, Rhode Island. As brilliant as Sarah was, she always felt socially inept and out-of-place in the rarified air inhabited by the Lamoureux family and their friends; even after nearly four years of exposure to the type at Harvard, where she landed on full scholarship, and recently being bolstered by the confidence which came from her acceptance to the prestigious Stanford Medical School.

"They're in The Senator's study, Sarah," Libby said, her eyes moving up toward the next level. "I am certain they will be coming down shortly." She gestured toward the great room assemblage with a small sweep of her arm. "Please, Sarah, make yourself at home, I am certain you already know some of the people here." Several more guests arrived at the door. "I don't mean to run you off, dear, understand, but I'm all alone here welcoming our friends since the girls, and now even Mary Rose, have abandoned the duty." She offered a harried smile.

Sarah returned an open and genuine smile and began to walk into what Dace had always jokingly referred to as the Lion's Den. Just then, she saw Dave Saunders moving along the outside ring of guests, a glass of beer in his hand. The big man was pulling uncomfortably at his collar, which Sarah noted did look a tad bit small. When he saw her, he smiled broadly, waved, and came over to meet her halfway.

"Sarah," he said, surprising her by lifting her off the floor and turning her around with him in a big, one-armed, bear hug.

"Um, Dave," Sarah said with slightly embarrassed surprise, her hosed and heeled toes dangling under her dress.

He looked across the elevated hug at her, as if waiting for something.

"Ah, you can put me down any time, Dave." She smiled at him, but blushed when she noted some of the guests had begun tittering about the display.

Dave noted her embarrassment and stared back menacingly at some of the guests who didn't know him for the gentle giant he was. They all turned away. Dave smiled at Sarah.

"That was easy," he said out the side of his mouth and then in typical Dave fashion, changed the subject to beer. He held up his glass of brew and pointed to it. "Do you believe that they won't just give you a beer in a bottle or can inside the house? Has to be in the glass." He pushed a thumb point over his shoulder at the bartenders. "Dude said: 'If you want beer in a can or bottle, sir, you have to go out back with the rest of the beer crowd.' Beer crowd? What's that? People, huh?" He huffed in mock disdain for the bartender's comment, then looked her up and down again and let out a soft whistle; not a wolf whistle, but one appropriate between friends, and punctuated the positive appraisal with one of his characteristic, easy smiles. "You look absolutely gorgeous, Sarah. Dace told me the two of you had picked out something that would knock everybody's socks off tonight." He took a long draw from the glass, wiped his mouth with the back of his oversize hand, then raised a leg and lifted a pant leg to reveal a long stocking with clip and strap at the top of his ample calf. He shrugged and dropped his leg. "Well, maybe it's harder to knock these things off when they come with garters, cuz these things sure stayed put when they shouldn't have. You sure do look fantastic."

"Garters?" Sarah asked.

"Yup," Dave said, then finished off the glass of beer. "That's what my mom called 'em." He shook his head. "If it ever gets out that Dave Saunders wore garters..." He shrugged and smiled broadly. "I want a refill. You want me to bring you something?"

Sarah glanced around the room for any other friendly, familiar face, and seeing none decided it wasn't in her best interest to stand there alone.

"Yes, I'll have something with you." She took his arm. "Lead the way, Dave."

Dave did and parted the crowd like a battleship headed for harbor.

She felt safe at his side. Dave was a big man: six-foot-four and carried a bit over three hundred pounds, but solid as a block of granite. He played offensive tackle for Harvard, starting all four years and attracting some minor attention from the pro scouts even though in the NFL he'd be considered one of their smaller offensive linemen. As Dace had often noted to her, Dave was quick, smart, and most of all he had heart; and heart could make up for any number of physical shortfalls. Whether he made a run at the pros or not, Dave had his eyes ultimately set on an MBA degree and life in the boardrooms of global mega-corporations. Dace had said one time: 'Dave will offer an imposing physical presence as his first impression hoping they'll underestimate him as some dumb ex-jock there because of what he *was* and then blow them away with his brain.' Moving through the gathered throng, Dave's broad shoulders and height sheltered her. Sarah smiled. He was the perfect substitute for Dace at the moment.

Libby watched from her position in the foyer as Dave and Sarah passed through the crowd. Even though she truly liked Sarah, Libby wondered how the girl could survive the vicious social judgments and backbiting should she become a Lamoureux wife. Part of Libby thought Sarah fit better on the arm of someone like Dave Saunders than her son, but then she instantly regretted the judgment and chastised herself for making it. Thankfully, another set of guests arrived just then and distracted her mind momentarily from her concerned thoughts of, and for Sarah Avidago.

"Dad, you just have to listen to me," Dace repeated for what seemed the twentieth time since The Senator had closed the door behind Mary

Rose. "I am talking down the road for myself and Sarah's future, *after* law school, *after* she finishes medical school, *after* we become established in our chosen careers; but you really need to understand that I believe she is the one woman in the world for me. I truly love her."

The Senator's expressed reaction was the same the twentieth time as it had been the first time his son had spouted those words: he was unmoved, and he showed it, but had after the third time stopped spouting in retort his words of pragmatism.

From The Senator's perspective, his son's continuing return to the same fruitless plea reminded him of a floundering colleague who was out of debate points and had fallen to rest upon a fact-devoid, emotional appeal. In his heart, he hoped Dace could bring more to an argument than this tripe. He was, after all, a Lamoureux; and this argument was barely worthy of the least of his esteemed colleagues, most of whom The Senator judged as unimaginative twits swept into office by an equally unimaginative collective of everyday Americans who repeatedly bought into the same type of empty-headed salesmanship which sold them their clothes, overpriced sports shoes, and their cars.

From Dace's current perspective, he had witnessed The Senator's famed, derisive snort many times over the years, but his last one being the twentieth in the last hour was beginning to weigh upon his patience.

"Dace, you're twenty-one, what can you possibly know about love and life?" The Senator asked again. "I was out of school, admitted to the Bar, serving my first term in Congress, and considering the launch of my first run for the Senate before I asked your mother to marry me. And..."

"I know, Dad," Dace interrupted, "and, you had asked your father for his approval before you even discussed the matter with mother."

"That's correct," The Senator said, glancing at his watch. He had been hearing the guests arriving out front for nearly forty-five minutes, and seeing the reflections of headlights come and go in the drive and knew Libby would be growing impatient with this delay; so, he moved to wrap things up for the evening. He realized all he had to do was to keep his son from doing something stupid that night. He'd drive the points home in the morning and close the discussion for good and the rest would be resolved one way or another. He rose from his chair and moved to stand in front of his son still seated on the couch, which clearly signaled an end to the discussion. He placed a hand on Dace's shoulder. "Your next response is going to be that my situation was nearly fifty years ago and times are different now."

Dace visibly deflated. His father continued.

"We've covered the same ground over and over tonight, son; neither of us moving from our original position. We'll talk more of it tomorrow.

You have my word on it. I just ask you say nothing and take no further action this evening."

Dace looked up at his father. The Senator's face was still showing resolve, but Dace believed they would indeed speak of it tomorrow. He nodded. The Senator patted his son' shoulder, confirming the end to that night's communication on that subject between father and son. Dace rose to face his father. He was several inches taller than the older man, yet The Senator carried an extra fifty pounds, mainly of the good-living variety. The topic was an often repeated joke within the family. The public explanation for the paunch was always a little less aristocratic and was jokingly referred to as where The Senator kept his concerns for the collective future of the American people. For seven terms, nearly forty-two years in the Senate on top of six years in the House of Representatives before that, the Lamoureux family mythology had worked for The Senator with the voters of Connecticut, even though in much of the country he was lesser known, and once one arrived in flyover country, lesser liked.

Together, father and son left the office, and while The Senator excused himself to make a stop at the restroom, Dace descended the stairs headed toward the heart of the party already underway. As he rounded the turn at the mid-landing and looked over the assembled crowd, he spotted Sarah with Dave standing near the bar next to the circle of husbands. From his perspective, the pair displayed the only friendly faces in the room. They had not seen him, yet.

Dace smiled to himself because he couldn't locate any of his other high school friends in the crowd, although from the office window he had seen their cars outside. He concluded his mother had sent them off en masse to the back yard fire pit where she had insisted the bottled and canned beer could be self-served from a galvanized washtub filled with ice water. He had specifically invited the group of friends from the area, many of whom he hadn't seen since the summer after high school. They were Navy brats, mostly, as his father called them, and Dace had not extended the invitation because he had much of a fondness for the 'old gang', but because the separated group would give him a refuge to retreat to later on with Sarah and Dave. Dace smiled again at the thought that most of the high school crowd, apart from Dave, probably hadn't paid much attention to the black tie notation on the invitation.

Just then, Sarah spotted Dace paused on the landing, resplendent in his tailored tuxedo and courtly in his demeanor as he overlooked the crowd of well-wishers and friends below him. She smiled to him and he nodded, his eyes conveying the message that he needed to check in with his mother and do some mingling in the Lion's Den before he would be free to come over to officially greet her. Sarah nodded her understanding and her eyes glanced toward the second floor in an unspoken question about the mysterious meeting between father and son. Dace raised his eyebrows in response and mouthed the word 'later' to her. She slowly turned for him and he returned an admiring smile and was comforted she was safely tucked under Dave's wing.

Dace descended the last dozen carpeted steps and completed his entrance onto the marble of the first floor foyer, then moved to kiss his mother on the cheek. Her eyes probed his, a silent search of his well-being, and he responded with nothing but a smile which she could still penetrate. She provided him a quick review of who had arrived and who was obviously being fashionably late. The list for both categories was always the same: friends arrived on time, while dad's political colleagues always enjoyed arriving late, making grand entrances to crowded rooms to inflate their egos and reinforce their masters of the universe self-image. Dace momentarily wondered to which group his father and mother belonged when they arrived at the parties and gatherings of others, then nearly laughed out loud as he dismissed the answer as ridiculously obvious. His father, was, after all, Allard Lamoureux, the Lion of the United States Senate.

His father arrived at the mid-landing as Dace departed his mother's side and began moving into the crowd of gathered well-wishers. The Senator stood in the same place from where Dace had moments earlier surveyed the same scene and watched his son go forth amongst family, friends, and assorted strangers. He marveled at the seeming ease with which Dace handled the social maneuvering. Like his father, but more so, Dace indeed had a gift for making each person he met feel special. He also knew instinctively when to move on, when to linger for that extra moment, how long to hold a handshake and when and where to apply the second hand, and whom to approach next in order. The Senator had observed many elite politicians and captains of industry working a room over the decades, and so few could master the challenges of effectively massaging a crowd as well as his twenty-one-year-old son. He had only seen one person whom he considered equal to Dace in both ability and effectiveness at the endeavor, and that man had gone on to become the President of the United States of America.

However, that man had also been more than twice Dace's current age and quite practiced over twenty years in politics. Not even Jack Kennedy, shortly after whom he had arrived as a freshman in the United States Senate and then worked with several times over those fateful thirty-four months of his presidency, was as comfortable with mixed crowds as was Dace.

Not wishing to steal his son's thunder on his special day, The Senator paused and watched before resuming his descent and collecting his wife from welcoming duties so they could make their way into the party proper and begin mingling with their guests. He knew his colleagues would be arriving soon, so he wanted to be well situated as the king of this particular court, rather than as an anxious host perched at the door awaiting the important late arrivals, but first he wanted to take more note of his guests who were there. And his son.

Across the room, The Senator spotted Sarah standing with Dace's best friend, Dave Saunders. The girl was indeed lovely, and from their previous meetings, smart, and more socially adept than she herself believed. He momentarily wondered how formidable a force she could become with the addition of more confidence which had worked wonders for Libby in those early years. Yet, even in a beautiful designer dress and exquisite sable shrug, she was so obviously of such common stock. Too bad, he thought to himself, then he considered his son's earlier words regarding this girl and momentarily wondered if she could be molded, no, forged was the better word given the heat and fire she would have to face, and become what Dace needed for his future. He just as quickly dismissed that particular thought because accomplishing all that would be required would take years, and if he had his way, she'd not get the time or the chance.

The girl's Lusitanic heritage was obvious, and often confused with Hispanic, an ignorance of which any person of true Portuguese ancestry would quickly disabuse the confused person; she had long, thick, lustrous, black hair and expressive black eyes and her skin possessed a slight olive coloring which some would mistake for a tan. She was unusually tall and lithe for the genetics though, he thought, about five-foot-eight and maybe one-hundred-twenty-five pounds. As a total package, Sarah Avidago was a spectacularly attractive woman and he could understand what Dace saw in that, but to marry this girl? He thought not. A waiter spotted him and climbed the dozen steps up to the landing with two glasses on a silver tray. The Senator removed his glass of Scotch and the one containing white wine for Libby from the tray and thanked the young woman. He then descended the stairs ahead of the girl and crossed the foyer to his wife. Libby was looking deeply at him as she accepted the glass of wine.

"What?" he said in a low tone, lightly clinking his tumbler to her wine glass and then taking a large sip from his drink.

"I've been watching your eyes, Allard," she said. "I know what your mind is thinking." She shot a glance over his shoulder to Sarah. "She's a wonderful girl; beautiful and smart, and quite personable if you'd give her the chance. Sarah is also stronger than you may think, apart from the breeding, she reminds me much of me at that age. The one thing I beg you to remember before you do what you are wont to do, is that the girl makes Dace happy."

"We'll talk about it later, Libby. This is a party." He turned around and his eyes moved across the room. He strategically lifted the glass almost to his lips. "Remember, these people have curious ears."

Dace finally made his way to where Dave and Sarah stood.  First, he gave Dave a handshake which they pulled into a hug and then he turned and welcomed Sarah with a warm hug and light, chaste kiss on the cheek.  Their eyes met.  She understood, but didn't necessarily like it.

Then, unlike most twenty-one year olds celebrating their birthday, Dace asked the bartender for a glass of club soda with a twist of lime.  Alcohol wasn't the only vice of which Dace Lamoureux did not partake.  He didn't smoke and had never taken drugs of any kind, didn't even like aspirin, as he saw any chemical intrusion into his body as a thing to be avoided.  Lastly, he and Sarah had never been intimate.  Not that they hadn't come close to doing so on those nights when Dave would be out all night partying somewhere and they'd be in alone in the apartment.  By each pulling strength and resolve from the other, however, they had been able to abstain.  It was a technique of one relying on the other that he had learned from his parents for so many things couples needed to be in synch about.  Sex had been one of the first conversations Dace and Sarah had had, and both had been relieved to discover, on a college campus in the late 1990s, they each found someone who also saw premarital sex as something which was too freely given and too often regretted.  Sarah believed she had fallen in love with Dace when he had told her that the one thing he wanted in their relationship, no matter how long it lasted, was for there to be no regrets either of them would have to carry through the rest of their life.

Dave took passing note of his friend's continued abstinence, of alcohol, that is, and asked for another bottle of Miller Genuine Draft from the female bartender, which she promptly poured into a clean pilsner glass.  He accepted the drink, thanked her, and then threw his arm around Dace's shoulder.

"It's okay, buddy, you're legal now."

"I know, Dave.  I just don't have a desire for a drink."  He took a draw from his club soda and mimed a phony, exaggerated wincing expression.  "They do use *real carbonation* in this soda water, you know.  Yowsa."

Dave laughed and clinked his glass against Dace's.

"Just because you're a pussy, doesn't mean the rest of us have to suffer.  Tonight we celebrate Dace Lamoureux becoming a man, or so I'm told."

He winked and Dace grimaced.

The husbands were still huddling nearby and taking turns peering surreptitiously over their shoulders at Dave, Dace, and Sarah.  Dave had noted earlier that they had been stealing glimpses of Sarah ever since she and he had crossed the room.  He looked over at the circle.  Now there's three *real* pussies, he thought.  "Shooters, anyone?" he said to them just for fun.

They all looked around the party. Shook their heads in unison.

"Oh yeah," Dave said with a laugh. "I forgot where I am."

Sometime after dinner, Ashley and Ronnie had the idea that there would be no time like the present to test their new IDs. At eight o'clock, just after final bed check, they each grabbed a small duffel, exited their room, padded quietly along the semi-darkened and empty hall and down the stairwell to the first floor, sneaked out the back entry of the dormitory, climbed the ivy-covered brick fence near the service gate, crept along the outside of the wall in the direction of the distant river and then ran across the open ground to the road. They climbed into Ronnie's car which Bobby had idling with its lights off on the narrow shoulder.

"Hey, Bobby," Ashley said as he held the front passenger seat forward and she climbed into the back seat.

"Hey, Ashley," he said before giving Ronnie a deep kiss after she slid into the replaced front passenger seat and leaned over the center console to meet his lips.

Bobby put the car into gear, stepped on the gas and spun some gravel from the shoulder before the rear tires bit on the tar and chip roadway with a momentary squeal and then carried the trio east toward New Orleans. He turned on the headlights when they were out of view. After passing Manresa House several miles down the road, the girls began to relax a little and decided it was time to change into the clothes they had carefully selected and packed into the duffels. Ashley handed Ronnie's bag forward through the space between the seats, then unzipped hers and pulled out clothes, shoes, and a makeup pouch and laid them across the back seat. Bobby adjusted the mirror to an interior rear view and Ronnie promptly slapped him across the shoulder.

"Keep your eyes on the road, Bobby," she said.

"Yeah," said Ashley. "Anything back here is strictly off limits, you pervert." She looked into the rear view mirror and saw his eyes were playful. He winked at her and she tossed him the bird before leaning forward into the front seat and flipping the mirror up into a position which was fully unusable for anything.

"It isn't perverted to look at hot girls if you're a guy," he said. "Hell, I don't even think it would be perverted if you two girls wanted to sneak peeks at each other." He laughed, then reset the mirror to look out onto the roadway behind the car. "I've heard all about you Catholic school girls. All deprived, and such."

"Well, dream on, Bobby," Ronnie said. She was down to her bra and panties and modeled them briefly for him.

Bobby looked her up and down, momentarily forgetting that a similar show was going on in the back seat; one with a performer whose body he hadn't become somewhat familiar with. Yet.

"Those do not look like regulation underwear, Ronnie," he said with an admiring twinkle in his eyes. "I thought you were issued cotton tidy whiteys and locked bras at that school of yours." He winked at her and put his free hand up. "Not that I'm complaining, you understand. But I am glad you two waited until after we passed Manresa to start stripping down. Catching a glimpse of this little show might have caused one or two of those old Jesuits to break their vow of silence; along with other things."

Ronnie rolled her eyes as she stepped into her jeans and then lifted her bottom off the seat so she could pull them up over her butt. She zipped up the fly and buttoned the top, then turned to toss a teasing pout at Bobby. By the time the car was turned north toward the interstate, both girls were dressed in form-fitting jeans, high-heeled sandals, spandex tops and leather jackets. While Ronnie used the visor mirror on her side to finish her hair and makeup, Ashley sat forward and commandeered the rear view from Bobby to do the same.

As a finishing touch, both girls dabbed on some perfume to the napes of their necks, behind each ear, and on the inside of each wrist. They didn't know why those were the spots to put the stuff which, because of school rules, they hardly ever got the chance to wear, but that's where they had seen sultry women in movies apply it.

"Damn fire," Bobby exclaimed. "You two smell better than my granny's sweet tater pie."

"You're such a hick, Bobby," Ashley said from the back seat. "What's wrong with you?"

"That's the way them tourists from up north expect us all to talk down here. When I deliver fresh fish, oysters, and crawdads to the restaurants I always spice up my talkin' with some good bayou flavor. It gives 'em a cheap thrill."

Ronnie's mouth was agape.

"Seriously, Bobby?" Ronnie said finally. "You really go out of your way to make them think we're all stupid down here?"

"You means we ain't?" he said. "Cuz we's definitely all related and inbred, and such."

"Whatever," Ronnie said. She bounced and half-turned on the seat, changed the subject. "Where are we going, Bobby?"

"You'll see."

Forty minutes later, they were veering off the interstate for the Pontchartrain Expressway, passing the Superdome, and finally exiting from the elevated roadway down to St. Charles Avenue. Ten minutes after that, Bobby parked the car around the corner from one of the taverns he had decided to try. He wanted to stay off Bourbon Street and out of The French Quarter entirely on the girls' first outing, concluding it would 'suck big time', to steel one of their favorite off-school-premises sayings, if one of the bartenders over there were to confiscate their new IDs. The season and crowds were ramping up to Mardi Gras and that meant the cops would be running underage stings on the clubs to test the bartenders' vigilance. A week down the road, once the parties were in full swing, everyone - cops, bouncers, and bartenders - would be so busy they won't have time to check IDs.

The girls piled out of Ronnie's car, then Bobby locked the doors. Ronnie and Ashley stood together and posed for him on the sidewalk.

"So, do we look like hot twenty-one-year-olds?" Ashley asked.

Bobby looked them up and down. They both were hot, that anyone could see; but twenty-one? Eh, maybe, he thought. It would take some confidence and luck to totally pull it off.

"Oh yeah," he said. "And then some." He moved between them and whispered conspiratorially. "Just a few words of advice."

Ashley wondered why they should listen to Bobby. He was only nineteen himself, and it was only because of his six-foot-seven stature, the fact he had been shaving since the fifth grade, and he dressed in Bayou chic, that he didn't get carded everywhere he went in southern Louisiana.

"What's that?" Ronnie asked.

"Cut down on the sex-appeal," he said softly, his eyes darting around because someone had once told him that you could never tell when a narc was listening in the city. "Just remember, you want to look like adults, not like refugee hookers from The Quarter."

Ashley stuck out her tongue at him.

"Yeah," he said sarcastically. "Adult, like that."

They began walking, Bobby in the center. He took Ronnie's hand and the three moved out of the darkness of the side street and into the neon-dappled light of that section of St. Charles Avenue. Outside of the tavern, a mixed group of kids hung out together. The males of the crowd stared at the approaching girls and grinned broadly, but when they noticed Bobby, they tucked their hanging tongues back into their mouths so as not to offend the big country boy. Apart from his height, Bobby had a lean frame which hard work had filled with muscles; and even though he had shaved two days ago, he already sported a scraggly, down-home growth which gave him a rakish and slightly dangerous appearance.

Ashley returned the last of the lingering looks from the group with an uppity snort, then cast her gaze right through them, almost tripping on the broken and uneven sidewalk. She wasn't totally comfortable walking in high heels even though she and Ronnie had been practicing in their room for several weeks, and the stumble caused the last of the ogling to morph into chuckling. Even though Bobby's look quickly silenced the laughter, Ashley was immediately reminded she was just a sixteen going on seventeen-year-old kid. However, knowing the success of that night's outing depended upon she and Ronnie pulling off an act to convince people they were more than four years older than they truly were, she took a deep breath and did her best to banish the lack of confidence from her demeanor as they passed the street monkeys and walked through the door and into the tavern.

The jukebox inside was playing loudly. A stratus layer of yellow-gray smoke hung in the air above the crowd like a false ceiling while little trails rose to grow it from cigarettes scattered among the patrons. The crowd was two deep at the bar, both pool tables in the back were in use and circled by observers, and most of the tables were taken. From the looks of the crowd, it was mostly locals with a scattering of tourists thrown in for ambience. A few male heads turned at the opening of the door, checked out the two girls, but when they absorbed the image of Bobby moving in behind them, quickly went back to their conversations.

Ashley and Ronnie stayed close to Bobby as they flowed into the barroom mix. Out of the corner of her eye, Ashley noticed the female bartender looking them over. Ashley tossed the woman a snotty look and dragged Bobby and Ronnie farther down the bar to where the younger, male bartender was working. Bobby found an opening and wedged himself into it. Leaning forward and resting an elbow on the bar, he ordered a bottle of Dixie, dropped three dollars on the bar when it appeared, then turned to let the girls order on their own. The male bartender leaned forward, but neither girl moved into the spot Bobby had cleared, and like Mississippi River mud, people flowed back to fill the hole.

Ashley's eyes darted frantically from Bobby to Ronnie as she watched their opportunity quickly fading. Ronnie was just standing there, wide eyed, not saying a word. Bobby stood back near the first row of tables and chuckled to himself, then drained some of the Dixie down his throat. Ashley silently prayed she didn't look as frightened and confused as she felt and as did Ronnie at that moment. All the planning, all the thought, all the talking and role playing, and they never had taken a moment to consider what they would order when they finally had the chance?

"What he's having, a Dixie," Ashley finally said.

Ronnie held up two fingers toward the bartender indicating she'd have the same and he nodded and moved to one of the refrigerated cabinets behind the bar and removed two more brown bottles of Dixie. Thinking they were in the clear, both girls breathed a heavy sigh, unheard over Billy Idol wailing about his little sister's white wedding on the jukebox, and started to relax. Until, that is, they saw the female bartender sliding down the bar in their direction, followed closely by her male colleague now holding nothing but a bar rag in his hands.

The woman stretched out her arm across the bar and repeatedly coiled and uncoiled her finger at the girls, her long, sparkly, red polished nail beckoning them to step closer. When they both moved up to the crowded bar, the woman spoke.

"You girls have any ID?" she asked with a sly smile.

Ashley and Ronnie had played this scene through in their minds, and they each reached calmly into their small shoulder bag and pulled out the phony Louisiana driver's licenses, and offered them with as much confidence as they could muster, just like they'd seen on television. The woman snatched Ronnie's out of her trembling hand, and as she did, Ashley thought about holding firm to hers just in case the woman tried to confiscate them. Even if they didn't get served and got kicked out, she'd still have the ID, Ashley thought. She tightly held the card; until the woman pulled it from her grip, that was.

Both girls watched as the woman closely scrutinized each license. She held it to the light, angled it to view the color changes on the authentication holograms. She next looked hard at both girls, studied the photos and descriptions. They had each used the other's home address, just in case something turned up and someone came looking, but beyond that and the age the licenses reflected, they were totally accurate. Then she removed a little device about the size of a penlight out of her pocket and shined it onto each license, illuminating under ultraviolet light a series of normally invisible logos. Ashley's heart was beating hard, and she knew so was Ronnie's. The woman looked at them both one last time, her eyes darting back and forth, hoping they would fold; but her bluff didn't work when the girls held fast.

Defeated by the perfection of the genuine documents, she reluctantly handed the licenses back with an annoyed smile which belied her disappointment that she not caught a couple of phonies or better yet, beat a police sting, and nodded reluctantly to her coworker who then brought them each an ice-cold bottle of Dixie and flashed five fingers at them.

"Glasses?" he asked across the noise in the bar.

"What?" Ashley said, leaning toward him.

"Do you want glasses?"

She stared blankly at him.

"To drink out of. You know, glasses?"

"Oh, no," she laughed away the final bit of nervousness and handed over a five dollar bill. "Keep the change."

He gave her a small grin, shook his head because each beer cost two-fifty and walked away.

The girls moved closer to where Bobby was standing to observe them, clinked their bottles together and took a drink. The faces they made at the taste of their first beer made Bobby laugh.

"Don't worry, ladies, it gets better as you keep going," he said.

My name is William Langdon, and I'm a private investigator, a P.I., in the one of the best cities in the world, New Orleans. Together with my wife, Sandy, we run William Langdon Investigations from our building on Magazine Street. Sandy was an attorney, still is, I suppose. I'm an ex-cop. We'll get to all that in time.

To provide you with mental images until we do, allow me to describe myself as being a relatively large man at six-foot-six, about two-hundred-sixty pounds. I was raised in the small town of Sheboygan, Wisconsin, moved to Chicago after graduating high school and became a cop with the CPD when I was twenty. I came to New Orleans a couple of years ago, by way of the Cayman Islands in the Caribbean. Over the last five or six years, I've grown a bit of a paunch, and have thinning brown hair worn short, and brown eyes. With that burned into your brain, you're no doubt going to wonder how I landed someone like Sandy, who is absolutely gorgeous. You'll figure it out in time.

Sandy is five-foot-seven, one-hundred-twenty pounds, with light brown hair which she wears slightly past her shoulders and the most beautiful, expressive, deep blue eyes you've ever seen. She's got all her curves in all the right places and legs that just don't quit, but do end at beautiful, size seven feet. She looks incredible in heels. Heck, Sandy looks incredible in anything.

We met inauspiciously on the first day of high school after I made a joke about her name and she caught up to me in the hallway after class and told me what a jerk I was and that I shouldn't delude myself into thinking I was the first one to make the joke about her name. Sandy Beach? Come on. We first dated the summer between our junior and senior years, and lost touch after graduation. Years later we literally bumped into each other in the lobby of the Cook County Courthouse in Chicago, and both of us being single at the time, after I helped her pick up her things from the terrazzo floor we took a second run at a relationship. That one abruptly ended when I took an early medical retirement a year later and left the country. For Sandy and myself, however, the third time proved to indeed be the charm when she walked into the bar I co-owned on Grand Cayman in early 1995, and the rest, as they say, is history.

Just before sunset on the fourteenth of February 1998, Sandy and I shuffled across the uneven dirt floor of a dimly lit, ancient warehouse in trail of one of our clients who was giving us a little tour. There had been some work to be done at our office which had come first that day, and we had a romantic Valentine's Day evening planned which I was eager to get to, but Sandy had accepted this little tour invitation and where Sandy went, William follows. Or, something like that.

The city had experienced the fifth stormy day in a row, but by mid-afternoon, the low clouds yielded to a clearing line in the west which offered the welcome promise of a seasonally cool and dry evening. It was going to be a beautiful night for a parade, dinner at a favorite little spot in The French Quarter, and a stroll through the old, cobbled streets. Then home, just Sandy and me.

The nearly constant rainfall over the last work week appeared to have located and penetrated every possible leak in the old building's roof and had created expansive puddles on the compacted dirt floor. The rains had also saturated the normally soggy soil of the entire metropolitan area, much of which lies below sea level to begin with, to the point I doubted these puddles inside were going anywhere anytime soon. Because of the building's inadequate ventilation system, the air held an acrid, earthy smell of decay, as did much of the rest of the waterlogged city across the Mississippi.

As we wove our way between the colorful Mardi Gras floats, many fronted with massive, humanized faces attached to wildly contorted animal bodies, I was primarily focused on keeping my new shoes clean and dry. My wife, Sandy, however, appeared totally engrossed in the ongoing monologue of our tour guide, who was giving us this insider's view of the nearly perpetual home to the ornate floats belonging to one of New Orleans' oldest and most storied krewes. Next week the nearly fifteen-hundred members of the Krewe of Bacchus would come for these rolling monstrosities of the Carnival season, and they would breathe in - if one believed these grotesque plastic faces could draw breath - the relatively fresh air of the city for the first time in a year.

The client chattering away was a young attorney with a respected and multi-generational downtown firm for whom we had just wrapped up a small investigation. Upon our first meeting about a year ago, she had taken an immediate liking to Sandy, but seemed to have a bit of a different opinion of me. C'est la vie.

I probably wouldn't ever be the woman's favorite P.I., but Tracey Walker certainly wouldn't ever be my favorite client. In my opinion, she was the personification of the most dangerous paradigm for an attorney: ambitious, young, ruthless, and a know-it-all. Sandy, however, really liked her for some reason, and always reminded me to play nice whenever I interacted with Tracey. As suspenders added to her belt instructions, Sandy also insisted on being present whenever there was to be a face-to-face meeting including myself and the woman. Being closely monitored by my loving and loved wife, I always did the best I could to be sociable to Tracey Walker, but that didn't mean I couldn't toss a few good natured jibes her way from time to time. It's part of how I roll, and besides, if she liked Sandy, I came with the package.

On the positive side for Tracey Walker's career trajectory, she truly was smart, savvy to office politics, and relentless once she got an adversary in her sights. She was a tireless advocate for her clients, and in this man's humble opinion, that's the single key attribute one should look for when hiring an attorney. To make it through law school, they all have to be smart and driven and competitive, but advocacy comes from the heart, and I'll take heart over brain eight out of ten times. She was also easy on the eyes, which, sexist and shallow as it sounds on the surface, in the real world works for both men and women in any career field. Tracey was tall, thin, yet curvy, with bewitching green eyes and, according to Sandy, naturally blonde hair, which fell just above her shoulders. To top it all off, so to speak, she carried her own personal floatation devices should the airliner she be riding in ever have to put down in the middle of the ocean. Not that I've noticed.

More recently she had been accepted as a member of this particular krewe, whose parade was scheduled to pass down St. Charles Avenue in the Garden District and into downtown New Orleans on the morning of Fat Tuesday, the last day of the Mardi Gras season. Over the last several weeks, the floats had all been uncovered, cleaned and readied to roll out ten days hence, and our guide was going to be riding one; waving and tossing treats and the much-coveted strings of beads in the traditional gold, green, and purple of the season to throngs of cheering, curbside partygoers.

Sandy and I had wrangled a second floor porch spot along St. Charles Avenue for Fat Tuesday with friends, and I was frankly looking forward to the day of feasting, drinking, and otherwise absorbing the party atmosphere with Sandy and good people. Our perch would be out of bead tossing range, but we'd also be safely off the crowded street. Our guide was understandingly excited about having been accepted as a member of this particularly prestigious and historic krewe, and when we had stopped by her office earlier, she extended the invitation to share that excitement with Sandy, and by extension, me by giving us this little tour.

We had gone to see Tracey that afternoon so we could hand deliver an investigative report on some low-life who wouldn't pay his child support claiming indigency, but who had enough money to support and house not one, but two mistresses in downtown apartments and maintain a fifty-four foot power boat docked at the South Shore Harbor Marina on Lake Pontchartrain. Tracey had quickly scanned the document while we stood waiting in her office in the One Shell Square tower, and after she was satisfied we had gathered enough information to drag the shirker into the Parish courthouse on a Contempt warrant, she had asked if we had any plans for the evening.

I knew immediately the question was less about us than something Tracey had in mind, but before I could pull my wife to safety, Sandy had told Tracey we planned to walk the four blocks to Canal Street and wait for the evening's parade while doing some people watching or perhaps kill time at Canal Place doing some window shipping, and then walk a few more blocks into the French Quarter for dinner at The Gumbo Shop, then home. It was our two-year-old ritual for the first Saturday night of Carnival, which this year just happened to coincide with Valentine's Day.

'That sounds wonderful' Tracey had said absently as she put things in order on her already overly organized desk. It was her stock and trade reply to most anything said unrelated to a case, and I had seriously wondered at that moment if I had relayed our plan as: I am going to run a hot bath when I get home, then sink into it and open my veins with a razor, if she would have parroted the very same line. The conundrum in verbalizing that would be that I would never be certain if she just hadn't listened to me, as usual, or if she would have been on-board with the plan.

Instead, I had kept my mouth shut as she looked at her watch, performed some mental calculations, then offered to give us this little tour. Accepting the invitation had meant we needed to give up our primo, and validated, parking spot in the garage of One Shell Square and drive across the river to where we currently wandered: this rat-and-bug-infested, smelly building with the Swiss Cheese roof. Then, upon our return to the city, pay for parking - if we can find any - someplace else while we attended the parade and ate dinner. It also meant before Sandy and I could watch the Knights of Sparta krewe pass by on Canal Street to officially open our Mardi Gras season and then enjoy a nice, quiet meal in The Quarter, I'd have to endure an hour or so of Tracey Walker chattering away about *her* krewe's history and relating stories behind the various floats, all while keeping my new Oxfords clean of mud in this indoor swamp. It wasn't really that bad, but you get the idea of how quickly my mood can sometimes turn tepid.

Sandy appeared fascinated with the history and the name dropping of which celebrity had ridden which float during which year. Truth be told, I was kind of into it too, once we got going, but to show too much excitement would tarnish my cherished and hard-forged image of being standoffishly cool about such things. So, I took it all in, adopted an edgy posture, shot off a few barbed quips in Tracey's direction from time to time, and generally dawdled behind like a kid headed back to the daily grind of classes after the best summer ever. Yeah, I was too cool for school.

The previous year had been my first exposure to New Orleans' Mardi Gras parades and the carnival atmosphere the city adopts for the season which, to the local hardcores, officially began a week earlier with the Krewe du Vieux parade through The Quarter and ended at midnight seventeen days after that, on the Tuesday before Ash Wednesday. Fat Tuesday is what they call the last day of Carnival season and it is the literal translation of Mardi Gras. Sandy had been down in New Orleans for some of the season's festivities twenty years ago with her low-life first husband, what's his name, but I had never been.

While I've read that some historical purists argue the Carnival season really begins in January with the Bal Masque of the Twelfth Night Revelers on the Feast of the Epiphany and the ride of the Phunny Phorty Phellows in a decorated street car along St. Charles Avenue, much of the outside world considers the season in New Orleans as the condensed schedule of these next ten days ending with Fat Tuesday. People can argue over the technicalities of the beginning, but nobody argues that it all ends at the stroke of midnight on the day which dawns as Ash Wednesday, the beginning of Lent on the Catholic calendar. Regardless of what one calls this time of year around the world, Mardi Gras, Carnival, or something else, the season and New Orleans combine for one of the northern hemisphere's biggest series of parties, and I'm don't intend to spend any of it arguing about when to start celebrating.

As the tour progressed, I lagged further and further behind Sandy and Tracey. I had been enjoying immensely the poking of our hostess or asking her to repeat something she had just said, throwing off her obviously, well-rehearsed rhythm. By the third or fourth interruption, however, she had begun to simply ignore me, and even Sandy had stopped giving me grimaced looks over her shoulder which I, in accordance with my extremely adorable nature, had shrugged away in feigned innocence. Something told me, however, adorable or not, I'd be hearing about my little displays of petulance a bit later.

In truth, what was causing me to lag behind was neither Tracey's ignoring of me, nor the content of her talk, nor being too cool for school, but rather because I was finding the more the shadows crept in as building settled into the coming darkness, the more I was becoming haunted by the ghosts of another time.

The oversize incandescent bulbs hanging at the end of single black cords from the ceiling trusses had moments before only been supplemental to the last rays of sunshine which flowed through the ample skylights. Now, with that sunlight gone, the bulbs were left to handle the lighting duty on their own. They cast scattered, yellowish, mote-filled cones of light, which, in their lack of connection, created voids of blackness. As I paused there motionless, Sandy and Tracey were now several cones of light away from where I stood, but more than a thousand miles from where my mind wandered.

Memories flooded through me and even brought the hairs on the back of my neck to notice; and then, in an instant, in my mind, I was back there, reliving the events in another warehouse which took place on my last night as an active-duty narcotics detective with the Chicago Police Department.

My partner, Eric Mendez and I had been inside that warehouse several times before, doing simple recon and surveillance. That night, I looked down a cross aisle to watch him move into a crouched position along the opposite wall. The building was one of those architectural oddities drawn to fit the lot, which in that case was roughly triangular. We were halfway to the back. He nodded across to me. Because of the building's design, as we moved further toward the triangle's apex, the aisles of palletized racking and shelving grew shorter. When we started our move down opposing walls, there was roughly one hundred feet between us. By the time we entered the nearing edge of the light, we'd be separated by less than twenty feet. There was no center aisle splitting the triangle, so this was the best approach to take with only two detectives and no backup on scene: down those two long, dark aisles toward the apex.

As we drew closer to the illuminated point of the building, every exit to the outside now lay behind us. I signaled down the row to Eric. We began to move again; our weapons were drawn, and we each carried a back up piece in an ankle holster. Low voices came out of the light ahead and were swallowed by the darkness behind.

Just as we began to move again and without warning, angry flashes of white light and noise erupted from above. I reflexively dove behind a pallet of auto parts. Just as suddenly as it had been shattered, darkness reclaimed the silence. Instants evolved in slow motion and as I shifted into a defensive posture and listened for any telltale of the shooters, the darkness gave forth with nothing but the faint echo of my partner's moans. I began a careful move down the row toward Eric, sticking close to the stacks of boxed items and found him there, crumpled onto a pallet containing bags of oil absorbent. His face was an ashen orb and his eyes were wide and searching, but rapidly growing dim. I knelt down by him and assessed his condition while keeping watch for another attack. Eric had tried to speak and I leaned down to hear, but nothing came but wet, labored gasps, and then he was silent.

Today, for an instant, standing there amongst the Mardi Gras floats, I again felt the rush of adrenalin, smelled the cordite and blood, heard Eric's raspy moans, and felt a chill flow through my soul as if someone had just walked across my grave.

I took a deep breath; focused on the moment and fought my way back to this warehouse in this time. I shook off the memories and the visions of Eric dying, and again left that past behind. Then, like a frightened kid, I hustled to catch up to my wife, all the while stealing glances over my shoulders as the ghosts retreated again into the engulfing darkness. When I caught up, I took Sandy's hand in mine.

"You okay?" she said, her eyes probing and concerned. Sandy had seen that reflected mask before on many nights. "You look like you've seen a ghost, Will."

"I did," I said.

Sandy squeezed my hand. It was all I ever needed from her. She was my anchor, my lighthouse, my safe port, and she knew not to press me. Her eyes stayed fixed on my profile as I focused on Tracey's monologue and tried to remain in the moment. I suddenly felt sadness for this group of colorful, fanciful floats, which spent year after year locked up in this hot, dusty, old warehouse to be let out on one day to show themselves to the world, only to then be locked back inside this little prison. Eh, sucks to be a float, I thought, and at that internal utterance could tell I had made it back, this time.

"Hmm," I said.

"What?" Sandy asked.

"I said, 'Hmm'."

"Hmm, what?" she asked.

"I hope I don't come back in the next life as a Mardi Gras float."

"What?"

"Seems like such a lonely existence," I said. "You know I'm a people person. Right, Sandy?" I tossed a look toward Tracey.

"Geeze, Will," Sandy said, shaking her head and releasing my hand. "Can't you ever be serious."

"I have spent my whole life being serious, Sandy. Well, except for those years in the Caymans which were mostly wall-to-wall partying," I said. "You know me, honey, scratch just beneath the hard candy shell and you hit...," I smiled at her and winked before continuing, "...creamy milk chocolate..."

"Yeah, I know, and then a soft caramel center," my wife finished for me. "I've heard it before."

"Hmm," I said.

Sandy shook her head again, the sharing of our private joke welding me firmly to her and the present reality, and then she shot me a wry smile as she moved to catch up with Tracey, who through it all had just kept walking and talking to the empty air. As I watched my wife move, I realized she never even knew how important her just being there for me to reach for was to me. I followed along again, my thoughts turning to the more pleasant matters of the parade and culinary delights of The Gumbo Shop to come.

Even before we moved here, I had always loved to come to the city of New Orleans. The food, the culture, the music, the history, all combined for me to make the city and its surrounds into one magical place to visit, however, I always thought it would be a difficult place to live. When Sandy had initially suggested we leave the Caymans and begin a fresh life here, I was initially reluctant, but eventually bought into the idea, following a little unsolicited marital advise from my old friend, Teddy.

When I changed the focus from my desires to considering hers, I realized my hard-driving, lawyer wife had become restless living the numbing sameness of my beach bum, island lifestyle, albeit in the relatively lucrative reality as part-owner of a popular tavern in a wealthy resort area of the southern Caribbean.

Southern Louisiana had its negatives: the heat, the humidity, bugs the size of Volkswagens, but those can all be defeated by modern technology, and plenty of chemicals in the case of even the heartiest of pests. No place is perfect, and if you focus mostly on the negatives and forget about all the positives, no matter where you call home can quickly become just another place to live. Sandy and I strive to not let that happen here in New Orleans. This is *our* place now; Sandy's and mine. The Big Easy; and we try to make the most of every day here. Besides, if it gets too hot or muggy or buggy here, we can always catch a flight the Caymans for a week or two at our place on the beach at Snipe Point.

At its core, New Orleans is a city of contrasts. It thrives on coming alive with revelers, yet seems hopelessly rooted to the mysteries of the dead. It struggles to claw its way into the future, but ferociously clings to the past. New Orleans has intentionally cultivated the imagery as the singular destination for debauchery and excess and yet remains constrained by the inviolable foundations of the Church. To an old Catholic school kid like me, New Orleans embodies the dichotic mysteries that are the Faith's embracing of sin and belief in the power of forgiveness leading to salvation. The city fits me like a comfortable, well-worn, old shoe, and I love it.

I remained close to Sandy and Tracey, who were now standing at the side of a large, multilevel float in mostly red and white paint with a giant, clown head on the front. I had to admit, as lonely as it would be to be to wake up in the next life as a Mardi Gras float, when loaded with characters in costume interacting with cheering crowds, they did, for those hours, become larger than life on the streets of the city. That has to be worth something, to a float, I imagined. As I scanned the area while Tracey continued to prattle on about this or that, the shadows cast over some of the faces on the floats gave them an almost demonic appearance. A few of them suddenly gave me a case of the serious creeps. Sandy glanced at me and nodded. I got the message. Some of them gave her the creeps too.

I tuned into Tracey's ongoing monologue, because the stop seemed to be the herald of something important; perhaps even The End, I thought. I retook Sandy's hand.

"The symbiotic relationship between the Church and Carnival season, which has evolved into the amorphous and all-inclusive term of Mardi Gras, dates back, as with many religious holidays, to the early days of Christendom and the attempts to induce pagan or multi-theistic peoples into the realm of the Faithful. Carnival season equates to the mid-February *Lupercalia* celebrated by the ancient Romans. As the Church was growing in acceptance in Rome during the first centuries A.D., early leaders of the faith determined it was easier to incorporate parts of the pagan rituals into Christianity rather than abolish them outright and expect voluntary conversion. So, Carnival was born and became a period of abandon and merriment which ended with the beginning of Lent, the forty days of soul searching and repentance before Easter which corresponded to Jesus' forty days of fasting in the desert before His crucifixion. Carnival is the very essence of the Catholic Church's foundational paradigm involving the remorse and guilt of committed sin leading to confession and penance and thus, ultimately to forgiveness and redemption."

"Hey, I was just thinking the same thing," I said and Sandy shot me a look. "Really." Since it had been a while, I thought I'd toss Tracey an irreverent quip, so I did: "We Catholics sure do love our precious guilt, though."

Sandy dropped my hand and jabbed me in the ribs with her elbow, then grabbed my hand again. Tracey ignored me and assumed an unnatural pose with her arm extended parroting the move of a *The Price Is Right* model. I cocked my head to one side, felt a thought tumble from my brain and into my throat. Sandy squeezed my hand. Hard. I swallowed the thought.

"This is the float I'll be riding next week," Tracey said with a face which then lit up like a three-year-old whose wait to see Santa was just about over. "Of course, I'll be in costume."

"Hidden behind a mask, I hope," I said with an impish smile.

That time, Tracey shot me a look. I shrugged. My wife appeared quizzical about my remark. I wasn't even sure why I said it or what I had really meant by the jibe. Perhaps that's why Tracey feels like she does about me. Maybe verbalizing whatever falls out of my brain was a character flaw in yours truly. I dunno. Tracey waved it off a moment later and invited Sandy - yeah, Sandy only - up onto the stages of the float. I stood and watched them climb aboard, mesmerized by the glimpses of my wife's legs as she went higher and higher and suddenly realized sometimes it is good *not* to be invited. When the pair reached the main platform about eight feet above the ground, I gave Sandy a wink. She returned it with a smile and a very subtle movement which this husband could, and certainly did appreciate.

Ten long minutes later, as we exited the warehouse and made our way to our cars, I noticed darkness had also brought a heaven of stars high above the muted lights of the city. I could see the reflections of the lights of The Quarter and the downtown area shimmering across the glassine surface of the Mississippi River; and could feel a damp coolness coming with the night. The paddleboat Natchez was just then pulling away from its mooring at the Esplanade Plaza; its steam-powered calliope on the roof playing a festive tune.

I walked ahead of the women across the gravel lot. Sandy spoke quietly with Tracey while I leaned against the hood of my car and took in the sights and wafting sounds from across the river. I was certain Sandy wasn't defending me the way some women have wont to explain away or beg forgiveness for their husband's uncouth behavior. No, my Sandy normally did not even address my behavior and was most likely just congratulating Tracey for the honor of being invited to join the krewe and thanking her for the tour, leaving apologies needing to be delivered, if any, to me at some later date. In a couple of minutes, when we would be alone in our car, she'd let me know what I had decided on that account tonight.

Standing there, waiting on my wife, I checked my cell phone for the time: 5:15. I had to use the phone because I have never worn a wristwatch because I hate anything confining me. Not wearing a watch was a habit which used to tick off my CPD partners in the days before pocket-sized cell phones. One night, when I was a rookie, my first partner and giver of marital advice, Teddy, and I were riding a blue and white on patrol. I was filling in a report form and asked if he had noted the time we arrived on the last scene. It was a simple question desiring a simple answer, but in response, Teddy suddenly wheeled the car into a K-Mart parking lot and pulled up in front of the store. He said nothing to me before he got out of the squad and went inside. A few minutes later he came out carrying a white, paper bag marked with a big red K. He removed the cheap watch he had purchased, checked the time against his, and already knowing I wouldn't wear the thing, tore off the band and handed me the bare timepiece, which he told me to keep in my pocket.

Then Teddy looked me straight in the eye and told me if I ever asked him again what time it was he was going to shoot me. I looked back into his eyes and even as good friends as we already had become, I truly believed he would follow through with the threat; so, from that night to the day I bought my first cell phone, I carried that watch in my pocket everywhere I went. I still have the thing and keep it in a small box on my desk. Teddy and I remain very close friends, and while we haven't been partners for years, I have never again asked him for the time. Just to be on the safe side.

Teddy is perhaps my best friend in the world, apart from Sandy. I would do anything for him, and him for me. Teddy also loves Sandy, and he still carries several pieces of lead in his body to prove it, but that's another story for another time. I first introduced them to each other when Sandy and I began dating for the second time. In Chicago.

Teddy was then freshly divorced from his second wife and playing out the role of the older bull in that well-known joke, I was a vice squad detective and Sandy was a rapidly rising criminal attorney. I've often wondered, and teased her relentlessly about the term 'criminal attorney' being unnecessarily redundant, and while in some cases was certain it was, in Sandy's case it certainly wasn't.

My wife is probably the most scrupulously honest person I've ever known. She won't even let me pad my own expense reports. Our Chicago get together fell apart when I was offered and accepted an early medical retirement after Eric was killed and the perps wound up paying the ultimate penalty. I not only lost my friend and partner that night, but also a chunk of my soul; and not only because I was the only one who left that warehouse that night alive.

I left the force, and the city of Chicago, late one night shortly after and haven't been back since. I left the whole damn country behind, in fact, taking a job with another former cop friend who had retired to Grand Cayman and owned a tourist bar on the beach with his new wife. Eventually, I bought into the place, got myself a little shack on the beach on Snipe Point on nearby Little Cayman, and reigned in my drinking. I was happy as that proverbial clam, and then I looked up one day and Sandy was standing on the other side of my bar.

She had taken a short vacation after a rather stressful case representing a corrupt state legislator caught with his hand in the till and another part of his anatomy in a cooperating federal witness. The vacation turned into a short leave of absence as we began to spend days and nights together, and finally, after we got married on the beach one morning several weeks later, turned into an early retirement from the practice of criminal law. After another year or so of island living, we decided it was time for a change, as I've already told you.

Don't get me wrong, living in flip-flops and shorts is a great way of living life, but after a while, the world claws at you to accomplish something more than selling tourists overpriced umbrella drinks. By the time Sandy suggested we get back to the real world, I'd had several years of emotional recovery under my belt and had been itching to get back into investigative work, although I knew no cop shop in the country was going to hire me. Sandy was still burned out on the practice of law but needed to do something more than count waves and help out at the bar on occasion, so we decided to open our own little private investigation agency and settled upon New Orleans as the place to do it, mainly because we both loved visiting the place. That's mostly the whole story of how we ended up here, standing in the cooling night air outside of a Mardi Gras float warehouse across the river from probably the most fascinating city in the world.

I turned my head to see what was keeping the women and Sandy appeared to be finishing up with Tracey. They hugged briefly, looked in my direction and shared a laugh, then Sandy turned and walked toward me. Tracey tossed a brief wave and I returned it. I opened the passenger door for my wife and before she got in she gave me a kiss. I took that to mean I would not be needing to send flowers or chocolates to Tracey's office on Monday. I walked around the back of the car and slipped into the driver's seat, reached to turn the key, and then stopped and looked at Sandy.

"You know, I really didn't mean anything by that mask remark," I said. "It was a joke."

"I know," Sandy said and her profile morphed, then as she swiveled in her seat, revealed a huge smile. "Tracey knows, too." The smile turned a little conspiratorial. "She told me she loves keeping you guessing. That's her game, Will. You poke her, she never reacts as you think she should, and that keeps you off balance. She thinks it's hilarious."

Now it was my turn to smile as I looked out the windshield and watched the tail lights of Tracey's champagne BMW move through the gate. Nicely played, counselor, I thought.

"Is that so?" I said. "Hmm."

"Oh, boy," Sandy said, turning forward in her seat and pulling on the seat belt. "Maybe I shouldn't have told you. You know you're adorable when you think you're being bad, but now you're just going to be worse."

Sandy knew what I was thinking; and yes, that I would now escalate the game on the next occasion it was necessary for me to spend time with Tracey Walker. Perhaps it was those years of being a cop, mostly hanging around with other cops combined with a lifetime of being a hopeless cynic and irredeemable wisecracker, which had made me so good in the boyish game of 'breaking balls'. Not only was I an incessant player, but I judged a person by how they took to the game, how well they received the jibes and how good they were at giving them out. To me, it was a measure of character, and to my personal dismay, Tracey's stock had just ratcheted up a notch or two in the ranking. She had been pulling one over on me for the last year, and that doesn't happen very often.

"Chalk up one for Tracey," I said, licking my fingertip and making an imaginary vertical mark in the air.

"Now don't you dare let her know I told you that," Sandy warned. "Because if you do, she'll never trust me again. I just thought it was time you knew." She giggled.

I reached across and found that secret spot that makes her jump and squeal, which she did. I grinned.

"Don't worry, honey. It'll be our little secret," I said and touched the spot again. "If she finds out somehow, you can always tell her I tortured it out of you."

I withdrew my hand and turned the key in the ignition and put the car into gear while she settled down again.

"Ready for some fun?" I asked. "We should just make it in time to get a decent spot for the parade. Then how about a few beers and some gumbo before going home for a romantic evening?" I grinned in anticipation of the next line. "I think a *Maude* marathon is on TV Land."

Sandy unfastened her seatbelt, then leaned over and gave me a deep kiss, her hand finding one of my many secret spots: the inside of my shirt collar. Of course, I don't squeal and jump, which I believe is inappropriate for a man, and which she seems to find consistently disappointing for some reason. She pulled away and looked into my eyes.

"You *almost* read my mind, Will," she said, her expression deep and serious.

I returned the look into my wife's blue eyes, then reached over and put my hand on her leg as she settled back into her seat. How I love Sandy's legs; I'll use any excuse to have my hands or my eyes on them.

"Okay, how about *one* beer and some gumbo, and maybe I'll turn on *Maude* much, much later tonight?"

"That's better," she said, her eyes twinkling at me in that special way they do.

I hit the gas and accelerated toward the gate.

Ten minutes later, we rolled across the Greater New Orleans Bridge across the Mississippi and twenty minutes after that I had found us a spot in a cramped parking lot near the Jackson Brewery. We gathered a few items from the trunk and began our walk through Jackson Square into The Quarter. I guessed we could find a few feet of sidewalk along the parade route on Canal near Chartres and then beat any crowds to the Gumbo Shop on Saint Peter Street.

Sandy and I walked hand in hand through a thinning crowd in the square, mixed in with the flow along Chartres Street for six blocks and took our place amidst a growing throng lining both sides of Canal Street. I noted that when we passed through the Jackson Square the street artists and palm readers who normally packed up at sunset had extended their hours to capture some of the nighttime Carnival celebrants who would undoubtedly return to The Quarter after the parade.

All around us on the east side of Canal Street, fathers held kids on their shoulders, lovers held hands, and everyone buzzed with anticipation. Beads of all sizes and designs in the gold, green, and purple colors of Carnival, hung from the necks of almost everyone. Sandy and I sported a few strings we had bought for the celebration since last year we hadn't been quick or lucky enough to grab any of the aggregated tons which had been thrown from floats before they hit the ground, and I'm not putting anything around my neck that's touched the streets or gutters of the city of New Orleans.

Cops on foot and horseback roamed the streets which had been closed for the parade. They were watching for troublemakers, and my ex-cop's eyes also scanned the crowd for predator types, mostly pickpockets who can and do make a decent living during Mardi Gras. I didn't feel for my wallet at the thought, knowing a good pickpocket would always be watching the crowd for that tell.

We soon heard the approach of the Knights of Sparta and for the half hour after it arrived, we watched the passing of brass bands, floats, a wide variety of paraders in getups from painted-face skeletons to carnival royalty in robes adorned with fur and feathers. Sandy snagged a set of beads on the fly and promptly flung them around my neck, pulling me down for an unusually sensuous public kiss. As the end of the parade passed our spot, we sneaked around the corner into The Quarter and down to the Gumbo Shop where I had seafood and okra gumbo and Sandy ordered hers in the chicken and andouille variety. As promised, I had one beer and Sandy ordered a glass of Pinot Noir which she barely touched.

On the way back to the car after dinner, I stopped in at the St. Louis Cathedral and lit a couple of candles for my grandparents. It was a ritual I performed every time I have been in the area. There's something about the ambience of that old church which reminds me of the Sunday's when I was a kid and we'd go to Mass with grandma and grandpa. Whether or not they are now someplace where they know or care what I'm doing in their memory, I always envision them smiling down on me every time I light a candle in their memory, so it is good for my soul.

We were home an hour later and by the time we hit the bedroom, the only thing Sandy had on were last year's store bought beads.

The Langdon Mardi Gras season had officially opened.

Ashley and Ronnie left Bobby behind playing pool in the bar and rode the St. Charles line streetcar to Canal Street then wandered down Bourbon Street into The Quarter. The crowds were milling about and almost every imaginable variety of music was wafting from every other doorway. People wore Mardi Gras beads and masks adorned with feathers and everyone seemed to be in a party mood. Cop cars sat at every intersection, and police officers on foot and horseback patrolled the edges of the street scene.

"This is so freaking cool, Ash," Ronnie said as they walked along and mixed with the crowds along Rue Bourbon.

Ashley smiled at her best friend. It was indeed freaking cool, she thought. They had been served at two bars so far, the fake IDs were working like a key to a lock, opening the door for them to adult fun. For no particular reason, at that moment Ashley spun around three times, her arms wide and a huge smile on her face. At the end of the third turn, she stumbled and caught herself on Ronnie's shoulder.

"I am feeling weird, Ronnie," Ashley said. "Drunk, I guess."

"We've barely started, Ash, I want to get totally wasted." Ronnie took in the sight of Bourbon Street in full party mode, including the crowded balconies from which groups of buff young men offered strings of beads to women below. Why they offered the strands, she had no idea, yet it was all part of one big party and just being part of it was more intoxicating than anything she'd yet consumed.

"Not tonight, Ronnie. We still have to get back into the dorm and I'm not going to drag your drunk ass over the fence," Ashley said, and then saw the look of disappointment wash over her friend's face. "Don't pout, next weekend we'll rock it all night long and then crash at the Fairmont."

"You got the room?" Ronnie said, grabbing Ashley's hands in hers and jumping repeatedly.

"Yeah, Saturday through Fat Tuesday night," Ashley said with a big smile on her face. "I figure we'll sign out of school for home over the weekend, then plan to get back there on Ash Wednesday in time for the afternoon Mass. That should make Sister Regina happy and nobody will ever know where we spent the weekend. It's going to be so freaking cool, Ronnie."

They strolled hand-in-hand past the strip joints and jazz clubs and because they looked hot and might draw in the guys, were hustled by most of the sidewalk barkers. Feeling a little of their female oats, the girls put on a little extra swing in their walk and just continued on. At one of the kiosks tucked between saloons, Ronnie pulled Ashley by the arm into the alcove.

"Hey, Ash, let's do a shot," she said. Her eyes were wide with excitement. When she saw Ashley's expression turn reluctant she added a plea. "Aw, come on, Ash, it's Mardi Gras and I want to try everything I've never experienced. This is our year, Ash!"

Ronnie turned to the attendant and ordered two shots of tequila. He poured them into in little plastic cups after looking over their IDs. They retreated to the sidewalk holding the translucent dose cups filled with a light amber liquid. Ashley sniffed the booze and wrinkled her nose.

"Geeze, Ash, when you do that you look like a kid," Ronnie admonished. "Just take it and drink it all in one gulp. It's easy, I've seen them do it in the movies."

Ashley wasn't convinced by her friend's shot drinking expertise garnered from watching people doing it in movies where the tequila was probably colored water.

"You first," Ashley said, because while she liked Ronnie's idea of conquering all the things she had never done, after sniffing the liquor in the plastic cup, she wasn't so sure about tequila being high on that list.

"You big baby," Ronnie teased, and then tossed back the shot in one big gulp.

The coughing fit lasted several minutes, during which Ashley was certain Ronnie was going to puke right there on the street. People watched them with curiosity, sympathy, then levity, and Ashley wasn't sure what to do for her friend, but she did know she wanted to disappear from the looks and sniggers they were receiving. Not wanting them both bent over and helpless, Ashley handed her full shot glass to a passing man, who sniffed it, and then tossed it back. She watched in amazement as he didn't cough once and certainly didn't look like he was going to puke. He just turned back, smiled, and pulled several strands of beads from around his neck and tossed them to her.

A cop on horseback eventually took notice and navigated the animal through the crowd to the curb near where they were standing. He sat there, looking down at them astride a well-trained, large, brown stallion which stood patiently at the curb. Ashley did her best to smile back at his inquisitive, yet non-threatening stare.

"She's okay," Ashley offered nervously. "Just went down the wrong way."

She pulled Ronnie up so the cop could see she wasn't going to die or something. Ronnie's face was red and there were tears streaming down her cheeks, but she managed to put on a bit of a smile when she saw the cop's stare.

"I'm okay," she rasped through the last remnants of the coughing fit. She wiped her tears with her hand. She no longer felt like she would puke, but she wasn't feeling all that great.

The cop took one last look and then pulled the reigns to the left and turned his horse up the street and continued on.

"What did you do with yours, Ash?" Ronnie asked.

"Traded it for beads," she said with a tenuous laugh as the fear and embarrassment of the last several minutes morphed to relief. "Anything else you just *have* to try tonight, Ronnie?"

Ronnie shook her head.

"Well, I think you earned these more than I did tonight," Ashley said and hung the man's beads around Ronnie's neck.

Ronnie grinned and looked proudly down at the beads.

"My first Mardi Gras beads as an adult," she said, brightened by the reward, but still a bit unsteady. "Laissez les bons temps rouler."

"Oh, we will, Ronnie," Ashley said. "We'll let all the good times roll on our next trip down here." She looked at her watch. It was near one in the morning. "Hey, Ronnie, give Bobby a call and have him pick us up so we can get back. Tell him we'll meet him at the Cafe du Monde in the French Market. I want to get some beignets and a Coke for the ride home."

Ronnie pulled out her cell phone and hit the speed dial, but when she heard the word 'beignets' come out of Ashley's mouth she looked out of the tops of her eyes at her friend.

"Don't worry, Ronnie," Ashley said as she noticed the skeptical glance. "I won't get powdered sugar all over your precious car."

Dace's celebration wound down before midnight. That was a bit early for his partying high school acquaintances who reluctantly left the free beer to take the party to a bar in Groton, but after all, this was a birthday party at the parents' home, not a frat party at the Delta Tau Chi house. After doing his duty of seeing off the majority of his father's friends and colleagues, Dace rejoined Sarah and the remaining small group of his friends around the fire pit behind the house.

The evening had definitely turned colder, he noticed as he exited the house, and he saw there were a few flakes of light snow beginning to fall. He carried an extra blanket for Sarah, who was already wrapped in two but had still been cold, despite the roaring fire and sable shrug.

"How about this weather?" Dace said as he sat down next to Sarah. He wrapped the oversize blanket around her and huddled close. He held his hands toward the fire pit, then rubbed them together. "This afternoon I ran in shorts and a T-shirt, now it's back to freezing and the snow is coming."

He nestled close to Sarah and gave her a kiss. She smiled and leaned against him. Dave was entertaining himself making breath rings, the nonsmoking version of the smoker's game.

"Ah, Connecticut in the winter time," Dave said while hoisting a bottle of Corona in mock toast to Mother Nature. "I can't wait to sign with the Dolphins and only come up here to embarrass the Patriots every now and again."

"You're too small to play pro ball," Dace teased. "You did, however, bravely throw your puny ass in the path of danger to save my butt on more than one occasion over the last eight years, and for that, I'm forever in your debt." He hoisted a glass of club soda toward Dave. Dave drank from his bottle, Dace set his glass down on the paver stones.

"Me too," chimed Sarah. "It's a nice butt, too," she whispered to Dace as she slid her behind even closer to his.

Dave's ears picked up the whisper.

"Hey, I've seen more if it than you have, Sarah dear, from what I've been told," Dave said.

The group laughed, Dace and Sarah included. They felt no embarrassment by their coincidental choices as teenagers to remain celibate until after they were married. Their friends all knew they had chosen to do so, and frankly, they all respected them for it even though none seated around the fire had joined in the pledge. Dace glanced at each of his remaining handful of friends. They were his closest and dearest, the ones he hoped he would keep for the rest of his life. They were all real, genuine, and expected nothing from him or his father than a return of their friendship.

"I think I'm going to drive Dave home tonight," Dace whispered to Sarah. "I don't think he should drive himself. He can get his car tomorrow before we head back."

"Really?" she said. "Can't someone else do it? It's your birthday."

"None of this crowd is going that way. They're all headed south. I'd hate to impose."

"I'm going north," Sarah said. "Staying at my Grammy's tonight. Remember? You and Dave are picking me up tomorrow night on your way back to school."

"I remember, but taking him home will add an hour to your trip, and it's already late."

"It's done," she said, her sparkling dark eyes probing deeply into his. She touched his cheek and lightly kissed him, effectively ending the conversation on that topic.

Dace smiled at her, kissed her fingertips and then tucked her back under the blankets. He so loved this woman. He'd make his father understand, and eventually accept her as his wife, he thought. As Sarah put her head onto his shoulder, Dace squeezed her close.

He reached down and retrieved his club soda and went to take a drink. He noticed a light skin of ice had formed on the top. It really had gotten colder, he thought.

About two hours later, Sarah drove along the bluff above the Thames after dropping off Dave at his parents' home near Gale's Ferry, on the other side of the river from Dace's place. Her thoughts turned to the party and the private conversation she and Dace had had before she left. He had been honest with her about their chances for the future together given the tone of the conversation with his father, but she agreed to trust him when he had asked her to do so.  She really did love him. She knew that; and she believed he loved her, and would fight for them. In the end, what more did two people have in this world except for their love and trust in one another?  She smiled at the warmth of the thought.

Sarah glanced at the clock on the dashboard.  It was just after two-thirty in the morning as she began heading back through the quiet, winding road toward the expressway and calculated she'd be at her grandmother's place in Providence in an hour or so.  She considered phoning to let the woman know she was on her way, but knew Grammy would be asleep in her chair in the living room and decided to not wake her then just to wake her again in an hour.  Sarah yawned and thought about sleep.  She'd get a good night's rest, sleep until mid morning, attend late Mass with Grammy and then catch up on some reading while she waited for Dace and Dave to pick her up later in the afternoon for the drive back to Harvard for classes on Monday.  It had been a wonderful weekend, she thought. So much excitement and promise.

Sarah shifted in her seat and adjusted the rearview mirror to eliminate the reflected glare of the headlights of the car which pulled out of a driveway just after she passed.  She redirected her view to the roadway.  The road crews had repaved the surface with asphalt late last fall, Dave had said, but hadn't had time to put on the lane striping before winter came to call.  The effect was an enveloping darkness.  To the left, her headlights occasionally lit a portion of the bluff towering higher still, to the right, the nothingness beyond a single guardrail as the bluff dropped to the river, and in the distance, the lights of Groton and New London shimmering on the gently rippled river.

She accelerated slightly to open the distance between her and the other car which was following closely with its bright lights illuminated. With both hands on the wheel to navigate the turns, the other vehicle soon disappeared into darkness.  Suddenly, she felt a jolt from the rear. Then the car's high beam lights came back on, reflecting into her eyes from the side mirrors.  She fumbled to readjusted them and clear the glare.

She watched in the rearview as the car weaved and then almost hit her from behind again.  She reacted by unconsciously accelerating along the curvy road and her tires squealed around the next turn.  She applied the brakes to slow and cried out as the car bumped her from behind again.  Her heart began beating hard enough for her to perceive her own pulse in her ears.  She began breathing harder.  Her grip on the wheel tightened.  She glanced at the cell phone on the passenger seat and momentarily thought about calling Dace, but then realized he could do nothing.  She glanced across the river and saw the lights of his house on the other side.

Sarah looked into the rearview mirror again. Seconds were moving along as if minutes; everything happening in slow motion. The car was weaving again behind her, accelerating toward her and then backing off.

"What do you want?" she screamed inside the emptiness of her car.

Her hands gripped the wheel and her eyes moved from the dark and curvy road to the rearview mirror and back again. Should she pull over and let the obviously intoxicated driver pass? She was breathing harder now, her mind on the verge of a panic. She saw them backing off again and she began to breathe easier and accelerated to open the distance. Suddenly she saw them racing forward again and was prepared to be jolted in her seat again but instead she saw them brake quickly to a stop.

Her car hit the black ice an instant later and began to spin as she tapped the brakes. The day's thaw had created a river of water across the road and the night's freezing temperatures had turned that water to ice. Sarah fought for control, but the Corolla refused to cooperate. Each time she spun around she could see the headlights of the other car stopped in the roadway. Then she heard a screeching sound and felt herself falling as her car rolled and plummeted down the bluff toward the water.

Her last thought was of Dace.

# Chapter Three

Dace awoke on Sunday morning to his mother seated on the edge of his bed. She gently roused him and asked that he get up and go down to his father's office. She stroked the side of his face a moment and Dace saw a profound sadness in the woman's eyes. She then stood and walked out of the room without further word. Dace sat up and watched her go, shook his head, then slipped out of bed, put on robe and slippers against the slight chill in the house and padded downstairs to the second floor. He saw his mother ahead, continuing to the first floor and could hear echoes of low, indiscernible voices coming from the kitchen.

As he entered his father's office, knocking first as a formality at the door which had been left ajar, he found his father watching out the window, his back to the entry and his gaze across the river. The Senator was wearing pajamas, robe and slippers, and had both hands clasped behind his back and Dace noticed the right one was tightly clenched.

"What's up, dad?" Dace said as he entered the room, wiping remnants of sleep from his eyes.

"Sit down, son," he said.

Dace remained standing.

The Senator did not turn to address him.

"The police were here early this morning," he said. "As a courtesy."

"The police?" Dace asked. "Why? What type of courtesy?" He could feel a tension rise inside him. His father remained mute a moment longer. "Dad?"

"There was an accident last night," he said, finally turning to face his son. "A tragic accident."

Dace saw the pain in his father's eyes. His mind raced to assemble the puzzle pieces of his mother's touch on his face, her rapid departure, and the voices downstairs, muffled and low. He dropped into one of the tufted leather chairs near his father's desk and braced himself for the bad news he now knew was coming. He mentally ticked off the names of people who might cause this type of sadness on his father's face. Before he got to her name, his father said it.

"Sarah's dead, son," he said. "Her car slid on a patch of black ice and went over the bluff early this morning, shortly after she left the party."

Dace could feel his heart momentarily stop in his chest, then resume its beating in an accelerated, powerful rhythm. Had he heard his father correctly? It couldn't be. Was he still dreaming? He fought to awaken himself from this nightmare, but quickly discovered he could not; because this was real.

"Sarah?" he said, tears welling in his eyes. "Are you certain?" He saw his father was. "When? Where? What happened?"

His father closed the distance between them, leaned against the front of his desk, his arms hanging loosely at his side, his hands relaxed.

"From what the police reported to me, she had just dropped Dave off and then was heading back to the interstate..."

"Yeah, she was going to spend the night at her grandmother's house," Dace interrupted. "She volunteered to take Dave home because he had had a few too many and it was kind of on her way." His face flashed a revelation of horror. "My God, has anyone told her grandmother?"

"My understanding is she received word this morning from Rhode Island State Troopers," The Senator stated perfunctorily. "The police asked if she had been drinking at the party and I told them I didn't think so."

Dace's face was blank, his mind was operating at light speed, but not wasting the time or the energy to manipulate his face. He slouched back in the chair, his arms hanging free over the sides.

"Sarah doesn't drink," he said in a flat tone. "Never did. No drugs either."

"Regardless, they are going to run toxicology tests at the autopsy," The Senator said as he again moved to stare out the window before continuing. "Such a tragedy. Beautiful young girl. So much of a future, wasted. No, not wasted. Lost, stripped away."

Dace raised his eyes to see his father shaking his head absently. He thought the man sounded as if he was forming a statement for the media. He was certain his father had rehearsed every word in his mind; even the correction. He could feel the bile burning his guts. He wanted to throw up. 'Autopsy' he thought to himself and the energy without outlet took hold of him. He jumped to his feet and began speaking rapidly.

"Where is she? I want to see her. I need to see her. Father, I have to go to her." He began moving in nervous circles, but going nowhere. His mind didn't truly comprehend or accept this. He had never before had anyone he knew die, apart from the natural passing of elderly relatives.

His father turned to observe his son, but made no move toward him to either console or restrain his movements; his hands set firmly in the small of his back again. The Senator's heart felt a profound sadness for his son and his gut roiled with rage, but for different reasons. Even with all his experience in dealing with important and often emotional national matters, at that moment, he just didn't know how to express his empathy or sympathy effectively to his own son.

There was a solid, yet muted double knock on the closed office door and it swung open without invitation a moment later. The Senator's chief political advisor walked into the office and for a moment stood as the third corner of a distant triangle. Dace noticed the older men's eyes meeting and then settling upon him as if an unspoken signal had been passed to implement a prior arrangement.

Tom McDaniel approached Dace and extended his hand. Dace reflexively accepted the gesture. Tom placed his left hand over the top of Dace's in the shake and offered his condolences and apologies that he could not be in attendance last evening to have met Sarah. Dace nodded and was relieved the man had not offered birthday wishes. He could see in Tom's eyes a searching for something within *his* eyes as much as any offering of commiseration as Tom deftly used the handshake to maneuver Dace back into the chair. Tom then took up the position held moments earlier by his father: leaning against the front of The Senator's desk. He folded his arms and looked hard at Dace; it was a look of cold, analytical assessment rather than anything emotional. Dace felt uncomfortable.

Tom McDaniel was a bulky man of slightly less than six feet. Not fat, but stocky; *husky* was the word most often used to describe his physique. Built low to the ground, like a fire hydrant, Tom had played fullback in college for Michigan - the Wolverines, not the Spartans - and still held several game records for the Big Ten. He had shared many gridiron stories with Dace over the years, and closely followed the younger man's high school and college sports play. Dace knew Tom as his father's top political person, but also as a friend of the family.

Tom was a seventh generation American son of independent, hard-drinking, fiery, Irish stock, a man of few words who had the reputation as one of the country's most savvy political strategists. In his youth, Tom had sported pale, freckled skin and flaming red hair, but age and exposure to the sun on extended post-campaign vacations had toughened the skin and erased any evidence of freckles while lightening the fiery hair to a dirty reddish blonde with hints of gray at the temples. Though the man had started his adult life as a stereotypical, hard drinking Irishman, he had been sober for ten years.

"I'm so sorry about your loss, Dace," Tom said again. "I came right up from New York after your father called me with the sad news early this morning to see what I could do to help over the coming days."

He searched Dace's face for signs of understanding.

"I could always count on Tom," The Senator said, walking from the window and putting a hand on the other man's shoulder before moving behind the desk and taking up his chair. "Now, so can you, Dace."

Dace may have been new to all this manhood stuff and though his heart, mind, and soul were consumed in grief and disbelief, but he certainly maintained enough of a grip on reality to recognize a set up and a double team when he saw them. The question was: *Why?* His eyes moved between Tom and his father. Was his father truly that calculating about the death of the woman he loved, the woman he had intended to marry no matter what The Senator said? Dace could feel his head beginning to spin with the swirling emotional and logical contradictions.

"I want to go see her," Dace said as he started to rise out of the chair again. "I have to go see her."

Tom placed the palms of his hands on Dace's shoulders and put just enough resistance in his arms to gently guide him back into the seat.

"That would be the wrong thing to do," he said. "I understand how you feel, Dace, I truly do, but there's nothing to be gained by you rushing into the center of the police investigation and public spectacle which is taking place on the other side of the river. We feel there is a better way to handle all this. If you give us the time to review this all with you, I think you'll come to agree."

Dace's near frantic mind raced. Again his gaze shot between the noncommittal faces of people he saw at that moment, not as his father and a family friend, but as two detached professionals, and he pushed deep into their eyes where he eventually received the same unspoken message from each man: '*This has nothing to do with you.*' His mind reeled. Tom shifted his lean, then cleared his throat and continued.

"The girl is dead, Dace. It was a tragic accident which occurred after she attended a party here," Tom said in a matter-of-fact tone. "The press reports and photos coming out of all this will follow you for the rest of your life. How you and the family manage this matter must be carefully considered." He shifted a bit toward The Senator, who nodded, then squared himself again with Dace. "It's important to your future, um, prospects."

The last sentence took Dace a minute to process. He looked down at his slippered bare feet on the plush Oriental rug and when he raised his gaze, it moved past Tom's bulky frame and met his father's eyes.

"Politics?" he spat. "This is about politics? You two are afraid of this becoming another Chappaquiddick? Are you freaking kidding me?"

Dace angrily thrust himself against the back of the chair, then his body slumped. His hand cupped his chin, one finger covering his tight lips. His eyes focused on nothing as he slowly shook his head, letting everything process. He remained that way for several long moments, while the two elders remained stolid and mute. As his mind reached and clawed to a metaphorical rock in the middle of his racing river of emotions, Dace's eyes again moved between Tom and his father. Tom's eyes were patient, like those of a doctor who had just delivered bad news to a patient and was waiting out the rants and raves of the 'Why me?' stage to play out. From his father, he received nothing but a stony, emotionally disconnected stare. Dace then calmly spoke the conclusion his mind had understood even as his heart rejected the premise.

"Dad," Dace began, his voice a blend of disbelief and resignation, then paused. "Sarah is dead and you want to issue a press release?" He stared into his father's eyes, and because his heart would not allow him to yet condemn the man for this nonsense, his focus fixed upon Tom. "Is that it?"

"Son," The Senator began and a crack opened in his cold resolve for just an instant before force of will sealed it. "You have to consider your future in every action you take going forward. It's as we talked yesterday. You're a man now, and you're going to be judged as a man. What we are doing is not for us and certainly not against that young girl." He paused to allow the words to sink in. He stood, straightened up and walked again to stare out the window, finishing with his back to his son and a single loosely clenched hand in his back. "This is for your own good, Dace. For your future, and the future of this family."

Dace's temper boiled over at his father's seeming inability to say Sarah's name and referring to her as 'that young girl' now, and he leapt from the chair. Tom made a move to coax him back down and Dace's glare froze the older man. Dismissive of everything he had just heard, he move toward the closed office door.

"Screw the future, dad. And screw the family," he said in a raised voice, turning to point a finger at the end of a straightened arm at his father who turned his head to confront the statements, but remained silent. Dace held strong to his accusatory affront toward The Senator's authority and the family's legacy as long as he could, but soon wilted to desolation at the continued silent stare of his father. His arm fell limply to his side, and he continued in a low, slow, sorrowful tone. "I loved her, dad, and you tell me she's gone, and that's it?" The thought again solidified his resolve and he walked with newfound purpose toward the door. "I'm going to see her."

He placed his hand on the doorknob and turned it slowly as he considered additional words, but then quickly dismissed them. Instead he pulled open the office door to leave before anything more could be said by anyone, but stopped short of the hall as two very large gentlemen in suits moved to fill the opening. Dace slowly turned to see his father standing with his back to the window, his arms crossed over his chest.

"I'm afraid, in this case, son, you have no choice," The Senator said.

Sandy and I stopped about halfway between home and our office building about nine on Monday morning at Starbuck's to buy a Grande coffee for her, and while she sat at one of their umbrellaed outside tables and reveled in a second straight morning of sunshine and temperate, dry weather, I strolled next door and grabbed an ice cold Coke from the mom and pop store on Magazine Street for me because I refuse to pay two-and-a-half bucks for something I can get for ninety-nine cents around the corner. I returned, plastic bottle in hand, twisted off the cap, took a swig, issued forth a loud 'ah' in a blatant display to the coffee pushers inside behind the counter before settling my six-foot-six frame in the metal chair across from Sandy. She rolled her eyes to me, sipped her coffee then set the tall white cup with brown cardboard sleeve onto the table; she sat back with a warm, contented smile on her face, crossed her smooth, lithe, bare legs. She dangled her heeled pump on the tips of her naked toes. She knows I like that. Her distraction from my act of defiance toward overpriced drinks worked and I reached under the table and slid my fingertips on her calf. She smiled at me. I smiled at her. Does it get any better than this?

Sitting back in my chair to enjoy the relative calm of a Monday morning, I looked around at the nearby businesses all decorated for Carnival. Traffic flowed in the normal workday rhythm along the street, but there was a special buzz in the air. New Orleans had been sprouting all manner of gold, purple, and green decorations in anticipation of Mardi Gras festivities for weeks now, but I was amazed at how locals kept finding more places and ways with each passing year to display the season's frippery. There was also a perceptible pecuniary vibrance in the city as hotels, restaurants, and bars filled to capacity with visitors and the air of Carnival permeated every nook and cranny of the Parish. In nine days, it would all be over, and local Catholics would settle in to the relative quiet and fasting of Lent for the next forty-six days until Easter. Yes, I said forty-six days between Ash Wednesday and Easter.

See, though Lent consists of only forty days of fasting, which to Catholics honors the forty days Christ spent fasting in the desert in preparation for his trials and tribulations to come, it had only taken me a mere three decades to understand the math of the season. I don't recall the reasoning for the differential being taught to us in my eight years of Catholic grade school, so on a bet one year I had looked it up. I often tease Sandy that Catholicism is like that, we sit and listen, don't need to read our Bibles because the priests will tell us what we need to know, and never question the proclamations of the Faith. That facetious viewpoint is just one thing which exasperates her father about me, but that's another story for another time.

The story of the math of Lent, I learned, dates to early Church leaders who ran into some trouble in moving the Sabbath from the traditional Saturday under Judaism to Sunday under Christianity. With Christians considering every Sunday to be a day of celebration of Christ's resurrection, and since no fasting could occur on a day of celebration, to get to forty days of fasting, they eliminated Sundays from the count and ran the period of Lent from Ash Wednesday through Easter Sunday, a total of forty-six calendar days. Confused yet? Yeah, well, that's one of the reasons we Catholics just trust the priests to tell us what we need to know. It's easier that way. Now, don't go sending me letters. I'm just calling it like I see it; but if you do need to send me a letter to express your angst, please address it to Sandy at the office or I may never open it.

Sandy and I are full partners with distinctively different roles in our little private investigative agency. She's the research and administration type, and I'm the field investigative wing of the deal; it seems to be working quite well. Someone once said to me that a business partnership was like a marriage, and since we're doing them both at the same time, we are working harder than it may appear to a casual outsider at getting each of them right. Ours was a second marriage for each of us, and having screwed it up royally on my first go, I didn't enter into this one lightly. I couldn't be happier, though, and I try hard every day to make my wife just as happy. Some days I'm more successful at it than others, but what would a woman's life be without the occasional dozen roses showing up unannounced?

We operate our business from a building we own outright on what I call the poor side of Magazine Street. Windows of my second-floor office look across toward the multimillion dollar homes of the Garden District, while Sandy's seldom used private office windows watch over the working class shotgun-style homes of the city's blue collar types. The first floor area, which in a previous life was used to serve the needs of a gaggle of realtors, we have rented out to a middle-aged woman named Nellie who runs a thriving sundries and notions store.

We bought the building from the widow of the real estate broker who, one night after an office bash celebrating the closing of a large land deal, tried unsuccessfully to add an exit to the bridge over the middle of Lake Pontchartrain. He must have forgotten the prime rule of any real estate opportunity because, while he successfully exited the bridge, where he did it turned out not to be the best of locations. It took them two days to drag his car from the lake because of traffic on the bridge and the fact the first crane brought in for the recovery hadn't the muscle needed to extract the vehicle from the grip of the silty bottom, which seemed to want to keep the Porsche. Him, divers got out that first night.

After we finished our morning drinks outside the Starbuck's, we completed the short drive to the office. There are days when Sandy walked the trip, but if I'm going in, I'm taking my car. When we arrived, I unlocked the front door and we climbed the stairs to our second floor offices where I unlocked that door as well. I gave my wife a chaste kiss on the cheek and left her out front in the reception area and went into my private office to start the week. Now, I don't leave her out front to be the receptionist because she's the woman in the equation; I'm already going to get letters from my fellow Catholics, I don't need them from the feminists too, so understand she's there because that's how *she* prefers it. For the record, her private office is nearly as large and just as comfortable as is mine, but she rarely uses hers during the day because sitting out front is the way she likes it. Some people have commented it's her way of protecting me from myself by keeping an eye on me. I'm a sucker for anyone wandering in with a problem, but my patience wears thin quickly, so perhaps she's also protecting the unsuspecting public from me.

That morning, as usual, I closed my door against her talk radio which she switched on immediately after rounding the corner behind her desk. Though some would call them oldies now, I consider myself to be more of a classic rock kind of guy; and I like it loud, so if I listen during the day, my agreement with Sandy and our renter below is: closed door or iPod and ear phones. At night when I'm alone, I crank my amplified Bose system to max and open all the doors, just to convince myself of something I can't quite identify. Ours is a modification of the agreement I had with my mom when I was growing up, only back then it was a record player or 8-track tape machine plugged up with KOSS headphones. Music has always helped me to think and I'd often play it while cataloguing cases and writing or reading reports. Some may find working with noise in the background distracting or unprofessional, but I don't. For me, it's back brain, not front brain, so I have no problem staying focused with the tunes blaring in my ears. That morning was going to be a classic rock day.

Long story short about my day ahead. I had something to sort out before telling Sandy of my decision. I've never been too political, so it shouldn't bug me when I get approached by one side to keep an eye on the other side, especially in Louisiana, where political dirty tricks are a way of life in every election. For some reason, however, it *was* bugging me. Part of the reason was the party which wants to hire us offends Sandy's disposition on things political. She doesn't know the details of the job offer yet, and I'm not sure how to approach her, so I've been procrastinating, but the deadline for returning the contracts is drawing close. I slid into my judge's chair which fits my frame better than that spindly metal thing at Starbuck's, removed my iPod from the desk drawer, pushed play and Alice Cooper reminded me that he was eighteen and 'just don't know what he wants,' put my feet up on the corner of my desk and began pondering.

One part of me, the apolitical, crassly cynical, capitalist part, simply wanted to take the job. It would pay well for a one-week gig, and how hard was it to surveil politicians and their hired hacks in order to catch them with hookers, or drugs, or in drunken revelry while they hold their convention in the Superdome that coming summer all the while proclaiming to the country they hold the moral and ethical high ground? The job was a peripheral economic boom which benefits the investigative industry in whichever host state these windbags choose every four years. During the dog days of August in 1998, every P.I. in the state of Louisiana was going to be getting a chunk of this thing, so why not us?

It doesn't matter which side of the political fence you stand on, or even if you decide to sit on the fence itself, know that each side spies on the other side, and *both* sides spy on you fence sitters. Ever read Mad Magazine? Yeah, it's *Spy vs. Spy* stuff twenty-four/seven for these people, but especially every four years when time comes for them to sell us another incompetent dickhead who happens to look good in a suit to be our new president. Accept the fact. Welcome to modern day America.

Another part of me, the married guy who wants to keep his wife happy with him part, kept repeating the moral of the story told by Gene Hackman's character to the cabby in *Runaway Jury* who was pondering the dilemma of having his sick mother move in with him because his unsympathetic wife doesn't get along with the mother: 'It's better to have an unhappy mother than an unfriendly wife.' Not that Sandy would hold my decision against me, for long. I hoped.

With Carnival going on, most of our regular work had been put on hiatus as our clients told us they just wanted to party and feel good for a while. They've put down their swords and shields and traded them for masks and beads, at least for the next eight days. On Ash Wednesday, even though it will be the start of Lent leading to Easter, they'll put away the toys and trinkets, pick up the swords and shields and be back at each other's throats screaming for blood. It's *one* of the sides of life, I thought.

The last thing I remember was the Moody Blues singing about the other side.

The next thing I knew, Sandy kissed me lightly on the lips and woke me up, and then asked me, like she does almost every day, if I would like to take a walk with her over lunch.

"What time is it?" I asked trying to fake off the fact she caught me sleeping, again.

"Noon, a few minutes after," she said with a Cheshire Cat smile.

I took in the smile and briefly wondered about it, but I was quickly discovering upon waking that I was indeed hungry. Today, perhaps because I'm startled by the gentleness of her kiss or am still half asleep and carrying to wakefulness the sweet dreams of our Valentine's weekend we just enjoyed, I surprise her and agree to go out on the walk with two conditions: 1) that we walk on the shady side of the street; and, 2) that we walk to get a shrimp po' boy and ice cold beer. To my surprise, she readily agreed to both conditions.

We locked the office doors and descended the stairs, waved to Nellie, our renter, and walked out hand-in-hand into the sunny comfort of a New Orleans midday in February. We crossed over to the rich side of Magazine Street and I start to turn toward my favorite hole-in-the-wall place to get a po' boy which lies a mere couple of blocks away when Sandy, my loving wife, pulled my arm the other direction.

"Not so fast, Will," she said.

That playful glint in her eye was there, and that usually meant in my negotiations I had forgotten I was dealing with an attorney.

"We're going through the park to *my* favorite place for a sandwich."

"But, honey, I meant that great little place just two blocks away," I pled while gesturing with my free hand and lightly pulling against her grip.

"You should have said so. Verbal contract, you know."

I feign disgust and give up easily. Maybe too easily, I think to myself.

"Verbal contracts don't exist under Louisiana law," I said.

"You forget we were married under the laws of the Cayman Islands, and there they do."

"Lawyers," I said under my breath, defeated by my own argument, but thinking she was probably blowing smoke about the Caymans.

"What's that, dear?"

"Nothing."

I give her hand a little squeeze and we turn in the opposite direction, toward Audubon Park. After we take the first few steps, I recall that Sandy's favorite deli doesn't serve beer, so I'm thinking I may have her on a technicality. I'm about to say something to that effect, hoping to perhaps get her to turn around before we go too far in the wrong direction, but then that little voice in my head weighs in and I just keep walking.

As we strolled along, I decided to tell her that I was going to take the political spy gig that coming summer. I expected a battle, or at least a minor skirmish, but to my surprise she just said: 'Good'. As we got closer to the park entrance, I wondered if she's got an ulterior motive for agreeing to let me spy for the politicos Sandy considers the bad guys, or if something else has her mind right now.

"Hey," I said, looking over at her. "You really don't have a problem with me surveilling the good guys this summer?"

"I've begun to think there are no good guys anymore," she said with an uncharacteristic tone of resignation. "It's always the same, just the color of the jerseys change. The vitriol on both sides just keeps getting harsher and harsher. Nobody is listening to anyone anymore. Makes me afraid for the future."

"What brought this on?"

Sandy was never melancholy. She never gave up.

"I don't know, Will."

She squeezed my hand, moved a bit closer to me, put her other hand around the inside of my elbow and nestled her head against my shoulder as we continued walking along. Something was tingling my senses, but I had no idea what it was. Sandy was quiet, just walking next to me, slower than she normally does. I glanced down at her face and she was obviously thinking something over; and she was being affectionate and yet guarded at the same time. The little guy in my head who seems to know more about women than yours truly just shrugged his shoulders when I look to him for help; I'm on my own here, apparently, so I decide to change the subject.

"I talked to Teddy last night," I said. "He's made Captain and has put in for a central district downtown; north downtown."

"Mmm-hmm," she responds. "That's great."

It *was* great. Teddy has been slowly burning out on the street as a Robbery/Homicide Detective Lieutenant and landing the promotion and new assignment just may be what it took to get him through to retirement in ten or twelve years. I'm certain it would be just the thing to save his marriage. Valeria was his third. She was native Venezuelan, fifteen years younger than Teddy, and she was gorgeous, with thick black hair and bewitching green eyes, a body that just won't quit, and a fiery personality that surely kept Teddy on his toes.

Teddy first showed up with Valeria when they were still dating and we had hastily arranged a group vacation about three years ago when Sandy and I were newlyweds still living in the Caymans. We borrowed my bar partner's eighty-foot sailing catamaran for a couple of months to bounce around the south Caribbean together. It was that trip which started me hating the water, but like a couple other things, that's a story for another time; and no, living on an island has nothing to do with how someone feels about the water. It's two different things.

Sandy loved Teddy, really loved him just like I do, so her minimal response to what should be great news for our dear friend had me wondering what safe hanging by a fraying rope was above my head right then. In my ex-cop brain, I concluded I should just make her tell me what was on her mind. In my husband brain, I concluded it would be better to just let her come to it in her own time. So, we walked.

We turned into the gate at the back of Audubon Park. *Gate* was a misnomer, because it's really just an opening in a chain link fence and it always amuses me when I pass through it because it serves to further highlight the contrasts between the wealthy Garden District and the wrong side of the street where our office was. The front entrance to the park resides on St. Charles Avenue and serves the Garden District patrons and was an ornate affair with signs carved from stone slabs, palm trees, flower beds, and rock walls terminating at ornate, fifteen-foot-high carved stone pillars. On the Magazine Street side, which serves working stiffs like me, they give us a chain link fence with a gap. Now, I don't believe the contrast is intentional, or has anything to do with the city consciously making a social commentary; I just found it interesting.

"Remember when I mentioned the differences in the gates here at the park to your dad one time and he asked me if I was some kind of Communist?" I said.

"Yeah," she said, then paused for nearly a minute as we continued to walk along the path before adding: "Daddy thinks everyone is a Communist, Will."

It was then the little guy with the little voice in my head starts waving his arms and I think I understand. 'Of course,' I said to myself. There have been other clues over the last few weeks or so that her mind has been elsewhere and I was certain I knew then what was going on. I use the old cop trick of making the suspect think you know everything already and just need them to come clean. 'It's not like telling on yourself. I already know.' You parents know how the *psych* works with your kids, too.

"So when are you going to tell me about it, Sandy?" I asked.

She stopped walking immediately and let go of my hand, my arm, and removed her head from against my shoulder.

"Oh, Will," she said, her head and eyes downcast.

I moved around to face her, lifted her chin with my fingertips. Her eyes were moist.

"I'm so sorry," she said. "I never meant to do this to you. To us. It's all my fault."

So now my heart was racing because throwing out that little bit of bait obviously hooked me something I was not fishing for. Perhaps I didn't know what was going on. Fault? Do what to me? To us?

Time to retreat a bit.

"Are we talking about the same thing, Sandy?" I asked cautiously. My fingertips released her chin and she began to sob. Emotionally, I begin to prepare for the worst news a man can get. She's having an affair and I never saw it coming. My heart clenched.

"I don't know. What are you talking about?" she asked, calling my bluff, or maybe being truly confused. Her eyes searched mine; hers were moist. Mine would have been too had I not been a man, but seeing hers did cause mine to sting behind my sunglasses. Then, a tear traced down her cheek, collected at the base of her chin, and I could feel myself losing it.

Then a new look unveiled itself on her face. My heart unclenched.

"Just how would you know?" she said. "I only found out for certain this morning."

I let out a breath, it wasn't an affair. What was the second worst news a man can get from his wife, I thought. I drew a blank. I decided to just give up the ruse, and get the cards out on the table.

"Sandy, just tell me what you're talking about. Going in circles obviously isn't good for either of us here."

She shifted her feet, then swiped the beginnings of a new tear away.

"Well, you were sleeping at your desk when I left this morning," she said. "So I couldn't say anything to you then, and when I got back to the office, you were still sleeping..."

"Yeah, I know, I slept the morning away," I said, interrupting. "I'm sorry."

She looked at me curiously, then shook her head.

"No, I'm the one who needs to be sorry, Will. It's all my fault. I just know you're never going to forgive me."

This was starting to give me a headache, but that last sentence sure got my attention and I fell back into the thoughts of an affair. How could she do that to us? I removed my sunglasses and rubbed the bridge of my nose.

"Who is he?" I asked, perhaps a little too firmly in my attempt to get her to focus. If I was going to be hurt, I didn't feel like dancing before it happened. Inside I prepared for the next words out of my wife's mouth.

"What?" she said, looking at me like there were crawdads crawling out of my ears. "He? He, who? Dr. Simmons is a she. What are you talking about, Will?"

"Dr. Simmons?" I said. Breathe. "Your gynecologist?"

Sandy reached across the gap between us, took both of my hands in hers and looked up into my eyes. My heart was trying to beat its way out of my chest. I hadn't been as frightened about what could be coming next since gunfire erupted in that warehouse and Eric went down.

Then, a thought ran through my head. Gynecologist? Sandy and I had been together for four years, but we each had full adult lives before that. Then I remembered what the second worst news was a wife could give her husband. I held my breath, squeezed her hands in a show of support and solidarity. We could face anything together, I thought.

"Yeah, I saw her this morning. While you were sleeping."

"I remember the sleeping part," I said. "And?"

"I'm pregnant, Will."

The word hit me like a hammer in the chest, but at least it stopped my heart from wanting to beat its way out. My mind reeled. I looked at my wife. Sandy's expression had turned stolid, her eyes impenetrable. Slowly, I wrapped my mind around what she had just said to me.

"Pregnant." I searched her eyes for a glimmer of a gotcha, but saw none. "Pregnant?" I repeated. "How long?"

"Dr. Simmons says three-and-a-half months, about fifteen weeks." Sandy bit her lower lip and waited nervously.

"Pregnant." My head still spun, but was slowing down some. This wasn't the worst news, or even the second worst news that a wife could give a husband; truth be told, it was wonderful news. "Hmm," I said as my mind mulled this over.

"I changed birth control around Halloween, I guess we hit a gap." She looked at me, offered a hint of a hopeful smile, raised her eyebrows and shrugged her shoulders. "I think it was that weekend on South Padre Island."

Then a new wave of reality washed over me when I realized we were both turning forty later that year. Wasn't there something about the dangers of older people having babies on the news recently? I remember seeing something about it. I was certain.

"But we're middle aged, Sandy. People don't have babies when they are middle aged."

"Forty is not *middle age* anymore, Will," she said, her tone instructional. "Women safely have babies well into their forties these days. Some even later than that."

Babies? Did she just say *babies*? Plural?

"Babies?" I asked cautiously. "More than one?"

She laughed and a big smile flowed across her beautiful face, and then I saw it, the glow they get was there too. The subtle glow I had been noticing for weeks, but had been alternately discounting as just happiness over being married to me or fearing it meant something awful. Sandy put her hands to my cheeks. It was her way of telling me to focus.

"No, just one," she said.

She cocked her head, put her hands onto her hips and stuck one foot just in front of the other and looked deep into my eyes. That was her 'There it is, mister, now what are you going to do?' stance.

"Well?" she said.

"You're pregnant. One baby. Fifteen weeks."

"Those are the facts, detective."

"Out of how many weeks?"

"Forty."

I didn't know what more to say, what more to even think. I had three daughters from my first marriage, each of them a joy, but each of them a surprise. I hadn't planned any children in my life; and now a fourth? Was I some sort of anomaly of fatherhood? Never a plan; always a surprise from the blue? How could I be so lackadaisical as a man? Sandy started to shift her feet again, her smile dried up. Was I doing something wrong in how I was reacting? Can't I do anything right?

"Oh, Will, I'm sorry," she said.

Oh, my, she obviously concluded my thoughtful pause was some sort of expression of disappointment. When I didn't say anything again, she continued.

"I know we agreed when we got together neither of us were in a place in our lives where we wanted children. I took all the precautions, but then more studies were coming out about the dangers of long-term use of the birth control pills, especially in women nearing forty, and other non-chemical options were developing, so Dr. Simmons put me on something new around the end of October." She half-smiled. "Like I said, we just got lucky."

I smiled at her. It was all sinking in. My daughters were growing up. The oldest would graduate from college next year, the middle one from high school and the last one from the eighth grade, this year. Sandy, on the other hand, had never had children. When we married, we decided we were way past the having babies part of our life, so we took precautions, on her end. Before you ladies ask, even though I've been shot before, and stabbed twice, there is absolutely no way that this cowboy was going to submit for any snipping down in that general area.

"So, we're going to have a baby," I said. "When?"

"Dr. Simmons said end of July or first week of August."

It would be a Leo, just as we were.

"Are you angry?" my beautiful wife asked as she bit her lower lip in trepidation of the answer.

I smiled. She smiled.

"How could I be, Sandy?" I said. "You are giving me a wonderful gift, and even though it's a huge shock, there is nobody in this world I would want to have a child with more than you. I love you, Sandy."

Sandy's eyes misted again as trepidation turned to happiness. She jumped into my arms and I spun her around. She couldn't see my eyes, but they misted as well.

"And you, Will, are the only man in the world whose child I would want to have. I love you so, my darling," she whispered into my ear.

I set her down gently, a sudden look of concern on my face which Sandy noticed.

"Don't worry, Will. I won't break."

She tossed her head back in laughter, whether in joy or relief or just pure levity, I didn't know. Or care. Sandy's laughter always lit up my universe, whatever the cause; and she looked great doing it.

"I know," I said, although not convinced.

She hugged me again. I gently rocked her, kissed the top of her head, stroked her back with my big hands.

"What do you think the girls will say?" she asked.

"Girls?" I asked.

She pushed away a bit, but our arms remained encircling each other, and stared up at me.

"Your girls," she said in a tone which contained an unspoken 'duh'. "You know this news could come as quite the shock to them. I know the timing is bad because you're just making inroads into getting to know them again after those years of drifting apart."

I thought about Sandy's reasoned concern for a few moments to keep myself from just spouting a flippant male 'I've got it covered' response. Yes, my girls had just begun coming around again over the last eighteen months or so after about a half dozen years of minimal contact because I had issues with their mother, and she with me. When I had divorced their mother, it was fairly traumatic for each of them. The oldest had just turned fourteen and the youngest had just turned seven. My middle daughter was ten going on twenty-five at the time, or so it seemed because she handled the breakup of her parents with the least emotional distress, on the outside. It took me years to discover how devastated she had been, on the inside. They all loved Sandy from the beginning, and not just because she had been the catalyst which helped me rekindle the relationships between father and daughters. I really didn't know exactly how my girls would react to the news of a sister or brother on the way.

"I guess it's all going to depend on how we tell them and how we relate to them going forward," I said.

"Why would we relate to them any differently?" Sandy asked.

"No, no, we wouldn't, of course," I clarified. "I mean it's how they *perceive* the way we treat them going forward."

Sandy nodded.

"There are so many things we need to talk about, Will," Sandy said. "This is a life changing event for people our age. Your girls will need to feel secure in our love for them, and we'll both work on that. I promise."

"That's just one of the reasons I love you, Sandy."

My mind had forgotten food for the last few minutes, but now the hunger came roaring back with a vengeance.

"Are you hungry?" I asked.

"Famished," Sandy said in a tone like the worries of the world had just been lifted from her shoulders.

"Me, too. Starved."

We walked out the front gates of Audubon Park, hopped aboard the St. Charles line of the trolly and got off in the boulevard across from Sandy's favorite deli.

After lunch, back in the office, we called my girls.

The funeral mass for Sarah Maria Avidago was held at ten in the morning on Tuesday, the seventeenth day of February at Our Lady of the Rosary Catholic Church in Providence, Rhode Island.

Dace had not returned to classes before the funeral. He had also not been allowed the opportunity to see Sarah. Dave Saunders had come by on Sunday afternoon to retrieve his car and attempted to see his friend. The Senator would not allow Dave to see Dace, but didn't prevent him from saying hello to a very excited Mary Rose who hugged the big man and then passed him a note from her little brother.

On the day of the funeral mass, the Lamoureux family, meaning Dace, The Senator, and Libby, arrived at the church a mere fifteen minutes before the scheduled beginning of the service. On The Senator's orders, they had avoided both the wake the previous evening and the final viewing earlier that morning. The understated, black limousine which had transported them from New London to Providence pulled up alongside the black Cadillac hearse parked on Traverse Street in front of the church. Dace could see the blonde oak casket through the partially draped windows as he got out, held his hand to assist his mother, and awaited The Senator's exit from the car. He also could see the two large gentlemen who parked down the block in their black Lincoln Town Car.

The air was cool and crisp and the sky a cloudless, blue expanse. A strong breeze moved around the buildings and swirled dust devils down the street. Dace looked up at the faint humming sound the wind made as it moved through the louvered and screened openings of the twin bell towers high above the street. He absorbed the entire scene: the old neighborhood turned commercialized area bordering the highway beyond and the river and docks beyond that, the overflowing parking lots across the street. He wanted to remember every detail.

His father clapped him on the back and discreetly said something about being proud of his son, a remark Dace let flow in one ear and out the other. As he walked past the hearse, Dace lightly touched the roof above the glass. It was the closest he'd ever get to his Sarah again, he knew. Dace had become emotionally numbed by the two days of solitude and manipulation, but that one simple act of touching the cold, black steel found its way to his heart which tore just a bit more with fresh pain, and for a moment he felt a little more like himself again.

As they moved past the hearse and approached the stone steps of the church, Dace looked up again. The building itself was large, and while the bronze plaque proclaimed the congregation had been founded in

1886, the building was relatively modern in design and construction. The oddly irregular cut of the stone facing and the somewhat incongruous mixture of architectural details struck Dace as a structure assembled by committee. A grassed courtyard with a winterized fountain stood off to the right of the church. A walkway led past the fountain from the street to the rectory building beyond.

Several groups of other later arrivals also moved toward the doors while people spoke quietly to each other. The Lamoureux family, the men with Libby between them, allowed the others to precede them and then fell into line, finally ascending the broad steps and moving through the heavy, double oak doors in the centermost of the three lancet archway entries as a family unit. Dace held open the door to allow his parents through, then walked into the quiet of the church vestibule.

Just inside the doorway, Dace felt a rush of warm air carrying the hint of burning candles hit his face. He turned to see the six waiting pallbearers in black suits and ties standing off to one side of the foyer speaking in low tones to an older man who could only have been the funeral director. Dace recognized two of Sarah's older brothers in the group and he nodded an acknowledgement to them. Obviously confused by the lack of personal contact the family expected from Dace over the last several days, they returned only glares.

In the opposite corner of the foyer stood another shorter man in black suit attending the collapsable casket carrier. Folded on top was what Dace recognized as a Portuguese flag. On a small oak lectern with a letter-sized slot in the front for bereavement cards set slightly off to the right of the center aisle doors Dace noticed a guest book which had obviously been brought over from the funeral home. More than half of the pages were already filled in and a cheap black pen lay in the binding. In a pair of small, clear plastic containers he saw envelopes for donations to the family and Holy Cards with the Virgin Mary on the front. He felt his body reflexively stiffen and tears welled in his eyes, this in-church visual suddenly much more real to him than even the coffin lying in the hearse on the street outside. He reached over and pulled a couple of Holy Cards from the container, pushed them into his jacket pocket. He felt the touch of his mother's hand on his arm and he turned and looked down into her eyes. For the first time since she had come to his room on Sunday morning, he saw genuine pain and understanding looking back at him. She mouthed the words 'I love you, my son' to him and then he felt her subtle guidance to move him through the doors into the church.

Dace glimpsed his father's eyes staring straight down the wide main aisle of the church. Several steps inside the doors were two fonts of Holy Water and The Senator's eyes never wavered as he dipped his fingertips onto the small sponge in the center and used them to bless himself with the Sign of the Cross. His mother reached past her son and did the same with water from the opposite font.  The ushers were seating other people in the remarkably full church and the Lamoureux family waited their turn to be escorted to an open pew.  Dace could see Sarah's grandmother seated alone in the first pew on the left.   His eyes searched for Dave Saunders' oversize frame and he finally located him about halfway back on the left side.   There was ample space on the pew next to Dave, so when the usher returned, Dace asked if they could be seated next to his friend.

As they continued up the aisle led by the usher, some people turned to look and a few who recognized the group began to speak to their neighbors.  People who knew both Dace and Sarah shot quizzical looks at Dace.  He merely averted his eyes to the tiled floor, but inside his heart, a spark had ignited and he could feel the anger, sadness, and resentment which had taken root over the last several days begin to grow.   It was time, he knew, to not stifle the emotions as he had been doing since Sunday morning in his father's office.  As he slid into the pew next to his lifelong friend, his first tear for Sarah rolled down Dace's cheek.  Dave reached over and patted his friend's shoulder.  When Dace looked over, Dave flashed him a covert thumb's up signal with his left hand.  Dace looked into Dave's eyes and nodded once.

"Daddy," Ashley said in her best manipulative voice.  "Please say it's okay for me to spend the weekend at Ronnie's house until Wednesday.  I don't want to just hang around school all weekend again if you are going to be out of town.  Ronnie's parents already said it's okay."

She winked at Ronnie who sat cross-legged on the bed.  Ronnie had already made the same call to her parents a few minutes earlier, only asking if she could stay at Ashley's place for the weekend.   Both girls knew the parents would never compare notes.   In fact, Ronnie believed her parents were a bit afraid of ever crossing paths with Mr. Monreale.

Ronnie watched as Ashley listened on the phone.  Ash's eyes were sparkling more with every passing second, so Ronnie assumed the news was good, but she was also rocking her head from side to side so that meant the lecture was long.  Ashley only had her dad as family in her life and he was fiercely protective of her; and Ronnie knew her friend loved her father dearly.  Ashley's mom had died unexpectedly when Ashley was five, years before the two best friends had met, and while they never really spoke about it, Ronnie thought that may explain the closeness which exists between Ashley and her father and why her father had the need to always know where she was and who was with her.   Ronnie smiled and thought of their outing to New Orleans last Saturday night and briefly wondered how Ash's dad would have reacted to that.

Ronnie had learned about Ashley's family slowly over the course of the friendship.   Over the last couple of years, Ronnie had heard the whispers around school about Vincent Anthony Monreale and how he really made his living; it seemed to her that rumors and innuendo were all that ever surfaced about some of the real estate developer's alleged darker side of doing business since the newspapers were very careful not to point the finger too directly, and she never broached the subject with Ashley.

Ronnie had first announced the friendship at home during Thanksgiving break her freshman year, and later had overheard her father speaking to her mother about whether it was such a good idea for their daughter to be so cozy with the daughter of 'Tony Gators', but when she had asked who Tony Gators was, her parents had quickly changed the subject and Ronnie had let it drop.

Then, the next spring, the girls were at Ronnie's house working on a science competition project which involved creating a complex diorama of a swamp to explain how the food chain of an ecosystem develops and as Ronnie was putting a toy alligator into the setting, she had said offhandedly, 'How about we name this guy Tony the Gator?' Ash had freaked.

'That's *not* my father,' she had said, jumping to her feet, her face red with rage. Then pointing a shaking finger at the center of Ronnie's nose, Ashley had added: 'Don't ever use that name again.'

"Aw, daddy, thank you so much," Ashley said into the phone. She and Ronnie bounced on the bed is silent celebration. "I love you, daddy." Ashley rolled her eyes and added: "Yes, daddy, I'll be good. Bye."

She flipped the phone closed and tossed it onto the bed between her and Ronnie.

"Laissez les bons temps rouler," Ronnie said.

# Chapter Four

Dace arose with the rest of the attendees at the sound of the small bell announcing the cortege. He turned to see the short, stocky priest in deep violet vestments flanked by two young altar boys in black cassocks under white surplices entering the church from the foyer beyond. The trio were led by another similarly costumed altar boy carrying a gold and silver staff with a crucifix surrounded by a circle at the top. It was a Celtic Cross, Sarah had told him one time when he had accompanied her and her grandmother to church there one Sunday two years ago. The same design was used at the top of each spire and throughout the building. She had also explained to him some of the history of the Portuguese culture and how the Celts and the Lusitanic people were connected throughout history, but he had forgotten most of that, at least for this day. The priest and each of the flanking altar boys held their hands in proper prayerful position, fingers straight and pointed skyward, left thumb over right, as Dace recalled from his days serving mass at St. Joseph's in New London.

Next came Sarah, flanked by three somber pallbearers dressed entirely in black on each side of her honey blonde oak coffin with a carved Celtic Cross in a darker wood affixed to the top. The coffin was set upon the chrome carrier he had seen off to the side in the foyer. The two funeral directors Dace had noticed when they had entered, quietly closed the church doors as the procession moved slowly down the center aisle, the soft rubber wheels of the carrier thudding dully against the stone tiles. It was the only sound which echoed above the soft sobs of some of the mourners. The taller funeral director remained in the foyer area, while the shorter one moved down the right side aisle carrying the folded Portuguese flag under his left arm.

When the cortege reached the area of the communion rail at the terminus of the center aisle, the priest and the three boys ascended the several stairs and scattered into the altar area to complete their routines in preparation for the Mass, while the pallbearers received the folded flag from the funeral director and proceeded to slowly unfold and cover the casket with the national symbol of Portugal, the homeland of Sarah's ancestors. Sarah had been proud of her heritage, Dace remembered.

As the pallbearers took their seats in the pew with Sarah's grandmother, the priest descended the stairs from the altar and performed the Asperges by dipping a silver and gold aspergillum, a short, hand-held device with holes in the end to capture and then release the Holy Water, into the aspersory, the small, gold, pail-like vessel held by an accompanying altar boy and sprinkled it onto the flagged casket and then into the assembled mourners, most of whom understood the ritual and reverently blessed themselves as the priest recited the traditional words of Psalm 50.

The words he spoke were in Portuguese, familiar to the parishioners and regular attendees of Mass at Our Lade of the Rosary, where the Liturgy was still practiced in the language.

"Tu sprinke-me, ó Senhor, com hissopo e ficarei limpo; Tu lava-me, e eu me tornarei mais branco do que show. Tem misericórdia de mim, ó Deus, segundo a tua grande misericórdia," he repeated the verse softly until he was finished and the pair returned to the altar.

Dace remembered the words in English: 'Thou shalt sprinkle me, Oh Lord, with hyssop and I shall be cleansed; Thou shalt wash me, and I shall become whiter than show. Have mercy on me, Oh God, according to Thy great mercy.'

The next hour of the Mass was a blur for Dace. He participated, stood when he was supposed to, kneeled when everyone else did, sat when the assembled just needed to listen, prayed when told to, and accepted Communion at the foot of the altar next to Sarah's coffin. Sarah's younger brother, Trevor, the taller of the pall bearers who had glared at Dace in the foyer, read a eulogy which Dace noticed omitted any mention of his and Sarah's relationship. The omission stung his heart, but given the unexplained lack of communication since the accident, Dace understood. Understanding didn't assuage his pain, but it did perhaps beguile his heart. For the moment.

As suddenly as it had begun, it was over. The cortege reassembled, the pall bearers took to their places, and Sarah was moved up the center aisle of her lifelong church for the last time. As her coffin passed their pew, Dace felt the tears welling and his heart breaking again as his mind flew to a thought he and Sarah had very recently shared. Dace had broached the subject of their wedding - not the marriage, but rather the ceremony - with her a couple of weeks earlier and she had informed him her one insistence was going to be that their wedding ceremony be held in her grandmother's church. Her face had lit up with an almost childlike joy as she described to him how all her life she had dreamed of the day she would walk down that very aisle to join the man of her dreams, and then walk out with him after God had blessed and sealed their love and the promises they both had made to Him and each other. Dace felt a single tear roll down his cheek. He left it there. It felt good. Alive.

His father began to shift nervously in his place, obviously eager to get out of there. His mother lightly patted one of her husband's hands which tightly gripped the back of the forward pew. Inexplicably, the images of his father and mother at that moment transformed his pain for the loss of Sarah into a white-hot rage in the center of his soul aimed directly at the man to his right. Dace couldn't comprehend the emotion at that moment, but could understand the resentment which had been building slowly since Sunday morning was fueling the inferno which burned within him.

The Senator had informed Dace and his mother on the ride from New London that they would not be going to the cemetery for the burial, nor return to the basement of the church for the luncheon provided by Sarah's family. So, as Sarah's casket was rolled back out of the church into the foyer, Dace said his final farewell to her from a distance. The tears he had swallowed over the last days, and the one which now dried at the base of his chin were rapidly turning the wounds in his heart into scar tissue, hard and calloused, yet still tender to when touched. He knew the process was occurring, but he was unable to understand how or why.

The pews released from the front, and when Sarah's grandmother passed by the Lamoureux family she made eye contact with Dace; unlike the malice expressed by Sarah's brothers, Grammy's eyes contained nothing for him but sadness. He broke the connection by looking down, and understood that would be the last time he would ever see her. When their pew released, the three members of the Lamoureux family joined now by Dave Saunders fell in behind the other mourners in the slow walk back up the center aisle. The crowd filled the foyer area and spilled through the triplex of open doors onto the stairs outside. The chill of the day swirled into the church and freshened the air inside. Flames attached tenuously to wicks of candles in sconces along the back wall danced with every breeze, and as Dace approached the area, one of the candles extinguished, the smoke rising in a twisted ribbon and it dissipated as it floated toward the arched ceiling. Just before they passed through the doors into the foyer, Dave and Dace momentarily lingered together.

"Go down the stairwell off to your right when you get to the foyer," Dave whispered to Dace. "The bathrooms are down there. There's another stairwell off to the left, that's the one I'll go down before you tell your dad you have to piss." Dave suddenly looked a little embarrassed. "Geeze, I probably shouldn't say piss in church, should I?"

Dace almost laughed out loud, but disguised it with a cough. The Senator turned to look at him with a hint of disapproval. Dave cut through the last pew to the left and went out the side aisle door. Dace watched him exit the church. When the he and his parents had shuffled out into the foyer, Dace turned to someone who looked local and asked in a volume to ensure his father would hear where the bathrooms were. The man pointed toward the stairwell and told him the restrooms were downstairs in the back of the large hall.

"Dad, I've got to make a stop before we head back," Dace said, putting his hand on his father's shoulder.

His father nodded.

His mother looked Dace in the eyes; Dace disconnected the gaze a moment later, turned toward the stairwell off to the left. Over the heads of the crowd and through the open doors, Dace could see Sarah's coffin being loaded into the hearse.

"Meet us at the car, son," The Senator said, then he and Libby slowly wedged their way through the assemblage and out onto the sidewalk. Their driver spotted them and maneuvered the limousine onto a spot along the curb on the opposite side of the street, pointed in the direction out of the area for the quickest exit to the interstate. Further down the block, the two large gentlemen in the black Lincoln Town Car did a y-turn and prepared to follow the limo out of Providence. Libby and The Senator crossed the street behind the idling hearse. Sarah had already been loaded, Libby saw, the Portuguese flag still draping the casket. The pall bearers mingled and several shot angry glances toward the lone pair departing the scene.

Inside, Dace sprinted down the stairs and found Dave standing in the center of a large open area. He knew he didn't have much time before his father would begin to suspect something. They needed at least a ten minute head start, which would put them on the I-95, and then it would be anyone's guess where they had headed.

"What the hell is going on, dude?" Dave asked as Dace trotted up to him. Dave had already loosened his tie and opened the top button of his shirt. He stood there with his arms spread in the perfect pose for the question.

"I'll tell you all about it once we're out of here," Dace said. He surveyed the area, saw the men's room door and moved in its direction. "Hang on just a second."

Dave watched as Dace ducked into the men's room. He smirked to himself as he noted the symbols on the blue and white plastic cards identifying each restroom were caricatures of male and female angels. 'Catholics, man,' he mumbled to himself. Dave's family was Methodist and didn't believe in the existence of angels. When Dace reappeared a mere couple of moments later, Dave made a smart aleck comment. Dace returned a wry look before responding.

"No, but I did have to drop something off," Dace said.

Dace glanced around the room. This was obviously where the lunch was going to be held after the burial; it had been set with rows of long tables covered with paper and attended by brown, metal folding chairs. In the front of the room waited a group of tables set up as a buffet with stacks of disposable plates and napkins, containers of plastic silverware, chafing dishes waiting for the warm food and some Jell-O and cake pieces on Styrofoam plates already set out on the far end of one table.

"Okay, lets get out of here," Dace said. "Where are you parked?"

"Out in front of the rectory building, on Benefit Street," Dave said as he began moving toward the far end of the room. "Come on, exit's this way." He led his friend at a jog like he was pulling out in front on a quarterback sweep. Through a door, down a long hallway, out another set of doors, then up a stairwell and through a plain metal door and they arrived into the daylight on the opposite end of the church from the rest of the crowd, and what was more important, out of sight of both Dace's father and the two large gentlemen.

They ran to Dave's old Mustang GT Liftback. A parking ticket had been tucked under the windshield wiper, but Dave tore it loose and tossed it onto the back seat as he slid behind the wheel. Dace got in on the passenger side as Dave cranked the engine. A moment later, they were pulling from the curb; at the corner Dave turned left and drove over the bridge, then left at Eddy Street and left again at Thurbers Avenue swinging wide into the far right lane, the onramp for I-95 headed south.

Eight minutes after Dace had excused himself, the pair was gone. Six minutes later, two rather large gentlemen searched the basement men's room. The only thing they found was a cell phone.

"It's Dace's all right," said The Senator as he scrolled around the cell phone's menus. He slapped the phone closed and threw it onto the adjacent side-facing seat in the back of the limo. The two large gentlemen stood outside the door's open window. The Senator glanced at his watch, noting it was no more than twenty minutes since Dace had excused himself. He shook his head in irritation. "What the hell does he think he's doing, Libby?"

She knew the question was rhetorical and any response she may give would just further annoy her husband, so she remained silent and continued to stare out the window of the limousine at the rapidly emptying parking lot across from the church. The hearse and family cars had already departed to lead the procession to the cemetery.

"Dave Saunders was involved in this, to be certain," he said, again, rhetorically. He was thinking things through.

He moved to pick up Dace's phone from where it had landed and flipped it open again. He went to the address book and scrolled for Dave Saunders' entry then pressed the green Send button. Without ringing, the voicemail greeting picked up.

"Hi, this is Dave. I'm gonna be out of touch for a while, but I'll be checking in now and again with a couple of folks, just to keep my hand in, if you know what I mean." Self-amused laughter. "Don't leave a message, 'cause they'll just pile up. See you when I get back."

There was no 'leave a message after the beep' beep and the line simply went dead. The Senator slapped the phone closed again and this time heaved it toward the front of the compartment. When it hit the divider, he could see the chauffeur's annoyed eyes drift up toward the rearview momentarily, then disconnect. The driver didn't care if The Senator was a valued client, it was his job to clean up any messes and explain any damage to his boss. The Senator pushed a button on the overhead control panel which rolled down the smoked glass divider just a bit. The driver's eyes moved back to the rearview.

"Take us back to New London, driver," The Senator said.

"Yes, sir," came the reply as he slipped the car into gear and pulled away from the curb, leaving two large gentlemen to jog to their own car idling up the block.

"Oh, and sorry about the noise a moment ago."

"No problem, senator," he said as the divider was closed on his words.

The stretched Lincoln passed its smaller sibling as the two large gentlemen slid into their car and then it pulled out behind the limousine. Six minutes later, the convoy of two was headed south on I-95.

Before they were off the surface streets, The Senator was on his own cell phone with Tom McDaniel. If anyone could pull out all the stops and get done what needed to be done, it would be Tom. The Senator would never know all the details, and there were very good reasons for that. In the nation's capital-speak, the game was referred to as *plausible deniability*; it was an art form, and Senator Allard Lamoureux and Tom McDaniel were masters. Moments after The Senator disconnected, the Town Car with the two large gentlemen accelerated rapidly past the limo and disappeared into the distance a few minutes later.

In the back of the limousine, The Senator watched them, then sat back and smiled. Libby continued to gaze silently out her window as the city quickly gave way to countryside, with forested land stretching on rises as far as the eye could see. It always amazed her how quickly one could get out into the middle of nowhere along the hugely populated eastern seaboard.

"I'm so sorry, Dace," Dave said, breaking the silence which hovered inside the car since making their escape from Providence. "I should have..."

"Don't you dare start that," Dace interrupted and pointed a finger at Dave's surprised face.

The two sat in silence again and the miles fell behind them. Dave maneuvered the Mustang around the traffic, trying to put as much distance between him and The Senator's men, whom, he was certain, were looking for them by now. He strained to keep the car under eighty because he knew a traffic stop would quickly eat up any lead they currently held. When Dave did reembark upon the topic ten minutes later, Dace let him get more out, obviously understanding his big buddy just needed to say the words, whether Dace needed to hear them or not.

"Geeze, Dace, if I hadn't drank so much, she wouldn't have had to drive me home, man. Don't you see? She wouldn't have been on that road. She would have been on the clear, dry highway halfway to her grandmother's house, instead of babysitting me."

"Yeah, and if I hadn't been such a selfish asshole who allowed her to volunteer, I would have driven you home," Dace said as he watched out the passenger side window. He turned to look at his lifelong friend. "We can play these *what if* games forever, Dave. It won't bring Sarah back, and all it will do is heap worthless guilt on our shoulders. It'll be an endless circle, man. We'll feel better because we're taking responsibility and then we'll feel more guilty because of what we did or didn't do and around and around we'll go, but in the end what happened to Sarah was just a stupid accident. The police said so. A series of events in a chain. Hell, if the weather hadn't been so warm that day, the snow wouldn't have melted and created that patch of ice." He opened his arms, palms up. "Come on, man."

"I guess," Dave said, and the subject of 'who did and who didn't' was dropped as a topic of conversation. He knew that there would be more time to discuss Sarah and the accident while they were on their little journey, and that Dace would eventually need to do so, so he didn't further push the issue at that moment. Instead, he changed the subject to the aftermath. "You know I tried calling all day Sunday after I heard. At first your phone just went to voicemail, and then nothing. When I'd call the house, no matter who answered, I was told you were unavailable and not taking calls. So that's when I got a ride and came over to get my car." An evil grin came over his face. "How did you ever think to get a note out to me using Mary Rose?"

"You know she loves you, Dave," Dace said as he looked out the side window at the passing countryside and a conspiratorial smile slid onto his face. "I knew you'd come over, for your car, at least. They had me on lock down, and nobody else would dare have gone against father's wishes, so Mary Rose was the only option. They're never going to figure it out and it'll drive them all nuts."

They shared a much needed laugh.

Just then, Dave began to slow down, put on his right blinker and slid the white car with blue racing stripes onto the exit lane. Dace swung around in the seat to see if they were being pulled over, but their tail was clear.

"What's up?" Dace asked as he peered across to check the gas gauge which read nearly full.

The sign along the highway indicated the exit they were taking was for Highway 102 - the Victory Highway - at West Greenwich.

"You're not the only strategist in this thing, you know," Dave said, a sly grin again on his face. "I figured we'd have, at most twenty minutes before your old man had the dragnet starting to deploy. He knows my car, and even if he doesn't know the license number, he'd be able to have it with one phone call." Dave rounded the two-hundred-seventy degree turn faster than the signs said he should, but the little sportster hugged the road nicely. His eyes moved toward Dace. "So, I arranged something."

After the cloverleaf, they were headed east, then Dave suddenly jerked the wheel to the right and pulled into an old park which held about two dozen relatively dilapidated house trailers haphazardly parked at less than orderly angles. He drove down the first lane which curved and intersected the second drive, took a left and pulled around back of a trailer in the center of the half loop which then became the third and last gravel street of the complex. He parked the car, turned off the motor, popped the trunk using a button inside the glove box, jumped out and told Dace to sit tight.

Dace watched from the passenger seat as an extremely thin, middle aged woman with black and gray streaked hair pulled into a pony tail, dressed in pink, fluffy slippers, and a well-worn, matching robe cinched tight at the waist came out of the trailer and stood on the small, unpainted plywood and two-by-four porch. She smiled when she saw Dave, took a long drag from the cigarette in her hand and then expertly flipped a half-burned butt into a nearby pile of dirty snow pockmarked with gravel, pee stains, and dog crap.

Dave climbed the couple rickety steps onto the small porch and threw his big arms around the woman. She returned the hug and then clasped his cheeks in her hands when the two released. The ensuing conversation was short and sweet, and unheard in the car. Dace had no reason to want to overhear what was being said. If Dave wanted him to know, he'd tell him. The woman stepped back into the trailer and a moment later reappeared with an envelope and a set of keys, all of which she handed to Dave as she pointed over the top of her trailer toward the west. The greeting was repeated in reverse order, starting with deep, shared looks and cheek cupping and ending with another hug. Dace watched the woman wipe a tear from her face and then she reached into the pocket of the robe, removed and ignited another cigarette with a cheap, disposable lighter and disappeared for good inside the trailer. The inner door closed.

Dave was off the porch and signaled Dace to get out, which he did. Dave leaned into the trunk, removed two large duffels and tossed one to Dace.

"I grabbed you a bunch of stuff from the apartment at school that I figured you'd need, since I knew you couldn't exactly pack a bag today," he said. "The rest we can pick up along the way." He slammed the trunk, packed a couple of handfuls of snow over the rear license plate, and started around the trailer. Dace fell in behind, being careful not to step on anything but dirty snow.

"What do you think?" Dave said as the pair rounded the far end of the mobile home and stood face-to-face with a brand new, pearl white Cadillac Esplanade. Dave touched a button on the key and the tailgate opened automatically. He tossed his duffel inside and Dace threw his in alongside.

"What do I think?" Dace said, shaking his head slowly. "I think that lady needs to get her priorities in order. She lives in *that* but drives *this?*" He pointed first toward the trailer and then the SUV.

"She's my aunt, the black sheep of our family," Dave said. "This is my new car, well, my new leased car. I figured a corporate mogul or pro football star deserved something better than a twelve-year-old Mustang GT Liftback." He held up the key ring to Dace. "You want to drive?"

Dace smiled broadly and shook his head. Dave had indeed taken the ball and run with his simple request to help him get away for a while which he had written in the surreptitious note delivered by Mary Rose.

"You're doing great, buddy." He walked around to the passenger seat, stood on the running board and peered over the top at his best friend. "Let's get out of here. I can't wait to see what's next."

"You're gonna love it, dude."

Two minutes later, they rolled around another leaf of the clover and were back on I-95 headed south. A speeding black Lincoln Town Car blew past them before they passed the next exit. The two large gentlemen in the front seat never even glanced back.

Sandy and I called each of my girls in turn. They all seemed to take the news of the new baby in stride, mainly, I think, because Sandy made certain to reinforce our commitment to them. I believe Sandy speaking those words meant more to my girls than they would have coming from only from me, which gave yours truly something else to think about during those long, dark nights ahead.

When we had hung up with my oldest, the last of the three to get the news, I asked Sandy if she wanted to call her parents and my mother to give them the good news. It is then that she told me that my mother already knew. Sandy had called her before she had come in to wake me at lunch. One corner of my mouth raised in response to that news. It made sense. If a woman wants to know how to handle a son, who better to ask than the man's mother? Sandy winked at me.

As I sat across the couch with my wife, I reached along the back and took her hand in mine. Sandy really was glowing. I could see it now for what it was. Her eyes seemed bluer, and quicker to moisten when I looked deeply into them. Her smile, always ready to pop out, was quicker, and lasted longer. I ran my thumb over the back of her hand. Heck, even her skin seemed softer. I was beginning to become excited with the whole idea of becoming a middle-age dad. I had been a dad three times before - as far as I know, as the tired, old joke goes - but it had been a number of years since I had been in that position and everything about the experience seemed new, and bright, and fascinating.

"Well," Sandy said with a teasing smile on her lips. "You want to break the news of what you have done to me to my dad, or should I?"

"Feel free," I said, gently pushing forth ushering hands toward the telephone. It was a no brainer. I'm not even certain Sandy's father likes me; and I know he doesn't appreciate my sense of humor. I had no desire to tell him he's going to be even more closely related to a part of me now. "Although I do want to hear the reaction as it happens, so put the call on speaker again." Then, it was my turn for the smile, although mine was a little darker than the teasing kind.

Sandy punched in the number, placed the cell phone between us on the couch and we listened to the echo of the ringing back in Wisconsin. It rang five times.

"Maybe he's out shoveling snow," I said. "Wanna just text him?"

"Even if he is, mom should be home from work by now."

I looked over my shoulder and out through the plantation shutters on the side windows overlooking the narrow street below; it was just starting to get dark outside. It would be the same in Wisconsin, although much colder than our day had been.

"Hello?" came through interrupting the seventh ring.

"Hi, dad," Sandy said from above the phone. "It's Sandy, and I have Will here with me. We've got you on speaker phone."

"Is everything okay, honey?" he asked.

See? Not even an acknowledgment of me. I told you the guy doesn't like me.

"Just fine, dad," Sandy said.  She looked at me and conveyed in an instant what she was thinking and that was she had no intention of letting me slip through the net. "Say hello to Will, dad."

A pause.

"Hello, William," he said a moment later with about as much feeling as if the words had been delivered by a teenager interrupted in his video game playing by his mother so he could greet an elderly aunt.   Another pause. "How are you?"

"Just fine, Mr. Beach," I said. I still called him Mr. Beach after all the years I've known him, going back to high school.  Sandy's mom had wanted me to call her mom since the first time I met her when I was seventeen, but he had never offered the informality and I didn't assume. So, yeah, you got it, my in-laws to me are 'Mom and Mr. Beach'.

"Is mom there, dad?" Sandy asked.

"Just walked in, honey," her father replied. "You want to talk to your mother?"

"No, I want to talk to both of you," Sandy said. "Can you have her get on the extension?"

Several moments of what must have been frantic, yet silent, signaling and mouthing of the words 'It's Sandy', followed by a few more moments of silence and then the click of the extension being picked up. Anybody want to take a bet on whether Sandy's dad mentioned I was on the line too?

"Hi, dear," said Sandy's mom, a little out of breath, having climbed the stairs to the bedroom extension. "How are you?"  Breath. "To what do we owe this pleasant little surprise?"

"And Will, mom." Sandy rolled her eyes to me.

"Oh, hi, William," came the genuinely sweet addition. "Your father didn't mention William was on the line when he told me to pick up. Sorry.  How are you *both* then?"

From the barely repressed irritation in mom's voice, I wondered if Mr. Beach would hear further about leaving me out of the call announcement.  I hoped so.

"We're both fine, mom," I said. "How are you?"

Sandy flashed me a look.  I had done the unthinkable.  I had asked a septuagenarian who loves to tell everyone about her various medical maladies the moment someone opens the door, how she was.  Don't get me wrong, I love the woman.  My grandfather was the same way.  I shrugged my shoulders to my wife and silently mouthed 'I'm sorry'.

"Oh, William, thank you for asking," mom began. A sigh. "Really, I've been so tired lately.  I just don't know what's wrong, but since the holidays I have been exhausted.  The doctor says everything is fine, so don't you two worry.  You have your own lives to live.  No sense worrying about an old woman..."

"Jesus, Harriet, you make it sound as if you're dying," Mr. Beach injected from the other phone. "This is long distance and it must be costing these two a small fortune, and I don't think peeping around at people pays a lot, so let them get on with why they called. They don't want to hear your medical history."

"Dad, we're on a cell phone, and long distance is free these days," Sandy explained.

"Oh, I never thought about the cost, Thomas," mom said as if Sandy hadn't just clarified the situation. "Go ahead dear. Do you want us to call you back? Or do you want to reverse the charges?"

"No, mom," Sandy said. She had a patient smile on her glowing face. "We have some news we want to share with you."

"You aren't going back to that island again to live like cannibals, are you? See, I told you, Harriet, this little Peeping Tom thing of theirs wouldn't last. Spying through windows, what kind of job is that for a grown man?" Mr. Beach said.

I had to fight the thought that he would have been happiest if the news his daughter had for him had been that I was going back to the cannibal-infested Caymans alone and Sandy was coming home to Sheboygan. The beer I missed with lunch would have been handy right then, if it had been a glass of bourbon. Now that was a thought I didn't fight.

I got up, crossed the office, pulled open the bookshelves which hid my wet bar, and poured two fingers of Jim Beam Bourbon into a lowball glass. No ice, neat. I tossed it down, set the glass down and walked back to the couch. I left the bookcases open. I had a feeling I'd be back.

"No, dad," Sandy said, "and, there are no cannibals that I know of in the Cayman Islands. It's a rather civilized place."

"Yeah, flush toilets and everything," I said as I sat down.

A pause.

"Then what is the news, dear," mom asked.

"Well, we're very happy, and we wanted you to know we're going to have a baby at the end of July or early August," Sandy said.

She bit her lower lip and looked at me. My God, her eyes were blue.

Silence.

"Well, that's wonderful, dear," mom said. "Thomas?"

A beat.

"Yes, congratulations, honey," Mr. Beach said.

"And Will."

I think that last words had been spoken by Sandy, but I was so engrossed with staring at the phone in total disbelief by that point that I didn't quite see her lips moving.

"Yes, of course," Mr. Beach said. Then, in a tone which I heard as hopeful: "Are you certain, honey?"

What the hell did that mean? I thought.

"I saw my doctor this morning, dad," Sandy said. "There's no doubt about it."

I got up and walked over to my hidden wet bar again, glad I had left the book case open and downed another two fingers of Beam. Something in the way Mr. Beach said the word 'certain' stuck in my craw. Right then I wasn't just uncertain whether Sandy's dad liked me, I was certain the man hated me. I stood there, confused and getting pissed as the alcohol rushed to my brain. I discerned more discussion in the background but paid no attention, and a minute later felt Sandy's arms move around me from behind. I let her hug me backwards for a moment, then turned around and saw her smiling face looking up at me. I hugged her back and kissed her.

"They're happy for us," she said when I released her.

"How can you tell?"

"Phil Neufeldt was one of the cops who came to my house on Sunday morning."

Dace looked puzzled.

"You remember Phil. We went to grade school with him. He and his mother came to New London from Florida after his father had died. We were in the third grade. He left school after seventh grade, then came back to the area after high school when his mother passed away and is now working for the New London County Sheriff's Department."

Dace shook his head.

"No, don't remember him."

"Well, no matter. He remembers you. I remember he never liked you after you pushed him down on the school playground during that beanbag football game we were playing one day just before he left, and he apparently hasn't gotten over it."

"So, tell me," Dace said ignoring the last remark and twisting the top off a Mountain Dew he had bought when they stopped to fill up just outside of Hagerstown, Maryland. "Every detail after you left the house Saturday night."

Dave took a deep breath and his grip tightened on the leather-wrapped steering wheel. He punched a button on the center console and his heated seat stopped heating. His eyes focused on the lights of the cars in the road ahead as his mind fought through last Saturday night's alcohol fog to recall every possible detail for his friend. The drive had only taken twenty minutes or so from the Lamoureux estate to Dave's house, so it wasn't much of a period to remember. Even so, there wasn't much detail that Dave could recall apart from most of the drive he and Sarah had spent talking about a singular subject; one which Dave was certain would only reopen the fresh wound in his friend's heart. His mind raced through options which he could use to lessen the impact, but there was no ruse or misdirection which he could play on his lifelong buddy. The pair of men were closer than most brothers. Dace carefully observed Dave's dilemma playing out inside him.

"It's okay, Dave," he said. "I can take it. I want to know."

Dave broke his locked stare with the roadway and glanced across the darkened car at Dace. Dace nodded. It would be okay, Dave knew then.

"She was in great spirits when we left the party," Dave began, returning his attention to the road. "Apparently, you two shared a secret; and while she hinted at it enough the whole way home, she didn't let the cat out of the bag. She said that you two had talked about a future, and when the time was right, everyone would know. It was all she wanted to talk about, Dace. She went through it repeatedly, but never really said the words." He turned and looked Dace in the eye and smiled. "Not that I couldn't guess."

"I had asked her to marry me," Dace said with a thoughtful nod. "I told my entire family about my plans in my father's office shortly before guests began arriving Saturday night. I thought they all loved Sarah as much as I do. Did. Whatever." Dace's voice faded with those final words and out of the corner of his eye, Dave saw his face morph through several confused, pain-filled permutations and then drift to a distant focus.

Dave glanced across the car's cabin when the silence continued. Dace was staring out the windshield. Dave wasn't so sure he should have been so blunt, but what else was there to tell his friend? Sarah had really talked about nothing else on the ride home. He couldn't lie, make something up which would be less painful. That just wouldn't be right; and Dace would know. So, Dave changed the subject from what was lost into something more related to *why* they were where they were right then: on the interstate in the dark, moonless evening somewhere in northern Virginia on the day they buried his best friend's girlfriend.

"Let me guess, your old man didn't like the fact Sarah didn't come from Portuguese royalty or from some old money family from Boston, and was instead the orphaned daughter with two brothers each with minor criminal records, all raised by their paternal grandmother in blue-collar Providence. It didn't matter one whit to him that she had clawed herself out of that could-be dead end life and was a gonna be doctor with degrees from Harvard and Stanford. She still wasn't good enough for The Senator's kid."

Dace's expression changed again as his focus returned to the moment. He shot his old friend a look which conveyed what they both understood but which would, for the moment anyway, remain unspoken. In that instant, the loss of Sarah changed from an abstraction to a reality to Dave.

The young are unfamiliar with death and even though he had seen the spot where her car left the roadway, been in church that day at her funeral mass and had seen her closed coffin, he had not processed those things with the mental image of a young woman he had known, laughed with, plotted a surprise birthday party for Dace a year earlier together, and had hugged good-bye just three days ago, mere minutes before she was dead. Yet, he could now see it all in Dace's eyes. She was dead. Gone. Nobody would ever hear her voice again, or her contagious laugh. Dave felt a stabbing pain inside his chest and his eyes misted and he looked back to the roadway out the windshield again. He knew his friend felt a much deeper pain, and he also understood Dace would have to deal with it in his own way.

"I just don't want to believe she's gone," Dave said absently and more in response to his own thoughts than to anything exterior.

"Yeah, they took my phone, just gave it back this morning," Dace said in a response to Dave's question asked hours earlier. "They wouldn't let me out of the house, not even to take a run. My father's first reaction was to bring in his political advisor. Oh, and those two mountains posing as security men. I think The Senator considered it all to be some sort of political situation needing to be managed." He issued a derisive snort and looked out the side window into the dark emptiness. "I think he saw this as the Lamoureux family's version of Chappaquiddick. My father and Tom McDaniel have spent days in his office and on phone calls figuring the best way to put the proper spin to this so it could never come back to bite me."

"Spin it? What's there to spin?" Dave asked. "Chappaquiddick? That Kennedy thing from the 60s? What the hell, Dace? Even Phil said it was very clearly an accident; and you weren't even in the car. There's a truth to this tragic story that wasn't there for the Kennedy's when Ted drove his car off that bridge and left that young girl behind to drown while he saved his own skin and didn't have his lawyers call the police for eight hours or something like that, till he had sobered up. Had that piece of crap been anyone else, he would have served time, and not in the United States Senate."

"No, that's not it," Dace said, shifting in his seat and drinking down more of the Dew. "It doesn't matter that Sarah died in some stupid accident. She was only twenty, under age in Connecticut and had left a party where alcohol was available shortly before hitting that ice patch. She was my long-term girlfriend, and had left in the company of another man."

He was parroting the perceptions he had heard endlessly for the past three days from Tom and The Senator, not the reality.

"She left with *me*, Dace," Dave said with a strong tone of incredulity. "Me. I'm your best friend, not some *other man* for Christ's sake."

"My father's political enemies could spin this a hundred different ways. Besides, who cares what the truth is in politics? It matters what people believe the truth is, and that is controlled by managing the story." A pause. "At least that's the Lamoureux way, I'm told."

"You're talking like your father now," Dave said. "I think we need to get some rest. Roanoke is coming up; we'll get a hotel room there and start fresh in the morning."

Dace continued to stare into the nothingness.

"It's been made very clear to me that I had better start thinking more like my father and less like me," he said.

"You're not your father."

"No, but I am a Lamoureux."

"Yeah, a friggin' fortunate son, all right," Dave said under his breath, not intending Dace to hear.

"So they tell me," Dace said to the nothingness.


"Sandy, do you have any problem with that contract?" I asked from my office door.

She had taken the political party contract to her outer office desk to review it after we finished with the phone call to her parents, and before I blindly signed it and sent it back, I wanted her okay. I knew she could pick it apart and make it airtight and favorable to us, but my review had found it to be boilerplate stuff: identification of the parties, purposely two or three steps away from the 'Party', payment, agency, confidentiality, etc., and I would have just signed it as it was. Doing any modifications would take months of going back and forth and I just wanted to see if there was anything major I had missed.

"Nope, it's just boilerplate," she said. "I've attached our standard billing schedule, payment terms, and liability riders, which I don't think they'll have any issues with. It's all coming off the printer now. I'll bring it in so you can sign it, I'll witness and then we can fax it back and head for home. I'm done in today."

"Sounds good to me, Sandy." I looked at the wall clock in the outer office which showed six-thirty. I couldn't believe it was really that late and checked my cell phone. Yep, six-thirty. "Wanna stop for some Chinese takeout on the way home? I can call The Great Wall while you're putting it all together."

"If you really want to know, I have been craving chocolate ice cream and bread and butter pickles for days," Sandy said, a huge grin then breaking over her face.

A pause.

"Seriously?"

She put her elbows on her desk and cradled her chin in the palms of her hands and looked at me with a closed lip smile on her face.

'What?' I thought.

"You sure are gullible for an ex-cop," she said and she slowly shook her head, "but I still love ya."

"Funny." I turned to go back into my office. Once inside, a huge grin came over my face. 'A baby', I said under my breath.

"What?"

"Nothing," I said over my shoulder. "You want Singapore Noodles and Cashew Chicken?"

"That'll be great," she called after me.

"Okay," I said back and then settled into my chair and spun it around to face the desk. She was already standing there with the small stack of papers and scared the crap out of me as I came around and my eyes focused as quickly as they could with four fingers of Kentucky bourbon dumped into me an hour ago.

"Get some pot stickers and pork egg rolls," she said as she pointed out where I needed to sign. She had already signed as witnessing my signature and applied our corporate seal, I saw.

"Seriously?"

I scribbled my signature across the line.

"Yeah, I'm starved." She retrieved the executed stack and turned to walk out of the office. "I'll fax these and meet you out front."

I found the entry for The Great Wall restaurant in my cell phone directory and hit the green SEND button. While it was connecting, Sandy stuck her head back into my office.

"Oh, and can we stop at the Winn-Dixie and get some cream soda on the way home?" Then with a giggle, she was gone.

"Seriously?"

# Chapter Five

Dave awoke early the following morning. As he peered out the window, he saw the sun was just beginning to hint at a new day. He dressed in sweats and sports shoes before leaving Dace sleeping in the room while he headed for the motel's gym. A full eleven hours on the road yesterday had left his muscles knotted and begging for a workout before facing the promise of that many or more hours of driving today. As comfortable as the Escalade was, when you're six-foot-four and over three-hundred pounds, no automobile seat fits you well; and airline seats? Forget about it.

He was glad to see the motel's gym was more than the typical broken down treadmill and stepper machine with a television in the corner of some unventilated, oversize closet they had cleared out. As he learned later when he complimented the front desk staff on the facility, the CEO of that particular chain had suffered a near-fatal heart attack two years earlier and in the aftermath of re-embracing life he had issued orders his locations would provide their guests with a fully equipped workout room along with dietitian-approved, healthy breakfast items. The man predicted healthy would be the next trend as the country woke up to the growing problem of growing Americans. While complimentary of the gym, seeing no chocolate donuts on the breakfast bar a few minutes after concluding his workout, he found a bit disappointing.

When Dave was finishing up on the elliptical, Dace showed up and stood next to the machine, just watching. He was dressed in a pair of jeans and polo shirt Dave had packed in the duffel bag. Dace hadn't shaved and his hair was tousled and still wet from a shower.

"Not feeling like a workout this morning?" Dave teased as he climbed off the machine. "How can you ever think you're going to get this kind of body by slacking it?" He flexed and raised his arms to pump the biceps. Dave looked at his muscular arms. "Oh, yeah, that's what I'm talking about."

Dace smirked, shook his head, turned and began to walk to the door.

"I take it we have a ways to go today, buddy," Dace said over his shoulder. "I'm ready when you are. No hurry."

"Just gonna finish up with some free-weight curls, then grab a couple of donuts and a quick shower," Dave called after him, "and yeah, we've got a ways to go."

"You're the boss."

Dace looked around anxiously as he paused at the door. He seemed filled with nervous energy.

"Hey, I'm gonna walk across the street to that convenience store and grab a pack of smokes. I'll be out front whenever you're ready. Bring down my duffel, would you? It's ready to go."

"Smokes?"

Dace walked through the door.

"You don't smoke," Dave called after him.

"It's as if they've dropped right off the face of the earth," Tom McDaniel said. He was finishing the last of his Eggs Benedict which Caroline had prepared and brought to him in The Senator's office. Seated at the front of the edge of the leather couch, he was hunched over his plate set on the coffee table. The Senator watched him from his chair behind his desk.

"People just can't do that," The Senator protested. "Not these days. We know he's with Dave Saunders. Find him and you'll find Dace."

"That's what we've been trying to do, Allard," Tom said. "This isn't my people's first rodeo. Our teams are as good as anyone out there and we've been discreetly tapping into the various local, state, and federal agencies for information. I don't want to put anything into the official channels yet. We don't need some bureaucrat's file showing up down the road when we don't even know what the hell is going on with the boy yet."

"Of course not," The Senator said. "Just be careful how much you toss around Dave Saunders' name. It's no secret locally he's Dace's best friend and we don't need anyone putting two and two together." He rose from his desk and walked to the window and looked down the drive. It seemed like a lifetime ago when he last watched his son run out to the road on his birthday. "Whatever you do, don't use any strong arm stuff on anyone local. I don't trust the local cops, and I know that old man Saunders votes straight ticket on the other side. We don't need him pissed off and sniffing around or telling stories. We already are at a disadvantage because we don't know how much he knows, or suspects."

"The Saunders kid's parents don't know anything. I had one of our men approach them surreptitiously as you suggested, calling them last night and saying he was from Harvard. Our man spoke to each parent individually. A voice stress analyst was on the line and she said the parents each indicated levels which one would associate with getting an unanticipated call from a child's college rather than with deception over the questions about his whereabouts. As the call went on, the voice stress levels dropped even lower, further bolstering the expert's conclusion of truth telling. They don't know anything is awry."

"Maybe they know where Dave is and were merely comfortable with that fact," The Senator opined. "Did your expert consider that?"

Tom held his fork and knife out in a gesture of frustration with the question.

"We know the Saunders kid got a parking ticket outside the church rectory," Tom said with his mouth half full. "The fact he was parked on that side of the building means there was some planning done here. As far as we can tell, his car hasn't shown up anywhere yet. Maybe they are local, holed up someplace."

"I doubt it, but anything's possible at this point, I suppose," The Senator said. "What about their cell phones?"

"We'll have both their cell phone records in a couple of hours to see who they have been talking to recently. We already have tracking on them, courtesy of a technician who's a friend, but given Dace dumped his cell phone in the men's room of the church basement, I don't anticipate Dave Saunders would be dumb enough to be carrying his along with him to allow us to track him. Given what we have so far, which isn't much, we have to assume they have different phones, or have dropped completely off the grid."

"What about bank accounts, ATMs, credit card purchases?"

"We've tapped into all those we knew about last night. Nothing which points to where they are since yesterday morning, but Saunders withdrew a large amount of cash from one of his savings accounts on Tuesday morning. We're doing a deeper records sweep today to see if there are any accounts we've missed. Thank goodness everything financial is tied to Social Security numbers these days. If you've got access, it makes it easier; and we've got access."

"How large an amount of cash?"

"Nine-thousand-nine-hundred," Tom said, stuffing a large bite of his breakfast into his mouth and wiping it with the napkin. "Just under the IRS limit for mandatory bank reporting."

"I called the banks yesterday afternoon and froze Dace's access to any of his accounts, including credit cards," The Senator said. "I never removed myself as an administrator for his banking, so they had no problem locking things up. I was going to sign off this week, now that he's twenty-one, but thankfully hadn't gotten to it yet. Bottom line is, he won't get far before he runs out of funds."

"Unless the Saunders kid is going to underwrite him," Tom observed. "That would seem likely if he's pulled out ten grand in cash. You can go many places and do many things before running out of that much money, especially if you're frugal."

Tom forked his last bite, washed it down with a drink of coffee, set the cup back onto the tray and wiped his mouth, dropping the napkin onto the empty plate.

"In addition, there's no way you can lock up the Saunders kid's accounts, so we don't even know how much more is available to them," Tom said, sliding back onto the couch.

The Senator returned to his seat at the desk.

"Well, that can be dealt with as well. We've got friends at the IRS, right? They have innocent snafus all the time which eventually straighten themselves out, but until that happens we can tie up any individual's accounts in knots immediately, and on a whim, which the agency later can claim to have been the result of a bureaucratic oversight."

Tom jumped up from the couch and moved in front of the desk in one fluid motion and taking The Senator by surprise.

"Now just hold up, Allard," he said in an agitated tone as he pointed his finger across the expanse of polished leather inlay. "Using the IRS is a *huge* step, one we had better think long and hard about before we make a move we'll regret." He began to pace in front of the desk. "I mean, using agencies to obtain information is one thing, we can always spin that into our concern for finding the boy, but calling out the IRS to chomp down on someone outside the family is a whole 'nother ball game. That's a genie we have very little control over once we pop the cork on the bottle." He stopped, turned to stare down The Senator. "Remember Allard, I don't mind being out there pulling strings and working the back room for you, but in the end my main job is to protect your political ass and get you elected until you say stop, hopefully without either of us ending up in jail along the way."

"Ball games? Genies in bottles? You are full of metaphors this morning, aren't you? Relax, Tom," The Senator soothed, his voice calm and even. "I'm certain we can distance ourselves from the action, should it become necessary, and besides, the importance of what we are protecting down the road takes every priority. I will not allow my son's reputation to be tarnished, no matter what I have to do. The boy, as you call him, has a destiny to fulfill."

Many people, those charged to speak for the FBI included, said the Mafia in Louisiana scattered in the wind after the death of reputed, longtime boss Carlo Marcello in 1993. Many people can be wrong about many things. In reality, organized crime, a term often joked by those inside of it to be an oxymoron, never went away. Rather the activities of the Louisiana Mafia continued all the same after Don Carlo's death; rackets such as gambling, prostitution, drugs, protection, union manipulation, and cargo hijacking were just too profitable to not tempt someone from filling any void.    Following Marcello's death, and some would argue, before, the void in Louisiana south of Baton Rouge and east of Lafayette was filled by one Vincent Anthony 'Tony Gators' Monreale.

Tony Gators received the nickname during the early days of his criminal career when he would go beyond the orders of his bosses to merely kill and dispose of a victim in the swamps outside of New Orleans.    Back room stories claimed Tony discovered the terroristic barbarism of feeding his bound and more-often-alive-than-otherwise targets to the alligators would not only save the cost of a bullet, but also enhance his reputation as a feared, cold-blooded killer.  To Tony Gators, the practice was merely killing two birds with one Alligator Mississippiensis, so to speak.

Fifty-five-years old then, and to the legitimate world a landholder, investor, and real estate developer living outside of Thibodaux, Louisiana, he was also the unrivaled boss of everything illegal in southeast Louisiana, and some would suggest, beyond.   He'd spend his days cultivating the later-life reputation as the face of aboveboard business and real estate development, but more enjoyed his nights doing to southern Louisiana and the city of New Orleans in real life what Don Corleone did to New York City in fiction.  To the people who bought into his developments or invested in his legitimate deals, Mr. Monreale was a personable, honest, and hardworking man who just happened to have a bit of a whispered reputation.  That combination was nothing unusual in Louisiana history, even in modern days.   To those who worked the underbelly businesses, however, Tony Gators was a much-feared and iron-fisted boss who one never double-crossed or shorted on what was owed.

Standing five-foot-six and weighing one-hundred-forty-five pounds, whether he was Mr. Monreale or Tony Gators, the man hardly cast an imposing physical shadow.  It was, however, in his dark eyes that the real danger of the man could become most obvious.   When angered, his normally unreadable and unemotional eyes reputedly reflected utter soullessness, however, those who saw that transition take place, rarely returned to tell about it.   He dressed well, and in the latest fashion, however, his full head of black hair remained styled in the fashion of the early-1970s version of Elvis, although the pork chop sideburns he once wore were long gone.

Physically, he was overall unremarkable.   Take him out of the tailored suits and thousand dollar shoes, and put him in jeans and a work shirt and nobody would turn their head to take notice of him.   What people would always catch because he never hid the abnormality, however, was that the man was missing his index and middle fingers of his left hand. As the *official* story goes, he lost the fingers in an accident on a state-owned construction site. As the *unofficial* story goes, he lost the digits during the interrogation of a smalltime Lafayette loan shark suspected of turning snitch after his wife had been arrested with a large amount of cocaine and pills in her car in the early 1980s. Reputedly, one of Tony's gators decided on an appetizer before the main meal had been plated and snapped at its master. It was said, though injured, he concluded the questioning and then fed the live loan shark to the gator. According to back room whispers, he later shot the gator and for several years wore nothing on his feet but handmade shoes fashioned from its hide.

Emotionally, the man was said to truly love very few things, and even fewer people in this life; but at the very top of any list was his daughter, Ashley. He had raised the girl alone since her mother had died suddenly, shortly after undergoing a relatively new surgical procedure. The doctors called it a 'pallidotomy' and claimed it offered remarkable results in the treatment of the symptoms of her diagnosed, idiopathic Parkinson's Disease. For Tony's wife, the drug therapy and other treatments were having little or no effect upon either the symptoms or associated lifestyle problems of the malady. The brain surgery was what the doctors had called the woman's last chance for relief, and it failed miserably. Three weeks after undergoing the procedure, the woman's heart gave out one night and she died alone, collapsed against the wall between their bed and nightstand. Tony had found his wife the next morning.

The first time they had detected anything unusual was three years earlier when Tony noted to Anastasia she wasn't swinging her left arm naturally as she walked. Her right arm swung like it should, but the left arm remained limply in place. She had full movement and feeling in the limb, but the unconscious, anatomic reflex of swinging the arm when walking was not working properly on that one side. He would tease her during their strolls around their property, exaggeratedly swinging her left arm as he held her hand, at first thinking she just wasn't wanting to move it after he pointed it out. When numbness on the left side followed about a year later, however, he took her to the first of dozens of doctors and specialists all over the world.

Over the next couple of years, he watched helplessly as his Anastasia slowly descended into the hell of being locked inside her own failing body and there was little Tony could do about it. She became less and less ambulatory, had trouble swallowing food or drink, developed the posture and gait of a ninety-year-old, and would spontaneously lock in position, lose her balance and fall. Tony hired an aide to watch over Ashley and a nurse to stay with his wife anytime he needed to be away. When he could be home, he alone would take care of everything but housecleaning and laundry, for which he hired a local woman to come in several times a week. Ashley had been two at the time of the diagnosis, and five going on six when her mother died.

Tony didn't understand everything the doctors had said or done in the initial period of diagnosis or during their treatment of Anastasia. What he did understand was she was not getting better, or even stabilizing, no matter what they tried. They were the experts, the reputed best in their fields, and Tony trusted them because Anastasia trusted them. Finally, as things continued to negatively progress, the doctors suggested the relatively new-at-the-time pallidotomy option; the neurosurgeon described the procedure in a conference room at the hospital one day and while it seemed extreme and risky and yet too unproven to Tony, Anastasia became obsessed with the promise of being *normal* again and insisted on moving forward immediately. Positive results had been seen in the vast majority of patients, all the doctors had told them, and only a very small number suffered any ill-effects. From what the short-term studies were then indicating, longterm benefits could be prognosticated, *without* the receptor-numbing effects of extended drug therapy.

The day of the procedure, they checked into the hospital in Baton Rouge and the process began with the installation of a surgical stabilization device called a 'halo' onto her head. Pointed pins pressed into her skull and held the ringed device absolutely secure. Tony sat with her in her room, the medieval-looking device in place, for an hour before they took her to the surgery suite. Once there, while Anastasia was fully awake, a small hole was drilled into her skull and the neurosurgeon mapped her brain by tracking electrical activity during the performance of visual and aural testing and minor physical movements such as moving a finger or wiggling toes. Finally, a probe was inserted deep into the globus pallidus region of her brain and heated using radio frequency radiation to destroy certain tissues which were thought to be 'misfiring'. The goal was to restore Anastasia's brain chemistry balance; the processes which control nerve function and voluntary and involuntary muscle movement. The doctors had told them it wasn't unusual for patients to *figuratively* jump off the table afterward and move like they hadn't in years.

That didn't happen at all like that for Anastasia. Instead, she was returned to her room following the procedure, the halo gone and her head in turban-like bandages. She appeared devastated and drawn, her face affected as if she had suffered a stroke. In the coming hours of testing, each of her prior physical symptoms was more pronounced and others new problems surfaced. While Tony sat at her side and held her hand, she cried. For three days there had been no consoling her, and she would become agitated and frustrated whenever her husband saw her in that condition. Her face contorted, her mouth moved involuntarily, she couldn't feed herself, and she keened constantly. The medical staff suggested Tony leave, saying they believed many of her symptoms were self-imposed by her stress. They wanted to work with her alone and without distractions. So Tony left her there.

Two weeks later, they called him to come and get Anastasia. She was better, they said, had made progress, was more in control and less symptomatic after the physical therapy and careful adjustments to her medication. She was ready to leave the care of the hospital, they said. Tony drove alone to pick her up and bring her home. Not certain what he would find when he saw her, he had decided to send Ashley to her aunt's house in California for a couple of days.

When he walked into his wife's hospital room, she was up and about, packing some final items into a suitcase. She smiled when she saw him, and he hugged her and kissed her gently. He could feel the slight tremors in her lips, and as he held her, could feel how small and frail she had become. As he watched, she still moved tentatively, but appeared better than the last time he saw her. Her eyes were clear, and she was glad to be going home.

During the drive back to Thibodaux, she spoke little, seemed more inclined to rest with her eyes closed. Occasionally, Tony would take a hand off the steering wheel and hold hers or stroke her cheek. He could feel the tremor in her hand and an unnatural coolness in her face. She would respond with a small smile, often not even opening her eyes.

By the time they arrived home, she was exhausted, and Tony had to nearly carry her inside their home. Against his wishes, Anastasia insisted on remaining out of bed, so he placed her on the couch in the living room. The hospital had sent along enough of her medications for the remainder of the day and had phoned in the refill order to the local pharmacy which delivered a dozen pill bottles. She was scheduled to take thirty-two pills each day, each medication timed precisely. After taking her four p.m. dosage, she perked up and told Tony she was hungry.

He prepared a meal of things she especially loved, lobster tail, wild rice, and asparagus; and cut everything into smaller-than-bite-size portions for her because the nurses had reminded him she would still experience some trouble chewing and swallowing. The process was not new to him, as this had been the mealtime routine for at least a year by then. They sat together and Tony talked of their daughter while Anastasia slowly picked at the food. By the end of the meal, she had again grown fatigued and asked him to take her to bed. He supported her as she slowly climbed the stairs to their room, helped her undress and put on a nightgown, gave her the last of the day's medications and tucked her into their bed. He kissed her on the forehead, sat with her for a while and left his wife alone there after she fell asleep. Several house later, he dozed off watching television on the couch in the living room downstairs.

In the morning, he awoke early and went upstairs to check on her. As he walked down the hallway toward their room, he saw Anastasia through the open door, on her knees, wedged between the bed and nightstand. Her left cheek was pressed against the wall and her arms hung limply at her sides. Tony called her name and ran to her. The instant he touched her, he knew she was gone. Her face was cool and her body rigid and firm to the touch. As he pulled her away from the wall and gently laid her on the floor, her body moved as one solid object, having neither flexibility nor movement. Her left eye remained closed by the cheek having been pushed upward by the chair rail on the wall. Her right eye stared blankly into space, any sparkle it previously held forever extinguished.

An autopsy was performed, but the cause of her death remained undetermined; there was a police investigation, but no foul play was ever suspected and the case was quickly closed. Several months later, a Coroner's Inquest was held and ruled the manner of death as 'Natural', yet remained 'Undetermined' as to cause. A Death Certificate was issued stating those details. The coroner spoke to Tony after the inquest and opined that Anastasia had most likely suffered what he called Sudden Cardiac Death and was most likely gone before she fell to the floor, as if that could be any consolation. Even had Tony been right there, he could have done nothing to save her, the Coroner said, but had added there had been no way to scientifically confirm that scenario postmortem. It was merely his 'best guess'. 'Sometimes we just don't know exactly how people die,' the coroner concluded, a statement in which Tony had found no comfort.

Relatives and friends came and paid their respects for the funeral, then left him and Ashley alone in the house. He later hired a private pathologist to review the autopsy only to learn that somehow Anastasia's brain had been misplaced after it had been sent to the state university's medical school for further study. One fact his pathologist could share with him, however, was something which nobody else had dared: Anastasia never had Parkinson's Disease and the treatments and surgery were doomed to fail from the outset because of the misdiagnosis, which appeared to the hired expert to be merely rubber stamped by each successive specialist. And that pissed off Tony Gators.

The first doctor to go missing was Anastasia's neurologist who came up with the initial Parkinsonism diagnosis. Tony had reviewed Anastasia's medical records with his hired pathologist and they discovered the doctor had initially questioned his own diagnosis when she failed to respond to the standard set of Parkinson's medications, and had even referred in his notes to the Harvard Medical School study which concluded: '...in the class of patients where initial response to standard medication therapy is negative, the proper diagnosis may well be Multiple System Atrophy (MSA), a degenerative brain disorder which initially mimics the symptomatology of Parkinson's Disease, but is unresponsive to standard treatment protocols...'.   There was, at the time, only one diagnostic method for differentiating between the two maladies, and that was response to medication.   MSA patients do not respond to the dopamine treatments, his pathologist explained, because they do not suffer from a lack of natural dopamine production or have dopamine receptor damage.   Tony learned much after Anastasia's death about the diagnosis and medical treatments for brain disorders.

The last doctor to go missing was the neurosurgeon who performed the pallidotomy.   It wasn't so much that he did anything wrong in his procedures, but Tony learned he, too, had questioned the initial diagnosis, but performed the surgery anyway, even while suspecting it may do more harm than good and expressing that opinion in a letter to the original neurologist.

Now, more than ten years later, as he stood on the wide veranda on the second floor of his home outside of Thibodaux, having just given permission for Ashley to spend a weekend with her best friend, Ronnie, at her parent's home, he looked out over a sea of cypress trees.   The sun was moving lower in the horizon and turning the sky and a variegated veil of high clouds moving in from the west a pinky orange.   The sight brought him memories, but also an inner peace.

He had done what he had to do in this life to protect and provide for his family, he concluded.   He'd do it again with very little changed, he knew, had he the opportunity nobody else got.   He'd never apologize for any of his life.   He realized he overindulged Ashley, but she suffered from few of the behavioral problems which afflicted most sixteen year old girls.   Her grades were better than good, he liked Ronnie as her best friend, and the behavior reports from the school were excellent.   She was a good girl and he trusted her.   He'd done right by his daughter, he knew, given the challenges he faced when Anastasia fell ill and subsequently passed away.

"I have no regrets," he said to the cypress trees.


Dace was again uncharacteristically quiet as they drove out of the Roanoke area, still headed southwest.   Dave watched him out of the corner of his eye and wondered how deep inside himself Dace would eventually go before he turned around and came back to the surface. Longtime friends understand one another, and Dave thought he certainly understood Dace.

"Hey, I did think about waking you up this morning to go work out with me, but you were sleeping deeply," Dave said after they had been on the road for about thirty silent minutes.

"Thanks for that," Dace said, never taking his eyes off the passing landscape of southern Virginia.

"For thinking about it or for deciding to let you sleep?" Dave said with a bit of a teasing tone.

"Huh?" Dace said.

"I was wondering what you were thanking me for?"

"Can you pull off at the next exit?" Dace said. "I gotta piss."

Dave looked over at his friend and noted that Dace's right leg was bouncing nervously.

"Are you sure you're okay, Dace? I mean if you gotta pee that bad, I'll pull over right here."

"I told you, I gotta piss," Dace replied. He pointed at the truck stop sign high above the upcoming exit. "There, pull in there."

Dave wheeled the big SUV off the interstate and turned left at the stop sign at the end of the exit ramp. They passed under the four lane road and he pulled into a parking stall at the convenience store side of the expansive truck stop. Dace jumped out before the car was stopped and slammed the door. He walked into the store and disappeared from view. Dave locked the Escalade and followed him into the store. He took the same path he had seen Dace take, and once inside caught a glimpse of him entering the men's restroom. Not feeling the need himself, he returned to the front, grabbed a Milky Way bar from one of the display racks and a liter bottle of cherry Mountain Dew from the cooler.

"Anything else?" the young clerk asked as she began to ring up the two items.

"No, just this," Dave said as he dropped a five dollar bill onto the counter. He glanced around the store. "Is there a back way out of here?"

"Why? Is someone after you big fella?" the clerk teased and then winked at Dave as she handed over his change.

"Ah, no," he said, at first a little off balance, and then catching the wink and feeling a little less of a sting from the tease. "No, my friend just came in ahead of me..."

"The tall, skinny guy, brown hair, green eyes, jeans, green polo shirt?"

"Yeah, that's the guy," Dave said, a little amazed at her powers of observation and memory.

"No need to worry, he's still in the men's room."

"How do you know that?"

"Every inch of this place is under video surveillance," she said, pointing at rows of monitors above the counter. "The rear door is marked for emergency only. If it's opened, an alarm goes off. A real loud one."

Dave wondered if the woman took such detailed note of everyone who came and went at the store or if there had been something special which had her give Dace such attention. Sure, young women always seemed to notice him, but this level of detailed observation was unusual. He glanced over his shoulder, saw nobody standing in line behind him, then moved a little closer to the counter.

"I'm just curious," he said in a low tone. "Why did you take such a notice of my friend? It can't be something you do to everyone who comes and goes from this place."

"His eyes," she said. "I always look at the eyes when people walk in. It tells you a lot."

"The eyes?"

"Yeah, after you've been working a job like this for a while, you pick up on certain cues on who may be aiming to give you trouble, shop lifters and the like. Some clerks look at the way people are dressed, or how they are walking, if they're excessively nervous or something like that, but I just look at the eyes."

Dave glanced over his shoulder again, a dozen different thoughts ran through his head. He was minoring in psychology and everything he knew about human behavioral studies told him there was no way to effectively gauge another person's true inner workings with such anecdotal methodologies, but the way Dace had been acting since yesterday made him curious about what this clerk had seen in him as he walked through. So, he asked her.

"Why my friend? What did you see in his eyes that made you take such notice?"

She leaned forward across the counter and spoke in an even lower tone.

"There's a storm brewing inside him," she said. "A bad one."

Dave tucked the bills into his wallet and dropped the coins into a large plastic jug with a photograph of an obviously sick kid taped across the front and the words 'Please Help Amanda' written in black marker across the top. He took one last scan of the store for Dace and then went out to the Escalade.

Ten minutes later, Dave watched as Dace exited the store, looked in both directions as if making some sort of decision, then strolled casually over to the SUV and climbed into the passenger seat. He was carrying a brown paper bag in his hand which he set on the floor by his feet.

"That was quite a piss, my man," he said with a laugh. "What are you? The proverbial race horse?"

Dace turned to look across the cabin at him. Dave peered into the eyes which had interested the clerk. He saw something now, too. It was a distancing, yeah, that was the word, distancing.

"I needed a few things," he said. "That okay, officer?" He reached into the bag without further explanation and pulled out a pair of cheap sunglasses, black 'Buddy Holly' frames with deep blue lenses. He handed an identical pair across to Dave. "Since we're on a mission from God, so to speak, I thought we might as well look like Jake and Elwood."

Dave nodded and accepted the gift, then put them on. He glanced in the rear view mirror to check the fit, and smiled across at Dace.

"We've got a half tank of gas, you've got a pack of cigarettes, it's the middle of the morning and we're wearing sunglasses," Dave said channeling the Blues Brothers whom they now resembled.

"Close enough," Dace replied in character as Dave backed out of the parking spot. "Hit it."

Instead of peeling out in the caution-abandoned Elwood style, Dave pushed the remaining end of the candy bar into his mouth and took a long slug of Dew from the bottle as he carefully weaved the SUV through the gas pump area and headed back out to the road. It wasn't the movie departure reminiscent of Jake and Elwood in their old police cruiser, but what can you expect from a couple of guys from Harvard on the run?

Ashley was finding it hard to concentrate in Sister Magdalene's class. Physics was the only period in the school day which she didn't share with Ronnie who had to repeat second year chemistry after failing the class during their sophomore year and thus had been precluded from taking first year physics. The reason for the failure had been simple, Ronnie just didn't accept the theories of chemical bonding which formed the conceptual foundation of the course. That basic had to be taken on faith as being accurate or any further study of the subject matter would be lacking. No, Ashley thought, Ronnie understood the theories, she just didn't believe in it because nobody could see it happening.

Ashley smiled to herself at the thought as Sister Magdalene rambled on to the mostly blank faces surrounding her about Noether's Theorem on Symmetry. Ashley had read the material the night before and understood it well enough to regurgitate it back on a quiz or test, which was how she saw the process of formal education. Ashley always got it. Ronnie, on the other hand, endlessly wanted cold, hard proof and fought against that basic premise of the educational system: to get the grade, give them back what they gave you. That was hard for Ronnie, especially when theories were taught as facts, which often brought her to loggerheads with the instructors. It's not that Ronnie was less intelligent than Ashley; their IQs were nearly identical. The difference was, Ashley accepted their facts as facts, and Ronnie endlessly demanded proof.

Like the time when they were told in chemistry class that there were two main types of chemical bonding between atoms in our physical universe: ionic and covalent. Ashley accepted it and regurgitated it on tests, eventually passing the course with a solid A minus. Ronnie, however, refused to buy it and wound up with a failing mark. Ashley had tried to cheer her up by saying she should change her name to Thomas, in honor of the Apostle who just wouldn't believe Jesus had risen from the dead if he couldn't see Him and touch the wounds.

"How do they *know*, in all the universe, that these simplistic mechanisms are the *only* major two types of chemical bonds?" she had asked Ashley that night while the two studied the following day's lessons.

"They just do."

"Have you ever seen an electron, Ash? No, nobody has. They are almost infinitesimally small. Yet they *know* one travels around the nucleus of a hydrogen atom at *precisely* 2,200 kilometers per second and it is *exactly* 1,800 times lighter than that nucleus?"

"So they say."

"And that the speed of electrons varies in every one of the other elements?"

"That's what they're telling us."

"I just don't buy it, Ash."

"Just take it on faith, Ronnie.

So it would go. For hours. At first Ashley had tried to explain things to her friend, but then quickly realized Ronnie understood everything just as she did, and would do fine if only she would accept what she couldn't see. Eventually, every discussion would return to the basic question of: 'How do they know?'; and after a while, Ashley hit upon the simplest response: 'They just do.' That was the best answer she could think of to end the infinite loop.

Then there was the time a couple years ago when they were freshmen studying biology and a substituting lay instructor had introduced them to the idea of instantaneous cell death by using as a simple metaphor: the plucking of an apple from the tree. To Ronnie, it had seemed incomprehensible that anyone could assume, much less have the audacity to pass that assumption as absolute truth to a group of mush-brained teenagers, and had become absolutely recalcitrant with the woman.

"Are you telling us," Ronnie had begun, "that in the instant the physical connection between the tree and the apple is severed, the apple goes from a living thing to a dead thing? Just like that?" She had snapped her fingers to accentuate her point.

Ashley had known, of course, Ronnie had understood the woman was using a simple metaphor to represent the very complex stimuli and chemical changes which can cause or lead to instantaneous cell death. In that case, she apparently just objected to the metaphor.

The substitute teacher, uninitiated to the Thomasonian logic of Ronnie's arguments, made the first attempted block of the girl's question by using a quip to short-circuit further pointless discussion which would deflect the whole class from the major ideas of the lecture.

"Even faster than you snapped your fingers," she had said, gazing across the faces of the class with the hope of seeing nods so they could now move on.

The substitute didn't know Ronnie, though, who had, by that point, sat back in her chair and crossed her arms over her chest. The class, having seen that posture of Ronnie's before, almost in unison set down their pencils and began to wait out the oft-repeated back and forth which would end with the frustrated instructor closing the debate with a perfunctory 'Because that's just the way it is.'

"So, in that instant, *every* cell in that apple dies," Ashley had responded.

"Yes."

"Every cell?"

"Yes, every cell."

Ashley remembers the class holding its collective breath, each girl knowing what was coming next.

"How do you know?"

"What?"

"How do you *know*? You can't observe the physical activity of every cell in that instant? How do you know that some cells don't go on living for a time before they get the message they have been plucked?"

The instructor went slack-jawed.

So it went, for twenty pointless minutes, until the substitute instructor closed the discussion in the typical manner. After class, Ronnie had continued expressing her position to Ashley in the hall.

"That's bullshit, Ash," Ronnie had said in a hushed tone as Ashley took a drink from the water fountain. "They don't know. They're guessing. Why do you think they call them theorems?"

Ashley stood up and wiped her lips with the back of her hand and looked at her friend. Across he hall, Sister Regina, the principal of the school, passed by. Her rosary hung from her belt caught Ashley's eye, the black beads clattering softly above the black and silver crucifix and gave her an idea. Sister Regina smiled at the pair and tapped the crystal of her watch to indicate they needed to get to their next class. The girls nodded and smiled in return, and began to walk toward their next classroom.

"Do you believe in God, Ronnie?" Ashley asked just before they turned into the doorway. "I mean really believe."

"Of course," she said.

"Have you ever seen God?"

"No," Ronnie said, rolling her eyes.

"Yet you pray, participate in the Sacraments, confess your sins, and ask for forgiveness, just like they tell you we need to do so we can go to Heaven to be with God for eternity. Right?"

"Yeah."

"You do it all fully believing in your heart that what you're doing is right and true?" Ashley said, nearly closing the loop.

"Of course."

"How do they know, Ronnie? I mean, how do they know what God even wants us to do to get to Heaven? Some words mortal men have written into a book? Come on, really? How do we *know*?"

Ronnie rolled her eyes.

"I know, it's called Faith. What's your point, Ash?"

"Just give them what they want, Ronnie," Ashley said with a sly grin. "It's as simple as that. If they tell you blue is yellow, just put that answer on the test and move along, even though you know it's not correct. You have maybe sixteen or so years of schooling to merely get through; you've got the rest of your life to be right."

Ashley turned and walked to her desk in Sister Agnes' English class. From that day on, Ronnie had tried to play their game, but that hadn't saved her from having to repeat second year chemistry.

The next three hours were as quiet as the first half hour after leaving Roanoke had been. Dace, now wearing sunglasses, sat staring out the window and gave one word answers to any questions Dave would pose, and begrudging 'mmm-hmm' responses as his only participation on any topics of conversation he would broach from the driver's seat. The only difference between the two segments of the morning's travel, apart from the Blues Brothers look, was Dace had begun drinking from a pint bottle of cheap gin which had come out of the truck stop convenience store in the same brown bag as had the sunglasses.

Then, just outside of Knoxville, Tennessee, after draining the last of the bottle and tossing the empty out the window into the long grass of the ditch, Dace offered his first comment since the request for a piss stop.

"You hungry, buddy?" he asked. "I could sure go for some barbecue."

"Yeah, I could eat," Dave replied. "I wouldn't guarantee Knoxville has the best barbecue, but I bet we can find us some."

"I don't care how it tastes, I'm hungry." Dace's words were coming out with a hint of drink in them, but he wasn't slurring or overtly drunk as it had taken him well over two hours to down a pint of gin. "Besides, I want a smoke."

"What's the deal, Dace?" Dave asked. "Are you going to talk to me? You've never smoked and I know you've never even tasted alcohol in your life. I realize this is a rough time for you, and that's why we're here, doing what we're doing, but getting away for a while to think things through is a whole lot different from picking up some really nasty vices. What's next?"

Dace turned to look at his friend. He lowered the glasses to the tip of his nose and peered over the top of the wide black frame.

"I bought these glasses because they had blue lenses," Dace said. "Do you want to know why?"

"So we could do a bad, east coast version of the Blues Brothers?" Dave joked, not knowing to where the conversation had shifted.

"No. The Blues Brothers thing was just a fluky coincidence." He pushed the glasses back into place and scanned the scenery outside the car. "I got them because blue lenses don't do anything. They change nothing."

Dave was just about to ask what that meant, when Dace spun around in his seat and pointed to an upcoming billboard with a big, pink pig wearing a smile and sporting angel wings.

"There, let's go there," he said with the most animation Dave had seen in him since they sat around the fire pit at the end of his birthday party. "Sky Pig Barbecue."

Dave picked up on the directions off the interstate before they passed the sign which included the admonition to watch for the airplane. He also caught the slogan, 'Where Pigs Don't Fly, But They Are Quite Delicious'.

"Looks interesting," he said, sliding the Escalade onto the exit ramp. At the stop sign, he turned right as the billboard had instructed and drove about a mile before topping a ridge, after which he spotted it. "Sure shit, an airplane that's a barbecue joint."

He drove into the gravel parking lot followed closely by a cloud of dust and stopped between two other out-of-state cars in the front row. Dace and Dave looked at the joint. It was a white boxcar of an airplane with red and blue stripes running horizontally down the length of the fuselage. Above the stripes, the white paint shadowed the airline name: American Eagle. On the vertical tail, they could make out the faint outline of a stylized eagle decal long gone. On one of the wheel fairings, the words Shorts 360 proclaimed the type. The skinny wings, held up with struts each sported an engine with propeller which slowly rotated in the wind safely above head height. Just behind the cockpit was a counter cut through to the inside. A plywood sign served as a menu board and covered about half of the dozen or so windows running down the side of what had been the cabin area. All around in the grassy area were scattered picnic tables, two of which were occupied by families from the other cars in the lot. A well-sooted single metal stack towered above the fuselage on the far side of the airplane. About fifty feet west of the tail, a chemical toilet sat off by itself. The land sloped quickly away on the other side of the restaurant down into a wide expanse of forest land to the west and the city of Knoxville to the east. If a person were to squint and stand in just the right spot, one could almost picture the Sky Pig barbecue in flight.

"Well?" Dave asked, more to give Dace a last chance to change his mind and consider a more conventional restaurant.

"Looks great," Dace said. "I'm starved."

They exited the SUV and walked up toward the menu board. There was movement inside the airplane which they could see through the uncovered windows and a moment later, a skinny man in his early fifties popped his paper hat covered head through the sliding window which had a hand-painted sign above that instructed, 'Order & Pay Here.'

"Whenever you guys are ready, I'm ready," the attendant said with smile and midwestern accent.

"How are the ribs?" Dave asked.

"Excellent, it's all great," came the reply. "Of course, I am a bit biased. You guys missed the lunch rush, but I've still got some of just about everything except for brisket; that's gone until tomorrow."

Dave looked around, and it appeared from the garbage cans about to overflow with bones, corn cobs, well-used paper towels, and plastic silverware that they had indeed missed quite the lunch rush. If, that was, the little dude in the paper hat emptied his garbage cans every day.

"Okay, I'll have the rib plate, full rack, corn on the cob and macaroni salad," Dave said, reaching for his wallet. "Oh, and an iced tea, unsweetened."

"Gotcha," the attendant said. "For you?"

"Double it up, but do you have beer?"

"All in cans or bottles, what brand?" To Dave: "That'll be seventeen fifty with the beer." Dave handed him a twenty, told him to keep the change.

"Surprise me," Dace said back. "Just no light beer crap."

The attendant shrugged and smiled and pulled himself back through the small opening. Dace and Dave wandered off toward one of the unoccupied picnic tables and took seats on the benches opposite each other. Dave gazed out over the valley and then toward the city. Out of the corner of his eye he watched Dace, who seemed again to be pulling inside himself.

"Beautiful, ain't it," came the voice of the attendant from behind Dave. "Those are the Great Smoky Mountains in the distance, and this place is known as Sharp's Ridge. There were some folks around here who didn't want this old bird dragged up here, but once they tasted my barbecue, they stopped complaining, mostly." He set down the large tray on the table and passed out the plates heaped with food, tea, and an ice cold Miller Genuine Draft. "Glass?" he asked Dace.

"No, this is fine," Dace replied and took a long draw of the icy amber liquid from the already sweating bottle.

"Mind if I sit and jaw a bit with you two?" the attendant asked as Dave picked up a rib and took a bite. "I'm almost cleaned up in there for the day, and I know how it is when folks are traveling together, they sometimes run out of conversation."

"Oh, my, that's good," Dave said, his mouth still half full of succulent meat and just the right dose of sauce, then motioned with the naked bone for the man to have a seat. "Make yourself at home." Then, to Dace: "Man, you have to try this. Best damn barbecue I've ever had."

Dace looked down at the plate, took another long draw from the bottle of beer and then decided he was indeed ravenous and tore into the ribs with a vengeance. As the two men devoured their food, stopping only for the occasional wash down and drying of fingers sucked clean of any remnant of sauce or charred meat particles, the attendant, who introduced himself as Glenn, gave some history of the area.

"The Sharp family settled and owned this land in the nineteenth century; that's why it's called Sharp's Ridge. It runs a total of about seven miles, and is two to three hundred feet above the valley floor. Up that way, there's a memorial park. Off to the west there, that's the Cumberland Plateau.

"When I proposed to drag the Sky Pig up here, like I said, there were protests to the county, but I got past the board by pointing out that my little airplane wouldn't be any more against nature than that tower farm they have out yonder. So, that got it up here, and then the free barbecue I offered for our opening closed most of the rest of the mouths. Except those goddamn vegans." He belly laughed.

"I suppose they stopped complaining because they were too busy chewing," Dave said, tossing down a finished ear of sweet corn and wiping the butter from his cheeks. "Why Sky Pig?"

"Because that's what she is," Glenn said pointing a thumb at the airplane turned restaurant. "See, I used to be an airline pilot in Chicago. The company I flew for in the 1980s bought a whole slew of those old things and we flew the crap out of them. They were ugly and slow, but they went through just about anything without complaining. Because of that, the way they smelled, and other in sundry reasons, somebody coined the name "Sky Pig" one day, and it stuck. I just thought having one as a restaurant was unique and a bit clever when I came up with the idea of selling my barbecue. So, I tracked one down in the Arizona desert and had it shipped up here to Sharp's Ridge."

"Was that one from your airline?" Dave asked.

"In fact it was," Glenn said with pride. "Not the queen of the fleet, but one of the princesses. You can still see the N-number there, in front of the tail. I flew this thing all over the Midwest. She's ugly as hell, but she got me home every night."

Glenn let out a skewed laugh that Dave thought needed an insider's perspective to understand, so he just smiled and nodded. Dace finished the last of his plate, sopping up some fugitive sauce with the last of a cornbread muffin, wiped his fingers on the paper towel and silently rose from the bench. Dave and Glenn watched him walk off toward the portable toilet and go inside.

"Your friend's not much of a talker," Glenn said.

"Long story," he said, watching the closed green fiberglass door. "He lost his fiancé last weekend. Car accident."

"I'm sorry to hear that," Glenn said and his embarrassment caused him to get up and pile the trash onto the tray.

"No, it's okay, Glenn," Dave said. He felt a touch of guilt for even saying anything to a stranger.

"Where are you boys from?" Glenn asked, changing the subject.

"Uh, Ohio," Dave lied.

"Ohio, eh? Did you boys steal the car in Connecticut?" Glenn teased with a wink.

Dave gave a little smile and a you-got-me shrug, then turned around when he heard the outhouse door slam.

"I guess I shouldn't ask where y'all are headed then, should I?"

Dave felt a second pang of guilt over lying to the man, and decided to answer the unasked question.

"New Orleans, a bit of R&R," he said.

Dace walked past the table and continued toward the Escalade. He stood outside, lit a cigarette, took a newbie puff and stifled a cough.

"Your friend's not much of a smoker either, is he?" Glenn asked.

"Just started this morning," Dave said.

"It shows," Glenn said with a laugh, picking up the tray and wiping down the table with a wet rag he had brought along for the purpose. "You boys gonna hang around New Orleans for Mardi Gras after your long drive from, where was it, Ohio?"

"That's the plan," Dave said, then nodded toward Dace. "Depends on him."

Dave walked with Glenn toward the Sky Pig and thanked him for the great food and conversation, and Glenn thanked them for stopping by. "Tell your friends back in Ohio," he called as Dave walked off toward Dace and the car.

"Ohio?" Dace said as Dave rounded the front of the Escalade. He took a last drag from the cigarette, dropped the remains onto the gravel and scuffed the ember with the toe of his shoe.

"Long story," Dave said as he opened the door. Then, through the gap between the door and windshield frame he said to Dace, "Oh, and exhale before you get in."

"Yes, mother."

# Chapter Six

Sandy and I decided to treat ourselves to a hastily arranged getaway on South Padre Island; returning to the scene of the crime, as Sandy jokingly put it. Since we had nothing pressing our schedule, we decided to split the twelve hour drive into two easy days, left home on Tuesday morning and spent the first night on the road on the outskirts of Houston. By early afternoon on Wednesday, we had arrived and checked into the same bed and breakfast on the Gulf side of the island where we had stayed last time. Sandy had shared our good news with the owners when she called for the reservation, and they arranged for us to stay in the same accommodation.

Walking into the pinky beige room accented in deep green, wine, and gold striped and floral fabrics on overstuffed pillows and oversized chairs, I felt a rush of happiness flow into me. Perhaps it was the thrill of returning to the scene of the crime, but perhaps it was simply watching my wife move through the space and open the French doors to let in the sunny coolness of a February afternoon on the shores of the Gulf. She stepped out onto the small balcony and leaned against the ornate, white, wrought iron railing. I have always enjoyed looking at Sandy, for many reasons, but there were those special times when observing her simply fascinated me. She caught me much quicker these days than she had early on when I could go for minutes just enjoying the sight of her, her mind working, thinking, breathing, posing when even she didn't know that she was doing it, but I still had enough time to amaze in everything she did. Sandy was going to be an incredible mom. And I was going to be a better dad, I resolved.

"Hey, let's take a walk on the beach before dinner," she said, returning inside and kicking off her bright red pumps. She caught me watching her and performed a little turn for me on tiptoes causing the hemline of her flared, sleeveless, knee-length dress which I thought looked like a Jackson Pollack canvas in various shades of blue, black and red spatters and streaks to twist around her bare legs. She then padded over to me in bare feet, stood on her tiptoes to reach and threw her arms around my neck. "Please?"

"How could I resist any request from such a beautiful woman?" I said. "Are you ready?" She nodded and I kissed her gently and took her hand to lead her out of the room when I sensed a bit of resistance.

"You're not going like that, mister," she said, pointing at my shoes. "Bare feet and khakis rolled up a couple of times is the dress code of the afternoon."

I gave her a 'really' look which she returned, and I complied. I kicked off my loafers, slipped off my argyle socks and then rolled up my slacks to about mid-calf. While I transformed myself from respectable businessman to newly arrived beach nerd, Sandy pulled a light, cream colored shoulder wrap from one of the suitcases.

"That's better," she said, and took my hand and we walked out of the room.

"I feel like Huckleberry Finn in business casual," I said with feigned embarrassment, even though bare feet on the thick-pile wool carpet runner of the hallway and stairs did feel good after the long drive.

"I think you look adorable," my loving wife said, and pulled herself into my arm as we walked.

We were making the turn at the landing, about to descend the second flight of stairs when the sight of the legs of a little man who could only be Mr. Eugene under a large floral arrangement backed us up. The legged flower combination was followed closely by Mr. Eugene's wife, Anita, wearing a big Texas smile. A moment later, the five of us were crowded onto the small landing, the three of them, two owners and the flower arrangement which was large enough to deserved its own personage on one side, and Sandy and myself on the other like football captains facing each other for the coin toss.

"We wanted to surprise you with these," Anita said, apparently a bit disappointed we had caught them before they hauled the mini-botanical garden up to our room and knocked at our door.

"Well, you certainly did," I said. Sandy squeezed my hand.

"They're beautiful," Sandy said. "So thoughtful of you both."

"The driver was late," said Mr. Eugene, or perhaps the flowers.

"We were just stepping out to take a walk on the beach," Sandy told them. "It's such a gorgeous afternoon."

"Well, you two go ahead and enjoy your walk," said Anita. "We'll put these in your suite so you can enjoy them when you get back."

"We'll certainly look forward to that," I said. "Do you think there will be enough room?" Sandy squeezed my hand again.

Anita smiled. She got me. We maneuvered the landing, the three of them headed up, the two of us headed down and a minute later, Sandy and I walked out the back door of the B&B, scuffed across the stretch of grass, passed through an opening in the knee-high hedge and stepped onto soft white sand which squeezed between our toes and felt even more relaxing than the carpet had. The sand was warm on my feet and *really* felt good; for some reason, I thought to myself at that moment that I needed to get out more. I promised myself I'd work on that. The sun was moving off toward the western horizon, and the houses along the beach were casting shadows across the sand. It had been forecast to be an unseasonably warm day on the island, still topping eighty-six degrees on the car thermometer when we arrived, but the air was already cooling and Sandy slipped the wrap around her bare arms. She held the ends between her breasts with one hand and retook my hand in her other.

We walked north, Sandy closer to the water than I. The surf was light, the tide was low and the Gulf was massaging the beach with nothing more than a gentle roll onto the sand. There were scatterings of people enjoying the last of an afternoon spent in the late-winter sun, and at least one other couple taking a similar stroll a hundred yards or so ahead of us. None of the men had their pants rolled up. There was a light breeze from the west, more of a gentle movement of air over us than anything else. Sandy put her head against my shoulder and I kissed the top of it. I loved doing that.

"How are you feeling?" I asked, suddenly feeling like a father-to-be again.

"Contented," she said after a moment's search for the right word, "and happy."

I was happy, too; and contented. In a life often spent in one state of anxiety and stress or another from early childhood to approaching middle age, being contented at that very moment felt even better than warm, soft sand between my toes. Although, I must admit there had been a bit of a shock to the system when Sandy first broke the news to me in Audubon Park. For a forty-year-old with three grown and nearly so kids already, and who had messed up with them from time to time over the years, I concluded I would, at the very least, have to reassess a few things about how I approached the rest of my life.

Sandy shivered a bit at my side and I put my arm around her. The lower the sun set, the stronger the breeze became and the cooler the air felt. That time of year on the island, the drop to the mid-fifties at night happened quickly.

"We should turn around," she said. "I'm enjoying this, but I'm starting to feel the chill."

For the walk back south to the inn, we moved a bit further from the water's edge onto a dry, level stretch; even the dry sand, was losing the day's heat quickly. We retraced our steps into the rear entrance and returned to our room. Inside, we found the flowers taking up most of the top of a rather large side table and an accompanying note offering Anita and Mr. Eugene's congratulations and reminding us that dinner would be served promptly at six.

"That's really sweet of them," Sandy said after reading the note and then handing it off to me. "They're such wonderful people."

"It's the Southern way," I said. "We Midwesterners may be a relatively courteous lot, but when it comes to manners and hospitality, you can't beat a true Southerner."

"As I recall, Will, Mr. Eugene and Anita are relatively recent transplants here from Coeur d'Alene, Idaho. You can't get much more north than that."

I thought about that a second.

"Let's say they're fast learners," I said, never one to be wrong.

"You can't ever be anything but right, can you?" Sandy asked, a twinkle in her eye.

"I married you, didn't I?" I smiled at her.

She bent over to smell the flowers, and then stepped aside while I replaced the card on the table top. I turned to see her unzipping her dress and letting it fall to the floor. She stood there momentarily in her soft and delicate white lace bra and matching panties, then grabbed a day blanket from the foot of the canopied bed and asked if I'd like to take a quick nap as she slid across the thick comforter, making little effort to cover herself up. I eyed the clock on the nightstand, did some quick math to dinner time, and joined my wife.

A cell phone vibrated in Tom McDaniel's coat pocket and then began to ring, interrupting a discussion he was having in The Senator's home office which had become an informal Operations Center in the search for Dace. The Senator used the distraction to rise from the leather wingback chair and walked to the bar to refill his glass. He motioned to Tom with the cut crystal decanter half filled with Highlands single malt and received a silent shaking of the head in response as Tom answered the call after checking the number.

"Whatcha got?" Tom said. He listened for a moment and then told the caller to repeat what he had just said as he placed the phone into speaker mode and laid it onto the coffee table.

"Dave Saunders paid a little over five-thousand dollars in cash on Monday morning as downpayment on the three-year lease of a Cadillac Escalade at a dealership in Cambridge, Massachusetts, on the outskirts of Boston. He took possession of the vehicle then: a new, 1998, pearl white SUV with Massachusetts plates, license number 6449MN, but don't bother writing that down because that has been changed."

"Changed?" The Senator said from across the room. "Changed how?"

"Yes, sir. According to the salesperson in Cambridge we visited with several hours ago, the vehicle had been located by the dealership in New London for Mr. Saunders and was to be swapped between the two dealers by the week's end but Mr. Saunders told the people in New London that he was preparing for a cross-country trip and needed to have the vehicle ready to go by Tuesday morning. So, he made the trip to Boston to pick it up instead of waiting or trusting the dealerships to get it done in time. It was obviously quite important to him."

"No wonder we're having no luck tracking down his piece-of-crap Mustang," The Senator said.

Tom nodded and a small smile came to his lips. Part of him was starting to respect this Saunders kid, a bit.

"The law required the Cambridge dealership enter the registration information in Massachusetts because that's where it was originally titled, but the New London dealership nearly simultaneously applied for Connecticut licensing and registration since Mr. Saunders used his parent's house in Gales Ferry as the registry address. By the time Mr. Saunders returned to his parent's home, new plates had been issued. He picked them up on Tuesday morning about seven from the service desk."

"What's the license number on the vehicle now?" Tom asked.

"858DWF, Connecticut," came the response.

"Did he turn in the Massachusetts plates?" The Senator asked, retaking his seat and taking a draw from his glass.

"Sir?"

"Did he give the old plates to the dealership here, or is he running around with two sets of license plates?"

"Just a second, sir, I'll ask," the voice said. The sound of muffled voices could be heard through the scuffing noise of the covering of the mouthpiece. A moment later the voice returned. "No, sir, he did not turn over the Massachusetts plates to this dealer. He told the salesman that he'd return them to the dealership in Cambridge in a couple of weeks when he returned from the trip."

"Any idea what the destination is of this cross-country trip?" Tom asked.

"No, sir. Not from anyone we spoke with so far. The only descriptive we have is 'cross-country'."

"It's a big country," The Senator said. He paused a moment. "Okay, is that it?"

"One more thing," the voice on the phone said. "We're going to check it out after we get off the phone here," the voice said.

"That is?"

"The Escalade has GM's OnStar system installed and it last registered in an area just off the expressway in West Greenwich yesterday, but has been offline since then. We've been able to retrieve the GPS coordinates from a very cooperative maintenance tech here and have found the location on a map. The guy also tells us that with some access at OnStar, we could track the vehicle anywhere and operate the cellular phone link remotely to listen in on any conversations occurring in the vehicle without the occupants knowing."

"Well, that's promising," The Senator said to Tom, but the comment was heard over the phone.

"Problem is, sir, if it's gone offline, it could either be a simple fault which will reset the next time the vehicle is started and the system reboots, or it could be someone intentionally disabled it by pulling the fuse on the circuit which powers the system."

Tom shrugged his shoulders at The Senator.

"The last known position of the vehicle. What's in the area?" Tom asked.

"It appears to be a small trailer park, which we feel is better than some public area like a parking lot. If the SUV is gone, maybe someone living there saw the vehicle or knows where they are headed."

The Senator's eyebrows arched when he looked at Tom.

"Well, get on it," Tom said. "While you're out there, remember to maintain a low profile. There is to be no mention of who we are really looking for. So far as anyone believes you're tracking Dave Saunders, I don't care, but no mention of anyone else. Understood?"

"Yes, sir. Understood."

The line clicked off and Tom flipped his cell phone closed and returned it to his jacket pocket. He rose and walked to the bar to add a splash of Beefeater's to his glass along with two or three fresh cubes of ice. As he walked back to his chair, he swirled the gin over the ice and then took a draw. He set the glass on the coffee table where the cell phone had been and then sat forward on the chair, his elbows on his knees as he began to lay out some scenarios with The Senator.

"Mama, where's Dace?" Mary Rose said absently as she worked at prying out the mahogany chestnut from its brown shell she had discovered in the receding snow.

Libby and Mary Rose were enjoying yet another beautiful and unseasonably warm February late afternoon. Enough of the winter's snow had melted so that they were able to go on a walk along a pathway through the wooded area behind the house. The fresh air was doing them both good.

"Dace is with Dave, Mary Rose," Libby told her.

"I like Dave," Mary Rose said. "He gives the *best* hugs." She chewed on her cheek as she turned the shiny nugget in her hand and her mother noticed the tick which meant Mary Rose was thinking about something beyond the chestnut. "I hope he liked the note from Dace I gave him." A pause, more examining of the unshelled nut. "Mama, is it Friday yet?"

"Mary Rose, you gave a letter to Dave from Dace?"

"Yep. It's a secret. Just me and Dace and Dave."

"When did you do this?"

"I dunno. Will you tell me when it is Friday, Mama?"

"Why are you so interested in Friday, Mary Rose?"

"It's a secret."

Knoxville, as it turned out, was not only a good place to stop for lunch, but it also was a necessary stop for gas. Dave pulled off at one of the several interchangeable city exits and wheeled into the nearest gas station. As he prepared to fuel the tank, Dace walked into the convenience store.

"Hey, buddy," Dave called. "Pay for the gas while you're in there. Use cash since we're not using credit cards on this little getaway."

Dace's response was an over-the-head thumb's up as he kept walking without turning. Dave waited at the pump and a moment later, the dials reset and the pump went on. He poured twenty-two gallons into the Escalade, closed things up and got back into the SUV. Dace appeared a minute later carrying a register receipt in his right hand and a brown paper shopping bag in his left. He opened the door, put the bag on the floor and stepped onto the running board then slid inside.

"What did you buy me?" Dave said as he started the engine and put the Cadillac into gear.

"I got you glasses this morning," Dace said, shaking his head in mock disgust. "Kids. Always wanting something."

"Gee, dad, I didn't realize I was being so selfish."

Dave looked across at his best friend, and for the first time since last Saturday night at the birthday party, before Sarah's accident, the house arrest and The Senator's goons, and the odd new behaviors kicking in, they shared a truly uninhibited laugh.

Dave released the brake and maneuvered out of the lot and toward the interstate. Dace reached into the paper bag and pulled out one made of plastic. He ripped the seal and the vehicle filled instantly with the smell of teriyaki and artificial smoke.

"Beef jerky?" he said, holding the open container toward Dave.

"You just ate. You can't be hungry already." Dave reached into the container and grabbed a piece of the cured meat. He placed it between his teeth and ripped off a hunk and began chewing. "You know you're gonna lose your girlish figure if you keep this up."

Dace took out a piece and shoved it all into his mouth. He looked like a dog trying to chew peanut butter. Dave nearly spit out his half-chewed wad.

"You know I've never in my life had beef jerky," Dace managed to say through the bulging mouthful.

"You thought this was a good time to start, why?" Dave asked, swallowing the first chaw and inserting the rest of the piece into his mouth. "I hope you bought us something to drink. Do you have any idea how salty this stuff is?"

Dace again reached into the paper bag and pulled out a can of Red Label beer, popped the top and offered it across.

"You're kidding, right?" Dave said. "Am I wearing a shirt that says: 'I went to Tennessee and all I got was a night in jail and a new boyfriend named Bubba'?

Dace reached back into the bag and pulled out a liter bottle of cherry Mountain Dew. He handed it across to Dave who opened it and took a long draw. Dace drank down the entire can of Red Label and then reached into the bag and pulled out a half pint of Tequila, opened the bottle and took a slug.

"Oh, now it's tequila?" Dave said.

"Gin sucks," Dace replied. "I figured beer and tequila, how could I go wrong?"

"Normally, I'd agree with you, buddy; but you do realize we're driving and you can't buy beer, don't you? You can only rent it."

"Yeah, that's why I only got a six-pack. By the time I have to piss again, it'll be time to stop and buy more beer anyway." He tapped the tip of his index finger to his temple. "Smart, huh?"

Dave rolled his eyes, then put on the dark sunglasses again. Dace turned and looked out the side window again. Dave took another draw from the bottle of Dew and the Escalade again settled in with traffic on I-59. He tapped the cruise control, giving a thought to Bubba. He glanced across the cabin. From Dace's face after he took another swig from the pint, tequila was only a bit more palatable than had been the gin, and he quickly washed it down with more beer. Dave had suspected Dace would crash and rebel after Sarah's death and the way he was forced to handle it by his father, but this was all happening so fast. Dave had never seen this side of his best friend. Was it losing control or just a rebellion? Time would tell, Dave knew. Either way, Dave was glad to be there for him. He returned his eyes to the road, kept Dace in his peripheral vision, thankful to see he was drinking the second beer slower than the first.

"So, where are we headed?" Dace suddenly asked several minutes later.

Dave glanced into the rear view mirror, changed lanes to the right after passing a school bus doing fifty-nine.

"You remember Cindy Spagliano? I dated her last year"

Dace shook his head slowly, thinking, and then his eyes grew wider as the memory came into focus.

"Wait, you mean Ms. Double D's?" he said, putting his hands out in front of his chest a generous distance.

"That's her," Dave said. "Smart as a whip, witty as hell, but she'll always be prejudged by her tits."

"Hey, beats the alternative. Seems like we have more than our share of Itty Bitty Titty Committee members at Harvard."

"Ah, yeah, the IBTC must have been founded in the Ivy League," Dave observed. "Give me some of those healthy, Big Ten, corn fed types anytime."

"So, Cindy Spagliano?"

"Yeah, when I got your note about getting away from it all for a while, I remembered she had connections to a place outside of New Orleans. We had talked about going down there last year to hang out, get some food, screw on the big porch. You know, all the normal tourist things?"

"Yeah, all the high points," Dace said with a chuckle which he followed with the finishing of the second beer. He wiped his mouth with the back of his hand, put the empty back into the paper bag and to Dave's relief didn't bring out another full one just yet. "So, you looked her up again?"

"I did."

"Did what? What did you tell her?"

"That I was really stressed and needed to get away for a while. I asked her if she'd like to head south and get some good food and do that porch screwing thing we had talked about last year."

"Smooth. How many times did she hit you?"

"That's the great part, I did it over the phone," Dave said, this time he laughed. "No, seriously. She's really cool, like I said, witty as hell. She understands us guys. So, she got the joke and laughed it off."

"Why do I sense there's more to the story?" Dace said.

"Okay, so she busted my chops a bit, too."

"Here we go."

"Yeah, she said, 'Just consider it like when we had sex, Dave: I doubt I'll be able to come, but you feel free to use the place for as long as you need to.'"

"Oh, that's cold," Dace said, keeping his reaction to a small smile.

It was just after dark when the black Lincoln Town Car rolled slowly into the small trailer park outside of West Greenwich, Rhode Island. The two large gentlemen sitting in the front seat scanned the areas in and around the trailers. A brand new pearl white Cadillac Escalade would be an easy spot in this mix of hastily parked, ramshackle, wheeled homes and rust bucket cars dating to the Carter administration, they each thought.

"This must be the trailer park James Carville was referring to when he said that thing about dragging a hundred dollar bill through to see what you'd catch," the large gentleman in the passenger seat said with a derisive snort.

"Hell, a twenty in this place would have them fighting over it," his counterpart said.

They rounded the next curve, neared the back of the park.

"Whoa, what's that?" the passenger said.

"What?"

"Back up a bit."

The driver put the car into reverse, backed along the gravel drive.

"There, hold it," the passenger said. "That's it."

"Where, under the snow pile full of dog shit?"

"No, behind the snow pile full of dog shit."

"I hate to break it to you, pal, but that ain't a Cadillac," the driver said.

"No, it's not." He was checking through a pocket notebook for the page he wanted. Finding it, he looked back and forth twice to double check. "It *is* Dave Saunders' old car, though. Now, I ask you, why would he leave his old car here, if he wasn't swapping it out for the Escalade? We already know he had the Mustang at the church the day of the funeral because of the parking ticket."

"Whatcha say we start knocking on a few doors, beginning with this one?" the driver said, pointing to the trailer nearest the snow pile.

"I'd say, just what I was thinking, partner."

The driver maneuvered the car into a little spot of gravel off the roadway and turned off the ignition. They waited for a couple of moments before getting out, noted the movement of the blinds in one window of the darkened trailer, then slowly exited the vehicle and walked toward the rickety porch. The large gentleman who was in the passenger seat climbed the rickety stairs and knocked firmly.

"These folks are usually not the overly friendly type," said the driver when nobody came to the door. "They don't trust people they don't know; think everyone who comes to the door in a suit is either a cop or process server. They don't talk to cops. I bet she thinks we're cops."

His partner nodded and switched to Plan B. He knocked again.

"Hello, we're from the Cadillac dealership. We're here about Dave Saunders' old car," he called into the closed door.

Several moments later, the inside door opened a crack. The woman inside was smoking a cheap cigarette and the smoke swept outside like it was seeking fresh air.

"What about Dave's car?" she said in a raspy, distrustful voice. "He didn't tell me that anyone was comin' for the car."

"May we speak to you, ma'am?" the large gentleman on her porch said. "Please?"

Through the crack of the door, he could see the flaring of an orange ember at the end of her cigarette as she took another draw while thinking what to do next. Finally, she opened the door fully, leaving the screen door between them closed, and from what he could determine, latched with a rusted hook in an eyelet bored into the frame.

"I can't tell you nothin' about the car," she said. "He didn't tell me nothin'. Just came a coupla days ago with that other boy, took his new car and left that one here."

"So they're gone?"

She nodded, drew a deep drag.

"Did he leave you the keys for it?" the large gentleman who had been driving asked from the gravel below the porch.

"Keys?" she said, suspiciously and strained unsuccessfully behind the locked screen door to see from whom the voice had come. "I can't give you the keys." A beat passed. "I mean, if I had the keys I can't just give 'em to you. Not without something from Dave."

"Did Dave tell you where they were headed, ma'am?" the passenger asked. "Did he give you some way to get in touch with them? See, we've called his house, spoke to his parents and they don't know where we could find him."

The woman snorted.

"My sister couldn't find her ass with both hands," she said. Her face morphed into a look of deep suspicion. "So, how did you get to *here*, anyway?"

She backed away from the screen door a bit, moved toward a position partially behind the stouter inside door. He was losing her. The large gentleman on the porch smiled broadly. He considered moving for his wallet, which on the advice from his chiropractor he carried in the breast pocket of his suit jacket, but thought the motion may just frighten her enough to have her slam and lock the door in his face. Not that it would pose much of a barrier were he so inclined to enter the trailer, but they had been told to maintain a low profile and as common as broken in doors may be in this type of place, a splintered door and screaming woman was fairly far from operating with a low profile. So he smiled and expanded the storyline.

"I'll tell you the truth, ma'am," he said in a low, conspiratorial tone and leaning forward.

The near whisper forced her to lean forward to hear.

"See, I'm the salesman who did the lease deal on the Escalade with Mr. Saunders, and, well, I screwed up and my boss is looking to have my ass. I mean, butt. Pardon my French."

The deprecation was enough to ease her mind. She stepped from behind the inside door.

"Aw, shit, I've heard worse," she said with a laugh. "No virgin ears around here. My last boss was an asshole, too."

"Well, my boss is normally not a bad guy," he said. "Just that I messed up the paperwork and may have accidentally given Dave the copy of the lease which has to go to Cadillac along with his copy. They don't have it, we don't have it, and we can't get paid which means I won't get my commission until they have all the paperwork. So, we drove down here to see if we could catch Dave because we can't raise him on his cell phone." It was more detail than he needed to offer, but he had learned a long time ago that just about anybody would buy any kind of bullshit story if you piled it high enough.

"So, did he leave you the keys so we could maybe check inside his old car to see if he left the envelope with the paperwork inside?" asked the large gentleman down on the gravel.

That question coming from out of her sight line moved her even closer to the screen door, and when she couldn't see him still, she flipped the latch and opened the door a crack to get a better angle.

"My gosh, you guys are like bookends," she said with a raspy laugh. "I didn't even see you down there before."

Then she obviously remembered something and pulled the door closed and reached for the latch.

"Hey, so how did you know to come here?" she asked, fumbling to get the hook back in the eyelet.

The large gentlemen shared a discreet look between them, the one on the gravel shaking his head slightly indicating to his partner on the porch not to escalate the situation.

"Oh, geeze, no wonder you're confused," the man on the porch said. "See, the Escalade Dave leased has what we call the OnStar system on it. Have you ever seen the commercials?"

She nodded slowly as recognition came before cognition.

"Yeah, the thing that calls somebody if you get into an accident?"

"That's just part of it," he said. "It's truly a fantastic system. It works with cellular and GPS technology. Global Positioning System, I mean. It continuously sends out a location for the vehicle, which is great if the driver is unconscious after an accident or if they have to locate a stolen vehicle. They have a whole organization set up which monitors tens of thousands of vehicles twenty-four-seven; and it's only going to get bigger over time."

She was loosening up again, he could tell, so he continued. Thank God for piled up bullshit and television commercials, he thought.

"This is the last location we have for the vehicle. We were driving through because we had no other way to track him down, as I said, and payday is tomorrow, Thursday, and I could really use the commission because my rent's running a little late for this month."

"I've been there," she said, undoing the latch again. "Let me get you the keys so you can take a look." She disappeared into the darkness and returned a moment later without her cigarette but carrying a single key on a Porsche fob in her left hand. She handed it through to him.

He tossed the fob and key down to his partner, who caught it, sniggered to himself over a Porsche fob being attached to a key for a twelve-year-old Mustang GT Liftback, and began walking toward the car, being quite aware the dog crap in the yard most likely wasn't confined to the snow pile. He knew his partner would keep her attention occupied and her view blocked while he quickly went through every bit of the small car for any clue as to where the boys had gone. He was also planning to leave something behind, just in case they returned for the vehicle.

It didn't take much to block the woman's view. The man on the porch really was a large gentleman, and it was a relatively small door, but his partner did need a bit of time, so he kept up the conversation until his partner called over that he was done.

"Did you find the paperwork?" he called down from the porch.

"Sure did, in the glove box," said the other man as he slid into the driver's seat of the Town Car. "We can head out anytime you're ready."

"Just a second," the passenger at the trailer's door said with a bit of a wave. Then to the woman: "I want to thank you for helping me out today. If you talk to Mr. Saunders, please don't mention any of this mix up. I am hoping he'll send over some of his Harvard buddies to see me, and well, if he thought I was such an irresponsible idiot, he may not do it. I can use the commissions, believe me. Let me give you something for your trouble."

He reached into his jacket and pulled out his wallet, flipped it open and removed a crisp, new, one-hundred-dollar bill. She could see the cash pocket wasn't at all barren, like you'd expect from someone late on the rent and a chill ran through her.

"Mister? The key?" she said, hiding her now shaking hands by holding tightly to push bar on the aluminum storm door.

"Oh, geeze, yeah," he said and then he waved and signaled to his partner. "Key," he called.

His partner rolled down the window, tossed the key and fob up and he handed it back to the woman through the cracked screen door, along with the hundred. She protested slightly, but took the bill all the same, dropped the key and the bill into the pocket of her robe, and the man turned to leave. As he walked to the car, she stepped out onto the porch and memorized the license plate, then went back inside the trailer, locked both doors securely and wrote it down on a pad by the telephone as she heard them back out and drive away.

## Chapter Seven

Sandy pulled my big toe and woke me from a wonderful nap filled with dreams. Good ones.

"Time for dinner, sleepy head," she said. "You can continue the snore fest later."

I opened my eyes and saw it was dark outside the window, and Sandy was already dressed and made up for dinner. God, she was an eyeful, and then some.

"What time is it?" I asked. "And, I don't snore."

"I'll tell the folks next door that you're sawing railroad ties in here then," she said with a wink and grin. "It's ten to six," she said without wink or grin. "I know you take less time to look stunning than I do, so I let you sleep."

"Yeah, but look at what I start with," I said, tossing back the covers.

Sandy smiled broadly. Have I mentioned that I love it when Sandy smiles?

"Well, pack up the toolbox, Bob the Builder," she said. "You know how Anita is when she adds the word 'sharp' to meal time. Besides, I'm famished. I wonder if she's serving her fresh Gulf seafood pasta."

"Now you did it," I said, leaping from the bed and into my shorts and pants in one fell swoop. "You know I'm a sucker for both fresh seafood and pasta. Put 'em together and I'll bust down a door to get a dishful, or two."

Five minutes later, we were in the hallway. One more and I followed Sandy into the dining room. Have I mentioned how much I enjoy walking behind my wife? Tonight she was wearing a floral pattern dress. I wondered if Sandy's selecting it was perhaps inspired by the forest of flowers inhabiting our room. It had an azure background which sported a formfitting bodice and flowing skirt that ended just above the knee, and she wore matching deep blue, open-toed, sling-back pumps. A thought hit me as the aroma of what had to be Anita's fresh Gulf seafood pasta came from the kitchen and fought to overpower Sandy's subtle perfume and I hoped I never had to choose between *two* doors: one with Sandy behind, and one keeping me from seafood and pasta because I am not sure I'd get to the seafood and pasta before it got cold. That's just how I roll.

The dining room was filled with other guests, making about twenty of us in total. Ten rooms in the B&B, so that count made sense. It seemed to me that everyone had the same idea we had had to take a midwinter break to the island. Most of the other folks were from Texas, we learned when Anita did the introductions, although we were seated directly across from this interesting couple from Green Bay. We were William and Sandy Langdon of New Orleans in the introductions, but I quickly made the home state connection with the Wisconsinites.

Their name was John and Chrissy Baird, pronounced 'bird'. He was an engineer, and, of course, I made my train driving joke I reserve for engineers. He clarified he was a civil engineer. I was about to make a comment about hoping so since we were seated across from them, but Sandy pinched my leg under the table before I could. Chrissy taught third graders in the Green Bay public school system. They had renewed their vows after five years of marriage and were on a second honeymoon. From the bit of lingering tension between the couple and the fact that they had sought out the renewal of their vows after only five years told this old detective and P.I. that one of the two had cheated and the other was willing to take them back, for now.

When they asked, we told them about our lives. How we had briefly been high school sweethearts, had drifted apart during our senior year and then had both escaped the small town of Sheboygan right after graduation. Me, to the big city lights of Chicago to bounce around a while before joining the police department. Sandy, to the numbing boredom of small-town Iowa where she hooked up with some real loser, until she left him naked, face down, tied to a bed one night with the cattle prod he was so proud of sticking into a place, well, let's just say a place not made for holding a cattle prod, while promising him if he came near her again or raised his hand to any other woman, she'd come back and use the open straight razor she had strategically placed beneath him. I didn't share those last two details with John and Chrissy, not because it would embarrass my wife, it wouldn't, but it may give Chrissy an idea I didn't want to be responsible for. Sandy then had gone back to school and became a lawyer, landing a job and eventually becoming a partner at one of the most prestigious firms in the Midwest. Also in Chicago.

When I got to the part about living in the Caymans and running into Sandy again, out of the blue, John's eyes lit up. I was even more certain then that John was the cheater, and one day he'd leave the railroad and go chase his long lost love. Fortunately, because of their wedded outlook,

"The mnemonic," Ronnie said. "For remembering. From English."

Ashley shook her head, waved the detour away.

"Well, it began to mean less and less as time went on."

"What do you mean?"

"I asked her the same question."

Ashley smiled and Ronnie returned it.

"Great minds, eh, Ash?"

"Yep. She said it lost its value as an expression of love and that boys just didn't care about it as such anyway. She said she learned that a teenage boy would stick his pecker into a porcupine if he could get it to hold still long enough."

They both laughed.

"Then she said, for a girl, it's different. It's not that it's not fun, and it does feel good, she said, but it doesn't feel *right*; and giving in to some boy's pressure that first time when she wasn't really ready and in love was one of her biggest regrets in life."

"How old was she? Did she tell you?"

"She said she had been fifteen."

"That's younger than we are now."

"Wow, look at you. Without a calculator, even, Miss Einstein."

They broke out into exaggerated laughter and fell against each other, the convivial boisterousness due mostly to the abundance of blood sugar and lack of sleep because the line wasn't *that* hilarious. Moments later, they shushed each other when a light went on inside one of the rooms in the nun's quarters. They sat there frozen in place and watched with hands over their mouths for several minutes until the light was extinguished.

Ashley began again, in a lower volume.

"My aunt and a group of friends had been drinking and smoking pot at a party and the next thing she knew, she was alone in a bedroom with this guy she had just started seeing and that she really liked, and he talked her into going all the way. She said before she knew what was happening, it was over, and when it was, he changed. She knew that somehow she had changed in that instant, too, and would never be the same. After that, perhaps because she lost respect for herself, perhaps because she just didn't care, perhaps because everyone who was cool was doing it, but for whatever reason, it didn't matter who, what, when, where, and much less why.

"Later, she was *certain* she had lost all respect for herself. Of course, that was looking back at it all. At the time, it was fun, gave her a sense of being a grown up, of being part of the cool crowd. At least that's what she said. Her point was that a girl shouldn't do something just because it's fun at the moment or some guy is trying to talk her into it, because in that one seemingly unimportant instant, so many important things change. Forever."

"What about love? How did she say that played into it?"

"Geeze, Ronnie, hasn't your mom had the love talk with you either?"

"I think my mom knows less about love than she does about sex."

"Well, she knew enough about one of those things to have you."

"I was an accident. My mom told me so one time after she had had a really bad fight with my dad. The next day she apologized, said she had been drinking and hadn't meant it." Ronnie looked up at the sliver of a new moon overhead. "She apologized, but the arrow still stuck, you know?"

"Wow, Ronnie, we've known each other for nearly three years, and you've never told me that."

"There are some things you don't tell people about, Ash."

"Exactly."

Ronnie nodded slowly.

Ashley tapped Ronnie on the knee.

"Let's go in, it's starting to cool down. Feels like rain," Ashley said.

She stood up and Ronnie followed her back to the dorm. On the way, each wondered if anything had been settled in their discussion.

The two large gentlemen worked under the light of the open trunk at a highway rest area a few miles from the trailer park and sorted through the items recovered from Dave Saunders' old car.

"I'm just glad this wasn't a typical college kid's car," the driver said. "I was envisioning digging through piles of stinking Taco Bell wrappers and empty Slurpee cups. This kid is fairly neat."

"Hey, here's something which could be interesting," the passenger said as he held up a crumpled a small, yellow Post-it note. "The initials 'CS' and what looks like a phone number. Boston area code as I recall."

"Tag it and bag it," the driver said. "We'll call it in when we get back on the road." He pushed the small pile around again. "Let's get going, there's nothing else here."

Seated in a darkened room, the muted television playing in the far corner and illuminating a stratus layer of smoke hanging just below the plastic paneled ceiling, Dave's aunt replayed the encounter with the two large gentlemen in the black Town Car. From the pocket of her robe, she again removed the hundred-dollar-bill and looked at it. She dropped it onto the end table. Dave had warned her there may be a chance people would come looking for them, but had assured her he had taken every precaution to prevent that from that happening. She wondered what her long-estranged nephew had gotten himself into, and who that other boy with him was.

She reached into the robe pocket again and removed a small piece of paper on which Dave had written an emergency contact number. Was this an emergency? The cover story the man had used seemed believable enough when he had told it. When the man on the porch had pulled out his wallet and she saw all that cash after claiming poor and unable to make the month's rent the day before payday, however, she wondered about the truth of everything he had said. Then she had a Eureka moment: he never gave her his card. That alone was odd, especially for a car salesman. They're always forcing their card into your hand, even if you tell them you are just looking and could never afford what they were selling anyway. The standard comeback was always: 'You never know, here's my card. Just in case, or for a friend who might be in the market.'

Okay, so they were phonies. That was obvious to her now. That much realized, she now had to think about what to do. She sat in the well-worn, plaid cloth recliner and then snatched the pack of cigarettes off the side table and pulled one with her lips before tossing the pack down again. She picked up the cheap disposable lighter from the same table, flicked it for fire and lit and inhaled in a fluid motion honed by decades of practicing the habit. The lungfuls of exhaled smoke rose to the ceiling to join the stratus layer just below the yellowed ceiling.

Half an hour of thinking, and five cigarettes later, she picked up the phone and dialed Dave's emergency number. The phone was answered on the second ring.

"Hey, it's Cindy."

The voice came across as light and easygoing.

"Hi, ah, Cindy, is it?"

"Yep, who's this?"

"Um, hi, Cindy, this is Gloria Keller, ah, Dave Saunders' aunt."

"Hey, what's up?"

"I'm sorry to bother you, but Dave gave me this number in case there was an emergency while the boys were gone, and, well, I'm not really sure this qualifies, but there were a couple of men here earlier looking for Dave's new car."

"His new car? I didn't know he had a new car. What did he do with the Mustang?"

"The Mustang is here. The men went through it looking for papers on the new car, they said."

"Why would Dave put papers for a new car in his old car?"

Gloria was feeling really stupid now.

"Who were these two guys?" Cindy continued.

"They said they were salesmen from the dealership and that they thought they had mistakenly given Dave the wrong copies of the paperwork. The one said he needed to get it back so he could be paid his commission and catch up on his late rent. The other one looked through Dave's old car."

"Wow, that's a good one."

Gloria was almost afraid to ask why, but did anyway.

"A car salesperson doesn't get paid his commission off the contract paperwork. It's a totally different accounting system."

"How was I supposed to know this?"

"You weren't. A friend's family owns a string of GM dealerships in the Midwest. I worked a couple summers at one. I guess it's an insider thing."

"Well, shiny crappola. I guess I screwed up."

"What did the guy find in the old car? Any paperwork?"

"He didn't say; I didn't think to ask. Gosh, I feel stupid. They just left right after he was done looking." She took a drink from the plastic cup of the RC Cola and vodka she had been drinking from and refilling most of the afternoon. She lit another cigarette.

"Not to worry, Gloria. I'll let Dave know what you told me."

"Do you know where they're going, Cindy?"

"Sure do. Bye."


The next phone call came in ten minutes later. New York area code.

"Hey, it's Cindy."

"Yes, Ms. Spagliano, this is Cal Jameson from New London Cadillac, how are you this evening?"

"Just fine, Mr. Jameson, is it?"

"Yes, but you can just call me Cal."

"Well, you can call me Cindy, Cal."

"We'll just go ahead and call that a deal, Cindy."

Way too 'schmoozie', she thought. This guy *could* be a car salesman, or worse, a realtor. No wonder Gloria was taken in.

"What can I do for you, Cal? I'm not in the market for a Cadillac. I've got my eye on a sweet, older Mustang."

A pause.

"Is that so?"

"Yeah, a guy posted a Car For Sale notice with some pictures on the bulletin board at the Commons up here at school, and I called him on it. He was supposed to call me back, but I haven't heard from him yet. I hope he hasn't sold it."

A pause.

"Cal, are you there?"

"Yes." Another few beats. "Well, I guess we were misinformed as to your interest, Ms. Spagliano."

"Cindy."

"I'm sorry, Cindy."

"No problem, Cal. You have a good night."

The phone clicked off.

"Dipshits," Cindy said and she tossed the phone onto her small desk.

Dace had finished all six cans of beer and recycled some of it onto the side of the road when the urge overpowered the distance to the next offramp. He had also polished off the pint bottle of tequila and a healthy bit of the beef jerky. Dave had been grateful when Dace had slept through the next gas break twenty miles northeast of Birmingham. When filling the Escalade, Dave had dumped the empties into a trash bin lest any Alabama cop decide to take a look around. He didn't want to spend a night in an Alabama jail anymore than one in Tennessee.

Back on the interstate, Dave shook Dace by the shoulder.

"Hey, wake up, buddy."

Dace protested, rolled in the seat. Dave shook him again.

"Yo, Dace. We've got an executive decision to make here."

"What?" Dace didn't turn or look over. Dave wondered if he even opened his eyes, which he couldn't see because Dace was sleeping with his Blues Brothers sunglasses on.

"Well, it's about five-thirty in the afternoon, we've got about another six or seven hours to get to the house."

Dace sat up and looked out the side window.

"It's too dark for five-thirty, Dave."

"Take your glasses off." Dave let out a belly laugh. "Man, you are not a drinker, are you?"

"Working hard to learn, though," Dace said as he removed his glasses, folded them and tossed them into the storage area in the center console. "You know I'm what's called an overachiever."

"So, do you want to keep going or shack up somewhere along here for the night and finish up during the daylight tomorrow?"

"How much farther is it?"

"Like I said, about six or seven hours by the time we get out to the house, from what Cindy told me. According to the map, it's only about five hours to New Orleans from here."

"Let's finish it up tomorrow, then," Dace said, stretching in the seat. "You have any Tylenol?"

"There's a bottle in the glove box; how many you need?"

"How many do you have?"

An hour later, they had checked into an inexpensive chain motel just off the interstate on the southwest side of Birmingham, and had a pizza and wings ordered and on the way. The night manager had at first declined to accept a cash customer without a credit card imprint, but a call to the general manager had solved the problem with a driver's license photocopy. It seemed to Dave traveling off the grid was continuing to be a problematic effort; he wondered what had happened to people to make them not want to just take cash.

Once settled in the room, Dave jumped into the shower to wash the road off him. When he came out, Dace was gone.


"We must look at this thing pragmatically, Allard, before we go heading off into a place we cannot defend should the excrement hit the spinning airfoil," Tom McDaniel said with more than a hint of irritation.

The confines of The Senator's office and home, as comfortable as they were, had begun to close in on him. For the last four days he'd been holed up there, having come on Sunday morning as a friend first and a political advisor second. He had come to help his friend and most valued and longest-standing client and his family contend with a tragedy which could have ramifications to the political career of a fine young man. Since the funeral on Tuesday, however, he'd been wrestling a different monster, spending his time calming The Senator's escalating rants, managing an underground search for Dace and the Saunders kid, all while missing appointments with other clients, and even having to forego his speech to a gathering of party faithful the night before in New York, after which he had plans to meet privately with a charming and energetic blonde intern.

"Bullshit, Tom," The Senator said, stopping his endless pacing for a moment to point across the room with one of his fingers while the rest remained wrapped around his cut crystal tumbler. "How can a pair of college kids just drop off the face of the earth without a trace? We've got to pull out the big guns and get Dace's ass back here before he ruins everything I have worked and planned for him by doing something stupid. Do you realize how minor an error he could make which would ruin his career?" He huffed in emphasis and took another draw from his drink. "Goddammit, make it happen. Get that kid back here." He turned his back to the room and stared out the window.

Senator Lamoureux was drinking too much, in Tom's opinion, and was becoming increasingly angry and irrational with every glass consumed. Earlier in the day, Tom had surreptitiously approached Libby while The Senator had dozed on the leather couch in his office and asked for her assistance in redirecting her husband's emotions. He had also asked Libby to tell him if she knew anything which she was holding back; for Dace's sake, he had pled. She had said she would help in any way she could.

Tom had issued a press release which blamed The Senator's absence from sessions in Washington on a minor bout with the flu, but as the week transitioned toward another weekend and media types left the District for their homes, Tom was beginning to grow concerned some unfavorable rumors would be spun at parties. He realized news was made in Washington, but gossip and innuendo gathered at parties often fueled the search for the next breaking story. A number of The Senator's colleagues had attended the party Saturday evening last, and he had been in good health then. It also wasn't a secret Dace had known the girl in the accident, but to that point the tragic death of Sarah Avidago had remained a local story. Tom had been surprised, and frankly, relieved, that no national press inquiries had come in to either his or The Senator's offices about the connection between Dace and the dead girl.

On the other hand, Tom realized The Senator was correct to become increasingly concerned as the hours ticked away without word from Dace; but to begin pulling in favors from agencies like the FBI and IRS was dangerous ground which usually led to worse problems down the road. Everyone in DC wanted a 'Get Out of Jail Free' card in their pocket; the District ran on favors and paybacks of favors. They were the currency of the realm, and an IOU from a United States Senator was tough to beat on the list of good things to have in one's pocket.

What really was the bottom line problem here? So Dace and the girl had been dating. So she wasn't listed on the Society page. So she had died in a tragic automobile accident after leaving a party where alcohol had been served, but at which nobody had seen her consume any. The preliminary autopsy report confirmed the fact there were no drugs or alcohol in her system. Tom had felt from the first telephone call The Senator was overreacting, given the circumstances, but he had come up from the city anyway. As he sat in the office across the room from his agitated client, he considered not just the current crisis, but all the situations he had helped this man who now treated him not as a trusted and longterm advisor, or even as the friend he was, but rather as just another employee to be ordered about and chastised for things over which he had little control.

Tom was becoming angry and resentful, and that's not a good thing for either a professional relationship or a friendship. Over thirty years, six senatorial campaigns which were gimmes given the power of the Lamoureux name in that part of the country, and one flirtation with a run for the Oval Office when a wounded incumbent appeared for a time to be too weak to beat back a primary challenge, it would have been impossible for the pair not to have also developed a personal friendship. For all his egocentric proclivities, Senator Allard Lamoureux was generally an affable guy whom Tom genuinely liked; but after four days of close contact under stress, even an affable guy can begin to rub the best of friends the wrong way.

Tom's phone vibrated in his pocket and returned him to the moment; he was frankly glad for the interruption of his thoughts. A check of the caller ID revealed it was coming from one of his men's cellular phones.

"Yeah," Tom said after flipping the phone open and raising it to his ear. Tom tended to share everything with his client, however, given his current agitated state, he judged it smart to control what The Senator knew and when he knew it. "Update me."

"Sir, the taps and traps are in place on the phones of the aunt and Cindy Spagliano," came the voice of one of the large gentlemen. "We received notice of placement shortly after I spoke with the girl."

"Good," Tom said. "All lines?"

"Yes, sir, land line and cellular, both. Our contacts for both providers advise they can maintain them for a maximum of seventy-two hours before they will be required to either receive a Court Order or disengage."

"I would think three days should be enough time. Nobody wants to bother a federal judge at this point." Tom paused and thought a moment, then dismissed his next question unspoken. "All right, call me immediately if something turns up." He disconnected.

"What's that about?" The Senator asked when Tom tucked his phone away.

"That was my guys checking in," Tom said. "You don't need to know anything more at this point."

The Senator, understanding the game, simply nodded and then returned to staring out the window into the coming darkness.


Dace sat on small bench outside a truck stop restaurant watching the customers in big rigs and cars come and go. The night was cool, about fifty degrees. He wore a pair of jeans and a dark blue hoodie over his shirt. He had the hood up against the slight breeze. Every so often, he'd take a drink from a bottle held in a small paper bag. The Greyhound Bus Lines sign in the window behind him cast a bluish neon light to mix with the amber glow of the sodium vapor lights of the parking lot. The result was a small radius where colors could be seen as they really were with a sea of yellow wash beyond which cast everything in surreal, brownish hues.

His eyes followed an attractive woman in her early twenties as she exited the nearby convenience store doors and walked to her car at the gas pumps. New York plates on the car. Dace wondered which direction she was headed; and why. In the back seat, he noted a rack hung full with clothes. From the way the car rode low in the rear, he estimated every cubic inch of free space within it was packed full with her other belongings. He smiled to himself. He concluded she was exiting an old life, headed for a new one.

"Good luck," he said as he hoisted his bag in her direction.

As he brought the bag back down, he heard the squeak of rubber soles off to his left and sensed someone approaching him. He turned to see a pimply faced kid striding up; he was no more than Dace's age, dressed in polyester pants and a white shirt turned cream by the glow of sodium vapor lamps. In the wash of yellow light, the kid's pimples were brown, but as the kid entered the 'Blue Zone', as Dace had begun calling the arc of true colors, the pimples turned bright red while the kid's freckles remained brown. A silver badge was visible on his chest; Dace read the word 'Pinkerton' as he came to a stop in front of the bench.

"Are you waiting for something, sir?" the kid asked.

Dace returned a puzzled look while sizing him up: six or eight inches shorter than himself and carrying around an extra forty pounds of donuts in his midsection. Towheaded with gray eyes, his cheeks and neck sported scattered areas of unshaved growth along with the mix of pimples and freckles. His accent wasn't as thick as Dace had expected. The uniform was well-worn, the shirt sweat stained under the arms and beginning to fray at the collar. Dace watched as the kid's right hand moved to rest on what appeared to be a pepper spray canister on his belt.

After he had looked the kid over, Dace decided the rent-a-cop wasn't worthy of his attention, and he lowered his head and returned his gaze outward. He drank again from the bagged bottle. The hoodie blocked the kid from his peripheral vision. Dace waited. His body tensed.

"I said, are you waiting for something, sir?"

"Just enjoying the night air," Dace said without raising his head.

That seemed to catch the kid off-balance. He shifted into Dace's line of vision and stood squared to the bench. His feet were spread to shoulder breadth and his hand remained fixed upon the canister in his belt. To Dace's observation, the kid appeared slightly fearful as he began to shuffle slightly from foot to foot in his stance.

"You've been here for a while, sir. Do you have a vehicle in the lot or are you waiting for someone?"

"No, like I said, just enjoying the night air for a bit," Dace said before taking a purposefully long draw from the bagged bottle. "You need to learn to listen better."

"Sir, what's in the bag?"

"What bag?"

"The bag in your hand, sir. What's in it?"

"This bag?" Dace said pointing to the brown sack; a playful glimmer in his eye. "The lady inside gave me this bag when I bought my drink."

"I didn't ask you where you got it, or who gave it to you, sir. I asked what's in the bag?"

"My drink," Dace said, enjoying this even though he could see the kid becoming annoyed as his right hand twitched on the mace canister with each smart aleck response. "Like I told you. You have to learn to listen better, son."

"Sir, there is no consumption of alcohol in public areas in this state. It's the law."

"Now, that's a good law," Dace said with a slow nod, downed another swig, smiled at the kid and then looked past him into the night. "A very good law, indeed."

Dave parted the curtains and peered out across the expanse of parking lots surrounding the motel and other businesses geared toward the interstate traveler. Off to the east he could see the seemingly endless lines of red and white lights of the traffic moving along I-59. He moved away from the window and sat on his bed. He twisted the cap off a half-consumed, two-liter bottle of Pepsi, downed another healthy draw and followed that up with a hearty belch.

The pizza and wings had arrived half an hour before, and Dave had scarfed down half the pizza and a little over half the wings. The remains sat in grease stained boxes on Dace's bed. Dave muted the hockey game on the television and picked up the handset of the phone mounted to the nightstand between the beds. He browsed the calling instructions and then dialed the number he knew by heart with the added digits so the call would be billed to the room. In the distance he could hear the ringing.

"Hey, it's Cindy," said the cheery voice.

"Hey, it's me," he said.

"Well, well, my long lost brother," Cindy said.

It was their prearranged code to let Dave know someone had reached out to her. When they had made the arrangements for the little getaway, Dave had suggested the code to provide a warning in case someone had tracked Cindy down and had come looking for Dace. Dave was a little surprised they had found her so quickly, yet he played his predesigned role to hear what she could tell him.

"I know, I know, it's been a long time," Dave said. "How's my favorite sister?"

"Well, since I'm your only sister, I guess I'd be in trouble if I weren't your favorite."

"Anything new?" he asked.

"Hey, you're gonna love this," she began. "I got a call out of the blue from some Cadillac salesman earlier, wanting to sell me a car. Must have gotten my number from someone playing games because he knew my name and really thought I was in the market. Weird, huh?"

"That is weird," Dave said. A moment. "What did you say to him?"

"I told him I had my eye on a sweet, older Mustang some guy at school was selling, and that I was waiting for that callback."

"Eh, some people just have crappy jobs, sis," Dave said. Another pause. "Everything still okay?"

"As far as I know, it is."

"Well, listen, the kids need a bath and story before bed, so I best get going."

"Hey, before you go, let me give you a new number for Aunt Margie," Cindy said. "It's her birthday next week, so don't forget to give her a call. Got a pencil and paper?"

Dave grabbed the half pencil and small note pad from the night stand, pinched the handset to his ear with his shoulder.

"Yep, go ahead."

"Don't forget to dial the 'one' first," she said with a chuckle and then recited the number.

Dave copied the ten digits down, then read them back.

"That's it. Give the kiddies a hug from their auntie."

"You got it. Good night, sis."

"Catch ya later, bro'."

Dave hung up the phone. He looked at the ten numbers, then recopied them on a line below in reverse order and dialed out again. He heard the ringing in the distance.

"Hey," she said.

"Now who's paranoid?" Dave said.

"Yeah, yeah."

"So what makes you think they tracked you down?"

"Your aunt Gloria phoned me," Cindy said. "Not ten minutes before this so-called salesman called. They had been to see her. They've found the Mustang, I understand. She let them go through it looking for lease papers."

"Hmm, I gave her your number in case of emergency. I wonder if she gave it to them."

"I don't think she did. At least she said she didn't, so maybe they found it someplace."

Cindy recited the rest of the story as Gloria had passed it along.

"She's really sorry if she caused a problem, Dave," Cindy said.

"I know she is, Cindy. You know, it was a fairly good ruse they pulled. Anybody could have fallen for it." A pause. "It does sound like the security goons Dace described: two large gentlemen in a black Lincoln."

"Speaking of Dace, how is our dear Little Lord Fauntleroy?"

Dave laughed, tried for a moment to picture Dace in the Fauntleroy suit and ringlet curls described in the 1886 Burnett novel, a style originally captured on canvas by Gainsborough in his 1770 *Blue Boy* painting from which Burnett had probably been inspired.

"Right now, I'm not so sure. He disappeared while I was taking a shower, so I don't even know where he is at the moment." A pause. "Oh, here's one thing, he's taken up smoking and drinking."

"Dace? Smoking and drinking?"

"Yeah, and eating beef jerky," Dave said with a small laugh as he remembered Dace's earlier reaction to it. "Seriously, though, he's been really quiet on the drive so far. I think he's internalizing plenty right now. Strangers have begun seeing something in his eyes, though." He relayed what the cashier in the truck stop convenience store had observed. "He'll open up soon, I'm sure. He's got to. If he doesn't he's gonna explode."

"Well, there's nobody better to handle this than you, Dave. I know you love Dace and he loves you. Bro love, you know. Not the other kind. Oh, you're all set at the house," Cindy said. "If you have any problems, call me on this phone. I imagine it will be safe; for a while, anyway."

"I figure we'll be down there sometime tomorrow afternoon." A pause. "Sure you don't want to come down? After all, it's Mardi Gras."

"Good night, Dave," Cindy said, and the line went dead.

Dave hung up the phone, turned to sit on the bed with his legs stretched out and returned the sound to the hockey game.

A few moments later, the door opened, and in walked Dace, more the image of an *Our Gang* ruffian than Little Lord Fauntleroy.

# Chapter Eight

Tom's phone rattled his change on the nightstand in his room. After further discussions went nowhere with The Senator, Tom had decided to turn in early and nurse a headache. He grabbed the phone before the ringtone started and checked the caller ID.

"Yeah, what's up?" he said, propping himself on one elbow and reaching for the nightstand light.

"We've got something here, sir," one of the large gentlemen said. "I'm reading the transcript of a call which came in to Cindy Spagliano's phone about two hours ago."

"Read me the important segments," Tom said. He listened carefully. "So, the girl took a call from her brother."

"There are problems, sir."

"Such as?"

"Well, we did a background check and the girl does have a brother. A stepbrother who came with the guy who married her mother when Cindy was eight. Twenty-six years old now."

"And?"

"He lives in Michigan, in Muskegon. Married, two kids."

"Well, from what you read me, that would check," Tom said with a hint of irritation. "He said he was going to put the kids to bed."

"That's where it just doesn't fit. Muskegon is area code 231. The call came from a number in the 205 area code. That's Alabama. Northern Alabama. The exchange is Birmingham. We checked the number, it's a motel just off I-59. We also called the brother's house to see if perhaps he was traveling with the family, but got his wife and she indicated he was home."

"Hmm," Tom said. "I guess we should get on this. Could be our boys made their first mistake."

"The earliest commercial flight out of Newark would put us into Birmingham just before eight in the morning, sir. By the time we rented a car and made the drive to the motel, it could be after nine. We could miss them."

"No, let's put together a charter." Tom looked at his watch. "Call Missy on her cell. Tell her to charge it to The Senator's campaign fund, and get you guys out tonight. They should be able to pick you up right here in New London. Groton-NewLondon Airport has runways long enough for most charter jets. The crew can wait for you in Birmingham for a return trip, hopefully with Dace tucked under your arm. I would imagine your stay in the land of Dixie would be short, regardless of the outcome. Have her rent you a car down there, too, and get to the motel before sun up. They most likely still have that new Escalade of Dave's which won't be hard to spot in the parking lot, especially since we have both possible license plate numbers."

"What do you want us to do when we find them?"

"I don't care what you do with the Saunders kid, just don't kill him; but get Dace on the plane back here so we all can go on with our lives."

"Yes, sir."

"Call me with updates after you're situated down there."

"Will do."

The phone clicked off. Tom considered for a moment about finding The Senator to let him know what was happening, then overruled the thought. He had just extricated himself from another long day of tedious conversations in what was rapidly becoming a long week of tedious conversations and had little desire to spend the rest of the night in the same situation. This information was nothing but foam so far, he could bring the man up to date when he knew something solid, he concluded. He placed the phone back onto the nightstand and turned off the light and fell back asleep.

Dace was laughing when he came in, but looked a little worse for wear since Dave last saw him. His hoodie was torn and stained, the right leg of his jeans ripped open and the knee beneath abraded and bloodied. His eyes were red and watering. A trickle of blood had dried on the corner of his mouth and a faint bruise was beginning to form on his left cheek. The knuckles of both hands were scraped. Yet, he was laughing. Not the good joke kind of laugh, or the 'hey, we won the game' celebratory type either. To Dave, what was coming from his best friend sounded more guttural, more primitive, base.

"What the hell happened to you, Dace?" Dave asked.

"Got into a little disagreement with a couple of Pinkerton boys next door," Dace said before ducking into the bathroom to survey the damage. "Apparently, it's illegal to consume alcohol in public in this state." He laughed again. "Weird thing, I was just sitting and drinking a Gatorade." His smile became wry. "Out of a brown paper bag." He laughed again.

Dave thought it must be an inside joke, then a realization hit home.
"You instigated this on purpose?"

"I guess."

"Why would you do that?"

"I dunno, bored, I guess."

"Bored?"

Dace exited the bathroom, glanced at the television, then surveyed the items stacked on his bed.

"Yeah, hey I see the pizza made it.  I'm starved."  He pulled the hoodie over his head and plopped down onto his bed and opened the boxes.  "You ate already?"

"Uh-huh," Dave said with a nod and a stare.

"Where, oh where, are your manners, old boy?"

He had known Dace nearly all his life and never knew him to get into a fight; or smoke; or drink.  Again, he wondered what would come next.

"I dunno."  A pause.  "Maybe I left them at home with the real Dace Lamoureux.  Seen him lately?"

Dace smirked, then turned his attention to the television screen.

"Hey, who's winning the fight...I mean, hockey game?"

"Blackhawks, three to zip over the Canadiens.  Just about to start the third period."

As he watched Dace settle in and tear into the first piece of pizza, seemingly oblivious to the nature of what he had just done, Dave began to wonder if he was in over his head.  He could understand the drinking and even squint really hard and see the smoking, but violence?  For nothing?  Because he's bored?  Sure, Dace would play sports at the level of a fierce competitor, but when the whistle blew, he was the most generous of field or court sportsmen, whether in defeat or victory.  Dave sat on the edge of his bed and watched Dace wolfing down the remaining half of the pizza and rest of the wings, washing it all down with almost half the Pepsi directly from a new two-liter bottle.  It was a vision of ravenous feasting, almost animalistic.

"Dude, we need to talk," Dave said.

Just before three in the morning, a Learjet 45 touched down at the Groton-New London Airport and taxied up to the general aviation terminal.  The pilots had been told to prepare for a quick departure, so the captain only shut down the left engine while the copilot jumped out of the aircraft to help the two rather large gentlemen aboard.  The manifest said two passengers, minimal bags and that's exactly what they picked up.  With the door closed, by the time the first officer was climbing back into his seat in the small cockpit, the captain already had the left engine spinning again.  They rolled across the ramp moments later as the copilot chatted with Air Traffic Control and collected their clearance.

At six minutes after three, the aircraft departed on an instrument flight plan to Birmingham, Alabama. The estimated time en route was two hours and fourteen minutes. Because of the time of night, traffic in the normally congested eastern corridor north of New York was light. The first officer requested, and New York Center approved an unrestricted climb to their cruising altitude of thirty-eight-thousand feet.

Rudy and Travis dozed in the cabin. The seats were large, but they were still tucked into a Learjet, so things were still a bit cramped and uncomfortable for the oversized pair.

At ten minutes past five in the morning, the jet rolled to a stop at the general aviation terminal in Birmingham. A rented Crown Victoria pulled out onto the ramp as the engines spooled down and the clamshell doors opened. The rental car attendant opened both front doors and pointed to the map and directions lying on the front passenger seat. At fifteen minutes past five, just as the hint of a new day was dawning in the eastern sky, the midnight blue sedan containing two large gentlemen from up north drove off the airport property and headed southwest on I-59.

The cresting sun slowly changed the sky from gray to pink, and by the time they neared the exit for the motel, had painted it brilliant orange and the highway had begun to fill with traffic. Alabama was stirring to welcome the new day.

Dace pivoted the visor over to the side window. Even with the tinted windows in the Escalade, the first rays of the sunrise were intense in the corner of his eye. He drove along I-59 on a due south segment of an interstate which ran generally southwest toward Mississippi while he munched an Egg McMuffin as Dave tried to sleep in the reclined passenger seat. They had talked much of the night, and Dace volunteered to do some driving that morning. He arced around a sweeping curve back to the southwest and was surprised the big Cadillac SUV handled so easily; and rode even better on the left side than on the right.

Police squads had come to the motel several times during the night. Dace and Dave watched each time from their window as they arrived, then left fifteen minutes or so later. The cars cruised the lot slowly each time, but not slowly enough to be taking down license numbers. After leaving the motel lot, they would drive over to the truck stop, linger for a time, and then leave the area. The cops were obviously looking for a man on foot.

Around three in the morning, Dave wandered down to speak to the overnight desk clerk and find out what was going on. The woman had been pleasant in that chatty southern way, and had told him the police were looking for someone who had caused a ruckus at the truck stop. 'Beat up two of those security boys' she had told Dave. 'One fairly bad, had to go to the hospital for stitches and observation for a suspected concussion,' she had added.

The clerk told him they had dropped off some printed stills of the perpetrator taken from the truck stop's security camera. Dave had asked to see them, 'just in case', he said, and sure enough, it was Dace. Fortunately, the overnight desk clerk had not been on duty when they checked in, and Dave concluded the photos were just blurry enough to not give anyone enough detail to pick him out unless Dace walked through the lobby wearing his hoodie. The cops had told the woman they were working on a computer-enhanced photo and a composite drawing at the hospital and they'd be back with those by the morning.

Having no desire to see his friend hauled off to jail in Alabama for assaulting a couple of good old boys, Dave had suggested to Dace that they split before the cops came back again. Dace agreed and they packed their things and just before five in the morning, Dace sneaked out the side door and retrieved the Escalade while Dave checked out at the front desk.

The Crown Victoria slowly rolled through the parking lot of the motel on the outskirts of Birmingham. The two large gentlemen in the front seat quickly determined the pearl white Escalade was not there. On a hunch, they canvassed the nearby fast food places, the truck stop, and even the outlet mall lot. Nothing.

"They're gone," said the passenger, slamming a fist onto the dash. The Ford rattled in protest. "Friggin' Fords."

"What was your first clue, Sherlock?" said the driver.

"Let's go back to the motel and see what we can dig up before we call in," the passenger said, ignoring the ball-busting remark.

The two large gentlemen prowling the outskirts of Birmingham that early morning were longtime comrades and had known each other nearly half of the younger man's life. They had served together as Marines, had sold their services as mercenaries in several hotspots around the world after leaving the Corps, and upon returning home, had fallen into the lucrative private security business. Their clients had been Top 100 corporations, politicians, and they had even performed a bit of contract protection work for the government when high-ranking officials went into areas of the world which could be especially hot. For the last several years, they had worked almost exclusively for Tom McDaniel doing security and investigative work. Neither of the men could sustain marriages over their life of numerous deployments and each had begun to desire more of a personal life and perhaps a wife and family, so while it wasn't as adrenaline driven as some of their previous endeavors, working for Tom had meant more nights at home in New York, but had provided not much luck in finding true love for either man.

Through the years, their modus operandi had always been the same, whether in uniform or custom-made suits: intimidate with physical presence, run some variation of the good guy/bad guy program, and if neither fully did the job, crack a skull. Each had packed on fifty or so pounds since their Marine Corps days, but even with that added weight coming mostly from good living, what hung on their frames was still more muscle than fat. They were solid as tanks, and nearly as big.

Rudy, six years younger than his partner at thirty-six, always rode shotgun. He was the passenger. Six-foot-six and nearing three-hundred pounds, he cast a very large shadow for intimidation purposes and though smaller than his partner, was the more physically aggressive of the pair. Rudy had loved intimidating people with his stature his entire life, but he truly enjoyed getting physical. It was his unbridled predilection for physicality which had resulted in his being given a choice by his high school principal after he had beat up a physical education teacher his senior year. Join the military or have charges brought, he was told, and his parents agreed with the options. Being eighteen and realizing conviction on the assault charge was certain; the combination of the savageness of the beating and his violent juvenile history would surely have meant prison time, so Rudy chose the military, and without an adult criminal record, the Marine Corps accepted him.

His now receding hairline he camouflaged by shaving his head. His deep brown eyes were perpetually suspicious and focused on the moment; they were cops eyes and people often took him for one, and he used that assumption to his advantage on many occasions. He usually hid his eyes behind dark glasses, and when he'd remove them people would generally take even more careful note of the hulking man. As intimidating as his eyes could be, they were also capable of reflecting great compassion. His soft spot was children, and there had been a photograph of him carrying a badly injured child taken in Lebanon in 1982 which had made the cover of *Time* magazine. Tears had been streaming down the big man's cheeks.

Rudy's hands were the size of dinner plates, and he needed custom-made boots while serving in the Marines for his size eighteen feet. After mustering out of the Corps, and until he could afford the custom-crafted dress shoes made by a company in Wisconsin, he continued to wear his boots as a civilian.

His partner, Travis, always drove. Travis liked having control, and in the Marines had proven himself a natural leader, having risen to the rank of Gunnery Sergeant in the shortest enlistment time of anyone in the history of the Corps. At six-foot-eight, a special waiver had been required because he exceeded the Marines' height limit of seventy-eight inches. He currently weighed in at three-hundred-twenty-five pounds and his physical presence was even more intimidating than his partner, yet he was the more cerebral and soft-spoken of the pair. People who understood Travis as Rudy did, knew he was a gentle giant; but very few people knew Travis as well as Rudy did.

Travis had already held the rank of Sergeant when he first met Rudy shortly after the younger man had reported for recruit training on Parris Island, South Carolina. Even though Rudy was at the time considered lower than whale excrement, the two struck up a fast and solid friendship. Travis had stepped between Rudy and a new Lance Corporal who had a bit too much starch in his fresh stripes and had targeted the much larger recruit for some extra attention. It was under Travis' tutelage that Rudy had learned to harness his flash temper, which had surely saved him from doing his enlistment, and probably more, in Leavenworth.

"How do you want to play it?" Rudy asked as Travis pulled into a vacant spot out front and turned off the ignition.

"I figured we'd just go in and talk to 'em," Travis said. "My sense is these overnight folks are just eager to have someone to talk to. So let's just play it by ear, okay?"

"Makes sense to me," Rudy said, as he opened the door and slid himself out. He stood and stretched, then slammed the door and looked across the roof at Travis who was checking out the area. "I miss the Lincoln, man. I bet Missy rented us this piece of crap on purpose. I hate Fords. Built for the peewees of the world."

"Lincoln is a division of Ford," Travis said.

"Yeah, and Cadillac is a division of GM. Doesn't mean I want to ride around in a piece of shit Chevette. What's your point?"

"My point is that the Crown Victoria is Ford's version of the Lincoln Town Car. It's the same car, basically."

"Bullshit," Rudy said. "Ford can stick the *basically* where the sun don't shine." He stretched again. "Shit, my back is gonna be out of whack for weeks."

Travis looked across the roof of the car, shook his head and smirked. Then, he scanned the parking lot again, not looking for the Escalade which was clearly gone, but to take stock of the other vehicles. What he saw gave him an idea. He opened his door, removed his jacket and tie and tossed them onto the front seat, popped his cufflinks and pocketed them, then rolled the sleeves of his blue and white striped dress shirt.

"Whatcha doing?" Rudy asked.

"Take a look around."

Rudy did.

"Yeah, so?"

"Mostly pick ups, work trucks, Chevys, rice burners, and heavy on your despised Fords; every one of them a lesser model than this Crown Vic."

Rudy shrugged his shoulders, put his hands out to each side.

"Again, so?"

"These are just regular folks, Rudy." He looked at the number of lighted windows in the upper floors of the motel. "Look," he said, pointing. "I bet most of them are up already; and not from alarm clocks or wake up calls, but because this is when they get up. Think back to when you were just one of the people, and not some overpaid, excessively pampered elbow rubber to the rich and famous. Remember how you'd react to seeing some fancy boy after leaving the Island?"

Rudy smiled as the ideas gelled, although he sincerely doubted shedding half of their three-thousand dollar, hand-tailored suits and rolling the sleeves of two-hundred dollar, custom-fitted shirts would be enough to pull the wool over the eyes of the hayseeds his partner obviously expected to find inside. Whatever, he thought, giving in to Travis' better judgement, and he matched the look. Then they walked across the tired asphalt in six-hundred dollar loafers toward the motel entrance.

Rudy held the outer entrance door for Travis.

"Just a couple of working stiffs," Rudy said as Travis passed.

Travis shook his head again and then returned the door favor on the inner set.

"Don't worry, buddy," Rudy said in a hushed tone as he passed through, "I won't tell them about your Learjet parked out at the airport."

They entered an empty lobby. Anonymous furniture dotted hideous commercial carpeting and defined two separate sitting areas. A stack of USA Today newspapers were set on one end of the wide Formica counter. A basket of apples rested on the other end fifteen feet away. There was nobody visible behind the desk, so Travis tapped the small bell in the center of the counter next to a folded card which said, 'Welcome - For Service, Tap The Bell'. From down one nearby hallway, in the direction indicated by the 'Breakfast Room' sign, the sound of a television tuned to some news channel could be heard along with a mix of unintelligible chatter.

"Y'all just hang on a sec, I'll be right there," came the disembodied female voice from the rear office.

The voice was a moment later personified when a short, stout woman in her late fifties or early sixties with black hair cut close, wearing tight black capris, an oversized sweater of the same slimming color and orange flip-flops waddled from the back office. The woman's big brown eyes were bloodshot and appeared tired above silver framed half-glasses which were attached to a matching silver chain around the woman's ample neck. Travis' mother had called her similar pair of glasses 'cheaters'. The woman's smile was fresh and welcoming, despite the message sent by her eyes. The gold name tag pinned on the horizontal of her ample bosom identified her as 'Julie K'.

"You boys checking in or checking out?" she said without really looking at them while her fingers tapped the computer keyboard to bring up the screen for either eventuality.

"Actually, neither, ma'am" Travis said, "or do you prefer Julie?" He flashed a big smile.

"Either way, we're easy around these parts," Julie said returning the smile and then blushed as she realized the double entendre which had just tumbled out to a stranger.

Travis laughed and his expression communicated he understood the faux pas but took nothing untoward from it.

Rudy turned his head and rolled his eyes as he wandered about the small lobby for a few moments, playing the oblivious sidekick and leaving Travis to handle Julie K. He picked up the news section of a USA Today someone had left on the coffee table in the nearest-to-the-door sitting area and then slumped into a cheap low-back chair clad in gold corduroy and opened the paper and noisily ruffled through the pages.

"Popcorn for the mind," Rudy mumbled in a low tone.

"What's that Rudy?" Travis said as he turned to look over at his partner, giving Julie a clear view. "Did you say something?"

Rudy looked up and encouraged by Travis' facial expression unseen by Julie K continued in character.

"Um, I said, 'popcorn for the mind'." He held up the paper. "The USA Today. Newspaper for idiots."

A frown immediately came to Julie K's face as she glared over the top of her cheaters past Travis toward Rudy.

"Folks seem to like it," she said, a hint of defiance in her voice.

Travis thought, good, she doesn't like Rudy. They had done this so many times before, it was almost second nature. Travis' job would be to now put on the understanding, friendly face, and make Julie his emotional comrade, united against Rudy. Once that bond forged, which didn't take much time with most people, she'd tell him anything he wanted to know, while she'd swat Rudy's mitt with a ruler if he walked over and reached for one of the free apples in the basket.

"Some people's kids, eh, Julie?" Travis said, tossing a thumb point over his shoulder toward his partner.

Julie continued to shoot Rudy the stink eye. Then she leaned forward toward Travis, smiling up at him.

"Oh, I know the type," Julie said in a hushed tone and a dismissive wave of her hand. "I got family like that, on my husband's side, of course. Highfalutin, thinkin' they're better 'n most, when they ain't."

"Eh, what am I gonna do? He's my partner. I can't just shoot him."

Julie took a step back, crooked her head and her look shifted out the corners of her eyes at both men. Rudy had moved on to the Sports section.  Travis forced a grimace and then massaged his chin with his right hand to give a contemplative look.

"I'm sorry, Julie," he said, leaning forward a bit.  He spoke the next sentence in a low, confidential tone.  "I didn't mean to scare you.  See, we're government investigators from the northern Virginia area, you know, and please forget what I am about to tell you.  My partner and I are traveling undercover to meet a couple of gentlemen who may be witnesses in an investigation."

Julie nodded and visibly relaxed, a bit.

"And you are to meet them here?" she said.  Her tired eyes indicated interest, yet remained wary.  'Federal agents?  In Alabama?  It's been a long time,' she thought.

Rudy crumpled the Sports section and disgustedly tossed it onto the coffee table, picked up the Life section, mumbled something like 'Here we go' under his breath.  She tossed another irritated glance in Rudy's direction.

"Yes, but they don't seem to be where they said they'd be and we cannot reach their cell phones."  Travis leaned forward again and lowered his tone.  "See, they've been playing a bit of a game of cat and mouse over the last couple of days.  They haven't done anything wrong, mind you.  Just getting a little scared, I guess."

"I understand," she said.  "I think."

"Our intelligence reports they made a phone call from one of your rooms last evening."

Julie tapped some keys, ran a finger down the monitor.

"Lotta folks made a lotta of calls from here last night," she said.  "You have names for these witnesses?"

"Their real names are unimportant.  Besides, we believe they're traveling under aliases, but we've picked up on a couple they may be using.  One is Dave Saunders and, oh, here's a good one, Dace, ah..."  Turning to Rudy.  "Hey, what's the last name of that Dace alias."

"Huh?"

"That Dace alias.  What's the last name he's using?"

Out of the corner of his eye, Travis could see Julie glaring at Rudy, her lips pursed.  Rather than waiting on the irritant to remember, she rolled her eyes and began tapping away at the keys.

"Geeze, I can't remember.  Something French, as I recall.  It's written down out in the car.  You want me to go out and get it?"

"I suppose we should, so Julie..." Travis began.

"Here it is," Julie interrupted.  "Dave Saunders.  Room 314.  One night, checked in yesterday evening.  Paid cash.  Double, one other boy.  Checked out a little over an hour ago, though.  Seemed like a nice young man.  Never did meet the other boy, saw him though.  Chase, you said?"

"Yeah, that's right," Travis said.   "Did this Saunders character register a vehicle?   A pearl white Cadillac Escalade; Connecticut or Massachusetts plates, by chance?"

"Yes, exactly."

"What license number are they using?   I mentioned both because they have two sets of plates and they've been switching them out."

Julie shook her head absently and scanned the screen.

"Connecticut plates.  858DWF.  I know that's what they were driving, because when Mr. Saunders was checking out with me, the other boy pulled the vehicle up front.  He was driving when they left, but I never got a clean look at him.  Mr. Saunders, or whoever he is, got into the front passenger seat and off they went.  Drove out about thirty, forty-five · minutes ago."

"My, we could use observant people like you in the Bureau."

She shrugged and smiled.

"So, you're with the FBI?"

"Oops.  I didn't say that, you did, Julie."   He added another a big, disarming grin.

Julie returned the smile, now completely relaxed.  She scanned the screen, scrolling down the electronic page.  Travis had her just where he wanted her.  She'd give him anything he wanted now.

"It appears they made three calls from the room yesterday, by the way."

"I beg your pardon," Travis said, his distant thoughts interrupted.

"You said your office picked up on one call.  There were three."

"Do you have the numbers?"   He patted his empty shirt pocket for a pen and paper.

Julie handed him a cheap motel pen and half sheet of scrap paper from behind the desk.

"Let's see, first one is local: a pizza joint.  Know that one by heart.  Then we have two long distance calls billed to the room.  One in the 857 area code."   She read him the number.   "For about two minutes.  Then a couple of minutes later, one to a phone in the 339 area code."   She relayed that number as well.   "That second call was longer, about five minutes.  Then nothing."

Travis copied down and then stared at the two sets of numbers.  He recognized the first one as belonging to Cindy Spagliano's cell phone, the one they had tapped and trapped, but the second one seemed somehow familiar as well.  He looked at the set of digits over and over, but just couldn't place it.  Travis looked up from the paper and saw Julie staring at him, waiting.

"Anything else you can tell us, Julie?  This has all been very helpful; and, off course, we'll maintain your confidentiality..."   He felt the right side of his mouth curl upward into a half smile. "...as I hope you'll forget my couple of slips."

She eyed him, then her brain came to a conclusion and she began to slowly shake her head and her gaze narrowed.

"You don't slip."

Slowly wagging a finger in his direction would be the appropriate gesture, but she didn't do that. Travis received her message all the same.

"You've not even told me your name so I couldn't check on you if I wanted to." She smiled knowingly at him, and nodded as her brain came to a decision. "It's okay; tonight has been an exciting one around here and we don't get many of those beyond the usual noise complaints and occasional drunk and domestic. It was a pleasant change of pace, but not for those two boys across the way."

Travis knew she had him figured out and wondered if the information flow would now stop.

"So, more excitement than just me and giggles over there?"

Julie's eyes shot a dart at Rudy, then again connected with Travis.

"Some punk beat up two security guards over at the truck stop. Cops said people thought the guy came our direction after walking away. They were here three or four times through the night."

"Beat up a couple of guards?"

"Yep. Rent-a-cops, you know the type. Just kids, really. No training. More for show. Put one into the hospital. Broken ribs, stitches, possible concussion. Still in the there from what I hear. The other one, not so bad, mainly just bumps and bruises, but enough to put him down, from what the cops said."

"They catch the guy?"

"Not last I heard. White boy. Oversize sweatshirt with a hood like the black gang bangers wear, you know. Cops dropped off some security camera stills and a drawing done from the description the kid in the hospital gave a police artist, but I didn't recognize him."

"Would you mind if I took a look at the pictures?"

"Oh, it wasn't the Saunders boy. He was clean cut, different coloring, and no marks on his hands or face like he'd been in a fight. Cops told me the guy would be beat up some. Security guards said they got a few licks in, enough to mark him up. Who knows? I looked when Mr. Saunders checked out because he was about the right age. Early twenties. The second guard, the one not hurt so bad, said he got in some pepper spray and a few good blows before the punk in the hoodie sucker punched him and knocked him down. Wasn't the other boy with Mr. Saunders, neither. I'm sure of that. I gave him as much of a good look as I could through the car window." She paused, took a breath. "As far as looking at the pictures, I don't see nothing wrong with it. Cops are putting them up all over the area, and might make it onto the local news in a bit. I'll get them."

Julie waddled back into the office. Travis turned around toward Rudy who was just then shaking his head in disgust and scanning through the Money section of the paper. Playing the role to the end. Just then, Rudy looked up, raised his eyebrows and winked. Travis had to stifle a laugh. A moment later, Julie was back with a small stack of sheets.

"Here you go. Not much to go by."

Travis leafed casually through the grainy, dark, security photos and didn't need the artist's drawing to identify the face of Dace Lamoureux under the hoodie. His next thought was a simple one: 'What the fuck is this kid doing?'

Back in the car and driving toward the airport a short time later, Rudy placed the call while Travis drove. It rang once.

"Tell me you have good news," Tom said, hoping to make his first meeting of the day with The Senator a positive one.

"We've got news, not much of it good," Rudy said. He relayed the bad timing, much of the information from Julie K, and then paused.

Tom sighed.

"Okay, give with the bad news," he said.

"It appears that Dace was involved in some sort of altercation."

"Altercation? What does that mean?"

"It appears," Rudy said, then stopped with the soft sell. "Hell, Dace beat up two security guards at a truck stop last night. Put one into the hospital. Not life threatening from the description the desk clerk gave, but beat up fairly bad. I'd have to say if this was a random event between total strangers, the level of anger displayed by the described beating was extreme, bordering on out-of-control rage. Believe me, I know the pattern."

"Jesus," was all Tom managed. He hadn't expected something like that as the bad news. A beat or two passed. "I imagine the local police are involved."

"They are investigating, but from what we could get from the night clerk at the motel, Birmingham PD doesn't have much to go on yet. There are some blurry security camera images, a composite drawing which Travis says could be thousands of guys. The motel has Dave Saunders' name, but no record the roommate was Dace. The clerk may also be doing us a favor when she talks to cops again because she swore to us that the perpetrator wasn't Dave Saunders or his roommate."

"There's no doubt about the identity to you, though?" Tom asked.

"Not according to Travis. It was Dace; but to the general public, since the kid's face isn't everywhere like his old man's is, if this stays local, there should be no way to make him."

The line went quiet and Rudy pulled the phone from his ear to verify the connection still existed. Tom came back a moment later.

"All right, get back up here as fast as you can."

"You want us to put a tap and trap on this other phone number the Saunders kid called last night?"

"Yeah, do that; and see if they'll extend the others. Call in any favors you have to; give IOUs as you need to, but keep The Senator's name out of it, like we have been."

"Done. See you in a few hours."

"I'll brief The Senator. He's not going to be happy."

"Roger that."

The line went dead. Half an hour later, the white and nickel-striped Learjet 45 was climbing briskly into a crisp, blue, Alabama sky, pointed northeast.

Tom sat on the edge of his bed and reviewed the notes he had just made. Something familiar kept him coming back to the second phone number he'd written down. Then, he began to smile, and found the fax which had come in to his room overnight and contained the transcription of the recorded phone call between Dave Saunders and Cindy Spagliano.

"You're not as smart as you think you are, kid," he said to the empty room.

He stood, pulled on a robe over his pajamas, stuffed his feet into elk skin slippers and exited his room for the first time that morning. He strode down the hallway from his second floor guest room to The Senator's office. The door was closed, but then it was always closed. He knocked, no response. He turned the knob and slowly opened the door, announcing himself as he stepped inside. Over the years, with a couple of other clients, he'd opened doors when nobody had answered a knock only to see things he wished he hadn't. His clients aren't any different from other men, they are just more so, as the saying goes. Not that he suspected anything like that was going on with Allard Lamoureux, in his own home, but one never knew, and some images didn't easily purge from the memory.

The Senator wasn't in his office, and when he stepped back into the hallway, Tom could hear muted conversational noises and the sounds of cooking drifting from the first floor. He looked at his watch. Just after seven. His stomach, and the sudden arrival of the drifting smell of bacon and eggs frying and coffee percolating reminded him that he had skipped dinner the night before. He closed the office door and went downstairs.

The Senator, Libby, and Mary Rose were seated at the small table in the breakfast nook. A fourth place setting was out.

"Good morning, Mr. Mac," Mary Rose said, wriggling excitedly in her seat. "Breakfast time, bacon and eggs today."

"Good morning, Mary Rose," Tom said, making certain to give the girl his full attention, if only for a few moments. "I'm so hungry I could eat an elephant. Have you got any elephants around here?"

"There aren't any elephants around here, Mr. Mac," Mary Rose said with a big grin. "Only in the zoo; and you can't eat those."

"Okay, I guess I'll just have bacon and eggs like the rest of you."

The Senator and Libby waited patiently for the exchange to play out. They had always encouraged Mary Rose to interact with people outside the family and appreciated anyone who truly took the time and made the effort to not treat their daughter like a piece of furniture. All their friends did an excellent job with the girl. If they didn't, they didn't remain friends for long. More predictably, it would be the unfamiliar professional contact, so caught up with the ticking of the clock, who most often experienced the buzz saws that were The Senator or Libby when they dismissed or attempted to cut off Mary Rose.

Tom had been around the family all the girl's life, and he truly loved Mary Rose and her pure view of the world. In political circles, a true heart was hard to find, so Tom cherished every moment of the innocent times with her. Tom slid out the remaining empty chair and sat down. Caroline served him a cup of coffee and confirmed how he wanted his eggs before disappearing around the corner into the kitchen proper.

"Any word?" The Senator asked before stuffing the last of his egg along with a folded strip of bacon stacked on a corner of dry wheat toast into his mouth.

"Yes," Tom said as he distractedly stirred in some cream, blew across the surface and took a cautious sip of the steaming coffee. "It's been a busy night."

"Why didn't you wake me?"

"What would have been the point, Allard? We merely had a new lead to check out, my boys were able to handle things, and the mission still remains the same. Right?" His eyes moved to everyone at the table, the pause for effect.

The Senator nodded, a thoughtful look on his face, then wiped his mouth with a cloth napkin that matched the table cloth, tossed the napkin onto the plate and pushed the assemblage forward. He placed his elbows on the table, rubbed his hands together at the apex of a triangle created by his upwardly angled forearms. He shot a look at Libby, then a glance to Mary Rose, who was obviously finished with her breakfast too.

Tom took another sip of coffee then sat back in his chair as Caroline placed his plate of eggs, bacon, hash browns and English muffin onto the table in front of him. Tom slid the ring from the cloth napkin, placed it into his lap and began to inhale his breakfast.

"Caroline, would you mind taking Mary Rose up to get ready for the day?" Libby asked.

"Certainly, ma'am" Caroline said with a broad smile. Then to Mary Rose: "Come on, honey, time to get cleaned up and dressed for the day."

Mary Rose finished off her glass of milk, then wiped her face with the napkin, missing some jam on her cheek which Libby lovingly removed with the corner of her napkin. Mary Rose slid her chair back, gave her mother a big hug, then moved around the table to give one to The Senator. She didn't give Tom a hug, rather just waved and said: "See you later, Mr. Mac."

Tom smiled and told Mary Rose he'd see her later too. He pivoted in his chair and watched her walk off. The girl grabbed Caroline's hand and said: "Did you hear Mr. Mac, Caroline? My goodness, have you ever heard of someone so hungry they could eat an elephant?"

The pair gone, Tom squared himself in his chair again and briefly took in the eyes of his hosts while stuffing a piece of bacon into his mouth. He'd seen many a politician use the family as props for votes over the years, and witnessed enough dysfunction behind the scenes to fill a psychology textbook, but he knew genuine parental love and pride when he saw it; and that's exactly what he'd always seen with Libby and Allard Lamoureux toward every one of their children, especially Mary Rose and Dace. Tom also knew there were only six people on the planet that The Senator would lay down his own life for, or kill to protect. Three were his older set of daughters, one had just left the room, one sat off to Tom's right pouring them all a topper on their coffee from an insulated server, and another was headed away from Birmingham, Alabama to God knows where. To Senator Allard Lamoureux, family may be something to be molded to his Will, but it was never a prop.

"All right, Tom," The Senator said. "Bring me up to date."

Tom finished chewing the bacon. Washed it down with a slurp of coffee and grabbed a side of English muffin. Just the right amount of melting butter percolated into the nooks and crannies; Caroline was indeed getting to understand all his tastes. He held the muffin out horizontally, postponed the bite.

"We turned up something on one of the tap and traps late last evening, shortly after we got them set up," Tom said, then chomped on the muffin and chewed. He was more hungry than he had thought.

"The aunt?" asked The Senator, a bit perturbed at the delays in hearing the information.

"No," Tom said, swallowing the oversize bite. He put the muffin down and then swiped his hands together, brushing off crumbs from his fingertips onto the plate. "It was the other one, the Spagliano girl. A call came in to her cell phone from what turned out to be a motel in

Birmingham, Alabama. The recording and transcript seemed innocuous enough, a call from her brother."

The Senator sat back in his chair, spread his hands in an unspoken gesture of 'I assume there's more to this, so please get on with it'.

"Problem is, after we first identified her from the contact with the Saunders kid's aunt Gloria, the boys did some quick background work. She's a junior at Harvard. Her brother lives in Michigan and we verified he was home last evening, not in Alabama. So the call came from someone else in a motel down there, obviously the Saunders kid. I sent the boys to Birmingham on a chartered jet in the middle of the night to try to catch up to them early this morning, but they missed them by less than an hour. They had stayed at the motel overnight all right, but checked out about five this morning, destination unknown."

"Alabama?" The Senator asked.

Tom nodded, folded another piece of bacon onto the remains of the muffin half and put the combination into his mouth. He followed it up with a forkful of eggs sunny side up.

"That's right," Tom said, still chewing, the food only half down. He washed it the rest of the way with coffee before continuing. "Travis and Rudy arrived at the motel early this morning, found a relatively talkative overnight desk clerk, but our boys were gone. The clerk had no idea where the pair was headed from Birmingham, but had checked them out personally. Apparently Dace waited in the car while Dave did the paperwork. The night clerk reported she hadn't seen, or spoken to Dace at all, only the Saunders kid this morning. She wasn't on duty when they had checked in last evening."

The Senator looked at his watch: 7:14. He struggled to recall if Alabama was in the Eastern or Central time zone; Eastern, he concluded.

"It's only over two hours since Dace and the Saunders kid hit the road, Tom" he said with a level of irritation in his voice. "Have the boys gone after them?"

"After them where, Allard?" Tom said, spreading his hands with the question. "The motel, from what I could gather, sits just off I-59, and Birmingham has three or four other major highways shooting out from it in every direction. We had a one in eight chance of picking the right direction on the right highway, and they had sixty to eighty miles head start."

Libby placed her hand onto the table in the direction of her husband, who reached out and touched his fingers to hers. Tom watched the movement, noted its calming effect.

"Of course, you're right, Tom," The Senator said, more even-tempered than a moment ago. "I'm sorry. You understand. You're right it wouldn't have made any sense just lighting out on a wild goose chase based on what you say we had."

The Senator stood up and shuffled to the patio door to look out over the back yard. The combined effect of the stress and his age was becoming obvious in his demeanor. Outside, a light dusting of snow overnight had put a fresh layer of white on everything. The early morning shadows were long and pointing slightly north of west as the sun climbed into the new day's sky. He clasped his hands behind his back. "Anything else, Tom?"

"We may have caught an extra break."

The Senator turned to look at him. Tom knew he was feeding the man the sugar before the vinegar to come, and part of him wondered if the tack was wise; however, having already set it, he was committed, so he continued.

"Turns out the first call Saunders made to Spagliano may have used some kind of pre-planned code, because he cut it short and before disconnecting she gave the 'brother' a phone number to call some fictitious aunt for her birthday. When the boys got to the desk clerk this morning, she turned over the calls from the room and they show Saunders called that number almost immediately after disconnecting the first call. I noticed something interesting about it from the transcript after the boys gave me the second number the Saunders kid called from the motel. Seems that he and the girl must have had a system set up so the phone number she had given him needed to be reversed to use. It goes to a cell phone registered on the outskirts of Boston. We're setting a tap and trap on that one now."

"That doesn't put us any closer to knowing where Dace and Dave are headed, and why," The Senator said, returning his look to the outside.

"No, but it gives us access to a phone number that they think is secure," Tom said. "They're bound to use it again, and when they do they're certain to be less guarded. We'll learn something."

"Mm-hmm," The Senator grunted. "The problem is when; and from where."

Tom hesitated a beat; quickly thought about the ways to move on now to the second part of the story, only to conclude that the only way was to be blunt. Just lay it out there as facts as they knew them. The Senator had dealt with worse news over nearly half a century in politics, albeit none which struck so closely to his personal dream.

"There is one other thing, less positive," Tom said.

Libby sat back in her chair and put the fingertips of her right hand over her mouth, expecting the worst. The Senator returned to his chair and sat down and crossed his arms across his chest.

"Seems Dace was involved in a beating last evening," Tom said.

"My God," Libby exclaimed. "Is he all right?" Her eyes were wide.

"We believe he's fine, uninjured," Tom said in her direction, then looked at The Senator, "Dace beat up two security guards at a truck stop across from the motel, put one into the hospital. He was reportedly the aggressor. The local police are involved, but don't know the identity of the attacker at this point."

"Then how the hell do *we* know it was Dace?" The Senator said.

"Travis saw some security camera stills and a composite drawing the cops were passing around the area overnight. The assailant was wearing a sweatshirt and had the hood up to cover up much of his face from the overhead camera angles, and the photos are dark, shadowed, I am told. Travis tells me if you didn't know Dace, you'd never make him from what they have. There is no doubt in his mind, however, that it was Dace under the hood and behind the shadows. According to what the desk clerk told our boys, the kid had been loitering around the truck stop, watching cars and just acting suspiciously, smoking, and drinking from a bottle in a paper sack. So, security decided to check him out. The attack was unprovoked, from what the police told her, and 'extremely vicious, out-of-control, and rage-filled', was Rudy's assessment. The second security man who had come to the aid of his partner was less injured than the first, mostly cuts and bruises and a broken nose. The first one is still hospitalized with broken ribs, multiple cuts and bruises, and a possible concussion."

"Smoking and drinking?" Libby said. "My God. It can't be Dace. He doesn't smoke and has never drank alcohol. He even refused a drink to toast his own birthday with family."

"He's also never disappeared like this either," The Senator said to his wife, obviously believing it possible. "Who knows what's going on in the boy's mind?" Then, to Tom: "So what's the next move?"

Tom's thoughts momentarily latched upon the peripheral issue Libby had taken from the entirety of his description of Dace's unprovoked attack on the two kids. He shook it free, then continued.

"I see three prongs here, Allard: one action, one eventuality, and one contingency we need to address," Tom said, sliding his plate forward and leaning his elbows on the table. He ticked the prongs off one by one on his fingers. "One, we wait for them to get in touch with this Spagliano girl and then we track them down and send the boys to bring Dace home. Two, they get this out of their systems and come home on their own; hopefully, with little collateral damage to clean up. Three, which may be the most imperative of these: we pray that the story of this attack does not get out of Alabama and connected with Dace, but we need to develop a plan now for what we're going to do if it does."

"Why should that last matter?" Libby asked.

"Because," The Senator spoke before Tom could, "from what Tom's guys tell him, it's improbable that anyone in Alabama is going to be able to identify our son from the evidence they currently have, but, if the story should go national somehow, someone will surely recognize the photos or drawings of the perpetrator as Dace.    If our security men could immediately identify Dace in the photos, anyone who has met him could also pick him out.    Friends, and enemies.    Think of all the people who are looking to hurt me in any way they can.    It would be a political bloodbath.    I can live with a political firestorm, but something like this would end Dace's career before it's even begun; and, that is something I will *not* live with.    I agree we must have a plan ready.    What do you suggest, Tom?"

# Chapter Nine

Dace wheeled the car off the interstate at Slidell, Louisiana, a small city northeast of New Orleans at the tip of Lake Pontchartrain. He had to pee, and the Escalade was on empty. Dave was snoring in the passenger seat until they started rounding the cloverleaf, when he let out a snort and roused. He powered the seat up and blinked wildly in the sunshine until he found his Blues Brothers sunglasses on the top of his head.

"Where are we, bro?" Dave asked, stretching in the seat.

"Sign said Slidell," Dace replied. "I have to pee and this thing could use some gas."

Dave leaned across the center console to get a look at the gas gage which was grounded well below the E mark.

"Geeze, I guess so. Why didn't you stop earlier?"

"I didn't have to pee earlier."

"It really is always about you, isn't it?"

"Always."

They shared a laugh.

"You hungry?" Dace asked.

The cloverleaf exit led to another highway headed west.

"I could eat," Dave said through another stretch in his seat. "You thinking something in particular?"

"I saw a place called Fat Boyz as we pulled off the highway." Dace looked around as they moved further west, there were no easy exits into the city. The road appeared that it would simply sweep them back out into the country without a chance to get gas or food, or for Dace to pee, a call of nature which was becoming more urgent by the moment. "Geeze, whoever designed these highways must not have liked Slidell. I don't see an exit."

Dave peered over at the gas gauge again. The needle was lying dead at the bottom. The prospect of heading back out into the bayou and running out of gas in rural Louisiana was less than appealing. He looked out ahead, squinted against the cheap sunglasses. Then he pointed.

"There," Dave said. "An exit to the frontage road, just beyond that overpass."

"Yeah, that'll work," Dace said.

He steered off the highway at high speed and rocketed around the sweeping one-hundred-eighty degree ramp back toward the frontage road with the SUV's tires squealing. As the vehicle rolled back into the straightaway headed for the stoplights, the engine sputtered, surged, and then fell silent. The traffic light turned red when they were still about two hundred feet away; vehicles along the four-lane cross road began moving through the intersection. Dace spotted gas pumps on the far side. To Dave's white knuckle horror, he wasn't braking.

The Escalade shot through the intersection, still doing about forty, bounced across the two sets of crowned lanes, barely missed two minivans and a pickup truck with huge off-road tires and a shotgun rack in the rear window driven by a bearded dude whose baseball cap Dave could see said 'Dixie' on it, bounced again into the lot of the Kangaroo Express, and then slid sideways as Dace muscled the now unpowered steering wheel to the right, stomped on the brakes, and came to rest in perfect position next to the gas pump. A cloud of gravel dust arrived a moment later, moving northeast on the slight breeze.

"Wow, that was intense," Dace said, eyes wide and a huge grin.

Before Dave could respond, Dace was out, jogging toward the convenience store. Dave exited his side and stretched, his heart still pounding in his chest. The dude in the jacked pickup was glaring at him and slowly rolling south. Dave shrugged his shoulders and held his arms out and hands palms up, offering a gesture of apology and muttering to himself, 'Whatcha gonna do? The man had to pee.'

At about that same time, some thirteen hundred miles to the northeast, the Learjet 45 came to a stop on the ramp of the Groton-New London Airport. As he did nine hours earlier, the Captain shut down the left engine and kept the right engine running while the copilot pried himself from the cockpit and opened the clamshell doors for the two large gentlemen. The crew was assigned to return the jet to its home base in Burlington, Vermont, two-hundred-sixty miles and about forty minutes flying time to the north and once the doors were again closed, the captain turned the left engine for, what was in a Learjet, the short hop. Once there, for the pilots, after thirty-three hundred miles, and twelve hours after receiving the calls at home from dispatch, their duty would be done. The company would send out an invoice later in the day to the Reelect Senator Lamoureux Campaign Fund for nine-thousand dollars and change, which would be paid on time using tax-free funds and classified in Federal Election Commission reports as a Miscellaneous Travel Expense.

Tom remained at the kitchen table after Libby and The Senator had excused themselves and gone upstairs. He drank more coffee and stared transfixed through the windows and into the yard where a light snow had again begun to fall. Oversized flakes from last night hung on the bare branches of the deciduous trees and flocked the evergreens. The day outside was overcast, continuing in the alternating pattern of sun and clouds of the last week. Overnight, the temperature had dropped into the low twenties and forecasts expected it to remain there through the weekend. Tom took another sip of his coffee. Caroline had returned from her Mary Rose duties and was now busy removing the remaining dishes and attending to cleaning the kitchen. Unless there was some reason to take her somewhere, Mary Rose would most likely spend most of her day in her room, Tom knew.

His thoughts of Mary Rose drifted to how he had become so connected to this family. Had it truly been thirty years that he'd been working with The Senator? Indeed it had. There could be no denying that the years had passed; seemingly moving faster with every successive twelvemonth. He had been at the hospital when Mary Rose was born, standing in when The Senator had been delayed in Washington on a budget vote and was the first person outside of the nurses to hold the girl. It was nearly the same when Dace came, however, The Senator had arrived just in time and Tom had watched from across the room as The Senator had first held the newborn boy. His turn had come second.

Letting his memory take him back to the beginning, Tom had been fresh out of the University of Michigan, when he arrived in Washington in 1965, eager to break into a changing political game, not as a politician or staffer, but in the relatively new role of paid political consultant. The times had been much different then, and prospects for a young, unconnected man with an interest in politics but not in holding office were few outside volunteering as a member of staff, which didn't appeal to him at all. Most people would have given him little chance at longevity in the city since he came to D.C. with no prospects and only a few hundred dollars of graduation money in his pocket, but Tom McDaniel possessed a fire for change in his belly, a midwesterner's penchant for hard work, and a desire to personally make a difference in the world. At his core was an idealist, but not an ideologue, so his doors would be open to both political parties until the first client walked through the door.

Such were the late 1960s for many, but for him, helping change arrive was more than sitting around getting stoned and listening to antiwar records or attending peace rallies. He understood that to affect true change meant one had to work from the inside; to massage the craft of politics *and* the public perceptions. The defined role of paid political consultant was still on the far horizon, and, even so, for decades its limited opportunities were closed to outsiders. Politics was, and in far too many ways, remained a closeted, self-serving, incestuous system. Still, he came. It did not take him long to shed his idealism and replace it with realism as his core. There would be many more changes he'd make in his belief system over the coming years, and his would be a career choice for which he would dearly pay in his personal life.

California had experimented with ersatz political advisors who worked in the public eye as early as the 1930s, and President McKinley had employed the services of Mark Hanna for advice, a man widely recognized as probably the United States' first political consultant, but most students of the art realized it was the advent of television which shifted the campaigning paradigm and truly created the need for the services of image management professionals for politicians. For a time through the early 1960s, that work was handled by established advertising firms. Then, following the 1968 election, political rules changed and essentially created the professional political consultant overnight. Tom had been there to be in that forefront, even helping to establish the first association for himself and his growing number of colleagues in 1969.

A mere few years later, nearly everyone in the state and national political game employed a professional political advisor or team and even the lowliest rookie member of Congress dumped their local talent and upgraded to a DC-based firm the moment the election results were in. No one could afford to play the game anymore without the services of a talented and well-connected coach.

Over the years, Tom had become much more than a coach to The Senator; not that Allard Lamoureux had ever needed much coaching. By the time Tom had arrived in D.C. as an ambitious, but untested young man seeking work in a field which barely existed, The Senator had already been elected to federal office from Connecticut five times - thrice as congressman, and twice as senator. Nevertheless, Tom persisted in courting the man's business and in the years which had passed since Tom started working for The Senator shortly after he had won his third election to the United States Senate in late 1968, a professional and personal evolution had taken place in which Tom had become advisor, confidant, fixer, flak, and even friend to The Senator and his family.

Tom's early potential had been recognized by the founder of one of the first political consulting firms in Washington, begun by a former advertising executive who would later become a legend in the political consulting game with his behind-the-scenes managing of the resurrection of Richard Nixon's political career following the disastrous televised 1960 Presidential debates. Sitting in The Senator's kitchen that day, Tom felt a shadow of sadness pass over him as his reminiscences reminded him that the man had been deceased by that time for more than a decade.

Spotting talent had been only one of Tom's first boss' gifts; the man was a true visionary. There were no guidelines for how the profession would work under yet-to-be-developed laws, but once Tom had come on board in early 1966, together they had begun to define them. The man's second-greatest gift had been the ability to restrain his own ego and refrain from taking credit for the work of underlings, which was uncharacteristic to most in the District. That had allowed his people to shine in their own undiluted light, and that's how Tom McDaniel had come to the attention of Senator Allard Lamoureux.

Tom was twenty-five at the time and concluding his third year in Washington. Late in the 1968 election cycle, he had been assigned the beleaguered campaign of a first-term congressman seeking a second term from the people of Tom's old home state. The man's first term had been a disaster, and the tone from back home was to turn the bumbler's first term into his last. Tom conditionally accepted the challenge and took over the campaign in September with polls showing his man trailing a relatively unknown alderman by thirty-six points. As a first step, Tom advocated for a public purging of the man's small congressional staff, and an embracing of a revitalization of the populist, blue collar, union-only tone which had played so well in the man's first election, but which had been abandoned soon after the congressman had been sworn into office.

On Tom's advice, the client fired his five staffers, all holdovers tied to a corrupt political machine in the district's main city. Next, Tom initiated a whispering campaign and found within the media more than enough eager shills. Stories soon appeared lauding the congressman for his strength of conviction in standing up to the business machine which had corrupted his staff. Finally, Tom launched a personal attack against the congressman's equally flawed opponent. The voters in the district sent the man back to Congress that year, and fourteen times after that.

That particular client passed away in August of 1997; in a motel room in New York City. It was Tom to whom his widow had turned after the congressman's office had been called by a panicked collegian who was working as the congressman's traveling aide during the summer break. Even though Tom had not represented the man for nearly two decades, Tom answered the woman's call and he agreed to help. He arrived at the hotel room before the authorities had been called, and had ensured both the cocaine and the young lady had been cleared from the scene. After the NYPD arrived, it was Tom who had planted the story with the media which painted congressman as a hair shirt wearing populist who had suffered a massive cardiac event, alone in his room, while rereading the speeches of Dr. Martin Luther King. He was, as Tom leaked, doing research for an article on Dr. King which he was writing at the request of a minority-owned, upstart, online magazine. The work Tom did that day was dirty, and dishonest, and the young idealist who boarded a train in Lansing in June 1965 would have retched at the idea of being complicit in such acts, but the jaded old hand viewed it as just another reclamation project.

Immediately after the 1968 campaign season concluded, Tom had received a call from Senator Lamoureux's chief-of-staff. They wouldn't be facing an election for another six years then, and even though The Senator's ratings remained high, his margins of victory had been on the slight decline in each successive race. The opposition party sensed blood in the water with the 55% - 45% race that year and had pledged a candidate of 'monumental status' would give Senator Lamoureux the 'run of his lifetime in 1974'. The Senator's biggest fear, according to the chief-of-staff, was that, in the face of the massive social and political upheavals the country had been enduring over the recent years and the uncertain road the newly elected president would be traveling between inauguration and the next election, a legacy politician could become an anachronism. Tom had agreed to meet with The Senator the very next day.

"The rest, as they say, is history," Tom said to himself.

"What is history, Tom?" came the voice from behind him.

It was Libby, freshly scrubbed and made ready for the day. Tom was always amazed at how little enhancement it took for Libby Lamoureux to look like she had just stepped from the pages of a Glamour magazine. Even though she had turned seventy-one the past November, she often was still mistaken for a woman twenty-five years junior.

"Oh, Libby," Tom said, off-guard, "you merely caught the end of my reverie." He turned and smiled up at her. "I was watching the snow and just began thinking how times have changed over the last thirty years for this old political hack; about how much has been done and accomplished in the time I've been working with Allard, and, how you've always made me feel like a member of the family."

Libby touched Tom lightly on the shoulder, lingered the contact in an extended moment of unspoken familiarity, then, before his hand could move to cover hers, slipped away and retook her seat at the table to his right. Caroline brought a clean coffee mug and set it on the table a few moments later, then immediately retreated to the kitchen. Libby poured herself a cup from the insulated server. She offered Tom a top off, which he declined.

"The Senator will be down momentarily," Libby said.

"How is he handling this?" Tom asked. "In private times, I mean."

Libby added neither sugar nor cream to her cup. She had always drank it black, and preferred it stronger than most people would tolerate; certainly stronger than Caroline would brew for a family breakfast. She sipped from her cup. The coffee had cooled from breakfast. Tom watched as she crinkled her nose when the tepid liquid hit her mouth. He smiled to himself that he knew her so intimately he fully understood the wordless expression.

"Oh, he's coping," Libby said, sliding her chair back from the table, cupping her mug in her hands as she searched for the right words. "I think his overarching concern is for Dace's future, not his present. As for me..." She stopped mid-sentence, shook her head as if driving the thoughts out.

As she rose to reheat the coffee in the kitchen's microwave, Tom had time to consider his next words carefully. When Libby returned, he leaned close and spoke softly to her.

Gassed up, Dave maneuvered the Escalade to the edge of the parking lot. He eyed the Subway across the street.

"That okay?" he said, pointing to the familiar chain restaurant.

"No, go right, down the frontage road," Dace said, and pointed animatedly. "I asked the guy inside and he said that Fat Boyz - with a 'z' - has decent sub sandwiches with fresh, local ingredients like fried oysters and soft shell crabs. So much better than stamp-a-sub over there. They call them po' boys down here."

"What? The crabs?"

"No, the sandwiches. They call them po' boys."

"Why?"

"Who the hell knows?" Dace said, pointing off to the right. "Why do they call them hoagies in Philadelphia?"

Dave shrugged and turned right.

The woman behind the counter was large, really large. She wore a white apron which covered her from chest to knees. She smiled as Dave and Dace walked through the door. What appeared to be an equally large man peered through a pass-thru to the kitchen. He wore a paper hat and a net over his beard which was about the size of a small cat and didn't smile. A pair of middle-aged men in matching blue uniforms hunched at a small table along the wall over orange plastic baskets lined with paper containing french fries and crumbs and overflow fried shrimp from their already consumed sandwiches. The patrons slowly eyed the two newcomers from head to toe, then went back to devouring the remains of their lunch. An oversized menu board in red and black lettering over a white background was mounted on the back wall. Everything about the place was large, except the tables; and it smelled delicious inside, the perfect blending of spices and grease.

"How y'all doin'," the woman asked.

The man disappeared from the pass-thru.

"We're doing just fine," Dave said, moving slowly toward the counter as he perused the menu board. "How are you?"

"Just fine, thank you." A pause, then: "Where're y'all from?"

Dave looked into her round face framed by tight reddish blonde curls. She was still smiling. A gold crown capped one of her incisors, and its neighbors were stained yellow from either smoking or copious amounts of coffee. It definitely was a smile designed to be viewed from across the room, he decided. Her name tag read 'Candice'.

"Up north," Dave said, "just passing through."

Candice put her hands on her ample hips and pursed her lips.

"Well, I *knew* that, sweetie," she said. "I meant where up north are you from? We don't get many folks in here who are just passing through."

"No wonder," Dace said, bent at the waist and staring into the large fish tank off to one side. Crabs fought each other for the top position, although he thought if they knew what awaited them within such easy reach, they might fight for a different ranking. "Boston. Hey, are those the soft shell crabs?"

"Yep, straight from the Gulf, can't get 'em no fresher 'n that," Candice said with a touch of pride then her smile faded. "Whatcha mean 'no wonder'?"

"Hmm?" Dace said, still enjoying the crab ballet.

"No wonder. You said no wonder."

"Oh, that," he said and straightened up and looked at her. He pasted a smile on his face. "No offense. I meant it appeared to me that whoever designed the roads around here didn't want people getting off the highways at Slidell. You almost have to be local to get to you."

She crooked her head toward him.

"Oh, yeah, that. Story is somebody from Slidell ticked off the governor down in Nawlins one night."

"Nawlins?" Dave moved closer and asked.

She cleared up the contraction for him.

"Well, there's always the next election," Dace said with a smile.

Candice stared at him.

"What are you talkin' about, sweetie? That governor was Uncle Earl and that trouble down in Nawlins was in 1949. We hold a grudge down here." Candice chuckled, pulled a pencil from behind her ear and grabbed an order pad from the counter. "So, what y'all gonna have?"

"I think I'm going to have one of those soft shell crab po' boys. Footlong. Sweet potato fries," Dace said.

"Double it up," Dave said with a smile.

"Dressed or undressed?"

"Hmm?" in unison.

"Y'all gonna have them dressed or undressed?"

Blank stare.

"Sweetie, dressed is with lettuce, tomato, and mayonnaise. Even you boys from Boston should be able to figure out the undressed part."

"Dressed," in unison.

"Pickles, onions?"

"No," in unison.

"Anything to drink?"

"Iced tea, sweet," said Dave.

"I'd like a Barq's root beer," Dace said.

"Y'all have a seat. I'll bring it over when Clyde's got 'em ready," Candice said, ripping off the slip and sliding it onto a ring with springs.

Clyde popped his head up and pulled the slip down on his side of the wall then again vanished. Dave wandered over to a table and slid out a vinyl covered metal chair with his back toward the kitchen; Dace remained and watched as Candice moved over to the fish tank, pulled up a sleeve and snared six unlucky crabs one at a time, placing each one on a plastic tray which she then passed through to Clyde. Dace walked over to the table and slid out the other chair and sat down. Across the narrow aisle, the two other patrons were finishing their lunch and not caring if they were caught staring.

One of the men wiped his mouth on the sleeve of his well-worn work shirt, then drained the remains of his bottle of Dixie beer.

"Where you boys headed?" he asked. His belch which followed was unrestrained.

"New Orleans. Well, outside the city. Vacherie, to be exact." Dave said as he wiped the tabletop with a paper towel from the roll in the condiment holder. "A friend's family has a place there. Old plantation house."

"Ah, Vacherie," the man said with a smile and distinctive French accenting. When he said the name it sounded nothing like the way Dave had spoken it. "Mardi Gras?"

Dave wadded up the paper towel, looked for a place to stick it. Candice arrived with their drinks, set them onto the table, gave Dave an irritated glance as she snatched the used paper towel from his hand.

"Thank you, Candice," Dace said.

"You're welcome, sweetie," she said, then turned and shuffled back behind the counter.

"Well, maybe we'll check it out," Dave said to the men as he squeezed the lemon wedge into his tea and stirred the drink with the straw. "Mainly came down to chillax for a while."

"Ain? Chillax? Wat dat chillax?" the other man chimed in. His accenting was thicker, his cadence choppy but measured.

"It's a combination of chill and relax, chillax," Dave explained.

The two men looked at each other, shrugged, then pushed their chairs from the table. The second man mumbled something to his friend who then waved him off.

"It's been a tough week," Dace said absently, stretching to watch the crab tank. He took a slug from the root beer which he was glad to see had come in an old-style glass bottle.

The second man walked out of the restaurant while his partner moved to the counter, pulled a wallet on a chain from his back pocket. He unzipped the wallet, removed a bill and paid Candice, dropping a buck into the clear, plastic tip jar, then turned to leave.

"Well, you boys be good wit dat chillax," he said with a smile which revealed one missing incisor, laughed, and then left them alone with Candice and Clyde.

Dace took a slug of ice cold root beer, then spun the bottle around.

"Look at this," Dace said pointing to the enameled label. "Product of the Coca-Cola Company. Can you believe that?"

"Got a point?" Dave said, still half pondering the local pronunciation of Vacherie.

"Barq's is a product of legend, man. Created right here on the Gulf coast in 1898. One man's hard work and vision; one hundred years old this year. Now, it's nothing but pasteurized, homogenized, corporatized, global bullshit."

"You sound just like..." Dave stopped himself.

Dace looked up from the bottle to his friend. His eyes misted. The sandwiches arrived, along with a suggestion from Candice to add some Louisiana Hot Sauce, but only a few drops to each crab. The warning, she said with a big belly laugh, was reserved for Yankees from up north. Dave was glad for the interruption. Apart from his sharing of the events on the post-party ride home, Dace and he hadn't spoken one word about Sarah in life since shortly after they started out on this adventure. Dave could see his friend was right on the edge on that subject, and then he saw it again: Dace disconnected.

Dace popped a couple of sweet potato fries into his mouth, then opened his sandwich which contained three fresh soft shell crabs, neatly breaded and deep fried. He searched the limited condiments tray and found the hot sauce and dribbled some along the breaded crab. He handed the bottle over to Dave, who did the same. They both took huge bites.

"Oh, man, that's good," Dave said through a mouthful of fresh, crusty French bread, crab, and fixings.

"You know it," Dace said, biting off another chunk, stuffing in a couple more fries and washing it all down with a big slug of root beer. "Candice, can you bring me another Barq's?"

"Sure thing, sweetie."

"Corporatist," Dave said with a mouth half full of po' boy.

When they had finished their lunch, Dace sat back and looked across the small table at his lifelong best friend.

"You know, it's okay to say her name, Dave," he said, then he smiled. "You're right, my little rant earlier did sound a lot like Sarah."

Dave wiped his mouth and fingers with a paper towel, tossed it into his empty basket. He bought a moment by washing down the last bite of sandwich with a long draw from his iced tea. He set down the glass, rubbed his hands on his jeans and then looked Dace in the eyes.

"I guess I stopped myself because I have been waiting for you to broach the subject when you were ready. I didn't want to push you. You know I loved Sarah like a sister, Dace. More than that, maybe."

"I know you did, my brother." A pause and his eyes drifted to unfocused, then flashed with anger quickly covered. "What wasn't to love?"

The Senator arrived back at the breakfast nook a few minutes after Tom and Libby had concluded their muted, private conversation. They both agreed it had been far too long since they had taken the time to acknowledge the painful and intimate issues between them, but again the conversation ended with nothing being accomplished; save perhaps, the opening of old, deep, scabbed-over wounds. By the time The Senator entered the room, they both had retreated into their own thoughts. Libby stood as her husband came near, kissed him on the cheek and left.

"What's next, Tom?" The Senator asked.

Anyone watching from outside would have known the next question which the man should have been asked just by the distance in Tom and Libby's eyes. That The Senator wasn't overly observant of others, Tom was relieved.

After a big breakfast, Sandy conned me into another walk on the beach. I didn't think I would eat again when I had finally pushed myself from the table the evening before, but I was surprisingly hungry by the time I smelled the bacon frying the next morning. Maybe it was the perfect combination of soft and firm of the bed in our room, or resultant of the tangled mess we made of the covers last night, but I slept like a baby. Normally, I am a neat freak in bed, wanting the covers straight and even, the little fold of sheet over the blankets at the top, but by the time we finally were ready to sleep, I didn't care so long as Sandy was there, warm and snuggly beside me.

Thursday morning dawned with high clouds streaking from west to east and while we missed it, the other guests commented on the rare beauty of the red sunrise. I still don't understand why people want to get up to watch the sun come up on their vacation. Sunsets? Certainly, but sunrises? Besides, the morning's dreams were not worth leaving just to see something which happens every day, no matter how spectacularly the instance. That morning, while my fellow guests were marveling at the sunrise, I was dreaming of a picnic in Audubon Park with Sandy and my unborn son or daughter; of flying kites, and explaining leaves and bugs, and crossing the street to the zoo. I dreamt of my girls with us, and it was just too joyful a scene to leave - until Sandy's leg found mine under the rumpled covers, that was.

"Red sky at morning, sailors take warning," Mr. Eugene said to the group as he returned the refilled silver coffee urn to the sideboard in the dining room. "Storms are coming in this morning. Big ones."

Sandy had sold me on the idea of a post-breakfast walk while I was in a weakened state, enjoying my bacon and not really paying attention to Mr. Eugene's weather alerts. After all, we weren't sailors, were we? Of course, had the B & B installed televisions in the room, we'd have seen the line of thunderstorms charging hard toward the island on the local news. It hadn't, so we didn't.

By the time we left the inn, the high, thin clouds had thickened and lowered and the Gulf had begun to roll, its water reflecting the color of slate. Whitecaps churned far offshore to the east. The air was nearly motionless and hung heavy with stagnant moisture, yet pockets of alternately cooler and warmer air would surround us then move on as we walked along the dry sand well away from the rolling wash. Every Midwesterner's weather sense I had screamed at me to turn around and go back inside; then Sandy took my hand and I got lost in her eyes. I do that.

We walked south that time, and silent moments passed. Comfortable moments. To answer my nagging weather senses, however, every minute or two I glanced to the west where I had started to note the darker, grayer clouds in the distance.

"What a peaceful morning," Sandy said finally. "Barely a breath of wind."

"Something tells me that's coming," I said. "That sky off to the west looks a little daunting, don't you think?"

She shot a glance.

"You won't melt, my love. It's only a little rain, even if it does come before we get back."

She paused, hugged my arm and posed for a kiss, which I gladly supplied her.

"Ever want to get caught in the rain with me?" she asked. "I think it would be romantic."

"Are you sure about that?" I asked.

"Sure about what? That it would be romantic?"

"No, that I won't melt. Remember, I can't quite see my tag, and you know I'm not what most people would call outdoorsy."

She shook her head and exhibited that tight lipped smile of hers which I've come to learn means she isn't quite sure what she's going to do with me, but she's enjoying the time while she decides. I shrugged my shoulders and stopped looking off to the west. Her hand was warm and soft in mine. She gave my paw a squeeze. I looked into her eyes again. Yeah, it was romantic, I thought to myself; and though I don't admit it to Sandy, I'm reasonably certain I would not melt in the rain.

We were nearly to the geographically mandated turn around point: the breakwater which provides the northern boundary of, and protective barrier to the channel connecting the Gulf to the inland waterways, having just passed the Lerma Pavilion, when I felt the first drop hit the top of my head. I think it was big enough to splash, but it *was* only one. I peered up at the sky, suggesting with my best cop squint it not try that again, while simultaneously congratulating the aim. The clouds above us had begun to churn. The Gulf had begun to roll ashore more vigorously, forcing us to walk even further up on the beach so the larger surges wouldn't swamp our feet.

"Did you feel that?" I said wiping the top of my head. "I think that drop was big enough to leave a dent."

"Rumors to the contrary, your head isn't *that* soft, Will," Sandy said with a smirk which meant the second part of the jibe was coming. "Even though sometimes I wonder."

"Well, that drop was the size of a golf ball," I said, trying a second time for either her pity or her suggestion we turn back early.

She offered neither.

I readied for more drops to fall, but that first one seemed to be it. Nothing was even hitting the sand around us. So I kept walking. Sandy enjoys stormy days; I do too, but I prefer to be safely inside. I've watched my wife stand out in the rain, relishing the experience with childlike joy. She's never seen me do that. When I was a kid, we got caught in a tornado while driving in the country to my grandparents' house. We huddled in the ditch, my father on top of us all until the storm went past. I was four, so my mother tells me. It was the only time I can remember my father being overtly protective of our little family. The very next week, I was playing with a toy barn on the lawn in the back yard when he came home from work. He had been drinking and because he said I made the yard look messy by laying out there playing with my toys, he kicked my barn over the fence, ruining the metal toy. I learned from those two events that fathers are mercurial sometimes, but I never wanted to be like that, and I don't think I ever have been.

"What's the matter, Will?" Sandy asked, moving in front of me.

"Memories," I said. "You want to head back? I think this storm is getting uncomfortably close."

"No, let's go out on the breakwater," she said, a playful look in her eyes as she used both of her hands on one of mine to pull me along. "I want to watch the storm. I want to feel it. I feel so alive these days."

"I think we could watch it all the same from the inn," I said, resisting the pull of her hands on mine. I used my free hand to rub the top of my head. "I've already felt it, remember?"

"It's not the same as being in it. Come on, Will. It's only rain. Please?"

Again ignoring the Midwesterner's weather warnings in my head, I relented to my wife's wishes and we walked to the end of the beach, past the scattered stacks of tubular pilings and up to the sea wall and breakwater. That was there I decided we really should stop and turn back, seek shelter in the pavilion, but Sandy released my hand and climbed onto the concrete blocks of the breakwater and began moving eastward out into the roiling Gulf. The waves had begun to surge at the piled concrete toward the seaward end of the structure, yet Sandy walked east, waving for me to join her. I took another look at the sky over the countryside to the west just past Port Isabel on the opposite side of the narrow channel; it had turned an eerie shade of greenish gray, and far to the north, I saw the first bolt of lightning flash to the ground. The wind was the only indicator which hadn't shown up. Yet.

"How stupid is this?" I said to myself, just before I stepped onto the concrete blocks and walked out after my excessively adventurous wife.

Together, we stepped over the gaps of between the massive blocks of reinforced concrete and started to leave the shoreline behind. Seawater rose and fell in the gaps with the arrival and passing of each wave surge. As we ventured further out onto the breakwater with Sandy as the adventurer and me as the protector, I noticed the gaps between blocks were wider and more water surged through them. The waves grew larger with each passing minute and then I saw the first one break over the top of the pier toward the end.

"Okay, Sandy, it's time to head in," I said with a tone of authority and pointed out into the Gulf. "This is going to get far worse before it gets better. It's becoming dangerous. I'm not kidding."

Famous last words as it turned out.

We were about two football fields from shore when the sea lashed out at us for the first time. The surge which had topped the end of the pier and faded as it moved inland, was followed by another which did not fade as it raced toward shore and was throwing tons of seawater over the length of the structure and into the relatively calm channel to the south. I grabbed Sandy by the hand and pulled her behind one of the raised concrete blocks, shielded her with my body as the saltwater poured down upon us. I looked up to judge the next surge.

"We move now, Sandy," I yelled over the wind which had suddenly shown itself and begun to roar in some elemental competition with the sea.

When she looked at me, gone was the mirth of moments before, having been replaced by genuine fear. At first, she refused to move. I fought to keep my eyes calm for her in the face of the fastest and most violent change in the weather I had experienced since I was four. I knew I had to get us off that pile of rocks or we'd be swept off the pier and into the water by the vicious waves and roaring onshore wind. The leading edge of a line of thunderstorms was now visible running north to south over the island and was voraciously sucking the air off the Gulf, drawing in warmth and moisture and growing rapidly along the shore.

The next wave surge hit the end of the pier and moved quickly toward shore. I estimated the time between waves was roughly twenty-seconds. I scanned the pier toward land, and safety. We had reasonable protection from the force of the waves due to the irregular heights of the loosely stacked cement blocks for about two hundred feet. After that, we had to cross the relatively flat, unprotected concrete studded with the occasional round metal piling for the last four hundred feet to shore. I again pushed Sandy to the concrete block with my body. The instant the wave passed, I grabbed her hand and led her behind the surge, counting to fifteen in my head. I refused to look back.

"Will, next wave," she screamed.

We had covered roughly fifty feet and I pulled her behind another block and held tight as the water poured over us. Something carried in the surge struck my soft head, leaving a gash. I tasted seawater and blood. I pulled Sandy along again, repeating the duck and cover drill three more times before we were finally facing the last, long, unprotected segment to shore. We waited out two waves under cover and I told Sandy we'd have to cover at least half the distance between surges. I pointed out a pair of pilings about two hundred feet away. Fortunately, the intervals between surges had grown to about thirty-seconds, however, the waves they brought were much higher and moved faster along the pier. I wondered if we could cover two hundred feet in half a minute. I doubted it, but it was our only shot.

"We go after the next wave, Sandy, and we take shelter at those two higher pilings, regardless of where the next wave is. Then one more run to shore. Okay?"

She nodded. There was less fear in her eyes.

I heard the next wave approaching and squeezed her tightly between me and the concrete. It passed over us.

"Now, run," I hollered, yanking her up.

I pulled her along behind me, holding her hand harder than I think I ever have. Somehow, we made the pilings well ahead of the next wave and I momentarily thought of making the run for the rest of the distance, but knew if we got caught in the open we'd never hold to the pier. I wrapped my arms around Sandy and the pipe as best I could and braced for the hit; and what a hit it was. Tons of water pounded against us and felt like being trampled by the entire front line of the Green Bay Packers. Sandy screamed and hunched lower and I gripped the rusty, slippery steel with every bit of my strength. The attack of the wave seemed to go on forever as time stopped. I gasped and swallowed seawater. Sandy was coughing and screaming at the same time.

Then I lost my grip.

Dace and Dave stopped at the Metairie Wal-Mart on Jefferson Highway. They bought some supplies and food, and a prepaid cell phone. Dace had retreated into himself again and hadn't said much since the brief mention of Sarah at lunch. Dave un-boxed the cell phone while sitting in the car in the parking lot, opened it and punched in ten numbers. He heard a distant ringing.

"Hey, it's Cindy," came the answer.

"Hi, it's me," Dave said. "We're almost there. Stopped and picked up a prepaid cell phone and some other stuff to provision the place."

"Hey, you. Glad to hear you've almost made it. Call me when you get in, I'm just headed into my Astronomy class."

"Before you go, I can't remember where you said the key is."

"Uncle Jack said they'd leave it in a magnetic case under the lip of the molasses pot to the right of the front porch."

"That's why I didn't remember. What's a molasses pot?"

"It's a big, old, iron pot they used to boil sugar cane in to make molasses. This one is filled with dirt and flowers as I recall from photos Uncle Jack sent me. It appeared to be about six feet in diameter and, oh, about three feet high. You can't miss it."

"Okay, that should be easy enough."

"Yeah, but call me when you get settled. There's a small market just down the road for emergency stuff, food and whatnot, but for anything significant, it's suggested you head into the city."

"Okay. Talk to you later."

The phone clicked off and Dave dropped the phone onto the center console, then turned right out of the Wal-Mart parking lot and a block later made another right onto the extended approach to the Huey P. Long Bridge over the Mississippi River. The Escalade began the long climb to the apex of the approach where it met the bridge, one-hundred-fifty-three feet above the river.

The Huey P. Long Bridge opened in 1935 and was designed mainly as a railroad structure with two sets of tracks running in the trussed center sections of the bridge, while the two roadways outboard on each side seemed almost an afterthought. As the SUV completed the climb, they caught and began passing a slow-moving freight train on the viaduct off to their left. As they passed onto the bridge proper, they could feel the strong, shallow vibrations of the moving weight of the train. The view on the narrow roadway section was spectacular, but Dave moved to the left, inboard lane to give a little padding between him and the guardrails, which even with their size, number, and height, seemed somehow inadequate in comparison to the rest of the bridge structure. The train moved outward from New Orleans along the track closest to them; the bridge rumbled even more the further out onto the bridge they moved. Far below, nonstop river traffic flowed in both directions.

On the far side of the river, the roadway again descended below the elevated train tracks and dumped the SUV into Bridge City. The Great River Road ran east and west at the stop sign. Vacherie was to the west, so Dave turned right, glad to be back on solid ground.

In the early afternoon, Tom's phone vibrated in his pocket. He had escaped to his room to work on some things for other clients for a few hours after breakfast and his short discussion with The Senator. Frankly, he had told The Senator, until the boys surface again, they're looking for two needles in a very large haystack. Sure, they could assume they would continue heading south, but there was a tremendous chunk of country between Birmingham and the Gulf coast.

Tom scanned the caller ID. It was Rudy's cell. Tom had told him and Travis to get some rest after the overnight excursion to the land of Dixie and hadn't expected to have them check in until Friday morning, so he knew it had to be something important. He flipped the phone open and put it to his ear.

"Yeah, Rudy," Tom said.

"I just got off the phone with our contact at the cellular company," Rudy said with a bit of a raspy voice. "I had told him to call me if anything unusual showed up on the three trap and taps we have going, especially if it has to do with the new cell phone that Cindy Spagliano has. The one the Saunders kid got cute with the number."

"And?"

"Well, seems the girl's new phone line has received just one new call since last night. About an hour ago." Rudy read Tom the transcript of the conversation. "Came from a prepaid. Area code 504. I heard the recording, it's definitely the Saunders kid." He rattled off the rest of the number.

Tom scratched the number on the outside of a file folder.

"Where is 504?"

"New Orleans.  We were able to confirm the phone was bought at the Wal-Mart store on Jefferson Highway in Metairie, which is just outside New Orleans."

Tom circled the phone number several times as he thought.

"Well, based on the conversation you just read me, I'd say our boys are close to their final destination."

"That'd be my guess," Rudy confirmed.  "Problem is, that's a big area down there.  They could be anywhere.  Of course, the girl talks about a molasses pot in the front yard, so I'm assuming a house of some sort.  As I recall from some excursions through that area when I was in the Corps, they grow cane all over.  Those old boiling pots have to be everywhere, now as planters and such.  There was at least one sitting out front at every plantation house west and south of the city."

"I've seen them myself.  They are all over.  Not much of a clue."

"She does say there's not much around the place but a small store for emergencies, so it's got to be rural," Rudy observed.

"If this Uncle Jack is real and not another cutesy ruse," Tom said, "then the place is tied to the Spagliano woman and she's the key to finding them."

"So, are you thinking we go see the girl?"

"Makes sense, right?"

"We don't have a lot on her in the way of background yet, but I can see what can be dug up, maybe pay her a personal visit tomorrow."

"The sooner the better," Tom said.  "The Senator is starting to drive me nuts.  Email or fax me whatever you turn up on the girl or this Uncle Jack.  Spread it around; it's far enough removed from The Senator, so the more eyes we have looking, the better."

"You got it."

The line was disconnected and Tom closed his cell phone and returned it to his pocket.  He tossed the pen onto the folder with the prepaid cell phone number on the desk.  For a moment, he considered calling the phone to see who would answer and then just as quickly ruled it out.  The problem with doing that, he concluded, was Dave didn't know they had the Spagliano girl's other cell phone number and if he called the prepaid, Dave would easily spot the New York number on the caller ID.  Even if Tom blocked the number from the ID program, it may still spook the kid if the phone rang with a blocked number and then God only knew how they'd change things up.  No, he concluded, it would be best to keep a few cards close to the vest, at least for the time being. He slid his chair back on the hardwood floor, then stood, hiked his Dockers and walked out of his room and down the hallway to The Senator's office.

I tumbled against the pier after losing my grip on both Sandy and the large, round piling, and was rolled by the water toward the now surging, yet relatively protected waters of the inlet. Sandy screamed for me but held fast to the piling as the massive wave moved rapidly toward the beach. Somehow in the wash, I located and held fast to a smaller pipe protruding from the concrete pier about fifteen feet from the piling. I was retching on swallowed seawater, yet knew we'd have less than half a minute before the next wave. Sandy released her grip and moved toward me as I struggled to get up. My pants were torn at the knees and along with the cut on my head, I was now bleeding from both knees and the palms of my hands were scraped bare.

Sandy pulled me to my feet with a strength I had forgotten she possessed and we began running the last couple hundred feet to the beach. The rain began falling and even though we were already soaked to the bone, the sheets of water falling from the menacing storm somehow made me feel even wetter. At least the fresh water was washing the sting of saltwater and blood from my eyes. I seemed to gain strength as we ran and I kept Sandy going until we were well onto the beach where we jumped off the seawall and onto the sand, just ahead of the wave which rushed up the beach and tossed us like jetsam to the vegetation line. As the water receded around our heaving bodies, I could feel the sands shift underneath me and I struggled to sit up. I pulled Sandy from the mire and she sat next to me, eyes wide, but calming down quickly.

"Are you all right, Sandy," I asked through rapid, deep breaths. "Are you hurt, anywhere?"

She was breathing less hard than I - evidence of her more active lifestyle - I was certain I'd be reminded later. My eyes did a quick inventory of her body. Her light, yellow sundress was nearly translucent and glued to her skin by the water, and I could see no injuries, no evidence of bleeding.

"I'm fine, Will," she said, adding when she saw my continuing concern, "Really, I am."

The sky had opened and we were sitting on soft, wet sand in the hardest rain I had ever experienced. To the west just on the other side of the inland channel, a bolt of lightning flashed and a split-second later the boom of thunder rumbled through us. That flash was quickly followed by repeated cloud-to-ground strikes to the near north and south. The storms were right on top of us and even though we were now safe from the fury of the Gulf, we were in the open with violent lightning striking all around us. I looked up and watched the low, churning clouds moving quickly east, bringing even darker, more ominous replacements marching on us from the west.

"We've got to get to shelter," I said. "Can you walk to the pavilion?"

"I made it this far," she said. "I'm fine, really, Will."

"Both of you?" I asked, remembering for the first time since that initial surge that I was now responsible for two lives plus mine.

Sandy smiled reassuringly and took my hand as she stood up. Her face dripped water in sheets, her eyelashes briefly held and then dropped more rainwater onto her cheeks. She reached for my forehead, touched the wound. I could taste blood again. I stood up and felt momentarily lightheaded.

"That cut's not bad," she said. "I'm so sorry, Will."

Normally, I'd milk the combination of Sandy's remorse and my minor injury for every bit of easy sympathy I could, but at that moment, with the lightning intensifying and the waves washing up around my feet, sinking me into the wet sand with every pass, I decided it might be best to forego the pity party for a little while. At least until we were safely under shelter.

We began to move between the huge stacks of loose pilings laid on the beach. Each two-foot diameter metal tube was forty-feet long and rolled from half-inch steel sheeting. The pilings were used for driving into the seabed for various purposes - I've watched the cranes and huge pneumatic hammers working along the Mississippi - and they were tightly piled five or six rows high on what appeared to be railroad ties on the sand. The stacks were a more than adequate shelter, I thought, and the easier pathway toward the pavilion building was to for us to walk between them rather than in the open closer to the surging waves on the shoreline. However, I realized the piles consisted of tons of grounded steel which could work as a lightning rod, so my thinking was to clear them quickly. My ultimate goal was to get out to the nearby roadway, be fully off the beach and then walk along the asphalt to reach to the safety and shelter of the pavilion.

I held Sandy's hand tightly, and she gripped back just as hard. We wove our way between stacks while every half minute or so another wave would rush inland and stop us while we struggled to stand on the shifting stands. Walking when the water was onshore proved nearly impossible so we were essentially mired until it receded. We were about to emerge between two stacks when another surge rushed ashore, that one seemingly much larger than the ones we had battled on the pier.

The wave rushed past us and the water level rose to well above our knees before I felt the suction of the return. Sand churned under my feet as I tried to continue on; I could tell Sandy was having difficulty standing, let alone walking, so I again stopped and looked back to make certain she was still okay. Another flash of lightning drove into earth on the opposite shore of the inland waterway. The flash was blinding and the thunder was instantaneous as it drowned out every sound but Sandy's scream.

In my peripheral vision I sensed movement and I turned to see the stack of pilings to our left beginning to shift, its dunnage foundation in the sand undermined by the continuing wave surges. The stack began collapsing and the individual pilings rolled down toward us in the narrow passage. My feet were still gripped by the watery sand and we were still five or six feet from the end of the stacks, but with a lurch I slipped free and pulled Sandy out of the way of the tons of rolling steel, tossing her into the open sand clear of the danger. I then rolled myself away as the giant pipes filled the passage and crashed into the seaward grouping, which caused that pile to collapse as well and roll several pilings into the surf. Sandy lay on her face in the sand, not moving. I crawled through the last of the receding waters to her and rolled her onto her back. Her head lolled. Her eyes were closed. I called her name through the howling wind and rain but got no response. A trickle of blood appeared in the watery sand under her head. She appeared to be breathing normally and as I pulled her up to examine her wound, my peripheral vision again caught movement, that time out to sea and my eyes went wide as the largest wave yet was rushing toward shore, peeling along the pier and sending tens of thousands of gallons of seawater in a spray fifty feet into the air.

I scooped Sandy into my arms and began to run for the safety of the road. Moments later, I prayed as I ran through the gusts and sheets of rain along sand-drifted asphalt that there'd be a phone in the Lerma pavilion to call for help, if only I could outpace the advancing wave.

I prayed for Sandy; and our child.

# Chapter Ten

Dace strained to reach into the back seat and ripped open the case of Miller Genuine Draft and removed a can. On his insistence, not that Dave put up much of an objection, they had pulled six cases of beer from the Super Wal-Mart cooler and bottles of tequila, bourbon, vodka and assorted mixers from the shelves. He offered the still-cold beer across to Dave, who to Dace's surprise accepted it and popped the top. He held the sweating can between his thighs as he maneuvered along the roadway. Dace reached back for another can, opened it and took a deep draw.

They passed out of what Dace would consider urban areas of relatively dense housing and moved into countryside where the roadway began a series of meandering turns which mimicked the river beyond the levee. A huge industrial complex filled the horizon and turned out to be a chemical plant with acres of flat-topped storage tanks and miles of piping. As they drove closer, they could see aluminum jacketed pipelines running from the plant and over the road, terminating at a structural steel loading station on the far side of the levee. They left the plant behind and the landscape transformed into bayou, dusty fields of sugar cane or other crops, and scrub trees.

The temperature outside was reaching into the high seventies with partly cloudy skies. Dace pushed the button to roll down the window and tossed out his first empty, then retrieved another full one from the case. Dave declined, having yet to take a drink. The outside air smelled of a combination of fertile soil and hardworking river and Dace drew it in deeply. They cruised along at a leisurely fifty-miles-per-hour on the smooth asphalt. There was no rush. A jet coming off the New Orleans Airport on the other side of the river banked westward as it climbed away silently and then plowed into a puffy white cumulus cloud. Dace thought the logo had marked the airliner as one of the Continental livery, not that it much mattered to him.

There were two River Roads in that part of the country, one on each side of the Mississippi, and, having crossed the bridge, they drove along the southern one, known simply as the Great River Road. It was a continuation of the named roadway which started far to the north in Minnesota, where the river's headwaters originated. For over a thousand miles the Great River Road mimicked nearly every twist and turn the Mississippi had carved over the millennia. Because of the height of the levee standing between road and river in southern Louisiana, Dave and Dace hadn't seen the river for which the road had been named since rolling off the Huey P. Long bridge.

Most of the time, the roadway ran directly alongside the levee, but occasionally, it would take a few turns away from the river and pass through a gathering of ramshackle houses too few to be considered a town, and too many to be considered a subdivision. Every mile or two, a gravel road veered off the main highway and ran up the side of the levee. At odd intervals, tire tracks cut through the wide grass and mud shoulder and made their own path to the top of the earthen berm.

The fields inland of the road were laid out like fingers perpendicular to the waterway and stretched back to a tree line a mile or two south of the river. Many of the parcels were planted in sugar cane or other greenery and a few were lying fallow or showed signs of recent planting or harvesting. Some areas were populated in cypress, cedar, and mesquite trees which had reclaimed the land. A few plats had been developed into makeshift subdivisions, with homes or trailers planted in neat rows in lieu of cash crops. A bit further along, they passed a massive grain storage facility extruding large, covered conveyors which passed over the roadway to another style of river loading station. That was where Dace finished his second beer and tossed the can into the long grass of the shoulder. By that time, Dave had finished his beer and accepted a second can when offered. Dace tossed out Dave's empty.

"You know you've been littering since we left Rhode Island," Dave said. "Where's your ecological soul?"

Dace turned his head, shot a smirk over the center console, then raised a lone finger to accentuate the coming point.

"Ah, but you must have noticed I've only sent empty alcohol containers out into Mother Nature's wastebasket. Nothing else."

Dave cocked his head, his lips held in a noncommittal tightness.

"Okay, I'll bite," he said. "Why?"

"Because I thought it would be better to be busted for littering than for an open container of alcohol in your pretty, new Cadillac."

Dave took another drink of beer. He realized then that was one of Dace's sardonic mind-screws, but he had asked.

"Down here, us being a couple of Yankees from Harvard, do you really think the cops are going to find a distinction without a difference if they pull us over for *any* kind of lawbreaking?  Have you seen *My Cousin Vinny?*"

Dace drank more of his beer; let out a belch.

"Eh, we've got lawyers in my family, too," Dace said.  "Besides, that was set in Mississippi."

"This is Louisiana," Dave said.  "I submit, your honor, the ultimate distinction without a difference."

They passed over a narrow bridge spanning a dammed spillway which connected to the river through a break in the levee while its other end disappeared into the bayou and forest to the south.  A little further along, Dace told Dave to take one of the gravel roads to the top of the levee.  Dave grimaced at the thought of taking his new Cadillac off-road, but slowed and turned onto the surprisingly well-maintained gravel drive.  He ignored the federal government's warning signs, which each sported a series of bullet holes and stated people dare not enter the levee area under penalty of law, and drove up the embankment.  When they crested the berm, they were each surprised to see a similar gravel roadway topped the levee for as far as the eye could see.

"Stop here," Dace said.  "I've got to pee."

"What?  That's like two-and-a-half beers since you went at Wal-Mart.  You got a baby bladder, or what?" Dave teased.

"Some smart fellah told me recently that one couldn't buy beer, only rent it," Dace said with a smile.  "I'm just done renting it."

"That was one smart fellah.  I'd like to meet him someday.  I imagine he was handsome, too, right?"

"I saw this joke once," Dace said, "if three people having sex is a threesome, and two people having sex is a twosome, why do you think it's good to be called handsome?"

Dave braked the Escalade to a stop and turned off the ignition and peered over the top of his Blues Brothers sunglasses.  Dace smirked, got out, left the door open and walked across the top of the levee toward the river to pee.  At the risk of suffering a baby bladder comment coming back his way, Dave joined him.  The view of the river was tremendous.  They had stopped at a shallow U in the track of the river and could see for miles both upriver and downriver.  Set along the banks on both sides of the Mississippi, lashed to pilings driven in the riverbed outside of the navigable channel, were dozens of river barges.  Dace estimated each one at nearly two hundred feet long and thirty to forty feet wide.  A tugboat churned upriver pushing twenty barges in a stack four wide and five long, its powerful diesel engines belching out dual trails of black smoke and noise.  Another such setup glided silently downriver toward New Orleans, moving with the flow at a slightly faster speed than its counterpart, and with obviously much less effort.  A breeze from the southwest was at the boys' back, and rippled the surface of the brown waters.

Across the river was another expansive tank farm with multiple river loading stations. A tanker ship lay at dock at one of the stations, either loading or unloading. Dace recognized the flag on the boat's stern as that of Panama. He recalled overhearing conversations between his father and other senators on his Commerce, Science, and Transportation Committee about the sad state of the U.S. shipping industry a couple of summers ago when he'd played at being an assistant to The Senator for several weeks of summer vacation. The politicians had said, he recalled, the cost of a U.S. ship registry had long been unworkable for most companies. The United States, they had lamented, had lost the lucrative registry battle to countries such as Panama and Liberia decades earlier, and had little hope of bringing it back mainly because of overarching regulatory hurdles and associated taxes and fees imposed by our government.

"This is amazing," Dace said, his point spanning the river horizon. "When you're done emptying *your* baby bladder, why don't you grab us a couple of beers and let's watch for a while."

Dave suffered the retort in silence and shuffled across the gravel to the SUV and removed a half dozen cans from the open case. Dace had found a seat on the river side of the road on a raised concrete block along the exposed structural spine of the levee. Beyond, the grassy berm sloped down to the river. Below, the anchored rows of barges rubbed gently against their moorings as the wake from the tug headed upriver washed along the shore. The waters between the parked barges and shoreline were stagnant, a muddy brown color which was somehow less appealing than the rest of the muddy brown river and littered with flotsam and jetsam. Dave sat down on the opposite end of the large block of concrete, placed the six beers in the open space.

"I wish my dad could see that," Dace said as he popped a beer and gestured to the ship with the can.

"The boat?" Dave said. "Why would he want to see that old rust bucket?"

"No, the flag," Dace said. "Panama. My dad chairs the Senate committee which oversees the Coast Guard and international shipping issues and it pisses him off whenever he sees merchant ships in U.S. waters flying foreign flags. The U.S. has regulated itself out of any standing whatever in the international registry of merchant ships." Dace took a long draw from the slowly warming beer and a broad smile returned to his face. "They're called 'Flags of Convenience' in the industry, and Panama was where many shipowners moved their registry in the 1920s, but these days, a plurality of merchant ships are of Liberian registry. The United Kingdom maintained the largest registry of merchant vessels until 1968 when Liberia surpassed them. It's all bullshit, and dad's been trying to pass legislation for decades to lure them back, but the marine shipping industry just pisses on him every time he tries. They know a good deal when they have it, and with lower fees and lower regulations abroad, they have a good deal."

Dave cracked a beer and took a drink.

"I didn't think your old man ever lost at anything."

Dace let out a belly laugh. The second genuine laugh of the day.

"He doesn't think so either," he said. "Although, I would imagine he's rethinking that a bit right about now."

Dace drained his can, tossed it down the levee toward the water, popped the top on another. He held that one in his hands and stared into the distance.

Dave watched his friend. Dace would often flow seamlessly from conversation into deep, silent thought as long as Dave had known him. He had always been mercurial, but in a good way. Over the last couple days, Dave wondered if that personality trait could be affecting his friend's outward behaviors, making him dangerous to himself, or others, as evidenced by those security guys in Birmingham. Dave shook the thoughts from his head. After all, it was one of the reasons he was there, to help keep Dace fairly close to center as he contended with the phases of grief he'd be going through in the aftermath of Sarah's death, but Dave wasn't working with all the parameters, as he had yet to be made aware of the added pressures The Senator had heaped upon Dace's shoulders earlier on his birthday. Dave allowed his attention to drift to the passing barges, both of which he noted flew the stars and stripes. It was easier.

"Those are flying U.S. flags," Dave said, pointing.

Dace removed his Blues Brothers sunglasses from his pocket and put them on.

"Any ship or boat which operates solely in the inland waterways or coastal waters of the United States of America is required to be registered here. The government's got those dumb bastards by the balls. It's the international ships which skirt the system."

"Ah, I get it," Dave said. "Captive audience, squeeze. An audience with options, whine."

"Your government in action," Dace said with a resigned shrug.

"Things will be different when you're president," Dave said.

"Many have tried, all have failed," Dace said, then went silent.

Dave observed him again. While Dace was, over the recent days, sometimes befuddling to Dave, he always amazed him. He seemed to know so much about so many different subjects and was able to summon the knowledge at will. It's not that he spent an inordinate amount of time with his nose in books; he rarely took notes in class, just would sit and listen, sometimes passively as he worked on something totally unrelated. Teachers and professors through the years asserted he must possess a photographic or eidetic memory. Dace said his memory worked best by hearing things, an aural memory he called it in high school after doing some research. However it worked, to Dave, who struggled in almost every class and clawed to retain every bit of knowledge, his best friend seemed to pick up information through osmosis, and without effort.

Ten minutes later, just as the scene and the several beers had put Dave into a feeling of peace, Dace started talking again.

"This area was plantation land for hundreds of years, you know, and access to the river was essential for travel and the movement of goods," Dace said, his point spanning the horizon all around them. "That's why you see the layout of the land in long, thin rectangles; each landowner would be granted river frontage out of necessity. As generations inherited the lands, the parcels were divided into narrower and narrower slivers, always attempting to allow for access to the Mississippi. This unique layout extends all the way to Baton Rouge, and beyond, on both sides of the river."

"You know this, how?"

"I did a research paper on the Napoleonic Code last year and read a pile of ancillary material on Louisiana history."

"Napoleonic Code? As in Napoleon, the little French dude with the perpetually cold hand?"

"That's the guy. Louisiana is the only state which based its laws on the Napoleonic Code, what's known as a civil code. The other forty-nine follow English Common Law, what's known as precedent law."

"The difference being, professor?" Dave asked taking a healthy slug from his beer. "You're prelaw, I'm not."

"English Common Law is based on judicial precedent where judges rely on previous court rulings to guide their own conclusions; whereas the Napoleonic Code, which heralds back even further in history to roots in French, Spanish, and Roman law is based in legislative intent, leaving each judge free to consider the laws on their own merit and issue rulings based solely on his or her independent interpretation of the statute."

"Ah, laziness versus mind reading. I get it," Dave said. "I should care, why?"

"You probably shouldn't care," Dace said. "Seeing you've got your sights set on being drafted by the Dolphins this spring and will most likely settle down in Florida for the rest of your life."

"Florida, under English Common Law, right?"

"Mm-hmm, you got it."

"Okay, so how does this all tie in to your initial observation about the lay of the land down here in Napoleonland?"

"Because in Louisiana, they adhere to the practice of forced heirship, which means when a landowner dies, the estate is divided into two parts, the forced estate which flows into two equal shares: a spousal share and a share which is again divided between any children - legitimate or otherwise. The second part, or free estate, can be disposed of by terms of a Will. So, these parcels of land may have originally been huge, however, by the time they passed half a dozen times across a couple of centuries, they became increasingly subdivided. Everything goes into the estate for division. Normally, they'd work it out, but I read of one heir who had the family home cut apart and his share of the structure moved to his inherited land when his father passed. Decades later, and long after the death of the son, the house was put back together during a historical restoration."

"You're nothing if not a constant surprise, my friend," Dave said, hoisting a mock toast with his can of beer.

"You don't know the half of it," Dace said, accepting the toast, then taking a deep draw, crushing the can and tossing it down the bank toward the river.

They sat and drank beers, which grew to a total of four each, and talked, and watched the river and boat traffic move along at a seemingly glacial pace before they were ready to leave. Each empty can they tossed toward the mix of trash lining the shore fell far short of the river every time. Dave finally stood and stretched, looked toward the sky. The sun was moving westward toward the horizon, but he judged there was still plenty of daylight left to get to Vacherie before sunset.

"Shall we go, professor?" Dave said as he prepared to pee again. While he watered the bank, and Dace wandered back to the car, Dave said to himself, 'Geeze, you really can't buy beer.'

The rain fell in buckets, windswept sheets cascaded across the roadway and empty parking lot. I saw the few cars, which I had noticed parked outside the Lerma Pavilion when we first walked by were gone. Twice Sandy had coughed and retched in my arms as the rainwater flooded down her throat, although she did not regain consciousness. The wound on the back of her head was small, but the bump was growing larger each time I moved my hand to check the area. My heart was pounding in my chest, whether it was the result of exertion or fear for my wife I couldn't be certain. I kept running.

Finally, I reached the shelter of the pavilion, an open-air building of proportion and design which under normal circumstances, I'd find incongruous. The concrete columns were massive and rose to support an equally massive roof structure. I assumed they had built the thing to withstand the equally massive hurricanes which Mother Nature could hurl at that part of the Gulf coast with seasonal regularity. Once inside, I found a series of wide, flat slat-type benches in a relatively sheltered and dry area on the second floor on which to place Sandy, but instead I put her onto the concrete floor while I went in search of a public telephone. Normally, I didn't travel far from my cell phone, but that morning it was safe and dry on the dresser in our room.

Mounted on a column on the ground floor I found a pay phone. I picked up the receiver, which was still thankfully tethered to an intact metal-encased cord, and heard a dial tone. I dialed 9-1-1 and fought to catch my breath as I waited for the answer.

"9-1-1, what is your emergency?" came the calm voice.

"I'm at the Lerma Pavilion on South Padre Island and my wife has fallen and bumped her head and is unconscious; I need an ambulance," I said through bouts of breathlessness. I silently vowed to myself that I'd get more exercise after this. Hell, I thought, I'm only forty years old come August and I'm wheezing like an eighty year old man.

"Sir, Emergency Management has temporarily closed all bridges to the barrier islands because of an anticipated heavy sea surge moving into inland waters, but if you've got a true emergency need, we can possibly move something your way with a volunteer crew," she said.

Bureaucrats, I thought. I took a deep breath.

"As I said, my wife has hit her head and is bleeding from the wound, she's unconscious, but is breathing normally," I repeated as I silently wondered what exactly would constitute an emergency to this particular woman. "Anything you can do to get us medical attention would be appreciated."

A pause. I heard the beep of the call recording notice, so I held there a moment.

"Sir, my supervisor has just advised me that he has a crew willing to cross the bridge and they are currently en route to your location. You say you're at the Lerma Pavilion, is that correct?"

"Yes, on the second floor, in a central dry area. I need to get back and check on my wife, do you need anything else right now?"

"No sir, the crew should be there within ten minutes." A pause. "Good luck, sir."

"Thank you," I said, hanging up the phone and running back upstairs to where I had left Sandy.

Sandy hadn't moved since I placed her on the concrete floor; I hadn't left her on one of the nearby benches just in case she had rolled. I again checked her head wound as I lifted her onto one of the benches. The bleeding, which had seemed worse with all the water, had nearly stopped and the lump didn't appear to be growing any larger. I sat on the bench and cradled her head in my lap. I stroked my fingers gently across her face and moved her hair back. I spoke her name quietly, then took her hands in mine. They were cold and clammy and when I put them to my lips to kiss her palms, she moaned and moved her head.

"Sandy?" I said. "Can you hear me?"

The rain was pounding against the metal roof and I could see toward the Gulf the lightning was now out over the water as well, pounding away at an angry gray sea. In the distance, I thought I could detect the wailing of a siren cutting through the howling wind and pounding rain and I breathed a sigh of relief, but what I really wanted was for my wife to open her eyes.

"Sandy," I repeated, brushing my fingertips across her cheek. "Open your eyes, honey."

I scrutinized her face for any sign of movement, although beyond the moan and head movement when I kissed her palms there had been nothing. I began to wonder if I had imagined it.

Then, her eyelids began to flutter, and I could see her eyes moving behind them. She licked her lips; and then she said my name, which came out in a quiet and raspy voice, distant some would have said, but it was my Sandy saying my name. Tears of joy filled my eyes.

"It's okay, Sandy," I said. "You bumped your head hard on a rock in the sand, but you're safe and help is on the way. Don't try to move, sweetheart."

She opened her eyes then and looked into mine, and then they looked past me and grew wider.

"Sir," the voice said as a hand touched my shoulder.

I turned to see one short rotund man and one tall gangly man in EMT garb standing behind me. The shorter one was breathing as hard as I had been when I arrived at the pavilion. He was carrying a couple of medical kits in gray, metal boxes with handles, like large tool boxes. The taller one had his hand on my shoulder.

"That's a nasty little gash you've got there, sir," the man with his hand on my shoulder said and he pulled a thick pad of gauze from his pocket and pressed it to my forehead. "Sir, can you apply pressure here for me while we see to your wife?"

The other EMT moved around to Sandy and bent down over her, removing one of her hands from my grip and gently touching his fingertips to the inside of her wrist. He next checked her heart with a stethoscope he pulled from around his neck, and an instant later removed a small flashlight from his chest pocket, spread Sandy's eyelids a bit and flashed the light past to watch for the normal response from her pupils.

"Ma'am, don't try to move now. We'll do all that for you," said the first EMT as he moved around to her head. His fingers moved behind her and he obviously found the bump. "Can you tell me what happened, sir? I understand there has been a period of LOC? How long was that?"

I told them as they continued the triage work, beginning with the walk out on the pier to explain my injuries and then the falling pilings to explain how Sandy was injured. Their eye rolls in unison and the look they shared between themselves was enough of an affront to my intelligence, so I mentioned that I could never resist a request of my wife.

"Well, maybe next time you should give that some thought, sir," EMT number two - the short, fat one - said with a bit of a wry grin.

"Yeah, I'll do that," I said sheepishly.

Sandy was becoming increasingly responsive and the more she came around the more she fought the idea of going to the hospital for a complete check.

"Your husband is going to need a couple of stitches anyway, ma'am, so you might as well ride along and have the doc take a look at you too," EMT number one told her.

Sandy looked at me and then consented to go when I nodded. They strapped her to a backboard and lifted her onto the gurney, not wanting to take a chance with any neck injury, especially given the loss of consciousness. At least that's what they told us.

Me, they had walk down behind them, holding my own compress against what I imagined was a bit more than a little nick to my noggin as the pain was just now beginning to surge across my forehead. Three of us packed into the back of the small ambulance, and EMT number two hopped into the driver's seat. The downpour had given way to a lighter rainfall, what we in the Midwest called a gentle soaker; while out to sea, the Gulf was still getting pounded and even more churned up.

We rode to the hospital past Sheriff's squads at each end of the closed bridge, through flooded streets and around stranded cars, probably driven by my fellow Idiot Club members who just had to get to the store for Pop Tarts in the storm. Sandy asked the EMT if we could borrow a cell phone to call the B&B because they might be frantic that we hadn't returned from our beach walk when the storms ran through. That's my Sandy, always thinking about someone else's needs before her own. She looked at me and asked why I was smiling so adorably, and I told her I had no idea. She squeezed my hand.

I used the EMT's cell phone to call the inn and spoke to Mr. Eugene, who was indeed glad to hear from me, but seemed much more concerned about Sandy's condition than mine when I told him we were headed to the hospital. I told him we'd most likely see them later in the afternoon and certainly by dinner. He asked to talk to Sandy and I passed her the phone. She listened, laughed, which was another good sign, and said something about 'her hero', before closing the phone and handing it back to the EMT. He took the phone, smiled at Sandy, gave me a tight lipped, crooked grimace, pulled the gauze pack from my forehead and gave me a fresh one and told me to hold it against the wound.

At the hospital, they wheeled Sandy into the ER, lifted her to an exam table and offered me a stool on wheels. A nurse with a strong Hispanic accent and a hint of a mustache, pulled my hand with the gauze away from the wound and then pushed it back telling me to hold pressure.

They took down Sandy's medical history and recorded it on a chart. When they got to the question about pregnancy, Sandy's eyes sought mine and she smiled, then a thought passed through her defogging brain and she began to cry. The mustachioed nurse held her hands and spoke softly to her, then her hands moved to my wife's abdomen and she gently touched and asked something I couldn't quite hear; but each time Sandy responded with a 'no', which from everyone's reaction, appeared to be the correct answer.

Next, they hooked up leads to Sandy's chest and ankles, ran an EKG strip for about forty-five seconds. I strained to look. From what I could see, Sandy's heartbeat was normal.

"You've got excellent rhythm," said the nurse with a smile.

I paused for a moment, weighed the pros and cons, then decided to just go for it.

"Yet, she still can't play the piano," I said.

Well, they both looked at me for a moment, then they laughed. Nurse Mustache walked over to me, a smile in my direction on her face for the first time.

"Let's take a look at that cut," she said, pulling the gauze free. "Eh, that's not so bad, but it's going to need a couple of stitches. Can you walk, funny man?"

"I could when I came in here," I said.

"Well, come on, I'll get a doctor to stitch you up while your wife rests a bit." She helped me to my feet and we walked through the curtain to another exam area. She sat me on the end of an exam table and then lowered her voice. "I'm going to call an OB down. I'm sure they'll want to do an ultrasound just to make sure everything is fine with your little son or daughter."

Half an hour later, I had three new stitches in my skull covered by a less-than-manly bandaid and was standing next to Sandy, holding her hand while the OB doc was moving the ultrasound around on my wife's bare, and very slightly enlarged belly. Sandy hadn't needed stitches for her cut, rather they had used a medical version of Super Glue they called Dermabond, something experimental, but that they soon hoped would be fully approved by the FDA. It would be, later that year. She was sporting a small bandage on the back of her head and holding an ice pack to the area which helped reduce the swelling of the bump. On the monitor, we both stared in fascination at the images of our child. We could see the head, and arms and legs, even the fingers and toes. The arms were crossed over the chest and the legs were crossed at the ankles. They had also hooked up what they called a Doppler and for the first time we heard a new heartbeat over a small speaker. I thought it sounded like the rapid clicking of horse hooves. Sandy's eyes misted. I couldn't see mine, but it felt like my eyes did too. Sandy squeezed my hand.

"How far along does your OB say you are?" the doc asked.

"Fifteen weeks," Sandy said with a smile.

"Well, that's a bit early, but if you'd like I can take a look to see if we can tell if you're going to have a boy or girl."

"No," Sandy said. "I don't want to know. Not even a hint."

The OB smiled knowingly.

"I totally understand. My husband was always curious, but I never wanted to know with any of mine either."

"How big is he or she now?" I asked, fascinated.

The OB doc moved her fingers and thumb about three and a half inches apart.

"Amazing," I said, looking back at the monitor and squeezing Sandy's hand.

The doc maneuvered the transducer a bit more and I'd swear I saw evidence of my first son on one of the images, but I kept that to myself.

On the west side of Vacherie, just beyond Oak Alley Plantation and a small subdivision, where the road veers left as Dave's instructions from Cindy had said, a two-mile long, twelve-foot-high hedgerow came into view to mark their destination. A small gap about halfway down the flora barrier revealed a drive of crushed seashells and small gravel which led toward a two-story plantation home in the Grecian-style with large, round, white pillars along the perimeter of a twelve-foot-wide, double-deck veranda. The double front entry doors were ten-feet high, and made of hand-carved, polished cypress, hewn and crafted from the swampland beyond by slaves in the 1820s, although that fact Dave didn't have in his notes and would learn later.

As described, a large, round, riveted iron pot anchored the landscaping out front.

Dave maneuvered the Escalade to a stop at the end of the teardrop shaped drive about forty feet from the house. A pathway of red brick paver stones and bounded by knee-high hedges which also guarded the perimeter of the ground-level porch led up to the three porch steps. Two large oak trees held sentry positions on the two large patches of grassed yard on either side of the drive. Spanish moss hung from the limbs, the combination casting long shadows across the property as the deep orange sun paused just above the horizon.

"Honey, we're home," Dave said.

"You should have hung on to that girl," Dace said. "It appears the family has money."

"Oh, this isn't real family," Dave said.

"I thought you said the place belonged to her Uncle Jack," Dace said, opening his door and stepping onto the bleached white shells and gravel which crunched underfoot.

"He's more like a close family friend who Cindy grew up calling Uncle Jack. No blood ties to Cindy's family, from what I understand. This is one of his homes. He's got places all over the world, from what I'm told."

"Good to have rich uncles, blood or not," Dace said, admiring the house. "What's his last name?"

"I never asked, she never said."

Dave pressed a button on the key fob and the rear door of the Escalade unlatched and slowly drew open. Dave then walked up the red brick path, jumping the hedge to get to the old boiling kettle. He felt around the perimeter under the rolled lip until he found the magnetic key holder. He pulled the small box free, slid open the back and a set of three modern keys fell into his palm. He replaced the empty key box. As Dave turned and retraced his steps to the SUV, he noticed Dace standing on the driveway away from the Escalade, his back to the house.

"What the hell are you doing?" Dave asked.

"Keeping down the dust," Dace said with a chuckle.

"You couldn't wait?"

"I didn't think Uncle Jack would mind."

Dave shook his head. He wasn't sure he liked everything about this new Dace who was emerging. It's not just that he was peeing just about anywhere he wanted, it was the lashing out, the lack of respect for anything, the drinking and smoking, the barely contained anger and resentment. Dave hoped a few days of chilling in the country, far from the pressures of school and family would help Dace to accept the recent events and move forward.

Dace zipped up and stretched, his hands massaged his buttocks.

"Didn't Uncle Jack have any houses closer to Connecticut?" he asked as he met Dave at the rear of the SUV and grabbed his duffle.

"I didn't ask, but I would assume he does." He nodded toward the house, no country mansion was more appropriate. "You got a problem with this?"

"Not at all," Dace said. "This will do nicely."

Dave slid his duffle out, then pushed a button on the key fob and the rear door silently closed, sealed itself and latched. They walked up the path, onto the porch and Dave slid a key into the lock. Before he turned the key, he reached into his pocket and pulled out the paper with the directions on it.

"Seven, three, nine, six," Dave said. "Remember that."

"Security code?" Dace asked as Dave turned the key.

Dave nodded.

The lock tumbled open and Dave pushed the latch to open the righthand door. A light went on in the darkened hallway. Dave stepped inside, walked over to the wall, flipped open the panel and entered the four digit code. The flashing red LED light turned solid yellow and the numbers on the digital display were replaced by the abbreviated words STD BY. The LED turned solid green.

Dace closed the door behind them and they each dropped their duffles in the hallway and took a look around. It was obvious the house had been totally restored, and that money had been no option. The doors were all highly polished cypress, the hardware right down to the flat-head slotted screws, restored solid brass of period design which had either been shined to a luster or plated. Walls and ceilings of original plaster had been penetrated for running electrical, and plumbing, and HVAC equipment and expertly patched.

The central hallway, which was roughly twelve feet wide and ran straight through to the rear doorway seventy or eighty feet distant, was lit by a single antique brass and glass-globed chandelier. The single, modern spotlight flush mounted and hidden in the ceiling which had illuminated when the door had opened, automatically extinguished the instant the security system had been disarmed and the chandelier automatically came on at medium intensity. From their perspective, with rooms off to each side of the hallway, they could tell the house was rectangular in shape, a little deeper front to back than wide. That was not readily apparent from outside in the front where the house appeared to be a simple square. An open stairwell hugged the right wall and the rooms on the upper floor were connected by railed balconies on each side. The floors on the first level were wide cypress planks, aged to a deep amber, highly polished with a modern finish, but retaining the tool marks indicative of early nineteenth century hand hewing and finishing techniques. The home had been ultra-modernized, yet it was readily apparent the original craftsmanship had been maintained.

There were four large rooms, the central hallway and a single bathroom, an obvious twentieth century addition cut from the house's pantry space, which comprised the first floor. Each of the main rooms encompassed roughly one quarter of the floor space, although the dining room was a bit larger and the pantry a bit smaller, even had the bathroom not been cut from it. The interior walls were roughly eighteen inches thick and passing through the doorways felt like moving through a very short tunnel.

The front room off to the right was what the original owners would have considered the parlor or sitting room. Dave and Dace stepped into the room as sunlight outside faded, and table lamps and a single floor lamp in the corner came to life automatically, slowly shifting the room from growing darkness to a pleasant medium light over two or three-seconds.

"All the ambience of a classical plantation home with twenty-first century gadgets," Dace said. "Sweet."

"Cindy said Uncle Jack feels it's great to preserve the past, but much more pleasant to enjoy it in modern comfort," Dave said, looking around the large room. "Geeze, clear this out a bit and you could have one hell of a party in here."

Dace turned and looked at his friend, smiled and arched an eyebrow.

"Don't even think about it."

Flat panels and carved pilasters of black marble with wide striations of pewter and touches of white fronted, and an ornately carved, shadowy-white, calcite alabaster mantle topped the original fireplace set mid-depth in the room along the interior wall. An assortment of impeccably restored early to mid nineteenth century furnishings decorated the room. A vintage baby grand piano occupied the back right corner ahead of a wall of bookshelves populated by all manner of leather-bound tomes and first editions, and plush oriental rugs anchored the three main sitting areas. Period art hung from long, gold, braided cords tethered to hooks driven into the wall just under the horse hair and plaster crown moulding.

The doublewide, multi-paned, nearly floor-to-ceiling windows rose twelve feet above the floor. In the parlor, there were two sets on the front of the house, and the three down the side; and they were not merely windows, but fully operational doors. The arched crown above each was fixed, but the windows could swing open to allow for passage to the porch or air movement. From the depth of the passage, the exterior walls were easily three-feet thick, and made of bricks kilned on the plantation, skinned with plaster. The windows were framed with drapes made of heavy tapestry material which contrasted with the delicate, semitransparent ecru shears which hung across each opening. Both drape and shear were purposely long and cascaded out onto the floor. Dace moved aside a shear of one of the windows and discovered even the glass panels were of the original construction period, the finish wavy and pocked with tiny bubbles and flaws. Split shutters mounted on the outside of the house protected the windows from the occasional passing hurricane.

Dace and Dave strode back into the hallway through the other door at the far end of the room, checked out the relatively small and nondescript bathroom across the way. It was workmanlike and contained only a water closet and sink set on a vanity. No lights went on automatically when they opened the door.

The kitchen was located in the back of the house on the same side as the parlor. It was a gourmet chef's delight with a commercial grade gas range, one oversize refrigerator and one oversize freezer. The center island was larger than some cars, and contained two large sinks on opposite corners. Everything was first-class, made of stainless and cast iron and marble and mahogany. The floor was slate tile arranged on the bias and sealed with a semi-gloss finish. A lone microwave sat on the countertop, out of place and almost hidden in a remote corner.

"At least we can make Hot Pockets and popcorn," Dave said, pointing to the microwave. "We won't starve."

Dace opened the refrigerator to find it totally stocked, including a couple cases of Coke and some Dixie beer. He pulled out a couple of bottles of the Dixie, twisted off the caps and slid one across the marble counter to Dave. He also removed a note and read it aloud.

*Welcome,*

*Thought this would be the best place to leave a note. Where else are a couple of college kids going to head first when they get someplace? :)*

*I've taken the liberty to stock the refrigerator, freezer and pantry (across the hall) with food and drink I thought you'd like. Please make yourselves at home and help yourselves to whatever you need. Enjoy and relax.*

*The staff has been let off for a couple of weeks, so you won't be bothered.*

*Should you need anything, please call me.*

*I'm in New Orleans. 504-555-1819.*

*Samantha 'Sam' Mimieux*

*Assistant to 'Uncle Jack'*

"Cool," Dave said. "You always thought that Cindy was nothing but a sweet set of knockers. I'd say she came through for us, buddy."

"Hey, I never said that," Dace said, pointing across the room with the bottle of Dixie. "*You* said that."

Dave tipped his bottle back at his friend.

"Well, so long as one of us said it." Dave took a draw from the Dixie, made a face, looked at the label on the bottle. "Rebel piss water, but smooth, ain't it?"

"Not bad," Dace said. "Let's check out the rest of the place."

Across the hall, they found the pantry and a small staff office. It was nothing special. High gloss, painted shelving and utilitarian finishes and furnishings.

Toward the front of the house on that side was the dining room, which, like the parlor across the hall, had two entry doors. Antique sideboards, china cabinets, dining table which comfortably fit the twenty-four matching chairs, all built of quarter-sawn oak, made up the room's major furnishings. Under the long table lay an immense, plush oriental rug which extended out to the sideboards, while above it hung the fly chaser fans which, when the house was a plantation served by slaves, a young boy would operate with a rope pull from an unobtrusive crouch outside on the porch. There were no electric lights in the dining room, only an assortment of antique silver and gold candelabra, each polished and impeccably clean. They all held new candles, but each one had been lit and extinguished.

"Uncle Jack must be a tad bit superstitious," Dace said. "Caroline's the same way. Drives my father nuts."

"What are you talking about?"

"The candles. See how each one has been lit, but not burned?"

"Yeah, so?"

"It's an old superstition that it's bad luck to have new, unlit candles put out on display."

"Who says?"

"Caroline, but she can't say where it came from. That's why it pisses off my dad."

"No wonder you're so screwed up, buddy."

Back out in the hallway near the front door, the boys picked up their duffles and climbed the stairs. At the top, they found a relatively small, but comfortable room, obviously decorated for a woman. On the door frame, they found a second note from Sam. That time Dave read it aloud.

*Well, you've made it upstairs. :) That's a good sign.*
*This is my room when I stay out here. The one toward the front of the house on this side (above the parlor) is Uncle Jack's suite.*
*Please feel free to use the guest suites across the hall. I'm certain you'll find them more than comfortable.*
*Thanks for understanding.*
*Sam*

*P.S. You'll find a fresh pineapple on each bed. It's a southern tradition for welcoming visitors to one's home. Should you find a second pineapple on your bed in the future, it's our genteel way of saying, 'We've enjoyed your company, but it's time for you to leave now.' :)*
*S*

They stuck their heads into Sam's room and then just out of curiosity walked down the hall to scope out Uncle Jack's digs, which took up about seventy percent of that side of the house when you included his oversize bathroom with whirlpool tub which looked like it could fit four people. In the bedroom, the four-post bed appeared to have been specially made and was larger than even a king size bed. Antique armoires and dressers, along with a seating area and a large desk centered on one of the side windows comprised the furnishings. A small walk-in closet, the only one they found in the house, fit into the area bounded by the L-shaped bathroom.

Across the hall, they walked through both guest suites, each equipped with its own full bath and walk-in shower. In layout and furnishing, they were each much like Uncle Jack's suite, but on a smaller scale and neither had a closet, walk-in or otherwise. On each of the beds was indeed a fresh pineapple.

Dace took the front bedroom, leaving Dave with the back one.

After they unloaded the rest of the stuff from the Escalade, they returned to their rooms and each stretched out on their bed.

Dace fell asleep.

Dave used his prepaid phone to call Cindy.

Tom's phone vibrated. He fished it from his jacket pocket, glanced a the caller ID and flipped the phone open.

"Yeah."

"We lost the tap and trap on the girl's cell phones this afternoon," Rudy said.

"What happened?" Tom asked.

"Our phone company contact reports they had an unannounced security sweep and had to dump us."

"Are they going to reinstate?"

"According to our man inside, they can't reinstate for at least seventy-two hours because the protocols the security team use mean the sweep can continue unannounced over three days. It's part of some bullshit FCC accountability reporting or something so it's really out of the company's hands, he said. Bureaucratic bullshit."

Tom thought about the situation. He was currently having a drink with Libby and The Senator in the office. Mary Rose was nursing a 7up with maraschino cherry juice, what Tom remembered as a Kiddie Cocktail when he was growing up. The Senator was observing Tom over his shoulder from his familiar perch of watching out the window, while Libby was seated on the couch opposite Tom, seemingly lost in thought as she absently fixed her gaze in the direction of Mary Rose.

"Well, perhaps we should use the time to keep tabs on the girl," Tom said. "You know, in-place surveillance."

"The Spagliano girl?" Rudy confirmed.

"Yeah, she appears to be the only person having intermittent contact with them," Tom said, rolling his Beefeater's Gin over the cubes in his cut crystal tumbler as he thought. "We've got this Uncle Jack connection, so they're most likely staying at a place she has a connection to. At this point, just watch. If we have to make contact, I'll authorize that later."

"Understood. You know, we have that cellular phone scanner on hand. If we get close enough to the girl, we could get lucky."

"Good idea.  When will you leave?"

"Well, I'd say within the hour, but first we'll confirm she's still at her place in Cambridge."

"Okay."  Tom paused.  "Anything yet on this Uncle Jack?"

"Well, the girl's parents and stepdad - the mother is alive and well in Minnesota and living with her husband who is not the father of the girl on the birth certificate, the bio-dad is nowhere to be found, probably dead - have no siblings we could uncover, so we're digging deeper, but so far not any relatives anywhere with the name Jack or any customary variations.  If it's a nickname, we may never find it."

Tom considered the timing of everything.

"Why don't you guys hang around here overnight?  Get some rest," Tom said.  "You can pick up on her trail tomorrow.  I'd rather have you rested and hitting it in the morning than spinning your wheels tonight.  Plus, I want to speak with The Senator about all this before we make the next move."

"That's fine with us, boss," Rudy said, silently grateful for the opportunity to grab a decent meal and a good night's sleep, rather than fast food and catching Zs in the car overnight.  "We'll plan to head out in the morning unless we hear different."

"I'll be in touch," Tom said and flipped his phone closed before Rudy could respond.

"What's happening now?" The Senator said.

Tom's eyes moved to Libby and Mary Rose, the question not requiring verbalization.  The Senator took a seat in the wingback chair, made a churning motion with his drink, the response not requiring verbalization either.  Even with the green light, Tom considered how to phrase the information.

"The boys will be headed to surveil the girl in Cambridge in the morning, barring any change of plans after you and I speak privately a little later," Tom said.

"Cambridge, that's where Dace goes to school," Mary Rose said absently.

"That's right, Mary Rose," Libby said.  "We're looking for Dace."

"Dace is with Dave," Mary Rose said.  "They got the hell out."

"Mary Rose, that's not the way a lady speaks," Libby said.

"Sorry, mama."  Mary Rose made a confused face.  "Maybe that's just the way boys talk; and daddy."

Libby stifled a laugh, her eyes moved to The Senator.

"Well, honey, boys, and daddy, shouldn't speak like that either."

"Mama, is it Friday yet?"

"No, honey, not yet."

## Chapter Eleven

Dace awoke shortly after midnight, his head spun and he was momentarily disoriented as to where he was. The house was dark, and quiet. He rolled his legs off the side of the hand-carved mahogany four-poster bed, sat there a few moments before padding to the bathroom. He returned to the bedroom, pushed aside the shear from one of the floor to ceiling windows, unlatched the lock and opened the doorway, then walked out onto the second floor veranda.

The evening was cool and calm, yet there was a hint of change in the air. Forecasters on the radio on the drive in that afternoon said they had been watching a storm system which had pounded the east Texas Gulf shore region earlier in the day and had since moved offshore. If computer projections held, they said, the storm system would intensify over the warm waters and then move ashore again by morning somewhere between New Orleans and Biloxi. If it moved east, they'd get little or no effect out in the country west of the city, if it came ashore further west and the storm revitalized, they could be in for quite a blow. For now, things in Vacherie were quiet. The sounds of frogs and lizards croaking away down by the river floated in the still air. Beyond nature's night sounds, Dace could hear the distant rumbling of diesel engines, most likely more tugs pushing barges on the hardworking Mississippi. The moon was full and bright in the sky, casting night shadows of the house and trees over the lawn.

As he walked to the northwest corner of the veranda, outside Uncle Jacks' suite, he looked up to see the moon and noticed it had a large reflective halo around it. He remembered from high school science class that ice crystals in ultra-thin cirrus clouds above twenty-thousand feet created the optical illusion. The high clouds were often the harbinger of incoming rain or snow, he recalled, and like the old 'sailors take warning' adage, a ring around the moon meant rain was coming soon.

Dace walked back inside, re-latched the door and again sat on the bed. He located his tennis shoes, slid his socked feet inside and tied them up. From his duffel, he removed his hoodie sweatshirt, put it on and zipped it up. He opened the door, went out into the hallway, paused at Dave's door, heard him snoring away, then went downstairs. He turned toward the pantry and found the bottle of Tequila they had bought at Wal-Mart. It was some cheap off-brand, clear, and made of pure Mexican blue agave, according to the label. Dace twisted off the silver cap, pulled the plastic aerator from the bottle and took a healthy swig.

Replacing the cap as he crossed the hall to the kitchen, he opened the refrigerator and peered inside. It had been stocked with just about anything he could desire. He had a craving for a sandwich, but not the motivation to go through the effort to craft one. He reached into the meat compartment and grabbed a small deli bag marked 'Roast Beef' and another labeled 'Baby Swiss', stuffed them into the pockets of his hoodie and then searched for a breadbox. Opening a likely candidate, he located and snatched out a full loaf of French bread, squeezed it, and satisfied, carried it and the bottle of Tequila back into the hallway.

Outside, standing on the front porch a few moments later, Dace took another swig, then walked down the stairs, across the pavers and along the driveway to the main road, and after crossing that, climbed the levee rising along the Mississippi to find a seat on which to sit and eat and drink and watch the river traffic go by. The night air was chilly for the south, he thought, but the alcohol quickly warmed his insides. He flipped up the hood over his head and laid the French loaf and tequila alongside on the concrete slab. In the pocket of the sweatshirt, under the packages of meat and cheese, he found the pack of cigarettes and lighter that had somehow stayed put during his altercation with the two security guards in Birmingham. He smiled at the memory.

"Dumb motherfuckers," he said to the night in a low voice.

He shook the pack and a couple of filter ends extended. He pulled one from the pack with his lips, tucked the pack back into his pocket and sparked the cheap plastic lighter. He lit the cigarette and took a shallow inhale. He had learned a couple of days ago that deeply inhaling would just bring on a coughing fit, the sure indicator of a rookie smoker which was embarrassing, even if the only witnesses that time would be the frogs and crickets.

When he was finished with the cigarette, he tossed the butt down toward the river. It fell far short, in long grass and something moved. He momentarily wondered about snakes. He hated snakes, had a fear of them, in fact. He banished the thought with a long draw from the tequila. Next, he slid his thumb into the French loaf and slid it along, zipping open the crispy crust and soft inside. Placing the bread across his legs, Dace pulled the roast beef and baby Swiss packets from his sweatshirt pocket. He emptied each deli bag onto the bread and tossed the empty packages toward the river. Picking up the sandwich, he squeezed it closed and hoisted it to his mouth for a healthy bite. The bread yielded easily in its freshness, the meat and cheese, earthy, nutty, and slightly spicy at the same time. It was the perfect combination for his midnight craving. He washed down the bites with the nectar from the blue agave plant, his mind slowly emptying as his stomach filled. His face flushed with the combination of food and alcohol and he pulled the hood down and unzipped the sweatshirt to let out the generated body heat.

The moon had moved a bit further off to the west, and the barges had moved east around the next bend in the river. The night was back to holding only the sounds of nature's creatures. Dace watched over the calm surface of the river as it moved toward the Gulf of Mexico. It was unstoppable, a force which moved where it wanted, and consumed everything in its path. He considered the millennia this river had flowed from the headwaters in northern Minnesota, carving its way to the Gulf. He knew much of southern Louisiana had been created by the Mississippi, with uncountable millions of tons of dirt and silt washed to this place from nearly every state east of the Rocky Mountains and west of the Appalachians.

Dace had grown up along the Thames River in Connecticut. He had summered in watery places such as Hyannis Port, Martha's Vineyard, the beaches of the Hamptons on Long Island, and had made extended weekend trips to Kennebunkport in Maine when it had been the location of the weekend White House. Lakes generally bored him and the vastness of oceans overwhelmed his senses, but large, working rivers such as the Thames, the Ohio, and the Mississippi had always tugged at his soul. He could stand and watch them flowing for hours on end. His father had termed it useless leisure, and when Dace had tried to explain how the power and perpetuity provided him with a foundation of reference as to his place in the universe, his father had further chastised him for engaging in delusional, self-indulgent egoism. Dace had been twelve at the time, and really had had no idea what his father was talking about. It was the last time he had spoken of that particular fascination to The Senator.

He bit off more of the sandwich, wished momentarily for some deli mustard, then wet the mouthful with a slug of Tequila instead. A fish jumped, then another, out in the center of the river. The first fish had been larger, or at least the splash it made had been. The water reflected moonlight, which, in itself was reflected sunlight, and Dace watched as the ripples moved outward from the center of each splash and approached the other set, and suddenly he was filled with an inexplicable, white hot rage.

"Like that, you old, stupid, old son-of-a-bitch," he yelled into the night as he jumped up onto the concrete block and pointed toward the series of intersecting rings, their creators already long gone under the black, night waters. "It's *all* like that. Everything in God's universe is exactly like that. Yet you'll never see it, will you?"

Dace looked down to discover his hands were balled into tight fists and the remains of the sandwich lay below in the gravel. He stood there motionless for several moments, then bent down and reached for the bottle, drained a burning swallow, then a second, and finally a third before dropping his hand back to his side, the bottleneck gripped tightly. He was feeling a bit drunk already. Raising the bottle into the moonlight, he saw he had finished half its contents. He had the urge to laugh out loud, but instead his lips formed a tight smile which was masked by the rest of his unfathomable face as an idea formed.

He stepped off the concrete slab, sat again, reached down for the sandwich, inspected it in the moonlight and brushed off a few bits of sand and gravel.

"Forty-five second rule?" he asked the universe, then took a big bite, washed it down with more nectar of the desert flower. For a brief moment, he wondered who first would have thought of fermenting that unlikely looking plant, but then opined that if he were living in a time when every day was a struggle just to stay alive and everyone around you smelled like sweat and crap, he'd too probably try smoking or drinking everything he couldn't eat. Perhaps it was just that simple through the annals of time, he thought. No inspirations of genius, just a desire to escape the tedium and stench. Whatever, as to its origins, he thought, tequila was good stuff now. He finished all but the end of the sandwich and tossed the scraps toward the river. Something along the shore moved on it quickly, causing a momentary eruption of water and mud. He strained to see the phantom creature, but then something caught his attention off to the east.

He looked in the direction from which came the obnoxious rap of unmufflered exhaust, a pulsing engine and the sound of tires spinning and sliding on gravel. As he peered along the top of the levee, Dace spotted erratic headlights trailing a cloud of dust approaching in the distance. He sat there, drained the remains of the bottle, waited.

The lights moved around the bend in the levee, then pointed straight for him. He stood to watch the old, beat up Ford pickup close the distance, gravel flying, a cacophony of light and noise which he felt was an affront to the peace of the night. The lights held him for an instant, then released him into darkness and a dust cloud as the truck roared past. About a hundred feet down the levee, the truck slid to a stop, the brake lights turning the cloud of dust bright red. It sat there for a moment or two, then the reverse lights came on and as quickly as it has passed him, the truck returned. When it stopped in the middle of the gravel road across the concrete pads from where he sat, Dace could make out two men in the truck, which sat idling, spewing noise and bluish smoke from rusty black header pipes mounted under the running boards.

The truck was painted flat black and a confederate battle flag hung in the back window of the cab, just behind a gun rack which Dace saw held two long guns, what appeared to be a rifle and a double-barrel shotgun.

The passenger leered out the window. He was perhaps two or three years older than Dace and wore a week's growth on his face. Greasy black hair stuck out from under a dirty, green John Deere baseball cap. Before John Deere spoke, he pushed his arm further out the window, then his head followed.

"Hey, boy," he said in deep country drawl. "What in the hell are you doing out here on *our* levee?"

Dace stood up, holding the empty tequila bottle by the neck, and stared back at the men without answering the question, but slowly rotated his hand on the bottleneck from drinking grip to striking grip.

"You deaf, boy?" John Deere said, not noticing the shift of the grip, or the gleam creeping into the lone stranger's eyes. "Or just stupid?"

Dace watched warily as the man pulled himself back into the cab and said something to the driver. He saw the motions of something being passed from the driver to the passenger in the darkness. A moment later, the passenger door opened and the man slid out and stepped onto the gravel road. In his right hand, he held a long-barrel revolver which he tucked into his belt as his eyes took measure of Dace.

John Deere was shorter than himself by about six inches, and lighter by about thirty pounds, Dace estimated. His jeans were tucked into worn, black, work boots, his yellowed T-shirt spotted and grimy under the unbuttoned, faded, denim work shirt. He stood facing Dace across about twenty feet of concrete. Then the driver got out on the other side and walked around the truck to stand near its rear bumper. He was outfitted almost identically to John Deere, but sported a black, Harley-Davidson T-shirt and black, leather jacket and an Evinrude Outboard cap. He matched up with Dace physically, maybe even outweighed him by ten or twenty pounds, which would put Dace at a disadvantage, especially as drunk as he now was. Evinrude smiled when he saw the bottle in Dace's hand.

"Whatcha got there, boy?" Evinrude said with a grin which was two teeth short of a smile. "How 'bout sharin' a slug or two?" He moved along the bed of the truck to stand side-by-side with John Deere.

John Deere took a cautious first step toward Dace.

"Sorry, fellas," he said as he tipped the bottle bottom side up. "All gone."

"Well, ain't that a shame?"

"How so, Goober?" Dace said.

The pair shared a look, a smirk, and a subtle nod.

"So, now what, gator bait? You two retards have the balls to make trouble?" Dace challenged.

Their smirks fell and anger swept their faces. They moved as a unit. Obviously, they had done that kind of thing before. John Deere came on faster than his larger friend. As he crossed the concrete blocks, Dace slapped the empty bottle against his former seat and the bottom shattered, leaving a wickedly rough edged weapon in his hand. JD had committed his lunge, but was able to sidestep the worst of the thrust of the bottle's razor sharp, spiked edges as Dace lashed out. One of the spikes managed to catch the man's cheek and he yelped and rolled away, sliding down the slippery grass on the river side of the levee.

Dace had half an instant to enjoy the vision of the hick sliding down into the blackness before he felt Evinrude's fist catch him in the kidney. Stunned, but adequately medicated by a whole bottle of Mexico's finest, Dace barely reacted to a blow which normally would have doubled him over, but did cause him to drop the bottle into the grass. As Dace squared with the man, Evinrude telegraphed a roundhouse to Dace's head which he easily sidestepped and then allowed his opponent's momentum to carry him into a gut punch.

"Get hold of that sumbitch," JD called from down the levee. "I aim to gut him like a goddamn catfish."

Dace caught a glimpse of the smaller man clawing his way back up the slick grass embankment and momentarily considered knocking the bigger man down with his buddy and then embrace the better part of valor and make for home, but something deep inside him was white hot with anger and retreat was not going to be an option.

So, with a flurry of punches, well-placed knees, and doubled fists to the back of the neck while Evinrude doubled over and gasped for breath, Dace put the bigger man down. For good measure, he kicked Evinrude in the side of the head, but got no reaction, not even a reflexive grunt. He stood over the man, waited for any sign of aggressive movement, but none came.

Then JD was behind him, the barrel of the revolver sticking hard against Daces ribs. Dace raised his hands out to each side and slowly turned around. JD backed off a step, but held the pistol level with Dace's midsection. The bore looked relatively small, perhaps a .22, certainly not a large-caliber weapon. Regardless of the smaller bore, however, Dace instinctively understood that trying to outmaneuver any kind of bullet would be both pointless and stupid. So he stood there, facing JD. A trickle of a smile slowly grew into a wide grin which lit up Dace's face and finally flowed into a full belly laugh.

"What the fuck are you laughing at, shit head?" John Deere said.

"I'm laughing because you're such a stupid, inbred asshole, that's what," Dace said.

JD appeared confused at Dace's display of bravado while looking down the barrel of gun. Blood streamed from the slash in his cheek. Sweat from the effort of crawling back up the levee rolled from under his dirty, green cap. His hand began shaking slightly.

"Did you really bring an unloaded gun to this fight?" Dace asked and then raised his face to the moon and laughed harder. "You hillbilly fucks sure do make me laugh."

JD shifted his feet. When he looked down, Dace knew the man wasn't sure if this was a bluff or not. Then JD's face hardened as an idea formed and he drew the hammer back.

"Why don't we just see who the stupid motherfucker is?" he said. "We'll know when your guts are all over my levee." He extended his arm, licked his lips and aimed directly at Dace's belly. Dace saw the man's finger begin to tense.

Then Evinrude let out a moan, JD paused, and Dace moved. Dace spun around, his foot flying into JD's arm with such force the man pulled the trigger and then dropped the gun. The explosion of the hammer igniting the powder was less than what Dace had expected, but the blue and yellow flame which shot out of the barrel of the gun aimed in his general direction was a sight Dace didn't wish to be repeated in his lifetime. The bullet ricocheted off the side of the truck and spun off into the night and only Dace had tracked the gun as it slid under the cab. Dace and JD stood facing each other, waiting, each armed now only with his fists and wits.

Dace moved first, catching JD with a strong kick to the place no man wants someone else's foot placed in anger. JD's world transformed into a whirl of blackness and stars and indescribable pain as Dace's shoe hit home. He doubled over, fell to his knees, gripped his groin in pain. Dace momentarily considered leaving him like that, but then wondered what may happen should either of the men see where he went after he left *their* levee. The last thing he wanted was to see Uncle Jack's house go up in flames one night. He kicked JD in the jaw and the man tumbled over and fell silent. Just to be certain, Dace walked over to Evinrude lifted his head by a grip of hat and hair. The man was out cold, so Dace just dropped his face onto the concrete. He was about to leave when he turned and kicked the man in the kidney, just as a payback.

Before heading for home, Dace located the tequila bottle and tossed it into the river. Then he dropped down on one knee next to the idling truck and retrieved the revolver from under the cab; he stood and looked inside the truck, and just for grins, hooked the two empty loops of a six-pack and removed the four remaining cans of Dixie from the seat. On a final whim, he ripped down the small confederate battle flag and stuffed it into his back pocket.

"Sleep tight, gentlemen," he said over his shoulder as he started to make his way off the side of the levee toward Uncle Jack's place.

The old Ford pickup idled away in the night.

"What the hell is this?" Dave said, looking at the spread of items on the table in Dace's room.

Dace rolled in his bed. He was still dressed, shoes and all. His head pounded. He opened his eyes a crack then resealed them. Considering the level of light he had detected that instant, it was sometime between mid morning and late afternoon. Dace could smell bacon. His foggy mind thought of breakfast.

"What time is it," he said through a mouth lined in cheap cotton.

"Dace, what the hell is all this?" Dave said again. "Where did it all come from?"

"What time is it; and what are you talking about?"

"It's about nine," Dave said.

"Morning or night?"

"Morning." Dave moved a couple of steps closer to the bed. "What the hell, man? Are you drunk?"

Dace moved to sit up. He opened his eyes again, squinted around the room. His head swam; he moved his mouth to wet it.

"Yes, I would say I still am. Do I smell bacon?"

"When did you get drunk?"

"Last night, just after midnight. You were sleeping like a baby with apnea so I didn't invite you." Dace slid to the side of the bed and put his feet onto the floor and rested his elbows on his knees. He rubbed his eyes with the heels of his palms.

"Okay, but where did you get this stuff?" Dave motioned to the coffee table again.

Dace looked over, squinted, then smiled.

"Oh, *that* stuff," Dace said, leaving Dave hanging as he stood up, nearly fell backward onto the bed as his equilibrium fought the move, recovered and shuffled into the bathroom. He ran some water in a glass, opened a bottle of Advil, dumped out most of it onto the countertop and selected six or seven pills. He swallowed them in one handful and drank down the glass of water and returned to the bedroom. He stood in the middle of the room, weaving a bit as he gathered his foggy senses and worked out a few kinks in his body. The bacon was calling him. "I took that stuff off a couple of guys on the levee."

"Two cans of Dixie beer?"

"There were four. I drank two on the walk home."

"A Confederate flag?"

"Yeah, they had it hanging in the back window of their truck. It struck me as a bit racist, even for down here. Don't you think?"

"A six-shooter?"

"Well, technically now it's a five-shooter."

"Huh?"

"The smaller guy shot one of the bullets at me. That should leave five, right? A five-shooter." He managed a snort of a laugh. "Dammit, Dave, is someone cooking bacon?"

"Someone shot at you?

Dace moved toward the door, drawn by the thought of bacon.

"Dace, what the hell went on last night?"

"I'll be glad to tell you everything I remember, buddy." He moved out into the hallway and turned back. "First, though, I just gotta have some of that bacon."

Dave followed him downstairs.

Dace found the plate with the bacon stacked between sheets of paper towels. From the size of the stack, Dace estimated his ever-thoughtful friend had fried up several pounds of thick-cut, honey-smoked, Louisiana bacon. That's the way he remembered it had been marked on the butcher's paper package he'd seen in the refrigerator last night. It was real butcher shop bacon, not that processed, prepackaged crap from that outfit that sings songs about bologna; which was a product Dace felt was an abomination, even to the word 'lunchmeat'. Dace hopped up on the countertop and sat with the plate on his lap. Dave poured him a glass of orange juice from a carton in the refrigerator. He'd already eaten breakfast.

"Can you spike that up a bit?" Dace said after a sip of OJ.

Dave eyed his formerly teetotaling friend.

"I think you best drink it without spiking it up there, champ" he said. "How about we do it that way today?"

"All right, mother," Dace said. "Hey, would you mind frying me up some eggs? Maybe some toast?" Dace folded another strip of bacon and shoved it into his mouth. As he chewed he added a bit of comedic relief: "Kicking redneck ass is hungry work, old son."

Dave watched his friend smile as a memory obviously rambled around in his foggy brain, then shove more bacon into his mouth. Dave retrieved a carton of eggs and some sliced bread from the refrigerator, brought them to the griddle plate on the stove. He cracked the first egg on the already hot surface.

"Four, over easy, if you don't mind, my man; and dry whole grain toast, if you have it."

Dave finished cracking the eggs on the griddle, tossed two pieces of white bread down next to them.

"We don't have it."

Dace watched Dave move around the griddle.

"How did you learn to cook like that?" Dace asked.

"You remember those couple of summers in high school I'd work at Dean's Bar and Grill?"

Dace nodded.

"Well, it wasn't all just washing dishes and taking out the trash. Dean let me work the grill a few times. I kinda took to it. If I weren't going to be an NFL star, and then an international business mogul, I'd definitely consider fry cook as a career choice."

"Don't forget brain surgeon, astronaut, or double-naught spy, Jethro," Dace teased through a mouth full of bacon.

"You should be a comedian, buddy," Dave said, his eyes on the grill.

Dave expertly maneuvered the eggs and toast and when they were just perfectly done, he flopped them onto a plate and handed it to Dace with a fork. Dace dug in, dunked a corner of the toast into the yolk, then forked a mouthful of egg followed by another slice of bacon into his mouth and washed it all down with a healthy chug of OJ.

"Best I ever had, man," Dace said.

Dave half-smiled at the compliment.

"Okay, now tell me what went on here when I was sleeping."

Dace related the story beginning with him waking up around midnight and ending with his walk back from the levee, light one bottle of tequila, but heavy four cans of Dixie, one Confederate battle flag, and one five- or six-shooter, depending on how one looked at those things. As Dace continued to eat after relating the story, Dave wandered out onto the front lawn to see if he could spot the truck. It was gone. Apparently the pair had awoken at some point and high tailed it off the levee.

When Dave returned to the kitchen, he grabbed a Coke from the refrigerator and popped the top, took a long draw from the can. Dace eyed him in silence as he paced the kitchen. Dave thought about the events of the last days and how things were escalating, regardless of the couple of tiptoeing talks they had had on the way down. He wondered if this was the best time to broach the topic again but then decided to just ask his lifelong pal flat out about the changes he was witnessing.

"What's happening to you?" Dave asked. "This isn't you, Dace. You're becoming someone I don't even know anymore, man. One moment you're the old Dace, and the next, God only knows what."

Dace sopped up the last of the egg yolk with a piece of bacon, then stuffed it into his mouth. He smiled at his friend as he chewed, then set his empty plate off to the side on the countertop. He jumped down, stretched, issued a belch.

"I really don't know, Dave." He put his hand on Dave's shoulder. "I think I'm liking it, though. The new Dace Lamoureux. Large and in charge." He patted twice, looked Dave in the eye, turned to walk out. At the doorway, he turned. "Thanks for the breakfast."

Then he was gone.

Rudy tapped the speed dial for Tom on his phone as Travis drove the Lincoln northeast on I-95 toward Boston. The trip was a little over one-hundred miles, and at the rate Travis was moving, they'd make the Bean Town suburbs by late morning, unless the snow which the weather reporter had forecast began to fall as they moved up the coast and slowed down the relatively light morning flow.

"Yeah," came the answer to the ringing down the line.

"We're on the way," Rudy said. "Should be up there by eleven or so. We've got the girl's home address. She rents a room in a house rather than one of the student housing buildings. The place is located just a few blocks off-campus on Clinton Street."

"Clinton Street?" Tom repeated with a chuckle. "I wonder if that's a good omen or a bad omen."

"Well, it's got its pros and cons, I guess," Rudy said. "Narrow streets, too many local cars and we may stick out like sore thumbs in the neighborhood, although with a huge student population in the area, people won't pay much attention."

"No, I meant the street's *name*," Tom explained.

"Oh, I don't know. Maybe it's a great place to get blow jobs from young Jewish girls." A pause. "We'll let you know."

Laughter on both ends of the line.

"Did you get the satellite shots of the area from our friend at the Defense Department?"

"Yeah, those came in via email, although those DoD files were huge and took forever," Rudy said. "We printed out a couple sheets of the area, but we'll reconnoiter and set up a watch schedule once we get up there. Our plan is to obtain another vehicle to swap back and forth should this run into more than just a day or two."

"Okay." A pause. "Have you given more thought to that other thing we talked about?"

"You mean if cooperation is less than optimal?"

"Mm-hmm," Tom grunted.

"We'll make it happen," Rudy said. "Whatever it takes."

"Just so long as it can't come back in this direction," Tom said. "The Senator finally understands the possible minefields as this thing drags on, but given what you turned up in Birmingham, an escalation by the boy created an exigency requiring the quickest possible resolution."

"I think we're on the same page, sir" Rudy said. A pause. "We also would again strongly recommend you obtain additional assistance on the other end. We know the general area they're in, but perhaps some local eyes on the ground down there would be beneficial."

"You mean searching the entirety of southern Louisiana? Just because that's where they happened to buy a phone? They could be wandering around a thousand miles away from there by now."

"With all due respect, sir, we don't think so. They didn't pick up a phone anywhere along the way. The only contact they have made that we know about is to this Spagliano girl. She appears to be a central loci. They drove almost in a straight line between the church and that Wal-Mart in Metairie, Louisiana, so to us that indicates a known destination, not just some wandering about."

"Nobody has been able to turn any connections between the Spagliano woman and Louisiana, though." Tom stood up and walked to the window. His room looked out the back of the house and he spotted Libby and Mary Rose walking the pathway in the yard. "No, I think we'll go with things as they stand now. We'll be ready to play it on the fly, though, should anything change, okay? I'll put some feelers out for people we could use down there, but I'm keeping the work in-house for now."

"You're the boss," Rudy said in the resigned tone of someone used to taking orders. "If there's nothing else, we'll sign off now and call you once we're established."

"I'll brief The Senator."

Tom closed his phone and his attention returned to the two women moving along cleared paver bricks. He saw the closeness between them again, and momentarily wondered what would become of Mary Rose when Libby and The Senator were gone. The girl had outlived nearly every estimate the doctors had given when she was born. Loving care and medical advances had staved off many of the genetically related threats to the girl's health over the first twenty-four years of her life, and the outlook with new research made the horizon now look boundless. He knew that Mary Rose would never want for either care or money for her needs, but he also understood the health benefits of a mother's love for someone so dependent; and a father's for that matter.

Medically, the advances had been nothing short of miraculous since the turn of the twentieth century when the life expectancy for Down's Syndrome children was less than nine years. That had risen to over eighteen years by the early 1960s, and by the late 1990s nearly half could expect to become sexagenarians, although almost certainly Mary Rose would begin to suffer from dementia and Alzheimer's symptoms by the time she turned forty.

Tom knew well the horror of that malady. His mother had been diagnosed with Alzheimer's Disease when she had turned seventy, although she had begun to exhibit signs several years earlier. Once diagnosed, however, she had deteriorated rapidly and the family had been forced to place her into a professional care facility within a year. Regardless of how his brothers and sisters had tried, the dementia often manifested itself in panicked dissociation and violent outbursts and there was no way they had been physically, mentally, or emotionally equipped to deal with that. The guilt of putting their mother in a care facility had been tremendous, salved only marginally by the repeated assurances from the professionals that it was the right thing to be done for their mother. Once institutionalized, albeit in one of the best facilities in the country, their mother further deteriorated and passed away nine months later.

He had no desire to watch as the same thing happened to this treasure of a young woman. He continued to watch through his window as Libby took a seat on one of the carved granite benches. In the summertime, the gardens surrounding that particular bench would be drowning in flowers. First the tulips would come in spring, then California Bluebells, followed in turn by poppies, daisies in white and yellow, the Black-eyed Susans, Queen Anne's Lace, snapdragons and toadflax, and by midseason, the nasturtiums would take over, yielding eventually to the burnt orange and muted yellow of the fall daisies. The planting of perennials, which covered almost a quarter acre of the grounds, had been an anniversary gift from The Senator. Libby and Mary Rose would spend hours out there amongst the ever-changing, fragrant display. Libby would direct her daughter in picking fresh bouquets for the house. It was always a joy to watch as Mary Rose moved carefully through the flowers, gently cutting each one.

The garden was snow covered again. Spring seemed a long time away that morning, and every day that Dace was gone, Tom had watched the stress grow on Libby's face and the pain swell in her eyes. At times, looking into Libby's eyes was more than he could bear; and not just since Dace had disappeared. He now watched as mother and daughter talked, their heads together as they both sat on the bench. Suddenly, Mary Rose jumped up, became quite animated and a huge grin took over her face as she ran up the pathway toward the house. Tom could hear the door slam and the rapid heaviness of a grown woman's footfalls running with the energy of a young child as she cleared the kitchen, great room, and stairs to the third floor. Tom heard her door open and fly against the wall followed by noisy searching, then another slammed door, and the reverse of the footfalls, the bang of the back door and then he watched Mary Rose run back to Libby who hadn't moved from her seat.

Tom observed the pair as Mary Rose stood in front of the bench and handed Libby an envelope. Another of the girl's handmade cards, he thought. He began to turn away from the window when the neatness of the folded paper Libby withdrew from its cover drew back his interest.

Libby unfolded the pages, and began to read. From his perch, Tom knew the letter had come not from Mary Rose, but rather from her baby brother, Dace.

Friday had finally come for Mary Rose. Her mother had told her that it was indeed Friday, reminding her that they would be going to get their nails done later that morning and Fridays were the day for getting their nails done. Mary Rose had leapt from the bench and ran into the house hollering back over her shoulder: 'I'll be right back, mama. Don't move.' Libby had waited patiently for Mary Rose to return, hoping that some unrelated distraction inside the house wouldn't divert the girl's attention.

Nothing had, and as quickly as she had disappeared with the sound of a slamming door, she had reappeared announced by a second slam. When Mary Rose handed her mother the envelope, Libby saw Dace's handwriting on the front. Her heart pounded as she withdrew the letter, unfolded it and her eyes scanned the pages. It was Dace's handwriting, and as she began to read, she could hear his voice in her heart.

*My Dearest Mother:*

*There is nothing I can write which will allow you to forgive me for leaving as I did, and if you're reading this now, it means I have gotten away and you are frantic, but know I am sorry. Similarly, there is nothing which I could have said or done to persuade father to give me leave to go and struggle through everything which has happened over these past days, compounded by everything which has been expected of me my entire life. I had to get away for a while, that much I knew. As you now see, I was forced by circumstance to make my plans and leave you in such a dreadfully inconsiderate manner.*

*I wasn't certain where I would go, or for that matter, how long I would need to be away. That's why I instructed Mary Rose to hold this letter until Friday, should an early return negate the need to tell you these things in such an impersonal, written form. I can imagine she has been asking if each new day was Friday.*

*For twenty-one years I have acceded to my father's wishes. I have excelled in every endeavor to curry his favor. I have accepted his advice as if the words were written in the Gospel, for indeed, in this family, I understand there may be little difference between the two. I have subrogated every one of my wants and desires for the good of the family, for the honor of a legacy to which I am told I owe my first devotion.*

*I have never once tarnished the good name of Lamoureux. I have remained free of the lures of drugs and alcohol. I have even avoided the most engulfing of potential scandalous behavior by remaining chaste, even in my deep love for Sarah. To what end now that mutual sacrifice in pursuit of a wholesome and honest relationship?*

*What of Sarah in our memories, mother? I realize I pose a question you cannot possibly answer and one my father will refuse to even consider; but, what of the memory of this young woman who gave me nothing but joy and love? Isn't love allowed in our glorious family? Is that emotion reserved only for those who pass all imposed hurdles of status and breeding? Isn't the love of a good woman something you and father have always told me was necessary for a man to be truly a man? I imagine I just never understood that it had to be the 'right' woman. Perhaps I was blinded by love or the way the family seemingly embraced her before I became a man. What does it matter now? Sarah is dead. Cold, and in the ground by the time you read this. Never shall she again feel the sun upon her beautiful face, or the touch of my hand to hers. She did not deserve her fate any more than I am wanting mine at the moment. I miss her eternally, and I am utterly devastated by the loss of her.*

*Father tells me in his unassailable manner I shall love again. Tom parrots him. Father attempts to assuage my guilt for not having been with her or having personally taken on the task of driving a friend home with clichés such as 'accidents happen' and 'Fate took a hand'. Fate took a hand? What exactly can he mean by that? Does my father possess such a cold and distant soul that he truly believes those hollow words? Has he been so jaded by decades of empty speechifying and pandering, all while refusing to acknowledging things as they truly are? I hope to be able to answer these questions, and others while I am away from you all.*

*Please understand there is no other way for me to come to an accounting of the intrinsic value of everything I have thus far sacrificed in my life, or to budget for what is now expected of me since I have become a man by the mere action of turning a calendar page. For what price will I be willing to sell my soul to this family legacy? Thirty pieces of silver? That was enough to buy Judas so he would trade his soul to worldly masters and forsake his God. What will my price be? Will I be willing and able to pay it? Will I even be willing to accept the current deal, or find the strength to fashion the terms of a new bargain? Time will tell.*

*Dave has arranged everything. His friendship to me knows no bounds; but mine to him? That is something I thought I had known to be equally so, but under this new light father has shone upon life's most precious and personal of relationships during his talks to me, the idea of friendship and loyalty are now other things I have to investigate as a Lamoureux man. Father has spoken so many things to me over the last days. He has unveiled secrets, some of which I am certain even you are unaware; and he has established and related the rules for the rest of my life. MY life, mother!*

*Growing up as the only son in a family whose tapestry is woven from the gilded threads of history, honor, and duty of its male members, I had understood much of what would be expected of me when I became a man. But, do I owe this family the entirety of my being? My heart, my soul? How can I know the limits of what I must give, and am I willing to, and strong enough to simply hand it all over? How can I simply give over something so precious and necessary as life itself to the cold, ethereal, and consumptive, preternatural flesh of something deserving to be called a Legacy?*

*As I have said, Dave has arranged everything. I don't even know where we will go or what we will do when we eventually get there. He has put things together apart from his own family and will not share with them or anyone else the details of this little excursion. But, even as he prepares, he does not fully know the depth and breadth of my questions for which I need time and distance to discern the answers. Like the friend he is, I asked and he didn't question. Someday, I hope to be able to repay his loyalty, but as I write these words here I wonder if I am already too much my father's son seeing a favor done by a friend as being in need of return payment. Something tells me believing a quid pro quo for the kindness offered by a friend is warped thinking in the majority of the real world. Do you think it is, Mother?*

*I shall return to your loving embrace when I have discovered the answers to my questions and fashioned my bargain to be forged with father. Then, I shall either commit to my father's view of my life, or be strong enough to explain to him the course of the journey I have chosen for that very same life. I have only one life to give, or claim, and ultimately, I will do what I wish, not what I must. That much I assure you. It will be as I wish it to be in the end.*

*I am my father's son, but I am yours as well. You have taught me well, my dear Mother. You guided my first steps, and the lessons your heart instilled into mine I pray shall guide me now. My soul is engulfed by the dark shadows of pain and loss and uncertainty and I am off to search for the light of fulfillment and commitment. I hope that light exists for me, and that the current absence of it does not already damn me.*

*I may stumble in the darkness, but I am forever your loving son,*
*Dace*

# Chapter Twelve

"What do you think about stopping in to see the aunt?" Rudy said. He gestured out the windshield at the notice for the upcoming exit to West Greenwich in two miles. "With this shit, we're not going to make Boston until early afternoon. We may as well do something productive while the county crews clean up the roads."

Snowflakes had begun to fall from a low overcast far earlier than had been predicted, about twenty miles out of New London. There was no wind associated with the weak low pressure system, but it was loaded with moisture and cold air; the darkness of the clouds alone told the tale of extensive vertical development portending heavy snowfall. What fell from those clouds were large, often chaotic agglomerations of a half dozen snowflakes tossed together in repeated falls and updrafts before their amassed weight made them too heavy for yet another upward excursion and they found their way to the ground. The roadway had become slick and traffic volume had increased, a combination which caused Travis to slow the Lincoln accordingly. The wipers chased away the mega-flakes and generous use of the washer knocked down most of the spray on the windshield.

"Tell her what this time?" Travis asked. "Even a skanked out old alchy like that is going to remember us from a few days ago. Besides, Dave hasn't contacted his aunt since they left. We still have the tap and trap on her landline, you know, and that's been nothing but her bullshit."

"Just a thought," Rudy said. "I'm not married to it."

"Let me think about it for a minute or two."

"Before this shit started falling, a minute or two would have been about all you would have had to think about it." Rudy pointed to the speedometer which was now down to thirty miles an hour. "Now, take five."

"Hey, Ash, you wanna go watch a parade tonight?" Ronnie asked as she bounded into the room, slammed the door and belly flopped onto Ashley's bed. "Bobby will take us."

"Mardi Gras parade?" Ashley asked with a touch of irritation as she bent to pick up some of her clothes she had been packing which jumped off the bed when Ronnie had jumped onto it. "You want to drive in to New Orleans tonight? Without permission? Risk getting caught and having our whole weekend ruined? We'll be down there tomorrow through the morning of Ash Wednesday and there are plenty of parades every day."

"Yeah, but Bobby's boss has him doing an emergency delivery to a bar in Baton Rouge. He wants me to ride along."

"Baton Rouge? That's like an hour drive in the wrong direction."

"Yeah, but I already asked Sister Regina about it and she gave her blessing. So long as we're back by ten, we're golden."

Ashley sighed loudly, looked into Ronnie's big, brown, puppy dog eyes as she tossed the recovered and refolded clothes into the open suitcase on the floor and flopped down next to her begging friend. She knew there was usually no derailing Ronnie once she set her mind on something. Ashley rolled her eyes in Ronnie's direction and smiled.

"Okay," she said and then looked seriously at her friend. "No funny business that could get us put under house arrest for the weekend. Deal?"

"Deal," Ronnie said, jumping up off the bed. "Now put on your pants and let's go. Bobby's already out front."

"He's already here?" Ashley said. "Geeze, Ronnie, why didn't you ask me sooner?"

"I didn't want to give you much time to come up with reasons we couldn't go. I really *need* to see him, Ash. You know he's leaving on Monday for three months to go work for his uncle in Missouri."

Ashley rolled off the bed, kicked the top of her suitcase closed. She checked herself in the full-length mirror on the closet door, tousled her hair and smiled at the results. She pulled her jeans off the bedpost and slid them on, then slipped her bare feet into her black and white checkered, canvas slip-ons.

"Okay, let's go," Ashley said, grabbing her jeans jacket off the doorknob and her purse from the top of her dresser.

Ronnie was bouncing down the hallway in front of Ashley, who walked along swinging her purse trying to hit Ronnie in the butt. At the end of the hallway, they bumped into Ronnie's former roommate, Brittany Roberts - the girl who had squealed on them and ruined last year's plans - coming up the stairs, her arms full of books. Ronnie stuck out her tongue at the girl, sending a surprised Tiffany's fake smile back into her mouth. As they passed, Ashley smacked her purse into the girl's ample rump.

"Oops, sorry Britt," Ashley said over her shoulder.

Ronnie and Ash romped down the stairs, up the hallway and out the front door, then ran out into the circular drive toward the idling, faded red, Dodge pickup truck. A smiling Bobby reached over and opened the door and the pair slipped into the cab and along the vinyl-covered bench seat, Ronnie tight against Bobby's leg.

Rudy pointed to the exit slowly approaching as they made their way along the increasingly greasy roadway at a decreasing pace. The wipers were keeping the windshield clean, but the large, wet, flakes were being piled up at the ends of each stroke and the wipers protested with loud thuds each time before reversing direction. At the slower speeds, the surfaces of the car were being quickly becoming covered in accumulating snow. Rudy had the defrosters on high, but even with that, the interior side windows were beginning to fog. The outside temperature was hovering just below freezing and was forecast to drop overnight, meaning the snow would be hanging around for a while.

"Wow," Travis said. "This shit is really starting to come down."

"Time to decide, Travis," Rudy said. "You think we should drop in on the aunt?"

"Yeah, let's stop by and at least ask her a question or two," Travis said, rubbing his chin with his fingers. "We can come up with some kind of cover story, like we're following up on the lease but can't reach Dave, and were passing by and decided to take a break from the snow."

"If nothing else, it stirs the waters," Rudy said. "We might just cause her to reach out to her nephew, rile him up, maybe he'll make another mistake to help us pinpoint them."

Travis steered the car off to the right into the deceleration lane for the exit. He braked early and was glad he had since the Lincoln's tires immediately locked up and piled snow in front of them and the car began to slide. He remembered there was a gravel shoulder beyond the concrete one and as he progressed down the slight decline toward the crossroad, he eased two tires off the pavement and onto the gravel, then again touched the brakes. That time, the big sedan slowed without skidding and he rode the shoulder the rest of the way down the exit ramp. At the bottom of the hill, he stopped the car fully before turning right toward the trailer park. The wheels spun briefly before finding a bite and Travis moved along even slower, gauging the lay of the snow-covered and untracked roadway by the mailboxes on each side. The state highway was just as slick as had been the interstate, although with no tracks in the now heavily falling snow, much more treacherous.

As they moved along, the water-laden snow packed onto the tires which flung chunks against the wheel wells adding irregularly timed thuds to the wiper's rhythmic ones. Reflections from the headlights meant the bumpers were piling high with collected snow. The side windows were nearly opaque from the condensation on the inside and the snow piling up on the outside, and gave the feeling of riding in a cottony cocoon.

"Roll down your window," Travis said leaning forward, trying to obtain some peripheral vision through the windshield. "I can't make out the trailer park driveway, but I know it's right along here."

Rudy powered down his window slowly, pushing snow away from the opening as he did so it didn't fall into the vehicle. New falling flakes immediately found the inside of the car and began settling on his jacket and pants. He brushed them away, but they were replaced just as quickly as he could shed them, so he gave up and watched them quickly melt. The tires rolled more slowly, the sound of wet, packed snow crunching under the load added a new sound to the muffled silence.

"There it is," Rudy said. "Between the two barrels."

Travis turned into the drive, creating ruts in the virgin snowfall. He drove from memory along the gravel roadways. The thickening clouds had turned late morning into dusk. A few of the trailers had lights on, but most were dark, the inhabitants most likely off at work for the day. Rudy powered the window back up, wiped the remaining flakes from his clothes. A subtle odor of wet wool filled the vehicle.

They spotted a smaller pile of snow alongside Gloria Keller's trailer, recognized the shape underneath as Dave's Mustang.

"Well, the car's still here, but at least all the dog shit is gone," Rudy said.

"Oh, it's still there," Travis said with a laugh. "It's just more like land mines, now."

"Oh, yeah."

Travis eased the car into the small parking spot where he remembered the drive was beside Aunt Gloria's trailer and brought it to a stop. He doused the lights, then killed the ignition. Inside the darkened trailer, Rudy noted a curtain part, then fall together again.

"Well, looks like she's home," Rudy said. "Somebody just looked out the curtain."

"Who'd ever leave this place?" Travis joked. "Except, of course, for beer and cigarettes, and Friday night bowling."

"Careful, buddy, your snobbery is showing," Rudy said. "Remember you and I are not that far removed from these roots."

"Thanks for reminding me, Rudy, but I left all this behind when I joined the Corps. Never to look back."

Rudy nodded, then his hand moved to the door handle.

"Let's go with the following up on the lease storyline," Rudy said. "I'll take point. She knows me."

Rudy opened his door, looked for a shallower spot into which he could place his handmade loafer. Finding none, he cursed to himself and put his foot into the snow. It compacted beneath the weight. Water squeezed out under the leather sole and seeped into his sock.

"Aw shit," he said, standing up between the cabin and open door. "Oh well, it was not the first time I've had wet feet, and it won't be the last, I guess. Just wish I hadn't worn a brand new pair of *Edmunds* today."

Travis laughed out loud at the shorthand reference to the custom-made shoes from Allen Edmund in Wisconsin.

"Now whose snobbery is showing?"

"Cute," Rudy said, bending at the waist and peering back inside. "Come on out, buddy, it's beautiful out here." He straightened up again, slammed the door, hiked his coat collar and carefully walked up the porch steps and knocked lightly at the aluminum storm door. He turned when he heard the driver's door slam, which was more of a muted thud lost in the snow-saturated air, and watched as Travis tiptoed through the snow, pausing only to clear the headlights and taillights before returning to the warmth and shelter of the car.

Rudy knocked again. He heard the television go off inside, then saw a shadow pass behind the interior door's small frosted window.

"Semper fi, Mac," he said over his shoulder rapidly collecting snow.

"Hey, it's Cindy," came the response from the other end of the line.

"Cindy, it's Gloria Keller, you know, Dave's aunt," Gloria whispered into the phone. "Do you remember me?"

"I can barely hear you, Gloria," Cindy said. "Of course I remember you. What's up?"

"Have you heard more from Dave?"

The words came across the line as not only softly whispered, but breathless and deeply slurred. Cindy concluded the woman was either still drunk from last night or beginning the weekend a bit early. She had no idea where the conversation was going, but decided to go along, for Dave's sake.

"I did, just yesterday." Cindy wondered what had prompted the call and why Gloria sounded so breathless and frightened. "Gloria, is something wrong?"

Pause. Cindy heard knocking in the background.

"Those two men who said they were from the Cadillac place the other day are back again. They ain't no car salesmen. I know that now."

"Even if they were what they said they were, why would they need to come back?"

Cindy related the quick story of the phone call she had received from a claimed Cadillac salesman the same night she had heard from Gloria the first time.

"Sheesh, between that story, Dave's beating it out of town like he did, and them showing up here twice, makes me wonder what kind of trouble that boy has gotten himself into. His family hasn't been around me for years, and he shows up out of the blue, makes me wonder. Not that I wouldn't do anything in the world for him."

"I don't think Dave did anything, Gloria. I think they're after the friend he's with."

"Which friend?"

"I'm sworn to secrecy," Cindy said. "They're furiously beating the bushes, though, just to track them down."

"Well, it's weird-o-rama, that's for sure," Gloria said.

"Ms. Keller," the voice called through the closed doors. "It's the guys from the Cadillac dealership from the other day. Could we have a few moments with you?"

"Aw shit, they're hollering in the door now." Pause. Then in a conspiratorial whisper: "I think they saw me look out the window when they pulled up."

Cindy could here muffled noises in the background, but not make out any voice or words.

Then the man on the porch opened the storm door and knocked hard on the interior door.

"Oh my God, they're coming in," Gloria said in a panic-filled whisper. "They're coming in, Cindy. What do I do? Who are these men? They're huge. What will they do to me?"

"Stay calm, Gloria," Cindy said, her mind reeling. She didn't even know this woman or anything about her other than the fact she was Dave's aunt. "Can you get out a back door, get to a neighbor's? Get some help?"

"This is a trailer, girl. There ain't no back doors."

The pounding from the door sounded again, followed by a large crash.

"Oh my God, no..."

Cindy heard the something which sounded like struggling, falling, the phone dropping to the floor, and then nothing.

"Gloria?"

Nothing.

"Gloria, are you there?"

Cindy looked at her phone display. The call was still connected, but there was no response from Dave's aunt.

Rudy looked down, shook his head slowly as he shuffled his feet. Disgusted, he threw up his arms, turned and walked back down the porch steps. He tried to retrace his original steps, although for what purpose he didn't know. The snow was piling up so quickly, refilling the tracks and besides, his socks and feet were already wet.

Travis called through the rolled down window that Rudy should check the Mustang and make sure the GPS locator was still in place. Rudy tramped across to the car, reached under the wheel well and found the device in the right spot. Though their monitoring system had continuously reported the vehicle had not moved, by confirming the tracking device was still where Travis had placed it several days ago meant nobody had ditched the device.

Rudy got into the car. He stomped his feet clean of snow on the floorboard. Travis grinned across the cabin. He started the car, made certain all the defrosters were on high and started to back out.

"I don't know what we could have learned anyway," Travis said. "It was worth a try, though."

"Yeah, she was in there and the pot has been stirred. Let's get up to Boston. Maybe this shit will let up the further north we go."

"Optimist."

Rudy brushed his hand through his short cropped hair in the direction of his partner, spattering him with melted snow.

A few minutes later, they were back on I-95 headed toward Boston. The good news was, while they had made their fruitless stop, the plows and salt trucks had gone through. The interstate was now clear and just wet, even though the snow continued to fall. The bad news was the snow was falling even harder the further north they traveled.

In her rented attic room on Clinton Street in Cambridge, just beyond the official reaches of the Harvard University campus, Cindy Spagliano continued to speak into her cell phone. She listened. Nothing. Then perhaps a faint moaning came across. She called Gloria's name, softly. Then louder. No more sounds returned, but it was clear the phone line was still open. She strained to listen, checked the volume on her phone. Had the two men come into Gloria's house? Had Gloria merely gone silent for a few minutes so as not to further alert them? Who were these two guys? The one thing Cindy knew for certain was they were *not* car salesmen. Cindy rose from her desk chair and padded across the old, maple plank floor to the window and still holding the phone to her ear, parted the curtains and peered outside.

The storm they had warned about on the morning news shows, which had begun shortly after breakfast as a light drifting of ice pellets had since transformed into a full-blown blizzard. The local weather reporter on WCBB the night before had predicted a couple of inches of the fluffy stuff, as he put it, but his counterpart that morning had been a bit more pessimistic, saying the system had stalled and might just be one for the record books. What Cindy was witnessing out her creaky, leaky windows looked like the East Coast version of the Alberta Clipper storms she had lived through year after year growing up in White Bear Lake, Minnesota. The snow outside appeared wet and heavy, and fell from a slate gray sky with very little wind. With an ample supply of moisture off the nearby Atlantic, and cold air available over Canada feeding it, this little storm could sit and spin for days. Then the wind would come, along with falling temperatures. Having lived in the Boston area for three years while attending Harvard, she had seen how poorly East Coast types dealt with snowstorms. They didn't have the equipment to move a big snowfall or anyplace on the narrow streets to put it. The city crews often had to haul the stuff away in dump trucks and drop it into the harbor; a process that could take days, or weeks. This could really turn nasty, Cindy thought.

She knew how badly the people out there drove in snow and ice when they did get out but would more often just abandon their stranded cars on the narrow, already clogged streets and turn to walking or taking public transportation. That meant, when the plows finally did roll through the neighborhoods, cars would get buried under tons of snow, and with the combination of piled snow, cars and the original lack of space, many roads would be down to one barely passable lane. Often, people didn't return to dig out their vehicles for days, and the shoveled snow from sidewalks also had nowhere to be piled, so Boston turned into one unmoving drift of snow and metal. Then the garbage would begin to pile up. Fortunately, they don't get hit hard very often, Cindy thought; but from what she was seeing out her window, the one overhead now was what the locals called a 'whoppah'.

She spoke into the phone again. Nothing. Not a sound. Cindy walked over to sit on the edge of her still unmade bed, grabbed a pair of thick pink socks out from under the covers and slipped them over her chilled, naked feet. She rubbed her toes through the cotton. Normally, her feet were unnaturally hot, and she hated the confinement of socks, but when her feet did get cold, like they were now, they ached. Her mother always was quick to remind her the problems with her feet came from the time she 'nearly froze them' one afternoon while sledding. Sure, they had been cold, icy cold, and by the time she made it home that day, Cindy could barely feel her feet; but, *nearly froze?*

Back waiting on the phone, she wondered what should she do? She barely knew the woman on the other end of the line, but this was very strange. Gloria could be in trouble, hurt, or worse.

"Oh, don't be so dramatic, Cin," she said to herself. Being dramatic, and impulsive, was something Lorelei Cindy Spagliano got from her mother.    The same mother who would never let her forget she had 'nearly lost her feet to amputation because the girl hadn't the sense to come out of the cold', had named her daughter Lorelei simply because she became pregnant in the back of a converted van either on the way to, or from, or perhaps even in the parking lot of the Styx concert in Minneapolis in 1976.    *Lorelei* had been the group's new hit single then, and they had opened the show with it, then performed an extended version as an encore, or so the story went.    Weeks later when Cindy's mother had learned of the pregnancy - what the boyfriend at the time had called the 'oops moment' - the mommy-to-be and Styx fan had naturally harkened back to the concert as the focal event.    Nine months later, two days before Christmas, Lorelei Cynthia Spagliano came into the world.

Cindy hated the name, and the story of how it had come to her was an embarrassing tale her mother would tell everyone who listened, which in White Bear Lake, Minnesota was almost everybody.    Her mother insisted she go by her true first name, which wasn't so bad through grade school, but by high school, an awareness of the story details lead to incessant teasing and whispers behind her back.    She had lived with the name for eighteen years, and had decided to take a new identity with her new start at Harvard.    So, when she registered for classes, she was Cindy. When she met new friends, she was Cindy.    Even though her life in officialdom outside the university - Social Security, DMV, and the like - was still under the birth name of Lorelei, to everyone who knew her, she was just plain Cindy.    Thankfully, for the past three years, the story of Lorelei remained untold outside of the state boasting ten thousand lakes.

Her phone beeped, and when she looked at the display, the battery indicator was flashing.    Cindy scrambled to the desk and searched the top middle drawer for the charger and plugged the phone into the wall outlet.    The charge began.    She didn't want to lose the call just in case Gloria came back on the line.    She also didn't want to hang up because she thought she remembered that Gloria had told her this was her land line and if she disconnected there was a good chance a call back to Gloria would result in a busy signal if the phone was not physically replaced on the cradle.    Cindy set the charging cell phone on the desk and tapped the speaker key.

Into her computer, Cindy typed Gloria's phone number.    The address given by the internet site reported the number was registered in West Greenwich, Rhode Island and when Cindy queried that, she found the town was located just outside of Providence.    Cindy called up a map of the area.    West Greenwich lay right along I-95, the corridor between Dave's home in Gales Ferry and Boston.    She snugged her feet onto the chair and hugged her legs.    Her feet were hot again, so she pulled off the socks and tossed them over her shoulder back onto the bed.    She wiggled her toes as she thought what to do next. Wiggling her toes when she was deep in thought was one of her tells which Dave had pointed out to her one day. Cindy had always realized subconsciously she had done that, but Dave had been the first person to notice and she smiled at the memory.

She reached across the desk for the new phone she had obtained when Dave had first asked her to find out if he and a 'friend' could go down and use Uncle Jack's house near New Orleans so they could get away for a while. She knew the friend had to be Dace Lamoureux, even though Dave had never mentioned the name in that first conversation. That just made sense. The two were inseparable. Cindy had of course heard of the death of Sarah Avidago the past Saturday night, and though she had only met the girl once or twice before Cindy and Dave broke up, she knew Dace and Sarah had remained a fairly serious item around campus. Besides, Dave wasn't dating anyone as far as Cindy knew, and since Dave had jokingly asked her to come along so they could 'do it on the big, wide veranda', she had known the friend had to be his best buddy, Dace. When she had asked him directly in the next conversation, Dave had spilled the beans to her, about everything. Cindy knew he only did so because Dave knew he could trust her completely.

She flipped the phone open and hit redial to Dave's new, prepaid phone. He had used it to call her when they had gotten in to Uncle Jacks place and the number was still in memory. It was also the only other call her other cell phone had received since Dave had phoned her a couple of nights ago from the hotel somewhere in Alabama.

The call connected and Cindy sat waiting, listening to the echo of the distant ringing and watching the snow fall outside the window. By the sixth ring, an automated voice advised that the user had not yet set up the voicemail option and promptly disconnected. Cindy closed her phone and briefly smiled as she caught herself recalling Dave's repeat of her original 'big, wide veranda' remark she had said to him when they were still dating and she had proposed a trip for the two of them. She sat wiggling her toes at the thought. There was another reason Cindy unconsciously wiggled her toes, one which Dave, sadly, had never picked up on.

Her attention shifted back to the open phone and Gloria Keller and her toes stopped wiggling. She picked up the cell again, switched off the speaker and held it to her ear. She strained to hear any sound, but there was nothing. She whispered Gloria's name.

Putting the phone down again, Cindy picked up the new one and punched 9-1-1.

Ashley hugged the passenger door of the truck belonging to Bobby's boss. In the back were six burlap bags covered by a tarp. Each one-hundred-pound bag had been wet down to keep the cargo cool and mostly alive. The burlap sacks undulated as if each contained thousands of disembodied fingers, but in reality the contents were an equal number of live mud bugs; crawfish bound for an evening boil at a Baton Rouge tavern which had somehow missed a delivery and whose owners were about as irritated with the situation as were the tasty crustaceans at being confined in burlap. Bobby drove with one hand and had the other sliding over another undulating package in the vehicle, this one in the cab, warm, and clad in denim.

Ashley had never seen Ronnie acting that way. Her hand was under Bobby's untucked T-shirt, rubbing his chest and flat belly, and Ashley was certain, sliding down occasionally to explore unknown territories. She kissed his neck, and when the roadway was straight enough, the two locked lips and swapped spit like it was going out of style. Ashley knew now why she had been needed: the outing had to be sanctioned by Sister Regina and she'd never knowingly approve of Ronnie leaving the grounds alone with a boy. Ashley would do anything for her best friend, but she certainly was not happy about her current role as wing-girl. They were still about half an hour from Baton Rouge, and Ashley bristled at the knowledge she'd most likely get ditched at the parade, *if* there even was a parade that day.

Bobby was three years older than Ronnie, and he had been pressuring her about going all the way almost since they had begun dating. Ashley believed she understood the one track of the young male mind, especially when considering the bottom-line assessment by her aunt. She hoped Ronnie had also been considering the discussion they had shared on the topic the previous night. Bobby was leaving for a three-month stint to help his uncle in St. Louis, and this outing was most likely the last chance he and Ronnie would have together before he left, and that was an additional ingredient to the mix, but Ashley had never before seen Ronnie exhibit interest in this degree of physical contact, at least not in her presence.

A strange noise filtered across the cab. Ashley tore her eyes from the passing landscape out the passenger side window and sneaked a quick glance at the couple. *Gross* was the only word which her mind could articulate.

Cindy spoke to the emergency operator in Boston and explained the situation with the phone call from Gloria. The operator was as sympathetic over Cindy's dilemma as she could be, but was obviously becoming too overwhelmed with stress from the rising number of calls about the snowstorm in Boston to muster much concern for some woman in Rhode Island. Immediately after she had punched the numbers and the call had been answered by the female operator with a thick Bostonian accent, Cindy had regretted the decision to call the local emergency number. Frankly, she was a bit embarrassed. She could think clearer and more logically than that, and she had chastised herself, given the unknown situation was eighty or more miles away and in another state. So, after the brief interaction, Cindy apologized and hung up.

Her next call was to 4-1-1 on her cell phone for directory help with the phone number for law enforcement in the West Greenwich area. She scribbled down the number for the Rhode Island State Patrol and then punched in the numbers followed by the SEND button.

"Trooper Thomas," came the voice from the District #2 office she had called. "How may I help you?"

"Ah, Mr. Thomas, or do I call you Trooper?" Cindy said with a protocol self-consciousness.

"Either way, ma'am," came the curt yet courteous response. "What can I do for you today?"

"Well, Trooper Thomas, my name is Cindy Spagliano and I'm calling you from Boston, well, Cambridge, specifically."

"Yes, ma'am," he said, devoid of patience for the social courtesies. "I'm certain you're getting the same snowstorm we are down here so I know you understand we're a little busy right now. How may I help?"

"I really feel silly for calling," Cindy said, and then she related the whole story as concisely as possible, including the fact she judged Gloria to be either still, or already drunk.

"So, you currently have the line open to this Keller woman, but you've heard nothing further at all since the sound of the scuffle or falling?"

A pause. Toes wiggling. Thoughtful toes.

"I'm not even certain it was a scuffle I heard. As I told you, she said something about the two men opening the door and then there was a conflagration, and then nothing. Well, nothing after the bit of moaning right after the falling sound."

"Conflagration? There's a fire?"

"What? Oh no, that's the word my mother used when she was hollering at us kids about unknown noise." Cindy uttered a nervous chuckle. "'What's all that conflagration?' she'd holler up the stairs. I'm sorry, I know the word describes a large fire and has nothing to do with noise. It's just habit from childhood."

"It's all right, Ms. Spagliano," he said, the anecdote loosening him up a bit. "We all do it, especially when we're upset. I would use 'irregardless' because my mother used to say it all the time, until one day my Lieutenant called me on the carpet for repeatedly putting it in my reports, reminding me it was at best a double-negative, and at worst, not a word at all."

"Yeah, but I'm a junior working at a political science major at Harvard," she said with pride mixed with embarrassment, and then shuddered with horror when she realized how that sounded. "I'm sorry."

She was thankful when it sounded as if he missed her elitist faux pas.

"Well, we'll dispatch a cruiser to the trailer park over there and check on Ms. Keller when we can. Right now, I've got fender benders all up and down the interstate to sort out, so it may be a while. If you want to try the county boys, you may be able to roust a sheriff's deputy out there quicker than us, but they've probably got their hands full right now too."

"I understand, Trooper Thomas," Cindy said. "I'll leave it in your hands for the time being. Makes it simpler that way. Please call me at this number when you find something out, no matter the time." A pause. "As I told you, I really don't know the woman, but I do have a concern. I'll continue to keep the line open to her and I'll call you back should something change on this end. I don't know, maybe she thought she had hung up the phone and is making lunch right now." A small laugh.

"Thank you for calling, ma'am," he said. "I'll be in touch."

They closed the call and Cindy rocked back on the desk chair. She rechecked the other phone; spoke into it. Still nothing, not even background noise. She peered outside. If anything, the snow was coming down heavier than before. She thought about Gloria Keller. What else could she do? She didn't have a car to drive down there, and it would be stupid to set out on a day like that even if she did. Cindy had decided at Christmas that she was ready for a car and she truly did have an interest in Dave's old Mustang when he got back. That part of the story she had told the 'car salesman' had been true.

Who were these guys? Did Dave have a deep, dark secret? Because Dace was with Dave, could they be people working for The Senator? That made about as much sense as anything, she thought, and she caught her toes wiggling again under the desk. Now that she was conscious of it, she would be noticing it every time it happened for the next day or two. She was like that. Dramatic, impulsive, *and* obsessive, she thought, a great combination for a career in politics.

Her feet were hot again so she put them up against the outside wall which was cooler than the floor and continued to sort through the situation. How would Dace's father know to send people to the house of Dave's aunt, a woman he had never even bothered to mention to Cindy during the whole year they had dated? She understood why Dace wouldn't tell his parents where he was going, and how; under the circumstances described by Dave, she also understood how he would feel compelled to sneak off. She knew from Dave that Dace was under a huge burden with this family legacy stuff, and now the sudden death of a girl he had been dating exclusively for at least a couple of years was enough for anyone to need to take a step back. Or several.

Dave had always been mesmerized by his buddy Dace. Cindy once teased Dave that he had a man love for Dace, and he had just said, 'Maybe so. Not in a gay way, though, right?' He then had laughed in that uninhibited way he had. Cindy caught her toes wiggling again up against the wall, but not in the thoughtful way. She considered for a moment about calling Dave's parents and immediately decided against it.

She had met the elder Saunders' one time, after the Yale game their sophomore year; the Harvard Crimson had lost that game in a heartbreaker, 7-9. John and Debbie Saunders had driven up for the weekend to watch Dave play. He started the game as an offensive tackle; Dace, as she recalled, had held for the kicker on the extra point following Harvard's only touchdown. During a dinner out, Dave's parents had invited her for Thanksgiving and the following weekend at their home in Gales Ferry, but shortly after that game weekend, and without much of an explanation Dave had broken it off and they had become 'hi in the hallway' friends. Before the breakup, they had talked about going to Uncle Jack's place for Mardi Gras that following February, and going back to Minnesota so Dave could meet Cindy's mom over Christmas. Obviously, neither trip had ever happened.

She tried another call to Dave's new phone. No answer. No voicemail. Because Uncle Jack refused to have a landline installed in his vacation homes, all she could do now was wait, watch out the window, and perhaps get some studying done for the coming week to clear her mind over what may have happened to Gloria.

It was shortly after noon before Travis and Rudy made it through Providence. In between Gloria's place and the northeast side of the city, they had counted sixteen cars in the median and seven semi-trailers jackknifed on the shoulder. They were averaging twenty-five miles an hour by then, with the snowfall overtaking the roadway again and with traffic slowing in reaction to every spin out. At that rate, it would take them another two hours or more just to reach the outskirts of Boston.

Mr. Eugene had brought up a small television after we got back from the hospital so I had something do do while Sandy rested, he said. I had turned it on in the morning with muted sound. According to the closed captioning on the Weather Channel, a fast-moving storm which had moved up the coast of Florida and the southeastern seaboard had collided overnight with a relatively dry, cold weather system sweeping through the Midwest. The jet steam had split into a northern segment which roared directly west to east at nearly two hundred miles an hour at forty-thousand feet; while the southern branch dipped deep over northern Mississippi and then raced out of the southwest toward Newfoundland where it was again merging with the northern branch.

As a result, millions of tons of moisture packed into warm Gulf air was being sucked up the eastern seaboard and was already beginning to dump record snowfall amounts from Massachusetts to Maine. Virginia was getting freezing rain, and the Carolinas were bracing for flooding following the already heavy rains which were forecasted to continue unabated over the next couple of days.

The vacuum effect of the northern low had sucked every bit of clouds and moisture from much of the south and as I looked out the windows of our room into a now clear, blue sky and millpond calm waters of the Gulf of Mexico just beyond the beach, it was hard to believe the change from yesterday. The storm front which had hit us hard less than twenty-four hours earlier had weakened over the Gulf in a complex mix of other systems, been sucked dry of moisture, and was now wobbling onshore east of Biloxi, bringing nothing more than scattered clouds back home and the rest of the eastern Gulf shore.

Sandy lay sleeping as the bedside clock's mechanical display flipped to ten a.m. I had spend much of the night awake and watching her sleep. I didn't end up turning on the television until after sunrise. An hour ago, Mr. Eugene had knocked softly at the door to inquire whether Sandy and I would be coming down for breakfast. Weekday breakfast hours at the B&B were six to nine. When I told him my wife was still sleeping, he nodded and said he'd bring up a tray for us a bit later. From the light knock I now padded my way across the carpet to answer, a bit later must have meant ten on the dot.

I opened the door and Mr. Eugene entered the room carrying a large silver tray with two covered plates, a stack of multigrain toast, an assortment of condiments and cutlery along with glasses filled with orange juice for Sandy and tomato juice for me. He quietly excused himself, and at the door asked how Sandy had slept, to which I had responded 'like an angel'. I had no ideas how angels slept, or even if they did, but when Sandy slept, she continued to resemble my vision of an angel.

As I closed the door and turned, Sandy stirred under the covers. Her gorgeous blue eyes opened, found me, and then she smiled as she slid to sit up, pushing a pillow between her and the headboard.

"Good morning sunshine," I said. "Breakfast just arrived."

"Mr. Eugene and Anita are so thoughtful," Sandy said, reaching out a hand to me. "So are you, my darling. Thank you for letting me sleep. I know you didn't get much yourself."

I moved to her beckoning hand, sat on the edge of the bed by her, took her soft, little hand in mine and kissed her fingers as my eyes misted. Embarrassed, I lowered my head. Yesterday's scare had hit me hard when it was all over and we were back at the B&B last evening. Throughout the night, I kept hearing the sound of the baby's heartbeat on that monitor. When I'd close my eyes, I'd see the tiny arms and legs on the sonogram.

Knowing me as well as Sandy does, my reaction to her this morning seemed to break a dam inside my wife, because her head dropped too. She looked up and with her free hand, gently touched the bandage on my forehead just below my retreating hairline.

"I'm so very sorry about yesterday, Will," Sandy said, her eyes moist, her cheeks ruddier than usual. "I don't know what came over me. I felt a rush of power, of joy. I can't explain it and I'm embarrassed by my lack of judgement."

I shushed her words away. We had both been very lucky yesterday morning, and after all, I had gone along on the adventure out onto the pier as well.

"I should have known better myself," I said and glanced down at her belly. "We're all okay, all three of us. That's what matters." A thought struck me. "You know, Sandy, neither you nor I have ever been too cautious in living our lives. We've both taken so many chances through the years; you've leapt often without looking, and I've dodged so many bullets even when I did look, both literally and figuratively, that I'm surprised to find myself still above ground some days when I think about it. We're older now, though, and this new baby is a twist neither of us anticipated at this point in our lives. We both have to start thinking a bit differently."

I shook my head as everything I'd experienced flashed through my thoughts and then pulled an often repeated quote from my brain which truly fit my existence on this mortal coil: "This has been the strangest life I've ever known."

I know I had just blended Shakespeare with Jm Morrison. Sue me.

That brought a laugh.

"Just how many lives have you lived, dear?" Sandy said.

I smiled at her.

"You know me too well, Sandy," I said.

"You think?" she said. "Let me put it this way, I know fully well the smell of that breakfast has already gotten to you and this mutual apology session is over. How about let's eat and agree to forget about yesterday."

That was all I needed. I released her hand, stood up, walked to the tray and lifted the cover on one of the plates. I snared a slice of perfectly cooked, Texas smokehouse bacon and stuffed it into my salivating mouth. I felt my eyes roll. What is it about bacon that makes it so darn good, I thought.

"Thank you, dear," I said through a mouthful of smoky goodness. "It's so good to know that when there's bacon nearby, all our concerns simply melt away."

"You're welcome," Sandy said as she slid out from the covers and joined me. "Thank God for the forgiveness of bacon."

"I saw you with the letter in the garden this morning, Libby," Tom said when he had the chance to catch her alone.

She was seated in the breakfast nook, a mug in front of her and a flowered teapot oozing steam out its curved spout in her hand. Caroline had already left for the day, it was her weekend off. The Senator was in his office, and Mary Rose was in her room. Libby said nothing, but merely finished pouring steaming water from the ceramic pot onto the tea bag in her cup. He could immediately smell the release of the lavender as the blossoms in the bag rehydrated and surrendered their soothing essence into the hot water and vapor escaping the mug. She always drank lavender tea when her mind was anxious. Her expression stayed neutral at his remark and remained focused on the task of making for herself a perfect cup. Tom recognized the stalling technique. He'd seen it enough with Libby over the years.

"I am assuming it was from Dace," he said to her silence.

She worked the teabag in the boiling water, then placed it into a spoon, wrapped the string around the bag and spoon and drained it into the cup and set the spoon and bag combination onto a small paper napkin before she glanced up at him. As much as they'd shared over the years, she knew he could see right through her. There was no point in lying to him.

"Yes, it was," she admitted, then stood and walked past him to stare out the windows in the breakfast nook. She blew across the top of the cup, then took a cautious sip. "Apparently, he had given it to Mary Rose before we left for the funeral, with instructions to give it to me today. On Friday."

"Did you tell The Senator?" he asked. A pause. "A father should know."

Her head snapped around and she glared over her shoulder at him, then just as quickly she returned her stare outside.

"No, the letter was addressed to me, Tom." She took another sip of tea. "The contents are not meant for his father."

She turned her head around slower this time, her eyes found his, lingered, then again returned to the outside. Her thoughts drifted to the wildflower garden, the stone bench where she had found so much solace over the years. It had been a gift, the garden and the bench, but also an unspoken apology; a material representation of an ever-changing love, and an indiscretion uncovered. While the garden so often had soothed her over the subsequent years, it was also a perennial reminder of her pain, and his sin; and hers. It was the harsh, naked truth to the maxim that life is merely a series of transitions.

"Don't you think you should?" Tom asked.

"Share the contents of Dace's letter with The Senator?" A sip. Her stare fixed outside. "I'm thinking about it."

"He's hurting, you know."

She turned, her body square to him and looked into his eyes. Her eyes were moist.

"They both are, Tom," she said and then she set her mug onto the table and walked past him out of the room.

# Chapter Thirteen

Dave bounded downstairs after showering and getting dressed to find Dace in the front room, reading, still in his clothes from the previous night's outing. Both men felt uncomfortable even saying the word *parlor*, so they had decided for the tenure of their stay this would be the front room. Dace was lying on an antique, tapestry-clad couch, his head on a throw pillow of muted, striped, gold sateen with twisted, gold twine fringe wedged against one wood and lightly padded arm with his shoeless feet hanging over the other. A red, leather-bound volume was resting with its foot on his chest, held open by his left hand. His right hand was between his head and the pillow.

"Hey, I could use a Dew," Dave said from the back doorway. "You want one?"

"No thanks," Dace said, not taking his eyes from the pages.

Dave walked down the hallway to the kitchen, noticed Dace had cleaned up the breakfast mess while he had been upstairs showering, grabbed a can of Cherry Mountain Dew from the refrigerator, cracked the top and downed a healthy swig. He again glanced around the kitchen, shook his head and shrugged his shoulders, then walked back to the front room. Dace hadn't moved, although the book lay splayed across his chest.

Dave plopped down on one of the oversized, wingback chairs across the heavy woolen area rug from the couch, tossed a leg over the arm and took another drink from the can. Dace stared up toward the ceiling, seemingly disconnected.

"What are you reading?" Dave asked.

Dace closed the book with his finger marking the page he had been reading and showed the spine to his friend. Dave had to squint to read its gold lettering.

"*Presidential Inaugural Speeches?*"

"Yeah."

Dace replaced the book on his chest.

"What, getting in some light reading?"    Another slug of Dew.
"What's next *War and Peace*?"

"I found it on the bookshelf," he said with a motion over the back of
the couch to the wall of bookshelves, ignoring the quip.    "This Uncle
Jack has eclectic taste in books, and quite an assemblage of rare, first
editions."

"Uncle Jack has an eclectic taste in just about everything, I'd say from
looking around this place," Dave added.    "You know that old, busted
down building in the back?  Well, Cindy told me that is a state-of-the-art
garage and workshop on the inside.  He had the outside made to look like
a ramshackle, old machine shed to keep away the curious."

"Did you talk to her today?"

"Cindy? No, not yet, although I saw there were a couple of missed
calls on the new cell phone after I got out of the shower, which, by the
way, wouldn't be a bad idea for you, brother."    He waved his hand to
move away the air.    "She told me about the workshop before we left
knowing I'd get curious."

"So you gonna stay away?"

"Hell no," Dave said with a laugh.

Dace's mind remained distracted by his own subject matter.

"Did you know that Joseph P. Kennedy, the old man, had no plans
for John to be president?  He thought the boy was too weak and sickly to
carry the family banner into the White House.  It wasn't until Joe Junior
got himself blown to bits in a B-17 bomber loaded with explosives before
he could bail out, that second son John's future came into focus for his
father."

Dave studied his friend as he spoke.  He had always enjoyed how
Dace's mind worked.  Dace could break down complex subjects into
smaller, easy-to-understand components, and most importantly, clearly
explain it all to just about anyone.  It was how he had helped Dave get
through high school physics.  Now, however, Dace wasn't really talking to
Dave or explaining a complex issue, but rather speaking to the air as if
giving dictation to some phantom secretary or merely verbalizing his own
thoughts to himself.  There was no need for Dave to respond.  He was
superfluous.  Just listening almost made him feel like an interloper.

"Only after Joe's death, and following John's PT boat coming to a
split-in-two end on the bow of a Japanese destroyer and the heroics
which could be spun from that, did number two son merit the mantle of
the presidential ambitions of Joseph Senior.  Had those two critical events
not happened, the world may never have known much of John Fitzgerald
Kennedy.    So many aspects of our history may have unfolded so
differently: the escalation in Vietnam and Southeast Asia, the challenge
and subsequent race to the moon, the social and geopolitical upheavals of

the 1960s, forced integration, assassinations, and so many other situations all may never have occurred, or if they did, played out much differently; and all because of an electrical short on a flying bomb headed for the Fortress of Mimoyecques in Northern France, and a split second when two boats attempted to occupy the same spot on the vastness of the Pacific in the same instant. Did you know that, Dave?"

Dave didn't know that, wasn't sure he cared. He shrugged, took another shot of Dew, pondered a moment before responding in a way typical of what Dace referred to as a 'Davism'.

"I dunno," Dave said. "I guess it makes sense. The oldest son gets whacked, the role passes. It's like in *The Godfather* when Vito speaks to Michael after he became the Don and tells him, almost as an apology, that he had never intended that life for him." Then in a fairly decent imitation of Vito Corleone: "I knew Santino was going to have to go through all this and Fredo...well, Fredo was...but I, I never wanted this for you. I work my whole life, I don't apologize, to take care of my family. And I refused to be a fool dancing on the strings held by all of those big shots. That's my life, I don't apologize for that. But I always thought that when it was your time, that you would be the one to hold the strings. Senator Corleone, Governor Corleone, something." He scuffed his cheek with his fingernails to cap off the impression.

Daces eyes sliced slowly across the seating area.

"Sorry," Dave said with another shrug of his shoulders. "Remember your audience, buddy. Go ahead."

"I was reading Kennedy's inaugural speech this morning. As much as it's quoted from and paid glowing accolades by historians, it was one of the shortest given by any president: only 1,364 words, delivered in under fourteen minutes. My father was in the gallery behind him that day. He had entered the House and Senate as a freshman one cycle after Jack had won his first elections to each body and he and mother had received a handwritten invitation from Jackie. JFK and my dad didn't always see eye-to-eye on policy or politically, but my father always respected him; and, of course, mother adored Jackie." A pause. "Sometimes, I think my father sees me as the next JFK."

"Gee, ya think?" Dave said mockingly. "Your dad thinks that all the time about you, dude. He fantasizes about it. Drools at the thought. You're the Golden Child. The Fortunate Son." Dave drained the rest of the can of soda, crunched it, and let out a belch. "I hate to break the news to you so brutally and all, but there are worse things to be than future POTUS."

"Classy," Dace said referring to the belch. "What if it's not my goal for *my* life to be the President of the United States?"

"Classy, huh? You want to know what's classy? Your problems, my friend. Maybe someday I'll trade you mine for yours."

Dave felt a touch of irritation. He could handle every face of his best friend which had presented itself over the years, save one: the self-pitying Dace. While that version made few appearances over the years, when it did, Dave would find himself annoyed and agitated. He couldn't understand why, although when he spoke to it with Cindy one time, she suggested it was like Dave had seen behind the curtain, glimpsed a vision of the real wizard.

Dave felt a rush of nervous energy, and not just from the sugar and caffeine from the Mountain Dew. He placed the crushed can on the side table, pushed himself up from the chair, walked over to one of the double doors, opened the set and stepped out into the afternoon sun. The air was calm and cool, perhaps touching sixty degrees, but the sun was warm on his face. A few puffy clouds lay scattered across the sky. He looked back through the doors and saw Dace was back to reading. He knew he had been unnecessary to the lecture, and that was fine with him. Dace wouldn't even miss him when he was thinking like this, so Dave turned toward the back of the house and walked along the wide porch which wrapped all four sides of the house, on both floors, and turned the corner around the back. Standing next to the back door, he paused, and glanced across the lawn at the old barn, then padded down the steps. There was no pathway between the house and barn through the sprawling grassy area, so he created his own. Reaching in to his pocket as he walked, he removed the ring of house keys. There were three keys on the ring. He wondered if one of them worked on the shed.

Cindy pushed hard against the door. On the other side, two indistinct faces on top of two large, but otherwise nondescript, bodies did the same, and they were beginning to win the contest. She screamed for help, but her voice sounded small and distant, even to her ears. She knew the room held nothing the would-be intruders would want, save her, and the unknown limits of that thought frightened her beyond reason. She again strained against the immense force from the other side of the door. Then she heard it, in the distance, a rhythmic electronic pulse, growing louder with each cycling. Slowly, she turned her head to seek out the source of the sound and as she did, she lost focus on the door and it flew open, striking her and sending her sprawling across the hardwood floor. The two large men surged into the room with the sudden conversion of potential energy into momentum. They were inside. In an instant, she knew they'd be upon her. Instinctively she understood her only hope was to get to the source of the pulsing alarm.

She jerked in her bed. The dream evaporated instantly while reality seeped slowly into the void between sleep and wakefulness. Her heart was pounding. Her covers and the books and papers which had laid scattered across them when she had settled there to study were all pushed against the footboard. It had all been a nightmare, she thought, and a relieved smile cautiously moved across her lips as her heavy breathing began to subside. The only remaining remnant of the frightening adventure was the soft electronic pulsing emanating from somewhere in the pile. She dug through the covers and books and papers, finally finding the phone. She glanced at the caller ID, which showed as 'private' and flipped the phone open anyway.

"Hey, it's Cindy," she said into the phone.

"Ms. Spagliano, it's Trooper Thomas of the Rhode Island State Patrol, we spoke earlier." A pause. "Are you all right, Ms. Spagliano? You sound out of breath."

"Yes, yes, I'm fine." She drew in a single, deep, cleansing breath. "I was studying and must have fallen asleep. Had a nightmare. The phone startled me awake; but, yes, Trooper Thomas, of course I remember you."

Cindy then remembered the other phone on the desk. The one with the open line to Gloria Keller. She rolled off the bed and padded across the bare wood floor to the desk, picked up the other phone and held it to her unattended ear. The connection had been broken. The display read 'Call Ended' and showed the length at one hour fifty-six minutes forty-two seconds. She quickly thought back and estimated she must have been asleep for nearly forty-five minutes.

"When I couldn't free up any of our units to do a drive by, I contacted the West Greenwich Town Constable who then contacted the Sheriff's Department which dispatched a deputy to Ms. Keller's address."

"Yes," Cindy said, sensing the worst.

"Well, Ms. Spagliano, when the deputy could not raise anyone inside the trailer with his knocking and calling at the door, he requested, and was granted authority, by his supervisor to enter the trailer. He had to force the door; it was intact and locked from the inside."

"Yes," she said, wishing the man would just get to it

"Well, I'm afraid I've some bad news for you. The deputy located a middle-aged, white female in the back bedroom on the floor, and subsequently located the woman's identification." A pause as he took a deep, cleansing breath. "Ma'am, Ms. Keller is deceased."

"Oh my," Cindy said, somehow anticipating that news but still finding herself not ready to hear it as fact. "Can you tell me how she died, Trooper?"

"There are no reported apparent injuries, Ms. Spagliano. The coroner now has custody of the body and I'm certain she'll do an autopsy to see if a cause of death can be determined. Preliminarily, she's suspecting a heart attack."

"The two men?" Cindy asked. "Any sign of them; or that they had been inside the house?"

"All I have is the deputy's verbal report relayed to me by the Sheriff's Department Shift Supervisor at this time, and there was no mention of any evidence that anyone else had been inside the trailer today. I'm not certain they even know about the two men. My message to the Constable was only that Ms. Keller had been talking to someone out of state and then the line had gone unresponsive and I had received a suspicious situation call from you in Boston. I don't think I mentioned anything about the two men. I will relay that item to the investigating agency when we are finished here."

Cindy rolled her eyes and shook her head. She parted her curtains and peered outside. The storm was still dumping on Boston. She could see the plows had made at least one pass on Clinton Street, but saw no evidence that any of the parked cars had yet ventured forth since they were all looking like those Hostess igloo-shaped cupcakes, the ones with the marshmallow and coconut topping.

"Ms. Spagliano?"

"Yes, I'm here," she said, not really knowing what else to say to the man. "If there's anything I can do, please call me."

"Well, frankly, we'd like to get a formal statement from you."

"You want me to come down there?"

"No, no, that's not necessary. Someone will get in touch with your local authorities over the next day or two and they'll make contact. I don't see any reason at this point to further inconvenience you."

"Oh, okay. I'll do whatever I can."

The trooper asked for any contact information she may have for Gloria's family and Cindy found the entry for Dave's parents in her address book, which she relayed to him. The Saunders' would be able to direct the police to Gloria's next of kin and help with the family notifications. After all, Cindy had never even met the woman. When she disconnected from Trooper Thomas, she called Dave's new cell again.


"I was just about to call you," Dave said after pulling the prepaid cell from his pocket and flipping it open. "Sorry I missed your calls earlier, but I was in the shower." He paused. "Does that do anything for you?"

"Shut up, Dave," Cindy said. "I'm calling to give you some bad news."

Dave stopped his walk across the lawn.

"Now what?"

"I received another call from your aunt Gloria earlier today," she said. "She phoned because those two guys who had posed as Cadillac salesmen the other day were at her door again and she was frightened to answer their knocks, then she said something in panic and the phone went dead, but stayed connected. I heard nothing further from her."

"She does that sometimes. You know she drinks. I mean a lot. She's been known to fall asleep while she's talking to someone. She used to do it all the time to my mom, until my mother kinda walked away from her. That's probably it. She fell asleep. She won't even remember talking to you when she does wake up is my guess."

Cindy took a deep breath.

"Dave, she's dead. Coroner suspects a heart attack, but I'm worried because I'm suspecting you're down there with Dace Lamoureux and these guys may just be the security types you told me about, and this is just too coincidental. Regardless of how much your aunt's health had been affected by drink, I'm afraid her death may not have been entirely natural."

Rudy had called from the road and reserved a four-wheel drive Jeep Grand Cherokee from a south Boston Enterprise location. He and Travis arrived there fifteen minutes earlier and were now split up into separate vehicles. Rudy made his way along the city streets toward the girl's apartment while Travis found a nearby hotel where they could take their breaks and get some sleep when off duty. On the drive from New London, they had determined that to give the surveillance the best chance of picking up another clue to Dace's whereabouts would be to monitor the girl's both known cell phones and keep their fingers crossed.

For that type of electronic surveillance, they didn't need to see or watch the girl, just be certain her cellular phones remained within the range of their scanner. That made things a little easier and simpler from an operational standpoint, since they could continually relocate throughout a general area centered on her apartment. Doing so lowered the risk of being seen by the subject, or having some nosy neighbor call the local cops about a suspicious man in a vehicle remaining in the area for extended periods of time. To further lower the risk of being discovered, they planned to alternate in relatively short shifts using the two very different vehicles.

Rudy had won the coin flip at the Enterprise outlet and decided he would take the first four-hour shift. Since the key would be maintaining surveillance on the girl's cell phones, they decided to call them when he was set up, just to make certain the girl and the phones were where they thought they were at the outset. Rudy glanced over at the cellular phone scanner on the passenger seat. It was plugged into the cigarette lighter jack, although a fully charged onboard battery allowed the unit to operate autonomously for up to thirty-six hours. The panel glowed with neon blue LED numeric displays and a row of red lights flashed as each operational cellular phone frequency was searched and released.

The scanner automatically sought out the strongest cellular signals, which usually meant the closest phones. However, the operation wasn't foolproof and required a trained and alert operator to properly accomplish the initial setup. Within a few milliseconds of locking on to a transmission, the number of an intercepted phone would display across the LED screen, and the operator could either lock the call or release it and allow the unit to continue scanning. The unit would detect the phone number on the other end of the call in a few more seconds as data needed to be exchanged with the cellular system itself, and would also collect all the discrete electronic information from the nearby cellular phone. The machine could do the searching, however it was the skill and luck of the operator which would provide the initial results. Once the electronic ID was locked into the system, however, the operator's job became passive, a matter of sitting back and waiting for the phone to be used again.

From their information, the area near Clinton and Harvard streets consisted of densely packed student housing. Rudy realized there could be hundreds of cellular phones within the scanner's limited range, so to help narrow things down, he would park as close as possible to the girl's physical location. To further refine the surveillance, he had brought along the directional antenna for the scanner which would allow the unit's sensitivity to be limited to a small arc rather than a circumference. The problem with the antenna was it was highly visible to people walking by the vehicle, and its shape made it a curiosity. Thankfully, he wouldn't need to use it for long.

Rudy turned right from Harvard Street onto Clinton Street and immediately spotted the bright red house, four in from the corner where a large apartment building stood. He knew the attic apartment would be Cindy Spagliano's place. Windows on that level overlooked Clinton Street and to the southwest. There were no windows he could see on that floor to the northeast. He could not determine if she had any view looking out toward the back yard, but that wouldn't really matter since there was no alley in that particular block and numerous trees to break up the view should he choose to move one block over for a while.

After driving past, he turned right on Massachusetts Avenue, then another right on Lee Street, which in keeping with Bostonian practice to best use the narrow streets, was one-way in the opposite direction to Clinton Street's flow. He worked his way back to Clinton and parked under a large, leafless tree just beyond the house. Normally, people don't think they're being watched out the back windows of cars, so that was an ideal initial location.

The two vehicles bracketing him on the street had obviously not been moved for a long period, certainly not since before the storm had begun, and were completely covered in snow and blocked in by a plowed ridge. The Jeep easily climbed the piled snow and he parked. Rudy considered whether to interrupt Travis' rest and call and tell him to rent another four-wheeler. The Lincoln would never make it into the parking spots in the neighborhood, even then, and it was still snowing just as heavily as before, perhaps heavier. Over the coming hours, there would be more snowplow runs, and higher ridges to climb over. He decided he'd call his partner and tell him to get himself another Jeep, but first he'd set up the directional antenna on the scanner and call one of Cindy's phones. Then, since he'd be calling anyway, he'd have Travis call Cindy's other phone from a local land line which wouldn't raise as much suspicion as two quick calls coming from a blocked number. With any luck, he'd be able to capture the coded ID and electronic fingerprints of both Cindy's phones in the scanner right off.

Dave stood in the middle of the yard, stunned by the words he had just heard. He thought about his mother. She was Gloria's sister, well, half sister; they shared a mother. Dave's mother had always said Gloria would drink herself to death one day, so he realized the news wouldn't come as much of a surprise to his parents, but hearing of anyone's sudden death was always a shock. Dave and his aunt had never been really that close, mainly because his parents had kept them apart through the years. He had to strain to remember the last time he had seen Aunt Gloria before that past week at her trailer. It had been so many years, but he still felt bad about her passing. She may have been the black sheep of the family, an embarrassment at any gathering, and lived a life continually on the edge of disaster, but she always had been warm and loving to him.

After clicking off with Cindy, he considered calling his parents to relay the news, but then remembered Cindy had said she had passed along the contact information to the Rhode Island Trooper. Chances were they would not have yet had time to send local police to the house. He looked back toward the house. His mother needed to know her half-sister was dead, but he had other considerations. He looked at his watch, paced out circles as he thought about his next actions.

If he contacted his parents, there would be many questions, and there would be a chance someone would be listening in and then this phone would be blown. He may not have been all that worldly yet at twenty-two, but he certainly was not naive. Dace had made it clear in the note not to tell a soul about where they were going because The Senator would turn over Heaven and earth to track them down. It was why he hadn't even initially shared with whom he was traveling with Cindy. She had figured it out, and he had filled her in, but he hadn't revealed most of Dace's confidence, and Cindy had agreed she would keep secret what she knew.

Dave understood he'd eventually have to check in with his parents, but doing so from this new cell phone was not an option. He already knew the house didn't have a landline.  He could perhaps use a pay phone from the nearby convenience store, but if anyone had a trace on his parents' phone, they'd certainly be able to narrow the search area by tracking the number to the small country store.  That wouldn't be an option either, he concluded.  The only phones he trusted were the two new ones he and Cindy had.  He'd have to get to a more distant public place when making the call to his mother and father, perhaps back toward more populated greater New Orleans area.

Then he thought about the suspicious two men who had visited his aunt, had probably called Cindy under false pretenses, and then had again showed up at his aunt's trailer earlier that day.  It was an easy leap of logic to know the two large men were the same two security people Dace had said appeared at his house on the Sunday Sarah had died.  Dave stopped his pacing. Sarah? Aunt Gloria? Both dead. Could there be a connection?  No, that was crazy thinking, he concluded, and immediately dismissed the thought.  The Senator was a wealthy and powerful man, but murder?  To what end?  On the other hand, Dace had talked about how displeased The Senator had been with the pre-party disclosure of his plans of marrying Sarah.  *Could* there be a connection?  No, that's just too conspiratorial. Dave shook his head.  At that point, he wouldn't allow the ideas to sprout, but he certainly had allowed the seed to be planted.

"Shit," he exclaimed.  Suddenly his leg was on fire and he jumped from the stinging pain.  Dave looked down to see hundreds of ants swarming over his tennis shoes and moving up his sock.  He moved away from the area instinctively and began swatting the insects.  He could feel them biting his leg, moving higher and higher.  His hands brushed over his pants, but the pain just got worse as the invading creatures under the jeans had begun a life or death struggle.  Others had begun clinging to his hands each time he went to swat them off the outside.

"Better get them britches off, boy," came the voice, "and get away from that nest."

Dave didn't care where the disembodied voice had come from, he had arrived at the same conclusion himself and was quickly undoing his belt and sliding the pants off, then tossed them away as he jumped and jogged from the area where the pain had begun.  He swatted the swarming ants on his leg, finding they didn't just brush off; he had to kill them to get them to stop biting him.  He'd never in his life had ants swarm him like that.  What kind of monster bugs do they have down here, he thought.

"Stand still, boy," the voice came again.

It was then Dave saw the elderly black woman who had come to his rescue and who was now bent over and helping pull the biting ants from his legs.

"You feel any in them shorts?" she asked. "Cause if you do, you best shed them too. You don't want 'em bitin' you there, do ya boy?" She looked up at him and showed a toothless grin. "Don't be shy, I seen it all afore; and if'n I ain't seen it, I promise to tell ya afore I go and swat it."

"No," Dave said. "I don't think so."

"Okay, looks like we got 'em all." She motioned to the jeans lying in a crumpled pile ten feet away, swarming with thousands of the tiny, devil creatures. "Just leave them britches for now. The others will soon realize you're not in 'em anymore and they'll go back to the nest."

"I've never seen ants act like that before."

"Where you from, boy?"

"Connecticut."

"This your first time down here?"

"Yeah, it is."

"Well, boy, this here is Louisiana, and you better learn quick that we gots lotsa things you ain't got up in Connecticut. Some of 'em is far worse to go stumblin' over in the grass than them fire ants. You need to watch where you is walkin' down here, boy." She gave him the quick once over, evaluating his stock as much as anything. "Come on up to the house, we'll get somethin' on them stings."

She began slowly making her way toward the house.

"Just watch where you is walking from now on," she said, looking over her shoulder.

Dave jogged to catch up.

"Where did you come from, ma'am?" he said, the fire in his leg changing to a deep throbbing as he moved.

"I'm Desiree, but folks 'round here just call me Auntie D for long as I can remember," she said. "My people have lived on this land for over two hundred years. I was born here, and since I'm the end of my line, I'm gonna be the last of my people to die here."

"Well, to say that I'm glad to meet you would be a gross understatement, Auntie D," Dave said. "Thank you for coming to my rescue."

She just nodded and kept walking. The incongruous pair padded up the back stairs together. Dave began to turn to walk around the porch to the front room doors he had exited but Auntie D reached into her skirt and pulled out a key and unlocked the back door.

"Come on, boy," she said, walking in and turning into the pantry.

Dave followed her to the pantry doorway, watched as she moved around the room as if she knew it intimately. She gathered items into her arms and then came toward the door. Dave moved out of the way, then reached down and started scratching at a few of the bites.

"Don't do that, boy," Auntie D said. "Come on into the kitchen and we'll get somethin' on them welts."

Auntie D worked for half an hour, finding and treating every sting on Dave's massive legs. As she worked, she explained how, unlike most ants, fire ants didn't just bite, they stung; they grab the victim with their mandibles and then sting from the abdomen, injecting venom from multiple hits. She used vinegar, a couple of pastes she whipped up at the sink, and then topped them with her own homemade combination of tea tree oil and other secret ingredients. All the while she told him stories about the plantation, the owners through the generations and the slaves who had worked the land and built the main house. Dave was so engrossed with the woman's tales that he didn't hear the footfalls coming down the hallway.

Dace walked into the kitchen and stopped short, his mind fighting to make sense of the image of Dave standing there without pants and an old black woman with close-cropped white hair in a full-length, deep green house dress sitting on a chair and dabbing at his legs with cotton balls.

"Fire ants," Dave said, turning his head. "I stumbled onto one of their nests in the back yard."

Dace nodded slowly, his eyes drifted toward the woman.

"This is Auntie D, she lives on the property," Dave said to the unverbalized question.

Dace smiled to the woman. She nodded to him, flashed a toothless grin and then finished up her work.

"It's a pleasure to meet you, ma'am," Dace said. "I'm Dace."

She stood up, arched her back and stretched.

"I heard you was coming, boy," she said, pointing a bony finger at Dave, "from that Sam woman. I was to make myself scarce, leave you two alone. I thought a young lady was gonna be with you, coupla lovers what Sam said." She peered at Dace. "I don't judge, mind ya. Then I seen this one here through my window, walkin' 'round them fire ant nests like he ain't got no care in the world for where he was goin'. He finally kicked one over 'bout the time I gots myself downstairs and outside. I live over Uncle Jack's workshop, that building this boy was headed toward what looks like a fallin' down shed. Uncle Jack done said I can live there long as I like, rent free. He a good man." She smiled at a memory. "And he do love my gumbo and corn bread."

Dave smiled and looked down at his legs, which now no longer burned or throbbed. The bites were still there, still reddish, but not getting any bigger, and not itching anymore.

"Well, Auntie D, I for one am glad you were here today," Dave said. "I didn't realize those things were out there."

"No thanks needed, boy," she said. "I already done told you this is Louisiana, not Connecticut. We look where we is goin' down here." She shook her head again. Then, to Dace: "Pleased to meet you. Dace is it?"

"Yes, ma'am, it's..."

"French, I know. This here was a Creole plantation most of its time. Only French spoke here until shortly afore I was born. Mama and daddy raised me knowin' French and English. They mamas and daddies was the last folk to be born as slaves here, and the first to be free workers on this place after Mr. Lincoln done said they was free. They was share croppers after the war. So was my daddy, and my husband, afore God called him home. Now, it just be me left here."

Auntie D continued to speak as she moved about the kitchen, cleaning up the dishes with the pastes, putting the caps back on the ingredients bottles and tossing out the cotton balls.

"She's got some amazing stories, Dace," Dave said. "She's one hell, I mean, heck of a nurse, too."

"What's your name, boy?" she asked Dave. "I think it's about time you and me was properly introduced."

"Oh, I'm Dave," he said, a flush of embarrassment coming to his cheeks.

"No need to turn all red faced now, boy," she said. "The time for that was when you kicked over that ant nest and had to shed your britches in front of a strange, old woman."

Dave gave a weak smile.

"Dave and Dace," she said. "People get you boys confused?"

Dace laughed, which left behind a wide smile. People often called it his 'Million Dollar Smile' and when he was running for class president over the years, his 'Election Smile'.

"Not when they have seen or know us, Auntie D, but we have had some fun with strangers because of the names sounding so alike over the years," Dace said.

"You boys eat yet today?" Auntie D asked.

"Breakfast, late," Dave said. "Haven't decided on dinner."

Auntie D glanced around the kitchen.

"Tell you what," she said. "I know Sam stocked the house, and I don't get much call to cook for a couple of young boys anymore, so why don't y'all go sit in the parlor and I'll whip up some good old fashioned country cookin'?"

Dace and Dave shared a look and then each nodded. There would have been no use in arguing. Auntie D had already strapped on an apron from one of the cabinets and was taking down a couple of old iron pots. Dace looked into the refrigerator and pulled out a can of regular Mountain Dew, looked at Dave who nodded, so he grabbed one of Cherry and tossed it across to him.

"Now you boys git," she said, and then pointed a bony finger toward Dave. "You, go git your britches. Them ants should have moved on by now. Look 'em over real good and shake 'em out, but pay heed you do that outside; and, for the Good Lord's sake, stay away from the nest, boy."

Rudy and Travis confirmed Cindy's known phones were in the area by placing calls to both numbers. When he was in position and set up, Rudy had called first, spoke in Spanish and asked for Sonia. Cindy told him there was no Sonia there. Frustrated by his repeated requests to speak to the woman followed by several moments of feigned confusion borne of the language barrier coming back at her, Cindy spat 'wrongo numero' and clicked off. Travis called her ten minutes later on the other phone and asked if Cindy cared to participate in a survey regarding health insurance; she politely declined and hung up.

For the purposes of identifying and locating her phones, it didn't really matter that each phone call was of a very short duration. The need to keep people on the line until a trace could be established through the telephone company had been long relegated to the category of Hollywood hokum and was just a rather cheesy device to build tension in the movies. Since the early 1960s, telecommunication companies had been in a transition from analog to digital technology which allowed them to eliminate the massive banks of mechanical dialers and replace those with smaller, highly efficient, and more reliable computerized switchboards. Cellular phones had always used the newer digital technology meaning any trace was instantaneous, and records of each call were stored on computers for billing purposes and documentation.

The scanner Rudy and Travis owned was technically illegal for them to possess, having been obtained through a cooperative soul at an alphabet agency in the federal government. Sure, there were knockoffs available all over on the electronics black market; *Popular Electronics* had even supplied plans for readers to build their own 'radio phone scanner' years ago, but those black market or homemade units lacked many of the more interesting upgrades available on the liberated unit which blinked on the passenger seat of Rudy's rented Jeep.

Their device identified *both* phone numbers on the call and the coded identification from the SIMM card of the captured cellular. It was capable of recording the conversations of up to six trapped calls simultaneously, but most importantly, it recorded the electronic fingerprint - known as the *radio fingerprint* to the technically savvy - of the surveilled cellular phone. While he didn't fully understand all the jargon the cooperative technician had used when explaining the guts of the scanner, Rudy knew it wasn't the just the phone number or even the SIMM card, but rather the radio fingerprint which made each phone uniquely identifiable to the telephone company equipment. By storing the radio fingerprint of an individual phone and tying it to the assigned phone number and SIMM card, the computers could immediately detect and disallow a fraudulent or cloned phone. They were working on a method of 'zapping' or 'tagging' the fraudulent phone, but that program had been plagued by policy pitfalls and technical problems.

How the technician had explained the fundamentals of the radio fingerprint to them was that each radio transmitter, phone, or other device that sent out a signal contained slight variations in its component values during manufacture which created a unique *rise time* signature when the device was keyed to transmit which could not be easily duplicated or faked. It was what could be viewed as the brain waves of the phone. Just as human brain waves are all unique to the individual, so was the rise time signature of every electronic transmitter.

If a phone were cloned, for instance, it could have the same numeric identifiers tied to the phone and SIMM card, but would not have the same electronic fingerprint, thus making it identifiable as a duplicate or fraudulent device. Federal regulatory and spy agencies, as well as the military, used systems similar to Rudy and Travis' liberated unit for tracking down suspect or specifically targeted transmitters, but it was illegal for a private citizen to possess such a device. What made Rudy always able to breathe easier when they used the scanner was that it was radiation passive, that is, it didn't transmit any signals; it merely listened, and was therefore theoretically undetectable.

With the electronic fingerprint data of Cindy Spagliano's cell phones captured and locked into the device after Rudy manually tagged them, the unit would automatically prioritize anything further coming from, or going to them, and quickly dispose of any nearby phone snagged which wasn't an exact match. From then on, the directional antenna was not necessary, nor was line-of-sight surveillance.

The snow continued to fall heavily as Rudy stowed the antenna in the back seat of his rented Jeep. In less than half an hour of his arrival, the SUV was completely covered in a thickening white blanket, with only the hood partially cleared by melting from the residual heat of the engine, and now, even that was filling in with snow. Inside, the windows were fogging with condensation due to the temperature difference and Rudy's exhalations. The cellular scanner was busy flashing away as it captured and quickly disposed of numerous calls within its range, but there was nothing further coming from either of Cindy's units. So long as the phones remained within range of the scanning unit, they'd be assured of not missing any calls made to or from them. There was nothing more he, or Travis when he relieved him in three hours, would have to do. They were now like the scanner, passive, just waiting for something to happen.

Rudy twisted the top off a plastic bottle of Pepsi and drained a healthy slug, then reached into a brown paper bag and pulled out a wrapped, cold-cut submarine sandwich he had picked up from a local deli on the way to Cindy's place. He placed the Pepsi back into a cup holder in the center console, rolled the sandwich wrapper open on his lap, pulled out a napkin from the bag and stuffed an end into his shirt collar. He wriggled himself in the leather seat. The Jeep's version of a luxury leather seat wasn't all that uncomfortable for a man his size, but he'd been doing an awful lot of sitting in the last few days and he really needed to move more. After years of being used to much more daily physical exertion, or at the very least the opportunity to work out, he was becoming physically restless with the sedentary routine, and when the broken sleep of the past week was factored in, a tad irritable.

He tore a big bite from the sandwich, washed it down with another slug of Pepsi. He was about to take a second bite when the cab interior was flooded with flashing yellow light reflected from every direction. The light was quickly followed by a heavy scraping sound and moments later a snowplow rumbled past, packing a high ridge of snow against the side of the Jeep. He chewed as he watched the rig roll down the street, pushing tons of snow against dozens of cars.

Half an hour later, he was finished with the sandwich and the Pepsi had been drained. He shifted in the seat again, felt like ants were crawling on his body. This was the part of the job Rudy hated: the sitting and waiting for something to happen. He looked at his watch. Just under three hours until Travis would relieve him. He cracked his neck to relieve some of the tension locked inside. The sandwich and soda had bloated him and Rudy knew his hunger and thirst hadn't come from physical need, but from boredom, which was the worst way to eat, he knew, and yet he continued to feed that craving these days. He'd gained fifty pounds since leaving the Corps and some of his muscle tone was turning soft. That irritated him too. He checked his watch again.

Dace and Dave took their soft drinks out onto the back porch rather than back to the front room. The sun was moving lower to the horizon, leaving perhaps an hour of daylight until darkness fell. They each took a seat in one of a pair of high backed wicker rocking chairs. They were large and sturdy with a perfectly tapered back, each with a cotton-covered cushion on the seat and wide arm rests with an integral glass holder and they quickly discovered they were as comfortable as anything in the house. They left the inside door open, and through the screen door they could hear the sounds of Auntie D clanking around in the kitchen as she hummed a recognizable spiritual song.

It wasn't long before the humming was accompanied by a blend of aromas began to waft from the kitchen. Oil and onions came first, followed shortly after by some kind of pork, identifiable, but subtly different from bacon. Then green peppers, paprika, garlic, celery, and finally, cayenne pepper. After that, the individual ingredients blended into a unique and seductive aroma medley. Like the spiritual she hummed, the food she was preparing was a classic tune being played by the experienced person of the mysterious Auntie D.

"Are you going to get your pants?" Dace asked.

Dave looked a bit uncomfortable, shifted in his seat.

"Aw, come on, don't tell me you're afraid of an ant," Dace teased. "Really?"

"Not ant, man; *ants*. No, of course not," Dave said. "It's just that I've never had such a voracious attack into my pants since I dated Cindy Spagliano."

Dace laughed. So did Dave.

"I feel sorry for you, man," Dace said. "That's been done for over a year, right? Nobody since?"

He knew the answers, but they were talking about easy stuff, so Dace wanted it to continue.

"About, and no," Dave admitted, eager to change the subject he had introduced. "You should have seen those little bastards attack. Vicious. Auntie D says they are just one of the nasty creatures lurking out there." He pointed back toward the swamp. "Snakes, alligators, heck, who knows what else."

"The Klan," Dace injected, drank and stared into the distance.

Dave stared at him. Had he really just said that? He shook the image from his mind and hoped that Auntie D had not picked up on it.

"Want me to go with you?" Dace asked. "Because I have to tell you, buddy, you're looking awfully cute over there and I don't know if I can hold myself back if you don't get your pants back on." Big smile.

"Funny," Dave said. "You can laugh all you want, but you haven't had those things in your pants."

"Ms. Double Ds either," Dace said with a laugh. "Am I missing anything?"

Dave shot Dace a mocking grin. After a pause for another thought to move through his brain, he stood slowly, hesitated for another few moments, hiked his boxers with determination and walked off the porch. He quickly crossed the narrow pathway of paver stones, then moved slowly into the grass, reconnoitering each step before he took it. To Dace, his friend appeared as if he were mapping a mine field.

The screen door opened. Dace turned to see Auntie D standing there in her housedress and apron over the top, a large, wooden spoon in her right hand. The end of the spoon was lightly coated in a translucent, reddish sauce speckled with spices. She placed her left hand on her hip and shook her head slowly as she watched Dave moving carefully across the grass.

"You know, boy, if you don't move a little quicker, it'll be dark before you get them pants back here, and the snakes come out at dark. The bad ones," she hollered, then cupped her free hand to cover a snicker.

Dave froze as if he had just stepped on a land mine and any further movement would cause the thing to explode. His head turned to look back at the porch. Dace was struggling to hold back the laughter. Auntie D was just shaking her head, a big toothless grin on her face.

"Is that boy always so, um, what's the word?"

"Gullible?" Dace said.

She nodded.

"Yep, pretty much."

"Just don't get near any mounds that look like turned up dirt," she called out, "and you'll be fine, boy." Then she turned to go back inside to the kitchen and Dace heard her mumbling something about 'so-called smart, city kids from Connecticut'. The screen door slammed behind her.

The last words of local advice seemed to help Dave make better time. After that, he was out by his pants in no time. He looked them over, turned them inside out and shook them hard. Then, he carefully retraced his steps back to the stairs. Once back standing on the relative safety of the porch, he double checked his pants before sitting on the top step to pull them on.

"That effort deserves a beer, at least," Dace said, rising from his rocking chair. He grabbed Dave's nearly empty can of Cherry Dew from the cup holder on his chair, shook it a bit. "You want the rest of this?"

Dave shook his head, continued to pull on his pants. They went hard over his shoe and he was wondering how he had shed them so fast.

"No, a beer would be great, thanks," Dave said to Dace's back.

The screen door slammed. A few moments later, Dace was back with two icy bottles of Dixie beer in his hand. He set one down next to Dave, who was busy removing his shoe to more easily get the second leg though the jeans. Dace clinked his bottle against Dave's, then moved to sit down again in his rocker. He took a long draw from the bottle. The beer chilled his throat going down and the combination of cold and carbonation brought a momentary grimace on his face.

"You know, Dave, the blackmail price for not telling the story of you falling prey to a gang of Louisiana ants is going to be quite high when we get back on campus." He grinned and took another draw of beer. "Yep, I may never do another load of wash again."

Dave finished retying his shoe, picked up his beer and returned to his chair. He took a long drink from the bottle. His face was sweating in the cooling air.

"You know, this stuff isn't half bad," Dave said, ignoring the blackmail remark, but refusing to let the second comment go unanswered. "I'm not doing your laundry, pal. I thought you had *people* for that?"

"We do," Dace said. "Then, I guess you're off the hook, buddy, until I think of something else."

The screen door opened halfway and interrupted Dave's coming retort. Auntie D stood there in the opening, no spoon in her hand that time.

"You boys wash up now, then come into the kitchen for supper," she said. "I ain't dirtying up the dinin' room. Y'all can eat like normal folk tonight."

She then moved back inside. Dave and Dace, lured by the perfect orchestration of aromas and driven by the emptiness of their bellies, rushed inside and went to the bathroom to wash their hands. Dave was first out, drying his hands on his jeans. He walked into the kitchen and was greeted by the most delicious looking and smelling spread of food he had ever encountered. Dace came up behind him a moment later.

Auntie D was removing an iron skillet from the oven. The aroma of hot corn bread momentarily displaced, then joined those of the other food into the perfect melange; Dave thought the addition of the cornbread was like an oboe being gently drawn in to complete an opus by Mozart.

"Come on, now," Auntie D said, motioning to the small table in the corner set for two. "Sit yourselves down."

In the center of the table sat two more iron pans on small hot pads made of unadorned terra cotta squares. Deep, wooden spoons rested across each skillet. Glasses of cold milk had been poured, three of them. A pot of honey rested on the table next to where Auntie D placed the fresh-baked cornbread. She left a potholder on the handle of the pan. As the boys drew closer, they noticed the skillet was cast to segment the cornbread into six pieces. One of the other pans held seasoned rice; long-grained and 'dirty', Auntie D called it. The other held a bubbling reddish gravy filled with chunks of celery, green pepper, red pepper, okra, shrimp and crawfish. Not just the tails, but the whole shrimp and the whole crawfish.

"I made ever'thing with a medium heat," she said. "Since y'all is from up north and are not used to Louisiana yet." She winked at Dave. "Now, dig in; and don't be shy."

She took a seat on a third chair at the table, where the extra glass of milk stood but no place had been set.

"Aren't you joining us, Auntie D?" Dave said.

"Me eat this? Boy, is you tryin' to kill me? I can't eat that no mo'. Just a piece of corn bread with honey and milk for me. Otherwise I won't sleep a wink all night, and if'n I do, may not wake in the mornin'."

Dace looked around on the table, then started to get up.

"Whatchu need, Dace?" Auntie D asked. "A little Louisiana hot sauce? I'd taste it first, were I you."

He had paused partway up.

"No, I was going to get a napkin, or paper towel."

She gently pushed him down by the shoulder.

"Boy, you go wastin' my good, country cookin' wiped on a piece of cloth or worse yet, paper, I ain't gonna be happy." She held up her splayed fingers. "The Good Lord give ya five fingers on each hand and you'll find they each fit quite nice into your mouth for cleanin'. Whatever you got left after that, you can wash away in the sink later."

At her instruction, they each scooped two heaping spoonfuls of rice onto their plates and then topped that with healthy helpings from the seafood skillet. The shrimp and crawfish were cooked whole, Auntie D said, so the flavor could get between the meat and shell and percolate in there. Everything was sprinkled with bits of seasoning, and coated in the light, red sauce. There were no tomatoes in the dish, the coloring came naturally from the seasonings, she said.

Once they started eating, sopping up extra gravy with bits of fresh corn bread, the only conversation at the table came from Auntie D. She showed them how to disassemble a crawfish, how to suck the tail meat from the segmented shell without too much muss or fuss, and then how to remove the fat from inside the head with their little finger. She told them they could eat the entire shrimp just as they were, but neither of them were yet so bold, so they twisted off the head and removed the legs and shells. Dace quickly realized what the old woman had meant about using their God-given mouths to clean their fingers. He didn't want to waste a drip of the perfectly seasoned goodness and eagerly sucked his fingers clean.

Auntie D's stories were the perfect wine for the meal. She told them how, through records given to her by Uncle Jack several years ago, she was able to find her ancestors had come to the plantation through the auction block in New Orleans, after having been snatched from their homes in Africa, an area which in 1998 was Senegal, were transported on Dutch ships to the West Indies in the Caribbean, and then finally on French ships to New Orleans. They arrived amidst a gaggle of slaves bought in July 1789 by Phillippe Charbenneaux, the son of the founder of the plantation, who by then had risen to be the master of the land. The first coupling which eventually led to Auntie D generations down the line were two slaves by the names of Francois and Delphine, common names in those days, given by the plantation owner, she said.

She told plantation stories which had been handed down through generations of slaves and later free people of color who remained there, told originally in *patois*, a sort of cobbled together language. To preserve her people's history as it had been lived, she said they maintained the homespun language with each retelling. She related one such story to the boys in the original patois, who even with rapt attention had a hard time following along.

Soon, the empty 'skins bowl' which Auntie D had set on the edge of the table was as overflowing with shrimp parts and crawfish rinds as were the two boys' stomachs with the rest of her delicious meal.

"That was some of the best food I've ever had," Dace said, sitting back in the chair. "Thank you."

He noted his fingers carried a slight ruddy tinge, and beyond that there wasn't a morsel to wash off in the sink.

"Same here, Auntie D. I don't suppose we could get you to do more of this for us while we're here," Dave added. "Your cooking and stories are good for the soul."

"Well, thank you, boys," she said. Rising from her chair. "It did me good to cook for two hungry young men again. It's been too long since I been able to do that." A pause as she stretched out a couple of kinks. "Way too long."

The three worked together to clean up the kitchen. Auntie D packaged up the few leftovers and then showed the boys how to dry clean cast iron skillets, telling them that getting water on them was as near to a sin as any cook could commit. She packed the crawfish and shrimp shells into a plastic bag and placed it into the freezer, telling them when she had enough saved up she's make a wonderful stock out of them. She told the city boys: 'In the country, we don't waste nothin'.'

When they were finished, she said her good-byes and then walked out into the night, eschewing their assistance to get home. Dave and Dace went back out to the whicker chairs on the back porch and watched her cross the lawn with hardly a downward glance and disappear around the corner of the shed.

A short time later, a light came on in an upstairs window. Dace looked hard, and would swear the light was a flickering candle. He contemplated the light while considering the old woman's words of a history preserved in the most common of terms, and how, his family's lineage could similarly be tracked back over two-hundred years in this country; but how his clan had traveled a much different road, solely because of skin color and the pure luck of how and where people were born. What was it that Dave had said to him earlier? Oh, yeah, about him being a Fortunate Son. Indeed, he thought.

He readily accepted an offered bottle of Dixie when Dave returned from a kitchen run a minute later.

# Chapter Fourteen

Dave and Dace sat long into the evening in the rocking chairs on the back porch. One beer after dinner had turned into six, then ten, then who remembered? Somewhere along the way, evening turned to night, and then night to early morning. They talked of their lives, their friendship, their parents, the future, and, finally, Sarah; they communicated on levels they had never before even approached.

Bobby maneuvered his boss' old red pickup up the drive of the Immaculate Conception Catholic Girls Preparatory School at five minutes before ten. Ronnie snuggled against Bobby. Ashley hugged the passenger door. When the truck stopped, Ashley opened her door, hopped out and slammed it so hard that the whole truck rattled. She stomped around the front of the old Dodge, her eyes focused straight ahead, and began to cross the drive toward the central entrance to the old, white, plaster-covered-brick dorm building. The barely muffled engine rumbled away, insulting the still of the night.

"Hey, no good bye?" Bobby called out his window.

Ashley turned to see Bobby grinning at her, his left arm perched on the door out the rolled-down window, his right around Ronnie, his hand slowly stroking her back side. Ronnie hadn't moved from her snuggle position.

"Good night, asshole," Ashley spat. Then past him: "Are you coming, Ronnie?"

"She already did, twice, as I recall," Bobby leered, then tossed a wink out the window.

Ashley glared at him. He smiled back at her, then opened the door and climbed out, Ronnie close behind. He turned to her and she edged close to him, her head tossed back and her big brown eyes dreamily crossing the one-foot difference in their heights to find his.

"I'll drop off your car in the parking lot first thing in the morning on my way to the airport, babe," Bobby said. "You girls have a good time. I'll call you soon." He kissed her chastely, after all he was standing on holy ground. "Love you, baby."

"I love you, Bobby," Ronnie said, stars in her eyes and honey in her voice. "I'm gonna miss you."

She jumped up on him, threw her arms over his neck and wrapped her legs around his hips and gave him a deep kiss. Ashley roughly pulled her off him by her belt. Ronnie turned over her shoulder to look hard at her best friend.

"Gee, thanks, Ash," Ronnie said.

"It's ten o'clock, Ronnie, and I'm not going to have my plans ruined for this weekend because you discovered the joys of giving it up to some walking hard-on." Her stare was hard and cold and then she began to drag Ronnie by the back of her pants. Ronnie's shoes scuffled backwards in protest across the crushed oyster shells of the drive.

"Okay, okay," Ronnie protested in a loud voice.

Ashley held tight to her belt line.

"She's right, babe," Bobby said to calm the situation before he had to be answering to a nun come out to check the racket. Then, mockingly as he looked past Ronnie into Ashley's eyes: "Let Mother Hubbard take you in and put you back in her cupboard."

"Screw you, Bobby," Ashley said as she turned and dragged Ronnie backward again toward the steps.

"Been there, done that, Ash," Bobby said, purposely using the nickname Ashley only allowed Ronnie to get away with. "Good night, babe. I'll be through here in the morning before sun up."

"Not if my prayers come true tonight, pencil dick" Ashley spat over her shoulder.

Ronnie had struggled free of Ashley's belt grip and turned to follow and walk behind her up the stairs and into the open portal. At the door, she paused, turned, and blew Bobby a kiss. The clock in the tower attached to the chapel began to peel off ten strokes of the bell.

Bobby jumped back into the truck and slammed the door as the girls disappeared inside. He grinned to himself as he spun shells out the back tires and headed for home.

Ronnie jogged to catch up to Ashley in the semi-darkened hallway. Her shoes squeaked out each contact with the highly polished, terrazzo floor.

"Geeze, Ash, you didn't have to be so rude to Bobby," Ronnie said in a low tone as they moved along toward the back stairwell. "He didn't do anything to you."

"Just drop it, Ronnie," Ashley hissed as she continued along at a quickened pace. "After all we talked about, you just go and give it up. If you were just going to do that, why did you bother dragging me along to Baton Rouge? Why didn't you just go rut in the tall grass out back?"

The tone of the words stung Ronnie to her core. She stopped dead in her tracks, her eyes followed Ashley's steps. Finally, Ashley stopped too, turned around to face her. Ronnie began to shake her head slowly, her eyes misted, and though the light was low, Ronnie could see her friend well enough. Her head dropped. She studied the floor, her shoes, anything she could make out down there so she could avoid Ashley's painfully accusing eyes. Slowly, she moved her gaze upward. Ashley stood there, arms hanging at her side, waiting.

Ronnie's mouth moved to begin to form the first word of the next sentence between them.

"Did you girls have a good time at the parade?" came the lowered voice of Sister Regina as she moved silently out of the complete darkness of the small alcove at the door to her office. She stood between the two girls. "You just made curfew, you realize."

"Yes, Sister," Ashley said, her eyes fixed on Ronnie. "We had a wonderful time. Thank you for giving us special permission. We're sorry we cut the curfew so close, but Bobby was driving very carefully."

"Ah, the boy with the truck who just spun his tires on the roadway out there? I'm certain he's a very cautious driver." Her lips pursed, although the girls couldn't make out the facial expression in the lowered light. "Did I hear you two quarreling when you came in?" She paused, her eyes moving between the Ashley and Ronnie, then fixing on one of them. "Veronica, is there something you need to tell me?"

"No, Sister," Ronnie said, embarrassed, her cheeks flushing.

"Ashley?" Sister Regina asked.

"No, nothing, Sister," Ashley said. Her eyes flicked toward the Head Mother and quickly returned to Ronnie.

Ronnie moved toward Ashley slowly. She refused to make eye contact with the nun as she passed her, then stood next to Ashley. A united front. Sister Regina, being well used to the machinations and manipulations of teen-aged girls, allowed her pursed lips to form a shallow smile. She unfolded her arms and removed her hands from the opposite sleeves of her full-length, black habit.

"All right, then, ladies, if that's all, I'll bid you a good night," she said as she turned to move down the hallway in the opposite direction her young charges were headed.

"Good night, Sister," the girls chimed in unison and they turned and made for the back stairs.

"Girls, one last thing," Sister Regina called from near the front door. "Morning chapel before Mass would not be a bad idea.   For both of you."

"Yes, Sister," they chimed again before walking slowly into the stairwell, then taking two steps at a time in a race to the safety of their second-floor room.

Tom again found Libby downstairs at the kitchen table, this time she was rereading Dace's letter.  The clock on the wall announced it to be a bit after two in the morning.  The Senator had left home shortly after last evening's dinner to travel to Washington for a number of important committee meetings and votes in the Senate over the coming days.  Tom had asked if The Senator wanted him to make the trip as well, but he had said he would feel better if Tom stayed with Libby while the matter with Dace was still unresolved.  He intended to be home late in the week, he assured, but reminded them both that he was always reachable should something turn up.

Tom was relieved The Senator had made the decisions he did.  He always had enjoyed spending time alone with Libby, and given the events of the last week, he could use some less stressful interactions with both Libby and The Senator.  The daily office sessions with The Senator and late night operational consultations with his main two operatives - Travis and Rudy - had worn his nerves to a frazzle, quite a feat to have done to a grizzled political advisor.  Word on the street in D.C. was they *had* no feelings, possessed no soul, and while Tom realized he had sold his soul long ago, he still laid claim to the emotions and feelings of any normal man.   With Caroline gone for the weekend, the next couple of days alone, apart from Mary Rose being in the house, would give he and Libby more of an opportunity to talk about Dace's letter, and other things, without fear of being interrupted or overheard.   Tom had questions, and as he sat down at the table with his cup of warm milk, he hoped Libby would have some answers.

"I couldn't sleep," Tom said and shifted forward on his chair, placed his elbows on the table, hands cupping the warm mug.  "I was hoping some warm milk would do the trick. Always has worked in the past."

Libby folded the letter, slid it under the corner of a woven placemat, made no attempt to either hide it or keep it out of Tom's reach.  She knew he wouldn't be so rude as to try to read it without her permission, but understood with it so visible he'd question her about it further.  She had, so far, kept the existence of the letter a secret from her husband. She knew he was under enough stress, and while he continued to manage it with either drink or bouts of lashing out, Allard was no longer a young man at seventy-five and didn't need to spend time dissecting and analyzing the words of her son to her.

"Warm milk never works for me," Libby said, removing her reading glasses, folding them and setting them at the head of the placemat. "Never has."

Tom rotated the mug in his hands, drawing warmth from it, but not taking a drink. Libby smiled as she recognized the tell.

"Are you going to drink it, or just play with it?" she said.

He smiled. He could feel the gentleness of the jibe, and it felt good.

"So many years, Libby," he said. "Has it really been that long?"

She sat back in her chair and looked across the table toward the windows, which reflected her image but revealed nothing outside but the blackness of a starless night.

"Obviously, from the reflection, it has been," she sighed.

Tom followed her gaze, saw the same image in the glass. He reached across to hold her hands with one of his. He felt an initial flinch of retreat, but then she settled and allowed the contact.

"Not judging from that reflection, Libby," he said. "You're still as beautiful as the first time I laid eyes upon you."

"Tom..." She drew her hands from underneath his. "Don't. It's been over twenty years..." She stood and began walking toward the kitchen. At the wide portal, she turned. "Read the letter, Tom. You were correct earlier. A father should know. I'll leave the final decision in your hands, for now. I'm going to bed."

His head whirled, but she was gone. From the darkness of the great room, her slow footfalls echoed in the quiet house as she headed toward the stairs.

In the darkened master suite of his secluded home outside of Washington in McClean, Virginia, The Senator lay in a sweat, his heart pounding inside his chest. He labored for breath and slowly turned his head, searching the night with his eyes. The blue electronic numbers on the bedside clock showed 2:23. His head swirled, he was thirsty, with only the meager remains of his night cap of single malt in a glass on the nightstand, barely within reach. Interrupting his gasping breaths, his dry tongue licked his even drier lips.

"Are you okay, Senator?" the young blonde woman who had just rolled off him cooed. She lay on her stomach, naked, resting on her elbows. Her blonde hair was tousled, and hung loosely around her shoulders. She was neither sweating nor breathing heavily. "Can I get you something?"

"A glass of water from the bathroom, if you don't mind," he said. "I'm a bit thirsty. You've worn me to a nub, my dear."

She watched him across the darkness a moment without moving. Without his glasses, all The Senator could make out of her was an outline and a preternatural set of brilliant teeth formed in a smile. She rolled out of bed, tossing the covers back as she left. He slid up to sit, reached for his glasses and placed them on his nose. It was still near total darkness in the room, the only light coming from the neon blue numbers on the clock, but he could at least see her shapely form as it moved toward the bathroom.

The woman possessed the lithe and effortless movements of the young, he thought as she walked across the thick carpet. Her round buttocks were firm and high and lifted and fell with each step without bouncing; her legs were long and lean. At the door, she touched the correct switch to provide a minimal, nightlight illumination in the bathroom. She had been there many times before and knew that part of the house nearly as well as its absent matron.

In the low light, she was even more remarkable. Her breasts were firm, and like her buttocks, perky and full, with small, pink nipples which pointed skyward as if giving homage to Heaven itself. Her belly was flat, and as she turned, The Senator saw her perfectly waxed nether region. She filled a glass, shut off the light and padded back to bed. She sat on the edge, one leg crooked underneath her, the other off the side, foot on the floor. A gentle aroma drifted in the lightly disturbed air. She handed the glass across to The Senator, remembered his last comment, and smiled knowing she had done her job.

"Why, Senator, you could never be worn down to a nub," she said, teasingly lifting the covers from his lap. "Nope, not at chance of that happening."

He smiled. He knew the game, but she was spectacular, and well worth the knowledge she said the same things to dozens of other rich and powerful men in Washington. He sipped from the glass, the water refreshing him instantly. His breathing came easier, his heartbeat nearly back to normal.

"Shall I stay?" she asked. "Think you've got a third in you tonight?"

Even with his glasses, he couldn't see the contents of her eyes across the darkness, thankfully so for his ego.

"No, I think twice is all I have in me tonight," he said. "It's been a very stressful week. I'm frankly amazed you could coax that much from me, my dear."

Sensing an opening to extricate herself cleanly, she rose onto all fours on the mattress and leaned to him, giving him a light kiss on the cheek. He moved his mouth toward hers - they always tried that move - but she expertly sidestepped his attempt and retreated. Even though she had just had unprotected sex with the man, twice, she wouldn't kiss him on the lips. It was a whore's code that, she guessed, went back perhaps to the trade's first practitioners. She had done everything else possible to him with her mouth, but still would never kiss a client. When she began in the business seven years ago, another girl had told her that kissing was just too intimate to share with a paying customer. 'That should be reserved for the man, or woman, you love,' the mentor had said. So went the code.

She slid off the bed, leaving him sitting there with his glass of water and sweaty, old man's body and began slipping on her clothes which she had carefully laid on a nearby chair before the evening's festivities had begun. Anyone could undress in the dark, but Saxony - her trade name, not her real one - was an expert at dressing in total darkness.

"On the dresser, Hon?" she asked, as she tied her one-piece dress across her now off-rent body.

"Yes, as always," he said.

Saxony was also an expert at finding her cash in the dark. Under a small nicknack, she found the twenty crisp hundred dollar bills, her fee for two hours of her time, plus travel. She didn't approach him again, merely blew him a kiss across the distance in the dark. She knew the way out. A couple of minutes later, she slid into the leather seat of her BMW and wheeled around the drive back out to the main road. Twenty minutes after that, she would be home in Alexandria.

The Senator heard her go, heard her car start and leave the driveway. He slid himself down in the bed, decided to sleep naked, something he rarely did with Libby anymore.

Suddenly he laughed out loud as he thought of the old ball breaking jibe often told in the Senate cloakroom, 'We all know *what* you are, the question is how much? Yes, he thought, Washington was inhabited by many a whore; Saxony represented merely one category of them.

Fifteen minutes later, The Senator drifted off to sleep.


Two hours earlier, shortly after they saw the light extinguish in Auntie D's window, Dave and Dace stopped going inside to relieve themselves, instead taking the short cut to the edge of the porch. It currently was Dave's turn.

"I hope this doesn't wind up killing Uncle Jack's hedges," Dave said, as most of him was concentrating on standing on the edge after...how many beers was it?

"Nah," Dace said. "Worst it will do is brown them a bit. Won't kill 'em."

"You sure?" Dave asked, letting loose with an accompanying 'ah'.

"No."

"Oh well, too late now."

"Hey, I just thought of something," Dace said.

"Yeah?"

Dave shook it, tucked it, and zipped it in, then returned to his chair and plopped down, his left hand plunging simultaneously into the small wash tub they had found earlier and filled with ice and beer. He rummaged around in the now icy water, found a full one, uncapped it and took a swig.

"What did you just think of?" Dave said.

"Huh?"

"You said you just thought of something." Dave took another drink, refunded a belch. "What did you just think of?"

"Oh, that. When you left, before the attack of the Dave-eating ants, you said you were headed to check out the shed."

"Yeah, I was."

"Well, Auntie D said you were in the middle of the yard pacing in circles." Dace followed in Dave's footsteps with the drink and belch. "I never knew you to get lost when going in a straight line, old chum."

"Oh, that," Dave said, having seriously forgotten all about Cindy's call for the last eight or nine hours. "Cindy called. My Aunt Gloria is dead."

"What?"

"You remember my Aunt Gloria. The woman whose trailer we swapped cars at on Tuesday."

"Of course, I remember," Dace said, suddenly feeling more sober than a moment ago. "She's dead?"

"Today, um, I mean yesterday, if tomorrow yesterday is now today," Dave said, his fingers leapfrogging to points in space and smiling to himself over knowing that the explanation made perfect sense. "Heart attack, Cindy said."

"Geeze, I'm sorry, Dave," Dace said. "She was your mother's sister, right?"

"Half-sister, same mother, different fathers. Thanks, but we were never that close even though she's been just up the road, so to speak, for years. My mom never liked her much, and thought her lifestyle was a bad example, so we just stayed away."

"Still, it sucks," Dace said. "Heart attack?"

"That's what Cindy said. They're gonna do an autopsy to make sure."

Something struck Dace wrong, his beer-addled brain struggled with it for a few moments before he put his finger on it.

"Wait, how did Cindy know your Aunt Gloria?"

"Oh, they didn't know each other."

"Then how did Cindy know about your aunt passing away today?"

"Yesterday."

"Okay, yesterday. How did Cindy know?"

"The cops called her."

"The cops called Cindy?" A pause. "Why would the cops call Cindy?"

"Because Cindy called them to check on Aunt Gloria after the guys showed up again."

"Guys? What guys?"

"The said they were car salesmen looking for my lease paperwork when they stopped in by Aunt Gloria on, let's see, Wednesday afternoon, the night you acted up with the security dudes in Alabama. Big dudes, in expensive suits, driving a black Lincoln Town Car. I think they were your dad's guys."

"They showed up again today?"

"That's what they tell me," Dave said. "Don't worry, buddy, we're safe down here. Nobody knows where we are except Cindy, and she wouldn't tell anyone if they were going to pull out her toenails. She's got cute toenails, and toes, by the way. My aunt didn't have a clue who you are. Poor, old, Aunt Gloria."

Dave toasted his bottle at the star-filled sky.

"She's home now, and at peace," Dave said. "With Sarah."

"What?" Dace asked, his mind racing, well as much as it could race in its current condition.

"I said, 'with Sarah'," Dave said.

Something clicked in Dace's mind.

"Son of a bitch," he said under his breath.


Ronnie lay awake in her bed. Her mind was filled with thoughts of the day. She knew Ashley was awake in her bed, too, but wondered whether it was best to try to talk things out, or just let them settle until morning. Ashley had been really rude to Bobby, Ronnie thought. Of course, Bobby had asked for it. A little. Ronnie also wondered what Sister Regina had overheard; and what was that comment about chapel being good for them?

"Ronnie?" Ashley whispered. "Are you awake?"

"You know I am, Diddle Brain," Ronnie replied.

"Oh, we're going back to freshman year?"

'Diddle Brain' and 'Noodle Doodle' had been their code names for each other when they'd pass notes during their first year at the school, just in case anyone had gotten their hands on their ultra-secret missives.

"Don't hate me, Ash," Ronnie said. "Please?"

"How could I hate you, Noodle Doodle?" Ashley said. "You're my BFF, no matter what."

"BFF?"

"Best friend forever," Ashley explained. "B. F. F."

"I've never heard that before," Ronnie said. "BFF. I like that."

"You've never heard it before, because I just made it up, Noodle Doodle."

"Cool. Let's keep it just between us. Never tell anyone else what it means. Okay?"

"Deal."

That's the moment they both knew things would be okay between them. They each drifted off to sleep minutes later.

Dace lay awake in his bed. The room had begun to spin the moment he laid down, but he remembered something he'd overheard from friends in high school: to stop the bed from spinning when you've been drinking, put one foot on the floor. He tried it, and was happily surprised when it worked. He didn't get sick to his stomach. A short time later, he had pulled his leg under the light covers so he could roll over into a more comfortable position, but the bed immediately began to spin again. So, he lay awake, one foot on the floor, staring at the ceiling. Down the hall he could hear Dave snoring away like a chainsaw with hiccoughs.

It wasn't just the spinning bed and the uncomfortable position he had to maintain to keep himself from becoming sick which was keeping him awake. He was wondering what in the world his father was doing sending the two security thugs out to intimidate innocent people to track them down. Had Cindy told Dave everything? Come to think of it, since this was the first he's heard of any of this, was Dave? He'd talk to his best friend more in the morning, when clearer heads prevailed. Okay, maybe in the afternoon. Did Travis and Rudy have anything to do with Gloria's untimely demise, or was it just a coincidence? Heart attacks can be triggered by intense fear, can't they? Then again, according to Dave, the woman had been abusing her body for decades with drugs and alcohol and that must have taken a toll on her heart. It had to be a coincidence, Dace concluded, as sleep began to creep in. His father wasn't a monster, after all.

The snow let up overnight as the low pressure system lost its grip on Massachusetts and slid up the coast toward Maine. The promised colder air moved in to replace the snowfall as Boston's number one least wanted, and that turned the sixteen inches of wet, packed, snow just perfect for making snowmen, into heavy, ragged, clusters of solid ice.

Travis had relieved Rudy for the second time in the wee hours, and now sat shivering in his rented four-wheel-drive Subaru Outback, which was all they had left at the rental car place, and watched the sun turn the sky to the east shades of red. On their shifts, they had moved their setup location, meeting to hand over the scanner two blocks away. So far, there had been no activity on either of Cindy's cellphones. Travis looked at his watch and stomped his feet on the floorboards to try to warm them up. What he really wanted to do was start the car and fire up the heater for a while, but nothing brought more attention than the vapor cloud generated by an idling car in subzero temperatures. So, instead, he cursed the assignment and decided he'd sacrifice some sleep for a chance to buy some insulated boots and coveralls for his next shift.

Half an hour later, Travis' cellphone vibrated then chirped with a call from Rudy. He punched the answer key with a shaking finger and grunted a greeting.

"Hey, Grumpy, you want me to bring you some coffee?" Rudy asked.

"Funny," Travis said, looking at his watch. Rudy's shift was to begin in fifteen minutes. "Are you on your way?"

"Yeah, be there in ten. Just running through the McDonald's drive-thru. So, you want coffee or not?"

"Okay, I'm gonna start up and move around the block, then run the heater for a few minutes and try to thaw my feet. Meet me on Lee Street. I'll be the one under my own cloud."

"Will do. Coffee?"

"Yeah, coffee."

"Man, you're getting cranky," Rudy said. "I can't wait to see you after a couple of days of this shit."

"I'm not freezing my nuts off for days here, buddy. If we don't turn something by tonight, we're moving to Plan B."

"Sounds good to me," Rudy said. "Have you bounced that off Tom?"

"Screw Tom," Travis snapped. "He's not sitting here like a penguin on an ice pile." A pause. "Bring me a couple of Egg McMuffins, too."

Travis disconnected, started the car, put it in gear and hoped the four-wheel drive would help it get over the rock hard snowbank made by the plow on its last run before the temperature took a plunge.

Cindy awoke with the sun. It was cold in her room. Darn cold. The floorboards, which normally felt good to her often overheated feet, wicked the heat right out of her legs as she padded the few steps to grab her robe off the hook on the bathroom door. Once at the window and having parted the lightweight curtain, she immediately understood the reason her room was now cold soaked. The snow which had last evening fallen against the glass and then slowly melted and slid down to build little ridges of water and flakes at the base of each horizontal glazing bar in the near-freezing temperature, was now solid blocks of ice, and there was a light frost layer on the *inside* of the windows. The temperature must have plummeted overnight, she thought.

She used her breath and fingers to create a small hole in the frost so she could see outside. In the distance, she could see ragged, low clouds moving fast along the horizon. She could also hear the wind rattling the phone and entertainment cables attached to the side of the house. From the snow piled on the roof of the building across the street, she gauged at least a foot and a half had fallen since yesterday; Boston had indeed been hit by a *whoppah*, not by Minnesota standards, but certainly by the benchmarks of Bean Town. Down in the street, the cars which had been there overnight were still covered and now were securely blocked in by ridges of what she knew was solid, ice-laden snow standing three feet high and five feet wide. A blue station wagon which she hadn't noticed as being there when she had turned in, was rocking back and forth and slowly breaching the snowbank.

"Good luck, buddy," she said to herself.

A moment later, the low riding car did indeed break free, its bottom scraping firmly on snow and ice as she watched both front and rear wheels spin on the slick roadway. 'Hmm, four wheel drive station wagon. That's a new one on me.' She watched the vehicle drive to the southeast on Clinton Street then disappear from view.

Cindy looked at both of her cell phones resting on her desk. Her laptop computer, a steel-gray, Apple PowerBook 3400c sat dormant alongside. She had several projects to finish up that day, then needed to get to the Student Services department to print and assemble them. She silently hoped they'd get things cleared out by afternoon and have the building open. She really needed to bite the bullet and buy her own printer, she thought. Maybe next year. Fifteen hundred dollars was a lot of money.

She considered calling Dave, just to see how he was doing. She wondered momentarily about his Aunt Gloria and if the family now knew what had happened. A wave of sadness washed over her heart, and then was gone. It's sad when someone dies, but she had never met the woman. No matter how normal someone appeared on the periphery of human contact such as a phone call, Cindy was savvy enough to know that couldn't be a true measure of the person. Dave had told her his aunt was the black sheep of the family, shunned even by her own half-sister who lived less than an hour distant, purportedly because of Gloria's bad personal choices. So sad.

She concluded she'd wait to hear from Dave.

Cindy peered out the window again, the little hole in the frost she had made was slowly filling in again, and she wondered when the Boston police department would call so she could give them a full statement about what she heard in the last conversation with Gloria. Somehow she understood it wouldn't be that wintry day.

Sandy and I were back to normal, or as close as the two of us can get to it, when we awoke on Saturday morning. We had slept with the patio doors open the night before because as the weather system cleared, it had brought in cool, dry air. In the morning, out of a clear sky, the sun came up and light flooded into the room. Since we had rested much of the day before, and had taken all three meals in our room, we were both ready to venture forth into the world, and I was hungry as all get out.

We dressed in something casual and made our way downstairs to the dining room. John and Chrissy Baird were the only other guests who were up as early as we were, although they were sitting on opposite ends of the table and not exchanging much conversation between them. I didn't feel like taking sides, and obviously Sandy didn't either, so we took chairs across the table from each other as nearly in the middle as we could. Breakfast on the weekend at the B&B was an a la carte affair, and Anita had the sideboard set with a line of covered chafing dishes, a fruit bowl, milk and juices, two urns of coffee: one watery decaf, the other 'Texas Regular' as Anita termed it.

After laying claim to our chairs, and bidding good morning to both ends of the table, Sandy and I packed plates with Anita's good home cooking. The conversation at the table remained nonexistent. Not even any questions from either Baird about our incident of the other day, or comments about the bandage and betadyne stain on my forehead. We had just sat down again and began to eat when Mr. Eugene appeared at the portal from the front room.

"Cab's here," he said. "Got your bags loaded."

My eyes moved to either end of the table, then stopped in the middle again when they caught Sandy's across the way. Her mouth was full of eggs, yet she got my unspoken question, and her eyes darted to her left, toward Chrissy Baird. I nodded that was my vote too, and sure enough, that's when Chrissy arose silently, never looked over at John and followed Mr. Eugene out of the room. I arched my eyebrow at Sandy. That one was a draw, and way too easy a call. We all heard the door slam.

"Sorry," I said to John. I'd seen it coming, but I was still sorry to see it happening.

"It was inevitable," he said. "Some things just can't be forgiven."

"Everything can be forgiven, John," Sandy injected. "Some things just can't be forgotten. Maybe she's just not ready. Give her time."

John looked at Sandy and me like we had just landed our space ship out front and walked in wearing silver suits.

"She's the one who had the affair, not me," he said. "She's going back to him. I tried to forgive, and I tried to forget." An evil grin came to his face with the realization. "You two knew all along something like that had happened between us, yet you assumed it just had to have been me who cheated. Why is it society always jumps to the conclusion that it's the man who has to be the monster when something goes wrong in a marriage?"

He slid his chair back and stormed from the room.

"Wow," I said when I was certain he was out of earshot. "Any of that seem just a bit light in the loafers to you?"

"Only all of it," Sandy said as she put half a sausage link into her mouth. "We didn't have a bet on that, did we?"

I shook my head.

Mr. Eugene's distinctive footsteps approached from the front room. I had just shoved a stack of toast corner, eggs, and sausage into my mouth when he came over to stand next to me.

"That's a shame," he said. "It happens, I guess." He leaned closer to us. "Me and Anita thought for sure it was him who had cheated on that dear young thing."

"Mm-hmm," I said with an eager nod, my mouth busy chewing, and waved my fork between Sandy and myself.

Mr. Eugene exited to the kitchen.

"We're not alone in the world, Sandy," I said.

My wife eyed me suspiciously across the table.

"Well, I'm not, anyway," she said.

# Chapter Fifteen

An hour later, Sandy and I had left a sobbing John Baird and our favorite B&B behind and were on the road for home. Our original plan had been to stay along the road overnight and get home on Sunday, but as we drove, I suggested we keep going straight through and get home late that night. If traffic moved along, we could make the trip in under twelve hours, putting us in our own bed before ten o'clock.

We had driven Sandy's Oldsmobile Bravada on the trip. It was a brand new 1999 model which had just come out that month and had less than a thousand miles on it when we left South Padre headed for home and plenty of that new car smell. I am old enough to remember when model years changed in the fall, and my dad had thought that had been rushing things. Now Detroit was bringing out the new model year earlier and earlier. Sandy had been lucky enough to get one of the first deliveries to the dealership out in Metairie and we had picked it up on Sunday last, leaving her well-used and beloved VW Rabbit behind. Her new Bravada was forest green with gold pinstripes, sported a camel-colored, leather interior with heated seats and it drove as nicely as I thought it would.

Sandy wore another light sundress for the trip home. Is that what those are? Lightweight, cotton, thin straps over the shoulders, one piece with a form-fitting top and flowing skirt. Well, it's what I call them. It's what my mother had called them. Sandy was able to fix her hair normally that day and added just a touch of makeup, not that she really needed it. She looked gorgeous, which on top of everything else less superficial about her, completed the package which constantly reminded me of how lucky I really was. I watched out of the corner of my eye as she slipped off her shoes and tucked her feet up under her skirt. She powered her seat back a bit so her eyes were behind mine, wiggled around a bit and rested on her left side. She tossed her sunglasses into the little storage area on the center console, folded her hands on her lap.

"Gonna take a nap, babe?" I asked.

I reached over and rubbed her thigh on top of her skirt.

"Just getting comfortable, Will," she said. "I'm not tired."

"A few more months and you won't be able to do that so easily," I said, indicating her posture. "Then it just gets worse, or so I'm told."

I glanced across the car. Sandy smiled, closed her eyes. I rested my hand on her thigh, her hand moved to cover mine. I normally would have slipped my hand from under hers because I don't like being confined like that, but that time the reward of her warm thigh coming through the thin cotton skirt and the coolness of her hand on mine was worth the minor psychological discomfort.

"Mind if I turn on the radio?" I asked. "No Zydeco, I promise, but maybe we'll draw some twangy Texas country and western for a while."

Sandy opened one eye, then closed it again. That usually meant: 'Okay, but not too loud'. I pushed the power button on the radio, hit the SCAN and set forth on an east Texas radio programming adventure. Finally, I settled on a Corpus Christi station which played a blend of easy listening covers of early rock songs mixed with 70s stuff from the likes of Donny Osmond, The Carpenters, and the Jackson Five with the occasional Tammy Wynette and Patsy Klein. The eclectic combination seemed to meet with Sandy's approval, because she neither protested nor reached to turn the volume down. A short time later, she was asleep. I carefully slipped my hand from under hers, she shifted a little, then settled into her nap. I maneuvered the various twists and exits through the city with the radio station and successfully found my way back onto Route 77 northeast of the Corpus Christi.

In Victoria, I took an exit for a gas station and Sandy stirred, reached for my arm and then woke up with a smile on her face.

"Just getting gas, babe," I said.

"I had the best dreams, Will," Sandy said, straightening in her seat, raising the back and tousling her hair. She stretched as best she could, flexed her ankles and pointed her toes, then settled and reached for my hand, held it in both of hers against her chest. "What do you want our baby to be?"

"Human," I said, then gave her a wry smile. "If you're asking whether I'd like a boy or a girl, Sandy, you had better word your question with more precision, counselor."

She bit my finger.

"Ouch," I said.

Sandy released the bite on my protest, then held my finger with her warm, moist lips. Her eyes sparkled and she winked.

"Okay, okay," I said, realizing again I'd certainly cave very quickly under any type of torture or enticement were I ever captured by the enemy.

I brought the Bravada to a stop next to the vacant gas pump, slid the shift into park and turned off the ignition with my free, left hand. When she released my finger from her lips, I took the cluster of my wife's hands and one of mine into the other one of mine and looked into her eyes. She waited, bit her lower lip. She does that when she's nervous.

"Honey, to me, whatever the baby growing inside of you turns out to be, doesn't matter because it's part of you and me. He or she is a product of our love and that's the greatest gift a man can ever receive from a woman. I have three fantastic girls now, and a boy would be a change, but truly, so long as you and the baby are healthy and happy, it's all good for me."

I watched her melt.

"I love you, William Langdon," she said.

"I love you, Sandy Langdon," I replied and I kissed her fingers. "Now, may I have my hand back? People are starting to stare."

Dave slept until nearly noon, in his clothes. Dace, to Dave's relief, was still in his room and hadn't added to his trophy collection overnight, and was sleeping soundly with one foot on the floor.

Dave went downstairs after using the bathroom and taking six Advil for the headache which was lurking behind a beer hangover. As his feet moved down the steps he silently thanked God he had resisted Dace's suggestion they do some shots just after midnight. He was hungry, and in the kitchen he found a lone piece of Auntie D's leftover cornbread, dribble some honey on top and washed it down with a Pepsi. He unlocked the back door, went through the screen and settled into the whicker rocking chair he had seemingly just vacated.

The sun was high in the sky. It was another clear day in southern Louisiana with the temperature somewhere in the mid-seventies, he guessed. There was a haze on the horizon to the south. A slight breeze stirred the air just enough to move wisps of the gentle perfume of azaleas which had seemingly bloomed overnight in planting islands on the east side of the house. Dave pushed himself out of the chair and walked in that direction. He hadn't really noticed the low-hedged, paver-walked garden area over there before, but that morning the azalea bushes were abloom in whites, pinks, reds, and purples and he went to explore.

The garden was about sixty feet square and lay to the east of the house, off the dining room and pantry, and although it also lay underneath his and Dace's rooms, Dave just hadn't taken notice. As he moved closer, the fragrance of the blooms became thicker. He descended the three steps from the veranda and moved across the blood-red, clay pavers. He recalled Auntie D telling them yesterday about the bricks which had been used to build the core of the house being made right on the plantation of clay from the backlands and hardened in kilns fired by scrub mesquite.  Those bricks were well hidden under layers of plaster. He wondered if the pavers on which he now trod had been cast and laid by the slaves and ancestors of Auntie D.  The walkway was in such good shape, he guessed they would have been relaid over time, but there was something ghostly, and ghastly which flowed through Dave with every step.

"Thinking of taking up gardening today, boy?" Auntie D said from behind him.

Dave spun around, startled.  In his thoughts he hadn't heard the old woman moving across the porch.

"Good morning, Auntie D," he said.  "No, I hadn't noticed the azaleas had bloomed until this morning."

"They hadn't," she said.  "Oh, they was peakin' out a bit the last few days, but somethin' sparked 'em overnight and here they is.  I was comin' over to clip a few branches for my table."  She held up a large set of shears.  In the other hand she held a basket.

Auntie D moved to join him on the pathway.  When she descended the steps, he saw how he hadn't heard her walking across the porch: she was barefoot.

"Aren't you worried about walking around barefoot with those ants and other creatures out there in the grass, Auntie D?"

She looked at him.

"Boy, I've been walkin' this country since your granddaddy was just a gleam in *his* daddy's eyes, the first sixteen years of this life spent barefoot 'ceptin' for the winters.  I done stepped on ever'thin' what crawls, swims, or walks from the grasslands and cane fields to the bayous and nothin' ever bothered to take much more than a tiny taste of me.  And that was when I was young and tender; I don't think nothin' out there wants to go gnawin' on this old leather and bones now."

Dave laughed, then he helped her clip some flowers for her table.

"Where's that other one?" Auntie D asked.

"Dace?"

She nodded.

"You know that one is itchin' for trouble, boy," she said.  "He's smooth as silk underdrawers, but he got him a dark side."  She looked up toward Dace's room.  "You watch he don't drag you down wit' him."

Dave considered her words and wondered how he wasn't seeing things about his best friend that others lately seemed to discern almost at just seeing him pass by or first meeting him.  He'd never heard anything like that before about Dace from anyone, but he'd also not seen the type of mercurial behavior he'd been exhibiting from his friend before. Maybe the girl in the truck stop was right.  Maybe there was something going on in Dace's eyes.  A storm brewing.

They walked back along the porch. Auntie D stopped by the chairs, looked at the wash tub, now half filled with water and mostly floating beer bottles. Caps littered its bottom.

"You boys had quite a time out here last night," she said.

"It started out as just a beer or two while the sun went down after your great dinner." He started to count the empty bottles, gave up at the case mark. "I guess we got talking."

"Well, so long as you boys clean up your messes and don't go disturbin' the country peace, I ain't gonna judge y'all for taking a bit of a nip and havin' a little fun." She looked Dave over. "You et yet today, boy?"

"Not yet, just got up," he said. "Dace is still sleeping, last I checked."

Auntie D clucked her tongue and shook her head in disapproval.

"Such a waste of a beautiful day; sleepin'. I baked some bread this mornin', I'll go fetch a loaf and come back and make you boys somethin' to stick to your ribs and chase away them liquor vapors." She nodded toward the upstairs. "You go wake that other one, get yo'selves cleaned up, and meet me in the kitchen."

He watched her walk off the porch and out across the lawn, hardly looking down, but obviously not hitting any anthills or other trouble. Then he picked up the tub, took it through the door to the kitchen counter, emptied the bottles and caps, then went back outside and poured the water over the hedges.

Dave tucked the empty tub into the pantry where they had discovered it, then walked upstairs, across the balcony to Dace's room and saw that he hadn't moved. He found a long-stemmed, dry flower in one of the vases on a side table, then took the thing and began to tickle under Dace's nose. It took a few seconds, but the first flinch was a doozy as Dace swatted himself in the mouth. A couple more, and he was glaring at a raucously laughing Dave through bleary and bloodshot eyes. He sat up, fell backward onto the pillow, then lurched forward again as his stiff leg gave him another jab. He rubbed his eyes.

"What the hell, man?" he said. "What is that?"

"Dried flower, buddy," Dave said, replacing it in the vase.

"What time is it?"

"Half past noon," Dave said. "Lunch time. I ran into Auntie D in the garden, she's bringing some homemade bread and is gonna feed us again. We've got to be the luckiest dudes in Louisiana, man."

Dace looked toward the windows, the overhanging roof on the big porch and the window sheers thankfully keeping most of the harsh daylight from penetrating his room. He sat up, swung his second leg over the side of the bed.

"What garden?" he asked.

"There's a garden right outside the windows," Dave said, pointing east. He moved the sheer on the window in that direction. Light flowed across the floor and into Dace's watering eyes. "Wanna see?"

"No, dammit, shut that."

Dave was enjoying this a bit, even as bad as he felt himself, his hangover was obviously much lighter than Dace's.

"Get your butt out of bed, clean up, take something for the headache, and come down to the kitchen for lunch."

He left Dace there to get ready, then took his own advice and jumped into the shower, shaved, and dressed in clean clothes, then went downstairs to find Auntie D in the kitchen searching the refrigerator. A huge loaf of fresh bread lay on the center island amongst a scattering of tiny, yellow-gold grains which she said was small bits of cornmeal having fallen from its bottom. He sniffed the loaf, hefted it. Dave loved bread, and his mouth watered at just the smell and feel of Auntie D's substantial loaf.

"That's whole grain," she said. "Dense and soft inside, thick crust. I only eat the centers, give the crust to the birds."

She closed the refrigerator, folded her arms. Dave watched her thinking.

"Let's go downstairs, boy," she said, moving toward the hallway door. "See what Uncle Jack's got tucked away down there."

"Uh, Auntie D, we are downstairs," he said.

"No, we ain't boy," she said, moving toward the pantry. "Follow me."

He followed her across the hall. Dace was just coming downstairs, looking more human than the last time Dave had seen him. Dave motioned for him to follow along. Auntie D passed around the shelves to a doorway at the rear of the room. The boys had seen the door, assumed it was access behind the bathroom's plumbing, maybe a closed-off door to the dining room. She felt around behind some pottery canisters on one of the shelves along the wall, found an old skeleton key and worked the ancient lock and pulled open the door. A slight musty, earthy smell floated into the pantry.

"You city boys is in for a treat," she said as she flipped a light switch inside the doorway and disappeared.

Dave and Dace followed, looked through the doorway to see Auntie D descending into a basement they had no idea existed. They followed, moving down the wooden steps and treading onto a packed dirt floor, their heads in the timbers of the floor above.

"Y'all bend low," she said. "Folks was a lot smaller than you two when this was dug."

They hunched over, peered out across a basement they each judged must run under the entire house. Black, decorative, cast iron oval grates spaced at even intervals near the tops of each stone and plaster wall let in dappled light and air from the outside. They were hidden from exterior view by the short hedgerow. Four-foot-square columns of raw brick which were not topped with plaster but finely set, were set in two rows of four along the center of the room, and supported the interior walls of the hallway. Four smaller brick columns were set on each side in the space under the rooms. Huge cypress beams ran lengthwise over the hallway columns creating the house's dual, structural spines, from which smaller beams ran perpendicular like ribs. The beams appeared perfectly dimensional, yet there were no saw marks, just very subtle hewing imprints.

"Look at this," Dave said to Dace, pointing out a finely cut joint into which he imagined they would be hard pressed to insert even a playing card between the beams. "All held together by dowels. No nails."

Dace moved his head around the timbers, then squatted like he was in a football huddle calling plays and took it all in.

"Amazing," Dave said, rising to touch the timbers. "Look at these markings at each joint, Dace."

"That there was done by true African craftsmen, boys," Auntie D injected, her eyes growing distant. "Slaves, what had been boat builders over to Africa cut all them from cypress logs out in the swamp. No power saws back then, just axes and hand tools. Them marks is so they could put it all back together when they hauled the pieces out."

"You mean this was all done by hand?" Dave said. "To such perfection?"

Auntie D smiled and nodded.

"You won't find a nail anywhere in the skeleton of this old house. Nails was scarce in them days. Those old slaves used wooden pegs. This cypress will last a thousand years after they have been gone and forgotten. It don't rot and no bugs will eat it."

"Cypress is like cedar that way," Dave said. "Natural oils keep the wood from rotting and insects such as termites, which they have by the ton down here, won't touch it."

"Come here, boy, grab a ham," Auntie D said to Dave. Then to Dace: "And you, go over there and lift the lid on that pottery and grab a small wheel of cheese. Mind you, a small one. We don't wanna go testin' Uncle Jack's hospitality too much, now."

Dave moved to where she was pointing at hams of various sizes hanging in the open air. They were thickly crusted with salt and other spices and wrapped in a cheesecloth mesh tied with a loop for hanging. She pointed to one about the size of a volley ball and he removed it from the the protruding peg.

"That there is dry-cured, country ham, boy," she said as Dave moved back to stand by her. "This one's been hangin' down here for nearly a year. You boys ain't never had none better in your lives."

Dace crouched across the room above a heavy, square pottery top sitting on the dirt floor. He pointed, looked over at Auntie D and she nodded.

"Just lift it up," she said. "Ain't nothin' there gonna bite ya, boy."

He displaced the cover and revealed a pottery cask buried in the floor. The pungent and raw aroma of curing cheese seeped out. He reached inside and removed a crusty looking wheel about six inches across and three inches thick. It was the smallest he could see.

"This okay?" he said, holding up the aromatic wheel.

Auntie D nodded and then urged them upstairs for lunch. Dace ascended the steps first, his hangover hurting bad again with the continued bending over. They heard him move across the floor to the kitchen.

Dave took one last look around the basement and moved to follow with the ham in his hands. Auntie D blocked the stairs, stared into his eyes. She pointed toward the columns.

"Them bricks you was studyin' so close, boy," she said, "the clay for each one dug from the ground by slaves, formed with slave hands and cooked in wood ovens fed by slaves and hauled out of the backlands on the backs of slaves."

He looked hard at her.

"The answer to your question you was pondering earlier out to the garden is yes," she said, returning his hard look. "Them bricks you was walkin' on, the same as these here." She looked up and toward the kitchen. "This is just an old house to that one, but I know you understand this here is all hallowed ground. A sacred place. Uncle Jack be a good man. He done right when he bought this place and fixed it up. You don't sully sacred ground. Pay heed to that." She pointed a finger directly between his eyes. "Uncle Jack understands and respects this place; and you must too, boy."

She turned and slowly made her way up the steps, leaving Dave behind to consider her words.

Ashley and Ronnie rolled suitcases along the hallway on the first floor of the dorm. They each also lugged a backpack slung over one shoulder and a purse tangled in. It was far too much stuff for a long weekend at home, but they had a cover story already planned should someone in authority make that observation. They would have preferred to take the back exit to the dorm to avoid running into any of the nuns, but didn't wish to drag their heavy bags through the grass and over a couple of short hedgerows. This path was easier, but it also led them past Sister Regina's office door, which they could see was open as they approached.

Most of the other girls had already departed for home, or mini-vacations with parents who had picked them up on Friday after classes ended or after Saturday Mass that morning at eight. Most of the sisters had retired to their rooms after lunch for study or chores or meditation. The hallways were darkened, quiet, and empty. There was no casting of light from Sister's office, and the girls breathed easier as they approached; then, as they began to pass, they wished themselves invisible and looked straight ahead. Even were it possible, they should have learned by then that one cannot be invisible enough when a nun was watching for you. Especially, Sister Regina. And she had been watching for the pair.

"We missed you girls at morning chapel," she said from behind her desk.

The girls stopped dead in their tracks. When both Ashley and Ronnie turned to look into the office, they saw the woman writing in files, not even peering up.

"We're leaving now, Sister," Ashley said, hoping to sidestep the remark.

Ronnie swallowed hard. Said nothing.

"I know, I heard your caravan coming from upstairs." The nun set down her pen, closed the file folder, kept her eyes on the desk. "That information, however, is not pertinent to my statement about missing you at morning chapel." She peered over her reading glasses. "But, you knew that, didn't you, Ashley?"

The girl turned her head to look at Ronnie, but received no support; so, she squared herself with the doorway, allowed her wheeled suitcase to sit at ease, took three steps forward to stand in the portal.

"We're sorry, Sister," she began, "but we overslept this morning. Yesterday was a long day for both of us, but you hopefully noticed we did make it to Mass after chapel prayers. On time, today." She beamed a huge smile, a mix of apology and manipulation.

An upturned corner came to pursed lips on the old nun's face. Fortunately for the girls at the school, she could remember being young, her own school days, the feelings and emotions coursing through her in a constant flux. She could recall as if it were yesterday how she and her friends had always tried to push the system, to mold it to their needs. Things had been different then, during the early 1940s, the world was at war, the Church was a much more stern, humorless, and inflexible taskmaster, and the Sisters who oversaw them seemed like alien beings. She wondered now as she peered into Ashley Monreale's eyes, which were lit with so much mirth and youthful resonance, yet chastened by a humility the girl must have determined was necessary, if that's how these girls now viewed her. Did they see her as an anachronism? She had always tried to be different in many ways from the unsmiling, harsh nuns of her youth, pledging to herself, and God, on the day as a novitiate when she took her first vows, that she would always strive to remember how it was to be young. On the other hand, years on the other side of the fence had given her the understanding of the responsibilities which fell to her role as the Head Mistress of the school. She had a responsibility to the girls, and to their parents who had placed their trust with her. She also had a responsibility to the Church, and to God. Sometimes, she thought, it was a difficult juggling act.

"No matter," she said and rose from her desk to approach Ashley in the doorway. The girl took a couple steps backward into the hall, nearly tumbled over her massive suitcase. "God was watching as you slept, and He knows your hearts." Her eyes moved to each of the girls, and she decided that was enough. "May I walk you out?"

"Um, sure, Sister," Ronnie said.

The girls moved silently with the nun toward the front doors.

"That's quite a passel of clothes for four days," Sister Regina observed.

"Spring is coming, Sister," Ronnie said. "A girl can't wear winter clothes in the spring, and our closets here are not big enough for everything. It's time to change things around."

It was the misdirection they had decided to use in the circumstance. Not really a lie, not necessarily the whole truth.

"I don't have those problems," Sister said. "I do, however, remember when I did. Not that we had the resources of you girls these days, but we still found it important when we were your age to remain in fashion outside of school as best we could."

They moved through the doors into the early afternoon. The air was fresh and clean, the sun just beyond its highest point for the day. Each girl carefully maneuvered her bags in turn through the portal as Sister waited on the landing.

"You girls have a wonderful time at home this weekend," she said. "I'll look forward to seeing you for Mass on Ash Wednesday."

"We will, Sister," Ashley said.

"Yes, we're looking forward to it," Ronnie added.

They carried their suitcases off the steps. Had Sister Regina not been standing there, they would have just thumped them down the stairs. They stood in the drive, wondering for a moment whether there was more of a lecture, or if they were free to go. Sister looked over their heads toward the levee in the distance. The river was not visible, even from their slight elevation.

"I was thinking this morning," she said, just as both girls had begun to drag their suitcases across the crushed seashells of the drive.

"Yes, Sister?" Ashley asked.

"Wasn't it a year ago that you two had plans for a weekend in New Orleans which were uncovered at the last minute?"

Ronnie and Ashley shared a glance. Older and wiser now, they didn't give it away. Ashley hung her head.

"Yes, Sister," she said. "It was us last year."

Ronnie shuffled from foot to foot. She wanted to just run to her car and make a break for it, deal with the consequences later. Something inside screamed that someone, somehow, had found them out again and Sister was toying with them like a cat with a mouse who momentarily sees an escape route where none really exists. Sister stood with her gaze fixed into the distance over their heads. Both girls waited for the ax to fall.

"God go with you," Sister said. "My greetings to your parents."

She turned and went back inside, leaving Ashley and Ronnie standing in slack-jawed disbelief.

"Let's get out of here, Ash," Ronnie said, wasting no time and beginning a quick walk toward her car, "before she comes back."

Ashley stood for a moment. A smile came to her as thoughts gelled.

"Oh, you're good, Sister," she said to herself.

Ronnie was almost jogging to her car, the wheeled suitcase plowing through the loose, white, shell fragments. Every dozen steps or so, she had to lift it up and pull it free from the added weight of dragged driveway. Ronnie looked over her shoulder and called again; Ashley picked up her suitcase and began to walk.

Is there anything more powerfully coercive than Catholic guilt, she thought as she moved away from the dorm. She didn't think there was, but then added out loud as her pace quickened: "Just not this weekend."

A short minute later, the pair of friends were out the drive and headed east along the River Road toward New Orleans. They smiled and began to sing with the radio, the conflict of last night, the disappointment of one in the other washed away by light hearts, the clean, cool breeze through the open windows, and the harmony of two best friends singing along to Usher's mellow hit, *Climax,* which just went number one on the charts.


Dace and Dave took perches on one end of the center island and watched Auntie D work at opening the ham and cheese. The lure of more beer was muted by the aftereffects of last night's drinking, so they each held a bottle of Peach Snapple on the counter between their legs. It was one of the drink choices stocked by Sam. Dave shook his bottle and opened the twist-top, then looked underneath and read the cap.

"Did you know crows are the smartest birds?" Dave asked.

"I did," Dace said, then added: "Ironically, highly regarded owls are near the bottom on that scale."

"What does yours say?" Dave said, his curiosity, especially for trivia never satiated.

Dace removed the cap again, since he hadn't looked when he first opened the Snapple.

"Mine says: 'Kiss guitarist Gene Simmons did NOT have part of a cow's tongue attached to his own'."

"Geeze, that's a weird one?" Dave said.

"It's how rumors get started, my friend," he said and dropped his cap onto the marble countertop.

Dave picked up Dace's discarded cap, turned it over and read.

"It doesn't say that," he said. "It says: 'Nearly three hundred million Frisbees have been sold worldwide'."

Dace grinned, drank another swig from his bottle.

The aromas from the ham and cheese Auntie D was unleashing were nearly as intoxicating as her seafood stew and cornbread had been the night before. They watched as if hypnotized as she carved off slices of ham so thin that the boys were surprised they stayed together. She then slid the knife into the cheese and removed equally thin slices. Dave's mouth began to water. He recalled watching a cooking show on television where the chef was speaking to thick cut versus thin cut, saying taste was all about surface area. He swallowed and licked his lips.

Next, she removed a serrated bread knife from the wooden block on the counter and began sawing off thick slices of her homemade loaf. Again, the blend of aromas was a superb melody.

"This ain't fancy," she said, "but it'll stick to your ribs. This here is just a simple down home, country lunch." She pointed the bread knife in Dace's direction. "Boy, go into that icebox and see if there is any course ground mustard. That will be the best for this mix of meat and cheese."

Dace slid off the counter and opened the refrigerator. He peered at every container in the door, saw only yellow mustard in a plastic squeeze bottle. He held it for Auntie D's inspection. She wrinkled her nose.

"No, no, look in the back on the bottom shelf," she said. "I knows Uncle Jack likes a local brand and always hides a jar down there."

Dace replaced the yellow mustard, bent down and rummaged through the items on the lower shelf, finally standing with a small, spherical glass jar in his hand. It had a gold and green twist off cap, and he removed it and inhaled.

"Oh, now I'm no expert on condiments, but this stuff is something else," he said. He replaced the cap when Auntie D nodded and placed it onto the counter next to her cutting board filled with sandwich ingredients.

She spread a thin layer of butter from an earthen crock on one side of two pieces of dense, brown bread, each slice an inch thick. Then on one piece, she placed a layer of thinly sliced cheese followed by a stack of the ham, then another layer of cheese. On top of the cheese, she smeared the mustard, its large grains sliding across the slice of cured curd in the golden mortar. She capped the sandwich with the second slice of bread, cut the sandwich in half, slid both halves onto a plate and then worked to create a duplicate. Onto a third plate, she placed two or three thin slices of ham, a small wedge of cheese, and one unbuttered slice of her bread.

"Come and get it, you two," she said, then followed them with her plate to the table they had shared last evening.

Dave was the first to try the sandwich and his eyes rolled as the blend of the perfect bread, sweet country butter, salty ham, and creamy, nutty, cheese combined with a mustard like he'd never tasted before into, dare he compare it to, an orgasm of culinary experience? The flavors were so intense and complex, he didn't even consider washing the bite down with something as pedestrian as Peach Snapple.

"Aw, man," Dave said. "This is the best sandwich I've ever had in my life."

"You ain't lived that long, boy," Auntie D said as she gummed tiny bits of ham and cheese. "Though, I will wager you'll never have one near as good from here on out either."

Dace appeared a bit skeptical of both statements, but quickly became a believer when he took his first bite. The boys ate in near silence after that, enjoying the combined rapture of the sandwiches and more of Auntie D's stories of plantation life in between her nibbling as she picked the center portion of the single slice of bread and blended it with small pieces of ham and cheese. Every second or third bite, she'd dip the ham into a dollop of mustard she had dropped on the corner of her plate. She smiled broadly and continued her stories as she prepared another set when each of the boys requested a second sandwich.

"So, whatchu boys doin' with the rest of your day, now that you done wasted the best part of it?" she asked, rising and removing their plates to the sink.

"Haven't decided yet," Dace said. "Maybe head into New Orleans tonight, rest up today."

"Rest?" Auntie D said in a disgusted tone. "From what I've seen, all you two do is sleep and drink. You gonna have plenty of time to rest when you is dead."

Auntie D shook her head and opened the refrigerator. She brought out a medium-sized bowl and small pitcher. She instructed Dave to fetch three small bowls and three spoons from the cupboard. She shuffled to the table with her items just after he completed the assigned chore and distributed the bowls and spoons to the three place settings. Auntie D set down the small pitcher first. A thick, white cream coated the glazed side of the vessel. Next she set down a bowl containing berries, some the size of half dollars, some the size of dimes. The small ones were dark purple, while the larger ones were midnight black.

"Blackberries and dewberries," she said. "They grow wild on the property, way out back. These are from last summer's crop. Put 'em up for the winter."

She used her spoon to divide the contents of the larger bowl into three equal portions, then sniffed the heavy cream just to be certain, and poured it over the berries. Dave and Dace attacked the concoction like they had the sandwiches, then slowed and savored the uniqueness of each berry. Auntie D smiled to herself as a thought gelled.

"Nope, I think you boys should spend the afternoon exploring the country 'round here," she said, squishing an extra-large blackberry with her gums. "Take a chance. Get off the main roads and go lookin' 'round the country. That's what you should do." She pointed a finger at Dave while spying Dace out the corner of her eye. "Just mind you don't wander onto private property. I'm beginning to like you too much to go pickin' rock salt out of your behind."

Ronnie turned right off Canal Street and wheeled her car up to the grand, ornate, towering, white marble front entrance of the Fairmont Hotel on Baronne Street in New Orleans. In contrast, though it was only mid-afternoon and sunny in the city, that block of Baronne Street was a shadowed, narrow, urban canyon. Treble coach lights in cast brass and integral square columns of white stone with brass inlay guarded the entrance, the glowing lamps providing an oasis of artificial light. Polished brass revolving doors gleamed beyond well-used white marble steps and a chandeliered exterior vestibule. A doorman in charcoal slacks, black shoes as highly polished as the entry doors, long royal purple greatcoat with gold-braid adornments and brass buttons with matching cap opened the passenger door before Ashley's hand could reach the handle.

"Welcome to the Fairmont," he said cheerfully, touching a gloved hand to the brim of his cap. "Checking in, ladies?"

Ashley took his other offered hand and slid out of her seat and stepped onto the sidewalk and looked up. A massive canopy bearing half a dozen flags reached nearly to the street. She smiled and nodded.

Ronnie opened her door and was standing on the cobblestone street before the doorman could make his move to the other side of the car. Her eyes moved up the massive structure; she sensed her jaw hanging and consciously closed her mouth. There were taller hotels in New Orleans and smaller ones with more decadent grandeur, but the Fairmont - originally the Grunewald, later the Roosevelt - was a historied Louisiana landmark which, including the fourteen-story annex built in 1907, encompassed nearly an entire city block. One could enter on Baronne Street and walk straight through the lobby hallway to exit a block away on University Place.

The doorman inquired about luggage, requested the car keys from Ronnie and traded them for one end of a numbered, blue, card-stock tag. He directed the girls through the revolving entry and toward the front desk, assuring them their luggage would follow, and that the car would be secured in the parking garage shortly by a valet who was at that time accomplishing the task for the previous arrival and advising the vehicle would be available anytime day or night with a simple phone call. Ashley reached into her purse and slipped a ten dollar bill into the man's offered hand, which elicited a broad smile.

Inside, the girls glided soundlessly across the wide, thick, carpet runner which revealed ancient mosaic tile floor and base beyond the edges. A large, round, mahogany table in the Victorian style, topped with a cut-crystal vase and oversize flower display marked the halfway point to the front desk. They could see a twin of the table and flowers toward the far entrance. Octagonal columns in ochre plaster with carved corners and crowned with decorative, sculpted beams painted in accents of red, blue, and gold against honey-colored wood stood as silent sentinels at intervals down the lobby hallway. Half-chandelier sconces marked the four corners of each segment. Further along on the right, they passed an elevator lobby gleaming in yet more polished brass, painted plaster walls and cast crown moldings under a smoked, mirror-panel ceiling.

At the small, out-of-scale, front desk crafted in mahogany panels and moldings they were greeted by another smiling face welcoming them to the Fairmont and asking if they had a reservation.

"Reservation under Ashley Monreale," Ashley said. "Four nights, checking out on Wednesday morning."

The clerk typed into her computer and located the reservation. She removed a prepared card from an adjacent file box, slipped it across the marble countertop with a pen, asking Ashley to verify the information, initial the rate, and sign at the bottom. She asked for her credit card and photo ID which Ashley removed from her purse and laid upon the variegated green marble counter. A couple more questions confirmed a couple more things, and then the clerk spoke beyond them and handed a white envelope with an ornate green 'F' to a gloved hand which reached from behind Ronnie. The girls turned to see a young bellman who was about the age their IDs claimed them to be and dressed in a less ostentatious, inside version of the doorman's uniform standing by a wheeled cart containing their bags from the car. A brass plate on his chest proclaimed him to be 'Kris'.

"This way, ladies," he said, ushering them back toward the elevator lobby. "Is this your first time with us at the Fairmont?" he asked as he pushed the button for one of the four elevators.

"Yes, it is," Ashley said.

"Well, I won't ask where you're from," he said. "I can tell you girls are from down here."

"How can you tell?" Ronnie said, annoyed by her inference of his assumption.

"No accents," he said, with a disarming laugh. "Everyone down here from someplace else has an accent."

"We're from a little west of here. I'm from Thibodaux. Ronnie's from White Castle."

"Down here for Maris Gras?" he asked.

"Something like that," Ronnie said.

Quickly over her annoyance with Kris, she flashed a flirtatious smile which he returned. Ashley rolled her eyes. The elevator doors opened and he held them for their entry, then followed with the cart. He punched the button for the tenth floor.

"I imagine you already know all about this hotel, if you're from the area," he said.

The girls shook their heads in unison.

"Really? Well let me give you the tourist's welcome then. We've got a bit of a walk ahead of us once we get up to the tenth floor, so it kills the time."

Kris had a great smile, Ronnie thought. Ashley thought so, too. As the doors closed and the lift started slowly upward, Ronnie wondered how she could let him know she had an interest. Ashley noticed her friend's mind working and from the way she was acting knew exactly what Ronnie was thinking. She mouthed the question 'Seriously?' to Ronnie who merely smirked and shrugged. The bellman watched the interplay in the reflection of the elevator's doors, then began his tourist welcome speech.

"As early as the 1830s, this land was home to the state capitol, Charity Hospital, Christ Episcopal Church and the mansions of famed Louisianans. In 1893, Bavarian-born businessman Louis Grunewald opened the Grunewald Hotel replacing the Grunewald Hall, which was a performing arts center. Fourteen years later, at the stroke of midnight on New Year's Eve in 1907, the annex opened. It contained four-hundred additional rooms in its fourteen stories. Locals of the era would find entertainment and libation in the hotel's infamous nightclub known as The Cave. It was a much rumored and scandalous place decorated in plaster rock formations, stalactites, and waterfalls to give the impression of an underground grotto populated by nymphs and gnomes. The true inhabitants were party goers entertained by chorus girls dancing to Dixieland, and later, during the early days of Prohibition, the place was a notorious speakeasy. Everyone knew about it, including politicians and the big shots with the police department, but some of them were the place's best customers." He caught their eyes in the reflection and adapted slightly the next line. "New Orleans never changes, does it?"

The elevator continued its slow climb. Ronnie continued to consider the bellman. Ashley continued to wonder what had gotten into Ronnie since Bobby had.

"That all changed in 1923 when new owners demolished the adjacent Baronne Street hotel, built the new addition, and renamed the whole thing The Roosevelt, in honor of President Teddy Roosevelt. You can still see the original Grunewald Hotel name on the entrance on University Place, but from 1923 to 1965, this was *The Roosevelt*. Many locals still refer to it as such, even though it's been The Fairmont since 1965. Whatever the name on the front of the building which greeted guests and visitors through the decades, it was perhaps a former barbershop manager, Seymour Weiss, who made the hotel a New Orleans landmark known throughout the country."

The bell dinged and the doors slid open. Kris held his hand across the opening, bade the girls exit first, then followed them out with the cart.

"If you ladies will follow me, please, we've got several turns to make on the way to your room," he said. "It's usually easier if people follow."

"You lead, I'll follow," Ronnie said, then her face flushed.

"Now there's an offer," Kris said with a warm smile, then returned to his monologue as the small caravan turned right. "Seymour Weiss moved from Bunkie, Louisiana to New Orleans at the age of 20 and worked as a shoe store clerk before accepting the job of managing the barbershop here in 1923. Back then, being the Roosevelt's barber shop manager was a coveted position in the cultural hierarchy which brought the opportunity to rub elbows with all the movers and shakers of Louisiana business, society, and politics. He eventually was promoted to assistant manager of the hotel, then manager, and in 1931 took over ownership of The Roosevelt.

Along the way, Mr. Weiss became a trusted member of the inner circle of cronies of Governor Huey P. Long, whom people called the 'Kingfish', and the governor would often come from Baton Rouge to stay in a perpetually reserved suite on the twelfth floor. It's rumored he had ordered the building of what's now known as the Airline Highway between the capital to New Orleans so he could make the drive in just over an hour. When he was elected to the United State Senate, The Roosevelt was the Kingfish's Louisiana address of record. Until he was assassinated, that is."

They maneuvered down long, wide, high, hallways. The design and craftsmanship showed everywhere in the details. Cornices of moulded plaster, carved columns and beams, white-painted mahogany frames forming every nine-foot-high room portal protected by immense doors of similar foundation and finish and thick wool carpet underfoot which carried a subtle, natural aroma fringed with heat and age combined to give even the hallways a sense of long-storied ambience and elegance.

"Since you're from down here, you know how Louisiana works. In the days of Huey P. Long, it worked the same way, only more so. Patronage jobs were handed out, and paybacks were expected; and nobody would dare short The Kingfish, it has been said. Those who knew the man intimately claimed he had a short memory for friends, but a long memory for enemies. Well, in Louisiana, the words kickback and bribe are in the class of winked-at dirty words, so they created their own language to shadow the practice. So, along with his duties as owner of the hotel, Mr. Weiss also became the governor's 'Funds' manager, and was responsible for ensuring people who had received jobs from the governor would make the expected 'deductions' to the governor's campaign fund. The going rate was between five and ten percent of their state salaries, which didn't much matter since many appointed positions were jobs in name only, and the people appointed to them often held other real work. In the lobby you'll find a re-creation of the original dropping place for the cash-filled envelopes which is marked 'Deduct Box'. It's been rumored the practice raised over one million dollars a year for the governor. That's a lot of money, in those days."

"That's a lot of money in any days," Ashley said with a forced smile.

"I guess so," Kris said with a smile over his shoulder as he wheeled the cart around yet another corner.

"Is the room much further?" Ashley asked, becoming bored with the history lesson and exasperated by Ronnie's growing obsession with Kris' butt. "I'm getting lost."

"Don't worry, you'll be able to find your way back. We haven't lost a guest in over a hundred years."

"I'm enjoying the walk," Ronnie said, "and the history lesson."

"Thank you," Kris said, tossing his smile directly to Ronnie. "Over the decades, the hotel has been temporary home to several presidents, including Coolidge, Eisenhower, Ford, and just last year, Clinton. Stars of stage and screen have also stayed here; Douglas Fairbanks, Jr., Sonny and Cher, Frank Sinatra, Judy Garland, Bob Hope and Marilyn Monroe, to name a few. It's been rumored JFK dropped in on Ms. Monroe here on the tenth floor, but I wouldn't know anything about that."

He turned and winked; then stopped at a door.

"Here we are, ladies," he said, inserting the key and pushing open the heavy, oversized door. "After you."

They girls entered the room. It was a simple accommodation, but huge by normal hotel standards. Two queen-sized beds appeared dwarfed against one massive wall, the ceilings were a good twelve feet above the floor, and a set of four, old-style, multi-paned, double-hung windows stood behind sheers and tied back striped curtains. Antique light fixtures on the wall aided the lone modern lamp on a single night stand between the beds. A desk and chair sat in front of one of the windows. A desk lamp was the last of the powered light in the large space.

The bathroom alone was nearly as large as some modern motel rooms, with white, pink, and black wall tiles, and mosaic tile floor, all which dated back to a 1940s remodel. On one end of the room, next to an old-style toilet with separate water tank high on the wall above, rested a huge, cast-iron bathtub on legs. A modern addition which may have dated to the 1950s, was a slightly rusted, chromed, oval shower curtain rod suspended from the ceiling in four places by rusted hangers. Thankfully, a clean, white, and much more recent iteration of a shower curtain hung from plastic rings and cascaded into the tub. Along the outside wall below the lone window, a cast-iron radiator stood, a smaller version of the one in the bedroom.

The accommodation was dated and a bit tired, but clean, functional, and in decent repair, and like the hallways they had traversed, very different from the ostentatiousness of the main-level public areas of the hotel. Ronnie was a bit disappointed. As Kris brought their bags in and set them on benches at the foot of each bed, Ronnie picked up the small pad of paper and pen from the nightstand. She scribbled something on the first sheet, tore it off. Ashley was pushing aside the sheers and taking in their view across a small, dirty rectangle of air toward matching windows across the way and didn't notice. Across the way, the exterior walls were not white granite like the facade out front, but rather painted and peeling red brick. She formed her face into a resigned grimace. It would do just fine, she thought. They weren't in New Orleans to hang in the room.

Kris prattled on about restaurant times and suggested reservations for all but the cafe near the main floor entrance, then mentioned there were some Mardi Gras krewes having balls and parties at the hotel over the next several nights and warned there may be some noise which he promised they'd work to keep at a minimum. He instructed them how to reach the parking valet, bell services, and concierge on the phone and thanked them for staying at The Fairmont. The final words were the punctuation of his greeting and speech and the moment he expected to be tipped for his efforts.

He moved with deliberate slowness to the door and Ashley and Ronnie both moved toward him. Ashley reached into her purse and removed another ten dollar bill and placed it into his hand. He smiled and thanked her again. At the door, Ronnie reached around and handed him the slip of paper with her cell phone number on it and said he should use it if he felt the need. She winked at him. He smiled and pushed the paper and bill into his pants pocket, and then exited quickly.

# Chapter Sixteen

Auntie D was cutting some extra ham and cheese and folding the slices into paper towels, then wrapping the bulk remains in plastic and putting them into the refrigerator when Dave reentered the kitchen.

"I thought you boys was goin' explorin'," she said with a hint of embarrassment. "Just taking some shavings for later."

Dave let the remark pass without comment, but something told him her reaction was more deeply rooted to something which he could not fully comprehend.

"We are," Dave said. "Dace is taking care of some business."

"Always a good idea," Auntie D said. "You didn't come back here to tell me *that*, did you boy?" She scraped some breadcrumbs from the counter onto one of her hands, dropped them into the sink, then rinsed them down. She washed off her hands and waited. "Well?" she asked when he didn't start.

"I was wondering how you knew," he said, shifting from foot to foot. "How you knew what I was thinking in the garden this morning as I walked across those paver bricks."

She eyed him and a small smile came to her lips.

"I done seen it in your eyes, boy," she said. "I heard it in your heart. You be a good boy; you gots a carin' soul and a curious mind. That be how I knew."

Dave studied her for a moment, as if he were seeking something more from the old woman but didn't know how to ask. Then the truth of her words hit home, and he slowly nodded his understanding.

"It's not something I admit to myself, let alone others," he said, his eyes searching his shoes. "You know, I've always lived in Dace's shadow; from the first time we met back in grade school. Sometimes I have thought that we're two halves of the same person. He was out front, I was behind, backing him up."

She looked into nothingness across the room; shook her head slowly.

"No, boy, you ain't half of that one," she said. "He be walkin' his road all alone. Always has. Always will. Mind you let him stay that way. You got yourself somethin' that one will never have. Somethin' he ain't never had. You got's a selfless and loyal heart, boy."

"I'm not certain I understand, Auntie D," Dave said.

"The pain he be feelin' ain't for that girl. It be for him. That's the reason he be here. For him; and him alone. Ever'thin' always be about him. His soul be dark; and his heart be silent and loyal to nothin' but hisself."

Auntie D picked up her wrapped packages of meat and cheese, placed them into the bowl which had transported the berries and set the pitcher with the left over cream on top and began to move slowly toward the door. As she came next to Dave she reached out with her free hand and touched him on the forearm. He looked down into her eyes.

"You take heed what I say, boy," she said. "Don't you go allowin' that boy to drag you down to the evil comin' to him. Remember, boy, evil don't come if'n it ain't invited in." Her eyes grew hard and held his.

Dace appeared in the doorway about the time she removed her touch from Dave's arm.

"You ready?" he said. Then to Auntie D as she passed: "Thank you again for the food you've made for us the last couple of days. I don't know when I've had better."

"Glad to do it, boy," she said as she walked through the screen door. After it closed, she turned, peered through the mesh at Dave and pointed a finger. "Mind you pay heed, boy." Then she walked from the porch and set off across the grass.

"What was that all about?" Dace said. "Pay heed?"

Dave pulled himself from his thoughts.

"Ah, nothing," he said.

"You know, she's been great with the food and stories, but there's something about that old woman that I just don't care for," Dace said, watching Dave close and lock the back doors. "I can't put my finger on it, but it's there."

"The feeling's mutual, buddy," Dave said under his breath, surprising himself at not only the consideration, but by the uttering of the words.

"Huh?"

"Nothing."

"Okay, let's go out and see this country she's talking about," Dace said, slapping Dave on the back. "Let's go learn us some stuff, boy." He laughed.

A few minutes later, they had the front closed and locked up, and Dave had the Escalade at the end of the drive.

"Which way?" Dave asked. "You got a preference?"

"Let's make my dad happy and veer left for starters," Dace said.

It didn't take long to get off the beaten path. Starting with a left turn out the drive, they ambled generally south. When they'd come to an intersection, they'd take the new road. Several times, they ran into dead ends at a house or cabin set upon pilings on the edge of the bayou and did a quick turn around. At one of the last cane fields before they hit the upcoming forest and swamp, Dave slowed down, stopped across the road from a narrow, dirt path extending into the field. Something had caught his eye.

"What is it?" Dace said, looking across the road through Dave's window.

Dave was out the door before the words made it over to him. He stood there on the parched, tar and chip road, looked both ways and crossed. Dace joined him at the junction of the narrow road and even narrower cut into the field.

"What a shithole," Dace said, peering through the drooping, arched leaves of sugar cane stalks at the unpainted house on concrete blocks. "That's why we stopped?"

"Yep," Dave said and he walked in a couple dozen steps, brushing aside the broad, green leaves.

The shack was bare wood which had been grayed by years of neglect and exposure; the metal roof rusted by the same causes. The building had a small porch out front and an old couch took up most of the space under the tin covered awning. There were yellowed, lace curtains which hung at one of the open, unscreened windows and another set had been covered over with newspaper pasted to the glass. A door, split into a top half of rusty screen containing a large diagonal gash and a wood panel below which had once been a deep green judging from the flaking remnants in some of the corners and grooves, bumped in the breeze.

Dace stepped closer, stood next to Dave at the edge of the clearing, about twenty feet from the porch.

"You think someone really lives here?" Dace asked.

Dave pointed to the fresh tire tracks in the parched, reddish dirt.

"How can people live like that?" Dace said.

"I don't know, man," Dave replied.

A face appeared in the window without the curtain. It was a small face, belonging to a child, perhaps four or five. Then it was gone. A moment later, a skinny man in blue work pants and stained and yellowed T-shirt appeared at the door, glared at the pair of intruders, threw the door open which slammed against the wall, then stepped out onto the porch. His worn work boots were unlaced, the tongues flapped forward in the image of an unspoken insult which matched the words which came next from his mouth. The child, bear footed and wearing what appeared to be a clean, but well-worn, hand-me-down dress, joined the man on the porch. She stood behind him, a finger in her mouth.

"What the hell do y'all want?" the man called. "This here is private property."

Dave ignored the man and looked into the little girl's eyes. In the reflection he saw a mind already dulled by boredom and poverty and the image tugged at his heart. He pulled himself from the connection and looked to the man whose eyes were similarly dulled, but also contained a dangerous anger and resentment.

"Just passing by," Dave said. "Didn't mean any harm."

The man eyed them suspiciously.

"Well, just keep passin' then," he said warily. He looked off both sides of the porch, as if he were expecting people to suddenly come around the corners of the small house. "Like I said, this here is private property. Y'all got no call here."

Dave lifted a hand, turned to leave the same way he had come into the tiny clearing in a sea of cane. Dace followed. Back at the road, Dave turned and watched through the blowing leaves as the man ushered the girl inside the house, looked over his shoulder then disappeared behind the torn, rusty screen. The door was slammed shut, then again resumed its bumping in the breeze which brought a shiver to Dave's spine as he considered the noise to be the ticking of some hideous clock. The little girl's face reappeared in the window for a moment, then was gone.

Dave joined Dace in the Escalade. He turned the ignition and the engine fired, then slid the shift into Drive and moved slowly down the road. The more they saw on their tour of the country life, the more agitated and sullen Dace became, while Dave settled into his own thoughts. After a while, Dave stopped listening to Dace's rants about hicks and rednecks; and those were the kindest of the words he used.

Just as the shadows had stretched themselves to as long as they could get before they evaporated into the coming dusk, Dave wheeled around a curve in a heavily wooded and unpopulated area. The road they were on was in good condition, two-lane and paved. He wondered how even the backroads avoided potholes, and then remembered that up north the pits were generally caused by freeze/thaw cycles which swelled the base and popped the roadway. Of course, some of the dirt roads they explored had evidence of washouts, but the paved roads were in remarkable condition for the limited amount of maintenance they most likely saw. At the midpoint of the long, arcing curve, Dave slowed as something again caught his eye.

"Now what?" Dace asked in a sarcastic tone. "More depressing poverty? Or did you spot an interesting patch of mushrooms?"

Dave pointed out his window, then crossed the opposing lane and rolled the SUV onto an overgrown, abandoned drive which intersected the arc at a right angle. In the shadows of the towering trees and in defiance to the clawing undergrowth about a hundred feet in, stood an old church, barely larger than the tiny house in the cane field. It had once been white, and had a short steeple above the entry door which had long ago fallen from its hinges. If there had once been a cross at the steeple's apex, it had either gone with the last of the congregation or had fallen to the earth over time. No glass remained in the single, narrow, lancet-style windows on each side.

Dave stepped out and moved in front of the car. Dace didn't follow. The short stub of gravel quickly gave way to forest floor, broadleaf ferns, grasses, and other brush. The soil ahead was dark and rich, and when he took a step, it emitted a damp, earthy odor. The footing was solid underneath, so he continued on. As he moved nearer to the building, he began to discern the remains of a graveyard off to the right. A scattered mix of small, stone markers remained. They were moss covered, weathered, broken, and stood their posts with all the precision of the last remaining platoon of drunken soldiers of a forgotten and defeated army.

Dave inched closer. Not knowing what had been there over time, he trod carefully, each step measured and reverently placed. He moved toward the main portal of the building. At the small landing two rotted steps barred his closer approach but neither did he trust the planking on the porch beyond to hold his bulk, so he peered inside. Through the opening, he could see the inside walls consisted of rough structure which held slightly more paint than did the exterior. There obviously had been no finished surface inside, just the exposed construction, repeatedly whitewashed. Rough-sawn, irregularly dimensioned beams supported what remained of a shake roof. Large holes had long ago given the torrential rains of southern Louisiana entry into God's old house. There remained no floor planking, most likely having been scavenged over time, Dave thought, as he saw no evidence of it having rotted in place. Only floor joists, similar to their elevated brethren in quality and condition, lay to rot. Many had fallen askew. The shadow of a cross could be seen in the whitewash on the back wall. The ropes still hung into the base of the steeple, but whatever bell they had been attached to was gone.

He crossed over toward the graveyard. Behind him, Dave heard the car door slam and turned to see Dace standing there, arms crossed. The ground of the old graveyard was wildly uneven in areas. Dave realized that happened in old cemeteries as the wood coffins collapsed over time and the earth settled into the void, but this more violent topography appeared to be the result of some of the graves having been dug up and relocated, the old holes only partly refilled by time. There were no headstones remaining on the emptied graves; only those left behind when the congregation abandoned the site still held markers. He squatted down at the nearest one; a weatherworn and white stone only about an inch thick. He guessed it to be limestone, not marble, and certainly not granite. The etching, which he could feel under his fingertips, had long ago given up most of its information to the elements. The person resting there would be unknown in the universe but to God, he thought.

Further back, he found more robust stones with deeper etching which still held the names and dates. In some cases, the date of birth was preceded by the letters 'Est' which he concluded by the mid-1800 dates of death to mean the it had been estimated. Most of the stones in this area contained only a first name, no surname. He turned to see where Dace was, and saw him moving toward the graveyard. As he neared the back corner of the church, his eyes caught something in the undergrowth.

Dave walked about fifty feet behind the building and brushed aside a large, broadleaf fern. The marker he revealed was brownish, deeply embedded with moss, and softer than the others. He crouched to get a better look. When he scratched the top with a fingernail, the surface crumbled. Sandstone, he thought. He inched around the marker, which was square, about six by six inches, and extended out of the ground about a foot. It had the appearance of a flat-topped obelisk. There was one date he could discern: 1801.

Dace approached and stood above him. As Dave's view scanned the area, he could see there were other markers of similar age and material, most of the others being not modified obelisks but typical, flat stones. The several he moved close to had been worn smooth. He stood up, wiped his palms on his jeans.

"Most likely a black church," Dace said. "Black cemetery."

"You think?" Dave said.

"It makes sense. First names only on the stones. Estimated birth dates going back to the late 1700s. The old church is obviously of this century, though."

"It's fascinating," Dave said. "I'd love to explore this more." He looked up through the forest canopy. "Not much daylight left, though."

"Yeah, in a while, we won't be able to see anything, unless they all start smiling," Dace said with one of his own.

Dave stared at him. He had never heard Dace use any kind of racial slur.

"Really? Did you just say that?"

"What?"

"You know what. I can't believe you just said that."

Dace shrugged his shoulders. He looked around absently.

The Senator called home unexpectedly, spoke to Libby in the late afternoon. She said nothing of the letter from Dace, and doubted Tom would have. What purpose would it serve?

She was surprised to hear from her husband, and as he spoke, she detected something familiar in his words and tone which stung her heart. It was as if he was calling to tell her something, but couldn't. She had picked up on the ritual decades earlier, after she had caught him in what he had claimed was his first, and swore would be his last, dalliance. It had been November 1952, shortly before Thanksgiving, and he had just won his second term as a United States Congressman. He had returned to Washington, on business he said, and he had called her in the afternoon, she remembered. He said he was just phoning to make certain everything was okay. They had been married four months at the time. He sounded like he did today, and hundreds of times since that day in 1952.

Shortly after Libby hung up the phone, she gathered Mary Rose and two small suitcases, exited the front door and walked across the arched drive to her car. Under her arm, she carried a thick album in green cover with gold etching and black-edged pages. In her other hand, she had a wooden container about the size of a shoebox. Libby carefully placed the album and box on the top of the car then she and Mary Rose placed their suitcases into the trunk. The pair of women walked around to the passenger side where Libby buckled Mary Rose into the seat, then went to the driver's side, opened her door and placed the album and wood box onto the back seat. Before sliding into her seat, she turned to glance back at the house. A minute later, they rolled down the drive.

Tom watched them go.

As the sun set and twilight crept upon southern Louisiana, Dave trailed Dace back through the undergrowth to the waiting Escalade. Dace's words echoed in Dave's mind. He backed the SUV onto the roadway and drove north in silence, attempting to retrace their path from memory, but without the directional aid of the sun, and the fact they had been roaming the countryside for more than four hours, he quickly became disoriented.

"I knew I should have picked up a map," he said as he stopped at an intersection. Behind them lay bayou land, to the right and left, fields of sugar cane. Ahead, the two lane road stretched into darkness. "Any ideas?"

Dace leaned forward in his seat.

"I say go forward," he said. "What's the worst that can happen?"

"Ever seen *Deliverance*?"

"Now who's being politically incorrect?" Dace said with a laugh.

Half an hour later, the soft glow of neon appeared in the darkness, and a minute after that, a Pabst Blue Ribbon sign came into focus in the blacked-out window of a compact, one-story, concrete block building on the edge of the road. Dave wheeled the SUV off the tar and chip and onto the small, gravel parking lot just wide enough for a single row of vehicles and came to a stop next to a battered, black, Ford pickup truck. A gun rack holding two long guns was visible in the truck's rear window.

"Great, I could use a cool one," Dace said as he hopped out.

They walked across the gravel to the aluminum and painted-glass door under a smaller neon sign which read simply BAR, pulled it open and stepped onto dirty linoleum tile into glaring fluorescent light. Three sets of unsmiling eyes welcomed them as the door closed behind them, re-ringing the small cowbell hung on the frame. The two male patrons returned their attention forward after giving the strangers the once over. The bartender continued to eye them. Dave and Dace stood there for a moment and glanced around. Finally, they began to cross the narrow distance between door and bar where ten empty stools of chrome and red vinyl waited.

"Glad they didn't over advertise by labeling this place TAVERN," Dace said out of the side of his mouth. "I would have been wildly disappointed."

They selected a couple of empty stools down the way from the two other drinkers and slid onto them, hooking their heels on the rails and placing their elbows on the bar. The bartender leaned forward on palms braced against the bar and eyed them, but didn't move, rather returned his look to the other two patrons and inched his head closer and spoke in a low tone. Dace commented to Dave that the man must have just delivered the punchline to a joke they had interrupted because the two patrons immediately broke out in belly laughter. Laughing himself, the man straightened and moved six or seven steps to stand in front of his new guests, big hands spread on the back edge of the Formica-topped bar. His fingernails were long and dirty. He wore dark blue work pants and a vintage, black, Harley Davidson T-shirt. His greasy, gray hair was disheveled from the previous night's sleep and his face hadn't seen a razor in days; his eyes were dark and unwelcoming under a single eyebrow.

"Whatcha'll have?" he said.

"How about we start with a couple of beers?" Dace said, flashing his glad-handing smile.

"What kind?"

"Well, how about a Pabst?" Dace said as he leaned back and looked around. He tossed a thumb over his shoulder. "Saw the sign."

"We don't got no Pabst. Ain't had for years."

"What do you have?"

"Dixie and Coors."

Dace's glance moved to the other two patrons. Each had a bottle of Dixie sitting on the bar alongside of a pair of empty shot glasses and a small pile of crumpled dollar bills. His eyes returned to the bartender.

"Well, how about we keep it simple for you and have a couple of Dixie's then?" Dace said.

The man behind he bar moved slowly as he considered whether he had just been insulted, walked to a stainless steel cooler, slid the door, removed two bottles, popped off the caps and dropped them in front of the newcomers.

"Two bucks," he said.

"Cheap at twice the price, my good man," Dace said.

The bartender eyed Dace suspiciously as Dave pulled his wallet and laid out a couple of singles. He snatched the bills off the bar and tossed them on the ledge of a closed cash register. He then walked six or seven steps and returned to his muted conversation with the other patrons.

Dace picked up his beer, took a long draw; then leaned forward and replaced his elbows on the bar to match Dave's posture.

The bar was brightly lit, and that was an understatement. A row of double-bulb fluorescent lights ran nearly the length of the rectangular room. Toward the back was a well-used pool table, its green felt thin, faded, and splotched with stains and scuffs of blue chalk. The back bar was a duplicate of the front bar, except its gray Formica top was home to the cash register and an assortment of about two-dozen liquor bottles. An ancient jukebox, which proclaimed itself to hold '200 Hi-Fidelity Selections' stood idle against the wall opposite the pool table. A red cooler with sliding glass doors on the front and Coke signage guarded the open end of the bar and was packed with an assortment of beers in six-packs, including, Dace saw, a stack with the familiar blue and white badge of Pabst Blue Ribbon. The bathroom doors guarded the far end of the bar.

Dace downed the rest of his beer, waved over the bartender.

"Yeah," the man said. "Two more?"

"Of course, but I've got a question."

The bartender glanced down at the other two customers who were taking an interest, then pointed to a backlit clock with a red neon band on the wall above the cash register. The black hands indicated the time as six-thirty.

"It's after six, I charge double for answers after six. What's your question, Yankee boy?"

The other patrons snickered.

"Well, I hope it's Happy Hour for questions because I've got two. First, do you always keep it so bright in here? Second," he said as he pointed to the cooler, "I thought you said you didn't have Pabst."

"Them are to go," the bartender said. "We got Dixie and Coors for drinking here. You want a PBR, you gotta take it with you."

He slapped down two fresh bottles of Dixie, collected the two dollars Dave again laid out. Then he reached behind the bar and flipped off the overhead lights, plunging the place into near darkness.

"That better? We call it mood lighting."

The only light in the place now came from the clock, the light over the pool table, the jukebox and several strings of multi-colored Christmas lights strung haphazardly above the back bar.

"Perfect," Dace said, toasting the man with his beer bottle. "I knew all this place needed was ambience."

The bartender eyed him menacingly.

"Don't crack wise with me, Yankee boy," he said, pointing a fat, dirty finger at him.

"My friend was just making a joke, mister," Dave said. "He didn't mean any harm."

The bartender's eyes moved warily between Dave and Dace, his mind calculating the potential with his now doubled patron base against tolerating the wise cracks of some smart-ass kid from up north. Greed won out, and he returned to the other end of the bar.

"What the hell is with you, man?" Dave said in a low tone.

"What?" Dace said, then drank from his bottle.

"This isn't you, Dace," Dave said. "We've talked about this. The aggression, the anger, the racial slurs, the generally being an asshole to people who haven't done anything to you. That's no way to grieve for Sarah, man."

Dace glared at him.

"Well, this *is* all about me, isn't it?"

"What?"

"Isn't that what Auntie D told you earlier?"

Dave shifted uncomfortably on his vinyl-topped stool.

I watched the sun set in the rearview mirror as we traveled nearly directly east between Houston and New Orleans. Sandy was reading a book she had picked up about a year ago, not so much that the subject matter appealed to her, but rather because it had been written by a guy we had graduated with from high school.

"How's the book?" I asked as she tucked the cover flap into the page she was at and closed it in the rapidly fading light.

"It's a good read," she said, rubbing her eyes. "The technical stuff is a bit beyond me, but he explains it fairly well."

"You should really get your eyes checked, babe," I said. "You're doing that more and more when you read."

I looked down at the book in her lap. A torn photograph of an airliner and the title in red outlined in black jumped boldly from the white jacket: *Unheeded Warning*.

Sandy swiveled in her seat, placed the side of her head against the back and gazed across at me with those gorgeous baby blues.

"I always knew you had a thing for girls in glasses," she teased.

"I'm a sucker for the studious types," I played back.

"Boys seldom make passes, at girls who wear glasses," she said.

"What's that?"

"Some of my mother's sage wisdom," Sandy said with a flicker in her eyes. "She also said: 'Never fall for a man who carries a gun. They're usually the wrong caliber.'"

She chuckled and slid her right hand inside the arm of my polo shirt.

"Well, that's okay," I said, placing my hand on her knee. "I carry two. That makes at least one of them, and me, just the right caliber for you in my book."

"Mine too," she cooed, then took a very deep breath.

Realizing that we still had three hours to home, I changed the subject.

"Do you want to stop for dinner?" I asked, "or, just drive right through."

She closed her eyes, settled in a little more.

"Let's get home," she said. "What I'm hungry for, I can't get in a roadside diner."

"Mm," I said and sped up a bit. "Tapioca?"

My wife opened her right eye.

"Yeah, tapioca, that's it."


Ashley and Ronnie each dressed casually in fitted jeans, heeled boots, a formfitting top, and leather jacket. They tucked their fake driver's license and some cash, a few cosmetics, cell phone, and a room key into small purses which they each hung diagonally over their shoulder. Before leaving the room, they checked themselves, and each other, in the full length mirror attached to the bathroom door.

Ronnie licked her fingertip and then touched it to her extended behind, adding a hissing sound.

"Hot," she said, then located the Mardi Gras beads she had received the previous weekend and added them to her ensemble.

Ashley walked away without comment. She was becoming annoyed with Ronnie's newfound sexuality. Heck, she'd only done it once; well, twice if Bobby could be believed, and because of that she was turning into a what...a nympho? As she rechecked the contents of her purse, Ashley suddenly wondered if her growing frustration wasn't because Ronnie was changing, but rather that she herself was turning into a prude. She shook off the thought. One of them was changing, that was the key point; and the biggest thing Ashley feared as she watched Ronnie strut to the door, was it would eventually tear apart their friendship.


Dace waved the bartender over with another round of Dixie's. As a peace offering, he bought a pair of beers for the other two patrons, and a round of shots of Wild Turkey for everyone in the bar. The bartender collected the offered ten dollars and even accepted the shot of Wild Turkey for himself. The five of them embraced a cease fire with a toast of the shot glasses, and together, downed the Kentucky whiskey.

Dave marveled at how easily they came across to Dace's outreach. Perhaps it was the free booze, but Dave had seen the same thing happen countless times over the years he and Dace had been friends. Of course, most of those other occasions were with people who Dace hadn't first pissed off or insulted. He had a natural gift, Dave couldn't deny it.

For Dave, the most positive aspect of the sudden generosity was it had distracted Dace from his pointed inquiry about Auntie D's comments he had obviously overheard. Dave knew Dace had inherited his mother's keen sense of hearing, but he never thought he could have picked up the old woman's hushed tone from outside the kitchen earlier. When Dace tossed his arm around him after downing the shot, however, Dave realized he wasn't going to get off that easily.

"So, buddy," Dace said, the two downed beers and shot already loosening him up a bit. "About this shit from Auntie D. What's up with that?"

Dave thought about the old woman's comments for a moment. He blended those thoughts with his concerns over Dace's escalating behavior and considered how he could best help his friend to understand and accept what he and others were seeing. Perhaps, he concluded, the conversation would do some good, this time. He looked into Dace's eyes when he began to speak.

Dave went through it all again, just as he had done the previous night on the back porch with a tub of beers between them. He enumerated the changes he'd seen since Sarah's death, the strangers who have commented during their trip down, and now added Auntie D's observations and warnings. He knew the real Dace was in there, listening, or at least hearing the words, underneath all that anger and resentment. He just had to be, Dave thought; people don't change overnight. Do they? Dace listened intently, like he always did, but Dave wondered how much was getting through and how much was just his old friend's previously undisplayed skill at making someone think he really cared about what was being said. Dave wasn't really certain he could tell the difference anymore. When he finished, Dace nodded, said nothing, then waved over another round of drinks.

"Make it for the bar, again, my good man," he said, then slapped another ten down onto the bar.

The bartender snapped up the bill, poured the five shots, dropped off four new bottles of Dixie and brought no change. The other two patrons wandered over with their shots in their hands to clink glasses and thank their benefactor for the continued flow of drinks. They smiled with the newcomers now, and even the bartender held less of a scowl on his face. Dace had won them over with less than twenty bucks in free drinks.

"Where you boys from," said the bartender as the whiskey warmed him a little more.

"Boston," Dace said.   "We were down here in the boonies this afternoon, and frankly, boys, we're a little lost.  We wandered a little too far from our home away from home today."

"Where's that?" said one of the patrons.

"A little place in Vacherie," Dace said.  "Think you boys can point us in the right direction?"

"Y'all ain't leaving just yet, are ya?" said the other patron.  "Hell, we ain't even drank to Boston, yet."

Dace turned to smile across his shoulder at Dave.

"Whatever, man," Dave said, starting to feel the beers and bourbon and forgetting he still had to drive them home.  "You know I'm always game for a party."

Almost on cue, were this a movie, the cowbell on the door clanked and two women walked in.  The first one was tall and thin, about five-nine and maybe one-hundred-twenty pounds.  She had fine, blonde hair which fell about her shoulders.  The other was a foot shorter, and heavier. Not really fat, but plump, with that round-faced fullness that provided an eternal youthful look and promised skintight sweatpants down the road. She wore her black hair short, framing her face and accentuating the effect.   They each wore jeans which appeared painted on, not really a good look for either one, and T-shirts under fringed leather jackets.  The taller one had her jeans tucked into white, heeled, western-style boots with fringes, while the plump one sported dirty, white tennis shoes.  They each called the bartender by name: 'Rupe' was what Dace thought he heard.  They tossed a glance past the locals and lingered a longer look toward the strangers, and then took seats in between where the two pairs of men had staked their claims.

"Well, things are looking up a bit," Dace said to the group of four men.

He watched as 'Rupe' filled two tall glasses with long shots of brandy and topped them with sour, dropped in thin straws and slid them to the girls.  They each tossed out a handful of crumpled dollar bills onto the bar, took out their cigarettes and lighters and set them out as well.

"That's Colleen and Angel," one of the patrons said.

"Which is which?" Dave said.

"It don't matter," came the reply from the other with a dirty laugh.

Dace eyed the girls as his mind worked on something for a moment.

"Does the jukebox work?" Dace said.

Not waiting for an answer, he wandered over to the two girls, introduced himself and asked Rupe to change up a five so the ladies could play some music for the place, adding, with a wink to the skinny one, that it would give more ambience to the joint. The girls were delighted by the attention from someone like Dace and eagerly grabbed the handfuls of quarters Rupe dropped onto the bar and headed off to plug them into the old Rock-Ola.

Dace used the opportunity of new blood in the place to make better friends with the bartender. He offered a hand across the bar and introduced himself simply as Dace. Rupe did indeed turn out to be the shorthand for the man's real name: Rupert. Dace then pulled a twenty from his wallet, told the man to fill another round for everyone, including the ladies, and asked he give him a few bucks in quarters for the pool table. Rupe did so, this time he brought several dollars in change. The girls' music rotation began with Jerry Lee Lewis' *Great Balls of Fire*, which seemed to please Rupe, and seemed fitting for getting the night started.

Dace walked down the bar, downed his refilled shot, grabbed the new bottle of Dixie and continued toward the pool table.

"Anybody want to shoot some pool?" he said as he passed the other three guys.

They all followed him the twenty feet to the table, set their drinks on a couple of small shelves along the wall, and each selected a cue. Dace rolled a cue on the table after he plugged two quarters into the table and dropped the balls. Dave started to rack. Dace's smile at seeing the locals interested in a few games momentarily vanished amidst animated laughter when Dave claimed the only cue remaining in the rack next to the bridge, rolled it on the ancient felt which confirmed the 'Old Maid' stick had a distinct curve. Dave and Dace shared a look. They had done this before.

Then Dace's smile returned.

The girls came over to watch, thanked Dace for the drinks and introduced themselves to Dave, whose shyness had begun to fade with each bottle of Dixie and shot of Wild Turkey he drained. Dace heard the names but didn't see which name went to which woman, not that it mattered, but guessed the taller girl was Colleen and the plump one was Angelica and went by Angel. He was right.

First, the four guys played for the next round of drinks, which Dave and Dace congenially lost. Then they started to play for five bucks a game. They were playing for ten bucks a rack about the time several other people wandered in, allowing Rupe to get into the action with a few side bets. Just about then, in a perfect metaphor for the July 1863 turning points at Vicksburg and Gettysburg during the War of Northern Aggression, the Yankees began winning.

Dace and Dave did manage to lose one now and again just to keep things on friendly terms, but even with Dave's warped cue they were easily lightening the wallets of their new local friends. Somewhere along the line, Dave saw Dace *accidentally* stumble into one of the locals and in one simple move, his hand lifted something off the man's belt. Dace slid the item into the front pocket of his jeans. Several drinks in, Colleen began to hang on Dace when he wasn't shooting. At first hesitant, Dace discovered the joys of rubbing his hand over her skinny ass a few minutes later. Dave started to chat up Angel. What the hell, he thought.

Around ten, the pool game petered out. Dave and Angel reclaimed his and Dace's stool on the bar and were getting friendly. The two locals, still smiling even after giving up about a hundred bucks each, re-found their stools along with their wives who had arrived about an hour earlier. Dace wondered if they would still be smiling when they went to accounting for the evening. No matter, he thought as he drained the last of a Dixie and then whispered something to Colleen, who nodded and walked hand-in-hand with him out the door.

They were gone for about twenty minutes.

## Chapter Seventeen

Cindy didn't make it to the Student Services building to print her papers until that evening. On her walk back to her house, she passed a Jeep around the corner on Harvard Street parked in the identical spot she had seen the four-wheel drive station wagon sitting when she walked to the Union. She normally wouldn't have paid attention, but the Subaru Outback had caught her attention that morning when it had climbed the snowbank to get out of the spot on Clinton Street just down from her apartment, and now the Jeep taking its place around the corner. A large man was sitting in the driver's seat; the car was idling, although the windows were thoroughly fogged and just beginning to clear with the running defrosters. She remembered now that the Subaru also had a large man sitting inside. She quickened her step, walked around the corner on Clinton Street and then crossed the road when she was out of sight of the man in the Jeep. She returned to the intersection, jogged across Harvard Street and then ducked into the entryway of an apartment building.

As the SUV idled, the windows continued to defog and she eventually got a better look at the man: short hair, tall, burly, mid-thirties or so. He was similar, but definitely different from the man in the Subaru from a couple of hours earlier. She tossed her scarf over her mouth and nose, jaywalked across Harvard Street. She passed behind the Jeep, climbed the snowbanks onto the sidewalk, then glanced inside as she went by. On the passenger seat a small electronic box sat, red LED lights flashing. In the backseat of the vehicle, a couple of different styles of antennae and loops of cable lay scattered, along with an assortment of fast food containers, empty soda bottles, newspapers, and coffee cups which littered the floor. She'd seen enough cop shows and movies to recognize a stakeout vehicle when she saw one.

That second time past, she didn't turn at Clinton Street, just in case the man had taken notice of her earlier. She instead went the additional block, then came around. Once back home, she entered the back yard, walked up the enclosed stairway which took her directly to her door and went inside. Cindy left the lights off, then moved to each window and peered out. She couldn't see the Jeep, which meant the man inside couldn't see her, but pulled down the roller blinds anyway, then turned on the desk lamp. She lifted the strap to her computer bag over her head and laid the padded, nylon satchel on the desk, then sat down in her chair, took off her hat and scarf and tossed them onto the bed. Snow melted off her boots and puddled onto the wide-planked floor as the Harvard junior began to put the puzzle pieces together. She didn't like the picture which was beginning to be revealed.

Libby and Mary Rose drove the two hours to New York City in the afternoon. Her oldest daughter, Miriam, and her husband, Richard lived in a high-rise apartment downtown. When Libby got close to their building, she phoned Miriam and Richard met them on the street. He had the doorman unload their two overnight bags from the trunk and take them upstairs while he parked the car at a lot several blocks away. The twins were off at school, so Miriam and Richard had two spare bedrooms at the time for a couple of guests. When Libby had called and said she and Mary Rose were coming down, Miriam told Richard that something must be wrong for such a visit on short notice; she almost never did something like that. Her mother hated New York City, found it dirty and increasingly crude, the people increasingly rude.

Miriam suspected something juicy was going on, and hoped to pull it from her mother when they arrived. She thrived on drama, real and imagined. She had been in bed in the afternoon with another one of her migraines and not feeling up to company when her mother had phoned and asked if she and Mary Rose could use the boys' rooms for a night or two. Caught off-guard, what else could Miriam say but yes?

Miriam waited for her mother, Mary Rose, and the doorman in the apartment while Richard went down. As she ensured everything outside of Richard's den was in 'company condition' since the maid was already gone for the day, she let out a heavy, pained sigh as she surveyed the living room. In addition to her penchant for drama, Miriam could also be quite put upon at times.

Their unit wasn't quite the penthouse, Miriam often lamented, but Richard's job at Chase Manhattan Bank had been enough to obtain for them this three-thousand square foot, 'Classic Eight' apartment in the fashionable high rise in the heart of the city as well as a reasonable place out on Long Island for weekends. Richard was satisfied. She was not. Yet. Miriam had never worked, even insisted on live-in nannies when the boys were little. She enjoyed the boys - especially when they were clean, quiet, and behaving - just not the associated work. They had shipped off

Chad and Terrance to preparatory schools in the eighth grade. While Richard labored, Miriam played the role of the metropolitan, socialite housewife; and because she was a Lamoureux woman, she played it very well.

They set up Mary Rose in Chad's room and left her alone watching a video and doing what she called 'her paperwork': crayons and colored pencils, pads of paper and books with drawings to fill in. After parking the car, Richard returned upstairs and immediately went back to the den and the basketball game which was just about to begin on the big plasma flatscreen. The Knicks were playing in Chicago against the Bulls that night, against the returned and revitalized Michael Jordan. Richard had called his bookie that afternoon while Miriam was resting and had a bet riding on the game: ten large - ten thousand dollars. The Bulls needed to cover the eight-point spread, though, for him to win. He needed a break, he thought as he pulled the heavy pocket doors closed. Soon.

Libby and Miriam found seats in the living room. The floor-to-ceiling windows presented a breathtaking view of the New York City skyline coming alive in the darkening sky. They sat on the long, white leather couch which faced the windows. Miriam had noticed that, while the doorman had brought up the overnight bags, her mother had insisted on carrying the thick album and small box on her own and wouldn't even turn them over to Miriam at the door. Perhaps her mother had just not been convinced by her admittedly weak offer, Miriam thought. No matter, after all, it was Miriam who was going the extra mile here; however, she was curious about them. She watched as her mother set them both down reverently on the coffee table and then Libby suggested they share a cup of tea.

"Are you hungry, too, mom?" Miriam asked with a thin mask over her annoyance at the thought of having to get up again when she had just sat down. In typical Miriam fashion, the next thing out of her mouth was passive/aggressive with a generous sprinkling of 'Do you have *any* idea how hard it is to be me?': "The chef left an hour ago, but I could fix you something, I think. Richard and I already ate since he had that silly game he wanted to watch." A sigh. "You know how men are."

A wry half smile came to Libby's lips.

"I certainly do know how men are, Miriam," she said, ignoring most of her daughter's lamenting tone. "Nearly fifty years of living with your father has sometimes taught me more than I ever cared to have learned." When Miriam's eyebrows raised and silently posed the question, Libby waved it away unspoken and unanswered. "No, thank you on the food. We stopped for Mary Rose at a McDonald's on the way down and I had some of her leftovers." She paused, gazed out at the city lights coming to life. That was one thing she did like about New York, the nighttime skyline. "Your brother has disappeared."

"What?" Miriam said, caught off-guard. "Dace has disappeared? How? When?"

I wonder what the Golden Boy is up to now, she silently wondered.

"After the funeral on Tuesday, he and Dave Saunders...can I say it this way of a twenty-one year old man? He ran away."

"Oh, my goodness," Miriam said, shaking her head and momentarily forgetting the requested tea. She turned to face her mother across the couch. "Have you heard from him? Where is he? What's to run away from?"

"Your father thinks they are somewhere down south, perhaps the New Orleans area. They had planned it somehow, using Mary Rose as a courier over the weekend. They both abandoned their phones, left after the funeral in Dave's car which he had parked on the backside of the church. They had it all set up. God only knows what he's up to; however, I did receive a letter from your brother yesterday, again, through Mary Rose."

A letter? Her father had not mentioned anything about a letter when she had called the McClean house and told him that her mother and sister were on their way to New York. Miriam wondered why he had failed to do that. Maybe he didn't know about it, she thought. Interesting. That could be worth something; if she had more to trade. Her migraine began to fade and she smiled warmly at her mother.

"What did the letter say, mom?"

Libby recognized the affectation and looked beyond her daughter and again through the windows at the awakening lights of the city. A small smile came to her lips and her voice became as distant as her gaze. She'd play Miriam's game, she thought.

"He's off to absorb everything which has happened over the last week. From your father's talk with him about the responsibilities which go with becoming a Lamoureux man and *his* future, to the shock of Sarah's tragic and sudden death, to the pressures of just becoming a man in these times, and a host of other issues which have come to a boil. I'm certain he's fine, although I understand there was some type of incident in Alabama."

"An incident? In Alabama?"

That, Miriam did know about. Brother Dace beating up a couple of security guards? What, oh what are you up to my dear baby brother, she thought.

"Well, your father isn't telling me everything he and Tom are learning, but he was very upset about whatever the incident was. Tom is saying even less. Sometimes I think Tom is pumping me for information, thinking perhaps I am holding back and not telling everything I know."

Miriam eyed her mother as she considered how she could help her father by finding out whatever Tom had been fishing for but coming up empty.    Just the knowledge of the letter's existence would be worth something to her from her father, of that she was certain, but if she could ferret out more information or wangle the contents of Dace's secret missive, she might just get that vacation to the Greek Isles Richard had said they couldn't quite afford until next year; 'Perhaps,' he had said.

"Well, are you, mom?"

"Telling everything I know?"    She unflinchingly looked her eldest daughter in the eye.  "Of course, I am, dear.  Now, how about that tea?"

Colleen sauntered back into the bar with a smile and an unmasked look of satisfaction on her face.  She sidled up to Angel and Dave, who used the interruption to come up for air.  The girls made some excuse Dave didn't fully hear and then left him there on his stool, alone, as they walked the several feet from the bar to the ladies' room.  The music from the old Rock-Ola was still playing loudly; something about Rocky Top, Tennessee, Dave then noticed.  He was impressed at how many songs five dollars in quarters bought down there.  In the bars around campus, five dollars was five songs.  He glanced across the slowly growing number of patrons for Dace, who just then reentered the bar.  He was grinning, Dave saw, and then he crossed the distance and stood rather than sat.  He picked up a bottle of Dixie from the bar and drained it.

"Hey, that was my beer, buddy," Dave mock complained.  Then he smiled and pulled Dace down to ear level.  "So, how was it?"  His eyes sparkled like his wide grin.

Dace returned the smile and absently scanned the room.

"Everything I thought it would be, buddy," he said.

Dave took on a thoughtful look.  He pointed a slightly inebriated finger at his friend.

"So, future President Dace G. Lamoureux loses his virginity in the parking lot of a rat hole bar in south Louisiana..."  He looked at his watch.  "At approximately ten-twenty, on Saturday, February 21, 1998, on the hood of a...what was it?"

"Green Dodge Charger."

"Make sure that all makes the book," Dave said.  "Including the part about how your dick falls off a week from now.  That way your political opponents won't be able to use it against you."

They shared a laugh.

Dace waved Rupe over.  The bartender had become much more friendly, and a little drunk, like most of his swelling crowd.

"A couple more shots, Rupe, and a pair of Dixie beers; and whatever the ladies were having, and have one for yourself."

Rupe nodded and returned shortly with the new round.  He poured himself a shot and clinked the miniature glasses with each of the boys.

Dave and Rupe slammed the shot. Dace was about to slam his back, when there was a pause in between songs and he heard the cowbell on the door. He turned partially to see who was joining the party, the glass poised at his lips, which curled into a smile when he recognized who had just walked into the bar. Standing there in the semidarkness were John Deere and Evinrude, each looking a bit bruised and battered from the other night. John Deere wore a bandage on his cheek. Dace drank down the Wild Turkey with deliberate slowness as he eyed the newcomers, who then noticed other friends in the low light and crossed the dirty linoleum tile and pulled up spots about ten feet away.

Dace turned his back on that end of the bar and began to think.

I wheeled into our driveway just before eleven. There had been some sort of accident along Highway 10 west of Metairie, and traffic going eastbound had come to a standstill. The biggest problem was we were stuck on a long section where the highway crosses wetlands on elevated piers and there were no exits for miles along that stretch. So, we sat in one spot for nearly ninety minutes. Ironically, my bladder didn't decide it urgently needed attention until after we started moving again.

Sandy remained curled up in the seat and sound asleep as we waited out the clearing of the accident and only awoke when I made the high-speed exit at Williams Boulevard near the airport and bounced her new SUV into the first gas station I saw. After my rest stop, we had moved along briskly with normal Saturday night traffic headed into the city. All the parade traffic had dissipated by then, much of it outbound anyway, and the party had shifted into the streets, restaurants, and taverns of The Quarter, from which most of the attendees wouldn't be headed for hours.

Sandy had fallen asleep again shortly after my little stop. I was happy she was getting her rest, but had begun to wonder about the soundness of her naps. Perhaps it was the pregnancy and the excitement and not the aftereffects of the blow to her head. After all, the doctors in Port Isabel had said she was fine. I pushed it out of my mind.

I tapped the button on the overhead for the garage door opener, drove in and parked next to my car. I turned off the lights and the ignition and removed the keys, then bent across and kissed Sandy on the shoulder. That's her favorite way for me to awaken her, and certainly much less distressing than the g-forces imposed by doing seventy around the arc of an interstate exit. She was warm to my lips and stirred gently on the third kiss, each successive one closer to the nape of her neck. I watched a smile begin to form on her lips followed by the emission of a long string of Mms; then she turned her head, opened her eyes and looked at me.

"You know, my darling, the first kiss always wakes me up," she said, allowing the smile to grow to fruition. "It takes all my willpower to not react until at least the third one."

I knew that.

She unfolded herself in the seat and stretched all the way to her toes. I watched her. I've often wondered if she knew how much I enjoyed just watching her; how fascinated I was by the way she moved. I was even enthralled with her when she wasn't moving. I never before in my life have been so mesmerized by a woman. Well, that was not entirely true, even if semantically it was. There had been a *girl* once, but that was a long time ago.

We worked the doors and met at the tailgate. She padded across the concrete floor in bare feet, her heels hooked on two fingers. I passed her the keys and watched her move toward our back door.

"I'll get the bags," I said after her. "I'll meet you in the kitchen for that tapioca."

The last words must have gone unheard, because when I came in, Sandy wasn't in the kitchen; and there quite obviously wasn't any tapioca.

Cindy tugged on a different coat, mittens, hat, and scarf and walked out of her apartment. She descended the stairway and moved into the night. There was no gate in the fence, so she scaled it and dropped onto the other side. The snow was knee high and she made tracks across the virgin fall toward the house. She didn't know the neighbors; she had just moved in to her apartment September last, but she did know they didn't have a dog. She edged along the building. The occupants had not been out to remove the snow from the walkway which ran there; nor, she discovered when she hit the street side, had they been out to clear the sidewalk. She turned right toward Harvard Street.

It had been two hours since she had been out and spotted the man in the Jeep parked there. At the corner, she wrapped her scarf across her face, partly because she didn't want to be recognized, but also because the wind had begun to pick up, adding a chill factor to the already frigid temperature. She peered down the street through the slit between knit cap and scarf. Along the block on Harvard Street, there were a dozen snow piles with cars underneath them, but the Jeep was gone. She started to walk in the direction of where it had been when she heard cars crunching on icy snow and coming up Lee Street. Cindy turned to look and then wondered if she should make a run for it when she saw the Jeep followed closely by the Subaru Outback. Instead, she reversed direction back toward campus and crossed Lee in that direction. There was a bus stop on that corner. Earlier, she had heard on the radio the buses had begun running again. She entered the glassed shelter.

The Jeep and Subaru Outback pulled off to the side of Lee Street into a clear area about three quarters of the way to Harvard Street. The headlights went off in both vehicles yet they continued to idle. Clouds of vapor rose up, threatening to engulf them were it not for the intermittent breeze moving the cloud in her direction. Between the filthy plastic walls of the bus stop and the circling vapor, she struggled to see. From her pocket she removed a pair of small binoculars one of her boyfriends had left behind at her place after they had gone to see a Red Sox game at Fenway near the end of the season. She had tucked them into the jacket pocket before leaving the apartment so she could get a better look at the men and the devices in their car.

The driver's door of the Jeep opened, the interior light came on, and Cindy got her first real good look at one of the large gentlemen Gloria had described. It had to be him, she thought. After all, how many guys of his size were lingering near her house? He glanced around, his eyes sweeping right past Cindy, then his look returned and lingered upon her. She had dropped the binoculars to her side just in time, then turned around stomping her feet to appear as if she was merely trying to stay warm. When she turned back, the man had stuck his upper body inside the Jeep; and when she looked again, he was just emerging and stood upright again, holding the electronic device she had seen earlier. He closed the Jeep's door and the light extinguished.

Cindy raised the binoculars and watched him walk the device to the second vehicle and hand it through the open window of the Subaru. The first man began speaking with the driver of the Outback, then raised his arm and appeared to check his wristwatch. He nodded. She wished at that moment she could read lips. In the darkness of the Subaru's cab, she had a hard time making out the features of the driver, but he was clearly a large man with close-cropped hair like his partner. The Subaru's lights came on and the driver pulled from the curb as the other man walked back to his Jeep. As the Outback approached the corner, Cindy again lowered the binoculars. She could discern more details of the man's appearance in the low glow of the dashboard lights. Perhaps it was just the size difference in their vehicles but this man looked even larger than his partner. She shivered, and not because she was cold. The driver paused at the stop sign, turned the car right on Harvard, then made another right on Clinton a block later. Cindy returned her look down the street toward the driver of the Jeep. She watched through the binoculars as he stood at the driver's door and made a series of stretching moves. Cindy estimated the guy went about three-hundred pounds and stood at least six-six.

A moment later, an icy chill ran through her, and that also had nothing to do with the subzero temperature. As the man opened his door, his jacket fell open, and Cindy saw a the flash of a stainless-steel, semiautomatic pistol dangling from a holster under the man's left arm. Her mouth felt as dry as the cotton scarf covering it, and her heart tried to pound its way out of her chest. She could feel her feet begin to sweat.

Moments later, she turned her back to the approaching headlights of the Jeep, which stopped momentarily at the corner, then turned left on Harvard and drove toward the campus. In the light of the street she could see the driver holding a cell phone to his ear. Then, she lost him behind the MBTA bus coming in her direction. The driver stopped the bus and the doors opened. She stood there unmoving for several seconds, as she considered getting on the bus and leaving the area to think about her next move. The driver waved at her, but she remained where she stood. He shook his head and closed the door and drove off just as she waved her hand for him to do exactly that. When the bus cleared, the Jeep was nowhere to be seen.

Cindy reached into her pocket and removed her cell phone. It was her normal phone. She had left the one she and Dave had arranged on her desk. She knew it was probably stupid to use a phone that by now had most likely been compromised as Dave had warned, but Cindy didn't know what else to do at the moment, so she flipped it open, went to the phone book, found the number for Al Smith, a friend of a friend who was an engineering student attending MIT. She pressed the SEND button on her phone, then almost immediately pressed the END button as a thought hit her. She dropped the phone back into her pocket, exited the shelter of the bus stop and walked across Lee Street along Harvard back toward home.

In his cramped Subaru Outback parked near the far end of Clinton Street, well beyond Cindy Spagliano's building, Travis' eyes shifted to the dormant scanner as it beeped. Two sets of numbers appeared on the display, one on top of the other. An instant later, they both disappeared and the machine returned to its former idle state. Travis shifted in his seat, pressed a button and both numbers came back from system memory to again illuminate on the display. He immediately recognized the top number as that of Cindy Spagliano's original phone. He wrote down the second number on a pad from his breast pocket. A moment later, he was dialing a contact at the telephone company, the one they had used to set up the initial tap and trap. He got voicemail and left a message, then dialed Rudy.

With his back toward her apartment, and his attention otherwise occupied, he never saw the girl from the bus stop wearing the burnt orange down jacket and striped scarf which covered her face come around the corner at Harvard and Clinton, walk leisurely partway down the block, then quickly dart behind a fence toward the back of the red house with the white trim.

Cindy Spagliano ran up the stairs two at a time to her apartment door. Once inside, she shed her hat, scarf, and coat and tossed them onto the still unmade bed. She slid the chair from the desk, sat down, opened her Mac PowerBook and launched AOL. As the program loaded, she silently thanked God for bringing her the thought before she connected to Al on the phone. She typed her password into the AOL sign-on box underneath her stored screen name 'GoodByeLorelei' and hit ENTER.

The program rotated through several screens and she could hear through the computer's internal speakers the chain of dial tone, electronic beeps as it dialed the local AOL access number, the handshake static and squeals, followed finally by the appearance of the Home screen and a cheerful voice proclaiming, 'You've Got Mail!' Cindy ignored the mailbox and went instead to her Buddy List and found Al Smith's screen name. She whispered a quick prayer that he was indeed online. She clicked on his name and an Instant Message dialog box appeared on the screen. She typed in a greeting, pressed ENTER and waited. Inside thick socks inside her boots, her toes began to wiggle.

Dace leaned in close to speak to Dave. He kept his back to John Deere and Evinrude, who were at that moment ordering shots and beers from Rupe. They downed the first round and Rupe poured them refills as the newcomers began chatting it up with the locals Dace had hustled at pool at the far end of the bar. Dace knew eventually their conversation would touch on the two Yankees who stopped in, shared some drinks, shot some pool, and had hit on Colleen (successfully) and Angel (results pending). Eventually, he knew the pair would recognize him, and though he would never run from a fight, given their status as Yankees on Confederate soil, he didn't really care for the odds.

Dave stole a glance past Dace's shoulder toward the other end of the bar; then drew his focus back into his friend's eyes and nodded. He picked up his Dixie and drained the bottle. As the song on the Rock-Ola faded, a shaft of harsh light penetrated the bar as the ladies' room door opened and the chattering gaggle of two barflies reappeared. Several heads in the place turned to see Colleen and Angel take positions next to the two Yankees. John Deere and Evinrude's were among them. A moment later, however, every head was back into their conversation and drinking. It was an old show. Every local had seen Colleen and Angel working their rear ends in the place hundreds of times before.

The juke box began to pound out the opening chords of the Billy Joel song *That's Not Her Style*. Dave slipped his arm around an undulating Angel's waist. He swiveled on the vinyl-topped stool, pulled her close between his legs. Colleen had moved to face Dace, her arms around him just above the hips. Dace smiled, and kept his back toward the far end of the bar.

Dave was already regretting the plan as Angel's plump, yet still relatively firm, hips gyrated against his groin. It had been a long time for him; since Cindy, if memory served him, and in that arena it always did. He whispered something to the girl. She kissed him deeply, then moved so he could slide off the stool. Angel slid herself onto Dave's vacant spot, pulled across her new drink and took a long draw through the thin straw. Dave moved toward the door and slipped outside. Angel smiled and waved past Dace and Colleen toward another friend. Dace and Colleen were talking softly and seemingly off in their own world. Dace reached into his pocket, found the item he was seeking and removed it, keeping it cupped in the palm of his hand. He whispered in her ear, then pulled away, slid off the chair.

At that point, Colleen became agitated and began yelling at Dace. People turned in their direction and took notice, including John Deere and Evinrude. Dace moved back slowly from the now angry woman who grabbed at his jacket with enough force to spin him around and held tight to his sleeve. Hell hath no fury, right? Dace glanced to his left and saw Evinrude nudge John Deere in the ribs as recognition lit his eyes. An instant later both men were staring directly at him and Dace fully knew he needed to break free from Colleen's grip and make an immediate exit. The pair of capped buddies began to move off their stools in unison and shouted to their friends while pointing toward the Yankee. Everything began to move in slow motion for Dace and his eyes shot across the bar at Rupe whose confused glances were moving between him and the two hollering locals now just steps away.

Dace spun around which tossed Colleen into the outstretched arms of John Deere and Evinrude. She was either too drunk or just didn't care who her claws tore into at that moment because she lit into both locals like a cornered mountain lion. Behind them, Dace noticed other patrons were standing and some had started moving in his direction; their faces reflecting the dangerous blend of hostility and confusion. Dace caught one last glimpse of Angel whose face reflected nothing but wide-eyed bemusement, the straw still clenched in her teeth. He assumed she was unconcerned because she still thought Dave would be coming back for her. He ran quickly toward the exit door and double-checked the item in his palm. With his other hand, he pulled the blade from the handle.

Dave was outside, as planned, the Escalade stopped behind the black pickup pointed in the direction Rupe had earlier said would take them toward Vacherie when Dace shot through the door and bounced off the front of the old Ford. A flash of reflected neon from the Pabst Blue Ribbon sign briefly reflected off something shiny in his hand. Dave reached across the cab and pushed open the passenger door. Daces' eyes shot right and then left. To Dave's horror, Dace moved off to the left instead of coming toward the waiting getaway car. Dave hollered for him, wondering if Dace hadn't seen him. An instant later, a crowd of bodies led by John Deere and Evinrude crashed through the door. Their furious eyes darted around the darkness, then drew a bead on the open door of the idling SUV.

Dace plunged the Buck knife into the sidewall of the front left tire of the old, flat-black Ford pickup truck with the Confederate battle flag missing from the back window. The gun rack, and the two long guns it held, were all still there. In a quick move, he also slashed the left rear tire just as the crowd crashed through the door and searched the night for him. He watched in horror as they began moving toward the open door of Dave's SUV. Dace froze the group for a moment with a 'Hey fuckheads' call from between the pickup and Colleen's green Dodge Charger. Like a scene from an old slapstick movie, the group reversed upon itself and when it did Dace made a sprint to the Escalade's open door, jumped in, and yelled 'Go' while he broke out in a fit of uncontrolled laughter.

Dave floored the accelerator and spun gravel at the pursuers who, even in the momentary confusion, had drawn dangerously close. Dave heard the impact of stones on the vehicle, but was uncertain if it was gravel he was spitting up into his wheel wells or if the crowd had begun throwing rocks at them. An instant later, his spinning tires hit asphalt, chirped, and bit. He accelerated the big SUV into the darkness of a Louisiana night.

The crowd from the bar gathered outside and separated slightly into chattering, small clusters, many still uncertain what they had just witnessed. John Deere and Evinrude ran to their truck.

"That sumbitch cut your tires," John Deere wailed in disgust as he kicked the deflated rubber. "I'm gonna kill that motherfucker."

"Not if I get to him first," Evinrude said.

The crowd ebbed toward them. Both men tried to solicit keys from the others, and immediately failing at that, attempted to get someone to drive them after the Escalade. Nobody volunteered.

Rupe walked over and peered down at the punctured tires. Colleen and Angel came up behind him, then the girls got into the Charger. John Deere and Evinrude grinned at each other and attempted to get in, too. Until, that is, Colleen told them both to fuck off. She spun the tires and backed the car out of its spot and took off up the road in the direction she had seen the Escalade go, leaving a dust cloud and a trail of bluish smoke behind.

John Deere and Evinrude threw their hands in the air, stood there in the darkness and shot curses and threats into the night. Rupe strode up to them, shaking his head slowly and rubbing his stubbled chin.

"I knew there was something I didn't like about that Yankee right from the start," Rupe said as an evil grin overtook his face. "I can tell you two things, though. They're staying someplace in Vacherie; and it won't be hard to find that big, white, elephant up there. Right?"

Cindy's toes wiggled. It seemed as if an eternity passed before Al responded to her IM. She quickly gave him the highlights of what had been going on, then got to the point of why she had reached out to him. She described the machine and antennae she had seen in the Jeep, how the machine alone had been transferred to the other vehicle, which was now parked down her block. It would have been easier to talk to the man on the phone, but as he responded, Cindy was glad she had decided at the last moment not to do that and cancel the call. She told Al about that decision, and her heart skipped a beat when he replied that if the call had been initiated, there was a good chance it had registered with nearby cellular towers, even if she had cancelled it before the connection was established.

He also informed her that from the description of the electronic device, it was some sort of cellular phone scanner. The style of the antennae were directional and omnidirectional, he wrote, and briefly explained the function of each type. If they were not hooked to the machine, he said, it was because they had already established where the devices in question were located and had just programed their equipment to watch for those particular phones. He asked her if she had received any unusual calls within the last day or two since she first noticed the Subaru. She described the two which had been received: the guy speaking Spanish, and the insurance survey.

There was a pause in his responding. Her toes continued wiggling, and she began tapping her index fingernail on the desktop.

'IF THEY ARE WATCHING YOU LIKE YOU DESCRIBE, THEN THEY'VE GOT YOUR PHONES TAGGED' he typed finally.

'WHAT CAN I DO, AL???' she typed in and sent the message.

'FIRST, <u>DO NOT</u> USE THE PHONES, AND <u>DO NOT</u> TAKE THEM WITH YOU IF YOU LEAVE WHERE YOU ARE.'

When she asked him to clarify that last statement, he replied if they were pros, and it appeared to him by the unlawful equipment they possessed that they indeed were not amateurs, they could very well also have a tap and trap on her lines, and perhaps even have tagged her phone with GPS tracking so they could follow her phones as they were moved from cell to cell, whether she used them or not.

Cindy collapsed into the back of the chair. First she was frightened, but then she got downright pissed off. She momentarily considered calling Dave, but if they had *both* of her phones, they very well could have his prepaid as well. Her mind reeled. Her toes didn't wiggle when she was this angry, or that scared.

She thanked Al for the information and apologized for bothering him. He asked if there was anything he could do for her and she told him she'd be in touch if she needed anything more. She logged off, for an instant wondering if they had tagged her AOL account as well. Well, she shrugged, if they did, it was too late now. She thought of signing back on to warn Al to watch his back, but decided anyone who earned a scholastic free ride to MIT was probably smart enough to figure that out for themselves.

She rose from the desk, slapped her computer closed, then crossed the room to the bed. She grabbed her jacket and threw it on, then went down the stairs and across to the back porch. She knocked on Billy's door.

Libby checked on Mary Rose to make certain she had been able to go get to sleep in the strange bed. Mary Rose had a problem with sleeping in places unfamiliar to her, even sometimes had issues when they'd be in their McClean house, though they had identically decorated her rooms in both New London and McClean.

Mary Rose was sleeping soundly. Libby quietly closed the door and padded down the hallway to Terrance's room. Shortly after their discussion had ebbed, Miriam had claimed to have come down with another migraine and went to bed. Richard was still watching the end of the game in the den. Libby closed the door. Miriam had turned on the bedside lamps for her mother before retiring, and the boy's room was filled with a soft glow.

Libby placed the album and box on the bed. She used the small bathroom to clean her face, then changed into her nightgown from the suitcase which Richard had brought there during a break in the game. She turned down the covers, placed the two pillows against the headboard, slipped in between the sheets and pulled the top and blanket over her legs. She reached out and dragged the album over first.

Libby opened the cover. Inside the thick book were photographs, mostly of Dace and his father. She studied each page, reattached a handful of photos which had come loose over the last two decades, and retraced the path of her son's life. Occasionally, she would pause over a particular photograph and touch the faces in the captured moment out of time. As each year passed in the progression, the number of photographs added grew fewer and fewer. She wasn't surprised about that fact. She had taken most of the shots.

Libby recalled the time in her life immediately after Dace had been born and her heart again felt the familiar piercing and a sting came to her eyes, then suddenly she felt a surge of warmth as she turned a particular page.

Of course, Libby understood why she had taken fewer and fewer of these private shots of her Dace. She kept the reason in the wooden box on the shelf of her closet. Her secrets, and her reasons, were on a shelf she knew Allard would never search, in that box she knew he would never open, so she hid them in plain view; and every day, when she'd see that box on that shelf, she would remember both the joys and the pain of those times. Over the last several years, the memories of the box had lost focus for her as the sharpness of her mind had begun to slowly erode. She knew things were beginning to fog in her memory; perhaps that was the blessing of approaching the final years of one's life, she thought. Tonight, she was revisiting both the reason for the hiding, and the secrets she hid. As she slid the closed album onto the bedside next to her, she reached for the box. Inhaling a deep breath, for the first time in years, she opened it.

"Holy shit," Dace said, turning forward after seeing no lights coming after them. "That was a rush."

He pressed the blade release on the back of the handle and folded the Buck knife, then slid the pilfered item back into the pocket of his jeans.

Dave glanced at the actions across the cabin, but mainly stayed focused on the road because it was very dark and he was more than a little drunk. He felt momentarily embarrassed for running from a fight, but knew Dace was right in them doing so. He had, by his own report, beaten and robbed the two men who showed up in the bar on the levee two nights earlier, and they had had a gun which they not only drew on him, but fired. The last thing either of them needed was to be shot dead in Louisiana, although the more things escalated, the more he wondered if that just may happen in the end to his friend with the new Buck knife.

Forty minutes later, Dave wheeled the Escalade into the narrow opening in the twelve-foot-high hedge which blocked Uncle Jack's property from the view of traffic on the Great River Road. The adrenaline which had flooded his body had since evaporated from his blood stream and he experienced a physical exhaustion much like the way he felt following a football game. Dace remained agitated in the passenger seat, fidgeting while he repeatedly relived the entire event.

Dave stopped in the parking spot at the end of the drive, placed the car into PARK and killed the lights. He didn't turn off the ignition. A moment later, he put the SUV into DRIVE and maneuvered on the grass to the back of the house. There, he shut off the engine and removed the key from the ignition.

"That's a smart move," Dace said as he exited the passenger side. "I was going to suggest we lay low with this beast for a day or so. Remember we did tell Rupe where we were staying."

After getting out of the driver's side, Dave pushed a button on the key fob and the doors locked, the perimeter lights flashed and horn tooted briefly to indicate the security system had engaged. He climbed the back porch steps, used a key from the ring of three to unlock the back door. Dace followed him in.

"You have to admit, Dave, it *was* quite the rush," Dace said.

"Yeah," Dave said as he walked down the hall and started up the steps. "I can hardly wait to see what happens next."

# Chapter Eighteen

Cindy knocked a second time at Billy's door. She could hear his music playing inside, so she knew he was home. She padded from foot to foot, then finally opened the storm door and tried the inside door. It was unlocked. She hesitated. When she had first moved in last September, she had come downstairs to meet her neighbors. She found the second floor tenants, Brian and Kurt, sitting in lawn chairs and drinking white wine in the back yard. Billy had been inside with his music going. After talking with them for several minutes, she went up onto the porch to Billy's door and knocked. Brian and Kurt had suggested she just go in when Billy didn't responded to her repeated knocking. She should have known by the sniggers and shared whimsical looks between the gay roommates the joke was going to be on her that day, but she went in anyway.

This frigid February night with two strange men obviously on her tail, she decided the lesser of two evils would be if she again walked in on Billy unannounced. She slowly opened the interior door. She could immediately smell the combination of pot and cat piss in the overheated air. She stuck her head inside and called out to him. No answer was returned, although Chester, the cat, did look up at her from his perch on the kitchen counter, then immediately set its chin back onto the worn and outdated Formica. She stepped onto the rubberized mat just inside the door and then loudly stomped the snow off her boots. Still nothing. The blues song faded out and she used the opportunity to again call out and announce her presence before the next one began.

"Billy, it's Cindy, from up stairs." Nothing. "Dammit, Billy, if you and Charity are going at it, I sure don't want to see that again. Once is enough for anyone's lifetime." Silence.

Chester rolled onto his back, hung his head over the counter's edge.

The opening chords of the next song vibrated. Cindy swore under her breath, then walked across the kitchen into the front room, the whole way hoping she didn't find a naked three-hundred-fifty pound man on top of a naked three-hundred pound woman again tonight.

Billy and Charity were indeed in the living room, on the couch, fully clothed, playing a video game on the television. Each of them were vigorously working a PlayStation controller, and using their oversize bodies to add English. On the screen, race cars zipped along; on the coffee table, two bags of Doritos and two plastic mugs and a half-full, two-liter bottle of Dr. Pepper. Between the game audio and the blues on the stereo, the living room was an indecipherable maze of bouncing sound.

Cindy stood there unnoticed for several moments. Finally, she must have been perceived in Charity's peripheral vision, because the woman elbowed Billy in the ribs and reached forward to put the game on pause.

"Dammit Char, I was just about to make my move," Billy said, tossing his controller onto the coffee table. He looked over and saw Cindy standing there. "Oh, hey, Cin." He reached for the remote and muted the stereo. "Can you hear this upstairs? Sorry. We cranked the music a bit tonight because the boys are gone for the week. I never thought you could hear this in the attic."

"No, Billy," Cindy said. "I can't hear you at all. Hi, Charity."

"Hi, Cindy," the woman said.

"Then what's up?" Billy asked, obviously eager to clear the issue and get back to his game.

"I need a favor, Billy," Cindy said. "May I sit down?"

He nodded.

She sat, and began to talk.

Ashley and Ronnie stood in the middle of the intersection of Bourbon and St. Ann streets. It had taken them three hours to make one circuit up from Canal Street on Bourbon, ebbing and flowing with the crowd which overflowed onto every side street along the way. Police cruisers were parked at each intersection, and they noticed a command center and video cameras on an elevated lift positioned in the wide median between the street car tracks on Canal and Bourbon. Cops on horseback roamed the crowd's periphery, obviously having decided it was just too dangerous to move the large animals amongst so many people.

Not that there wasn't a strong uniformed and plain clothes contingent of New Orleans police throughout the throng. There was; and they were conspicuously moving people out of the street party for everything from indecent exposure to fighting. Bars overflowed into the street, and second floor balconies were packed with bead throwers and bead seekers.

Ronnie had been among the second group their entire circuit, readily flashing her bare breasts - small as they were - to anyone offering beads.

The several strings she had left the room with had multiplied a dozen fold. Her favorite trophy set consisted of gold, purple, and green bulbs the size of small Christmas tree ornaments which she had been given by man about as old as her father who not only got a look, but had negotiated a rather limited tactile sampling. Ashley, though much better endowed than her friend, had kept her shirt down and still hadn't yet earned her first Mardi Gras beads.

This wasn't at all the way Ashley had envisioned it, being out there with the crowds of drunks pushing and shoving just to move a few inches along a cobblestone sidewalk and street polluted with plastic cups, trash, beer, vomit, and urine; the latter three seeping down between the pavers to ripen. In the morning, they'd hose the entire strip down, and the smell of river water would temporarily replace the odor of waste. Buying drinks and getting into bars and clubs had been nearly impossible.

They had passed one altercation between a couple of guys which uniformed and plain clothes cops had quickly defused, taking down the main instigator face first into the gutter. Ashley almost lost her small dinner just thinking about the stench and filth as the officers pulled the guy up to walk him to a waiting police wagon bound for the drunk tank after they snared a full load. Ronnie had snapped a picture of the takedown, then defused with a coquettish smile the irritated cop who turned at the flash.

On Rue Bourbon, the intersection with St. Ann Street was known as the 'velvet line' under normal circumstances. It divided the world-famous Bourbon Street into the straight and predominantly gay areas, but during Mardi Gras, that line got blurred. As they stood there, drinking from plastic cups the remains of two Hurricane drinks they had bought at one of the hole-in-the-wall stops, the girls considered whether to start back or take in some of the gay nightclubs. Ronnie was all for checking it out, but Ashley resisted.

"Come on, Ash," Ronnie pled. "Let's check it out. I've heard the dance clubs on this end are the bomb." She pointed to the laser lights flashing in the upstairs windows of the club on the corner. "Look, there's Oz, let's check it out. Please?"

"You've heard? From whom have you heard?"

The question came too late as Ronnie had already turned her back and was making her way toward the head of the entry line. Ashley stared after her friend, finished the last of her Hurricane, looked around for a trash can, then just dropped the empty onto the street and followed.

Dave lay on his bed and called home. It would be the first contact with his parents since the day he left for Sarah's funeral, which at that moment in the darkness of his room, seemed a lifetime ago. His heart was heavy, and in the electronic vacuum, he heard the ring.

His mother answered on the second ring.  It was obvious she had been sound asleep, even though she tried to not reveal that fact in her chipper 'hello' to the yet unknown caller.

"Hi, mom.  It's me."

"Dave?" she asked.

He could hear her shifting in the bed, most likely sitting up and looking at the bedside clock, he pictured.

"Yeah, mom," Dave said.

"Honey, where are you?  Is Dace with you?  I imagine you've heard about your Aunt Gloria.  What's going on, Dave?"

Dave closed his eyes.  He realized he was drunk and didn't want his mother to hear it in his voice, but he needed to hear hers, and his father's.  He needed to reground himself, and he didn't want to lie to his parents.  He had made certain promises to Dace, and wanted to honor those.  His mother could be a relentless questioner when she wanted to get to the bottom of something, and she always knew when he was not being honest.    Like the fact you cannot buy beer, Dave also knew the other truism of the universe was you couldn't successfully lie to your mother.  He decided to respond to the easiest question first and hopefully move away from the more problematic issues of Dace and location.  Of course, if he let on that he had just seen Aunt Gloria earlier in the week, that would bring even more probing questions.

He drew a deep breath.  Just hearing his mother's voice was helping him reattach to the real world, where things still made sense.  He would be content just to listen to her and his father, but knew his mother wouldn't let that happen.

"Yes, mom, I have heard about Aunt Gloria," he said.    "I'm so sorry."

She said something about it only having been a matter of time with all the bad choices Gloria had made for herself, then added there'd be no funeral.  It had been Gloria's wish, she said.  His mother then repeated her other questions.  His attempt to beguile her had worked about as well as it usually did.

"Is dad awake?" he said, attempting one last ploy.

"He is now," his mother replied.

"Can I say hello to dad?"

He heard the phone being handed over, but not the muffled words of the exchange.  Dave knew his mother was annoyed with him, but he'd get his father to salve her for him.

"Dave?" his father said as a greeting.  "What's going on, son?"

"Dad, I know mom would have nothing but questions when I called tonight, and I don't ever want to lie to either of you, so when mom started, I knew you'd understand and trust me if I asked you.  Can you tell mom to just trust me?"

There was a long moment of silence. Were his father not in bed, he'd be pacing. Dave understood it was the way the man's mind worked; he moved when he was thinking, especially when faced with a conundrum.

"Of course I will trust you," he said, "and, so will your mother. You're a good son, Dave; you always have been. However, there's just one catch this time."

"Yes, dad?"

"I want your promise that if you need us, for anything, you'll call. Anytime of day or night."

"I promise, dad," Dave said. It was almost all of what he needed at the moment. "Good night, dad. I love you." He closed the phone.

He was grounded again, but Dave Saunders felt very much alone.

Travis had rolled down his window a bit to let in some cold, fresh air. Something smelled inside the rented Subaru and try as he might, he just couldn't find what it was. The odor was subtle, but it was there, and over time, it seemed to grow increasingly noticeable; like something small had crawled into the car and died in there. A mouse or some other animal, he thought. The wind had subsided and the night had grown quiet. He spun around at the sounds of tools impacting a solid object behind him and then peered through the partially fogged rear window to locate the source further up the street.

A snigger surfaced as he watched the two fat people in down jackets and stocking caps chopping away at the ice and snow which long ago had eaten their car. He wondered momentarily if they had risked exercise to go find more food, then considered his own growing girth and suddenly it wasn't so funny anymore. He rubbed his belly, then comforted himself with the knowledge that he wasn't five feet in every direction like the pair of car miners working up the road.

His phone vibrated, then chirped in his breast jacket pocket.

"Yeah, Rudy," he said, "I called you earlier because we had a momentary connection come through on one of the girl's phones and I want you to check a number."

He listened to Rudy's griping about needing to grab some shut eye followed by his reluctant assent that he'd check it out. Travis read him the number he had scribbled on the pad, then clicked off and adjusted the rearview mirror so he could watch the fatties digging out their car so they could drive to the nearest store for more Twinkies.

Cindy was back inside her small attic apartment, throwing things from drawers and her closet into a large duffle. She repacked her computer and some supplies into her shoulder bag. She double-checked the documents she had printed, and placed them each into folders.

Charity had graciously agreed to drop them with Cindy's professors on Monday morning. She also double-checked the two sets of directions she had hand copied from the internet and tucked the notes into the flap of her computer bag.

After a quick collecting trip through the bathroom, Cindy dropped her makeup case onto the pile of clothes and then zipped up the duffle. She hoisted the strap of the computer bag and her purse over her shoulder, pulled the duffle off the bed and headed for the door when she remembered one last thing.

'Shit,' she mumbled under her breath.

She set down the clothes bag and padded to the desk where she flicked on the lamp, grabbed a pad of paper and a pen, then adjusted the computer bag to the backside of her hip and bent over to write. She read the words, smiled, then tore off the sheet and stuck it under her two cell phones. She turned off the light and went downstairs. She set the duffle down in the snow, removed the reports from her computer bag and climbed the porch to Billy's door. This time she didn't bother knocking, but rather just opened the door and placed the folders onto the kitchen counter. Chester, the cat, was still lying on the counter across the room. He raised his head and watched her leave; after she was gone, he returned to his slumbering. She retrieved her bag from the snow-covered back walk and that time, instead of climbing the fence to the rear of the house, she cut through a different neighbor's yard and then walked to the same bus stop on Harvard Street.

Several minutes later, Billy and Charity drove up Lee Street and stopped at the intersection in Billy's rescued Honda Civic. Cindy exited the shelter and loaded her bags into the trunk area of the car. Charity stepped out of the passenger side, pulled the seat back forward and Cindy climbed past her into the rear seat. Charity reentered, slid her seat back into place and slammed the door.

"Ready?" Billy asked.

Cindy noticed they were both breathing heavily and rivulets of sweat originating under their stocking caps traced down their round faces. She smiled and nodded.

"All set, Billy," she said. "Let's go."

Dace couldn't sleep. He rolled off the bed and opened a set of doors, then moved out onto the veranda, walked to the rail and looked toward the river. The moon was out in the cloudless sky and he could see the reflections on the far side of the river from where he stood. He pulled one of the chairs over and sat down, then popped up almost immediately and walked back inside his room. He located the pistol and the couple of leftover cans of Dixie he had liberated from John Deere and Evinrude the other night and returned to the chair.

He popped the top on one of the cans and took a long draw. It was warm, and Dixie really needed to be ice cold. He made a face, but then drank the rest of the can and tossed it over the rail onto the grass below. Dace grabbed the last beer still wearing the plastic rings and tossed it as far as he could into the yard. In the moonlight, he could see the shine of the side of the can. He picked up the pistol, aimed it over the rail and squeezed off a shot. The twenty-two popped and just like the other night when he had been staring down the working end of the barrel, fire flashed as the bullet exited ahead of the hot gas created by the burning powder. It took him four shots to hit the can, which sprayed a fountain of foamy liquid into the night sky. Dace smiled to himself.

"That leaves one," he said. "Just enough...for now."

He looked the gun over carefully, then placed it on his lap. He stared into the darkness beyond the levee, then noticed the red navigation lights of a river barge moving slowly upriver in pitch blackness and wondered where it was headed.


I carefully rolled out of bed, moved the covers back up. Sandy mumbled something in her sleep, then rolled over. I located my underwear, tugged them on without falling over, and left our room. I descended the stairs, wanted to walk down the hall to our den and watch some television to put me to sleep, but rather turned the other direction at the base of the steps and went to raid the refrigerator.

Now, if any of you are thinking I was still looking for tapioca, you're wrong, and perhaps you need to rethink how you gauge some of the things I say here. No, there was no tapioca in our refrigerator, and I knew it the whole time. What we did have was some leftover fried chicken. I removed the paper bucket - which any good chef will tell you is the best way to store fried chicken - pulled the top and gave it a quick sniff. It still smelled okay. Sandy had mastered the art of making real Southern fried chicken, and storing it in the bucket keeps it both moist and crispy for days. Satisfied it wouldn't kill me in the short term, I placed the entire bucket into the microwave and zapped it for a minute, catching the door right before the timer sounded and tipped off my slumbering wife I was about to violate my new diet rule of no eating after bedtime.

I peered into the bucket, stuck my finger on the surface of one of the four legs left from the other night to test the temperature, then salted and peppered them right where they lay. Yes, of course, I licked my finger. I went back to the refrigerator and removed a Diet Sierra Mist and pulled a couple of paper towels off the roll on the counter, then lugged my cargo down the hall to the den. I pushed the door nearly closed, set the soda and bucket onto the end table next to my favorite chair, found the remote and turned on the television.

I was in my blue leather recliner with my feet up and had no sooner picked up the first leg from the bucket and moved it toward my watering mouth when the door behind me slowly pushed open. Turner Classic Movies was running *Westworld*, and Yul Brynner was in the process of shooting James Brolin, which was never a bad thing in my opinion, and once Jimmy Boy gets a few years with Babs under his belt, I would imagine he would agree. I was so deeply involved in my deep thoughts that I didn't hear either the normally creaky door move or the footsteps coming up behind me.

"Wasn't I enough for you?" she said.

I turned. I was busted. Sandy stood there, hands on hips, off to my right, clad in a light, white cotton top with spaghetti straps and loose, white cotton pajama bottoms which came down to mid-calf. She was bare footed, and from all indicators, a little chilled, yet she had braved the cold to come down and bust me anyway. I dropped the leg, unbitten, back into the bucket, placed the container onto the end table, licked my fingers, and reached out for her. She took my hand and climbed onto my lap, curled herself against my chest.

"Always," I said. "Your charms filled my ravenous heart, my sweet, as always, but my jealous stomach woke me anyway."

"You've earned it, papa," she said, lifting her head from my chest and looking into my big baby browns with her playful blue eyes.

Sandy reached across her legs and brought the bucket onto her lap. I grabbed a leg from inside and took a big bite. To my surprise, Sandy pulled my hand to her mouth as I chewed and took a big bite herself, leaving nothing but bone and knuckle behind. I was glad to see her eat something since she hadn't had anything since our late lunch, but was also a little sad that now there were only three legs left in the bucket.

A short time later, after sharing each of the three remaining legs, Sandy extricated herself from my lap, picked up the empty bucket and my used paper towels, took a long draw from my Sierra Mist, kissed me with cool, wet lips which tasted of seasonings and citrus, and went back to bed. The Black Knight had just slain - or is it slew? - the nerdy guest in my movie. It appeared to me Medieval World was having robot issues as was neighboring WestWorld. Bored with a quarter century ago's view of the future, I flipped around the channels, finally settling on Father of the Bride - the good version, with Spencer Tracy, not the cutesy, politically correct iteration with Steve Martin and that frustratingly annoying what's-her-name as the wife - and settled in to watch a true classic movie.

As I observed Spencer Tracy as George Banks go from shocked to concerned to semi-comforted to drunk to overwhelmed to displaced and finally to a mix of joyful and sad at the same time when he realizes his little girl is morphing from being his child to an independent, married woman in the seeming snap of fingers, I thought of my girls. They were all growing up so quickly, and for most of their lives, they had known me only as the sometimes dad; a role I had vowed I would never play after living with the pain of divorce when I was a child. Even losing a marginal father such as mine had been, at the time, a powerful blow to the psyche of this near teenage boy.

I reached for my soda and finished the last warmed drops, replaced the can on the coaster. Even with purposely distracting my brain, my thoughts quickly returned to the subject of fatherhood. Here I was, going on forty-years-old later that year, and yet again, facing another unplanned blessed event. Suddenly, the thought of a couple fingers of bourbon sounded good, perhaps it would do double duty in helping me to sleep while keeping the demons away. Who was I kidding? I always told people you can't kid a kidder, and I'm one of the biggest kidders I know. So I folded my recliner, picked up my soda can and padded to the kitchen and warmed myself some milk in an oversize mug, then in an admittedly contradictory diet move, stirred in a couple tablespoons of Nestle's chocolate syrup. I returned to my chair in the den and put my feet up again, having first pulled down a couple of photo albums from the shelf and switching on the side table lamp. I turned off the television.

I took my first drink of the warmed, chocolate-infused milk and opened the first book of old photographs across my lap. Years ago, my mother had parceled out the family pictures to my brother, my sister, and myself. The siblings had then gotten together sometime later and went through them all, making duplicates of ones we wanted and didn't have, and swapping out others like baseball cards. In total, they spanned the entire 'Wayne Years' and beyond when it was just mom and us kids.

Photos are supposed to show happy times, things you want to remember, but when you grow up with an alcoholic and physically and emotionally abusive father, they also include glimpses of things you only recognize later on, long after you've picked up the prints from the drug store and tucked them away in albums or the backs of drawers. Years later, long after you've lived enough away from it all to see things for the way they truly were, and you look again, you wonder how you missed it.

You see telltales in the eyes of the persons being photographed, and in the affected smiles; and those are the things I was looking for that night as I paged through the years of my childhood. There was one series taken during a Christmas Eve when I was about nine, which would have made it 1967. I had gone to Prange's - the department store on 8th Street in Sheboygan - by myself for the first time and bought a Dean Martin album for my father that year. I had bought my mother a big bottle of perfume, obviously believing bigger must have meant better. Thankfully, she never told me how awful it probably was and over the next year is slowly disappeared and then finally the bottle itself was gone from her dresser.

In the first of the series of pictures from that night, my father was unwrapping the album. In the background was my mother, whose eyes weren't watching the unwrapping, and it wasn't just her being distracted by some other action taking place off the film. The next picture was of my father dancing to the record along with my two-year-old sister and five-year-old brother following his lead. The man's eyes were already fogged by drink, and that was before he left the family and went to the tavern for the night. Merry Christmas, Wayne.

People may wonder why I saved photos like that. Well, I'll try to relate the reason as concisely as I possibly can: because it was part of my life. Sure, we'd all have loved to have had Norman Rockwell memories, but that idyllic view of the world isn't how most of us had it. Not that I'm complaining, understand, rather I'm explaining. Plus, I've lived long enough to know that many people had it much worse than we did. My father was why I vowed to be different for my kids, but life intrudes sometimes, and people don't always grow up as quickly as their promises to themselves would require them to. I know I've failed my own children often enough, but it was for very different reasons.

I never physically abused my kids or my ex-wife as my father had done to us. I never kicked a play farm over the fence because it made the yard look messy, or shook a four-year-old so violently that he pissed himself, passed out and nearly died from fright because he had turned the valve the wrong way and the sprinkler had sprayed a bit of water in the window one summer evening, or tried to push my wife from a car doing eighty on the drive home after having too much to drink on yet another Christmas, but I had made mistakes over the years. While my father had been a monster in every sense of the word, I had merely been a selfish husband and immature father. I think if you asked my kids, I'm certain they'd agree with that assessment. They love me and are secure in the knowledge that I love them, and ultimately, isn't that the best gauge for any childhood?

Then I thought of my yet-unborn child and how maturity may bring a difference in my being a father. Over the last few years, I had made great strides with reentering my girls' lives in the emotional aftermath of a rather devastating divorce, and much of that was due to Sandy's efforts and support. I cherish each of my children, would die for any of them, which is something I was certain was never in my father's heart, but I wondered if they fully understood that at this point in their lives. They had each seemed happy when Sandy and I had called with the news of a new brother or sister the other day, but had that merely been a forced emoting, like the images in some of the photos from my childhood? Were they merely covering for how they really felt? Were they insecure in anything? How could I be certain they were truly okay with this? How could I be certain I didn't make the same mistakes with this brand new human being now slumbering within my wife?

The truth was I couldn't be certain of any of it. The girls were all doing well externally, they seemed happy and secure in who they were. Their mother had moved on. I had done the same, although not without a bit of drama from time-to-time, and I was gloriously happy with Sandy in my life. I realized that I can't do anything about the past; the only thing I could do was my best going forward. We can't apologize away the little scars you unintentionally inflict upon someone's heart because we often don't know when we do it, but we can learn from our mistakes and try to be a better person the next time. I've been working on it, but understand I still have a way to go. Being the best we can be is something we all need a bit of help with from time to time, so I did something I hadn't done the right way in nearly thirty years. I prayed.

I set aside the photo albums and folded the recliner. I slid off the chair and got to my knees, the way I had seen my mother's parents do every night before they went to bed when we'd be staying over as kids. I folded my hands and closed my eyes, then asked for two things going forward in my life: guidance and mercy.

# Chapter Nineteen

Ninety minutes after they had turned right on Harvard Street and drove unnoticed past Clinton Street with the large man in the Subaru Outback parked down the block, Billy wheeled his overloaded Civic into the parking spot at the trailer which had been the home of the late Gloria Keller. The idling car's lights illuminated the area as the three piled out of the cramped vehicle and the springs and shocks extended with an audible gasp of relief.

Just beyond a snow pile sat Dave's Mustang GT Liftback covered in about six inches of snow. As they had traveled south from Boston, the snow piles along the road had steadily decreased. Cindy had wondered aloud if God had somehow just been pissed off at Bean Town that weekend. Neither of her traveling companions had commented. Cindy walked around the Honda and noticed with a touch of sadness the police sticker which sealed the trailer's door and frame and warned of unauthorized entry. She concluded they probably did that whenever there was an unattended home death with an initial uncertainty as to the cause.

Cindy approached the Mustang. Billy stuck his head inside the Civic and emerged holding a snow brush with an ice scraper on one end. He waddled to the Mustang and began to clear the snow and ice. Cindy bent down and began feeling inside the rear bumper and eventually located the small metal object which she pulled free.

Inside the magnetic keeper was an ignition key for the Mustang, which also worked for the door locks. Dave had locked himself out of his car several times over the months they had been dating, and once when he and Cindy had attended a Boston Bruins hockey game Dave had been forced to call a locksmith when they couldn't locate a wire coat hangar anywhere.

In what Cindy believed to be a typical Dave Saunders overreaction, he had immediately bought the key keeper and placed his extra key inside.  Of course, she thought as she now approached the driver's door and recalled the howling winds that frigid evening outside of the TD Arena, the two-hundred bucks the locksmith had charged Dave for coming out late on a Friday night to open the door - a feat which had taken him all of thirty-seconds to accomplish - may be justifiable reasoning for reclassification of Dave's reaction as smart economics.

Cindy placed the key in the door and after the crunch of ice breaking inside the lock, the knob rose and she was inside.  She slipped into the driver's seat with her feet in the snow and inserted the key into the ignition.  The car turned over enthusiastically and fired up, and she turned the fans on high to clear the windows as the engine warmed, then returned to the Civic for her duffle, purse, and computer bag.  She stuffed the large duffle into the Mustang's small rear seat and laid the computer bag on the passenger side.  She went into her purse and pulled out her wallet and unzipped the cash compartment.  She tried to hand forty dollars to Billy, who refused it, joking that it was his way of paying her back for the emotional scars inflicted by what she had walked in on last September.  Cindy hugged them both and said there still may be a balance due her on that one.  They all shared a laugh in the cold crisp air.

Minutes later, Cindy turned south on I-95 and Billy and Charity turned north.  The internet trip planner predicted she had about twenty-six hours of driving before she reached Uncle Jack's place.  She settled in for the trip, smiling that Dave had left the tank nearly full.

Rudy maneuvered the Jeep alongside the Subaru Outback just before midnight.  Travis got out, leaving the monitor behind to work on its own and climbed into the passenger seat of the Jeep.  As Rudy pulled away, Travis was immediately uncomfortable.  He couldn't ever remember being a passenger when Rudy drove.  Rudy smiled as he watched out the corner of his eye as his partner shifted in the seat.  At the corner, Rudy turned right and drove them to the International House of Pancakes on Eliot Street.

Once inside and stuffed into a booth, they each ordered a full breakfast and coffee.  The waitress returned moments later with an insulated urn, filled each of their mugs and then set the jug on the table between them.

"That number is registered to an Al Smith right here in Cambridge," Rudy said, dumping two packets of sugar and two thimbles of cream into his steaming coffee.

Travis drank his coffee black and as he blew across the top of the white ceramic mug he slowly shook his head.

"Doesn't ring a bell," he said.

"Nor should it," Rudy said, dropping his spoon onto the table.

Travis eyed the utensil, knew it would leave a stain at the base of the spoon's bowl.  Rudy left those little spots all over the kitchen of their apartment in New York.  He also did it in every hotel room they ever shared, only in hotels the stains were long and narrow from those tiny stir straws. It drove Travis nuts.  Rudy had stopped caring about that particular issue long ago.  Rudy sipped his coffee, set down the mug.

"Al Smith is a student at MIT," Rudy said.  "Nothing at all on him in any databases, other than some articles about him being some kind of engineering genius.  Our phone guy said there were one or two calls a month between the two numbers over the last couple of years."

"Old boyfriend?"

"Could be, I didn't dig any further."

The pancakes, eggs, hash browns, and ham arrived.

They both began to devour their food like they hadn't had a decent meal in days, not that either would consider IHOP's culinary fare as a decent meal.

Rudy's phone began to vibrate and he dug it out of his jacket pocket, silenced the coming ring and checked the caller ID.

"It's Mike from Accu-Track," he said, then answered the call.

Travis continued plowing through his breakfast as Rudy listened. When he concluded the call, Rudy sat with a look of consternation on his face.

"What did Mike want?" Travis asked, his mouth half full of pancake.

"The GPS tracker on Dave Saunders' Mustang is on the move," Rudy said.  "Mike says it's traveling south on I-95, just south of New London right now.  He said nobody called us earlier because they thought it might just be someone retrieving the car to the Saunders kid's house, but when it kept going past the Groton exit, he decided to make the call."

Travis settled back into his seat.  He chewed and thought.

"What kind of engineering?"

"Huh?"

"The kid from MIT.  What kind of engineering?"

"Oh, electronics.  Got a full-ride scholarship..."

"Son of a bitch," Travis said, dropping his fork onto his plate as he recalled the woman at the bus stop who appeared to be watching them when they switched out last time.  "She made us."

Twenty minutes later, Travis and Rudy had returned to Clinton Street.  They both exited the Jeep which Rudy parked right in front of the red house with white trim.  They could see no lights in any windows above the first floor, although some kind of night lights appeared to be on in the second floor apartment.  Cindy's attic apartment was blacked out, and they could see the roller blinds had been lowered.

Rudy searched through a small bag in the back seat, removed a set of lock picks then dropped them into his jacket pocket. He and Travis donned a pair of nearly clear latex gloves, then exited the vehicle. They each pulled down the ski mask portion of the stocking caps they wore and walked through the newly fallen snow at the side of the house. As they passed a set of bay windows, they noticed a cat walking along the sill inside the first floor apartment. Travis was tall enough to look inside without stretching, so he checked for any movement beyond the cat. He saw nothing.

They continued around the back, looked up the empty stairwell which led to the attic apartment and slowly climbed the steps. At the top, they quietly checked the door. Locked. Rudy pulled the lock pick set from his pocket, extracted the appropriate pick and torsion wrench for that type of cheap, residential-grade, five-tumbler lockset and within seconds had it unlocked. He returned the tools to his pocket, then slowly twisted the knob. The door opened and Travis shined a flashlight across the small space. There was nobody home, that was easy to ascertain. When she left and where she was going, they could venture a good guess.

They moved through the apartment, eschewing the use of interior lights and each illuminating their search with a small flashlight held in their mouths as their hands worked. At the desk, Rudy found her two cell phones. He extracted the note she had left underneath them, quickly read it, snorted a laugh, then held it up for Travis.

'BYE-BYE, ASSHOLES!' was all it said.

The lights of New York City came into view. Cindy connected to the Crosstown Expressway on the north side of Manhattan and drove across the George Washington Bridge into New Jersey. The adrenaline which had driven her early-on had dissipated and she suddenly felt exhausted. Her eyes felt heavy, her arms and legs like Jell-O. She turned up the radio and turned down the heat, even opened her window to let some cool, fresh air into the car. Nothing seemed to be helping her stave off that desire for sleep until she thought of Gloria Keller and the fact Cindy herself had been drawn into this mess simply because she was the friend of a friend of that asshole Dace Lamoureux. She felt an instant reinvigoration as anger drove her harder than could any other master.

She had never seemed to be able to get along with Dace while she was dating Dave. There was something about him which she found unsettling at her core, but she had been unable to put the feelings into words when Dave asked her about it. She respected the fact Dave and Dace were best friends and never felt she had done anything to attempt to come between them, but truth be told, she believed the ongoing tension between herself and Dace was one of the reasons she and Dave had split. The more she thought about it all, the more angry she became.

She wondered if she could maintain the anger to drive her for the next twenty-plus hours.

Mike called Rudy again after the GPS indicated the Mustang had traveled south of New York.

"She's got to be headed to Dave," Rudy said to Travis. "She's making a beeline in that direction, now past New York."

Travis nodded as he collected the car rental receipts from the clerk, then turned and walked toward the door.

"I think it's time to check in with the boss," Travis said.

Travis and Rudy had made a thorough search of Cindy Spagliano's tiny apartment and found nothing they could use to help them track down Dace Lamoureux, which was really the focus of their mission. The other superfluous issues had begun to cloud the true purpose of what they had been assigned to do and they refocused while going through the girl's tiny place. They had also made the decision to end the surveillance and head back to New London themselves. There was nothing more they could accomplish to further the mission goal in Boston with the girl gone; and unless she had discovered the GPS tracker and tucked it onto a Greyhound bus, she obviously wasn't coming back home anytime soon.

Travis flipped open his phone and punched the speed dial for Tom's cell while he waited for the cab which would take them from the rental car facility to their hotel so they could pick up the Lincoln. He looked at his watch as the phone connected through and began to ring. It was two-thirty on Sunday morning.

"Yeah," Tom said.

"The girl made us," Travis said. "She's gone."

"Gone?" Tom repeated, a tinge of wariness over the word.

"Not *gone* gone. She split."

Travis gave Tom all the details to bring him up to date with the Boston situation, including the fact the girl had dumped her cell phones, their only link now the GPS tracker in the wheel well of Dave's car. They could find her anywhere she went, the tracking was as good as anything the U.S. government had, with an accuracy which could pinpoint the vehicle within three feet of where it was anywhere on the globe. As long as the tracker stayed attached to the car, and she was, in fact, headed for the Saunders' kid, there'd be no problem with them eventually getting to Dace. If he was somewhere in southern Louisiana as they thought, Travis estimated they'd have the location in the next twenty-four hours. Maybe less, if Tom ordered them to intercept her along the way.

"We're headed back to New London," Travis said. "There's nothing more we can do here." He paused. "What we'd really like to do is get back to New York for a couple of days."

"Yeah, we'd all like that," Tom said irritably. "This should wrap up soon enough, Travis, so let's suck it up and finish the mission."

Tom thought for a moment on the other end of the line. During the phone's silence, the cab pulled up to the curb and Rudy and Travis climbed in while the driver dumped their equipment duffels into the trunk. The cab pulled away from the curb headed back to their hotel.

"I'll brief The Senator," Tom said, verbalizing his thoughts. "It's time for him make some decisions, but my sense of things is we let her get all the way to Dave which gives us a location on Dace. Once we know exactly where the kid is, we go get him and we all can get back to our normal lives. I'm going to let The Senator make the call, though. Just get back here for now. Call me when you get in."

Tom clicked off.


Libby padded in bare feet down the darkened hallway toward the kitchen to make a cup of tea. On the way past Chad's room, she peeked in on Mary Rose who was still sleeping soundly and snoring lightly. Miriam and Richard's door was closed and there was no light coming from underneath it. She turned on one light in the kitchen, lifted the tea kettle from the stovetop, shook it to test the amount of water already in there and then filled it a bit more from the tap. While the water heated, she found the tea bags and a mug in the cupboard. She removed a spoon from the drawer as wisps of vapor began to drift out of the spout, then stood at the stove closely watching over the teapot, wanting to catch its boil before the steam whistle could possibly wake anyone. Her mind drifted to her photo album and the letters in the wooden box, settling on happier time images of Dace...and, Tom.

"Mom?"

Libby turned to see Richard standing there in pajamas and robe. His hair was mussed and his eyes tired.

"Is everything okay, mom?" he asked.

"Just fine, Richard," she said with a disarming smile. "I couldn't sleep, so I thought I'd make some tea. Most people think warm milk, but tea usually works best for me. Care to join me?"

Richard went to the cupboard and pulled down a mug. He selected a tea bag from the box on the counter and dropped it in, retrieved a spoon and carried them to the table. He slid out a chair and sat, leaned forward on his elbows and rubbed his eyes. He hadn't been sleeping when he had heard the low sounds of activity in the kitchen, but rather lying there contemplating yet another gambling loss. The Bulls had won the game, but had not covered the spread meaning someone would be at his office in the morning looking for the ten thousand dollars he had bet. It wasn't a large amount of money, but it was the bottom of the well, and he had no idea how he was going to tell Miriam. A cup of tea with his mother-in-law seemed like a good distraction from his thoughts.

Libby brought the boiling water, filled each of their mugs and returned the pot to the stovetop. She took a seat across from her son-in-law, who was moving the bag in his hot water to steep the tea. Like his mother-in-law, Richard liked his tea strong, and without adulteration of any kind. Libby watched him as he nearly mimicked her every move in preparing his drink and realized there were times when she felt more of an affinity toward Richard than she did toward her eldest daughter.

Libby lifted her mug, cupped it with both hands and took a sip of the scorching liquid. Richard watched a contemplative smile slowly drift to her lips, although he could see something less than contentment in her eyes. This wasn't the first time over his twenty-five year marriage to Miriam that he and his mother-in-law had shared a late night alone at a kitchen table and they could recognize the tiniest tells each of them possessed. He thought how he felt closer to Libby than to his own wife and had often wondered how the two very different women could be mother and daughter. Perhaps Miriam was switched at birth, he thought, which brought a contemplative smile to his lips.

Richard and Miriam had married early, when she was just twenty and Richard had been twenty-six. They had met at an art gallery opening in the Village while Miriam had been at Columbia; Richard had just started as an anonymous vice president at one of the Manhattan branches on what would be his meteoric career with Chase Bank. It had been a whirlwind courtship and, according to Richard, a fairytale elopement and honeymoon in upstate New York. Miriam's categorization of the events depended upon how much wine she had consumed, and the state of her ever-threatening migraines.

Whether the courtship and elopement had been a fairytale was eternally at debate, however, the marriage for Richard had been much less so and everyone in the family knew it. Libby knew Miriam took a more pragmatic view on her entire endeavor with Richard Bertram: landing him secured her future social and economic position in New York City while her family name - which she hyphenated and appended to his in order to assuage Richard's lamentations - brought her continued recognition and event invitations which the simple Bertram may have not provided. The marriage to her was a simple matter: a merger. In contrast to his wife's cold and calculating soul, perhaps it was Richard's sense of romanticism which helped him so easily relate with his mother-in-law. Libby smiled at the thought, a Wall Street banker with a heart. Wouldn't the public be interested to know that one truly existed?

Libby had always been a bit of a romantic herself, and there is nothing which cuts a romantic more deeply than a betrayal by the one they love, which was another thing she and Richard Bertram shared. She wondered what he'd think of her at the moment, should he know the contents of the small wooden box in her room and the secrets of which they told. Would one scourged romantic grant another absolution for her own sins? Did it matter?

"Care to talk about anything, mom?" Richard said, his eyes receptive over the top of his mug.

"You could always read me like a book, Richard," Libby said. "It's *one* of the reasons I love you like a son."

Even though she and Richard had shared many secrets during these late night happenstances, Libby knew she needed to consider her next words very carefully. It was one thing to share some tea and feelings, it was another to lay bare deep, dark secrets across a kitchen table in the middle of the night. To the best of her remembrance, neither of them had ever betrayed the other's confidence, but her current musings were not of a subject with which to test the continuation of that fact. She mentally ticked her options and the associated risks carefully as she sipped more tea, knowing she could not allow her emotional upset of the last days, and the memories those events had evoked to overrule prudence. The secrets held by that wooden box with its now scattered contents which she had long ago placed on that shelf and not had the courage to take down for so many years could affect, and even ruin lives beyond her own. She had to tread carefully, yet she so needed to share her thoughts with another kindred spirit, and who better than her long-time confidant, Richard Bertram?

He watched her eyes and waited patiently across the table.

The landline number servicing the McClean home was dialed and the phone chirped on the bedside table. The Senator awoke on the first ring, but it took him three more to roll over and find his glasses. He noted the caller's ID on the phone's base display. The landline to the homes, both in McClean and New London, were securely hardwired all the way to the telephones and swept routinely, meaning no electronic signals floated out into the ether to be picked up by someone wishing to surveil a United States Senator. Of course, there was the potential of a legal wiretap being placed on either lines, but The Senator had people who watched his back for that contingency as well.

While the caller ID indicated the incoming call was coming from his home in New London, it didn't tell him who was waking him up in the middle of the night.

"Hello?" he said.

"It's me, Allard," came the response.

"This must be something good for you to not call from your cell, Tom," The Senator said. "Have you found Dace?"

"Not yet, but there is solid movement in that direction," Tom said.

Tom first relayed the negative news regarding the lack of any new information uncovered in the surveillance, the fact the girl had discovered the boys then bolted, but balanced that all off with the fact Cindy had run in the one direction they had hoped by taking Dave's old car and traveling south, obviously headed straight to Dave and Dace, both of whom Tom and the boys were relatively certain were still somewhere in the New Orleans area.

The Senator listened to the entire report before commenting. He had worked with Tom long enough to know the man would be complete in his brief. Interrupting people to ask questions was a cheap political trick he used during his committees' sessions when he wanted to make a point for the television cameras. He didn't need to do that with Tom. When Tom was finished, The Senator did have a few questions as it turned out, but Tom didn't have many additional answers beyond the briefing.

"What are the options right now, in your opinion, Tom?" The Senator asked, even though he had calculated most of them already.

"I say we have two at this point. You know we can track the vehicle to within three feet of its actual location and we can find it anytime we want, so long as the transmitter remains attached and undiscovered. While it doesn't happen often, transmitters do fall off, and if she should find it and ditches it, we could wind up on a wild goose chase. Time is not a friend in this type of operation. As I see it, we have two options. Option One gets us the information fastest and could be obtained if we send Travis and Rudy to intercept the girl on the road; she's between New York and Washington according to the last report. That's risky because she may refuse to talk no matter what methods we employ and we may have shot our load for nothing. Option Two is longer term in which we would be to let her get all the way to Dave and then move the boys in to get Dace back here. The negative of that option is we'd have to wait at least a day before she gets down there, *if* they're still in southern Louisiana and *if* Dave and Dace are still together."

"Oh, they're still together," The Senator said. "You can count on that. Dace wouldn't have set this all up just to split up with his perfect ally. Dace knows how to manipulate useful people, and in this situation there is no more conveniently useful person to him than Dave Saunders."

"Like father like son, eh?" Tom joked.

The Senator ignored the backhand compliment. Politics was a dirty business consisting of only two player types: users and useful idiots; and there was no need to state the obvious between such old hands at the game.

"We have a third option, Tom," The Senator said. "We could hire someone local to put eyes on them before we move the boys in. That way, we make certain Dace is there before we let Dave and the girl know we're on to them. Gives us a cushion just in case they have split up."

"Local eyes? What's wrong with sending Rudy and Travis?"

"Dace knows them, and if somehow he spots them before they see him, he could disappear before they ever got near him. Look how easily the girl made them, and she'd never seen them before. Forgive me for saying this about your boys, but while they are wonderfully equipped for some missions, they are far too physically conspicuous to be spies. What we need is someone who blends in better. Someone local."

"Any ideas?"

"Call the Party headquarters in the morning, speak to Susan Delp, she's spearheading the August Project for us this year. She's been doing background research and hiring nearly every P.I. in Louisiana to gather dirt on our esteemed colleagues across the aisle. She should have someone right for the job. Call her at home now, if you wish."

Tom checked his watch. While it already was technically morning, he'd let the woman sleep a few more hours before calling her. He told The Senator that.

"Yep, let the Spagliano girl run out the line before we start firming up the drag to set the hook," The Senator said.

"I concur, Allard, but I wanted you to make the final call."

There was a pause on the line.

"Anything else, Tom?"

"Um, yeah, Libby and Mary Rose left the house late yesterday afternoon," Tom said a bit reluctantly.

"I know."

Tom could hear The Senator smiling.

"They're at Miriam's in New York. Miriam called me last evening after they arrived. I would imagine they'll be there for a day or two, Tom. A friend never knows more than a husband, old boy." A pause. "Anything else, Tom?"

Tom considered the last bit of information he was holding and whether to pass it along. Of course, from the spiking of the last topic, Tom easily recognized the familiar cat and mouse game The Senator loved to play when the man already knew, although he was fairly certain Allard didn't know what he was about to tell him.

"Dace left behind a letter with Mary Rose," Tom said. "The girl had been so excited about Friday because that's the day Dace had told her to give it to their mother."

"I know, Tom. Miriam told me. Do you have any idea what the letter said?"

"No," Tom lied. "Not a clue."

There was a pause on the line and Tom momentarily wondered what else Libby had told Miriam which may have flowed directly to her father.

It was the first time Tom had directly lied to the man in thirty years of their association. Not that Tom had always shared one-hundred-percent of every truth with the man, but most of those secrets lay buried two decades ago.

"Okay, Tom. Good night."

The connection was broken.

Richard left his mother-in-law at the kitchen table, nursing a second cup of tea. He quietly slipped into bed alongside of Miriam; the last thing he needed right then was to awaken a woman with the skill of his wife at ferreting out information from him. As he was closing his eyes, Miriam stirred.

Ronnie sneaked into the room just before daybreak. Oz had been a disappointing bust because the bouncer had refused to let a pair of straight girls into the already overflowing gay nightclub. So, they had wandered back along Bourbon Street on the straight side of the velvet line, settling in at one of the bars which had a live Blues band. It didn't take long before they were each approached with invitations for some dancing, which they accepted. It wasn't long after that when they had each been propositioned. Ashley had walked off the dance floor in disgust. Ronnie had taken a different path, and had just twenty minutes earlier left two worn out college boys from LSU sleeping in their room at the Quality Inn on St. Charles Avenue near the Garden District. Fortunately for her, the street cars were running on a twenty-four hour schedule during Carnival, because getting a cab was an hours-long wait, even in the wee hours. She had caught a trolly in the median across from the boys' hotel and it had dropped her a couple blocks from the Fairmont on Canal Street.

Ashley lay sleeping when Ronnie came in, but rolled over when the doorknob accidentally slipped from Ronnie's hand and the big door closed louder than Ronnie had planned. Ashley propped herself on one elbow and glared at Ronnie who stood sheepishly just inside the door. Ronnie braced herself for what was to come. Instead, Ashley looked at the clock on the nightstand between the beds, rolled over and went back to sleep. For Ronnie, at that moment, being ignored by her best friend was worse than being chastised. She crawled under the covers and quietly cried herself to sleep.

Even with his interrupted sleep, The Senator felt fully rested when he arose before sunrise. He showered, shaved, and dressed for the day. A chauffeured car stood waiting for him in the drive as he exited the McClean house. In the back seat waiting was one of his more junior staffers, a cute young blonde a year older than his son, with a cup of coffee and bagel with cream cheese for him.

He was up and out early on a Sunday morning because his staff had arranged for his appearance on three news shows to speak about his titular role as the chairman of the party's Senate Election Committee, even though some junior senator from Wyoming was shouldering all the day-to-day responsibilities for the upcoming mid-term elections. The Senator was scheduled to do ABC's *This Week* and NBC's *Meet The Press* as remotes from his expansive office in the Russell Senate Office Building, and for the third he would be on the set of *Fox News Sunday* in their studios several blocks away on North Capitol Street. If everything went as planned on the first two, he would have enough time to walk the few blocks between Russell and the Fox News D.C Headquarters through Lower Senate Park. The Senator smiled at the thought of his day, all of it, then devoured the bagel, keeping the hosed knees of the young staffer in his peripheral vision.

The car moved easily in early Sunday morning traffic and twenty minutes later, The Senator and his aide were dropped at the gleaming white marble facade of the main entrance to the Russell Building on the corner of Constitution and Delaware.

The Russell Senate Office Building was the oldest and closest to the Capitol of the three current buildings where United States Senators had offices. It also contained several large meeting rooms, as well as other public and private areas. Opened in 1909, it had been originally known simply as the Senate Office Building and was often abbreviated as the S.O.B. For decades, letters would arrive for Senators with the simple addressing which included their name over the initials S.O.B and Washington, D.C.

When Congressman Allard Lamoureux had first taken the oath of office as a United States Senator in January of 1957, it was before the building he now surveyed had been named for former Georgia Senator Richard B. Russell, and was the only building to at the time to house the offices of the members of the United States Senate. Work had begun on a newer building to house the growing staffs and operations the year before, but it would not open until 1958. Washington insiders and satirically-minded letter writers could then address their letters with sniggers to either the 'Old S.O.B.' or the 'New S.O.B.' Both acronym names were later replaced by Russell, Dirksen, and finally Hart after completion of the third senate office building in 1982.

Russell not only had the closest proximity to the Capitol, but to history itself. Every senator from 1909 to 1958 had had their offices there, including five who went on to become president: JFK, Truman, Johnson, Harding, and Nixon. The Senator paused at the base of the ostentatious white marble stairway which led into an even more ostentatious, three-story, Corinthian columned and coffer domed rotunda with twin marble staircases that led from there to the Caucus Room, site of the Titanic hearings in 1912, the Teapot Dome investigation in 1923, and the Watergate investigation in 1973. No matter how long he had been coming to his offices there, which was forty-one years and counting, standing on those steps always reminded him of the importance of his and the Lamoureux family's role in the history of the nation, and the world.

As he ascended the stairs, he turned his attention to the Capitol dome across the street which was just beginning to reflect the morning sunrise. He stood there and watched for several minutes as the immense white dome first glowed red, then orange, then brilliant white-yellow as the sun climbed above the horizon. That was another site he never tired of witnessing and The Senator smiled at the thought that someday his son Dace would also climb those stairs to *his* offices; and then, eventually, enter the most sought after office addresses in the District, down the road on nearby Pennsylvania Avenue. He allowed the visions to evaporate, for the time being, and followed his young traveling companion through the doors to begin preparing himself for the day's tasks at hand.

Cindy had missed a turn in Newark, so she had continued south on I-95 through Baltimore and shortly after sunrise had arrived in the northern suburbs of Washington, D.C. Although she could not know it as she traveled the BeltLine around the north side of the city to connect to highway 66 which would take her west to I-81 south, at that very moment The Senator was seated in front of an American flag in his office and had just begun his first taped interview of the day. While he was advancing his party's political agenda, Cindy was unwittingly running out the line and advancing The Senator's personal one.

# Chapter Twenty

Dave didn't go into Dace's room to check on him in the morning. He didn't really care if his best friend was there, gone, had ripped off some more locals, or was merely still sleeping. He had reached a crossroads in his friendship with Dace Lamoureux, something Dave could never have envisioned since they had sealed a pact to be eternal blood brothers on the banks of the Thames River when they were eight years old. Dave did take notice Dace's door was closed, however, that was as far as his interest went that morning as he descended the stairs and walked down the hall toward the kitchen.

When he reached the end of the hallway, he heard a soft knock on the back door. Dave twisted the deadbolt and opened the inner door to find Auntie D standing there with a basket covered by a red and white checkered dish towel.

"Mornin' boy," she said as he held the screen door open for her entry. "I done brung y'all some fresh-baked pecan rolls for breakfast. I figured you'd be up by now." She moved into the kitchen, set the basket onto the small table and looked around. "Where's that other one?"

"Dace?" Dave asked, buying a moment. "I haven't seen him yet this morning."

She made a derisive snort, then pulled back the dish towel to reveal the half dozen oversized, plump, glazed and nutted dough rolls. The aroma of fresh baked, cinnamon tinged bread quickly filled the kitchen. Dave touched one, they were still warm. Auntie D pulled out a chair for herself. Dave gathered a couple of plates and the container of orange juice. He grabbed two glasses from the cupboard. He took a seat at the table, removed one of the rolls and took a huge bite. As he chewed and savored the sweet warmth with just the right dose of nutty crunch, he poured himself a glass of orange juice and offered some to Auntie D who said she'd just have water. Dave stood, still chewing, and ran some bottled water into her glass.

"You're spoiling us, Auntie D," Dave said before taking a second bite. "I'm not going to ever want to leave here."

She eyed him as she drank several sips from her glass.

"Really, boy?" she said. "You ain't ready to end this yet?"

It was now Dave's turn to eye her. He watched her face morph from curious to accusatory. She pointed a bony finger in the direction of Dace's room.

"That boy ain't gonna stop until he be in it so deep even you can't be gettin' him out," she said. "You ready for that, boy? You owe that one ever'thin' you gots?"

Dave set down the last of his roll onto his plate, licked his fingers, which made Auntie D grin.

"I've been meaning to ask you about this since yesterday," he began. "How do you see these things? How do you know what's going on?"

She sat back in her chair, sipped more water.

"Boy, you don't get to be old as me wit'out learnin' some things 'bout how folks is. I done seen mean ones, cheaters, liars, murderers, and I done seen me a passel o' good ones, too. Some of 'em I done seen it in 'em when they was still in their cradle. My husband was a good one. And Uncle Jack. And you, boy. But that other one is just plain wrong. They is somethin' missin' in him."

Dave watched her eyes go distant.

"When I was a girl, seven or eight, there was a boy come here one summer. White boy from Mobile, fourteen or fifteen that year. His mama was the sister of the man who owned this place then. He was a bad man, and would cheat my daddy on the 'countin'. Mama wanted Daddy to speak up, but daddy never did. This be his home, he say, no matter who live in the big house. 'Where we gonna go, woman?' he would say to her. Some thin's daddy knowed better'n mama; not ever'thin', but some thin's." Auntie D's eyes misted, then quickly dried. "But that don't make no matter now."

She picked a corner of pecan roll and placed it into her mouth.

"This boy, this kin from Mobile, I can see the bad in his eyes when he look at me and I tells my mama 'bout it. See, they was somethin' missin' in him too. Mama done tol' me to jus' stay away from him, that he be gone soon, but one day he find me out gatherin' wild strawberries for a surprise treat after dinner. He ride up on a pony they done had, and me in the brush with no place to go. He sit on that pony, watchin' me, smilin' that evil smile o' his. Then he say, 'Hey, girl, whatcha doin'?' and I tells him I is just gatherin' some wild strawberries. He slides off that pony and say for me to come over by him. I shake my head, cuz his eyes done gone dark. He say, 'I gots some sugar candies' and he show me a paper bag, white paper, what come from a fancy store, and for me to come and see.

"He show me inside that bag, and they was sugar candies in it. He left that pony go, and he come closer. All I seen then was them sugar candies. I ain't never had nothin' but cane to chew on, and mama done made pralines for Christmas, but I ain't never in my life had no store bought sugar candies; and that bag be so close and he say, 'Go on girl, take one' and when I put my hand in that bag, he done grab me. I try and pull my hand out of that bag, but he have a strong hol' a my hand. I try and call out, but he put his other hand 'cross my mouth."

She looked Dave in the eyes and he could see the pain still there some eight decades later. She took a deep breath to chase away the demons, then continued.

"I done all the fightin' I could, boy. I swear it. I done all I could, but that boy were so strong, and he done had his way with me out there in that wild strawberry brush, his way and more. A girl no bigger 'n seven or eight and he done it. That ain't right, boy, even if'n he be white and me jus' a colored girl. After it were over, he rode off, but first he throw that bag of sugar candies down at me like it was nothin' to him. Though they was ever'thin' to me, I leave them lay in that brush and make my way home and mama find me and she see right off what done happen. She say, 'Thank God I find you 'fore yo' daddy' and she done clean me and tol' me never tell him. And I never did."

"Why didn't you tell your father, or call the police?" Dave said.

Auntie D looked at him like he was crazy.

"Boy, this be Louisiana, now and then, and no matter what you do to black folk up north, this be the south. And we be talkin' back in 1919, boy. If'n I tol' my daddy, and he make trouble, they shoot him dead fo' sho' and run me and mama off, or worse. A black man don' go makin' no trouble in 1919 Louisiana, boy; not on 'count some white boy takin' 'vantage of no colored girl, least ways."

She patted Dave's clenched hand and gave him an appreciative look.

"Thank you fo' carin', boy," she said. "Long time ago, long time."

Dave sat and thought for a moment. Was she telling him that Dace had the same look? That he was capable of such evil? He knew the old black woman must have many more stories over nearly nine decades of living to make her point, but why did she choose that one? He watched her sip her water, then look out the window. What was he supposed to do? Save himself and let Dace hurt someone? Or worse? He had so much to think about. He was about to ask her advice when she pushed herself up from the table and put her frail hand on his shoulder. He looked at her, almost straight across because of her height. He wanted to say something, but couldn't find the words.

She spoke for him with an answer to his unspoken question.

"Mark my words, boy. That other one gonna come to a bad end; and them 'round him too." She patted his shoulder then glanced at his half-eaten pecan roll. "Ain't you hungry no mo', boy?"

Dave shook his head. He had lost his appetite.

Tom waited until seven in the morning to call Susan Delp's cell phone. She answered on the first ring. He told her the minimum he needed to explain in order to extract a recommendation from her. Susan knew Tom McDaniel, so it wasn't much that he needed to say. She told him what he already knew from his internet research: there were more than enough private investigators in Louisiana to select from, most in Baton Rouge and New Orleans and Lafayette. When he asked her for a single name, she fell back onto one for whom she had just received back the contract for the August Project. To Susan Delp, that lateness in replying meant two things: the person had given the operation some consideration beyond pecuniary advantage which meant he most likely had ethical standards; and they weren't starving for business which meant they were good. She had also just spoken to the man two or three days before about this very contingency and he had seemed cautiously receptive, which meant he was thoughtful and professional.

"William Langdon," she said without equivocation. "Ex-Chicago cop, runs a sole investigator office with his wife, Sandy, an attorney."

Tom silently balked at both the ex-cop and the attorney qualifications, but he trusted Susan's judgement. She wouldn't steer him wrong. She was not only a very competent Party executive, but she was one of the true believers, which meant she would keep her mouth shut. Additionally, she knew, or should have known, whom Tom was representing here, and that carried more than just weight in the Party. So he asked her for the contact particulars and that she fax him the entire file on this William Langdon, including anything she may have on the attorney wife. She took down The Senator's home fax number and said he'd have it all shortly.

Tom read the pages as they came off the fax machine five minutes later. He smiled as he noted the particulars of William Langdon's meteoric rise and shooting star fall in the Chicago P.D. Sandy Langdon had walked away from a promising practice in criminal defense work to marry William. It was a second marriage for both. The only children were from William's first marriage which had ended a couple of years before he left the department and moved to Grand Cayman.

He judged from what was publicly known about William Langdon's career that this was a man who may have a very strong sense of right and wrong and not be afraid to act upon it. On the other hand, he had demonstrated an ability to keep a secret. According to the research they had done on him, he had never divulged the full details of what had happened the night his partner had been killed in that warehouse shooting. One of his former bosses who was very supportive of the man, was quoted as saying: 'Detective Langdon told me personally that what happened after Detective Mendez went down was a blur, then he winked at me and added it was a blur he would take to his grave.' Tom saw him as that perfect combination of lone wolf and team player, something akin to how he viewed himself.

Tom set the rest of the papers aside and called the cell phone number for William Langdon. He checked his watch as he listened to the rings come through the line. Then he remembered that New Orleans was an hour behind him and was about to hang up when a sleepy voice answered.

"This had better be important," came the greeting.

"Mr. Langdon?" Tom said.

"Yes. Who is this?"

"I'm sorry to disturb you so early on a Sunday morning, but I'm calling from Connecticut and I forgot you were an hour behind us."

"That still doesn't answer my question."

The typical cop response. Tom smiled for nobody and introduced himself across the telephone line and explained that he had obtained Mr. Langdon's contact information from Susan Delp at Party headquarters. There was no acknowledgement, so Tom told William he had something of a rather delicate personal matter with which he needed help.

"What type of rather delicate personal matter, Mr. McDaniel?" William said while strains in his voice indicated to Tom he had gotten out of bed and was walking somewhere.

Tom explained with a bit more specificity than he had needed with Susan Delp, but did not mention the Lamoureux name. He also told William that he anticipated the job to involve some surveillance in the New Orleans area, and location of a missing family member, all requiring the utmost in discretion.

"Is this person in danger, as is someone chasing them, or did someone make off with them; or are they missing of their own volition?" William asked, now obviously making notes.

"No danger, Mr. Langdon," Tom said, purposely being vague. "I'd say more the second situation."

"A minor?"

"No, twenty-one year old male college student," Tom said.

"That person is an adult in every state, Mr. McDaniel," William stated. "Last I heard, an adult who's not a danger to themselves or others can go wherever they want, whenever they want in this country." William paused. "Is this person a danger to himself or others?

Tom thought of the Birmingham incident that they knew of and wondered what else had been going on since they lost track of them several days ago, but decided that was information not needed by the man to perform this particular job.

"No, Mr. Langdon, neither."

"You said the person is in the New Orleans area? Can you be more specific? I know this is fly-over country to you East Coast types, but you realize it's a fairly large geographic area you're referring to."

Tom laughed and then explained that he was born and raised in Michigan, which was also considered part of fly-over country to these so-called East Coast types he worked for. He knew from William's dossier that he had come out of small-town Wisconsin and had thrown his mother state out there to plow some common Midwesterner ground.

"We anticipate narrowing that area down for you a bit within twenty-four hours, Mr. Langdon."

"Just how are you going to do that?"

Tom saw no reason to lie to the man about that particular, so he told him about the GPS locator on the car heading in his direction.

"So why not just come down yourself when the car arrives and bring the boy home? What do you need me for?"

"Mr. Langdon, I realize I'm being a bit vague, but I represent an important client, and I am attempting to maintain some level of confidentiality at that person's request. At this point, my client merely wishes for you to confirm the location of the boy and keep an eye on him for a short time until he can do just that. You will not be required to make any type of contact with the boy, just keep him in sight until my client's people can come for him. My client is concerned for the well-being of his son, and, I am certain you know how it was to be a young man stretching your wings for the first time, and my client also wishes to not intervene in the boy's, um, explorations, unless it's absolutely necessary."

"The young man is a bit fragile, is he? Daddy doesn't wish to upset the boy's tender psyche?" William said, making no attempt to veil the sarcasm.

Tom silently appreciated the man's forthrightness and ability to cut to the core, but he wasn't certain this was going to be a match made in heaven.

"Okay, let's say it's like that, Mr. Langdon," Tom said, not wishing to be goaded, and already wondering who Susan Delp's second choice would be. "Of course, we'll be relying on your complete discretion, now and in the future."

There was a pause on the line and Tom looked at his phone's display to confirm the connection still existed. It did. So, he waited.

"All right, Mr. McDaniel, I'll take the case and snoop on your client's sensitive, prodigal son," William said. "My wife is the administrative half of this operation, however, so give me a fax number where she can send over the contract when she gets up. When you sign and return it, and wire the required retainer to our bank in the morning, we'll open a file and consider we have an established a confidential agency relationship."

Tom relayed The Senator's home fax number, then regretted it when he realized all William had to do to learn his client's identity was do a reverse phone look up. He considered saying something, but didn't want to insult the man's integrity. He'd already implicitly given his word.

"Don't worry about me digging deeply as to the identity of your client, Mr. McDaniel," William said as if reading Tom's mind. "So long as there is nothing blatantly illegal going on here, there will be no reason for me to need to go beyond you. I'm assuming the father may be as fragile as is the son."

Tom smiled without comment at the proffered discretion and frankly had some concurrence with the quip, then merely confirmed that he'd be in touch when they had the location pinpointed.

I disconnected, then used the toilet and went back to bed. I spooned Sandy who asked who had been on the phone, and I told her we'd talk about it a little later, nuzzled her ear, and she snuggled closer. She was back asleep in minutes. It took me a bit longer.

By late morning, Cindy had reached the outskirts of Roanoke, Virginia and the anger which had driven her through the night was slowly losing the battle to her need for sleep. She didn't want to check into a motel, so instead she found a wayside, pulled in, and found a parking spot which was remote, yet safe. She locked the doors, slid the seat all the way back, cracked both windows, then laid the back of the seat down. She left her sunglasses on. In her lap, she held a tire iron. She was asleep in minutes.

Dave slid his chair back and rose to walk out with Auntie D. Her pecan rolls, like everything else she had been making for them, were the best he had ever tasted, and he told her so as he held the screen door for her. She seemed pleased with the compliment and returned a closed-mouth grin, touched him on the arm and thanked him. She said she hoped he'd get his appetite back in a bit, and to forget about the story she told him, but remember its moral.

"It be eighty years, boy," she said as they paused on the porch. "That boy be long dead. I done hear he shot hisself. Jesus teached us to forgive, and I done that long ago." She grinned at him and her eyes twinkled as she leaned closer to speak quietly. "Asides, the devil been pokin' at his backside for a long time now for what he done in life."

Dave smiled at the thought and hoped it was true; of course, he also believed in forgiveness, but only if one truly repented for their sins. It was beyond his mortal's brain and heart to know what eventually happened to the boy rapist in the afterlife, but Dave trusted God's judgement was always correct.   He walked onto the rear veranda with her.

Auntie D pointed at the Escalade parked on the grass.

"You know, boy, Uncle Jack'd skin you if he seen that.  Was you boys a little drunk last night and lose the drive up front?"

Dave shook his head slowly as he looked at his SUV and pondered the events of last night.  For days, he had been cut off from everyone but Dace, save the couple of short conversations with Cindy days ago, and the walking the tightrope call to his parents last night which grounded him, but he really needed to vent, or share, or both.  He liked Auntie D, he trusted her, he knew she'd never talk to anyone about anything he told her, especially anyone who could hurt Dace's reputation.  He made an executive decision.

He told her the entire story, beginning with Dace's birthday party a week ago and ending with the return to the house last night.  Once he began talking it was like the floodgates had opened, releasing his emotions in finally sharing with another human being the reasons for his growing concern for, and his growing disappointment in, his best friend in the world.  He blushed a bit when he mentioned Dace's encounter with Colleen, but Auntie D took it all in stride.  Somewhere during his monologue, they each took seats in the wicker rockers where he and Dace had sat and drank beer the other night.  He told the details of the story, but he also shared his innermost thoughts and fears.  He had never before felt so comfortable in sharing himself with another person and told her so, adding an exception for how he *used* to feel when talking to Dace.  He was suddenly sad when he uttered those last words, knowing his relationship with Dace truly had forever changed.

Dave wasn't exactly certain how long he had been talking, but Auntie D had listened intently and without interruption.  Nobody had ever done that for him before, not even his parents, who always would insert their questions and advice long before he was ever able to tell an entire story or completely detail a problem to them.  Auntie D just sat there, slowly rocking, her gnarled hands clasped in her lap.  On the few occasions he braved making eye contact, he found her eyes distantly focused, giving him the feeling she was fully there with his words, not just as a listener, but as what he truly needed: a companion on the lonely, barren road he currently found himself upon.

When he finished, he felt as if a thousand ton burden had been lifted from his shoulders.  He didn't let the essence of it go, he couldn't do that and still be a friend to Dace, or true to himself, but he did allow the weight of it to drift away.  They sat without talking for several minutes; comfortable silence embracing comfortable moments.  When she finally did speak, it wasn't to chastise him, or salve him, or absolve him. Her words were merely a gentle reminder of her earlier assessments of himself and of Dace, not merely a pointless repetition of them. Then she slowly pushed herself up from the rocker, everything between them having been shared, which from her perspective left nothing more to be said in that moment.

Auntie D shuffled to the stairs and took each step one at a time. She walked across the lawn. Dave watched her go, suddenly feeling physically exhausted, a condition which matched his spiritual state until a few moments ago. Eventually, he pushed himself up from the rocker, walked inside and found Dace sitting at the kitchen table, ravenously eating pecan rolls. When Dace's eyes met his, Dave felt them pass like projectiles right through him, the poison contained in the darts nearly seizing his heart.

"Feeling better now, buddy?" Dace said sliding his chair from the table, then picking up the remains of the roll from Dave's abandoned plate. "You're probably not going to eat this, right? Lost your appetite with the boohoo stories, right? I'll take it from here, old friend."

Dave found no words within him and slowly moved aside as Dace stepped into the hallway. Dace made no more comment and didn't look at his lifelong friend as he turned his back and walked toward the front of the house. Dave's eyes followed him as he walked straight out the front door.

The Senator stepped from the building which housed the Fox News Washington Bureau near the six-corner intersection of North Capitol, Louisiana, and D streets. He paused under the canvas awning as the young staffer with the great knees attached to even better legs caught up with him. It was a beautiful morning in D.C., and he smiled at the glory of it all and was glad he had decided to walk back the same way they had come an hour earlier, through Lower Senate Park. Together, they moved along North Capitol to the corner, then across Louisiana to the triangular pad in the center of the intersection, and then without regard for the traffic or lights, he set out across D Street and onto the broad, tree-lined walk of the park. A taxi screeched its brakes and its driver cursed. The staffer flinched and waved and mouthed an apology while The Senator merely kept walking, his eyes fixed on the Capitol dome across the park.

The reflecting pond off to their left was a smaller version of the more famous one near the Washington Monument and that time of year was only three-quarters full of dirty water and not doing much reflecting. The massive, ornate fountain had also been shut down for the winter, but its grand scale and ornate stone carvings rendered it still an impressive sight in the foreground. Other Washingtonians and visitors sat scattered along the benches on the outside of the pedestrian boulevard. The

Senator wondered how many of them recognized him, but he kept his visage thoughtful, yet neutral, his eyes he held forward and high; in his mind's eye, he projected the image of an unapproachable deity of political power. His pace was leisurely, yet purposeful.

Past the fountain, he bore left, taking the walk on the other side of the grassed boulevard beyond, then angling off under the trees on a spur which led directly to a marked crosswalk at Delaware and then up the steps of the Russell Building. When they entered the rotunda, his cell phone vibrated. He had silenced the ringer for his television appearances. He reached into his suit jacket's breast pocket and removed the phone and checked the caller ID before answering.

"Yeah, Tom," he said. "Did you catch any of the shows?"

"Yes, I did, Senator," Tom said, performing his least favorite aspect of his job: reinforcing the already inflated ego of a client. "You were strong, inspired, in control, unflappable, even at Fox. The message, clear and concise."

"Thank you, Tom," The Senator said, already knowing. "That's what I pay you for." He watched his young staffer casually pacing and nearly forgot about Tom for a moment as he enjoyed the view and contemplated asking her out for lunch, and perhaps plying her with a few drinks, then a ride back to McClean...

"I've hired a P.I. in New Orleans. The girl is still headed that way, but has stopped at a highway rest area near Roanoke for the last hour. Probably catching some sleep. She drove through the night."

"This P.I., he's trustworthy?"

The staffer stood with her back to The Senator across the rotunda, her feet apart. Aside for the Capitol police at the security scanner who were trained to see nothing beyond their job, they were alone in the area. The Senator's lips formed a shallow smile as he now knew there would be no *perhaps* about his afternoon. He fought to remember if he had any Viagra left in his office; no sense getting to McClean only to need to wait an hour.

"I would say he can be trusted. He's an ex-cop from Chicago, has an interesting history, but is used to taking orders. I can fax you the full background information we have in the file if you'd like to review it."

The last thing The Senator wanted to do that afternoon was to be stuck reviewing a file.

"No, that's okay, Tom. I trust your judgement. It's another reason why I pay you, right?"

He covered the phone and instructed Tiffany to send for the car. He'd suggest a lunch stop once they were on their way. Then he was suddenly struck by the thought of why parents would name their daughter Tiffany. Didn't they expect the girl to ever grow up, and when she did, not have a career outside of male entertainment? Tiffany was a name girls used; it wasn't the name for a serious career woman. Of course, he reminded himself, the girl he was discretely ogling across the way was just twenty-two. She could wait until her forties to be embarrassed by her name, and by that time he' be a distant, and hopefully wonderful, memory.

"Tom, just let me know when we have any development on that matter," The Senator said. "You know where to reach me this afternoon should something urgent come up."

"Let me guess," Tom said. "Tiffany?"

"You know me too well, Tom." He chuckled. "I'm not so certain that's a good thing."

He clicked off, then walked to his office to check his desk drawer for one of those little blue pills.


Early in the afternoon, I was driving Sandy to the airport. She had decided since I'd be doing some surveillance work for a couple of days, and perhaps nights, that she'd use the time to go visit her parents. She had prepared the contract, faxed it over with instructions for the wire transfer of the retainer, then called the airline and made reservations into Milwaukee. She'd rent a car there and drive the last sixty miles to her parents' place in Sheboygan. She checked the weather, but being born and raised in Wisconsin, she already knew mid-February would mean winter clothes and boots.

I had propped myself on the bed and watched her pack a couple days of clothes. Had we been going down to our place at Snipe Point on Little Cayman, she could have packed her flip-flops and a couple of bikinis in her purse, but since she was headed into the heart of winter, she needed a big suitcase for the bulky boots, sweaters and coats. New Orleans was headed for a comfortable seventy-two degrees that Sunday, so she had dressed comfortably for that and had packed the rest.

We took my Corvette, the trunk just barely adequate for her suitcase. I left the T-Tops at home so we could enjoy the fresh air. I looked across at my wife as we drove the more leisurely Airline Highway rather than jumping out to I-10. Her shoulder length, light brown hair was being tousled by the wind, her ankles were crossed, and though she normally displayed them bare, she had worn hose and a pair of brown suede boots which came halfway up her calves. She wore oversize sunglasses and I could see her baby blues from the side. Her face was glowing, no, all of her was glowing. I was going to miss her the next couple of days, but I understood her desire to spend some time with her folks. This time was about being focused on family, and that included mom and Mr. Beach.

I took the wide swoop off Airline Highway into the airport, found a parking spot in the multilevel garage, and we walked across to check her in. I wheeled her bag, held her hand with my other hand. United would take her to Chicago, then United Express would take her to Milwaukee. We checked her bag, then walked to security. I hugged and kissed my wife good-bye and wished her a safe and pleasant trip, reminding her to please drive carefully on those icy winter roads. She discreetly touched her hand to her barely-showing belly and promised me she'd take care of both of them for me. I put on my sunglasses because I had to, then watched her go through the screening, blow me a final kiss on the other side and disappear down the concourse.

The Palace Cafe on Canal Street was a New Orleans downtown landmark, even after only seven short years in existence, mainly because of the pedigrees of the owners and chef, and Ashley had made a reservation for brunch there a week ago. She and Ronnie walked out of the Fairmont, over to Canal and then three blocks toward the river before crossing the boulevard to the crowded restaurant. Street-side diners on the cobblestone walk under a green awning topped with gold letters, seated at tables shrouded in starched, white cotton cloths and fussed over waiters in black pants and immaculate white shirts and black bow ties enjoyed the clear, temperate day, and proved car exhaust and road noise could not keep people away from exquisite food. Ronnie opened the door and the pair was greeted by an outflow of aromas carried on the waves of live jazz music; the former an every day occurrence, the latter a Sunday brunch tradition.

Ashley followed her in, then announced themselves to the hostess at the podium. Her name was located on the list, then a waiter led them through the crowded room. Their heels clicked upon the black, white, and gold mosaic tile floor set to give the appearance of larger tile laid on a bias with an ornate border around the room, and they were seated across from each other in a booth with black padded seats, a green marble tabletop and plenty of tension between them. It was the first time they had looked at each other since Ronnie returned to the room early that morning. Perhaps it would be more accurate to say that Ronnie had tried to catch Ashley's eyes several times but without success. For her part, Ashley was avoiding Ronnie's gazes because she was still fighting herself over whether what she felt was concern for her friend's welfare or negative judgement when it was really none of her business, and didn't want to get caught swinging too far one way or the other.

They were left with large menus which Ashley quickly used to shield her face. A busboy promptly replaced the waiter and filled their glasses with ice water. Ronnie felt her heart breaking, and had no idea that Ashley was feeling the same. Regardless of their age on the phony driver's licenses, they were still just shy of seventeen, and had yet to develop all the necessary social skills to maneuver this delicate situation which had grown up between them, seemingly overnight.

Ronnie reached her feet across the booth, wrapped them around Ashley's legs. She held them there, resolved to do so until Ashley put down the menu and looked at her. When Ashley finally did lower the menu and look across the table, her eyes contained a blend of equal parts of sadness and disappointment. What Ashley saw peering back at her was a mixture of rebellion and regret, but mostly rebellion.

The jazz music in the background was restaurant volume, not bar volume, and even with the other conversations and clattering of cutlery on china, the restaurant provided a comfortable ambience. Finally, Ashley smiled across the table which disengaged Ronnie's foothold and wordlessly relayed the message that Ronnie needed to start things off or risk Ashley saying something which may fatally damage something they each cherished. Ronnie took a deep breath and opened her mouth to speak.

"Welcome to the Palace Cafe, I'm Yolanda, I'll be your waitress today. Have you dined with us before?"

The girls looked up and shook their heads in unison.

"Okay, we're serving the Brunch menu now, and I see you're looking at it. Everything is delicious, in case you're going to ask. May I bring you girls something to drink along with the water? Iced tea? Soda?"

Ashley pointed to an item near the bottom of the Brunch menu.

"Two of these, please," she said.

Yolanda struck a pose with her body back and one foot pointed forward, her hands on her hips. Before she could verbalize the question, both girls had produced their IDs which she scrutinized, then forced a smile, nodded, and toddled off.

"Peter's Planters Punch?" Ronnie said. "You sure?"

"Why not?" Ashley said. "It fixed her clock, and that alone was worth the price of admission, don't ya think?"

"Iced tea, soda?" Ronnie mocked.

They settled back in their seats, their shoulders relaxed and they laughed. Oftentimes that's all it takes with friends; even though there remained in the room the proverbial elephant which they both understood would need to be addressed. Sometime.

The drinks arrived. Ronnie toasted 'to best friends forever'. Ashley accepted the toast and they each drank through straws.

"That's good," Ronnie said. "Really good. Fruity. Not too strong."

"Yeah, I could get to like these," Ashley added.

Yolanda returned for their food order, seemingly a little less miffed. Ronnie thought the woman must have remembered the matter of her ultimate tip. Since they had each slept through breakfast and hadn't eaten anything since dinner the night before, Ashley ordered a shrimp remoulade appetizer that they'd split, a spinach salad, and lyonnaise Gulf fish. Ronnie ordered the Cafe Cobb Salad with Gulf shrimp. Yolanda smiled, congratulated them on making wonderful selections, then toddled off again.

"So, we gonna clear the air and move on?" Ashley said.

Over their meal, and a shared dessert of Bananas Foster which was a dish the Brennan family made famous at their namesake restaurant just a few blocks away, the girls each had their turn to talk. Ronnie maintained her decisions and any consequences were hers alone. Ashley agreed. Ashley maintained she only worried about Ronnie's health and well-being, physically and spiritually. Ronnie thanked her for that.

"I still think it's wrong," Ashley said. "It's your life, though, Ronnie."

"I see nothing wrong with having a little fun, but I appreciate your concern, Ash," Ronnie said.

Ashley picked up her third Peter's Planters Punch and drained the last of the ice-diluted liquid through the straw. She didn't know what else to say, so the action served to punctuate the discussion. She loudly drew in the final drops, including a lot of air, then belched, which caused them both to erupt in childish laughter that lasted several seconds and further banished any lingering tension.

"Hey, Ronnie, wanna have your palm read?" Ashley said setting down the glass as her eyes turned playful. "Of course, that might not be as much fun as you say sex is, but it could still be something neat to do this afternoon."

"You bet, maybe we can get a drawing made of us, too?" Ronnie said. "And sex is fun, by the way. Lots of fun." She stuck out her tongue.

"Yeah, yeah, let's hit Jackson Square," Ashley said pulling a hundred dollar bill from her wallet and leaving it on the table.

They slid out of the booth and left the restaurant. On Canal Street, in the sunshine, they turned left and walked toward the river. On the corner with Chartres Street, they made another left and did some window shopping at the antique and jewelry stores on their way to the palm readers, fortune tellers, and artists ringing Jackson Square.

Dace walked along the Great River Road. He passed Oak Alley and continued on toward Vacherie. He felt betrayed by Dave. He was angry and hurt and standing precariously on the edge of self-pity. Didn't Dave understand what he was going through? Didn't his lifelong friend comprehend what pressures were being heaped upon his shoulders? Didn't *anyone* care what he was feeling? His thoughts momentarily touched upon Sarah, and his anger skyrocketed. Even she abandoned me, he thought, then kicked a flattened beer can lying on the edge of the road. It skittered across the asphalt, then flipped into the air right in front of an oncoming car, striking the front bumper and ricocheting into the grass. The driver honked and hollered something out his window which Dace couldn't understand but he flipped the guy the bird anyway.

The driver slammed on the brakes, coming to a quick, screeching halt in the traffic lane. Dace looked over his shoulder, reached into his pocket. He watched an argument going on in the front seat of the car between the two adults. In the rear seat sat two kids in their early teens: one boy, one girl. They turned to look at him out the back window, their eyes wide, their mouths agape. The driver's door opened and one foot touched the pavement. Dace turned and faced the car. There was no other traffic along the road. The man stepped out. The woman in the front seat grabbed for him. Dace removed the buck knife from his pocket. He unfolded the blade, held it at the ready. It flashed in the sunlight.

"Come on, asshole," Dace challenged. "If you got the guts. I've been waiting days for the likes of you to cross my path, tough guy."

The driver shuffled his feet, looked into the car's back seat. The kids had joined the wife in pleading for him to get back inside. Dace laughed out loud, folded the knife and turned and walked down the road. He didn't look over his shoulder when he heard the car door slam and the wheels chirp as the car sped away.

The temperature was in the low seventies with relatively low humidity for southern Louisiana, but the sun was scorching. Dace wore jeans and a deep blue T-shirt. The black asphalt threatened to cook his feet through his running shoes so he moved over to walk in the grassy shoulder. Sweat rolled down his neck and trickled down his back. He wiped his face with a hand, tossed off the sweat. By the time he reached Vacherie, the sugar in Auntie D's pecan rolls and the sense of universal betrayal which had driven him along the road had all been used up, replaced by a voracious thirst and a seething anger.

At Church Street he spotted a small, single-story, concrete block building with a pitched, metal roof, much akin to Rupe's bar from the previous night. He shuffled across the gravel parking lot. Three old, wooden doors painted brown and containing no knobs or pulls on the outside and three windows, two containing air conditioners and the third displaying an unlighted beer sign dotted the west side. Two, small, high windows bearing beer signs and an old, decaying timber and plywood entry extended an unwelcoming invitation to people passing on the Great River Road. The place was definitely another locals only bar. The air conditioners were pumping away, dripping water onto concrete aprons. The parking lot was empty, although Dace had no doubt locals merely walked on down.

He pulled the door open and unlike Rupe's place with its overpowering fluorescent daytime lighting, the place without a name as of that moment, was darkened and cool. A few regulars had already staked out their spots at the bar. A handful of tables of chrome and plastic with mismatched vinyl-topped chairs sat unattended along the opposite wall. In the back, Dace could see a pair of well-worn pool tables under cheap brass and faux stained-glass light fixtures. The floor was painted concrete. Heads turned at the intrusion of light, eyes looked him over, then returned their attention to the basketball game on the television hung over the corner of the bar. Like Rupe's before, Dace assumed the joint started to jump later in the evening, but during the day, this was a boys only affair. The conditioned air was very cool, and a chill ran through him as the sweat leapt from him. The bar smelled like hard work and old beer, tinged with a hint of piss and urinal cakes. Dace smiled to himself as he tabulated the ambience.

The bartender, a twenty-something kid with his baseball cap turned backwards gave him as much initial attention as did the patrons, but when he obviously had decided to stay, the kid dropped a cardboard coaster on the old wood bar and asked in a heavy, slow drawl what he wanted. Dace ordered a tap beer and a shot of Jack - the Wild Turkey last night had been sour, oaky rotgut, in his opinion - and dropped a twenty on the bar. He downed the Jack, asked for another, and took a draw of the beer. The bartender returned eighteen dollars in change.

"Who's playing?" Dace said.

Cindy awoke out of a deep sleep with a start. She focused her eyes and checked her watch. It was two in the afternoon, although she had to fight to remember if Roanoke was on eastern or central time. She tossed the tire iron onto the floor on the passenger side, stretched from fingertips to toes. The rest area visitor's center was a short walk away, so she slid her feet into her boots, grabbed her purse, and exited the car. She closed and locked the door with the only key she had, stretched again and cracked her neck, then fell in behind a family making the same little walk.

The clock on the wall inside the visitor's building confirmed she was still on eastern time. She went into the bathroom, used the facilities, then washed her hands and face. She ran a brush through her hair, then brushed her teeth. The youngest girl from the family she had followed in stared at her from over the last sink in the row. Cindy smiled and the girl did the same and then ran out.

Back out in the center gallery, Cindy found a United States map in a display case, with a 'You Are Here' dot. A chart listed distances to various major cities. She still had over eight-hundred miles to go to New Orleans. Fourteen hours, if she drove straight through, she thought. Maybe less if traffic, and speed traps, allowed.

She returned to the old Mustang, and headed back onto the interstate. At the next exit, she bought some fast food, and resumed the trek.

Ashley and Ronnie fit themselves onto a single folding chair. The artist they selected had a prime spot on the St. Ann Street side of Jackson Square, across from the 1850 House. The afternoon sun filtered through full trees and dappled the cobblestones with light and shadow. An aroma of caramelized sugar drifted from a nearby praline shop. Wafting conversations blended with the clip-clops of horse-drawn carriages on nearby Decatur Street into a peaceful, slow-paced harmony which contrasted against the bustling cacophony of the previous night's Bourbon Street.

The girls had circled the square several times, watching and judging the artists before finally settling on the young man in goatee and top hat seated across from them. His hands worked quickly; his nails and fingers were stained with charcoal and chalk. He was commissioned to do two drawings for them: one a real life, the other a caricature. From his displayed works hung behind him along the wrought iron railings at the square's perimeter, he was a master at both styles.

They weren't certain which style he was doing first, but the admiring smiles of the curious passersby who paused for a moment to watch from behind him assured them he was doing a fine job. Ronnie alternated between smiling and making silly faces, hoping to draw Ashley from her continuing deep thoughts.

Earlier, they had stopped at a Tarot reader who had a card table set up near the entrance to St. Louis Cathedral. Ashley had selected a card reading for herself, while Ronnie wanted both the cards and a palm reading, as the woman also claimed to be a gifted soothsayer.

The woman asked if they wished an open or question reading, and explained the differences between the two. An open reading, she said, tells of one's life, upcoming changes, or issues such as health or career or marriage, but is not meant to foretell the future, rather to help as a guide in the decisions the person will make. A question reading addresses a single, specific decision, but rather than reveal an answer, also serves merely as a guide for reaching a conclusion.

Ashley realized that card and palm readings, and soothsaying, were occult arts, but she concluded there was always time for contrition and absolution on Ash Wednesday. She also thought they had as much truth to them as did the slips of paper inside fortune cookies. But it was fun.

The woman handed the Tarot deck to Ronnie and asked her to shuffle the cards while she concentrated on the areas of her life for which she sought guidance. She said while Ronnie handled the cards, her life's energy would be transferred to the deck, thus giving the power over to the cards, and the reader. The deck contained what were known as Minor and Major Arcana cards. The Minor Arcana being represented by four suits: wands, swords, cups, and circles or pentacles. Each suit had meaning regarding the specific approach to life, and addressed the practical, the daily ups and downs. The Major Arcana represented principles, ideals, and concepts, and spoke to strong, long-term energy, or big events.

Ronnie cut the deck, and the woman laid out the ten cards in what she called the 'Celtic Cross Spread', describing the meaning of each position as she went along.

"The first card covers you at this time," she said. 'The Seven of Cups, means your head is in the clouds."

"That sounds about right," Ashley said with a laugh.

The woman shot her a scornful look, then dealt the second card.

"The Queen of Swords is crossing you, advising you to let your mind rule your spirit."

The woman raised an eyebrow in Ashley's direction.

"Your foundation is the Five of Cups, meaning disenchantment and loss. There are times when you feel that you can have everything, but then disappointment happens. A relationship falls apart, you lose someone close to you."

Ronnie eyes went distant and she sat back in the rickety folding chair, hugged herself. Ashley thought she saw her friend shiver. She hoped Ronnie was listening, because some of this was applicable to the current situation. For an instant she gave the woman some credit. Just for an instant, though.

"The Eight of Cups in the fourth position means you are beginning to feel differently, you are coming to a change of heart. The bloom is off the rose, so to speak, and you are unable to get it back again. You'll never get it back.

"The Queen of Cups provides you with soft counsel; only a person close to you can truly understand your concerns, and this person shall provide you with suggestions which come from their heart and they will ring true in your soul.

"The Knight of Swords advises you to act quickly, leap before you look, and encourages you to accept the rash suggestions of a young man."

"Hmm," Ashley grunted, but only Ronnie heard.

"The Chariot is your Self card. This seventh card describes you at this very moment and advises it's time to take the reigns, to fly solo. Life is dynamic and needs to remain in motion; think of how you cannot balance on a bicycle when it's standing still.

"You live in an environment of Justice, your eighth card which advises you to consider all the possibilities in your life. Be flexible in your judgement, but once you have made a decision, you will be best served by standing behind your convictions.

"Your hopes and fears are represented by the King of Pentacles and tells you to enjoy your worldly success to come.

"The Moon in the tenth position portends a future which you alone must come to judge as either reality or illusion. Allow your dreams to wander each evening, but in the new dawn you must seek your true path. Avoid the beguiling beacon, for it is merely reflected light."

The woman had made the mistake of asking if Ronnie had any questions, and finally had to cut her off when Ronnie kept going on and on. Ashley viewed her reading as pure hokum, then decided she'd have to neither be contrite about, nor confess what she viewed as an exercise in arbitrariness rather than a dabbling in the occult. Ronnie, on the other hand, had become so wrapped up in the Tarot reading she had forgotten about the palm reading. Ashley paid the woman, and as they started to walk away, the woman touched Ashley's sleeve.

"I know you don't believe, but be careful, my dear, I see danger stalking your aura," she said, then she had released her.

The artist finished the first drawing and a group of older women who had been watching for several minutes complimented his work. He placed it aside without showing it to the girls and began the second piece. His dusty hands worked even faster on that one than they had the first.

The Senator washed his hands and face. He took his time with the towel. In the multiple reflections of the master bathroom mirrors, he watched Tiffany collecting her clothes. She stepped both feet into her panties - if such small bits of cloth could be called panties - and pulled them up over her perfect hips and gorgeous ass. She then sat at on the edge of the bed and pulled on her thigh-high stockings. She had worn no bra, even though her firm, ample breasts could have used one for longevity's sake. Finally, she stepped into her dress, pulled it up around her body, buttoned it and fixed the belt. She found her handbag on the dresser, picked up her heels and padded out into the hallway and down the stairs. The Senator emerged from the bathroom when he heard the closing of the front door.

The bedside clock read 5:38 p.m.

He picked up his cell phone and tapped the key to speed dial Libby's cell. He assumed she and Mary Rose were still at Miriam's since he hadn't heard any different. There phone connected to voicemail.

"Good afternoon, Libby. I just concluded a meeting in case you were looking for me earlier. No more word from Tom regarding Dace, but there's something brewing and I believe this will all be over and we'll be back to normal very soon." He paused, annoyed that *he* had to deal with the discourtesy of voicemail. "The day's appearances wore me out and I'll be turning in early tonight, so no need to call back. Another big day

tomorrow, you know.    I hope you caught some of today's shows."
Another pause. "Oh, I love you."

He closed the phone, disconnecting the call.

# Chapter Twenty-one

The edge of night crept across Manhattan, and as Libby stood in the floor-to-ceiling window and watched the rare sight of the earth's shadow moving though the sky, she felt twilight enveloping her soul. She had carefully repacked the small wooden box, gathered up her album, collected Mary Rose and their luggage and thanked Miriam and Richard for their hospitality. Richard had gone to retrieve her car. She turned when she heard him return.

"Which way are you headed, mom?" Richard asked.

She smiled obliquely.

"Back to New London," she said as her eyes caught Mary Rose curled up on the couch. She reached out and touched Richard's hand. "There's not much sense in any of it, but there remains a foundation, and sometimes that's all one needs to get through to the finish. Thank you for listening, again, Richard."

"Are you certain you don't want to stay the night and start out tomorrow in the daylight?"

"No, Richard, the cover of darkness is more appropriate for this journey, don't you think?"

With Sandy gone, I had the chance to reclaim my man cave. Not that I don't cherish my time with my wife and would never want to go back to the bachelor's life, but there's something comforting to me about having some alone time. I grabbed a bag of Lay's potato chips from the cupboard, made myself a drink of Jim Beam bourbon over ice, and put my feet up in my favorite recliner. I flipped on the television and found the Milwaukee Bucks were playing the Lakers.

I sipped some bourbon, tore open the bag of chips. For me, this was a vacation. Sandy loves to go places. I'd rather just sit at home, relax, hibernate. Sometimes I make concessions, and sometimes she does. It works. If I had to guess, I'd say we're both truly happy and contented souls these days. Okay, so the 'Vette was a bit of a cliched midlife crisis, but if we can't treat ourselves to a toy now and again, what is there worthwhile to any stage of this existence?

The Lakers had an early lead in the game, and the old hometown team looked a little ragged on offense; and defense. I crunched a few chips and sipped more bourbon. It was warm going down, and while the Bucks continued to look ragged, I was less and less concerned about it. It's only a game, right?

When I was a kid and had my growth spurt to over six feet by the time I was thirteen, I had become obsessed with basketball and would shoot buckets for hours in the driveway and listen to the Bucks games broadcast on the radio. When they played west coast games against the Lakers or Warriors or Suns, I'd stay up late and listen to Eddie Doucette's announcing with a jack in my ear. Those were the days of Oscar 'The Big O' Robertson, and Lew Alcindor - before he became Kareem - and Jon 'Johnny Mac' McGlocklin, and Bobby Dandridge and Lucius Allen, the Sky Hook and the celebratory 'Bango' when they'd drain a long jumper. I could see every play in my imagination. Those were good times.

Apart from the way the Bucks were currently playing, so were these.

Dace caught a ride from one of his new buddies. They stopped outside the hedges, along the road, and he hopped, well, maybe hopped is a bit of an exaggeration, rather he tumbled out. In typical Dace Lamoureux fashion, he had won over the constituency, which that afternoon happened to be the patrons at the little locals bar, with his charm and some free drinks. They had shot pool, watched some basketball, ate some deep fried alligator, and drank the sun away.

Dace shuffled up the drive. The porch lights were on and he smirked to himself. The front door was unlocked. He pushed it open. The house was silent.

"Honey, I'm home," he called. "Don't pay the ransom."

Silence. Dace thought, had there been crickets, they'd have been the only ones to greet his triumphal return; but there were no crickets. He was hungry again. He wandered to the kitchen, hung his head inside the refrigerator. Nothing appealed to him so he crossed the hall and looked around the pantry.

He glanced out the window and saw the Escalade was still parked in back. It hadn't been moved since the previous night from what he could determine from where he stood. Across the lawn, he noted there was a light in the window of Auntie D's apartment over the workshop. He turned his attention back to his search for something to eat, but nothing in the pantry was really calling to him either. He climbed the stairs and poked his head into Dave's room. It was dark, and empty. He glanced across the hallway at Sam's room, wondered what she looked like. They had her number somewhere. He considered giving her a call, going out in New Orleans that night. Her handwriting was sexy enough. He laughed out loud as he thought how ridiculous that correlation sounded, even unuttered.

He trotted back downstairs and walked out onto the porch. He jumped down the steps, looked inside the Escalade to see if the keys were there, then tried the locked driver's door. He set off across the lawn; it was dark, but not so dark that he couldn't see the little anthill land mines in the grass as he went and he stepped carefully. At the workshop, he circled the building until he found a door. He knocked. A few moments later, Dave opened the door.

"Hey, buddy," Dace said. "You didn't pay the ransom, did you?"

"We thought about it," Dave said, stepping back to allow Dace into the stairwell which led up to Auntie D's apartment. "The problem we debated was which Dace Lamoureux we'd be getting back if we paid."

"I'm always the same old me, Dave. You should know that."

"Lately, I've begun to wonder."

Dace looked up the steps.

"You want to come up?" Dave said. "Auntie D might want to see that you're really alive and well."

"Nah," Dace said, wondering to himself if she'd more likely want to see him dead after what he'd overheard her telling Dave that morning. "I'm hungry. What do you say we head into New Orleans tonight? Get some oysters. A good meal. A few drinks, a few laughs. After all, it's Mardi Gras and all we've done is hang out in the country." His grin grew broad. "Not that it hasn't been fun, eh?"

"Fun? How about interesting as a more appropriate descriptive?"

"Okay, interesting then. See, I can compromise. What do you say?"

"I say you're gonna make a great politician," Dave said. He glanced up the stairs. "Listen, let me say good-bye to Auntie D, tell her we're heading into New Orleans. Sure you don't want to say hello at least?"

"I'm going to jump into the shower quick," Dace said opening the door and walking back into the evening. "You tell her I said 'hi'." He leaned in close to Dave. "You know, it's not easy for me not being the favorite."

Dave smirked at that. He thought about how he had been the one in Dace's shadows for thirteen years and suddenly wondered 'Why?' He closed the door and walked up the steps to say goodnight to Auntie D. She was seated in her rocking chair as she had been when the knock had come, and was now reading her Bible, an ancient set of half-rim spectacles perched on the tip of her nose. She looked up when she heard him return.

"That our boy?" she asked.

"Who else?"

Dave sat down across from her again. He leaned forward, set his elbows on his knees, hung his gaze on the floor, rubbed his hands together slowly as he thought and spoke.

"He's cooled off, but still has a razor's edge to him; things just seem to keep escalating and he's at least a little drunk. I'm starting to worry about him doing something worse before this is all over. I wonder if we should just pack up and go home. Getting away was his idea." Dave looked up at her. "Time to breathe, you know? Maybe he does have an alternate agenda, something darker, like you said."

She rocked, listened.

"Boy, you done been there for him near your entire life," she said. "Sometimes all you can do for somebody what is that set on destruction is to pick 'em up and brush 'em off when it's all over. You can't protect him if'n he don't wanna be, 'specially from his own self."

"You're right. You've been right all along. I just don't want you to be right in your final prediction for him. That just can't be."

He looked deep into her tired eyes. She returned no redemption for Dace, no easing of everything she said. Dave's heart sank and so did his gaze again.

"You go into Nawlins, boy. Have a good time. He gonna do what he gonna do. You a good friend. You a good man, Dave. I dunno, maybe you can save him after all."

He raised his gaze. It was the first time she had ever called him by his name. Until that moment he had been 'boy'. She had allowed him some degree of redemption, after all, perhaps even absolution. He felt less hopeless about the situation. Dave, the aspiring eternal optimist.


Ashley and Ronnie pushed their way through the throng gathered along Canal Street. They were all waiting the arrival of the Bacchus krewe's Sunday evening parade which began in the Garden District, wove its way down St. Charles Avenue, then showed itself for a couple of blocks on Canal before finishing at the Convention Center where their black-tie gala ball would be held. Finally, the girls staked out a couple of curbside spots and waited.

The music announced the approach before the first of the floats appeared.

Bacchus was one of the foundational krewes of the modern Carnival season, being founded in 1949 by Owen Brennan, the then owner of the Absinthe House bar on Bourbon Street and founder of the world-famous Brennan's Restaurant. His vision was to open up to the general public the previously closed and private Carnival balls and celebrations. Years later, in 1968, his son Owen, Jr. revitalized the krewe and decided to break tradition by staging their parade on Sunday night and bring to the cheering crowds of parade-goers the biggest, brightest, animated floats of any krewe. Its marching bands were large, loud, and full of heart-pounding, foot-stomping, hand-clapping energy. If you were in New Orleans during Carnival, the Bacchus parade was the one you didn't want to miss; and it was one of the events which the girls had long planned for.

The first float to appear was the King's float, that year carrying Drew Carey as Bacchus XXX and touting the parade's 'Where Y'at Dawlin'' theme. It was followed by nearly thirty others, including the longest float of Carnival: the one-hundred-five foot, three-segment Bacchagator, repainted just last year to resemble the rare, white, leucistic alligator which lived in the New Orleans' Aquarium of the Americas. That float alone sported nearly ninety riders tossing goodies.

When it was over, the crowd, including Ashley and Ronnie, flowed into The Quarter.

Tracey Walker, dressed in a red and white satin costume matching the float's Cupid theme, waved and tossed beads and treats from the top deck of the Baccha-Amore float near the end of the line. St. Charles Street was packed with cheering people of all ages and its buildings awash in lights and decorations in green, gold, and purple. Some spectators had waited all day for Bacchus to arrive. This was the beginning of her first parade from this perspective. She smiled from under her half-mask as she recalled William Langdon's smart-aleck remark about hoping she was going to wear a mask and wondered if he was in the crowd. She used to be fairly good at winging rocks as a kid.

I woke up in my chair in the den with a start as my cell phone vibrated then issued forth Sandy's distinctive ring tone. The game was over, and the station was replaying some old sitcom. I turned off the television and picked up the phone.

"Hey, baby," I said.

"Hi, sweetheart," she said.

"How was your flight?"

"First one was okay, but you know how much I hate those puddle jumpers. At least it was a little jet, not one of those turboprop nightmares. I finished *Unheeded Warning* on the flight to Chicago, and I don't think I'll get on one of those again, especially in the winter. Poor people on that flight that went down."

"You buys your ticket, you takes your chances," I said and then instantly regretted it. I remembered that flight on Halloween night in 1994. It had been a nasty day from all reports and had turned into a wicked night in Chicago. I was tending bar at my place on Grand Cayman and we had the Monday Night Football game on all the televisions; my team, the Green Bay Packers was playing the Bears at Soldier Field in Chicago.  The wind was blowing icy rain horizontally, and when they announced the news of the crash, I recall wondering just who would be crazy enough to be flying on a night like that.  "I'm sorry, Sandy," I said.

"It's just you being you, Will," she said.  "You're my eternal irreverent soul.  I know what's deeper, though, you know.  You can never fool me about how deep you run."

I decided to change the subject.  I get uncomfortable when anyone understands me, and if anyone does, it's Sandy.

"Were your parents surprised?"

"They were.  Daddy asked why you hadn't come along and I explained you had a big case to work on this week."

"Big case?" I laughed.  "Sounds more like a few days of sitting in my car trying to look inconspicuous while keeping watch on some kid whose parents think he's run away from home.  More like babysitting if you ask me.  I see nothing big case about it."

"You never know," she said.  "Remember the Massey case last year? Simple cheating wife situation turned nasty.  I know she was glad you were there when hubby showed up with a gun."

"Yeah, I suppose.  Of course, why the guy's divorce lawyer didn't tell him that I was keeping tabs on the soon-to-be-ex-missus I'll never know.  Of course, had I not been there, the guy would be waiting execution for capital murder up at Angola, instead of just doing five years for attempted.  He should be sending me fruitcakes at Christmas for what I did for him."

"Most people don't consider fruitcakes a gift you send friends, Will," Sandy said.

"Yeah, but I love fruitcakes," I said, teeing up the ball for myself.  "I even married one."

"Ha, ha."  A pause.  "So, see, there is no such thing as a routine surveillance case, Mr. Detective."

It was Sandy's way of making certain I stayed on my toes.  She was right.  You never knew how cases would unfold, and if you got careless, sometimes, even for us peeping in the windows types, you could get dead.

"I doubt junior is going to go out whacking anyone, but I hear you mother."

She paused.

"I've never been called that before," she said with a bit of emotion in her voice.  "I know you were just being silly, Will, but I'm finding the littlest things can hit me sometimes lately.  Can you understand that?"

I paused.

"Yeah, I can," I said with a bit of emotion in my voice.  "How are you feeling?"

"I'm good," she laughed. "You don't have to keep asking me that, you know. I'm certain there will be times down the road when I won't feel so hot, and there may also come a time during labor when I tell you how much I hate you for what you have done to me, but now, I'm fantastic." A beat. "I love you, you know."

"I love you too, Sandy."

"There's not much snow on the ground up here," she said.

"From what I heard, the east coast had taken the brunt of the last storm, Massachusetts to Maine got buried."

"Yeah, but daddy said they'd not had much snow all year. Not as cold as usual either."

"Global warming," I said, not believing it. "I hear that's the new catchall for any unusual weather. Al Gore is all over it, the new Chicken Little with his own 'the sky is falling' mantra."

"Be nice," she said.

"Ah, it's just you and me here," I said.

"Okay, Will, I just wanted to check in, say goodnight and tell you how much I love you and miss you already. Mom's calling me, they want to play cards; three-handed Cribbage, penny a point, double on the skunk."

"Go get 'em, Diamond Jane," I said. "Goodnight, Sandy."

"Goodnight, Will."

I was just about to click off when I heard her saying something more.

"No sleeping in your chair all night, either. Go up to bed. You can watch television as loud as you want up there since I'm not home."

"Yes, mother," I said, and closed my phone.

Parking in The Quarter was a nightmare. The public lots were overflowing, the streets were packed. People were everywhere, even on the poorly lit side streets which most folks tended to avoid after dark. Dave was about to give up and head further out when a group of four guys staggered up Toulouse Street, toppled into a Chevy Blazer and took off like a bat out of hell, leaving the perfect spot for the Escalade.

He and Dace walked down Toulouse a minute later, the old cobblestone sidewalk uneven underfoot. The gutter was awash in used plastic cups, beer and God-knows-what. The sounds of revelry drifted from Bourbon Street several blocks away. The odors of the season were a pungent medley. They could already see the main party thoroughfare was plugged with people, so having discussed their first stop on the drive in, they made a right on Dauphine Street and four blocks later took a left on Iberville Street and approached the Acme Oyster House on a less crowded route.

There were two brightly lit areas of the Acme Oyster House in which one could savor some of New Orleans' fare, including Acme's namesake

Gulf oysters: the sit down dining room, and the high, standup, granite-topped bar with the brass foot rail with room for about thirty patrons and half a dozen shuckers on the other side. It was not a fancy place, but it has long been a city landmark, and because of its location, often the starting spot for generations of visitors to The Quarter in search of fresh, ice-cold bivalves on the half-shell. The place was packed, but Dace and Dave shouldered themselves into a few feet of bar space.

When the shucker looked at them, they ordered 'two dozen on the bar' and a couple of Corona's with lime. The drinks arrived from a roaming bartender, and the oysters began arriving slid right across the granite on the half-shell.

"Fixins is at the end," the shucker said, never stopping his well-practiced motion and pointing a white-handled, bill-shaped knife toward the end of the bar.

Dace slithered his way through the crowd and mixed up some ketchup and horseradish in a couple of small paper cups, grabbed a handful of two-to-a-pack saltines and several wedges of lemon, then wove his way back to Dave who had done an excellent job of maintaining their space. Dace dropped the crackers and lemons onto the bar, placed the custom cocktail sauce in front of himself and Dave.

"Fixins," Dace said.

He pushed his lime down into the neck of the bottle of Corona, then picked up a seafood fork and stabbed the first oyster. He clinked bottles with Dave, who also had one of the creamy-tan critters on the end of his fork.

Dace hoisted his oyster and toasted it: "As I ate the oysters with their strong taste of the sea and their faint metallic taste that the cold white wine washed away, leaving only the sea taste and the succulent texture, and as I drank their cold liquid from each shell and washed it down with the crisp taste of the wine, I lost the empty feeling and began to be happy and to make plans." He smiled and glanced askew at Dave. "Ernest Hemingway." He looked at the oyster. "I hope ye go as well with beer." He gobbled the beast, chewed, and swallowed, then took a swig of ice-cold beer. "Aye, that ye do." He tossed Dave one of his disarming grins.

Dave was shaking his head, then dipped his tidbit in the cocktail sauce, and downed it before giving forth his own line in honor of the little creature.

"'He was a bold man that first eat an oyster.' Jonathon Swift."

Dace stared at his friend.

"I give you Hemingway and you come back with Jonathon Swift?" "And quoted in the old English, yet." He laughed and stabbed another oyster. He held it forth in a mock toast toward Dave. "You, sir, in heart, as well as stature and girth, are a giant amongst us Lilliputians."

They polished off the two dozen in no time, added an order for a dozen more and another couple of beers. When those were gone, they headed out to explore Bourbon Street.

Libby drove as Mary Rose slept in the back seat. On the front seat, Libby had placed the album and box of letters. Inside the album, but more so wrapped in envelopes and ribbons in the handcrafted African mahogany box, were memories and a secret which could change history were it ever to see the light of day. Richard had made it very clear to her the previous evening what his thoughts were on the subject. Libby wondered what her son-in-law thought of her now, if anything had changed between them, even though he swore to guard her confidence and had assured her that he not only understood, but empathized.

She glanced at the clock on the dashboard. 9:49 p.m. If Tom were still at the house, he was sure to be awake. Libby was certain there had been no news of Dace or Tom or Allard would have called her with that update, instead of Allard's message of intended self-absolution. Sometimes her husband, as much as she loved him, was infuriatingly transparent, especially with his calling home to make certain he was still viewed as a 'good boy' by his wife.

While the previous evening had been a time of introspection and retrospection, this evening she had determined to be her moment of purgation. She had long ago made the confession, and had received her absolution in the eyes of God. Her decision, carried to fruition when she arrived home that night, she well understood, would be irrevocable, but she had made it. It was time. When she exited the interstate, she headed toward home. In the driveway, she could see the lights in the house. Caroline would have come back that evening and had most likely spoken to Tom when she found Libby and Mary Rose gone. The porch lights were on. At the turn to the roundabout and garage, Libby bore left instead of right and drove down the narrow private access road which led to the boathouse on the river.

At the end of the crushed granite drive, she stopped the car, turned off the lights, put the transmission into PARK and left the car idling. Had she shut off the engine, Mary Rose would have awakened, the sudden absence of motor noise and vibration was like an alarm clock to the girl. Libby didn't want her daughter to see what she had to do. She reached behind her seat, touched Mary Rose's face, brushed several stray hairs from her cheek. The girl stirred briefly, but quickly resettled. Libby kissed her fingertips and applied them to Mary Rose's cheek.

She opened her door and stepped onto the gravel drive. She gazed up into the night sky, then lowered her look toward the house on the hill above. Tom's bedroom faced the other direction, Caroline's on the lower level had no windows. She drew in a deep breath of cool air, then returned her upper body to the car, reached across and collected the album and box, and quietly closed the door. She turned to face the river and began to walk slowly toward it.

Dave talked Dace out of doing shots that night, however, there was one idea he couldn't talk his friend out of, not that he really tried too hard. The crowd in the street ebbed and flowed and passage to anywhere along Bourbon Street was nearly impossible except along the periphery, hugging the buildings on the sidewalks. They made their way to place with the girl on the swing. The red brick building seemed to vibrate with activity. Men in groups, or pairs, some with women, moved up and down the stairs to the main door. A bouncer who normally would be also hawking clients curbside, had no need for his secondary skills during Carnival. The club had more than its share of business and Dave and Dace took their place in the ingress queue.

"Three drink minimum tonight, gentlemen," the bouncer said to them as they passed the portal.

They nodded and stepped inside. There were three stages, and were girls on each one, and four more who were parading on the bar in heels and lingerie. The girls on stage were in various stages of becoming fully recognizable to the audience.

"What'll it be, buddy?" Dace said and then pointed to each stage in turn and concluded with the bar. "Blonde, brunette, red head, or smorgasbroad?"

"I've always preferred blondes," Dave said, beaming a smile across the room at the young woman with the oblivious look on her face who had just removed her bra.

They began to step in that direction when another woman, slightly more dressed and much less oblivious and carrying a tray encircled by a purple glow light stopped them, and directed them to follow her as she led them to a couple of seats at the foot of the stage occupied by the red head. The music was loud and distorted by the poor acoustics of the room and topped by general reverie. Dace had to shout for the waitress to hear him.

"My friend prefers the blonde," he said, flashing a smile.

"Dude, they all make the rounds," she said. "It's already been a long night, do you want to see the show or not?"

Dace nodded and he and Dave took the seats.

The girl with the tray bent over between them and placed two paper napkins on the little counter area and asked what they would have. They ordered bottle beer, Coronas with limes, and she wove her way through the crowd toward the bar. A few minutes later, just after the red head had removed her bra, revealing a perkier, yet smaller and obviously more natural set than the blonde across the room sported, the waitress returned with six bottles of beer, each topped with a wedge of lime, and requested sixty dollars.  Dace pulled out four twenties and told her to keep the change.  She smiled perfunctorily, then stuffed the folded bills into some type of pouch around her waist and quickly departed back into the crowd.

Outside, at the outskirts of the crowd on the other side of Bourbon Street, just about to walk into a T-shirt and souvenir shop, Ashley and Ronnie dropped their empty plastic cups onto the sidewalk.  Ashley carried the cardboard tube with their drawings rolled up inside; Ronnie displayed yet another impressive set of accumulated beads.  The girl sure does love showing her boobs to strangers, Ashley thought, then wondered if there was some sort of T-shirt inside she could buy her friend which echoed that insight.  Based on what they'd seen at other stores, she had no doubt there was some sort of boob flashing T-shirt hanging on one of the brightly lit walls.

Libby cradled the album and the African mahogany box in her arms. Her face was neutral, her mind resolved, her heart at ease and becoming more so with every step she took toward *her* river.  She crossed the gravel, then took three steps down onto the concrete pier which contained the boathouse and dock extending into the water.  The night was again crisp and cold and she could see her exhalations hanging then dissipating, but the recent snow had melted away with the rain and a couple days of above-freezing temperatures.  An old song played in her head as she rounded the boathouse and made her way along the concrete walk. Beyond the rails of the dock, she could see the silent roils of the river, and as they churned, the gently burbling surface reflected a waning gibbous moon high overhead.  The subdued lights of Gales Ferry, and the spot just to the east where Sarah Avidago had died eight nights ago, marked the opposite shore.  Further off to the east, the more intense reflections of New London and Groton lit the sky and seeped onto the river as it flowed toward the nearby Long Island Sound.

It was quiet out there at that spot on the Thames any time of day, but always seemed more so at night.  That night, it was nearly soundless as not even a breath of wind stirred the still dormant trees.  Peaceful and eternal, was the way Libby had always viewed her river and standing so near the quiet display of its awesome power, she invariably felt both safe and contented.  She couldn't suppress a muted smile as her gaze spanned the water and took in its reflecting blackness, because like herself, the Thames rarely revealed what was deeply concealed inside.  In so many ways, Libby had often considered herself much like the old river: she was powerful, yet did not seek outward display; she ran deep; she quietly roiled, yet always flowed on; and she, too, contained her secrets, never revealing to outsiders what she carried within her. On that night, as the lights of God and man reflected upon the river, Elizabeth Granuaile Mcintire Lamoureux understood, she, too, ultimately, had for almost all of her seventy-one years been merely the reflections of others: her father; her husband; her children; even her single, illicit lover.

As she approached the railing at the end of the walkway, then moved out onto the unprotected pier, a deep chill, mostly not having anything to do with the frigidity of the night, pierced her soul and she momentarily reconsidered her action. Fighting back the hesitation and affirming her resolve, Libby stepped to the very edge of the dock. There, she stood motionless for several ticks of God's eternal clock as she drank in the serenity of the moment. Finally, mesmerized and soothed by the black water flowing slowly past, her decision unchangeable, her will immovable, she understood what was to be done was not an emotional whim but contained an ultimate irrevocability. Once begun, the deed could not be undone. She drew in a deep breath, held it. It was time. She shuffled her feet forward slightly, her toes in her flat shoes hung in space above the icy Thames. For history's legacy, her arms began to unfold.

"Libby?"

She started, nearly lost her balance, shuffled backwards a step. She didn't need to turn to see who it was; she recognized the voice well enough. She turned around anyway. She faced him. His eyes searched her.

"Tom," she said.

"I caught a glimpse of taillights moving around the backside of the house, when I saw them go off down here, I thought I'd come check it out. I didn't recognize it was your car in the darkness until I got closer and saw it was running with Mary Rose sleeping in the back seat."

He took several steps further out onto the pier. His eyes contained concern and continued to search hers, then fixed upon the items in her arms.

"What are you doing out here in the middle of the night, Libby?" he asked, then took another step closer to her as something inside tugged at him. "What are you holding there?"

Libby quickly considered her options, then lighted upon the simplest. Tom worked for her husband, and by extension, her. Regardless of what he had meant to her personally, and still did in some respects, he was merely an employee and could be treated as such, to a point. He wasn't stupid, though, and notwithstanding what had occurred between him and her, he had always been totally loyal to Allard. She knew she couldn't just dismiss Tom with an abrupt wave-off like one could the janitor who walked into the office unannounced to empty the trash containers without risking a mention by Tom and then questions from her husband.

"Tom, this is my private business," she said. "I wish you'd leave me to it, and honor my request for discretion." Her face softened when his still held concern. "Thank you for caring, Tom, but I'll be fine. Really."

Tom knew he could never refuse Libby anything. Working for The Senator had fed his career, however, being proximate to Libby over the past three decades had nourished his soul. She may judge Tom eternally loyal to her husband, and professionally he was and would remain, but the secrets shared between his heart and Libby's meant he would never, could never, betray her.

"You know I will always keep your secrets, Libby," Tom said. "I always have."

Libby's eyes misted, glistened in the moonlight.

"As I have yours, Tom," she said, and then looked down at the items in her arms. "Forever."

Tom slowly nodded once. In that instant, looking into Libby's eyes, he realized just how much of life he had sacrificed for his clients over the years, and reluctantly understood that he was now firmly embarked on the third act of his life. He no longer felt the chill of the night air, but rather now was touched by the same icy fingers which raked his soul that had touched Libby's moments earlier. He turned and slowly made his way to the shoreline. He passed the idling car, peered inside to see Mary Rose still wrapped in her peaceful slumber, walked up the drive back to the house.

From the edge of the pier, Libby watched him first disappear behind the boathouse, then reappear as a shadow halfway up the drive. She watched him be swallowed by the gauzy darkness, then turned around again to face the river. It had waited for her; it was always there. Eternal. As she fully unfolded her arms that time, there was neither hesitation nor interruption, and the album and box tumbled through space and plunged into the blackness of her river. She looked down, saw them momentarily reflected in the moonlight, then like the figure of Tom McDaniel, they too were swallowed by the gauzy darkness.

After what seemed an eternity on the road, Cindy crossed from Mississippi into Louisiana. For the past five hours, since leaving the Birmingham, Alabama area following a gas stop and bathroom break, and having grabbed a microwaved burrito and frozen Coke for a late dinner, her mind had been reeling. As she had waited in line to pay for her gas and dinner, her attention had been caught by a grainy set of photographs and a sketch of a man wanted for the assault of two security guards at a local truck stop several nights earlier. She recalled the night Dave had called her, he and Dace had been somewhere outside of

Birmingham, he had said.    While the photography, which she had assumed had come from surveillance cameras were of medium quality, and were certainly ambiguous as to the identity of the man, there could be no mistaking the identity of the person in the police sketch.    It was Dace Lamoureux.

Cindy searched her purse in the darkness for the package of antacids she had bought near Hattiesburg, Mississippi, located them and removed two more.    The burrito had been a bad choice in so many ways, she thought as she chewed two more of the chalky tablets with an anonymous fruit flavoring.    She washed the residue down with a swig from a bottle of water.    Leaving the lights of Picayune in the rear view mirror, she crossed into the darkness of the no-man's land that was the Bogue Chitto National Wildlife Refuge, with the combined glow of Slidell on the horizon and New Orleans just a bit further on.

She gripped the wheel firmly.    She had tried a call from a pay phone to Dave's new cell number several times over the last ten hours, but he hadn't answered.    She wished he would set up the voicemail, knowing he'd not recognize the numbers from which the calls had originated and might freak out.    Just then, a bug the size of a Volkswagen splattered against the windshield right in front of her face, smearing flecks of brown exoskeleton amidst a spreading blob of greenish-yellow insides on the glass.    She looked around the remains of the bug and sprayed the windshield with washer fluid.    The wipers made more of a mess before eventually clearing the view with the assist of copious amounts of washer fluid.  Cindy smiled at the metaphor.

Behind pursed lips, she cursed the thought of the images of Dace Lamoureux hanging in businesses across Alabama at the same time her heart feared for Dave Saunders.    Not that Dace would ever hurt Dave, but Dave was sometimes a bit naive, and always easily led by his best friend.    In addition to never really liking him, Cindy had never fully trusted Dace, but there had been no daylight between the two boys for her to wedge herself between them, even for Dave's own good. Sometimes she wondered if the reason she and Dave had split up was because of that lack of daylight between him and Dace or if it had been Dace's reaction to what he may have perceived as her subtle - mostly - attempts to wedge herself between them.    Not that it mattered, really.  It wouldn't have worked in the long run.    She was too strong for Dave, and she discerned what he did not.    In the final analysis, Cindy wanted a knight in shining armor astride a snarling, white stallion with eyes as challenging and fearless as those of its rider to scoop her up to safety and drag her to his castle, not someone who would, once she was on the horse with him, hand her the reins.

She stifled a yawn, mentally calculated how long she had to go, measuring the last of the trip in time rather than distance.    She straightened and stretched in the seat, thought of what she had left behind in Boston. Cindy wondered if the two large gentlemen had gone into her apartment yet. She fully anticipated they would, eventually, and had warned Billy and Charity. The last thing she wanted was for Billy to try to play hero with two unknowns. That reminded her that she hadn't heard from metro police before she left for a statement on Dave's aunt Gloria. She knew they suspected natural causes in the death, but she had read many true crime books over the years in which even people of relatively modest means had come up with nearly foolproof ways of doing someone in. But why do in Dave's Aunt Gloria? If these brutes worked for Dace's father as she suspected they did, was there really any limit to what they could do and hide from authorities?

Naturally, Cindy had heard of Sarah Avidago's death a little over a week ago. The story had reached campus gossip mills and spread like wildfire. Of course, there was rumor and speculation given the disparity of their social positions, especially with Dace nowhere to be found, but there were also enough people loyal to the Lamoureux family who spiked any conjecture and reminded people that Sarah had been the victim of a tragic accident. Nothing more, nothing less. The car had reportedly left the road after an encounter with black ice, hardly circumstances for which The Senator could be responsible. Could he?

Cindy shook her head vigorously, opened the window to let in some air. She passed around Slidell and set off across the bridge on the eastern side of Lake Pontchartrain. An orangish glow filled the horizon. She had never been to New Orleans or Uncle Jack's place west of the city in old plantation country. For an instant she wondered what she would do if Dave and Dace had already left and headed somewhere else or were on their way home. She hadn't considered that possibility for over fifteen-hundred miles and she mentally kicked herself; but then what was she to do if nobody answered Dave's new phone for the last two days? She remembered there was an assistant living down in the area she could call, and of course, she could always reach out to Uncle Jack for that number, but she didn't really want to bother him.

Uncle Jack wasn't really her uncle, rather a friend of the family who seemed to have a special affection for her and her mother. He was a wealthy international financier after an eclectic professional life which included everything from sweeping floors to selling vacuums door-to-door, who now owned homes on four continents and at least two islands and traveled frequently. Occasionally, he'd send her cards or small gifts from places he visited for work or pleasure, never forgot her birthday, and he always made certain to add a postscript to remind her that she could call him anytime, for anything. She carried a phone number in her wallet for his private offices in New York City which she could call day or night and they'd track him down for her. She rarely reached out to him, not wanting to be a bother, but she had a week ago and had reached him in Singapore. It was how she had obtained permission for Dave to use the Vacherie house for his little getaway.

After the bridge, Cindy stayed on I-10 which skirted the north side of the city, but used the 610 bypass to avoid the dip into downtown traffic and reconnected with the interstate a little further west. It was after midnight and there was still a heavy flow of traffic out from the city. Red lights going her way outnumbered by three or fourfold the white headlights coming at her across the median. In Metairie, she pulled off for another bathroom break, and bought a Snickers bar and liter bottle of Pepsi. She needed the sugar and the caffeine for the last hour. When asked, the attendant suggested she stay north of the river on the interstate and then get off at highway 641 and use that bridge just east of Vacherie. It would be faster even if it took her a few more miles. She was frankly relieved to not see any photos or WANTED posters for Dace in the place.

As she made her way the last hour or so, she worked her mind on everything that had taken place in her life since she took that call from Dave a week ago. He had been quite secretive, but she could have wangled any information from him she had wanted. She just hadn't wanted to. He was an ex-boyfriend, and still a friend who needed a favor and she was happy to help out. How he had remembered that her Uncle Jack had a place down there she never would know...oh, wait, the sex on the porch thing, that's how he remembered. She smiled, finished the last of the Snickers and washed it down with cola. The sugar had done its trick for the first half hour, but now she was feeling tired again, and a little agitated by the caffeine. She stretched in her seat again, caught herself wiggling her toes, wrote that last action off to a combination of the good wiggling and the thinking wiggling.

She easily picked up the Great River Road on the south side of the Mississippi, noted the mileage at the turn and knew she had about seven miles to go. She remembered relaying to Dave what Uncle Jack had said about the place being behind an expanse of high hedges, and that the driveway could be hard to spot if you weren't watching, so she closely noted the odometer clicking off the tenths of a mile. She passed Oak Alley, remembered the place from the movie *Interview with the Vampire*. She wasn't much of a fan of Tom Cruise or Brad Pitt, but loved the writings of Anne Rice and had enjoyed the movie even with the odd casting of leading men. She slowed, knew Uncle Jack's place would be coming up soon. The hedgerow came into view just beyond a small subdivision in the middle of nowhere, and just as advertised one-point-one miles later, the small break.

She wheeled Dave's Mustang off the asphalt and onto the private drive. The tires crunched on what she would discover in the daylight was mainly crushed oyster shells and not gravel. There were lights on in the house, but she didn't see this Escalade Dave talked about picking up before they left parked anywhere. She pulled to the end of the drive, circled the roundabout, parked and shut off the engine. She saw the old iron boiling pot turned planter and walked over to check the rim for the magnetic key holder. She found the key holder, but it was empty. Next, she climbed the porch steps and knocked, rang the bell. No answer. She walked the veranda, smiled to herself at how big it really was, and that it had a very private mate complete with a sturdy, balustered railing on the second floor. She spotted the old, rickety barn in the back which she knew was a high-tech garage and workshop made to look like a building which should be condemned. The apartment lights were dark. She wondered if she had mentioned the tenant to Dave. No matter, she thought. She tried the back door. It was locked, just like the front one had been.

She checked her watch. 2:09 a.m., Monday, February the twenty-third. She was exhausted, and by then even the caffeine wasn't working and she came back around to the front. It was a pleasant evening outside, crickets and toads serenading her from the nearby fields and swamp and there wasn't a bit of wind. Vacherie's weather was much nicer than what she had left in Boston twenty-eight hours ago. She retrieved her bags from the car, dropped them next to an oversized whicker chair near the front door, pulled a second chair over to act as a footrest, covered herself with a small blanket Dave kept in the car and quickly drifted off to sleep.

# Chapter Twenty-two

Dave dragged Dace out of the bars on Bourbon Street around four in the morning. He had been expecting them to call bar time and flash the lights, but was surprised at the time when he checked his watch because that seemed not to be happening. Over the last hours, they had seen at least thirty sets of boobs, a few expertly revealed flashes of other things, and had spent at least six hundred dollars on alcohol and tips. At the end of the night, they had been listening to a live jazz band in the small, dark, and crowded Absinthe House bar. Dace had still been drinking, Dave had stopped shortly after midnight. On the way to the car, Dace bought them a couple of hot dogs from a guy with a cart shaped like a hot dog.

As they walked down Bourbon to Toulouse, they each devoured their two dogs. Dave was surprised he had been that hungry. Dace was weaving, the worst Dave had seen him, and Dave silently prayed Dace wouldn't decorate the inside of the Escalade with the combination of the night's beer and hot dogs. At least he'd talked Dace out of doing shots tonight, he thought. Dave could still feel a little buzz as he buckled into the car, but he felt fine to drive. Dace located a 60s music station and began to sing along for a while; but by the time they hit the highway, he was asleep.

An hour later, Dave maneuvered off the main road into the nearly hidden lane Auntie D had told him existed just where the hedgerow began and followed the rarely used trail which skirted the edge of several fields and eventually led directly to the workshop building. He drove around to the back of the building even though none of it was probably visible from off the property, and certainly not from the Great River Road. It wasn't that Dave was afraid of the locals Dace had made into enemies, necessarily, but why risk a further hassle?

He turned off the ignition, left the keys hanging and walked around to the passenger door to rouse Dace who wasn't really responding to the shoulder shake he applied from across the cabin.    Dace was leaning against the door, so Dave concluded at worst he'd awaken when he began to tumble out.    Dave opened the door and Dace indeed began to fall, reached out instinctively as Dave caught him.    Dace's eyes flashed from surprise to anger and back to confusion as he looked around.

"Where are we?" he asked.

"Behind the workshop," Dave said as he pulled Dace out of the car and steadied him on his feet.    "There's a path that goes from the road right to here.    Starts at the far end of the hedgerow.    Auntie D told me about it."

Dace wobbled, nearly fell backward into the car again, but Dave caught him, held him upright.

"Behind the workshop?"    Dace's eyes brightened with an idea.    He smiled broadly.    "Why, Dave are you afraid of them old boys who are looking for me?"    His eyes tried to focus.    "Are you, buddy?"

Dave shook his head, held Dace around the waist with one arm.

"Not afraid, Dace, just don't want to invite something bad to this place, or perhaps Auntie D, should they drive by and spot the Escalade. If you haven't noticed, there are very few of these out here in the country."

He began to lead Dace across the lawn.

"Watch out for those devil ants," Dace said.    He looked up at Dave. "By the way, how are your little legs, Davie?"

"Fine, just fine," he said.    "I know what to watch for, don't worry."

"Oh, I'm not worried, buddy," Dace said, his smile returning.    "I just want to get back to my dreams of that blonde's tits and ass and not have the image of you shedding your jeans and jumping around with your spindly legs poking out of tidy-whiteys coming into the picture."    He laughed.

"Which blonde?"

"Huh?"

"Which blonde?"

"Oh, any of them.    All of them.    Brunettes, even the redheads, too. When it comes to love, though, I'm loyal as an old hound dog, a metaphor which I am certain that old, black woman would be proud.    I loved Sarah.    I don't wander, buddy.    I love you, too, Dave.    Now that Colleen has introduced me to the joys of lust on a car hood, though, well, lust is a very different matter."

"You tell, 'em, Jimmy Carter," Dave said.

They walked up the steps to the back porch, Dave propped Dace against the doorway, unlocked the inside door.    He hadn't been setting the alarm system, so there was no rush getting in and disarming it.    He walked Dace down the hallway, neglected to lock the door behind them. Upstairs, he plopped Dace onto his bed, took off his shoes and tossed a blanket over the top of him. Dace mumbled some type of appreciation and fell asleep. He was snoring before Dave made it out of the room. He walked back downstairs and grabbed a cherry Mountain Dew from the refrigerator. The hot dogs were repeaters, he discovered, and had been loaded with sodium, so he was thirsty and hoped the Dew would settle his stomach down. As he was returning to the foot of the stairs he noticed something in the driveway through the door sidelight. He turned off the inside light and crept along the wall, then ducked down and pushed aside the bottom corner of the sidelight window cover.

It took him a few moments to recognize the vehicle parked in the roundabout, but even when he did, the confusion remained. He unlocked the front door, opened it and walked out onto the veranda.

"What the heck?" he said.

Dave detected some movement off to his right and turned quickly to face it. A smile overrode his concern and lit up his face. He closed the distance, went down to one knee and lightly jostled her shoulder. Her eyes opened with a start.

"Hey, Cindy," Dave said. "What the heck brings you down here? And in my car, no less."

"Hey, Dave," Cindy said, pushing herself into a sitting position and dropping her feet to the floor. "Do I have a story to tell you. Why haven't you been answering your phone for the last two days?"

Dave pulled the phone from his pocket, pushed a button, but the screen remained dark.

"Must've died," he said. "My old one would go a week between charges. I guess I just forgot."

Cindy rolled her eyes. He'd never change, she thought. To which she added, maybe that was not such a bad thing, overall.

"Pull up a seat, old son," Cindy said, shoving the second chair a bit with her foot.

She proceeded to fill him in on the two large gentlemen, the whole story behind the Aunt Gloria situation, the speculation which had been going around campus, how she couldn't reach him and became concerned, what she saw hanging in the gas station in Birmingham, and the rest, but by the time she had laid it all out, neither of them could really answer the question as to why she had blindly undertaken a twenty-five hour drive. Dave listened, then filled her in on what he had been living with and seeing since last Sunday morning when the police had come by his house. When all the stories were told, each of them still may not have understood the reasoning behind Cindy's trek, but they both were glad she was there.

About six-thirty in the morning, just as the eastern sky was coming alive, they went inside and upstairs. Dave carried Cindy's duffle. Dace was still snoring in his room. At the top of the stairs, Dave stopped and pointed in four directions as he spoke.

"There's four bedrooms up here," he said. "You can hear which one Dace is using, this one in the back is mine for the duration. Across the hall up front is your Uncle Jack's and the last one is Samantha's, your uncle's local assistant who's currently at her place in the city." He looked at Cindy. "Where to?"

She walked into his room.


Tom's phone vibrated on his nightstand. He was just coming out of the shower, and grabbed it as it began to ring.

"Yeah," Tom said. "Anything?"

"Something," Travis said. "Just heard from our guy doing the GPS tracking and he says the unit has been stationary for about six hours at a location near Vacherie, Louisiana. I think our girl has made it."

"That could very well be where they are," Tom said. "Give me the location." He grabbed a pen and pad.

"29 - 59 - 25.173 north latitude, 90 - 47 - 36.927 west longitude," Travis read off. "That's about five or six miles outside of Vacherie, to the west, on the south side of the river. Satellite map shows a plantation-style house on the site. Rural as hell, and private. My understanding from our friend at DoD is we don't have any live shots available for those coordinates."

Tom read back the numbers.

"No need for live shots," Tom said. He remembered Vacherie as a hot, mosquito-infested little place west of New Orleans, out on the river. Old plantation territory, now a mix of tourist spots at the restored antebellum locations, and abandoned wrecks where relatives had torn apart the places over the years in search of the families' rumored hidden treasure. "At The Senator's direction, I've already contacted a local P.I. who is going to put eyes on the place and confirm for us that the boys are still there."

"Do you want Rudy and me to get on a plane?"

Tom thought about that. He hadn't discussed the closure operation with The Senator, and needed to. It would be the cleanest to get Travis and Rudy onto a private plane into New Orleans, get out to Vacherie, put hands on Dace and bring him home and end this crap. He knew there could always be complications in that type of recovery, though. If Dace wouldn't come willingly, what were the limits on his team? Could they drug or manhandle the boy or would The Senator draw the line at that? When they got them in their sights, could he simply be talked back home by his father? There was too much which needed to be authorized and Tom decided it was premature to send out the Cavalry at this point.

"No, hold tight for now, but be ready to go on short notice. I want someone above my pay grade to make the calls on how we deal with the boy once we get eyes on him. We've been lucky in keeping this in the family so far, even with the garbage in Birmingham. I don't think The Senator will want to risk something getting out now."

"Roger that," Travis said.

"I'll call you back later." He thought of something else. "One last thing. Let me know right away if the car moves."

"Wilco," Travis said and the line disconnected.

I wrote down the GPS coordinates and then asked if the client had directions, a physical location or address from which a civilian could work. Tom did. I wrote that down, too, and I knew the general vicinity. If it all went well, it would be about an hour drive out there, recon the area, confirm the subject vehicle was there, put eyes on the kid, wham-bam, and I'm home before three. Since the banks weren't yet open, I agreed to allow the client a couple of hours to make the wire transfer of the retainer while I loaded up and saddled up. As I showered and shaved and dressed, I couldn't help thanking God I didn't have 'rich people's troubles'. I mean, a middle class kid runs away, you call the cops, they drag the little bugger home. Hopefully. All this rigamarole these people go through to hide the family's dirty laundry seems just plain silly to a small-town boy from Wisconsin. It all pays the bills, though, I guess.

I removed the anticipated papers off the fax machine and was out of the house by eight-forty. I'd review the information on the drive and call the bank in an hour to make certain the retainer had come in. No, it's not that I didn't trust the guy; after all, I knew how to reach him if he stiffed us, but Sandy is a stickler for policy and our policy was simple: no retainer, no case; no final payment, no final report. It was a policy which had worked well so far, but as I backed Sandy's Bravada out of the garage, I convinced myself I was capable of making this executive decision on my own, at the same time I hoped I wouldn't have to tell her about it.

I stopped off at a little deli near our house and bought some food and drinks for the day, just in case. There's nothing worse than being out on a surveillance job and not being able to think about anything other than how hungry or thirsty you are. Well, there is one thing that's worse, and that's the food doing a number on your innards. I checked the time on my cell phone and based on the amount of traffic I was mixed with heading out of the city, I estimated arriving near Vacherie by ten-thirty. Not wanting to be put into a position where I had to mislead my wife on this retainer thing, I decided to put off calling her until later that night. Okay, so there are some things about which Sandy scares me. Satisfied?

Tom called The Senator using the landline to the McClean house. He answered on the third ring. Tom briefed him on the GPS location and they discussed various options for getting Dace back home without any more problems. The Senator asked for an estimated timeline and Tom outlined things as he saw them currently. If they put Travis and Rudy on a private jet, they were talking about a three-hour flight between New London and New Orleans. Arranging for a jet could take up to four hours. Then getting out to Vacherie for the recovery would take at least another hour. The Senator told Tom to check if there were other airports which were less visible than Louis Armstrong International in New Orleans, and closer to the plantation. Any way they looked at it, however, they were looking at a minimum of eight hours between giving the 'Go' and getting the boys within arm's reach of Dace.

Tom assured The Senator that the local P.I. they had hired was reliable and had agreed to complete confidentiality in the matter, and was indeed already on the way out to put eyes on the scene.

When they concluded the conversation, nothing had been resolved, which left Tom a bit uncomfortable should things take an unexpected turn on short notice. The Senator, however, had agreed to consider each of Tom's scenarios while driving in to the Capitol, and to get back to him later that morning with his decisions. It left Travis and Rudy hanging, but it was the best Tom could wrangle from the man.

Tom finished dressing, and then went down to breakfast. As he descended the stairs, his thoughts turned to Libby, and the encounter he had with her last evening. His mind had sifted and culled all the possibilities of what she was doing on the pier the previous night, and what her oddly cryptic statements to him of recent have meant. When he walked into the breakfast room and found Libby and Mary Rose already dressed for the day, sitting at the table, he was as uncertain as to Libby's mysteries as he ever had been.

"Good morning, Mary Rose," Tom said with a big smile as he took a seat. "How's my best girl this morning?"

Mary Rose smiled at him.

"I'm great, Mr. Mac, and it's going to be a great day" she said, a dribble of blueberry pancake syrup on her chin. "Caroline made pancakes this morning, and wouldn't you agree that any day that starts with pancakes is a great day?"

"That I would, Mary Rose," he said as Libby reached across and wiped away the syrup dribbling on the girl's chin. Tom reflected that there were days when one could marvel at what Mary Rose said, and how she spoke the words. Today was one of those days. Perhaps Mary Rose was correct: perhaps because of pancakes at the start, it was going to be a great day. "Good morning, Libby."

Caroline came in then with the coffee pot and poured him a cup. He accepted the offer of a plate of pancakes for breakfast, which she went off to create for him.

"How did you sleep, Tom?" Libby asked. "Well, I trust."

He looked into her eyes; saw only his silent inquiry reflected.

"Not as well as I would have liked," he said. "Lots on my mind, I guess."

"There's plenty of that going around lately, isn't there?" Libby said, sliding her chair back. "You'll excuse me, Tom, but I'm taking Mary Rose out for a ladies day. We'll be back later this afternoon."

Tom watched her as she hustled Mary Rose from the table. The girl turned and waved.

"Bye, Mr. Mac," she said, sliding from her chair. "It's ladies day, and that's almost as good as pancakes."

Tom returned the wave just as Caroline brought in his stack of buttermilk pancakes, a dollop of butter melting across the top.

"These look and smell great, Caroline," Tom said as he poured some Vermont maple syrup onto the stack. "I'm sure they'll be the best I've had since the last time you made them for me."

"Thank you, Tom," she said, and disappeared back into the kitchen.

Tom reached across and dragged the newspapers over to his side of the table. He began with the Washington Post, left the New York Times for later. He cut into the stack of pancakes, pushed the forkful of them into his mouth as he glanced over the front page of the Post. Stories of President Clinton's alleged sexual liaison with intern Monica Lewinsky nearly consumed the front page. The rumors of the alleged affair had become too hot of a potato *not* to be handled by the mainline media which had been embarrassed after the story was initially leaked by online journalist Matt Drudge who reported Newsweek had been sitting on the story being investigated by their own Michael Isikoff. In the eyes of the public, it merely served to confirm their suspicions that the press was in the tank for the populist democrat.

Pundits and politicos alike had begun suggesting Clinton get out of the country to let things cool down and the story blow over. The President, they said, was far too visible in Washington, and an international trip historically had worked wonders as even the most partisan of political foes resisted criticizing a sitting president when he was overseas. The old axiom of 'politics stops at the water's edge' had worked well for many previous embattled chief executives. One California congresswoman even suggested Clinton take over and head their upcoming Black Caucus junket to Africa to investigate claims of ethnic cleansing and confront developing nation economic issues.

"Sorry lady," Tom scoffed his mouth working on another forkful of pancakes. "This one isn't going to go away, even if the guy runs to

Antarctica and is photographed rescuing penguins." Tom stopped in mid-chew. He sat back in the chair as his mind's eye drifted back to images of Libby on the dock last night; more precisely to what she had held in her arms, and it struck him like a bolt of lightning. The box she had been clutching had been a gift from him some twenty years or more ago when he had traveled with The Senator to western Africa. The moment he had seen it displayed in the marketplace of a small town in Mali, he had become mesmerized by the grain, carvings, and chatoyant luster brought out by the careful hand polishing by the craftsman, and had known it would be the perfect gift for Libby.

'Sonofabitch,' Tom said under his breath and simultaneously slid his chair back and sprinted to the front door and out onto the porch, only to see Libby already driving out. He stood there thinking for a minute, then came back inside. He shuffled to the kitchen table and picked away at the remaining pancakes. He wasn't certain when our how or when, but he promised himself he was going to get to the bottom of all this.

I drove past the Oak Alley plantation with its double row of ancient oak trees creating an eight-hundred foot canopied passageway to the restored mansion and slowed for a tour bus which was turning in to the public entrance just beyond the main house. I knew the address for Oak Alley was 3645 Great River Road, and I was looking for 4209 Great River Road, so I knew it lay west a bit. How far exactly, only the Postmaster General knew, so I drove along.

There were generally no numbers on houses out there, and the mailboxes were few and far between, with the majority of them being poorly marked, so I kept an eye on the odometer. I drove along a half-dozen roads of a small subdivision just west of Oak Alley, realizing there was no way the house described by the client could be located in that mix of recent and older single-family homes, but since I was also looking for a white with blue racing stripes, 1986 Mustang GT Liftback with Connecticut plates, and a young man and young woman whose grainy, black and white driver's license photos had arrived over the fax that morning, I wanted to cover all my bases. The few minutes driving through the dusty subdivision didn't seem like a waste of my time, but I found what I truly expected: nothing.

There were several Mustangs in driveways along the roads of the subdivision, but most newer than the 1986 vintage, and none displaying Connecticut plates. I drove out again on the Great River Road, headed west. The day was bright and sunny and there was a warming trend heading in. Puffy cumulus clouds dotted the western horizon. I estimated they'd be covering the area over the next couple of hours, perhaps be the seeds of some rain showers or afternoon thunderstorms.

I rolled up the window and turned on the air conditioning as the coolness of the morning was quickly being overpowered.

Just to the west of the subdivision, after the road concluded a shallow S-turn, a well-maintained, twelve-foot high hedgerow began. There was a relatively fresh set of vehicle tracks leading off into the fields in the long grass off the road right where the hedges began. I made a mental note of it, just in case I'd need it later. There was nothing to see behind the hedgerow which appeared to stretch for another mile or more, so I sped up a bit, and that's when I almost missed it. There was a small gap, just wide enough for an automobile drive, cut into the hedge. Because the foliage was at least four feet thick, and obviously watered to maintain such fullness of leaf, the gap was very hard to spot while driving along the road at normal speed. I swung around a little further on, then drove back slower, only pausing a moment at the gap.

Sure enough, behind the hedgerow there was a well-restored antebellum plantation home set back about six-hundred feet off the road and parked at the end of a drive, in some sort of turnaround, was a white with blue racing stripes Mustang GT Liftback appearing to be of the proper vintage. I couldn't spot the plate from that position on the road, and my eyes aren't good enough to read a license plate at six-hundred feet even if I could, but it had to be the one I was looking for. How many could there be in the area? I drove on down the road and pulled off near the base of the S-turn.

I removed a bottle of water from the cooler set on the passenger seat, and the aromas of the rich Italian meats, nutty cheeses, olive relish with garlic and spices of the muffaletta sandwich I had picked up for lunch filled the car and my mouth began to water. I glanced askew at the clock on the dash of the Bravada and noted, sadly, it was way too early for lunch, so I closed the lid and merely savored the remnants of the aroma medley as they swirled in the conditioned air and blended with the new car smell. As I drank the water, and assured my stomach the muffaletta would eventually be headed its way, I formulated a plan to confirm the Mustang's ID without being seen from the house before I called the client.

I remembered a levee access road by the subdivision, and even though there was also one nearly across the street from the gap in the hedge, I drove east to avoid being seen by the people in the house. I felt a little bad about taking Sandy's brand new SUV up onto the levee, but I drove slowly and tried to avoid throwing up much gravel against the paint. Atop the embankment, at the base of the S-turn, I had the perfect angle into the yard where the car was parked. I stopped, went around to the back of the Bravada and opened up one of my newest toys: a SkyHawk 9600 forty-power binoculars. I set up the tripod behind the SUV, then mounted the device and after a little focusing, I could clearly

make out the Connecticut license plate on the back of the car.     I
confirmed the number with my notes, then scanned the rest of the
property.    Nobody was moving around outside, and I could not see
through any of the windows because of interior curtains, then I swung
the unit to look up river just in case anyone in the house was watching me
watching them and pulled out my cell phone.

The bank confirmed the wire receipt of our full retainer, so my next
call was to the client who answered on the first ring. I told him that I had
indeed located the car in question, but had seen no movement on the
property, and had not obtained a visual on the two persons of interest.

"Is there a 1998 Cadillac Escalade on the property?" Tom said.

"Not that I could see, just the Mustang," I replied. "Am I supposed
to know about an Escalade?"

"Well, there may be a second vehicle involved.    Pearl white,
Connecticut plates, DWF858."

I hate it when clients ration the information.

"Anything else I should know?" I asked, the irritation unmasked.

"Not at this time," Tom said.

The line went dead. I looked at my phone.

"People are the worst," I said to the river.

The location on the levee was the perfect spot to see what I needed to
see, but it was a lousy surveillance location.   First, it was forty or so feet
above the roadway, meaning Sandy's Bravada and me were the highest
things for miles.   Second, there was nothing for me to blend in with up
there.   Third, the federal authorities took a dim view of civilians camping
out on top of the levees for some reason.   Instead of leaving, however, I
thought I could risk hanging out for a while and I called Sandy.   If the
worst happened, and the Army Corps of Engineers drove up on me, I
could always say I was bird watching and didn't see the multiple No
Trespassing signs. It might work.

Sandy answered on the first ring.    That usually meant her parents
were driving her nuts.   Don't get me wrong, Mom and Mr. Beach (should
you be reading this) because your daughter loves you both, but your
family dynamic has a tendency to get on her nerves. Frankly, it drives me
a bit crazy, too, and I haven't loved you both for my whole life.

Sandy had gone out for a walk and she had made it all the way to the
end of Union Avenue where a bluff overlooked Lake Michigan and
where the city had installed a series of benches so people could sit and
look at the water.   It's Sheboygan's answer to, well, just about any other
place where you can sit on a bench and look at a body of water.   I told
her we had received the retainer, and that I had found the car they were
looking for, but had not seen either of the kids, whom I assumed were
inside the house.  Of course, they could be a thousand miles away from
Vacherie in an Escalade I just learned about, but I didn't mention that to

Sandy.    She asked me 'What's next?' and I really wanted to say 'muffaletta and a Dr. Pepper', but I told her I was going to hang tight and wait out the kids. After that, I had no idea.

Sandy suggested if I needed to lay eyes on them and wanted to speed things along, that I just go onto the property and knock on the door.

"Use Portman on them," she said.

It was brilliant in its simplicity. In 'Portman', she was referring to my alter ego, John Portman, a fast-talking Texan - is that an oxymoron? People have a tendency to open up to John Portman for some reason, and often tell him things they would never tell William Langdon.

"That may be a good idea," I said. "I think I'm going to just watch for a while, though. There's one way in and out of the place they are staying at, and I can snug in along the hedge down the road and watch that spot without a problem. Plus, I've also got to wait to find out from the client what I'm supposed to do if the kids do show."

She wasn't happy about the case limits not being clearly defined, and I told her to relax, that I had it under control. She seemed on edge, cranky. I assumed what was making her that way was the ants on her skin of being too close to her parents, so I next talked her off the ledge, so to speak, and suggested she get back to her parent's house and just try to enjoy the visit saying nothing but us was forever. Lastly, we exchanged some mushy stuff, and then disconnected. I did end up watching some birds across the river for a while, rechecked the house and property, then drove off the levee and parked along the hedge to the west. I chose to park down that direction because if the kids did leave, they'd most likely be headed east, toward New Orleans and civilization, and not notice me that far away.

An hour later, I tore into the muffaletta.

Dave rolled over just after two in the afternoon. His mind was a little foggy, but he certainly remembered the identity of the warm body lying next to him. He also remembered their sleeping together had been totally platonic, by mutual agreement. He raised himself on one elbow and looked over at Cindy. She lay on her back, one hand next to her head, the other under the covers. Her long blonde hair had tousled overnight and a few strands lay across her face. Dave reached over and carefully brushed them aside. Her face was peaceful, and as cherubic as always, and then she opened one of her green eyes.

"Morning, sunshine," Dave said. "I didn't mean to wake you, but I couldn't resist."

She pushed herself up in bed, stretched her arms above her head. Dave's eyes were drawn to the subtle, compelling movements of her breasts under the stretched T-shirt she had worn to sleep. She looked over at him with both eyes.

"What?" she asked with the hint of playfulness in her smile.

Dave rolled onto his back, made certain the covers were doing their job.

"You know what," he said.

Cindy rolled her eyes and tossed the covers off herself and slid her legs off the side of the bed. She stood and then padded toward the bathroom. Dave watched her go, her workout shorts bobbing up and down with each step. She closed the door and he heard it lock.

Dave checked the clock on the nightstand: 2:14 p.m. He tossed the covers off himself, straightened his own shorts and fluffed his Harvard football T-shirt over the top as he walked to the window overlooking the back yard. He peered out through the sheer curtain, then pushed it aside and opened the doors. A shot of warm, humid air rushed against him. It carried the smell of rain. He breathed in deeply, then stepped out onto the painted planks, which felt cool and damp under his feet, and walked to stand at the rail. He leaned forward, placed both palms onto the top stile and stretched his shoulders. From there, he couldn't see the Escalade, but he could see a flicker of light coming from one of Auntie D's windows. The afternoon was dark, and the bases of a puffy overcast were steel gray. Birds were chattering away in the nearby fields and trees, and he was certain he could detect the intermittent rumble of distant thunder.

He heard Cindy's approach, but didn't turn to watch. She joined him at the rail, a friendly distance separating them. She had tied her hair back into a pony tail, and had quite obviously put on a brassiere. The words they had shared on the front porch before sunrise pressed to enter Dave's thinking, but he purposely shuttered his mind. He wanted to savor this moment. There was something about an approaching stormy afternoon that soothed his soul. Ever since he was a child, he loved an overcast, rainy afternoon. It contented him, and he liked the thought of sharing this one with Cindy.

"I love days like this," he said without looking at her.

Cindy smiled. She loved them as well; experiencing nature's power while safely cocooned filled her with images of hearth and home. Her gaze went up to the clouds, then settled upon the old shed.

"Is that where Auntie D lives?" she asked. "Looks awful, like an old abandoned barn just as you described it, but somehow far worse than I had envisioned when I had heard about Uncle Jack's disguised workshop."

"You should see the inside," Dave said. "The detritus is a facade, the building behind it is modern and incredible. I got inside the workshop and garage yesterday morning and your Uncle Jack has got a dozen cars stored in there, from antiques to sports cars, but the most interesting is a fully restored 1935 Duesenberg SSJ Coupe. It's gorgeous, and Auntie D said the actor who played Rhett Butler in *Gone With The Wind* owned one."

"Clark Gable?"

"That's the guy," he exclaimed like he was hollering 'Eureka!' and he straightened up and looked at her, a broad grin on his face. "You know that I tried all afternoon to remember that name yesterday? Thank you."

She smiled across at him. Dave enjoyed how the corners of her eyes crinkled and her dimples protruded when she *really* smiled. So often Cindy would paste a smile on her face to fit the occasion, but when she really smiled, her entire face beamed. Dave could feel something more compelling than gravity pulling at him in that moment, but because he couldn't be certain Cindy felt the same grip, he resisted the impulse it brought. Cindy broke the moment by looking back toward the house and shuffling her feet. She had felt it too.

"I'm starved," she said as she nearly bounced from the railing. "You guys have anything but beer in the fridge?"

She walked back into the bedroom. Dave watched her go. He then turned and looked out over the expanse of nature and smiled. The first drops of rain began to fall from the swirling clouds and were quickly followed by more. A flash of lightning struck far off to the southwest and was followed by a clap of thunder seconds later. By the time Dave closed the bedroom doors, a downpour was washing the dust from Vacherie.

There are two types of weather I hate sitting surveillance in: one is in the freezing cold, the other is during Louisiana thunderstorms. The only good thing about sitting in the rain is that I'm able to run the engine without attracting too much attention to myself and can have some air conditioning and defogging going. The scattered white clouds of that morning's horizon had become a solid overcast of puffy gray and moments ago, it had begun dumping rain. I rolled up the windows, started the engine and turned on the air conditioning as the vehicle had quickly became both stifling and humid.

There had been no comings or goings at the plantation house behind the hedge. Either the people I was hoping to find there had already gone out for the day in this phantom Escalade, or they were staying comfortable and dry inside. I considered my options, and the limits of my instructions. Sandy's suggestion fell neatly into the mix. As of that moment, I was merely hired to confirm the location of a vehicle and a pair of college-aged kids. I really had nothing more to do until the scope of my contract was expanded, so perhaps it was indeed time to dust off John Portman and move this thing along. In my car I carry a western hat to complete the persona, and I've discovered if I'm distracting enough with it, such as moving it around while I talked, using it for a pointer, things like that, most people had a hard time recognizing me when they saw me again as William Langdon. Unfortunately, I only had a baseball cap with a name and logo of my old bar on Grand Cayman in Sandy's Bravada, and I doubted that would work well as a tool of distraction for John Portman of Houston, Texas.

I glanced at the radio's clock. It was nearly two-thirty, my goal of being home by three was gone with the rain, so to speak, and so I put Sandy's Bravada into gear and rolled back onto the roadway which was giving off vapor as the first rain cooled the asphalt. I drove the several hundred yards up to the opening in the hedge and rehearsed a few reasons why I, I mean, John Portman was stopping by. Had Sandy been home, she would have pulled all sorts of ancillary information about the property for me by now, as well as traced back the license numbers of both the Mustang and the Escalade. I'd be sitting on a binder of printed pages or a plethora of notes from which I could shake loose an excuse for a big Texan standing at someone's door in the middle of rural Louisiana.

As I turned into the gap and crunched along the drive in a downpour with the wipers slapping water from the windshield, I still had no idea why John Portman had dropped in on total strangers. The Mustang hadn't moved since I had confirmed the ID on it earlier, but I already knew that. Once inside the hedge, I was granted a broader look of the front grounds, much of which had been shaded from view by two giant oak trees, and the far side of the house. There were no other cars that I could spot anywhere. I pulled the Bravada alongside the old Mustang and shut off the engine. With no solid excuse coming to mind for my being there, I opened the door and jogged along the pavers up onto the wide veranda and figured my keen wit would serve me well as it had many times before.

I was even more impressed with the restoration of the old plantation home a I came closer; money had obviously been no limitation to the owner. There were details I spotted which told me the place had been faithfully restored, but also had been brought into the twentieth century with security and technology. If that was all evident just by stepping onto the front porch, I wondered how interesting the interior might be.

I rang the doorbell rather than operate the ornate, antique, bronze clapper mounted to the center of the oversized double front door. As I waited for a response, I shifted my position so as to peer through one of the sidelights. A needlepointed curtain hung behind the glass, but I could still make out glimpses of the unlit interior hallway. From what I could see, the house was even more spectacular on the inside than out. I noted no movement, so I rang the bell again, and then saw a barefoot young man wearing shorts and a T-shirt exit a room toward the back right of the house and walk toward the front door. As he neared, a similarly dressed young woman with blonde hair pulled into a pony tail appeared at the doorway from which he had come. She held her right hand behind her back, in a manner which I'd find suspicious were I there as a cop.

The door opened. The young man standing in the opening was a couple inches shorter than me, perhaps six-foot-four, and well-built for the three-hundred pounds he probably carried. His face held a wariness, yet his body language, and how he widely opened the door revealed just the opposite, perhaps a cross between confidence and trust. The girl down the hallway was short and chubby, perhaps five-five or so, maybe pushing one-seventy. The look on her face displayed no trust and bordered on the lower limits of fear. Her right hand remained tucked into the small of her back.

A purpose for my standing there appeared in my brain.

"Howdy," I said when no verbalized greeting was offered by the young man. "I hate to be botherin' you good folks on such a day, but I thought y'all was open ever' day of the year, come rain or shine; 'cept Christmas, of course."

The man cocked his head, the wariness morphing to confusion. I stepped onto the threshold, the woman down the hall backed against the doorway, her eyes flashed a moment of alarm.

"Open?" the young man said.

"Yeah, for tours and such," I said. "I never do this kinda thing on my own, you know, but the missus said, 'John, if you can't go golfing today, why don't you just go out and have you a look around.' So, that's what I'm doing, having me a look around." I turned in the portal and pointed out to two oak trees. "You know, son, those are some perty decent specimens of red oak trees, but I surely would be embarrassed were I to call that area between 'em an alley. Though that row of bushes you folks got out front is somethin' we don't see ever' day in Texas."

A relieved smile came to the young man's face.

"Are you looking for Oak Alley? The tourist place?"

"Sure am, son," I said with a big grin, then cocked an eye to him. "Are you sayin' I done knocked at the wrong door? Aw, shoot, I am sorry." I nodded to the young woman, a gesture which would have been much more effective for John Portman had I my western hat to tip. "Ma'am."

The young man took a step forward, the shift in personal space effectively backed me out of the doorway and onto the porch. I could see the woman down the hall relax and then go back into the room from which they had both come.

"What you want to do is go a mile or so down the road in that direction," he said pointing off to the east. "You'll see a parking lot entrance before you get to the house itself. They've got a set of oak trees formed up into two rows in between which you'd be proud to call an alley, even by Texas standards."

"Well, I'm much obliged," I said, again wishing for my hat, but instead offering my hand. "John Portman, Houston. Texas."

He shook my hand. Strong grip. Honest eyes looking back at me.

"Dave, Mr. Portman," he said.

"Harvard, I take it," I said, reading his T-shirt. "You play football for them?"

He smiled.

"Yes, sir," Dave said, a proud smile coming to his face. "Last season for me ended in November, though; I graduate this spring. I was an offensive tackle. Started all four years."

"Well, ain't that somethin'," I said. "I was more a basketball type, played forward for A&M. Good school. Not Ivy League, like y'all, but still done all right by me."

He shifted his feet. My welcome was wearing thin, even with the good cheer.

"Okay, Dave," I said, turning to go. "Please apologize to your wife for me bustin' in on y'all."

"Oh, Cindy's not my wife; just a friend."

I winked at him and leaned forward a bit.

"Good to have cute friends like that, eh" I said moving toward the steps. "All right, bye, now. Y'all have a wonderful day."

I walked off the porch and into the pouring rain. When I had reentered the shelter of the Bravada and turned to look, I saw he had already gone back inside and had closed the front door. From their initial wariness, I assumed he had already locked it and was now arming the alarm system. Behind the sidelight curtain, I saw the shadows change as the boy peered out at me. I sat for a moment and wondered what could cause such suspicious behavior exhibited by the pair, and what the girl had been holding behind her back. A knife? A gun? These kids weren't panicked, but they obviously knew someone was looking for them, and that thought was of some concern. I turned the ignition, put the car into reverse just to get a longer look at the Mustang, then drove out to the main road, where I turned right toward Oak Alley just in case they were still watching. Whether the lost tourist ruse held up, I'd never know, but this whole case certainly contained much more interest and elicited many more questions now that I'd met the subjects and witnessed their demeanor.

Approaching the real Oak Alley's parking lot, a place I had been several times before, I reached for my cell phone and dialed the client.

Tom briefed The Senator following the call from William Langdon. He informed him that the P.I. had indeed found Dave's Mustang and had for some reason made personal contact with Dave Saunders and the girl. There had been no mention of Dace, or the Escalade. Tom also relayed the questions William Langdon had expressed. He waited patiently on the line for direction, but just then The Senator was called to the floor for a vote on one of his pet Bills and Tom was told he'd have to wait a while longer to further the matters at hand.

Cindy was shaking when she put the knife back into the butcher's block. Dave walked into the kitchen to find her near tears. He moved behind her, put his arms around her shoulders.

The Senator sat peacefully at his desk on the Senate floor. His legs were crossed and his hands were clasped in his lap. His piercing blue eyes were unfocused in thought as a junior senator from the state of Idaho prattled on in opposition to one of The Senator's Bills up now up for a cloture vote. His cloakroom count had this as an easy pass, but the other side was still allowed time to make one last appeal, weak as this one was. He sensed a presence and then felt a hand on his shoulder.

"Little pissant certainly enjoys the sound of his own voice, doesn't he?"

The senior senator from New York was currently bent over and whispering toward The Senator's ear. He was a longtime ally even though the two were from different sides of the aisle. Being from neighboring states, with much the same constituency base to be pandered to - apart from the upstate voters in the larger state - they had mutual interests and approached them pragmatically to get things done. The Senator just nodded at the comment, and then his eyes came to a focussed intensity upon the young colleague, who at that moment seemed to lose his point and stumbled to regain the argument. The Senator smiled.

"By the way," the New Yorker said. "How's Dace?"

"Dace? He's just fine. Why?"

"Because I heard from my daughter that he's not been back to school yet, and while I certainly can understand, given the accident, there have been some unusual rumors circulating around campus. A real doozy popped up today, in fact."

The Senator looked his friend from the other party in the eye.

"Rumors? What rumors?"

Tom's phone vibrated and he opened it. Before he could verbalize a hello, The Senator was speaking.

"Get the boys on a plane. Now." The Senator said. "This horse crap ends today."

The man was breathless, almost as agitated as Tom had ever heard him.

"I can do that," Tom said. "Just take a breath, Allard. Relax. You'll give yourself a heart attack. Tell me what happened."

"Get the boys moving," The Senator ordered. "Then call me back. Use the office line."

The phone went dead.

# Chapter Twenty-three

I sat parked in the Oak Alley parking lot, waiting for a return phone call in the pouring rain, the Bravada angled so I could at least keep an eye on the main road. The intervening subdivision and the rainfall effectively combined to block any possible view of the plantation house I had just left. I was beginning to stew; this was usually the point in a case that Sandy would step in to calm me down, but since I had just recently talked her off the ledge over stress at her folks' house, I didn't think it would be fair to add my irritation to her current burdens. After all, I wanted our baby to be born with a smile, instead of my perpetual furrowed brow. I have never liked working with an intermediary, so this waiting on further instructions to be relayed from someone I couldn't speak to firsthand was particularly grating on my nerves. My skin had begun to itch from the annoyance, but I was, so far, successfully fighting the urge to scratch.

I shifted in my seat. The next moment, my phone buzzed on the console, but when I picked it up to check the call, the screen indicated the caller ID had been blocked. Normally that meant telemarketer or some other type of loathsome undesirable on the other end of the line, but I picked it up anyway. I decided it was either going to be the call I was awaiting, or I'd get the chance to vent at some unsuspecting anonymous person. Either way, I figured I'd win, so I flipped open the phone and took the call.

"Mr. Langdon, this is Tom McDaniel," the caller said.

"Hello, Tom," I said. "I almost let you drift off to voicemail since the caller ID said blocked." Normally I wouldn't be so brazen with a client, but as I indicated a moment ago, something about this case was starting to make my skin itch. "What can you tell me? I'm sitting in the rain and I've already eaten my lunch *and* dinner and it's not even four o'clock."

"I'm calling from the client's home phone, Mr. Langdon, and, well, you said previously that you understood and respected our need for confidentiality. It's why I blocked the caller ID."

"That's fine, Tom," I said, only half meaning it. I really have no problem with giving someone my word about confidentiality, but I do have a problem when they don't trust me at my word. Tom's New York heritage, based upon the area code for his cell phone and putting aside his claimed Michigan roots, obviously contrasted with my Wisconsin upbringing and continuing values. Given how they treat each other up there and the fact this involves politics somehow, I could understand the distrust and added security. When you are a snake, and are surrounded by snakes, you operate like the rest of the world is just more snakes, but understanding that didn't mean I had to like what I inferred to be an affront to *my* ethics. "Do you have anything for me? By the way, you can feel free to call me, William. The Mr. Langdon thing makes me look around for my father when I hear it, and my father wasn't someone I often relished finding standing over my shoulder."

"Okay, William, it is," Tom said.

I could hear him relax a bit, and he gave a chuckle at the line. Not that I found the thought of my lurking father all that funny.

"Listen, William, I've spoken to the client and he wishes to bring in his own people on this one going forward. Um, now that we know the two kids and the car are there, well, we can bring this to conclusion ourselves." A pause. "By the way, you didn't mention the Escalade or seeing anyone else in the house when we spoke earlier. Is that correct?"

Something in his voice told me he was still playing games.

"No, I didn't mention the Escalade because I didn't find it at the location. Your instructions and photos only included two kids, a man and a woman, both of whom I did find, along with their Mustang." I paused. "You never mentioned another person of interest potentially being on the scene."

"Well, it really doesn't much matter," he said. "We were merely curious."

Okay, now the guy was outright lying to me.

"So, Mr. Langdon, I would imagine this means you're released."

"As you wish, Tom," I said. "We'll process the invoice and return the balance of the retainer with a full accounting within the next week. Is that acceptable?"

"No, no," he said. "Just go ahead and keep the balance for your trouble, mister...ah, William."

"I don't accept tips, Tom," I said. The guy was beginning to annoy me. "It's not how we work. An honest fee for an honest payment is how we do things."

"It's not a tip, William," he said, attempting to cajole. "Consider it a balance on account, if you wish. I'm certain we'll have some sort of additional need for your services in the future."

"Balance on account?" I said. Sandy was going to hate that, and I was still insulted. I never took a payoff in my life, and that's what this appeared to be. A 'thanks for your help, young man, now go away and don't look back'. I knew he wasn't going to back off on it, so rather than prolong the matter, I agreed and immediately felt slimy about how he must now perceive me. "All right, Tom, we'll keep things open until we settle accounts."

Something told me those words would come back to haunt me. Rather than argue the point on the phone, I'd just do what I had said I would initially, then close the case out and send him a check for his balance. Additionally, since he's succeeded in piquing my interest here, I just may do a bit of peeking over my shoulder, no charge.

We ended with some obligatory pleasantries which included an invitation to have a beer together someday which we both knew would never happen, and after we disconnected, I tossed the phone onto the passenger seat. I started the car, pulled out to the Great River Road for the drive back to New Orleans. I was over to the right at the end of Oak Alley's driveway, my blinker on and ready to go home when I paused for a moment.

Then I turned left.

Maybe I'd take that peek now, I thought.


"I'm exhausted," Ronnie said as she came in and dropped onto her bed without making eye contact. Her hair was wet.

She initially plopped down on the bed with her face toward the wall, then slowly turned to look at Ashley seated on the other bed, reading a book.

"Hi, Ash," she said sheepishly, then when she saw exactly what she expected in Ashley's glare, added: "Sorry, Ash, I fell asleep. We didn't leave the party until nearly dawn." She fluffed back her hair. "I took a shower in Gil's room."

Ashley dogeared a page and closed the book. She set it to her side on the comforter. She folded her hands on her lap.

"Your mother called," Ashley said. "She called my phone because yours keeps going directly to voicemail."

"My mother?" Ronnie said, her eyes going wide. "When? What did she want?"

"She wanted to talk to you. Duh." Ashley's eyes moved to the clock which was approaching five in the afternoon. "She called this morning, around ten."

"What did you tell her, Ash?"

"I told her you were in some guy's room you met a party last night letting him bang your brains out."

Ronnie sat up on the bed, her eyes showing alarm. Ashley's mouth slowly morphed into an evil grin.

"What do you think I told her?" Ashley said. "I told her your phone died and we needed to get you a new charger because you accidentally dropped the old one into the toilet. I told her you were fine, having a wonderful time, and that we were just on our way out for the day. I said I'd have you call her when we got back."

Ronnie exhaled a sigh.

"You think she bought it?" she asked.

"Why wouldn't she?" Ashley said. "I'm a good Catholic girl. I'll just have to add a couple of lies to my sins list on Ash Wednesday at Mass, but I know God will forgive me. That's the neat thing about being a Catholic, the absolution."

"That's only if you're truly sorry, in your heart," Ronnie said. "You can't fool a fellow Catholic, you know. We all know how the rules work."

Ashley shrugged her shoulders.

"Yeah, I guess." She paused. "So, Noodle Doodle, you had best think of something clean you and I were doing all afternoon and give your mom a call; and, by the way, taking a shower with Gilbert doesn't count as being clean." Then Ashley had another thought, and expressed it. "You know, your nickname for me is rapidly becoming much more appropriate for you."

"Diddle Brain?"

"Uh-huh, that's you," Ashley said slowly shaking her head, then picked up her book and began to read again. "Nothing but diddling on your brain."

Late in the afternoon, Dave and Cindy took the opportunity of a break in the rains and strolled across the lawn toward the old building out back. Dave pointed to the water soaked mounds of fire ant nests and told Cindy the story of how he had first met the old black woman who lived in the apartment on the faux barn's second floor. He couldn't remember if he had already told her the story. He had, but Cindy enjoyed hearing it again.

An hour earlier, Auntie D had come by the main house to check on the boys but had found only Dave up and about; Dace was still in his room, or so they assumed since they hadn't seen him yet and Dave hadn't bothered to check on his friend since he put him to bed early that morning right before finding Cindy asleep on the front porch.

Auntie D had smiled and shook hands with the young woman Dave had introduced merely as Cindy, then appended the status as his ex-girlfriend to the introduction. The old woman had only one question about the whereabouts of 'that other one' as she set about to collect several items from the pantry into a basket she had carried with her, then asked if the ex-couple would like to come to her place for dinner. His stomach was already growling despite the gathering of things they's munched for a late lunch, so it was an invitation Dave eagerly accepted for the two of them.

"This place looks even more dilapidated the closer you get," Cindy said.

"Before we go up, let me show you something really cool," Dave said. "Your Uncle Jack, I'm discovering, is a bit of an eccentric, but he certainly has good taste in cars. He must be rich as hell."

Cindy laughed.

"I don't know how rich hell is, Dave, but Uncle Jack has been said to have nearly as much money as God."

Dave's eyes grew wide to match the smile he'd been wearing since he had first laid eyes on Cindy curled up in the two chairs on the front porch early that morning.

"I'd like to meet him some day; your Uncle Jack, that is, and well, God, too, I suppose, but much, much further down the road," Dave said as he moved a small panel he had been shown by Auntie D the day earlier and inserted one of the three keys on the ring they had retrieved from the magnetic keeper stuck to the old, sugar boiling pot the day they had arrived. He pushed open the door which seemed to appear out of nowhere. "Entrez vous, mon cher," he said adding a small bow and sweeping arm motion.

Cindy took his fingers in hers and stepped into the garage like a princess into a ballroom; the lights came on automatically, adding a royal effect and revealing a meticulously clean and organized garage and workshop. Two rows of old and new cars glistened under the fluorescent lights. In front of each car was a portal to the outside, but Cindy hadn't noticed any evidence of them on the exterior walls of the barn.

"Wow, Dave," she said. "This *is* really cool."

Dave took her on the tour of the assembled automotive history, going from newest: a 1998 Ferrari convertible; to the oldest: an 1884 de Dion Bouton et Trepardoux Dos-a-Dos Steam Runabout. Dave told her that a similar Runabout had won the first known automobile race in 1887, achieving the blistering speed of 37 miles per hour. The tour was an event Dave obviously relished more than she, but Cindy enjoyed how talking about one of his cherished hobbies made him beam, so she smiled and maintained her interest which had truly waned shortly after the initial survey of the assembled collection. Cars, she knew, had always been a passion for Dave, ever since he was five and attended his first auto show with his dad. It was a story he had told her several times when they had dated. He took pride in his model collection and encyclopedic knowledge of everything on four wheels, even if he had made the most horrible of choices for his first car: the white and blue 1986 Mustang GT Liftback parked out front of the main house.

Her stomach let out a growl. Dave was going on about an old Mercedes Benz.

"I'm sorry, Dave," she said. "I guess I'm hungry. Wonder what Auntie D is going to make for us. You've been raving about everything she cooks or bakes since she invited us over, my mouth is watering and my stomach is getting restless."

"Okay, okay, Cindy," he said, "but, do you understand this car, a 1930 Mercedes Benz Nurburg 460 was the first Popemobile? The first. For Pope Pius XI, I think, presented by Mercedes as a gift to the Pontiff himself. There are photos of the event."

"This very car?" she asked, her hunger momentarily quelled by a new historical curiosity.

"Um, no, I mean, probably not," Dave said. "I would think the real one is stored somewhere in the Vatican; but this is exactly the same, a precise duplicate 1930 Nurburg 460, right down to the pin-striping." His eyes went from her to the car several times as the thought struck him. "Unless you think your Uncle Jack has that kind of pull."

She just shrugged.

Dave's face always lit when he talked about the things in life most important to him, and Cindy smiled. She normally wasn't much impressed by the stuff other people thought was cool, but something in Dave's boyish grin and unbridled enthusiasm always touched her heart. She posed another question, which set him telling his stories for another ten minutes while she did the best she could to keep her stomach quiet. When he was done speaking and almost breathless, he escorted her back outside.

"Thank you for at least pretending to be interested, Cindy," Dave said, as he replaced the small panel after locking the door. "It meant a lot."

"You noticed?" she said, her face doing one of its rare blushes.

"Yeah," he said. "I know you better than you think, Cindy." He turned toward the backside of the shed.

She followed a few steps behind him.

"I just want to check on the Escalade," he said over his shoulder. I think I forgot to lock it and must have left the keys inside this morning when we got back because they weren't in my pocket when I checked after we got up. When we got back here from New Orleans, I was too busy getting Dace out before he puked all over my interior or fell and hurt himself, that I must have just forgot."

They rounded the corner of the building. Dave stopped, then ran around to the other side, thinking perhaps he had been more drunk than he had thought.

"Darn it," he said, then he ran past Cindy. "Wait here."

He ran toward the main house, not dodging the anthills, but not lighting upon any of them long enough to give the ants a chance to defend the nest. Cindy watched him jump up the three steps in one bound, fling open the screen door and push into the house. A minute later, he walked back out onto the back porch with a slumped posture and a dispirited look on his face that Cindy could discern from the distance. He plodded across the lawn, his footsteps a bit more carefully placed at the slower pace. His hands were in the pockets of his jeans, his head down, and his face carrying an expression best described as hangdog.

"He's gone," Dave said, his unfocused eyes moving from side to side along the grass as he thought. "Dace is gone."

"He took your car?" Cindy said, her hands moving to her hips as she slowly shook her head. She disliked Dace now even more than she had, were that possible. "Without asking? Where do you think he went?"

Dave's eyes settled and then raised to focus upon her.

"I have no idea," he said. "I hope he's okay."

Cindy's lips pursed as she contained her next words for a moment of consideration intended to forestall the emotional explosion she felt percolating. She began to count to five in her head, only made it to three.

"Jesus, Dave," she said as she threw her hands in the air. "That asshole steals your car, takes off while he's probably still drunk, and you hope *he's* okay? What about your feelings? What about your rights? Dace Lamoureux is a self-absorbed asshole. He always has been. I'm sorry, Dave, I know he's your best friend, but dammit. You've got to get over this puppy-like fascination you have with this guy." She crossed her arms defiantly, stood her ground as he paced anxiously. "I think we should call the police. Maybe a night or two in jail will sober this jerk to reality, although I truly doubt it. More likely, he'll just call senator daddy and before you know it they'll be serving him tea and crumpets in the Police Chief's office."

Her eyes dared him to contradict her.

She waited. He thought, then made a decision.

"Let's go up to Auntie D's," he said finally. "She's waiting on us, and besides, you're hungry." He smiled weakly.

Cindy took his hand in hers and they walked around to the door leading to Auntie D's apartment.

"What am I going to do with you, Dave Saunders?" Cindy asked while slowly shaking her head and looking up at him.

"I don't know, Cindy," he said.  A few steps later, he added: "Maybe I'm just that last sucker people often talk about, but I'm going to give Dace another chance."

Dave squeezed her soft, warm hand with his.  She squeezed back.

In my opinion, there are two professions which require a person be possessed of a natural curiosity to perform at an exceptional level in the job.  One is a reporter.  The other is a cop.  I never could have been a reporter; my English grades were nothing spectacular in high school and I never went very far in college.  I couldn't turn a phrase on paper to save my life, although skill at firing verbal witticisms are another matter.  Besides, the idea of following around and pandering to the world's movers and shakers, allowing them to make the news while I simply sat on the sidelines and then told others about what had happened never appealed to me.  I am much more happy being a part of the action, even to be the subject of a news story every now and again.

I also have a strong sense of justice, and not just as in the sense of right and wrong.  To me, *justice* is a much more expansive term; it involves not only the settling of the right versus wrong issue, but brings to bear the appropriate consequences.  As a cop, and now as a different type of P.I., I have always believed my role was to assist Justice in her endeavors.  Sure, being a *normal* P.I. is much more akin to a reporter's job and less the cop's when you get right down to it, but as I said, I'm a different type of P.I.  The cop in me won't allow the P.I. I am to just observe and report to a client.  When my dander is ruffled or my abundant curiosity aroused, I tend to sometimes overstep my boundaries in the pursuit of justice.  Maybe it's a fault, but I don't see it that way; and neither do most of my clients.  I wasn't so sure how Tom would feel, but that wasn't my concern at the moment.  I had been fired, after all.

Everyone who knows us, believes Sandy plays the role of my foundation, and largely, they are correct.  She often counsels me on how she sees a case unfolding and is never shy in giving me her sense of the client.  But, while Sandy often arrives at her conclusions quickly, coming to my own judgment often takes a bit more time.  Once I do, however, the action will follow rapidly; it's what Teddy calls my 'long match, short fuse' problem.  I think it's just how I'm wired.

I had found a place further upriver to perch on the levee which gave me a complete view of the compound using regular field binoculars.  I had been up there for a couple of hours and had seen very little activity.  First, an old, black woman had appeared from the backside of a ramshackle barn and walked to and from the main house carrying a basket which had been filled with items on the return trip.  Then, an hour or so later, the two kids had exited the house and walked to the barn.  They had opened a door on the side closest to me, gone inside for a while, come out, then walked around the side facing toward the swamp. The boy had run back into the house alone, then walked slowly out again a minute later. The pair had spoken for a while, then hand-in-hand walked around the east side of the building and had disappeared for over an hour now. Obviously, there was an entry on that side I couldn't observe from my current position.

It was late in the day with sunset rapidly approaching. My cooler was nearly empty, my stomach was growling, and my curiosity was growing. What was in that building, I wondered. The door the kids had accessed had appeared ultramodern when they opened it, and lights went on inside automatically when they had entered. If there was some kind of operation going on inside, they certainly had the building camouflaged well. I wondered if it could be some kind of drug lab. That explanation would make some sense of the subterfuge and secrecy of my client if they suspected their politically connected kids were involved in something illegal down in Louisiana. It wouldn't be the first time something like that had happened.

I brought my field binoculars up to my eyes again. The last of the sun had begun peeping out below the clouds in the western sky as the rain clouds had moved east. The on-and-off drizzle of the last hour or so had become more of a hanging mist. There was a feeling of drying and cooling in the air. February in Louisiana. I twisted the focus on the binoculars, ran the wipers a single pass to clear the windshield. In the changing light and shadows, I thought I could see something in the lawn near where the pair of kids had been standing just before the boy had run back into the house. I returned the binoculars to the passenger seat, then stepped out onto the gravel levee service road and moved around to the back of the Bravada to set up the SkyHawk 9600 again. Focusing in, I definitely saw there was something there, in the grass. Depressions. Tire tracks from the look of them, looping back on themselves as if a vehicle had done a one-eighty behind the barn. I could see no mud mixed into the fresh depressions, which meant whatever had been back there had left today, but before the rain had started.

"I bet that's where the Escalade was," I said to nobody.

I thought about it. There was little chance I could have seen that area behind the barn from my first position on the levee near the S-turn, and no chance I could view the area while I was on the property or parked hugging the hedge to the west.

"So there *is* at least one other person there," I said.

Standing in the coming darkness, under a cooling mist, I ticked off what I knew and what I suspected. That's why Tom had asked me if I had seen a second man. He knows exactly who was down there, or at least he suspected it. The question was, what would three presumably rich kids from the northeast be doing in rural Louisiana in a place like this, with that disguised building in the back? Who was the *real* client in this? The parents of one of the kids made the most sense. Of course, this contact and case had all begun as a referral from the political party planning the August project later in the year; or, so Tom had said. Politically connected kids? Is that the reason for the covert tactics and confidentiality concerns? What was going to happen next with 'their own people' coming in on this? Tom had seemed far too eager to get me to back off the case once I confirmed the kids were there. My cop senses had been correct in telling me not to just pick up and leave when Tom had told me the client was sending in his own people. I glanced at my cell phone for the time. It would be dark soon, and I silently cursed my natural curiosity because I was now obviously going to be spending my night doing a look-see on this property rather than in my recliner watching basketball on the big screen.

My stomach growled again and I wondered what Vacherie might have for places I could grab some food and restock my water. I packed up the SkyHawk and drove down off the levee. I thought I had seen a small bar in town. As I drove past the gap in the hedgerow, I slowed, saw nothing new in the front yard, and continued down the road.

Dace awoke in the back seat of the Escalade. The rain had stopped in the city of New Orleans and darkness was approaching. The pint of tequila he had bought for a bit of hair of the dog lay drained on the floor next to the long-barreled revolver he had taken off John Deere and Evinrude several nights ago. He smiled as he saw it and remembered the look on their faces when they discovered he had outwitted them again by flattening their tires outside of Rupe's bar. The buck knife he had used for the deed was in his pocket, and in a paper bag from Wal-Mart on the passenger seat, was a box of five hundred .22 caliber long rifle bullets to restock the pistol. He pulled himself up in the seat. He felt hot and sticky, his mouth was dry and his head pounded. He found the bottle of Tylenol next to the box of bullets in the Wal-Mart bag and he twisted off the top and withdrew four caplets which he swallowed dry. His eyes focused outside the window and slowly panned across the puddle-strewn, gravel lot which provided the employee parking for the adjacent warehouses and container loading facility and had seemed a reasonable place to stop that morning for some sleep.

He stretched and yawned, then reached for the empty tequila bottle, screwed off the top and drained the remaining drops. The amber liquid burned his tongue, but didn't make it to his parched throat. He tossed the bottle out the window, it splashed into a nearby puddle, then floated to the far side.

"Message in a bottle," Dace said as his stare unfocused. "Let me see. What's the message I'd write? And who would find it in time?"

He opened the door, pulled himself out of the back seat, ran his fingers through his hair as he stood outside the Escalade. He felt as if he needed a shower and understood he really should get himself something to eat, but there were other desires pulling at him. He looked around, saw nothing of interest, tucked the pistol into the back of his pants, then set off walking.

Libby returned with Mary Rose shortly after Tom had hung up for the third time that day with The Senator. Caroline had put a pot roast into the crock pot earlier, had added carrots and potatoes shortly after lunch, and now the full, rich aromas were carrying throughout the house, even finding their way under the door into Tom's room on the second floor. Tom heard Mary Rose's unmistakeable bounding coming up the stairs, then traced her progress with his eyes on the ceiling as she ran to her room on the floor above. The girl had the limitless energy of a child, yet the body of a full-grown woman. He smiled.

In between the aborted or abbreviated calls with The Senator, passing orders to Travis and Rudy, dealing with the P.I. in Louisiana, and handling some early election year issues for a couple of other clients, Tom had surprisingly been able to do a great deal of thinking over how and what he was he going to say to Libby when she arrived home. He had, over the last several days, dealt with her erratic schedule, accepted her quick departing comments on their face, and generally ignored her innuendos. She had been in control. He had decided when they spoke the next time, however, it would be on his timetable and under his rules. Following dinner would be the perfect moment, he had decided earlier; when Caroline was helping Mary Rose get bathed and ready for bed. He envisioned himself and Libby alone in the dining room, which was a much more quiet and private room than the breakfast nook where anyone could overhear their discussion. It's why he had asked Caroline to set places in there for dinner, instead of the nook where the family would traditionally take most of its routine meals, especially when The Senator was away.

Tom had it all worked out, even with all the distractions of the day. He even had refined and rehearsed his opening line to her. He was going to extend his hand across the corner of the table and cup hers. He wanted to look directly into Libby's eyes when he spoke the words. Then he would say...

A soft knock came upon his closed door.

"Tom?" she said. "May I speak with you?"

Tom surveyed the room, quickly, stood, checked himself in the mirror.

"Certainly, Libby, please come in."

She opened the door and stood there a moment, then entered, closed the door, mostly, but left it unlatched. Her eyes moved around the room.

"You know, Tom, you really should ask Caroline to come in here and change the bedding, straighten up, clean the bathroom, run a vacuum around, and do your laundry. You've been here over a week now, and this is beginning to look a bit like a dorm room." She sniffed, wrinkled her nose. "It's starting to smell like one, too, frankly."

She took a seat on a chair across from the bed. She crossed her legs. Her skirt covered her knees. She wore heels that were low, sensible, and she still wore hose, going a bit against the convention of modern feminism. Tom attributed that to Libby's sense of style and womanhood. Libby had not shared most of the radical feminist views often espoused by her husband's political party, especially when it came to matters of femininity and long-established gender roles. She folded her hands in her lap.

"Have you spoken to Allard since I left?" she asked.

Her eyes looked directly at him. Her mask was one of contented satisfaction.

Tom brought her up to date on the progress they'd made in tracking down Dace and told her they hoped to reach the boy in the next several hours. He didn't mention that Travis and Rudy had already been dispatched to bring him home, in whatever condition, by whatever means. He also didn't tell her, that the home they were instructed to bring the boy back to was in McClean, not in New London; nor did he mention the rumors swirling around Harvard's campus, and that some of them were making their way to parents, including the honorable gentleman from the great state of New York.

She seemed to take it all in with the same level of distracted interest as if she were watching a movie she had seen several times before. When he was finished, she spoke succinctly.

"Thank you, Tom. I imagine his father is the best one to handle this all," she said, and she rose from the chair and began to leave.

"Libby, I have something to ask you," he said.

She stopped at the doorway, her hand on the knob, her back to him. She waited, but said nothing. He admired her silhouette for an instant, silently wondered if she still possessed the same athletic firmness to her body she had twenty-five years ago, then dismissed the thought as unimportant to the issue at hand.

"Libby," he said. "You've been making cryptic remarks about Dace's father should this, and Dace's father should that, for days now."

She peered at him over her unturned shoulder. Her eyes were like closed gates in a castle: unchallenging, yet uninviting.

"Cryptic?" she said. "I thought I have been making myself quite clear, Tom."

She turned her head back, opened the door wide.

"Libby," Tom said, his tone low with the door no longer containing their conversation. "Dace's father..."

He saw her hand tighten on the doorknob, her soft, pink fingers going white. She remained silent. Waited.

"Am I to understand that I'm the boy's father? That you haven't told me for all these years and now want me to know for some unfathomable purpose?"

He noticed her hand relax, saw her head slowly drop forward. When she turned this time, her eyes were glistening just as they sometimes would during their four-year affair, when guilt and remorse would invade her soul, and confusion would spear her heart.

She walked out of the room without saying another word, leaving him standing there, the question answered, but really not. He thought of following her into the hall, grabbing her by the shoulders and turning her, forcing her to look him in the eye and make her tell him outright, but his courage could not be stirred to the moment. Rather, he sat on the edge of the bed and hung his head.

Travis and Rudy arrived at Louis Armstrong International Airport on the outskirts of New Orleans as full darkness fell upon that Monday. There had been no amazing sunset which preceded it, no extended, magical twilight, just the sudden falling of darkness, like a heavy curtain dropping across a glowing window. Their private jet, a larger Gulfstream that trip, taxied to the general aviation ramp and parked at the direction of a young black man holding orange-tipped flashlights.

The attendant maneuvered the rented black SUV next to the aircraft as the engines were spooling down; the Lincoln Navigator's brilliant, blue-white, xenon lights piercing the darkness. Their green, military-style duffles were offloaded from the Gulfstream's cargo compartment under the tail and placed into the back of the vehicle. They each carried their own overnight bags from inside the cabin. Travis came down the steps with a nylon laptop case slung over his shoulder. Rudy carried a small, black, leather medical bag.

The final instructions to the crew were to remain on twenty-four hour standby with a one hour notice to depart. Travis drove out of the airport area, then navigated to highway 48 heading west, crossed the Mississippi at the 310 bridge and picked up the Great River Road west to Vacherie. Neither he nor Rudy did much talking on the drive; they had discussed every foreseeable contingency on the plane and now had their thoughts focused on the mission. Rudy turned on the radio and found a Jazz station.

After a greasy cheeseburger and surprisingly great French fries and a beer or two to wash it all down with at the little corner bar in Vacherie, I drove back toward the plantation house. I slowed going past the gap in the hedgerow and took a quick glimpse up the driveway. The main house was completely dark, save a few landscaping lamps near the walk to the front porch. The Mustang was in the same spot. I kept driving, and eventually found the far end of the hedgerow about a mile west of the plantation home. The other end I had pegged at about a mile east, so crossing onto the property by foot was about an even shot either way. Of course, as dark as the night was under the remaining cloud cover, I concluded I could probably just walk in the driveway opening without being seen, especially dressed in all black at a distance of nearly two-hundred yards. The problem was I didn't know what type of security they may have on the main point of entry whereas there are very few people, and that includes even the most paranoid of types, who will place sensors out a mile from their monitored center point.

Even given its grandiose name, the Great River Road was not anyone's idea of a busy thoroughfare during the day, and after all the locals got home from work and the tourists had fled the countryside for New Orleans or Baton Rouge, the nighttime traffic on the highway was even more sparse. It's for that reason that I felt fairly comfortable stripping down and changing into my blackout clothes at the road's edge. I had earlier decided to take a closer look at things on the property, mainly out of that pesky natural curiosity; and while being done out in all black from head to toe, including face paint wouldn't exactly transform my six-foot-six, barrel-chested frame into the profile of a wiry ninja, it would keep me from lighting up the windows like Jason Voorhees in goalie mask when I peeped inside. A smile came to my face when I recalled how my father-in-law classified my work as paid window peeping. That night, I guess he'd be correct.

The only equipment I decided I would need to carry on my little recon mission was a compact set of night vision goggles which also can detect most types of security lasers used for trip beams. Once I was dressed, I tucked Willie into the small of my back, and Sam I strapped to my ankle. For those of you who may not already know, Willie is what I named my 10mm SIG Sauer semiautomatic, and Sam is my .38 snub-nose revolver backup. I really *like* Willie, it's light, smooth, reliable, and has successfully retrieved my ass from some fairly sticky situations over the years, but I have come to *love* Sam, because Sam has saved my life. Those are some great stories, but best reserved for another time. I truly didn't expect any trouble on that easy recon outing, but as my dear wife reminded me earlier, the simple missions are sometimes the ones when trouble likes to come calling. Last, I slipped on a pair of black gloves; no sense leaving my fingerprints anywhere if the place turns out to be a crime scene later on.

I had Sandy's new ride parked well off the road, snugged up to the hedge. I locked up the Bravada and took one last look around. Then, as a precautionary afterthought, I unlocked the driver's door and retrieved a leather wallet from the center console storage where I had left the rest of my valuables, flipped it open and set it in plain sight on the dash. If anyone looked closely, they'd see it was a Chicago Police Detective's shield which I had never turned in when I took the early retirement deal after the media brouhaha over the warehouse shootings, but I was playing the odds that any locals bent on trashing or looting the SUV wouldn't look that close and just might think twice when they saw the flash of gold in the window. I relocked the car, tucked the keys inside the rear bumper and set off around the end of the hedgerow.

I crouched down just inside the property. I was now officially trespassing. Call the newspapers. I pulled my night vision goggles down into position, and scanned for laser trips. Seeing none, I began my walk, keeping close to the backside of the hedge. I hoped they didn't have dogs; many a drug operation had pit bulls or other surly and territorial types set to freely roam the place, especially after dark. I had seen no evidence of dog keeping, but reminded myself the estate was a fairly large place. I scanned the horizon for angry, bright eyes coming in my direction, but saw none.

The field off to my right was planted in soybeans, and the furrows were relatively shallow should I have to make an excursion that direction. The day's rain had saturated the ground and the mud would make walking - or running - tedious in the field, but along the backside of the hedge, just like on the road side, was a reasonably cared-for width of grass. Trekking onto the property was like taking an evening stroll around the neighborhood, only in black face and really large ninja clothes.

I still saw no lights on inside the house, although I did see a low, shimmering light coming from an upstairs window in the back building. The more I thought about it, I was certain that's where the old black woman probably lived. Not a bad cover if you're brewing meth in the shop below, I thought.

About a half mile along, I again stopped, crouched, and used the night goggles to sweep the area ahead. Nothing. The soybeans ran all the way to within about two hundred yards of the house, where lawn took over. I guessed that area would be the most likely for trespasser monitoring, so I planned to check the landscape well and tread more carefully from that point on. Did I mention that I hoped they didn't have dogs? I hate guard dogs. Out there in the open, along that massive, impenetrable hedgerow, I would be extremely vulnerable. With increasing age and decreasing day-to-day physical activity, there was also no way I could outrun any breed - save perhaps a Chihuahua, however, most people don't find them very useful guard types. In addition, my normal ace-in-the-hole card, Teddy, wasn't there, rendering moot the longstanding jibe between us of: 'I don't have to outrun the dogs, I just have to outrun you.'

Unexpectedly, the breeze started to pick up, and the lingering, moist stagnancy began to be swirled by cooler, dryer air coming down from the north. The increasing wind began rustling the branches of the oaks in the front yard and cascaded over the top of the hedge. Even the maturing soybean plants began dancing. For someone approaching an unknown target by stealth, that type of noise and natural movement enhanced the chances of moving in and out without detection. People inside the buildings tended to write off any alarms or unusual noises, including creaking floorboards on the porches as being the result of the wind. I picked up the pace a bit.

Dace made his way along Prytania Street. In the distance, he could hear the raucous cheers of crowds blended with the clashing, jazzed-up music of several marching bands of yet another Mardi Gras parade over on St. Charles Avenue headed downtown, but Prytania Street, apart from the occasional car passing by, was dark, quiet, and nearly deserted. He had been walking the streets of the city's south side for hours, and wasn't even certain then where he was, or how he'd get back to the Escalade. During his exploration, when he had been thirsty, he found a liquor or convenience store along his meanderings and bought another pint of tequila or an aptly named refreshment called Smirnoff Ice. When he had been hungry, he stopped in at a Popeye's chicken joint. The heat and humidity of the rainy day had given way to refreshing cool and dry air, and a few minutes ago, the wind had picked up. He tossed the hood of his sweatshirt up over his head, took another swig from his bagged bottle. He winced: tequila.

He wasn't certain as to the time, and the combination of alcohol and weariness made even the thought of looking at his watch too much to consider. What did it matter, anyway? Time was just an arbitrary measurement of the span between then and now, or now and when, wasn't it? Besides, petty clerks concerned themselves with, and recorded the time for the purposes of history, he and his family crafted the history. He smiled at the irony of finally discerning with approaching lucidity his importance to the world, and what a wonder to have it happen first when glimpsed through the fog of alcohol, something he had so long avoided. He was a Lamoureux, he could do anything he wanted.

His vision was beginning to blur, and his strides had become leaden and growingly uncertain. He was beyond tired. He was exhausted. His emotions were worn thin by all the thinking he'd been doing while distilling his twenty-one years on this planet into the basest of human emotions: a white-hot rage which pulsed through him with his every step. He felt the pistol against his back, tucked into the waistline of his jeans.

He was just aching for the wrong person to say the wrong thing or cross his path in the wrong direction. He took another swig, emoted another wince, and kept walking.

Auntie D sat silently in her rocking chair, her hands were folded in her lap. The old woman's eyes were soft and attentive, as Dave and Cindy, seated on a large, rag rug in the center of her living room, spoke and debated and interacted. The focus of their discussion was Dace Lamoureux, and had not strayed too far afield over the past several hours, before, during, and after dinner. Auntie D said nothing which would either fuel or dampen the debate going on between the two young people; her face remained noncommittal and impassive, yet she was fully engaged. Finally, she could take it no longer.

"Enough," Auntie D said, stopping in mid-rock and slapping her hands on the arm rests of her chair. When she had their wide-eyed attention, she pointed her finger at each of them. "You two have bigger things to do in this life than to waste your time focusing on that boy. Y'all are young; your whole life is waitin' for ya. Yet y'all spend so much time and energy on this other one. He ain't worth a second of it." Her last words came out almost as a spit at the evil she saw, then her eyes moved deliberately to each of them ensuring her point had hit home. "He ain't worth it, children, and don't go frettin' about him, neither. That boy love hisself so much, he don't need nobody else lovin' him or fussin' over him. He gonna come to no good, that one, and you best be no place near him when it happen or he gonna take you down wit' him. Where'er he be tonight, I garn'tee he ain't wastin' his time worryin' 'bout the likes of you."

Her agitation and the abrupt forcefulness of her words shocked them both and their mouths hung agape as she went on.

"He a bad seed. Y'all know what a bad seed is?"

They both nodded; they had each read William March's novel and seen the namesake movies.

"Now, no ways I can tell if'n he been made that way o'er the years, or if'n he come outta his mama that way. Sometimes nobody can tell. It don't matter nohow, do it? He be what he be."

They each slowly shook their head.

I was about to cross the barrier between farmland and landscaping after surveying the remaining ground with my night vision goggles, when the whole world exploded into a fireball in my eyes.

"Dammit," I said, ripping the goggles from my head and tumbling from my crouch onto my butt.

I scrambled to my knees. It took several seconds before my regular vision returned, and when it did, I watched a black SUV slide into the drive, its xenon head lights piercing the darkness, then immediately extinguish as the vehicle continued the two hundred yards to the house and parked next to the Mustang.

I picked my goggles off the ground and placed them back onto my head and surveyed the new arrivals. There were two men inside the vehicle, big guys, my size or better. They appeared to be having a conversation in the now parked car. I wondered if these two were the 'client's own people' that Tom had spoken of, and if so, why the semi-stealthy approach? If they weren't the client's people, this could add an interesting dimension to the puzzle, I thought. It had been a number of years since I had been involved with drug types as a narcotics cop in Chicago, but I still remembered how they behaved.

We were separated by about three-hundred yards point-to-point, and they continued to sit in the vehicle, so I decided to close the distance, moving low and fast while still hugging the hedge. There was no way they could pick me up visually, unless they, too, had night vision and I was watching closely for that as I moved along. Because the hedgerow ran along the road, when I was even with them on an east-west line, I was still about two-hundred yards from them on the north-south axis. Using one of the big oak trees as a shield between them and me, I closed three-quarters of that distance. Moving any closer would have meant having nothing as a visual screen, and since the human eye is sensitized to motion, even in the darkness, I wasn't quite ready to risk crossing open terrain until I knew who these guys were and what they were doing. I went prone and slithered - as well as this body can slither - behind one of the tree's aboveground roots, and watched.

As I lay there and scanned the open area between us, I noticed something cylindrical lying about fifty feet away, in the grass on the other side of the drive. I increased the magnification setting on the goggles, smiled to myself as I recognized the familiar logo of a Dixie beer can, this one still attached to the six-pack rings. The smile quickly faded when I spotted the bullet holes.

"No Escalade," Rudy said, "and no lights in the house. Think they've gone out?"

Travis looked at his watch. It was just past eight.

"Unless they turned in really early." Travis peered out at the house. "Of course, they could have parked the Escalade around back."

"Only one drive," Rudy said. "Ends here."

Travis looked out the corner of his eye at his partner, but said nothing. He depressed the button on the dash to override the automatic illumination function of the interior lights when the doors were opened, then unlatched and slowly pushed open his door.

"Only one way to find out," Travis said as he stepped onto the driveway. "Let's take a look around."


From my position, I watched the pair exit the vehicle then quietly close the doors; acting in a way that I'd still classify as semi-stealthy. The men were dressed similarly, in regular street clothes: dress slacks, button down shirts open at the collars, loafers, and sports jackets. Compared to me in black ninja outfit, semi-stealthy. It's not as if they seemed concerned about being spotted by the people in the house because their monster SUV parked right out front would be hard to miss by anyone looking. They clearly were just not wanting to be spotted too early. They stood motionless for several moments, communicated by hand signals before splitting up, one circling the house to the east, the other to the west. They walked in the grass, not on the veranda, and they moved with the discipline and precision which indicated they had either been through police or military training.

Once they had moved out of sight, I left the shelter of the oak tree root, and crossed the remaining distance toward their SUV. I looked inside, spotted a medical bag, a computer case, a couple of overnight-style pieces of luggage stacked onto the back seat, and in the rear compartment, two well-stuffed, military-style duffles. I made a mental note of the vehicle's make and license number. It had Louisiana plates. Then I spotted the rental car company's bar code sticker in the lower left of the windshield, which meant nothing other than these guys were probably from out of town. I could make a call in the morning to find out who they were. One of the things I've learned in this business was that you always made friends at the airport with the airline counter people, and have at least one friendly contact at each of the rental car companies. I knew Mary Ann would be happy to pull a record for me in the morning.

I moved toward the east, figuring I could use the garden area I had spotted on that side earlier as cover. I swung wide coming around the front of the house, and as I did, I saw the guy who had gone that direction was making his way to the back. I moved around the perimeter of the garden, separating myself from the house. As I approached the southeast corner of the garden, I again went prone and poked my head around the to look. The only artificial light still came from the second-floor window of the old barn, and it cast a delicate glow across the lawn below.  From the way the light flickered, I assumed it was either the glow of a fire, although there was no chimney I could discern, or candles.

The two men stood away from the porch in the back.  I could hear them debating whether to risk entering the house; obviously, they didn't belong there any more than I did.  Finally, they reached consensus, then climbed the steps, crossed the porch, opened the screen door, then tried the inner door.  It opened freely.  I assumed whether the kids were still in there or not, they wouldn't be expecting unwanted company.  Each of the intruders removed a small LED flashlight from a front pants pocket, then disappeared inside.  From my perspective on how they lined up at the door frame, I calculated they were my size or perhaps a bit taller, but each carried more bulk than I did.  Whether it was muscle or fat, I wasn't too eager to test at that point.

I didn't need the night vision goggles to track their progress through the house.  They moved rapidly through the first floor rooms, then minutes later I watched their lights flashing around through the upstairs windows.  They went through the entire house quickly, then returned and spent ten minutes in the upstairs rooms on the east side of the house.  I debated whether to leave them to their search while I checked out the old barn, but in the end, I concluded I didn't want to be surprised out there, so I held fast and waited for these guys to finish up in the main house.  There would be plenty of time, I hoped, to recon the barn.

"She's here, all right," Rudy said, illuminating a pair of panties that he had removed from a suitcase in the back bedroom with his flashlight.  "Either that or our boys have taken up cross-dressing."  He laughed, looked over his shoulder to make certain Travis wasn't looking, then discretely sniffed the panties and slid them into his pants pocket.

Travis opened the drawer in one of the night stands and removed a cheap cellular phone.  He held it up, shined the light on it.  Rudy nodded from across the room.    Travis scrolled through the recently called numbers, saw only a handful of calls.

"Looks like his parents and one of Cindy's cells are the only calls," he said.  He replaced the phone in the drawer.

After looking through the bathroom, and going through the luggage they located, the pair moved out of the back bedroom and went to the front bedroom.

"What do you make of this?" Rudy said, holding a miniature Confederate battle flag he had found lying on a center table.  "This wouldn't make daddy very happy."

Travis nodded.    He checked the bathroom, then searched the drawers in the nightstands and dresser, found nothing unusual.  Rudy flipped through the duffle on the floor in the corner.

"Dirty clothes, clean clothes," he said. "Nothing out of the ordinary. No cross-dressing potential with Dace, that I see, anyway."

"Takes one to know one, eh, buddy?" Travis said.

It was Travis' turn to laugh.

The two men exited the house less than fifteen minutes after they had entered. They stood just off the porch and discussed whether to check the barn, noting the flickering light in the upstairs window. They eventually decided to leave the barn alone, basing their decision on the fact they had determined who they were looking for was indeed staying in the house. From what I could discern by their conversation, which seemed to rule out my two prime targets indicated by Tom McDaniel, these two guys were most concerned with the mystery male, not the kids I had seen earlier that day. Information like that only served as enticing nourishment to my natural curiosity.

Dace finished another bottle, tossed the empty in its paper sack into the gutter and heard the bottle break. He returned to the convenience store on Magazine Street and bought a replacement, along with an oversized Snickers bar, then came back to Prytania Street. Something had caught his eye as he had meandered by earlier.

He located the twelve-foot-high white plaster wall again, and walked around each of the four sides of the city block enclosure. An aqua and white building with matching awnings across Washington Street he had spotted earlier turned out to be a restaurant called The Commander's Palace and it had constant comings and goings directly across from the white-walled compound's wrought iron gates; the Prytania Street side was carrying more automobile traffic than it had before, but the other two sides bordered homes, and the streets were fairly dark and remained quiet. While there were wrought iron gates on all four sides, they were securely locked. He had peered inside the compound at each of the gates and each time was moved to remember the rapid-cut, LSD-inspired scene from the movie, *Easy Rider*.

He was as drunk as he had ever been; almost seeing double everything. As he rounded the corner onto the Coliseum Street side for the second time, he stumbled on the pavement made uneven by the growth of large oak trees, tumbled to the ground and skinned his hands in the fall. He tore a hole in his jeans at the right knee, but didn't notice. He cursed, checked his bottle and found it thankfully uninjured, and as he stood up, repositioned the revolver in his pants at the small of his back. He smirked to himself at the feel of the hard steel of the long barrel between his ass cheeks.

Feeling suddenly sick to his stomach, he eased himself down in the grass and leaned against the white plaster. The gun jabbed him in an uncomfortable way, so he removed it and placed it under his leg. He wondered for a moment what it felt like to shoot another human being. He imagined there may be an initial recoiling from the finality of the act after the trigger had been pulled, but then considered the holding of that kind of power in his hands might well be quite exciting. His hooded head fell back against the wall, and lolled from side to side as he flirted with an impending unconsciousness, then he forced himself to focus for several moments longer as he surveyed the darkened street in each direction. He saw nobody.

Dace removed the Snickers candy bar from the bag, tore open one end and took a bite. The sweetness immediately surged into his system and he felt a rush of tingling energy, which he tamped down with a slug from the bottle. His face contorted into a wince as the cheap tequila bit his throat as it went down. Next time, he thought, I'll get the Smirnoff Ice to go with Snickers. He took another bite of the candy bar.

His musings drifted to his parents. His mother had days ago received his letter from Mary Rose and he wondered if she had shared the contents with his father. Not that it mattered, he concluded. His father, he thought with contempt and derision, the man who would be kingmaker. He laughed out loud, even as he was becoming increasingly inured to the idea, but nobody was there to share the irony of the moment save the occupants on the other side of the wall, and he was certain they wouldn't care one whit.

He returned to the moment and looked around. The earlier din in the distance had faded into Mardi Gras history, and now the party had obviously moved into The Quarter as it had the previous night when he and Dave had come into town. The thought reminded him of the blonde from last night, the one with the vacant stare and succulent tits, and he felt himself stirring at the thought of taking her, not seducing her, but making her his, bending her to his Will. It was a violent thought, one of taking what he wanted, of controlling the woman and wiping that disconnected look she had wore from her face, the one she affected as she moved for the lustful gazes of the men at her feet and replacing it with one of respectful awe at his power and strength. Dace was surprised to discover the entire idea excited him on a whole new level. There was now even more for him to ponder.

In the next moment, he found himself wondering what it would have been like to have had Sarah like he had had that Colleen girl. Well, not on the hood of a car, which had been disgustingly base, but in a bed, each experiencing for the first time the joys of making love, not just the carnal pleasures of having sex as it had been with the bar slut. He felt a sting come to his eyes and he fought back the tears with another swig from the bottle, followed by the final bite of the candy bar. The reverse order of consumption of the odd pairing, he discovered, was just barely more palatable than had been the first sequencing.

Dace closed his eyes. He could feel sleep coming - or if not sleep the threat of unconsciousness - but he was determined to resist its siren's call until he had entered the walled compound and selected an appropriate bed for his respite. Only then would he allow the darkness to overtake him.

I watched the two men return to their vehicle and pull away, their SUV's xenon headlights again illuminating the night as they headed out the drive. Surprisingly, they turned west and I wondered if they'd take any notice of Sandy's Bravada parked at the end of the hedgerow. For a moment, I regretted leaving my old badge in the windshield.

After they had departed, I crossed the lawn toward the old barn, avoiding the wedge of light which fell upon the grass from the second floor window. I circled the building slowly, confirmed the suspected tire tracks on the back side I had seen from a distance, inspected the location of the doorway I had seen earlier when the kids had gone inside. The passage was expertly camouflaged, externally made to look like the wall of a dilapidated structure, but under closer scrutiny revealed a modern, secure, steel doorway below the facade. The only item which was not misleading as to purpose on the entire structure was the unremarkable doorway to a staircase on the east face of the building which I assumed led up to the old black woman's apartment.

Satisfied I had seen what I could see without getting into the disguised building, I retraced my steps and returned to my car. The entire time I was lost in thought. Something intriguing was happening at that old plantation, that much being clear. I wondered who the mystery male component was and considered calling my now ex-client in an attempt to pull some information, but decided against it. I was tired, and surprisingly, hungry again. Once at Sandy's Bravada, I looked it over and determined nobody had been around it since I had left. I unlocked the door, stowed my gear and removed my hat and gloves. I momentarily considered changing back into my non-ninja clothes for the drive home, but decided against it.

However, it being Louisiana, I did wipe off the black face.

# Chapter Twenty-four

I awoke in my recliner. Fifteen minutes later, Sandy phoned and asked if I had slept in my recliner. I dodged the question. She also asked how the case was going. I informed her we'd been fired; then continued to fill her in on what I had done and seen the day before, including my little covert op that night. She took it all in stride, understanding like no other outsider to the cop world, my theory regarding natural curiosity. Finally, after admitting to already potentially violating it, I asked her if the confidentiality agreement I had signed specifically precluded me from looking into things after I was technically dismissed from the case.

"Whenever you ask me that type of question, it means you've got your teeth into something that you don't want to let go, so why do you bother?" she said.

"Because I believe it's better to ask forgiveness than to ask permission?" I said.

"I think you've got that backwards, my dear husband," Sandy said. "To answer your question: Specifically? No. However, the spirit of the agreement may tie us up in knots if you keep digging then uncover unlawful activity which I, as an officer of the court, will be duty-bound to report. That type of thing never ends well. Just promise me if you keep sniffing around, we're not going to wind up needing a good lawyer."

"You're a good lawyer," I said. She didn't seem amused, so I changed the subject. "So when are you coming home?"

"Tomorrow afternoon," she said. "You want to pick me up?"

"What's in it for me?"

"I refuse to talk dirty on my parents' phone," she teased.

"Bad girl," I said with a laugh, "and, yes, I'll pick you up." I copied down her flight information. "I'll see you tomorrow afternoon. I love you."

"I love you too. So, stay out of trouble," she said, well knowing it was too late for that admonition.

"Moi?" I said, using my adorableness as a shield.

The rest was mushy stuff.

After we disconnected, I showered and dressed and headed out to Metairie in my Corvette to the IHOP for a late breakfast; I'd been craving Belgian Waffles.

As I approached the Causeway Boulevard exit on I-10, traffic had slowed to a crawl as droves of people attempted to go north on the Causeway. I maneuvered around the jam by staying longer in the left lane, then took the second Causeway exit to the south and drove to the IHOP, the whole time wondering what the attraction was up north.

The waitress in the nearly deserted restaurant cleared up the mystery.

"Happy Mardi Gras," she said with a forced smile underneath tired eyes. "What can I get for you?"

"Ah, Mardi Gras," I said. "Fat Tuesday. The last day. It's today. I nearly forgot. No wonder the traffic going north on the Causeway was jammed."

"Yep," she said. "Parades over on Veterans Boulevard have got that whole side of town tied up in knots this morning. Frankly, this year, I'll be glad when it's all over."

Dace awoke inside the Lafayette Cemetery No. 1, lying on top of a moldering platform tomb. He opened his eyes to sunshine, badly muffled engines, and the odors of oily exhaust and fresh cut lawn; the maintenance crew was mowing the scattered patches of scrub grass. He issued a slight moan and rolled his aching body off the low, domed top and slid to his feet down onto the adjacent box grave. He stumbled back against the crumbling masonry which had been his bed for the night. His head pounded and swirled and his eyes ached and he reached into his hoodie pocket and removed his Blues Brothers glasses. His body was stiff and sore from sleeping on brick and plaster and he attempted a bit of stretching to work out the kinks and stumbled forward. The paper bag he had fallen asleep holding had slid down into the small gap between the two graves. He retrieved it, slipped the bottle from inside, saw there was a swallow or two left; he swirled the amber liquid, it reflected sparkles of sunlight. Dace crumpled the bag and tossed it back between the graves. The bottle, he set on top of the upper tomb, mock saluted it, then weaved through the maze of the markers and crypts of the dead, past the oblivious groundskeepers and out the now open Washington Avenue gate back into the world of the living.

Dave and Cindy awoke in each other's arms, naked, just as they had fallen asleep. The wedges of sunlight silently crept across the planked wood floor, and for the first time in over a week, Dace Lamoureux was not the first thought to enter Dave's mind as he opened his eyes. Cindy pulled closer, whispered a 'good morning', then rolled over and spooned against him. She felt good in his arms, and for the first time since he and Cindy had first begun dating, he didn't care what Dace thought of her. He was at peace. He was happy.

His arms scooped her even closer. Her long blonde hair cascaded across her pillow, tickled his face, yet he nuzzled against it, inhaled its freshness. Cindy purred softly at the attention. Dave's left hand explored her curves beginning at her bare shoulder then moved over her ample, warm breasts tipped by a special firmness, across her tight little belly then along the outline of her soft hips and smooth thighs. It was a magically sensual trip moving down, but it was as his hand moved in the other direction over the inner lines of her body that things began to really get exciting.

They made love that morning in the big, soft bed for the fourth time since they had left Auntie D's the night before.

The stroll back to the main house the previous evening had been quiet as they each had processed the old woman's words about living their own lives and not wasting it on insignificant things, or people who don't care enough about them to matter. On the back porch, Dave had stopped her and turned her toward him. Cindy had looked up at him with an excited newness, as if he, and the concept of *them*, had been reborn in her heart. She realized at that moment Dave had begun to cast his own light, no longer needing to be a reflection of Dace Lamoureux's. In that instant, she had fallen in love with him all over again.

And him with her, not that Dave had ever been far from it during the time they had been apart.

That's when he had kissed her, and she had kissed him back. What followed had not been a frantic rush of animalistic passion like they show in the movies; what happened between them overnight had been the simple, genuine act of two people making love.

Ronnie and Ashley awoke in the same room, at the same time, for the first time in several days. They had a big day planned, beginning with breakfast in the little cafe off the hotel's lobby, and then a trolley ride into the Garden District to stake out a spot along St. Charles Avenue for the last few parades. They had reservations for lunch at The Commander's Palace, then would experience everything the city had to offer on the last day of Carnival. Regardless of how things had gone thus far, it was the culminating day of the adventure they had planned for over a year, and they were both eager to make this day one they would remember for the rest of their lives.

In the little town of Thibodaux, some twenty miles south of Vacherie, a black Lincoln Navigator sat angle parked amidst Ford and

Chevy and Dodge pick up trucks outside a single-story, yellow-brick building. The vehicle was as out of place outside the working class motel as were the two large gentlemen from up north who had checked into room B3 the night before.

Travis rolled over and bumped into Rudy, again. Rudy pushed back, again. The motel had only one room left when they had arrived in town: a single with a double bed. When they discovered they needed a room for the night, Tom's assistant informed them everything between New Orleans and Baton Rouge was booked solid. After a single night of bumping into each other they both were wondering if there was any way they could sleep in the jet if another night turned out to be necessary.

Their orders were now clear and concise: Bring Dace home without any public display, and bring him directly to The Senator's home in McClean. If Dace refused to cooperate, then medical assistance, which was a euphemism for an injection of sedatives which had already been drawn into a syringe tucked into Rudy's black leather bag, had been sanctioned by The Senator, so long as doing so created no possibility of drawing public scrutiny. Though, time was of the essence, covertness was the priority. Simple.

Rudy and Travis had decided during their planning that it would be allowable to aggressively question both Cindy Spagliano and Dave Saunders to pinpoint Dace's whereabouts should he not be in the house with them anymore. Every indication from their entry the evening before, however, had confirmed the three kids were still staying together in the old plantation home, Rudy's cross-dressing canard recognized by them both for what it was.

Travis sat up, his feet on the floor. Rudy did the same on the other side. Rudy stood, stretched, scratched himself through his red and white striped boxers.

"Let's get breakfast and pluck that kid today," Rudy said. "I'm not sleeping on this bed with you another night."

"I offered you the couch," Travis said with an evil grin as he picked up his cell phone and pushed an autodial number.

Rudy again looked at the short, narrow, well-worn couch option and glanced about the bare-bones accommodation. He shook his head and shuffled his bare feet across the old linoleum tile toward the bathroom. At the door he turned. "I'll probably get that lung disease from the asbestos in this tile alone. If the mold in the shower doesn't get me first, that is."

"Mesothelioma?" Travis said, turning his head to look at Rudy.

"What?"

"That's the lung disease you get from asbestos. Mesothelioma. Lighten up, man, it's not that bad. We've stayed in worse."

"Not in a long time, brother. I guess I've gone soft."

"Just do me one favor, okay?" Travis said.

"What's that?"

"If we have to stay here again tonight," Travis said, his eyes twinkling, "don't go homo."

Travis laughed and Rudy threw him a one-finger salute and slammed the bathroom door.

Travis was still chuckling when Tom answered the phone.

Tom hadn't slept well. Libby and Mary Rose had taken their dinners in Libby's room. Caroline had played the role of messenger, informing him when he asked: 'Mrs. Lamoureux was not feeling well, and asks not to be disturbed.' He hadn't yet gone down for breakfast when the phone rang on his bedside table. He checked the caller ID and flipped open the phone.

"Whatcha got, Travis?" he said.

"They're all here, we entered last night. There was nobody home at the time, but we found their clothes and personal stuff to indicate it's all three now. We assumed they had gone out for the night, so we just came to the motel and planned to catch them this morning."

"Fine," Tom said, his mind foggy from lack of sleep and Libby's continued odd behavior. "Anything else?"

"Yeah, we rolled out of there last night and came across a vehicle parked about a mile down. The place has about a two-mile hedgerow which runs along the main road with a gap in the middle for a driveway as the only direct access to the main house. Well, at one end of the hedge, we came across a green, 1998 Oldsmobile Bravada parked off the road. We didn't think much of it, you know, maybe a couple of kids parking or maybe some fishermen over the levee, but Rudy gets out and walks around the thing. No people, no fishing gear, but a couple of duffles in the back, some street clothes on the floor of the passenger side, and a badge displayed in plain sight on the dash."

"Badge?" Tom said.

"Yeah, detective's shield," Travis said, "but, get this, it was Chicago PD issue."

I finished my breakfast, downed the last of my Coke, tucked a couple of twenties into the black folder the waitress had left on her final check if everything was okay and slid out of the booth. I walked across the restaurant, nodded to the woman just exiting the kitchen area toting a large, plastic tray loaded with seven breakfasts for the couple which had come in and had thankfully been parked along with their five overactive kids at a table well away from me. She returned another forced smile from under tired eyes. I hoped the tip I'd left would help her mood.

My cell phone vibrated in my jacket pocket as I was crossing the parking lot. I pulled it out, checked the caller ID and smiled. I let it go to voicemail.

On the drive out to Vacherie, I called Anne Marie, my contact at the company who rented the Lincoln Navigator I had seen the night before. She was working and agreed to pull the rental contract and relay the details, the core of which I already suspected. I wrote down the rental information while I steered with my knees. Then she added a detail which piqued my interest even more. The SUV had been delivered to the general aviation ramp at the airport about an hour before it had turned up at the plantation house. The kid who had driven it over had reportedly volunteered for the duty because he was an airplane nut, and returned all wide-eyed. It had been his first close encounter with a Gulfstream III jet. The crew had given him the tour after the passengers had departed. They had told the kid they had flown in from New London, Connecticut and would be on indefinite standby for a return to Washington, D.C. They brought down the two large gentlemen I had seen, and were told to anticipate a third person on the way home, possibly in some sort of medical condition.

I was frankly surprised by the amount of detailed information the crew had told the kid, but not that he had repeated it to anyone who would listen when he got back. Mary Anne said he was just seventeen, a part-timer and was so enamored with airplanes that they often had to track him down somewhere in the terminal. I remembered being that wide-eyed about things when I was a kid, but when I was his age, it was girls and cars which tugged my string.

I thanked Mary Anne, told her I owed her one and I'd pay off next time I was by the airport, which I remembered would be the following afternoon to pick up my wife. Since I had been south of the interstate at the IHOP, I had continued in that direction, mainly because the northbound Causeway was still backed up. I connected to the Huey P. Long Bridge over the Mississippi and headed west on the Great River Road back out to see what was happening at Vacherie.

Dave and Cindy showered together, dressed for the day and went down to find Auntie D making them a real country breakfast of eggs, bacon, potatoes fried with peppers, onions, and mushrooms, and fresh-baked biscuits. Dave had thought he'd heard some rattling around downstairs when they had come out of the shower, and had thought for a moment that Dace may have come back, but when he had opened the bedroom door and smelled the cooking, he was certain it had to be Auntie D. The aromas were amazing rising up the staircase, and even more intense in the kitchen.

"I trust, y'all slept good," Auntie D said as they entered. Her eyes moved over their faces. "Cindy, you is glowin' this mornin', honey." She winked at Dave. "And so is you, boy."

They each blushed, perhaps Dave a bit more than Cindy. Auntie D returned her attention to the frying eggs. There were two places set at the table with poured orange juice and a third plate with a glass of water.

"Sit, you two," Auntie D instructed.

They did.

"Long time since I gots to wait on two young folks in love," she said. She slid two over easy eggs onto Cindy's plate, four of the same onto Dave's. "Does this old heart good." She patted Dave on the shoulder. She returned with the plate of bacon and the biscuits under a red and white checkered dish towel in a basket. "I tol' you this was a good boy, Cindy. I knowed they was somethin' going on with you two last night when you left." She returned to the stove and retrieved the skillet with the fried potatoes, dished them out, made one more trip to drop the pan and returned to sit. "Go on, you two, eat. From the looks of it, you worked up an appetite." She smiled and flipped open the flaps of the towel inside the basket, revealing her homemade biscuits.

"I don't know what to say," Dave said, a slice of bacon and half a fried egg in his mouth. "Again you've amazed me, Auntie D. You've thoroughly spoiled me. I still say I may not ever want to leave."

Auntie D waved away the compliment. For her, having a couple of good people around who'd listen to her stories, and who enjoyed her food was reward enough. She broke small pieces off a biscuit, fletcherized each with her gums and washed the bits down with the water. They ate, and talked about nothing, and laughed.

"That other one ain't back yet," Auntie D said, when she felt the time was right, her eyes moving to Dave. "But ain't no matter. Today be Mardi Gras, Fat Tuesday, y'know. Ever'body be hootin' it up." She winked at Cindy. "You gonna take this beautiful, young lady to Nawlins for the party?"

Dave looked across the small table at Cindy. Auntie D was right, she was glowing, Dave thought. A smile grew on his face. At that point, he couldn't care less if Dace was back or not; Dace Lamoureux was the last thing he wanted to think about. His leased Escalade, now that was a bit of a different matter, but that would all work out in the end.

"Do you want to go, Cindy?" he said. "With you, it could be a blast."

"Why not?" she said. "We're here, we might as well have some fun. I've never been to a Mardi Gras parade, or New Orleans, for that matter. Other than driving through on the interstate a couple nights ago, that is."

"Good," Auntie D said. "You two go. Have fun. I'll clean up." She pushed her chair back and took their plates to the sink.

Dave and Cindy went upstairs to grab a few things. Cindy pulled a yellow hoodie from her bag and tossed it onto the bed. She checked her makeup in the bathroom mirror and found Dave writing on a pad when she returned to the bedroom.

"What's that?" she said.

"A note for Dace," he said. "In case he comes back. I want him to know we've gone into the city."

She read his words upside down, then smiled at him, shook her head, kissed him on top of his, grabbed her hoodie and went downstairs. Dave sat on the edge of the bed and reread the note:

> *Dace,*
>
> *Cindy came down. She and I are headed to New Orleans for Mardi Gras. Hope you are well, and safe. I understand your taking the car. Sorry I have not been friend enough for you. I did my best.*
> *We'll be back later. Hope to see you tonight.*
> *Dave*

Dave walked down the hall, then balanced the notepad on the handle to Dace's closed door. He went downstairs, found Cindy speaking to Auntie D in a low tone. Dave moved past her to give Auntie D a hug, whispered something to her which she acknowledged with a nod, then took Cindy by the hand and the pair walked out of the kitchen, up the hall, out the front door, and to the Mustang.

"I thought my days with you were over, girl," Dave said as he trotted down the steps and approached the old car.

"Me or the car?" Cindy said.

Dave opened the passenger door for her. The hinges creaked. He kissed Cindy, then watched her get in before closing the door and walking around to the driver's side.

"Both," he said to himself before opening the door.

He had to slide the seat back before he could fit inside.

"Sorry," Cindy said.

Dave got in, started the engine, clipped his seat belt, reminded Cindy to do the same. He maneuvered the remainder of the circle and rolled up the drive to the main road. He nosed the Mustang out to the road, looked both ways. The only traffic came from the east, a red Corvette moving along at a speed slower than he would have expected for the highway. He watched the car slide by, took no note of the driver. Dave turned right.

I had slowed to take a peek approaching the drive when the nose of the Mustang suddenly appeared at the opening of the hedge. I sped up, but wondered as I went past if the kid had noticed me moving so slowly.

He appeared to observe the car closely as I passed from what I could tell with my peripheral vision, then I watched him turn right and head the other way in the rearview mirror. I cursed myself for not taking my SUV, the anonymous silver vehicle I drove most of the time on business assignments. The kid had seen Sandy's Bravada the day before, so I thought the Corvette was a safe play for the day, plus I enjoyed driving the country roads in it.

After they disappeared around the S-turn, I found a spot where the 'Vette could do a U-turn without bottoming out on the shoulder and headed east to follow. I laid back a distance. It wasn't my first rodeo, but it was the first time I could remember tailing someone in something as conspicuous as a brand new, cherry red Corvette. Behind the passenger seat, I found a baseball cap I remembered putting back there, then tossed it onto the floor. To add a cap with the full-color logo and motto of the FBI to the 'Vette probably didn't create the optimum combination for blending in. I cursed myself. Normally, I'm much more careful.

"Your locator is on the move," the caller told Travis.

"Where is it now?" Travis asked. He and Rudy were about five miles south of Vacherie on Highway 20. He accelerated slightly, signaled for Rudy to get out the map.

"Moving east on I-10, about two miles east of the 641 interchange."

Travis repeated the information and Rudy found the spot on the map. They were about twenty miles away as best he could tell. Travis clicked off after telling their guy in New York to keep them updated, especially as to any prolonged stops.

"They're probably headed into New Orleans," Rudy said.

"Maybe they're headed home," Travis said.

"What about the Escalade?"

"Perhaps they're in convoy, or maybe the Saunders kid got tired of it and turned it in. How am I supposed to know?"

Travis drummed his fingers on the wheel as he thought.

"Only one way to tell," Travis said. "We go in again."

"In the middle of the day?" Rudy said. "Remember the light in the old barn last night. What if someone else is there and sees us and calls the cops? Low profile, remember?"

"There's more than one way into that place," Travis said. "We'll just not use the back door. It's the only way we can tell if they have left for good, or maybe Dace is back at the house alone."

"Makes sense," Rudy said. "Let's do it."

Dace drove along the Great River Road in the Escalade. It had taken him a little over an hour to find his way back to it from the cemetery. After retrieving the SUV, he had picked up something to eat at a McDonald's drive-thru and took some Tylenol. He was feeling a little better than he had when he awoke. At least his head had stopped trying to explode.

He had just passed some type of naval shipyard facility in the town of Avondale. From what he could remember, he had about an hour drive back out to Vacherie.

I was thankful the kid had decided to take the interstate. It made surreptitiously following him easier than had he stayed to the rural roads. I was about five cars back in the opposite lane, and I was suddenly struck by the thought that the same uniqueness which made my Corvette stick out like a sore thumb as a tail, made him in the white and blue, 1986 Mustang GT Liftback a most conspicuous head. I smiled.

Just for grins, I called Teddy and asked him to run a make on a couple of out-of-state plates. During the small talk, I asked how Valeria had taken the news that Sandy and I were expecting a baby. Well, that had been the wrong thing to say when I needed something quickly. Teddy launched into a long diatribe about how Valeria, his third wife, had now begun talking about having a kid, saying something like 'her biological clock was ticking'. Valeria was five years younger than Sandy.

"What is it with women and this biological clock?" Teddy said.

I remembered the scene in *My Cousin Vinny* when Joe Pesci had to contend with the biological clock rant by Marisa Tomei. It hadn't been pretty for Joe, and I imagined Valeria replicating the role on Teddy. That was even less inviting. Valeria was possessed of a feisty Hispanic temperament which would put any Italian woman to shame. I could also commiserate a bit with my old partner on the age issue from a dad's perspective, but Teddy was ten years my senior, which meant he'd be in his early seventies when the kid graduated from college. He'd also never had kids with his first two wives so he had no idea what to expect should he give in. I didn't know what to say. I could hear the stress in his voice.

I heard him issue a curt 'thank you' to someone in the background, and then he got back to business, the dad thing left hanging. He gave me the registry information and I did my best to write it down while steering with my knees again. Wanting to avoid getting back to the sore subject of kids, I gave Teddy as short a thank you and sign off as I could and still look at myself in the mirror in the morning. I told him I was tailing a vehicle, knew he'd understand but hoped he wouldn't be hurt. I promised we'd talk about this kid thing soon.

"All right, Big Dog," he said. "Go get 'em, and stay safe out there. Give Sandy a big hug for me."

I agreed on the hug thing, then momentarily toyed with the idea of asking Teddy for the time, just to erase any remaining tension and get a laugh out of him. The problem was, I've never known Teddy to break a promise, and he had promised to shoot me if I ever asked him that question again. So instead of risking a bullet, I tossed the idea onto the scrap heap and just clicked off.

I glanced at my notes. The Mustang was registered to a Dave Saunders at an address in Gales Ferry, Connecticut. I didn't know where Gales Ferry was, but Connecticut wasn't that big of a state, and my two buddies in the Navigator had flown out of New London. That connection fit. The phantom, pearl white, 1998 Cadillac Escalade's plates were also registered to Dave Saunders, same address, but the title indicated the vehicle was a lease through GMAC and listed the principal location of the vehicle as Cambridge.

I wished Sandy was back so she could run these trails a little further for me. So, the kid's full name was Dave Saunders. I already knew the girl went by Cindy. He went to Harvard. Something told me that Harvard was in Cambridge.

"Okay, Dave Saunders and Cindy, where are you heading today?" I said toward the windshield, then switched back to the right lane because a semi hauling, yep, pigs, was riding my tail. The trucker passed and his passenger gave me a dirty look through my T-top. I looked down at my speedometer. "Where are we heading, and how long is it going to take at fifty-eight miles per hour?" The smell of the pigs added insult for the next ten miles.

Rudy and Travis pulled into the driveway at the plantation house. They made no pretense at being stealthy. The Mustang was indeed gone. There was still no sign of the Escalade. They got out of the Navigator, slammed the doors, and walked boldly up onto the front porch. Travis used the heavy, old door knocker in an attempt to summon someone inside. Rudy watched through the side light for any signs of life.

"Nothing," Rudy said. "No movement."

"See any security indications?" Travis asked.

"I can see the control panel on the wall that we saw last night," Rudy reported. He smiled. "Green light."

Travis tried the door handle and it operated freely. The door swung open. Travis' eyes moved to the security panel on the wall to watch for any changes. It remained showing only the steady green light. The pair stepped inside, closed the door. They could smell the remains of bacon and eggs hanging in the air.

"I'll take up, you take down," Travis said.

"Rog," Rudy said, making his way toward the back of the house first.

Travis ascended the stairs. He went into the back bedroom first, saw things had changed little since the previous night, except the bed had been slept in. Damp towels hung in the bathroom. Next, he walked down the hall toward the front bedroom where they had spotted Dace's things. On the doorknob, he found the pad of paper. He picked it up, read the note. Smiled. He opened the door. The room was unchanged, and the bed didn't appear that it had been slept in. He checked the towels in the bathroom and found them to be bone dry.

Travis froze as he heard the faint echo of a series of clicks. He turned, saw nothing through the door up the hallway. He retreated from the room, replaced the note as it had been, peered over the hallway railing toward the lower floor. He placed his hand inside his jacket and onto the butt of his .40 caliber Smith & Wesson semiautomatic. He descended the stairs. At the bottom, he removed his hand from inside his jacket.

"Man, this is the best biscuit I ever ate," Rudy said.

Rudy stood there in the middle of the hallway, holding a bacon sandwich and an open can of cherry Mountain Dew. The opening of the can had been the clicks Travis had heard echo through the house.

"Where'd you get that?" Travis said.

"Kitchen," Rudy said, his mouth full of another big bite. "There's more if you want some."

"Did you find anything besides the makings for your breakfast sandwich?" Travis said.

"Nope, but they were here this morning. Plates drying in the kitchen, which still smells like home cooking. You?"

"A note, on Dace's room door knob," Travis said. "Apparently, the kid's got the Escalade and has disappeared."

He briefed Rudy on the note and other things he'd seen upstairs. They stood in the center of the hallway and debated their next move. Rudy was for following the locator and putting eyes on Dave and Cindy. Travis held out for staking out the plantation house. He reasoned that if Dave and Cindy had gone to New Orleans and wound up parking the car someplace, there was little chance they'd pick them up in the Mardi Gras crowds. Whereas, if they staked out the plantation house, they knew Dave and Cindy would be returning later that night, as the note had indicated, and that Dace *may* be expected to show up. Pulling the kid home from a remote country house sure beat snatching him off the streets of New Orleans on the no fuss or muss scale. Rudy had to admit, Travis' reasoning was sound; as always, and he deferred to the older man.

Rudy finished the biscuit sandwich and drained the Dew. He belched, then made an inquiry.

"So, you want to wait them out in here? Maybe stash the car around back?"

Travis thought about it for a moment, then shook his head.

"No," he said. "If Dave and Cindy get back first, it could lead to a scene, cops being called. We don't need the grief, man."

"Yeah, but if Dace comes back alone first, we just bag him, and if the little shit gives us any lip, we give him the needle. Bing, bang, boom."

"I still say we watch the place, park out on the road or on the levee."

"Okay, but if we're going to sit out there the rest of the day and into the night, I'm grabbing us some food," Rudy said as he turned toward the kitchen. "You should see the stockpiles they have in there. They'll never miss it."

Travis followed him.

"What the hell," he said. "Spoils of war, I guess."

Dace drove the Escalade into the entry at the eastern edge of the hedgerow. As his head had partially cleared on the drive back to the country, he worked out the story he'd tell Dave when his friend confronted him about taking his new vehicle without permission: 'It wasn't my fault, man. You and that old woman talking crap about me pissed me off. I had to get away.' He smiled when he knew how certain he was that Dave would buy it without protest.

He followed the faint tracks around the fields and pulled up behind the old barn and parked the SUV. He had cleaned out the overnight trash in the McDonald's garbage can, so he grabbed his fresh junk, stuck the box of bullets and .22 pistol into the glove compartment, grabbed the garment bag from the men's store at the Metairie Mall, exited the vehicle and walked around the corner of the building. He stepped carefully moving across the lawn, seeing the fire ants had rebuilt their nests after yesterday's rain had most certainly flattened and flooded them.

"Must suck to be an ant," he said as he passed by. Dace felt eyes upon him as he neared the house and he turned to look up toward the darkened window of Auntie D's apartment. "Mind your own business, old woman." He glared at the empty window, then turned and climbed the three steps and crossed the porch. He opened the screen door, then pushed open the inner door.

The house was quiet. A scattering of crumbs littered the hallway about a third of the way down. He went into the kitchen, saw the dishes and silverware drying in the rack next to the sink. The room smelled of bacon and some kind of fresh-baked bread, and he was suddenly hungry again. He walked to the refrigerator, found no bacon, but removed the ham from the other day, along with a Pepsi. On the counter, he spotted the basket with the checkered napkin folded over. Dace flipped open the napkin, but found nothing but crumbs remaining. He dropped the ham onto the cutting board, drew a carving knife from the rack, and cut off several slices. He stuck the knife into the remaining wedge, picked up the slices and Pepsi and walked back out into the hallway.

Apparently, the place we were going at fifty-eight miles an hour was downtown New Orleans. I followed the Mustang into the outskirts of the French Quarter, but when Dave started taking side streets, obviously looking for parking for a night of partying on Fat Tuesday, I gave up the ghost and went home. There'd be no way to discretely follow them up and down the narrow streets, and no way I'd find them in The Quarter after they parked and mixed with the overflow crowds the final day of Carnival always attracted.

While Sandy and I viewed the Mardi Gras *season* as one of the fantastic benefits of being a part of the New Orleans community, we fortunately also agreed that Fat Tuesday was rookie night, much like going out on New Year's Eve in the rest of the world. We had planned to go to a friend's place on St. Charles Avenue to watch the parades and share some food, drink, and camaraderie, safely ensconced off the street, but with Sandy gone, I had little desire to go alone and hang out. There was no question I'd be much happier at home in my recliner watching a game, and besides, what could happen down there tonight which would be of interest to me on this case?


Travis picked up the cell phone and saw the incoming call was from their New York contact who was tracking the Mustang. He put it on speaker. He and Rudy were sitting in the Navigator on top of the levee west of the estate so they could keep an eye on things. They had 'liberated' a stash of food and drinks from the kitchen and Rudy was deep into another biscuit and bacon sandwich.

"Yeah," Travis said.

"The locator has been stationary for the past fifteen minutes," he said. "Downtown New Orleans, Ursulines Avenue just northwest of Rampart."

"What's down there?" Travis said.

"French Quarter," Rudy said in mid-chew.

Travis looked across the car.

"How do you know that?"

"I told you," Rudy said. "After graduation from the Island, I fled to New Orleans on my pass." His eyes took on a distant look. "I spent a week eating, drinking, and screwing my brains out."

"I must have forgotten," Travis said.

"You guys need me anymore here?" the New York caller asked.

"No, just keep us updated," Travis said and clicked off.

Rudy chewed and thought. He washed down the sandwich with another cherry Mountain Dew.

"You know, it could be Dace downtown with the Mustang. You're just assuming it was the Escalade he had taken. Dave's note could have meant it the other way around."

"Timing doesn't work," Travis said, popping the top on a can of Pepsi. "Remember when we got the call of the 'Stang on the move. About fifteen minutes before we got here."

"How does that not work?" Rudy said, and he began to tick points off on his greasy and crumb-laden fingers. "One, Dace takes off in the Mustang, destination unknown. Two, Dave leaves an apologetic note. Three, Dave and Cindy go into New Orleans. Four, we arrive, everybody's gone. Works out just fine."

"I still say Dace has the Escalade," Travis retorted. "He doesn't even know Cindy was there. The first line of the note read: 'Cindy came down'. Finally, Dave 'hopes Dace is well'. That tells me the kid has been gone for a while, perhaps a coupla days."

"Okay, assuming you're right," Rudy said. "Riddle me this, Batman. Why are we sitting here?"

"Whaddya mean?"

"If the little brat took off days ago, why would he come back here? Maybe he's a thousand miles away and we're just wasting our time."

Travis shook his head emphatically.

"No way," he said, his eyes focused on the distant plantation house. "That little brat, as you call him, doesn't have the balls to trail blaze. He's at the core a coward. I could see it in his eyes that first day. I've been reading men for decades, man; in and out of the Corps. He won't wander far from a lifeline, because he'll hide behind what he knows. Were he a Marine, he'd be the type of guy who would shield himself behind his best buddy while running to take a hill. He needs a fall guy, and you watch, when he finally comes home, he'll blame the whole deal on Dave Saunders; and daddy will pat him on the head and that will be it. There's never any consequences for people like him. All this wasted time and money just to protect the brat's reputation for some kind of political future daddy wants for him. You know there'll never be any justice for those couple of kids he put in the hospital in Birmingham. That's just one incident we know of. Who knows what else has been going on." He drank a deep draw of the Pepsi, belched, and stared out the window. "Makes me sick, man."

Rudy nodded as he wiped his fingers and mouth on a paper towel.

"I'm kinda hoping the fucker gives me an excuse, man," he said. "I've been waiting for that with assholes like him my whole life."

# Chapter Twenty-five

Dace showered and shaved. He walked out of the bathroom, a towel wrapped around his waist, and tossed his duffle of clothes onto the bed. He removed underwear, a new pair of jeans, a blue and white striped, long sleeve, Oxford dress shirt. He dressed while brushing his teeth, then checked himself in the mirror, and ran a brush through his hair, which seemed to know just where to fall. Pleased with the overall effect, the last thing he applied was his patented smile.

From the men's store bag hanging on the door, he removed a black cashmere sports jacket and slipped it on.

"Perfect," he said.

Outside, the shadows were growing long as the sun approached the horizon. Dace walked to the windows and peered out toward the river. It was deathly still outside, not a leaf moved on the two giant oak trees in the front yard. He was about to turn away when a reflection caught his eye far to the west on the levee. He smiled and pushed the sheer aside to get a better look. The vehicle stood at a good distance, and while he couldn't make out the faces, he could judge the size of the two men seated inside.

"Oh, not yet, boys," he said, his smile morphing into an evil grin. "There's one more thing yet to do."

Fifteen minutes later, Dace rolled the Escalade out the same way he had driven in, well out of the sight of the men watching from the levee. He had paid no attention to the old woman's window as he had walked by that time, but Auntie D had watched him go. Dace drove across the bridge over the Mississippi River east of Vacherie. Barge traffic pushed in each direction leaving aerated wakes in the twilight. By the time he reached I-10, the sun had set and darkness had crept across southern Louisiana.

An hour later, Dace Lamoureux strode across Canal Street into the French Quarter after leaving the Escalade with a valet at one of the downtown hotels. Initially, the kid in the misfitted uniform had protested when Dace admitted to not being a guest of the establishment, but a hundred dollar bill slipped into the kid's palm quickly solved the problem.

The downtown area was overflowing with people, and Bourbon Street, which had been packed a couple of nights ago when he and Dave had come in, was even more crowded, if that were possible. Police presence had also obviously increased, and now included an elevated observation platform placed in the median on Canal Street at Bourbon which he hadn't seen before. A string of police vans were parked in the same median, awaiting the anticipated supply of drunks and the disorderly, or worse, which the 1998 Carnival season's last night's party was certain to send forth from The Quarter.

Dace weaved his way through the first block on Bourbon, past the few remaining hustlers and panhandlers who hadn't been displaced by the ebbing and flowing crowd. Beyond that, individual people seemed not to exist, each absorbed into a single entity becoming like a shapeless single-cell creature high school biology students would observe in microscopes, its tendrils reaching down side streets and Dace, too, was quickly subsumed.

As he moved with directional purpose, his eyes scanned the faces of the Mardi Gras revelers. Some wore masks. Some wore smiles. Some showed nothing but the dulled eyes of drink. Dace felt anonymous, as if he went unnoticed with no eyes evaluating him. To the assembled masses, he thought, he was as unknown as they were to him. It was the perfect setting in which to accomplish his final plan and his eyes searched out that single perfect match. The rest he quickly discarded from his attention. He smiled at a thought. Someday he'd be recognized by everyone still alive in this mass of humanity, but tonight he was nobody to them, just a face in the crowd, like the character in that old movie of the same name.

His hand touched the Buck knife in his pocket. It was hard and cold, the spine of the tucked blade smooth as he ran his fingers over it. He felt powerful as he walked, no, beyond that: omnipotent, as God Himself. He envisioned himself as a wolf infiltrating a herd of unsuspecting sheep, his target for his final defiant act a single, young female whom he would lure from the group, then watch her eyes fill with terror as she realized far too late the danger she had encountered on that night. He felt a sexual stirring and his heart began to pound in his chest and echo in his ears; it was a blend of anticipation and fear, he concluded. He considered taking a drink to calm his nerves but immediately rejected the thought. His other acts had needed alcohol, this one did not.

Tonight would be his last chance, he knew. Tomorrow, he would return to his life, and its responsibilities to family and history, legacy and destiny. He had already made that decision; his run was over. In the not-too-distant future, he realized, his face would be far too well-known to do something like this. Tonight would also be the last time he'd be untethered, not tied to handlers and managers and security people. Employees all, true, yet people with eyes and ears and mouths all the same. Yes, it was tonight or never.

He pushed slowly through the crowd, occasionally being jostled and crushed in the waves of counter-movement. Midway down the second block, he saw an overweight man urinating against one of the brick walls of a restaurant packed with patrons on the other side of large windows, the urine stream making a trail between the sidewalk's pavers toward the gutter which was already overflowing with beer and trash, and other things too disgusting to discern. Further along, balconies were filled with taunting young men holding fistfuls of Mardi Gras beads, and young women flaunting their breasts to the crowd. Because there was more room for women to flash on the crammed balconies than on the streets below, more beads were being tossed up than were flying down. Dace studied the women who were exposing themselves and he nearly laughed at how cheaply some women could be bought. They, however, were safe from him tonight. What he wanted for his final act was an innocent.

Then he saw her. The perfect girl. She was young, beautiful, and had a body he would give anything and risk everything to possess. She was standing on the corner of Bourbon and Bienville, under the blue and white awnings of an establishment named, oh so appropriately, 'Desire'. The girl had long brown hair which she wore loose and it cascaded beyond her shoulders with a slight, natural curl. She was about five-feet-six, perhaps a hundred-twenty pounds, and her curves were alluring. Dace inched closer. She was standing with another girl of similar features but with much smaller breasts. There was something wrong, soiled about the other, but the first was indeed an innocent; a pure, white lamb which he would separate from the herd. At that instant, her fate was sealed. He smiled and shivered with the thrill.

Each girl held a plastic cup and they were drinking and talking and laughing and oblivious to his gaze. They both wore high heeled pumps on small feet, black tights on shapely legs which disappeared under short skirts, tight-fitting tops, and leather jackets which hung just to the waist. They were perfect physical bookends, apart from the breasts, but only one of them fit his more *refined* needs. Beyond her freshness, there was something in her eyes: a fire he wanted to extinguish on top of the innocence he wanted to corrupt. Dace also had a feeling these girls did not belong on Bourbon Street. They just looked too young; and that was even better, he thought.

His 'Desire', as he had begun to think of the girl, had two ruffles on her short, black skirt, and her top was hot pink. Just the right amount of cleavage protruded above the scooped neckline. A small gold cross hung between her firm and ample breasts from a simple chain. As he moved closer, he could better discern her eyes which became intoxicatingly animated green flashes under the nearby flickering gas lamp. For an instant he thought she had looked at him, too, and he perceived a slight smile come to her lips, then fade away. He managed to pass directly behind her and could smell the fruity freshness of her hair. He circled her. Yes, she was the one he was seeking, and he could not lose her.

Ashley took notice of an attractive young man as he had crossed Bienville Street. He was just over six-feet tall, possessed of a runner's build, wore jeans which fit perfectly and a striped dress shirt under a soft, black blazer. She found his having the topmost button on the jacket engaged a bit odd for the generally casual air of Bourbon Street on Mardi Gras, but dismissed the thought as quickly as it had formed. He had a full head of brushed back, light brown hair which barely topped his ears, and she judged him to be a college man. As he had moved closer to her, she could see his eyes, darker green than hers, with gold flecks. His gaze briefly touched hers and she felt her body react. She whispered something about him to Ronnie shortly after the man had moved behind them and disappeared, and Ashley wondered if he had been sucked up by the crowds behind her, just as effortlessly as the one in front of her had released him. Or perhaps, he was merely an apparition of the night.

Dace discovered he was able to flow with the crowd fairly easily then, his earlier directionality transformed into a slow arc behind his Desire. He discretely followed her and her friend for hours as they wandered Bourbon Street, buying drinks at little kiosks from vendors too busy raking in cash to check the IDs the pair surely lacked. The girls drank, stood in crowded doorways and listened to the music surging from within various bars, sometimes dancing on the sidewalk and always resisting the hawkers' endless entreaties to come inside. The small breasted one flashed her mosquito bites whenever called upon, and her collection of beads hanging from her neck expanded with the hours. While his Desire drank like a fish, and would dance about seductively to the different styles of music, Dace was glad to see she refused to participate in that revealing debauch.

He checked his watch: it was just before midnight. The girls had just queued up at a bar a half block off Bourbon on St. Peter Street displaying a small, circular, white sign featuring a green, four-leaf clover logo and carrying the out-of-place Irish moniker of Pat O'Brien's. The pair quickly caught the attention of the bouncer who pulled them from the line toward the door. Dace pushed through several layers of people to catch up to them, and with a hundred dollar bill pressed into a receptive hand was able to follow them inside. The girls were escorted through the darkened, crowded passageway. Pianos accompanied by club-quality voices punched out an old Elton John tune which echoed above the enveloping boisterousness of the hallway from a portal toward the back. Dace wasn't quite certain, but thought the tune was *Rocket Man*.

Desire and her friend were greeted by yet another escort and seated at an upfront table for two which currently serviced six while Dace separated from them and selected a section of brick wall toward the back room to lean against while he surveyed the overcrowded room. Smoke rose from individual tobacco chimneys and hung in the air just under the low ceiling like a yellow-gray stratus cloud. Along the opposite wall, reflected by two oversized, ornate, gilded-framed mirrors, were a pair of copper-clad grand pianos. At each of the keyboards sat a reasonably attractive blonde woman in her mid-thirties. They may have been younger, but Dace saw they had already been aged by the nights of secondhand smoke and the hard life of what some would consider honky-tonk performers. Standing center stage was a black man dressed as the model for the Blues Brothers, complete with dark glasses and felt fedora. Each of his fingers was tipped by a thimble and he cradled a silver tray topped with an assortment of coins. As the pair of women at the pianos belted out the melody, his fingers tapped the bottom of the tray in time with the music, causing the coins to dance and vibrate. It was a uniquely New Orleans version of an accompanying percussionist.

Waiters and waitresses moved amongst the seated crowd. A seemingly endless supply of short-stemmed, curvaceous glasses filled with ice and a syrupy, red concoction called a Hurricane flowed from a counter along the back wall. On the other side of the entry hall, Dace had noticed a regular bar, packed eight or ten deep with patrons, and out back, a packed patio area strung with cheap lights and heated by portable gas-fired torches also held patrons to near overflowing. Though the late February night had turned cool, there was no need for heat inside the building as the combination of overcrowded conditions and lack of air movement effectively turned the room into a hotbox. The performers struck up a Billy Joel song, *New York State of Mind*.

A waitress delivered a pair of Hurricanes to the girls. Desire dropped a twenty-dollar bill onto the tray and waved the server away. His Desire and mosquito bites clinked glasses, then eagerly drank from the red, soft-drink-sized straws. When a waiter approached him, Dace ordered a club soda with a wedge of lime, and to his surprise, got it just that way a couple of minutes later, in a tall glass. He gave the waiter a ten spot and not surprisingly the man made no effort to return any change. Dace squeezed the lime into the bubbling water then dropped the wedge onto the ice and took a draw. It was clean and crisp and cold; and it hit the spot after hours of not drinking and the distant lingering of a hangover from the previous night's imbibing.

Dace continued to survey the room. There was only one exit, and he was standing near it. He could relax a bit. There was no way his Desire could be lost from here. Dace next began his observation of the people seated and standing around him, each of them thoroughly engrossed in the party, well lubricated with alcohol, and enjoying the music interspersed with friendly banter from the pianists as they acknowledged requests and rested their fingers. The place was a microcosm of the street scene outside.

Dace lifted his drink to his lips again, then held it there as his gaze drifted to the table adjoining the one at which Desire and her friend were seated. Some of the icy bubbles went down the wrong way as he recognized one of the pairs seated there and he coughed quietly and smiled at the irony as he recalled a line from the movie *Casablanca*: 'Of all the gin joints in all the towns in all the world, she walks into mine.'

Dave and Cindy were relaxed, a little drunk, enjoying the show, and the community of folks at their table and nearby; they were happy, and rediscovering the endorphin-filled joys of falling in love. When the two new girls joined the next table, Cindy had leaned in to whisper in Dave's ear. He looked them over and nodded his concurrence they were far too young to be in a bar, then shrugged, as if to say, 'Whatcha gonna do?'

When Cindy leaned over and started a conversation with the newcomers, Dave knew the big sister in her was showing. In between songs, they had learned the girls were named Ashley and Ronnie and that they were local to Louisiana and claimed to be juniors at Tulane University. Cindy had sat back in her chair at the last bit of data and gave them the disbelieving eye. Dave watched with interest as their facade crumbled a bit, but remained in place as they scrambled to maintain their returned unblinking stare. He had to give them credit, they played the role of college kids well.

Dace watched from the back of the room as Cindy and Dave interacted with his Desire and her friend. He wondered what the odds were that they all could be whirled by Fate's vortex and dropped into this single place at this particular moment. He decided the odds were probably incalculable, even to those prognosticators in Las Vegas.

"Not even Zeus himself was immune to the touch of the Moirai," Dace said to himself below the din, drawing his reference from the Greek Mythology course he had taken during his freshman year. According to the ancient Greeks, Fate was the domain of the Moirai, three mythological sisters: Clotho, Lachesis, and Atropos.    Clotho was the spinner, and she spun the thread of life from her distaff onto her spindle. Lachesis was the drawer of lots who measured the thread of life allotted to each person with her measuring rod.    Atropos was the cutter of the thread of life, and when each person's time was up, she determined the manner of the death and cut their life's thread with her abhorred shears. They had power over both mortals and the gods.    Such was Fate; and Fate, by definition, was beyond the intervention of man or god.

Fate may have taken a hand in this, Dace thought, but he was focused upon Destiny, which was a universal force and term the uninformed often wrongly used interchangeably with fate, and one with which Dace had become quite familiar during the entirety of his life.  His destiny had been laid out before him and it was the vision of his father, however, he knew for his destiny to be fulfilled, it required *his* action, as well as the actions of others, to be fully realized, and that was why he was standing in that noisy bar on that noisy night.

While the Greeks and other ancients may have believed one's destiny was as preordained as was their fate, Dace was of the modern world and believed mortals had the ability and responsibility to take action for Destiny's hand to be fulfilled.  If one acted and lost, that was his destiny. If one failed to act and lost, that was his fate.  With the actions he was contemplating tonight, as he saw things, Dace was taking control of playing the hand of his own destiny.  Fate had already dealt the cards.

Two hours later, Dace's boredom was lifted when he observed his Desire yawn; which was followed by an elbow poke from her friend. The two women piano players had been replaced an hour before by a balding man and less attractive redheaded woman, although the quality of the music remained fairly static.  People continued to come and go, and even though it was closing time in many places, they were in New Orleans, and the dawn of Ash Wednesday and beginning of Lent notwithstanding, neither the crowd nor the pace of imbibing waned.  But Desire was slowing down, and she leaned to speak to her friend, who looked disappointed, but nodded and said something in return.

Dace watched the winding down of the seemingly endless, animated discussions between the girls and Cindy and Dave.  The four of them had formed up on a single table as spaces had become available by the comings and goings.  Together, the foursome had consumed over twenty Hurricanes.    His Desire then stood, wobbled slightly, was hugged by Cindy, shook Dave's hand and touched her friend on the shoulder, then wove her way toward the portal to the hallway.  Her alcohol-dulled eyes brushed past Dace who had pushed himself back into a shadow.   He watched her round the corner into the hall, then turn right and make her way toward the courtyard area. He followed to keep her in sight, and saw her enter through a door marked 'Ladies'. Minutes later, she emerged, still seemed a bit uncertain in her walk, took a deep breath, recrossed the courtyard, paused at the doorway, then began to move down the less-crowded hallway toward St. Peter Street.

Dace slithered around the corner into the passageway and followed at a safe distance, already knowing how he would first approach her when the time was right. At the sidewalk, she turned right, away from Bourbon Street and Dace smiled. The crowds outside had thinned, but as Dace looked left at the doorway, he could see New Orleans' best known party street still contained a substantial crowd and he was glad she had selected the opposite direction. By leaving alone and walking toward the less crowded streets toward the river, his Desire had made the correct decisions necessary for destiny; correctly for his, and wrongly for hers.

The next road toward the river to parallel Bourbon was Royal Street. His Desire turned right, headed for Canal Street. He closed the distance between them to mere steps two blocks later. The cobbled sidewalks of Royal Street were still lightly populated, even nearing half past two in the morning. His Desire's pace was measured, and slightly less wobbly as the cool, clean air refreshed her drink-addled brain. Dace watched her body move. His eyes played upon the distinct up-and-down movement of her buttocks beneath the black, ruffled skirt. He could feel his body stir at the thought of what must eventually reveal itself.

At the intersection with Bienville, ironically the same street he had first laid his gaze upon her and made her his selection, she paused to allow a trio of police cruisers to slowly pass from right to left. Dace stepped beside her. As they waited, he used the moment to say his first words to his Desire.

"Hi," he said. "Didn't I see you earlier?"

Ashley looked up at him. He had applied his patented smile which she returned as her brain recalled him.

"I think you did," she said.

"I never forget a beautiful face," he said.

She ignored the line. The last of the police cars passed by and she and Dace, along with a handful of others who had gathered, began to cross the street. As his Desire took a step onto the slippery cobbles, her heel slipped and she began to tumble. Dace caught her with one arm, righted her with ease. His arm briefly held her, their eyes made contact, then he slowly released her with a flourish of gentility and proffered words of concern. She responded by grasping his outstretched arm with both hands, then gently separated from him, her hands slipping down his soft, cashmere jacket arm to momentarily linger upon his warm hand.

"Thank you," she said, her face flushing, then she released his hand and turned to continue her walk.

"You are most welcome," Dace said. He fell in beside her again. "If we're going to dance like that, I imagine I should properly introduce myself."

Her face turned to him. He could see the confused fog of alcohol in her eyes, but her smile welcomed his advance.

"I'm Dace," he said.

"Dace?" she said, her small, perfect nose wrinkling.

"It's a family name," he said. "You can call me Sir Gawain, the most gallant of all the Knights of the Round Table, if you prefer, my lady."

His Desire stopped dead in her tracks.

"I suppose that would make me Dame Ragnelle?" she said, her stance comporting to the challenge.

He was frankly surprised at her response and her posture. The girl was obviously well-read, he thought, to know the legend of Gawain and Ragnelle; and her spirit held a natural fire, which made his Desire even more appealing.

"Ah, so you know the stories. Pardon me for being so clumsy in my implication. Obviously, were you a vision of Dame Ragnelle, you would most certainly be the post-wedding iteration," Dace said, flashing another big smile.

She had begun walking again. She talked as she walked, her thoughts surprisingly cogent, her words flowing without sluggishness or slur.

"The Round Table story wherein the gallant Sir Gawain was forced to make the Hobson's choice? To save the life of Arthur, his king, Sir Gawain must consent to his betrothal to the 'Loathly Lady', a horribly ugly woman known as Dame Ragnelle, in barter for her supplying the answer to the question: 'What women most desire'? I know it." She turned her head as she walked, contentedly smiled up at him. "Thank you for adding the post-wedding comment, though."

"Ah, yes, I felt it appropriate to compare you to Ragnelle on the wedding night because that's when she reveals her true form to be that of a beautiful young maiden, much to Sir Gawain's ultimate relief, I'm sure." He smiled, but she didn't look at him directly. "Fortunately for us, we don't have that original conundrum."

He laughed. They continued along. She said nothing, but her mind considered him. He was cute, and personable, and obviously an intelligent and articulate man, but she was in no mood for a street side pick up.

"And you are?" he said.

"Ashley," she said. "Unless you want to continue this medieval role playing."

They arrived at Canal Street. Again, she stopped, looked around.

"Which way are we going?" Dace asked.

"We?"

She turned right, alone.

Dace caught up again.

"Turns out we are going the same way," he said. "Fate?"

"I don't believe in fate," she said, not looking at him, her pace quickening.

"Ah, a metaphysical libertarian, is that it?"

Again, she stopped. Was this guy really wanting to get into a sidewalk debate over determinism in the guise of Fate versus Free Will? It was late, and she was a bit drunk, and while Ashley never shirked from a challenge, especially to argue points, she really had no interest. Then she looked into his eyes, which were soft, and warm, and inviting, and she reconsidered; a bit.

"How did we get into this?" Ashley said.

Dace could feel her eyes searching his. He knew this was his moment.

"You slipped, I caught you," Dace said. "The rest is just two strangers getting to know each other."

"I doubt that can happen on a six-block walk," she said, then left him there as she crossed Canal a half block before the still extensive police presence at the Bourbon Street intersection.

"Stranger things have happened in the history of the world, Ashley," he said as he jogged to catch up. "You intrigue me."

"You don't even know me," she said.

"Why don't we change that?" he said.

He saw her smile. There came the breach in her wall.

"You've got a block and a half," she said.

He walked and talked. She answered all his questions. As they turned left on Baronne Street, Dace couldn't believe his luck. Ashley may not believe in fate, but at that moment he certainly did.

She stopped in front of the Fairmont, paused at the base of the entryway steps. A doorman stood watch inside. He observed; made no move.

"This is me," she said.

"Don't believe in fate, do you?" He swept his arm upward toward the hotel. "This is me, too."

She squared herself to him. It was the confident posture of an adult which belied what Dace believed to be her true age.

"Fate, gallant Sir Dace, presupposes the inability of man to alter his path as determined by the three sisters. It's an ancient superstition, and one perpetuated through time by people who never seem to be able to win on their own merit. It's at worst an excuse, at best a coincidence; nothing else. With God's gift to us of Free Will, the power of Fate seems a bit overrated, doesn't it?"

Dace smiled. She smirked.

"You believe in God?" he said. "Isn't that a bit of an antiquated viewpoint these days?"

"When I get to Heaven, I'll ask Him His view on the matter," she said. "So, yes, I do believe in God."

She turned to leave, but it was Dace who led the way up the steps. The doorman came through the side door, stepped onto the landing and held it open for them.

"Hungry?" Dace said as they passed into the lobby.

"What?"

"Are you hungry?"

She glanced down at her shoes; toyed with the thought. He seemed pleasant enough, well dressed, educated, clever, funny. Her eyes met his.

"Are the restaurants in house still serving?" she asked the doorman who had returned to his post several steps away.

"No miss, they're not serving until breakfast," he said and he looked at his watch. "Two hours from now."

"Well, that solves that," she said to Dace.

"I know a place," he said.

From his pocket, he retrieved the card the valet had given him and handed it to the doorman along with a twenty-dollar bill.

"Can we make that happen?" Dace said.

The doorman read the handwritten note on the back of the card, nodded, placed a call from the nearby podium and requested the gentleman's car be brought to the Baronne Street entrance.

"Two minutes, sir," the doorman said.

Dace turned to Ashley, spread his arms wide.

"See how easy it is?" he said.

Ashley took a step closer to him and cocked her head.

"What place?

Dace checked his watch.

"It's nearly three in the morning," he said. "Does it really matter?"

Headlights appeared on the street. Ashley saw the pearl white Escalade come to a stop and the valet jump out from the driver's side and jog around the car. Her eyes moved to the doorman who had stopped paying attention. Dace stood there, waiting.

"Okay," Ashley said and then she walked past him and moved through the revolving door and back out onto the street.

The valet waited at the passenger side door and held it open for Ashley as she got inside. He closed the door. Dace pressed a twenty into the kid's palm and walked around to the driver's side. He got in, and pulled away from the curb before his Desire, who now had a name, could change her mind. For her part, Ashley settled into the big leather seat, and when reminded by Dace, buckled up. She looked across the cabin of the vehicle, watched this interesting man as he maneuvered out of the downtown area.   She was tired, and a bit drunk, but she really was hungry.

"Where are we going?" she asked, crossing her legs.

Dace watched her body move and smiled.

"You're gonna love it," he said.

"I trust you," Ashley said, settling in the seat.

Famous last words, Dace thought as he drove toward the only area of the city he really knew well, although much of what he remembered about it was a bit foggy.   Minutes later, the Escalade moved along St. Charles Avenue.   The parades were long gone for another year; scatterings of revelers still wandered the darkened streets, and trash was everywhere while strings of green, gold, and purple beads hung from the canopy of branches and utility lines.   Many would remain tangled there for years.

"I love the Garden District," Ashley said.   "So historic, and the romance is intoxicating.   Have you read Anne Rice's Mayfair witch chronicles?   She lives in the Garden District, and sets several of the stories in the area.   Very sensual, very romantic.   They're a follow-on to her vampire books, you know, *Interview With The Vampire, The Vampire Lestat*.   Those."

"I spent the last couple of days wandering the area around here," Dace said shaking his head.   "But, no, I haven't read her work."

"You should," Ashley said.   "They're wonderful."   A moment later, his wording struck her.   "Wandering?"

"Yes, but perhaps exploring would be a more appropriate descriptive," Dace said.   "I spent the night in one of the cemeteries around here."

"Spent the night *in* one of the cemeteries?"   She was sitting up now, had uncrossed her legs, placed her hand on the door handle.   "Don't they lock those up at night?"

"They do.   I had to climb the gates to get in.   I was much more drunk than you are now, if you can picture that.   Slept like the dead, to tell you the truth, on top of a crypt.   I had been overcome by an impending death, of sorts.   In the morning, this morning, to be factual, a rebirth occurred and out I walked.   Almost like Jesus Christ Himself."

Ashley may have been drunk, and perhaps she was misunderstanding, but the words coming from her companion had suddenly begun to give her the creeps.   She sat forward, looked around outside.   They were passing Tulane University, and there were few people remaining out on the street that far uptown.   The lights in the windows of the houses and nearby buildings were mostly dark.   Dace flipped a switch on his side panel which locked the doors, then toggled another which disabled the power locks to all doors but his own.   He watched Ashley's right hand find the inside door handle. He smiled in the darkness as she worked it, but found moving the handle did nothing.

They were approaching South Carrollton Avenue, the street on which Dace had found the Popeye's Chicken joint two days ago. Ahead, the street car tracks of the St. Charles line departed the wide median and crossed their lane on St. Charles to continue in the median on South Carrollton. Dace slowed. Ashley relaxed.

"I know where we're going," she said with a smile.

"You do?" Dace said. "Where?"

"The Camellia Grill," Ashley said, pointing beyond the intersection to the building with the white-columned entry. It was a Garden District landmark for over fifty years. "I love the Camellia Grill. I don't think it's open yet, though. Looks dark."

Dace followed her point, saw the restaurant, remembered passing by. It was indeed dark; but it was also not where he was headed. He had wandered the area for many hours over the last two days and had discovered any number of interesting places, and one of them was only two blocks away and it wasn't the grill.

"Hmm, I guess you're right," he said.

Dace placed his foot on the brake, Ashley braced for the right turn onto Carrollton, wondering where they'd go for something to eat now that her companion had discovered the Camellia was closed. Dace suddenly accelerated hard and wheeled the Escalade to the left, bounced the SUV across the street car tracks and then raced down Carrollton in the opposite direction at high speed. Ashley's body, anticipating a right turn, fell away and her head smacked the side window in the turn; a blow which dazed and disoriented her. A block later, Dace sped across a two-lane road, then onto a gravel patch, over a double set of train tracks, then up an access road to the top of the levee. At the apex, he turned off the headlights and lightly applied the brake just before they bounced over an asphalt pathway, and began the stomach-dropping plunge on the backside of the levee toward the black waters of the river beyond. Ashley screamed. She clawed repeatedly at the door handle, not seeming to realize all she had to do was manually move the lock to get out. Just before they flew off the ledge and into the water, Dace slammed on the brakes, wheeled hard to the right, and the Escalade skidded to a stop. Before Ashley had the chance to orient herself, Dace released her seatbelt, grabbed her jacket just below the collar, opened his door with his left hand and dragged her across the center console and out the driver's door.

As the night air and smell of the river hit her, Ashley began to scream. Dace held her fast by the jacket and his left hand went to cover her mouth. She bit him and he hit her, hard. Her head fell backward and her eyes rolled in her head and for an instant he felt afraid, the type of instantaneous fear a child feels when they break something valuable. Ashley roused from the daze moments later; but not the nightmare, which was only beginning.

She was on the ground, on her back.  He was on top of her, straddling her, his knees pinning down her wrists to the gravel, his left hand over her mouth, his right pulling at her top.  She struggled, attempted to use her legs alternately to roll herself and to fight back.  Her nails clawed impotently at his jeans.  She was as frightened as she had ever been in her life and her mind raced.  When she looked into his eyes, her fright turned to near madness; gone was the softness and warmth, replaced by the merciless ferocity of a predator.  The more she fought him, the harder he pressed her to the ground.  She tried to bite him again and he responded by repeatedly slamming her head against the rocks.

The rest she experienced as more of a dissociated, gauzy awareness. Her mind had overloaded and she would have floated away from everything were it not for the tether of severe pain to her body.  He ripped her clothes from her to the degree he required for the things he did; he tore her skirt and pulled it from under her.  Her tights he pulled down, pausing only to smile into her face when he discovered she had no panties underneath.  Her bare buttocks pressed into the gravel.  He tore the front of her shirt and pushed up her thin brassiere.

Dace amazed at the firmness and fullness of Ashley's breasts, the tightness of her body, the way the girl had obviously waxed all the delicate areas of a woman.  He felt the pressure inside his jeans, the hunger inside of himself.  His hands moved over her, explored all of her most intimate spots.  His mouth tasted the blood on her lips, the subtle saltiness of her breasts, and even touched on the mound between her thighs.  She could resist nothing since he had grabbed her hair and bounced her head off the ground several times.  He had feared she had gone unconscious, but he smiled as he still found her there, behind half-lidded eyes.  The fire within those eyes had flickered, but it still burned. He wanted her.  He craved her.  This was his ultimate moment.  His control of his own life.  His nuclear weapon against Destiny should he ever need it.  The control he now possessed for perhaps the first time in his existence excited him beyond any imaginings.

He pushed her legs apart, spit upon her womanhood and then released himself from his jeans.  His manhood was as firm and full as it had ever been.  Before he pushed inside her for the first time, he roughly grabbed her by the chin and forced her to face him.  Her eyes attempted to flee, but could not as his gaze gripped her soul.

"Look at me," he hissed.  "I want you to remember who did this to you before you die."

The girl's eyes went wide and then everything remaining of her that was Ashley seemed to evaporate.  Dace pushed himself inside her.  Her buttocks absorbed all the force of the pounding which followed, sharp stones and bits of shells cut into her. Her leather jacket protected her back, but was little consolation to the pain of the violation. Deep inside herself, Ashley began to pray. A tear welled in the corner of her eye, then slid down her cheek. Suddenly Dace cursed, then slapped her.

He withdrew himself then stood, grabbed her again around the collar of her jacket and dragged her along the ground toward the rear of the Escalade. A shard of bottle lodged in the gravel sliced a gash in her right thigh. He opened the tailgate of the SUV and hoisted her into the cavernous cargo area. He climbed inside with her, pushed her diagonally across the floor, closed the tailgate and resumed his violation of her body.

Yes, this was much more comfortable, Dace thought as he moved inside the girl. The gravel had bruised his knees through his jeans. His annoyance at the pain he felt he took out on Ashley as she moaned and he felt her womanhood lose its wetness. He felt the years of anger inside him building into a burning sensation in the base of his groin and moments later he exploded inside the young woman. He felt the warm slickness return the pleasure to him of being there.

Dace rested a while, seated across from her as she rolled into a tight ball. He stripped the remaining clothes from her body, left her nude in her coiling. She began to weep softly and he struck her with his fist in her lower back sending waves of new pain through her body. He watched her like that for well over an hour, touching her as he wished, whispering in her ear so she could know he was still there. When he was ready, he took her again; just as violently, just as angrily, and again he released his rage inside her. When he had finished the second time, he was emotionally drained and physically spent. The girl was unresponsive. Blood flowed from her nose and mouth, and sometime during the attack she had lost control of her bladder and bowels. Dace grabbed her by the hair and raised her head, looked into her eyes. The light was dull, but she was still there, he saw. He smiled.

"Time to die, Ashley," he said. "Are you ready to meet your God and ask Him your questions?"

She offered no response, and even less resistance. He opened the rear door, fixed his pants, recoiled at the sight of the evidence of her disgusting loss of control, then dragged her by her hair through the blood, body fluids, and excrement. She tumbled limply onto the ground. The impact elicited no sound from her. Dace dragged her toward the river near a copse of trees and area of long grass just downriver of the rows of barges tied at anchorage just offshore. He stood with her lying limply at his feet on a small ledge of earth and gravel, then kicked her in the head twice. She gave no reaction, and when he spread the lids of her eyes, he could tell she was gone. The dull light of moments ago had extinguished. With his foot, he rolled Ashley's limp body down the small, grassy knob toward the river and turned his back on her. He knew the river would swallow her, then tumble her in its current toward the Gulf, and eventually regurgitate what was left of the body he had craved and possessed somewhere far away from there.

Back at the Escalade, he reached into the cargo area and retrieved her clothes. He wiped the mess with her jacket, scraped the bits of excrement with the only thing he could find fit for the purpose and threw everything in the direction of the river. Inside the passenger compartment, he removed her purse and shoes from the floor and threw those toward the Mississippi as well; he heard the sound of splashes.

A minute later, he was in the driver's seat with the Escalade climbing the levee to the road. The eastern sky was lightening. He looked at his watch. Just before six in the morning. The attack had lasted nearly three hours. He drove to the juncture with St. Charles Avenue, saw the lights go on inside the Camellia Grill just beyond the intersection. He drove around the median, parked out front, checked himself in the visor mirror, then went inside. He asked for the restrooms, was directed toward the back by a cook preparing his griddle. He cleaned himself up in the bathroom. On his way back to the counter, he spied a pay phone. He called home, knowing he'd only wake his mother if his father was there, which he doubted since the Senate was in session that week. If his father were home and his parents were still asleep, he knew Caroline would pick up.

"Hello?" his mother said.

"Hi, mom," he said. "I want to come home now."

The conversation was short. His mother cried when she heard something hauntingly familiar in her son's voice. Dace took the reaction as merely the emotion of finally hearing from him. When she informed him his father was in McClean, he said he'd call him there in an hour. He asked if she would help pave the way and tell The Senator that he was ready to end this thing. 'It is over,' he had said.

After he had hung up, he returned to the serpentine, Formica topped counter trimmed in stainless steel banding applied by tacks and took a stool. The place had the ambience of old-style cafe. A black waiter offered him coffee, which he accepted. Dace removed a laminated menu from a nearby condiment station and ordered breakfast. The waiter repeated the order to the cook in diner shorthand who responded in kind. Minutes later, just after being poured a refill of his coffee, the waiter slid the heavy china platter in front of him. Dace tore into the food. The flavors were exquisite for ham and eggs, almost as good as the breakfast Auntie D had made for him and Dave days ago.

'Yes, Ashley, I guess I will come to love the Camellia Grill, too,' he said to himself.

"Sir?"

Dace looked up at the waiter.

"Nothing," he said. "Just thanking a friend for recommending your fine establishment."

The waiter smiled and moved down the line to a new customer.

# Chapter Twenty-six

The coolness of the overnight, still air, and recent heavy rains created the meteorological trifecta necessary for early morning fog developing in the low-lying areas outside of New Orleans. As the sun peeked over the horizon, the Mississippi River for thirty miles each side of the city became shadowed by a thin cloud which climbed inside the levees then gently spilled out over the top to roll down the other side in fragile wisps. River traffic slowed through the area, even though onboard radar units were fairly effective at charting the channel and spotting other vessels; except for the smaller fishing craft which often were too low to the surface to be discerned from the clutter.

Jose, and his brother, Javier, had no idea about the river fog when they walked out of their room in the low-rent, transient hotel just off Airline Highway on the city's west side for a morning of fishing at a spot they had heard about from coworkers which was reputed to be good for small catfish, the good eating size. They loaded their rods and tackle, and a couple of plastic containers of what the locals called 'stink bait' which they had picked up the previous evening at a shop just down the road. Javier returned to their room for a cooler which contained beer and some food for later as Jose loaded the gear. Neither of the brothers had to work that day because their boss was a devout Catholic who had closed his upholstery business for Ash Wednesday. The boys were Catholics too, but with a loss of a day's pay, they also needed to put food on their table, so they decided to go fishing. They'd get to Mass in the evening.

Loaded up, they left the parking lot, made their way out to Airline Highway, then down Monticello toward the river where Jose made a left on Leake Avenue which parallels the levee. Right where they had been told it was, at the intersection with South Carrollton, they spotted the roadway which bisected the levee. Two sets of several cars each belonging to river barge workers were parked between the roadway and railroad tracks. Jose maneuvered between them, eased the old truck over the metal rails, then climbed the steep side of the earthen berm. They noticed the wisps of fog slowly flowing down the outside of the levee, and at the top of the climb, the truck entered a cloud. They could barely see the ground beyond the truck's hood from up there, and Jose carefully rolled down the back side, wishing he and Javier had checked out the place before they were forced to explore the area with such limited visibility. The last thing he wanted to do was to run his new truck - new to him - into the Mississippi.

Once they rolled onto a flat patch, Jose stopped the pickup, engaged the parking brake and turned off the motor.

"The fog is good for the fish," Javier said with a laugh. "Same as back home. They can't see us coming for them."

Jose shared the laugh, then they opened their doors and stepped onto the gravel shelf. They could see the edge of the river down there and smell it too. Somewhere in the fog, they heard the strain of diesel engines running lower than usual and the splashes which was the creation of a squared wake, but they could not see the barges or the tugboat which pushed them. The couldn't even tell if the combination was headed up or down river, the fog-dampened noise echoing off the levees on both sides to give no sense of movement. The brothers grabbed their fishing gear from the back of the truck, along with a couple of five-gallon plastic buckets which would serve the dual purpose of seats while fishing and later hold the catch. Jose retrieved an old blanket from inside the cab to use as a pad between him and the bucket. They made their way toward the river's edge to where they could finally see the pilings just offshore in the shape of an inverted-V to the left where their friends said the small catfish gathered and fed.

They located a relatively flat spot amongst the scrub trees and grasses, rigged and set out their lines; two poles each. Half an hour later, with six good sized catfish in their buckets, Javier told his brother to watch his poles while he took care of some business. Jose told him to go downriver because he didn't want to eat a fish which had swum through his 'mierda', his crap. As with younger brothers everywhere, Javier ignored his older sibling and went upriver to do his business.

He found a secluded spot, dropped his trousers and squatted along the riverbank. Another unseen barge was working its way on the river. Those diesel engines were working harder than the previous tugboat's, the echoes in the fog louder than the first set. He heard them moving along, thought they were going upriver. The sound of the diesels died out just as he was finishing up the paperwork for his business, and that's when he heard something at the river's edge off to his left. Deathly afraid of alligators since coming to Louisiana from Texas and before that Mexico, Javier scrambled to get his pants up and began to move quickly back toward his brother. Then he heard it again. It wasn't the rustling of something moving out of the water, it was a moaning. Soft and low. He inched toward the sound, stepped upon a flat ledge. He heard it again. Javier looked down toward the river. The wake of the barges was just reaching the shore, sending small waves over the body of a nude, young woman tangled in saplings on the river's edge.

He hollered for Jose, who, like older brothers everywhere, ignored the urgency of the call and took his sweet time walking over. When Jose joined Javier on the ledge, the younger brother was visibly shaken and pointed a trembling finger down toward the river. What they were each looking at was unmistakable. The brothers each crossed themselves. Then the woman moved slightly, and moaned again. The brothers looked at each other. They were in the country without documentation, having crossed into the United States one night two years earlier outside of Laredo, Texas. They had found decent employment in a craft with which they were familiar and enjoyed, and currently worked for a man who treated them fairly. Finding a dead, or nearly dead, naked woman would mean police, and after that, the INS, and ultimate deportation back to Mexico. They spoke to each other in frantic Spanish.

"Help me," the woman pleaded in a voice which barely had the strength to carry up the small knob of earth. "Please."

It was Javier who moved first, sliding down the incline. The woman was small, and young, and badly beaten. Javier rolled her over. She cried out weakly.

"Jose, go get the blanket," he called.

Jose hesitated a moment, then ran off toward their fishing spot, grabbed the blanket from his bucket and quickly returned. As he arrived, he watched Javier scramble up the incline, the injured woman over his shoulder. Jose reached out a hand and helped his brother onto the ledge, then unrolled the blanket on the ground. Javier gently lowered the woman onto the middle of it. They covered her up with both sides. This was no woman, they decided at the same time. This was a young girl, perhaps sixteen or seventeen. The brothers recalled their sisters still in Mexico, twins about this girl's age and anger overcame their fear. Who would do such a thing, was the question each asked themselves, but neither verbalized.

The girl tried to speak. Her left eye was bruised and swollen shut, the right merely a slit under which a flicker of life showed in a green iris. She was shivering uncontrollably. Javier knelt beside her, lowered his ear toward her mouth. She spoke with all her strength, but the words came out as a raspy whisper. Javier listened intently while Jose waited quietly. Javier nodded, stroked her matted and muddy hair. He stood.

"What did she say?" Jose asked.

"Her name is Ashley," Javier said, his voice cracking, "and she wants to go home."

Jose looked down at the girl. She had passed out.

"Home?" Jose said. "What are you talking about Javier? We cannot take this girl anywhere but to a hospital, leave her there, and drive away and hope nobody sees us. This is not our problem, my brother."

"Then what, Jose?" Javier said. "What if she dies? The police come find us? Not only do they want to send us back to Mexico, but they maybe think we did this. Send us to prison here."

Jose paced on the small landing.

"I told you to go downriver, Javier," he screamed. "This is your fault. Madre Maria nos ayuda."

Javier ignored the assignation and began rustling through the bushes and brush nearby."

"What are you doing now? Jose said.

"Looking," Javier replied.

"For what?"

"Anything," Javier said, then reached down and picked up a torn black skirt with ruffles which he held up for his brother to see. "This."

Jose knew his brother enjoyed the American detective shows. He'd watch them on the small black and white television in their room after work. His current favorite was Magnum P.I., which a local station had been showing as reruns after the late news. He had often talked to Jose about one day becoming a private investigator in Hawaii.

Javier continued his search, then told Jose to go and pull in their lines, dump the fish back for another day and find a plastic garbage bag or something from the truck. He bent down and picked up part of a torn pair of hosiery. Each item he held by a small corner. Jose continued to stare, unmoving.

"Jose, vamanos," he said, waving his free hand. "Go."

Jose took another look down at the girl, then he reluctantly returned to their fishing spot, thinking the whole time what they were doing was all a big mistake. He reeled in the lines, two of which had small catfish on the hook. He released them, dumped the others back. He returned the gear to the truck, then searched through the cab, under the seats, finally locating a plastic bag which had once held foam for the upholstery shop.

By the time he returned, Javier had collected more clothing from the brush. The items he had set out on the blanket on top of the girl, who had thankfully stopped shivering. Jose knelt next to her, touched her on the neck. Her pulse was strong, regular. Her temperature was warming. He crossed himself, thanked Mother Mary that the girl appeared no longer on the verge of death. Perhaps Javier was right, he thought. They should just take her home. No questions, no police. Let the family deal with it. There is only so much of a good deed they can do without being punished for it, and perhaps that was the limit, he concluded.

"Okay, Javier," Jose said standing up. "We take her home, but where is home?"

Javier was carefully reaching into the pockets of a short, leather jacket. There were smears of liquid and mud, he thought, as if the jacket had been used to wipe something. In the second pocket he checked, he found a wad of folded bills, a total of four-hundred-twenty-seven dollars, he later counted. Inside the fold of bills he found a Louisiana driver's license with the name Ashley Monreale. He looked at the picture, then at the bruised and battered face. He wondered again what kind of animal could do this to such a beautiful girl; and, apart from the obvious reasons, why? Just for sex? His mouth filled with liquid as bile formed in the back of his throat and he fought the urge to be sick.

He stood, showed Jose the money and license. He handed Jose the license, knelt down and replaced the wad of cash in the jacket pocket. From Jose's other hand, Javier snatched the bag, then carefully placed all the items of the clothing he had found. It was everything he expected a girl to wear, except for underpants and shoes. He stood, and handed the bag to Jose, then bent down to scoop up the girl in the blanket.

"Let's go, Jose," he said. "It's time to take this girl home."

Javier lead the way with Jose close behind. Jose jumped ahead at the truck, opened the passenger door, then the half-door to the back seat of the min-crew cab. Javier easily laid the girl onto the seat. He placed the bag with her clothes on the floor, closed the half door. Jose went around to the driver's door, reached across the cab to the glove box and retrieved a Louisiana map. He searched the city index, noted the cross coordinates and ran his fingers from the edges of the map. He pointed to the small town.

"White Castle," he said to Javier. "That's seventy or eighty miles, Javier." He glared across the cab.

"Then you had better start driving, Jose."

Javier slammed his door as Jose started the engine. He tossed the map onto Javier's lap, then backed out and ascended the levee. The girl said something from the back seat and Javier turned and rose up and leaned toward her. When he returned to his seat his eyes were wet. Jose drove out onto South Carrollton toward the highway.

"What did she say?" Jose asked, dividing his attention between Javier and the road.

"She said, 'God bless you'," Javier said.

Dave and Cindy left Pat O'Brien's shortly after Ashley had left when a man moved in on a willing Ronnie. When they arrived home an hour later, Cindy went to take a shower, and Dave checked Dace's room. He found the pad with the note he had left lying on Dace's bed. An empty garment bag hung from the bathroom door. Damp towels lay scattered on the floor. He shook his head and then joined Cindy in the shower.

Dace had spoken to his father following breakfast, and then waited for Travis and Rudy in the general aviation parking lot at the New Orleans airport. He had been waiting over an hour and was becoming impatient. During the first half hour of waiting, he had wiped down the interior of the Escalade. In the cargo compartment, he had used rags and water he had talked out of the janitor inside the airport building to further clean up the girl's mess and had deposited the used rags into a nearby garbage can.

He had searched every inch of the vehicle for anything of Ashley's he had missed when tossing things out in the dark at the river. He found nothing, but his heart skipped a beat when he had discovered there was only one Massachusetts license plate in the cargo area. He recalled having used it one to scrape her soil from the carpeting and had thought he had wiped it clean with her jacket and then replaced it inside.

'Could I have tossed it?' he said to himself.

He had no answer. He considered going back to search, but only for an instant. The risks were just too great, even though he was certain the girl's body had long ago floated down river. He recalled seeing a true crime program one time in which a detective of some sort had said that a dead body will sink initially, then, as it decomposes and gasses are trapped inside, will again surface. He shuddered when he thought about it. He had done it, and he now possessed the power to destroy everything should he ever wish to; he thrilled at everything about the memory and the power the truth possessed, but he took no pleasure in the reality of a dead young girl used to serve his purposes. She had been a means to an end, nothing more, and in order to beguile himself, he refused to think of her as ever having been human.

A van from a Hampton Inn arrived at the portico of the building across the way. Dace watched as two pilots in uniform exited with their bags. They each tipped the driver, then the younger man with three stripes on his sleeves followed the older man with four through the glass doors. The van departed.

Dace wiped the vehicles keys with the edge of his jacket and placed them on top of the visor. When he saw Rudy and Travis pull into the parking lot in a black Lincoln Navigator and drive through a gate to the ramp, Dace exited the vehicle, used his jacket sleeve to close the door, then walked toward the portico and through the same glass doors the pilots had entered. He strolled past the reception desk, smiled at the fetching young woman behind the counter, saw the Navigator parked alongside a Gulfstream jet on the ramp, pointed at it and said to the girl, 'I guess that's me,' then walked out another set of glass doors.

Attendants loaded the bags of cargo as Dace walked empty handed across the tarmac toward the red carpet leading to the air stairs where Rudy was standing, holding a black medical bag. Travis was speaking to another attendant who soon departed with the Navigator, then moved and stood next to his partner just as Dace crossed in front of the nose of the jet. The right engine was spooling up. The younger pilot descended the steps. The four came together on the red carpet.

"Boys," Dace said as he nodded to Travis and Rudy and then ascended the stairs and disappeared into the cabin.

Rudy and Travis exchanged annoyed glances.

"Dulles?" the junior pilot said.

"Dulles," Travis said and then climbed the stairs.

Minutes later, the gleaming white jet with silver stripes sped down the runway and jumped into the clear, blue sky. They turned left over the river. Dace looked out his large, oval window at the fog-shrouded Mississippi as it snaked its way east to west, headed for the city of New Orleans. He pulled the shade, reclined his oversized leather seat and a footrest automatically extended. He slipped off his loafers, closed his eyes and went to sleep.

With Sandy coming home that afternoon, I picked up around the house a bit. It's amazing how much clutter I can scatter in the matter of a few days. Not that I'm a slob, far from it. Rather, the items I was collecting and putting into the proper receptacles: trash, laundry hamper, dishwasher, was merely my stuff, the things Sandy referred to as 'man cave detritus'. I made one final pass through. Having Sandy coming home filled my thoughts, even pushed out of my mind the case of the kids out in Vacherie. When I had turned in last night, I was intending going back out there this morning. I was still curious, but finally realized what could I really do? Sit out there and wait for something to happen? Whatever was going on, it would resolve itself eventually. Of that I was certain. If it was still on my mind, I could always go out and snoop around more after I brought my bride home.

As I passed through the kitchen to drop yet another glass I had found into the dishwasher, I glanced at the clock. Three hours until Sandy's flight arrived. It was Ash Wednesday, and I thought we'd stop in at church before coming home. I knew they had a Mass at 5:30. The timing would be perfect. During my first marriage, nourishment of the kids' souls had been the purview of my wife as I slept in most Sunday mornings, but this time, I had already decided things were going to be different. We'd be a family, one grounded in a Faith I hadn't been close to for decades. I knew it would make Sandy happy, and what better time to restart than Ash Wednesday, the first day of Lent leading to Easter's rebirth?

I was removing some turkey breast, lettuce, a tomato and the Miracle Whip from the refrigerator to go with the two slices of whole grain bread I had just sliced from a fresh loaf I had picked up from the corner bakery that morning when my cell phone vibrated and rang. It was Sandy. My eyes went to the clock on the wall. Still two hours away from the time she had given me. I pulled the slip of paper from my pocket upon which I had written the information when she had given it to me. I double checked the times.

"Hey, honey," I said. "Did I mess up?"

"No, Will," she said. "I'm in Memphis between flights."

"Well, then, it's good to hear your voice, Sandy." I tried to ignore the something I detected in her few words. "What's up? Flight issues?"

"No," she said. A pause. A deep breath.

Oh-oh.

She continued. I wondered what I had done, couldn't think of anything.

"I just returned a call to Tracey Walker," she said.

"Okay," I said.

"She needs your help," Sandy said.

"She's got my number, Sandy. Why didn't she just call me?"

"Because she needed to speak to me first. Woman to woman."

Oh-oh.

"Listen, Sandy, whoever she was, she meant nothing to me. Nothing, you hear?"

"Stop it, Will," she said. "It's nothing you did for God's sake. Sometimes I wonder about you. No, Tracey has a delicate situation for which she needs your help. I think you should do it."

Sandy went on to explain things to me. I missed the first few sentences as I congratulated myself for my not having done anything wrong, but as she continued, I quickly caught up with her.

"She doesn't need me," I said when Sandy took a breath. "She needs the police, real police. I'm not a cop anymore, Sandy."

"The victim doesn't want police involvement, Will. Absolutely refuses it. She's in and out of consciousness, dazed, but adamant about that one point."

I asked the stupid man question.

"Why?"

Ronnie marched into the room in full apology mode. It was shortly after noon, and she was certain Ashley would really be ticked with her that day. She stopped in mid-sentence as the door closed behind her. She stood in the center of the room, looked around. Ashley wasn't sitting there, stewing; her bed hadn't been slept in and their things were strewn about just they way they had been a night ago when they had dressed to go out.

She walked to the bathroom, looked around. Nothing had changed since she had last left it after having curled her hair the night before. Her curling iron still lay exactly as she had placed it. The tub and sink were dry.

"Come on out, Ash," she said as she emerged from the bathroom and opened the closet door. "Point made."

The room was silent. The closet empty.

Ronnie moved across the room, picked up her cell phone from the nightstand between the two beds. Fourteen missed calls and the voicemail icon showed in the corner. Her heart leapt into her throat. She flipped open the phone, checked the record of calls. She nearly jumped out of her skin when the thing began vibrating in her hand. The caller ID read: HOME. She cautiously pressed the green button to answer the call, uncertain what she would say beyond 'hello'.

"Hello?" Ronnie said.

Her mother's voice in response was a blend of franticness and relief.

"Oh, my god, Veronica," she said, then in rapid fire: "Where are you? Are you all right? What's going on?"

Her mother waited for no answers, instead went directly into a recitation. Ronnie slumped to sit on the bed as her mother described the events which had taken place that morning at home. Her heart beat like it wanted out of her chest, her mind whirled.

"Is she hurt bad, mom?" she said sheepishly and on the verge of tears, all adultness evaporated.

Her mother described to her daughter the injuries Ronnie's general practitioner father had discovered, including the evidence of a violent rape. He would have normally been in his Baton Rouge office when Ashley had been dropped off by two anonymous men, but it was closed for Ash Wednesday. It had been fortuitous he had been home, her mother said, because she had not known what she would have done without him there. Next her mother asked how they were going to tell Mr. Monreale about this. It was a question which worried her mother more than Ronnie's condition at the moment and the girl simply said she'd be home right away. She disconnected the call and ran out of the room.

Ten long minutes later, Ronnie was in her car, driving out of downtown New Orleans. Her shattered heart tore even more as the worn and weathered reminders of Mardi Gras combined with that year's fresh additions which hung in the midday sunlight from every building and lamp post.

She began to cry.

I spoke to Tracey Walker while en route to a small town I'd never heard of. White Castle, Louisiana was about eighty miles from home, along the Mississippi River and closer to Baton Rouge than to New Orleans. I steered with my knees on I-10 as I wrote down the street address of Dr. Broussard's home. I asked her why the family would need the services of an attorney and private detective rather than the police. Sandy hadn't had an answer to that question. Tracey told me they were friends, members of the same Mardi Gras krewe, and she would fill me in when I got there. Only because Sandy had asked me to go out there, did that satisfy me; for now. I clicked off after telling her I'd be there in about an hour.

I had taken the Corvette after calling Sandy back and telling her I was on my way out the door and that she'd have to take a cab home. Given the circumstances, that plan was okay with her. I told her I loved her and would see her later at the house. She told me to call if I needed anything. I asked how the little one was doing and then told her how much I loved her again. She said the boy or girl growing inside her would be proud his or her father was such a good man. I'm kinda uncomfortable with that after everything I've done in my life, but I didn't burst her bubble.

Risking a ticket, and to clear that last thought from my head, I accelerated to just under ninety.

At highway 70, I exited the interstate and headed south toward the last bridge over the Mississippi before Baton Rouge. In Donaldsonville, I picked up highway 1 and cut cross-country to White Castle. Finding the street was easy, and finding the Broussard estate was even easier, given the relatively modest homes of their neighbors. I entered through open, white, wrought iron gates between two stone piers and up a paved drive to the big, red-brick house on the hill. Like many plantation homes, the front was columned, but lacked the wraparound porches, instead sporting individual porches off the rooms on the sides. It was an eclectic blend of architectural designs and my conclusion was a battle between husband and wife had created a monstrosity for which no committee would accept blame.

I came to a stop behind Tracey Walker's champagne BMW, and before I could get out, she was outside on the porch. As I approached, she closed the door and met me halfway up the walk. She held me there by the elbow and spoke in low tones even though the nearest ears were most likely half a mile away. Some of what she was saying made sense, much did not. At the time, I chalked up the anxiety I detected to her personal attachment to the situation, although with everything between Tracey Walker and I, our underlying tension may also have played a role in the content and quality of her disjointed briefing. I accepted all that because Sandy had asked me to be nice, but when she asked me to sign a confidentiality agreement, I nearly lost it.

"What the hell, Tracey," I said, holding the paper in my hand. "You call Sandy asking for a personal favor. I allow myself to be dragged into the middle of what rightly should be a police investigation, and you have the stones to tell me you need to clear the paperwork before you'll let me in on everything? This is bullshit."

She stood there holding a pen. I again remembered Sandy's entreaty.

"Gimme the damn pen," I said, finally, snatching the thing from her grip, and then spun her around physically and placed the document on her shoulder where I signed it, dotting the i's in William hard. She turned and grabbed the document back, and the pen, with an annoyed look on her face.

I followed her into the house. In the parlor, I was introduced to Dr. and Mrs. Broussard. Dr. Broussard had the typical handshake of a physician, weak and short-lived, like he didn't really want to risk you hurting his precious, heeling hands or pick up any more of your germs than he had to. Mrs. Broussard's handshake was firmer, but her hand was cold and clammy. A fish. They didn't offer first names, so I made a mental note to get those from Tracey later. They asked me to have a seat. I looked around for something suitable, but frankly, the furnishings - like Mrs. Broussard - would have been warmed by the addition of plastic covers, so I begged off, claiming I needed a stretch of my legs after an hour plus in the car. Mrs. Broussard gave me a tightlipped smile. The good doctor went to get himself another drink. He didn't offer me one.

I reached into the breast pocket of my sports jacket and retrieved a note pad and pen. I began asking questions, most of which Tracey intercepted and provided the answers, to the point I saw little use for the Broussards to even be involved in the process. For parents of a sixteen-year-old daughter who had been raped and beaten and found seven hours ago along the banks of the Mississippi River, they came across more as frightened out of their wits than angry or worried. It was something else that wasn't making sense.

After a while, I decided to eliminate the middlemen and directed my questions straight to Tracey. I noticed she also had a drink. I was beginning to feel like the hired help, but because this was a favor to my wife, nobody was paying me. I scanned my notes as I thought of other questions. In the midst of that process, the front door burst open and a young girl dressed like she had just come in from a night on the town ran into the room. She had been crying. She bypassed her mother's arms and went directly to her father, who hugged her tightly.

"Mr. Langdon, if you could give us a minute," Mrs. Broussard said as she stood and approached the father/daughter hug. "Please let yourself down to the kitchen. I believe Marcella is back there and she will be happy to get you something soft to drink."

I tucked my notebook and pen away. Tracey was giving me finger directions and mouthing 'down the hall to the left'. I backed out of the room and removed myself to the kitchen. I heard the heavy pocket doors slide shut behind me. Marcella was indeed back there, and she was indeed happy to get me something soft to drink. I chose lemonade, assuming the sour pucker would help me blend in with the Broussards. I also took an offered seat at the kitchen table. Marcella was cautious about speaking to me, but eventually she opened up a bit. She was the one who had opened the door around eight-thirty that morning to find two Hispanic men on the stoop and an older, gray pickup truck in the driveway. She was the one who had called for the doctor to come out. Somehow, during my parlor questioning, these events had been attributed to Mrs. Broussard by Tracey. There had been no mention of Marcella's involvement.

I asked how she knew the men were Hispanic and she put her hands on her hips and glared at me.

"Oh, yeah," I said. "Illegals?"

She nodded.

"Do you know who these gentlemen are, Marcella?" I asked.

She shook her head.

I asked her more questions about the pickup truck. Her eyes appeared to look through the wall in the direction of the parlor. Other than the original timeline clarifications, she gave me little more than I already had, and with every answer, her voice became softer and her answers shorter. Finally, I tried something I had done several times in interrogation rooms which were wired for sound but not video: I passed her my notebook and pen. She looked down at them on the table for several moments, then picked up the pen and wrote down a series of numbers and letters. She then dropped the pen and stood up. She turned her back to me and returned to her stove duties.

I looked over her writing. Definitely Louisiana plates. When I had asked Tracey for this information, she said they didn't have it. Well, now I had something Tracey didn't; or wasn't willing to give just yet.

I stood up and prepared to walk out to the hallway.

"Do they know this, Marcella?" I asked, walking up behind her and tapping my notebook.

She shook her head.

I placed a hand on her shoulder. She twitched, then relaxed.

"Tu secreto esta a salve conmigo, Marcella," I said.

"Gracias," she said, looking at me over her shoulder.

I went out from the kitchen, down the hallway past the still-closed parlor doors and stepped outside and stood on the stoop just outside the front door, which I left open. What I was looking for, I was certain didn't exist, but I looked anyway. A minute or two later, the doors to the parlor slid open and Mrs. Broussard, along with the young girl walked out and climbed a set of stairs which circled the perimeter of the foyer to the second floor. Neither made eye contact with me. A moment after that, Tracey appeared in the portal to the outside. I showed her my glass of lemonade to prove I had indeed been in the kitchen and not snooping outside the parlor. She waved me back in.

There was little else which could be gained in questioning the good doctor. I had covered just about every detail, and without giving up a confidence to Marcella, I didn't further pursue anything more on the two fishermen who had brought his daughter home. I asked to see the girl and was told she was sleeping; heavily sedated. I put my notebook and pen back into my jacket pocket, and when I did, sensed a weight lift from Dr. Broussard's shoulders as he believed the inquiry was concluded. Inwardly, I smiled. It was a method which I had learned from watching Columbo when I was growing up. I called it the 'one last thing' technique.

"Who's the girl, doc?" I said.

He looked at me, blinked quickly, then his eyes darted to Tracey.

"The one who came running in here a few minutes ago," I said. "You remember, right? Cute, brown eyes, dressed like she had just come from a night on the town? About sixteen?"

He swallowed hard. Took a sip of his drink, said nothing.

I stared at him.

"Veronica's twin sister, Ashley," Tracey said. "She was at school when she heard the news."

"Which school?"

"Hmm?"

"Which school?" I repeated.

"Um, well, the..." Tracey sputtered.

"Immaculate Conception Catholic Girls Preparatory School is where the girls go, Mr. Langdon," Dr. Broussard said, the client saving the lawyer. "It's outside of Convent on the other side of the river. Both Ashley and Veronica board there."

"Twins?" I asked. I looked at the doctor. "Tracey didn't mention a twin sister in the mix. Identical?"

"No, fraternal," he said, his eyes studying his shoes.

"May I speak to Ashley?" I said. "She may have some ideas about what happened and who may have done this."

Again the doc played eye tag with Tracey.

"Ashley's a little upset right now, William," Tracey said. "Why don't we go with what we've got for now and leave the girl alone for a while?"

"What have we got, Tracey?" I asked. "A couple of fishermen drop off the girl wrapped in blanket, then disappear as quickly as they came. No contact information on them. A girl who's sleeping. No description of an assailant. Come on, I gotta have something to go on. What do you want me to do for you here? You've got to play ball if I'm going to help you." My eyes shifted to the doctor. "If you truly want my help, that is. Do you want to end the bullshit, or do you all want to just keep blowing smoke up my ass?"

He seemed to freeze at that. Tracey attempted to step between us. I kept my eyes on him.

"Doc?" I said. "What's it going to be?"

The Gulfstream landed at Dulles airport outside of Washington. Yet another rental vehicle was waiting on the ramp as the air stair touched down on yet another red carpet. Attendants unloaded the bags from the aircraft and placed them in the rear of the slate gray Cadillac Escalade. Dace had recognized the D.C. area when they flew in and smirked when he spotted the Escalade from the airplane's doorway. Travis nudged him to start down the stairs, something which irked Dace who turned and glared at him.

"Don't give me any grief, kid," Travis said. "I've lost enough of my life over your bullshit. Now, get your ass down the stairs and into the back seat. If you give us any lip, I'm going to hold your skinny ass down while Rudy violates your left ass cheek with one of his needles from inside the bag. Believe me, you won't like the headache you'll wake up with sometime tomorrow afternoon."

"Spare me, Bruiser," Dace said with a smirk, then did as he was instructed.

"I really hate that little fucker," Travis said over his shoulder to Rudy. "Part of me was hoping he'd take the needle."

"Spare me, Bruiser," Rudy said with a laugh and brushed past his older partner to get into the Escalade's passenger seat.

Tom received a call on his cell phone from The Senator to advise him that the boys were en route to McClean from Dulles and that he'd be able to handle things directly from there. The Senator thanked him for all his help, said he deserved a little vacation, then hung up the phone.

Tom felt dismissed, which he could absorb from The Senator. For two days, however, ever since walking from his room without answering the question she had raised in his mind, Libby has avoided him, and given everything they had once meant to each other, he could not absorb that. So, Tom wrote her a letter which he deposited in Caroline's safekeeping before leaving the Lamoureux home. He drove from New

London to New York. On the way, he strongly considered the suggested vacation.

Again I was cooling my heels, that time in the appropriately cold and clammy parlor of the Broussard's monster mansion. Marcella came to inquire if I needed any more lemonade. I declined and she removed my empty glass. Tracey and Dr. Broussard had gone upstairs. I used the free time to call Sandy's cell phone. She picked up on the first ring.

"Hi, Will," she said. "I'm in a cab on the way home. How's it going?"

I updated her and then asked her do to a little research for me when she got home. I could hear her making notes on my various requests. I told her I most likely would be heading back in that direction shortly, and to possibly expect me for dinner. I suggested Chinese take-out and she thought that would be a great idea.

"Are you being civil to Tracey?" she asked.

"I haven't killed her yet," I said. "That's about as far as I can go until everybody stops lying to me out here."

I hate being lied to. Ever since the first day I put on the uniform as a patrolman in Chicago, people have been lying to me. Day in, day out, that's all anyone does to a cop. 'No, I've not been drinking.' 'No, I wasn't speeding.' 'What drugs? Those aren't mine.' 'She fell.' I've gotten fairly good at spotting the tells, but I've gotten worse about tolerating the liars.

"Please don't kill her," Sandy teased.

"No promises."

I heard footsteps coming down and told Sandy I had to go, then clicked off. I checked the time on my cell phone.

Tracey walked into the parlor followed by the young girl identified as Ashley, the one who had come in crying. She had changed clothes and now wore a pair of hip-hugging, pink sweat pants and a matching T-shirt. They both sat on the couch. The girl looked at me through puffy and bloodshot eyes. She was scared. Tracey nodded to me and I began.

"My name is William Langdon," I said to her, not knowing if they had told her who I was. "I'm not a policeman, although years ago I was one in Chicago. I'm a private detective, and your parents have called me in to help find out who did this terrible thing to your sister."

The girl nodded. Her eyes began to well up.

I knelt down on one knee in front of her.

"Now, Ashley," I said, taking her hands in mine and looking into her eyes. "I'm a dad, too. Just like your father, only I've got three daughters whom I love very much. As much as your dad loves you and Veronica. Just like every father loves his daughters and will do anything to protect them."

She began to tremble.

"Whoa, Ashley, I'm here to help. The biggest thing you have to remember is your father says Veronica will fully recover in time. She's in no further physical danger, and from what Ms. Walker here tells me, your dad is a great doctor and if he says that, he knows what he's talking about. So, believing that everything is going to be all right, can you help me? I've only got a handful of questions for you right now. Okay?"

The girl nodded, but her hands were still shaking. I gave them a last squeeze, then let them go.

I began questioning her.

She began lying with the first answer.

I was really getting pissed off.

Three minutes later, I told Ashley I was done for now. She looked to Tracey who nodded to dismiss her and said she could return to be with her family. The girl walked out of the room and sprinted up the stairs.

When I heard the upstairs door slam, I grabbed Tracey by the elbow and pulled her off the couch. I walked her to the front door and out into the afternoon sun. I marched her across the lawn. Fifty feet from the house she wrenched her arm from my grip and pointed a finger in my chest and warned me never to touch her like that again.

"Do you know term 'word salad', Tracey?" I said, ignoring both the order and the finger.

"Word salad?" she said. "No, I'm sorry but I don't know the term."

"How about word salad served with a side order of fuck you?"

She glared at me, crossed her arms.

"When a crazy person comes into his shrink's office and starts rambling nonsense, it's known in the profession as the person speaking a word salad. So far that's what I've been getting out of every one of you sickos. Word Salad. None of it makes any sense. Dammit, there's a sixteen-year-old girl lying in a bed up there, reportedly raped, beaten, and left for dead along the banks of the goddamn Mississippi River, and every one of you has been lying to me from the get go and I've had enough."

She continued to glare at me, but I knew she was smart enough to understand what I was saying.

"See?" I said. "What you've given me after my missing picking up my wife at the airport and driving eighty miles out into the middle of no-freaking-where, is word salad with a side order of fuck you. You've even got that little girl in there lying to me. Now, either you come clean, and I mean all the way, or I'm walking right now. No matter how much it hurts me as a father to know there's a teenager up in one of those bedrooms who's had her life nearly ripped from her by some animal, or how much my wife wants me to help you, I can't work like this."

"You can't walk, William," she said.

I watched her eyes showing the first glimpse of humanity since I arrived, so I waited for her to continue.

"I know we've been lying to you, but we don't know what to do. I thought I could get you to help, find this animal, as you put it, and..."

"Then what, Tracey?" I said, interrupting. "To what end? To go to the police? Why not just call them in right now? They've got all the resources. I don't have to tell you that every minute that passes evidence is spoiling which means the chance we can tie someone to all this is vanishing before our eyes."

Her gaze fell. She studied her shoes on the grass.

"Come on, Tracey," I said, my voice more controlled. "Tell me what's really going on here."

I had given her the vinegar and the honey. It was her chance. I waited patiently for the medicine to work. It took about a minute.

"The girl upstairs, the victim, isn't the Broussard's daughter. They only have one child and she came home when you were first talking to the parents. That girl's name is Veronica Broussard."

Tracey began walking toward a small, white gazebo set amongst a copse of willow trees. I followed.

"The raped girl is Ashley Monreale; her father is Vincent Anthony Monreale." Her eyes were hard, and she was scared, too. "You may know him as Tony Gators, southern Louisiana's godfather."

"Son of a bitch," I said, suddenly feeling a very tiny bit of sympathy for the perp.

"Yeah," Tracey continued, thinking the same thing. "The Broussards are frightened beyond words, William. Until a couple of hours ago they couldn't reach their own daughter. They've been half out of their minds all day. Dr. Broussard knows me from the krewe, and that's why he called me. They didn't know which way to turn when the two fishermen showed up on their doorstep with the raped and badly beaten daughter of the man the whole of the medical profession in Louisiana suspects in the disappearance of two of his colleagues following the sudden death of Mr. Monreale's wife a decade or so ago.

She let that sink in before going on. It did.

"I got more of the story from Veronica - she goes by Ronnie - while we were upstairs. The girls are best friends and roommates at the prep school the doctor told you about, and had sneaked off to New Orleans for Mardi Gras, each having told their parents they were going to be spending the long weekend at the other's house. Tony Gators thinks his daughter has been safely tucked away here on a girl's weekend retreat since Saturday, while the Broussards thought Ronnie was safely tucked away outside Thibodaux at Ashley's house. Instead, they've been at the Fairmont Hotel on Baronne Street, playing adult. Here's the room key, the number's on it."

She handed it across; I flipped it over, dropped it into my jacket pocket.

"Last night, they watched a couple of parades downtown, then went out on Bourbon Street. The last time Ronnie saw Ashley was when she left Pat O'Brien's alone shortly after two in the morning. As for Ronnie, she met a guy and spent the rest of the night with him in his hotel, the Sheraton, I think she said. That last tidbit she only shared with me, not her parents. Ronnie returned to their room this morning, and that's when her mother finally got in touch with her through her cell phone."

"Ashley?" I said, starting at the beginning to square my thinking. "Is she really going to recover?"

"Physically, yes," Tracey said as she sat in the gazebo. "At least the doc says so. Emotionally, who knows. She's a real mess, William."

I paced in the enclosed space of the gazebo. Everyone who knew southern Louisiana knew the reputation of Tony Gators, and how he dealt with people who disappointed or betrayed him. The Broussards were now on that list, as was Tracey Walker, and now, me. And Sandy.

"Jesus, Tracey," I said, sliding the fingers of my right hand through my hair. "What is your plan here? Are you going to hide his daughter from the man and hope word doesn't get to him about this whole thing? If the Broussards are afraid they're in some sort of jeopardy now, just imagine how bad it would be for them, and for you, and me, and Sandy too, if this psychopath discovers the wool had been pulled over his eyes. Which he will. You can't keep the girl from her father for as long as it will take all the bruises and injuries to heal. And, what about her school? They're bound to call looking for her; and then what?"

Tracey again studied her shoes. Shit, she didn't have a plan.

"You don't have a plan, do you?" I said, walking in a tight circle. "Dammit, Tracey."

"No," she said. "I don't have a plan. It's why I called you. I didn't know which way to turn. I trust you, William; and I trust Sandy."

The mention of my wife's name was like a knife to my heart. This wasn't just my hide hanging out there now. I can always take care of myself, but Sandy could be in just as much danger as the rest of us if this wasn't handled just right. I sat down across the gazebo. I was feeling sick to my stomach.

"Jesus, Tracey," I repeated. It was the best thing I could think of at the moment. I leaned forward, my elbows on my knees. Inside my jacket pocket, I continued to flip the Fairmont room key in my fingers as I thought. "When is Ashley supposed to see her father next?" I asked.

Tracey shrugged her shoulders.

"All I know for certain is the girls were to be back at school today for evening Mass. It's Ash Wednesday, you know."

I stared at her.

"Well," she said. "I'm not exactly certain, William. From what Ronnie says, Ashley doesn't see her father a lot. He does quite a bit of traveling, on business, he tells the girl."

"Okay," I said. "Here's what I'm thinking. This animal deserves whatever he gets for what he did to this girl. Right?"

Tracey nodded.

"Let's say we have a couple of days to put this together."

"Jesus, William. You're not thinking of turning this guy over to Tony Gators, are you?"

"No, of course not," I said, even though the thought had crossed my mind. My sense of justice?

"Then what?" she asked.

Tracey's eyes moved as her mind sorted something through.

"We investigate this thing as best we can, then bring in the cops," I said. Even my sense of justice didn't go as far as turning this animal into gator chow.

"Think that's going to keep Tony Gators from coming after the Broussards?"

She was right. No one knew what this guy would do. Someone had done the worst thing a person can do to another man's daughter and Tony Gators didn't play by the rules. There were no guarantees here.

"The other option I see," I said, "is we call Tony now and tell him what happened. It's not gone too far. Maybe he'll understand."

"If he doesn't? We've got nothing to trade now."

I looked at her.

"Nothing to trade?" I said.

She waved her hand dismissively.

"Figure of speech, William. You know what I mean."

## Chapter Twenty-seven

I phoned Sandy from the car on the interstate headed back to New Orleans. The research I had initially wanted her to do for me was pointless now that Tracey and the family had come clean. Sandy listened intently as I described the entire situation and I could hear her taking notes. I wanted her to know everything I did, just in case. Chinese food was obviously off the table for the night; I wasn't certain I'd be getting back until late, if at all. She asked if I wanted her to go around with me, but I told her she was more use to me at home. In reality, I wanted her to get all the rest and remain clear of as much stress as possible. She thanked me for my concern and told me she was just fine. She was more concerned about me, she said, and the young girl out at the Broussard home. That's my Sandy.

Before I had left the Broussard's home, Tracey allowed me in to see Ashley Monreale. The girl was sleeping under sedation. She looked like hell. I was glad Marcus Broussard was the doctor he was, lacking handshake or not. He had carefully treated the girl, closed several of her wounds with expertly applied sutures, applied cold compresses to her bruises and contusions. He had an IV drip going to keep her hydrated and replace lost fluids. He had done a rape test on her as well. Her vitals looked good and he thought she was out of danger, physically, at least, although he said had the fishermen not found her when they did, there was a good chance she would not have survived the morning exposed to the elements as she was. From the way the fishermen had described her condition when they found her, Dr. Broussard said, she was clearly in the early stages of hypothermia, and then internal organs began to suffer damage as the core temperature drops. Death follows.

Her face and body were badly bruised, but I knew all too well that those type of injuries eventually heal. It was the inside scars on her heart and soul that we were all concerned with, and those we couldn't know the extent of yet.

I had asked the doc if it would be possible for the girl to be brought around and he said it was medically possible, but didn't understand for what reason we'd want to do that at this point. I told him. He looked at the girl, then nodded, and added, 'At some point, but not now.' I didn't want to stress the man by telling him the clock was ticking, but the look I shared with Tracey who stood in the corner conveyed the message. She had nodded and I took that to mean she understood the 'soon' in my eyes.

I had a sit down again with Ronnie. She was a sixteen-year-old girl - nearly seventeen as she had the gumption to tell me - who had for the past five days been toying at life as an adult. Now she could see the depth of the consequences of playing a game for which neither she nor her friend were yet equipped; not that the lesson needed be learned in such a brutal fashion, but sometimes we don't get to choose our homiletics. Sometimes the world serves us our morals with bitter herbs. Her father had pulled down the sheet to show his daughter the full extent of Ashley's injuries. While during our first exchange she had played a role, Ronnie had been much more forthcoming after we had left Ashley's bedside.

I now raced back to New Orleans. First I was going to check out the Fairmont. Somebody there may have seen something, even though I doubted the night crew would yet be back on duty. Next I was going to stop in and see a buddy who handled the security for Pat O'Brien's. He was a good guy, and wouldn't ask many questions if I told him not to. Stan would also keep his mouth shut about what I did tell him. He was to be my next call after I finished with Sandy. Then, I was going to find the fishermen. Sandy had located the address the license plate Marcella had provided linked to in the Louisiana DMV records. I just hoped it wasn't an empty field, given that the pair were illegals.

There were many things which had to be tracked down in the next hours for my plan to work. I realized the clock was ticking. To avoid any possible issues with the school, which included truancy calls going out to the Monreale house, before I left I had asked Debbie Broussard to call and tell them the girls had come down with some kind of bug and wouldn't be there for the evening's services or the rest of the week's scheduled classes. That would buy us a few days, if we needed it.

Before I hung up with my wife, I asked Sandy to do some research on Vincent Anthony Monreale; public stuff mostly, but I also said she could reach out to her friends in the prosecutor's office so long as she gave no details on the current situation. I wanted to know everything I could about the man if worse came to worst. I told her I would handle dealing with the cops, if, and when it was required. I stepped on the accelerator a little harder and the 'Vette clipped along smoothly at a little over ninety. The dashboard clock showed 4:53. The sun was on my back.

The Senator was waiting for Dace when he walked into the McClean house with Travis and Rudy in trail. He was in his office, seated behind his desk, writing in a bound book. Dace entered, stood in front of the desk, waited. The Senator finished his writing, put down his pen and closed the book. He removed his reading glasses, closed them and placed them carefully at the head of the blotter. He moved deliberately. Only then did he sit back in his chair and look across at his son. The reflection he saw returned was one he hadn't expected.

"You've had quite the little adventure," The Senator said.

Dace said nothing.

Then to Travis and Rudy: "You boys can wait outside, please."

The two large gentlemen left the room and closed the door.

The Senator pushed himself from behind the desk, walked around the front of it and approached his son. Dace squared himself, his eyes defiant, his arms at his side. The Senator slapped his son hard across the face. Dace took the blow, squared himself again. The next slap came from the other hand. When the third slap was on its way, Dace reached up and stopped it by grabbing his father's wrist. He held it stationary, The Senator's strength no match for his twenty-one-year-old son.

"Two I give you, father," Dace said. "Those will be the last."

He tossed his father's hand away.

"Now sit down, old man," Dace instructed, "but first, pour yourself a drink; and while you're at it, pour me one. Scotch, rocks. We've much to discuss. The rules have changed, father." Dace strode to the big leather wingback chair, the one previously reserved for The Senator and sat down. "Oh, boy, have they ever."

The Senator remained at the head of his desk and glared at his son, his temper barely restrained. Fifty years ago, the smirking punk would be lying on his back on the Oriental carpet right about then, but time had taught the elder Lamoureux man a thing or two; restraint in dealing with the unknown being one of them. So he walked to the bar and poured two glasses of single malt into cut crystal tumblers and added a couple of cubes of ice. He picked up both glasses and walked to the center of the room. He handed one down to his son, then took a seat at the end of the adjacent tufted-leather couch. He sipped his drink. He watched Dace swirl the amber liquid over the cubes. The Senator had long said in times like those, the man who speaks first loses. It was a lesson he had long ago relayed to his son. So they each waited.

I stayed on I-10 into the city, arced past the Superdome and then took the Basin Street exit to downtown. At Canal, I turned left. At Baronne, right. I pulled up to the Fairmont. With the sun nearly set for the day, the street was a shadowed canyon, but from what I remembered of this block of Baronne Street, it was like that much of the time for some reason. The wide-eyed valet, who appeared no more than Ronnie Broussard's age, snapped to the job of parking my 'Vette and opened my door for me almost before I had slid it into neutral and applied the parking brake.

I unfolded myself from the car and stood in front of him, blocking his entrance to my toy, and not yet taking the ticket he was offering.

"Can you drive a stick, Sport?" I said.

"Yes, sir," he said looking up at me.

"Okay," I said as I stepped out of his way and pressed a twenty into his hand in exchange for the parking stub.

He sank into my seat, reached to close the door. I bent down and pointed to a vacant spot twenty feet away at the end of the valet zone.

"See that spot right there?"

"Yes, sir."

"You drive it any further away than that and I'm going to come looking for you." I smiled. "Understand?"

He looked deflated.

"Yes, sir."

I left him there to move my 'Vette twenty feet and walked up to the waiting doorman. At the open door, I turned and smiled as I saw the kid could follow directions. He dejectedly returned to his position to await the arrival of the next Ford Escort.

I walked through the door, asked the doorman who would have been on duty at the doors around three that morning. He eyed me suspiciously.

"No trouble," I said, "but it could help a young lady. You a father?"

The guy nodded, seemed to get it.

I slipped him a twenty to make sure. He gave me two names; one for this entry, the other for the person working the University Place door. The valet, he said, floated at that time of morning. The shift started at seven, in about an hour, but he wasn't certain if that particular crew was working tonight.

I asked him if the Fairmont had security cameras outside. He told me they were in the process of installing extra cameras on the premises, including exterior shots, but at the time, recorded surveillance was limited to the lobby and front desk, elevators, and some hallways. I thanked him and walked away.

The Fairmont lobby was subdued. It usually was, but I was certain this was the calm after the storm, the hangover period, such as the rest of the city was experiencing on Ash Wednesday, another Carnival season having been survived. I strode to the elevator bank about mid-building, and rode the box to the tenth floor. The hallway was empty with even the maids having finished their duties for the day. The heavy wool carpeting was soft underfoot and absorbed most of the sound of my footfalls leaving me alone with my thoughts.   Thick plaster walls and heavy doors blocked any sound from escaping the rooms.  It was a lonely place to be walking.  I felt solitary, and weary, and this case had just begun.  My eyes sought out the cracks in the paint, the spiderwebbing of the plaster, the evidence of settling of the structure over the decades. The old Roosevelt Hotel was beginning to show its age in a heaviness of heart. At that moment, I knew how it felt.

I found the room, slid the key into the lock and pushed open the door.  Everything appeared just as Ronnie Broussard had described it. Neither bed had been slept in - something she had admitted only to me - and it looked to be in the condition which two young girls would leave a room after getting ready to go out. Clothes, shoes, makeup, and hair stuff was scattered everywhere.  Dirty clothes from the rest of their stay had been kicked into a couple of corners.  I recalled how the bedrooms and bathrooms looked in our family home when I was growing up and shook my head at the mess, wondering what was going wrong with the new generation of kids.

Going through things left behind, I found nothing which pointed me in any direction, and I concluded the assailant hadn't been in there, meaning the whole attack had taken place outside the hotel.  I hadn't thought differently, but wanted to see for myself. Whether he had *met* the girl inside the hotel was another matter, and one for which I was hoping the doormen or valet coming on that evening would be able to provide some information.  I left the room and bumped into a maid pushing her cart.  She looked exhausted and asked if I was checking out, that she had the room scheduled for check out cleaning on Wednesday.  I said I wasn't leaving and that the room didn't need any cleaning.  As she rolled her eyes, I told her I was sorry for the confusion and promised I'd arrange with the front desk about it.  I wouldn't.  An annoyed maid wasn't my biggest problem right then.

Five minutes later I was back outside.  I stopped by the valet stand and retrieved my key.   I think the kid's feelings were hurt by our interaction, but his feelings weren't my priority at the moment either.

As I pulled from the curb, I phoned my buddy at Pat O'Brien's.  We had spoken on the drive in, and now I asked him to meet me out front so I could leave the car at the curb without having a problem.  He said he'd do that. As I drove up to the St. Peter's Street entrance, I could see Stan's distinctive profile waiting near the curb for me.  Stan was a beach ball of a man, late forties, black, and may be the only person I've ever seen who truly appeared to measure the same in all three dimensions.  I left the keys in the ignition and Stan told the bouncer on duty to watch the car like it was his own.  The guy nodded.  I knew my car would be as safe as if it were in my garage.

I shook Stan's hand and we walked back to the metal spiral stairs and then up to his office on the second floor. The place was darkened and looked like the control room of a television network news show with monitors stacked four high along one wall. Stan offered me a Coke, which I accepted and he tossed a cold can from a small refrigerator behind his desk. I popped the top, took a sip. He sat. I sat.

"I pulled up the piano bar tapes for last night," he said. "Between midnight and three this morning, right?"

I nodded, took another sip of the Coke.

Stan indicated a large monitor on the wall behind me. The single screen was electronically split into six segments.

"We've got six cameras in the piano room," he said. "Every angle is covered. You wouldn't believe the stuff we've seen over the years." He laughed. "Things people wouldn't want to show up on the six o'clock news, and that's just for starters."

I smiled and nodded, wondered if they had any footage with me and Sandy in the archives. We'd occupied a dark corner of that room a time or two. Stan started the playback. The images were dark, but he indicated he could do some tweaking to enhance them if we needed to. My eyes darted around the segmented screen.

"This ain't the FBI lab," he said, "but, we've got some fairly good technology here."

Stan spent twenty years with the FBI in the Chicago field office. He was a techie, not a field agent. We had worked together a few times over the years when I was with CPD and we had exchanged a few favors. For the most part, we had found the relationship mutually rewarding and I was glad he had come to New Orleans. Stan was all right. A good Fibbie, which, from an ex-cop, can be saying a lot. He tapped some keys on his computer, the images shifted and froze.

"I'd suggest we start toward the end," he said, "ID your people, then go forward and backward on everything we have while they were here. It could take a while. How much time have you got?"

"As much as it takes, Stan," I said. "The less, the better, though, if you know what I mean."

"That I do, William, my man," he said and began tapping the keys. "That I do."

"Oh, and remember, nothing leaves this room, no matter what we find, okay?" I said.

"No problem," he said. "I love having you owe me one. My wife's been giving me some grief lately, and..."

I held up my hand, signaling that was for another place and time. I pointed to the screen. We got back to business. The digital clocks on each of the six segments displayed the same chronological information along the bottom: WED 02/25/98 03:01:23. I immediately focused upon the segments with angles which showed the front row beyond the pianos which is where Ronnie said they had been sitting. I moved my chair closer to the screen. I couldn't see either of the girls anywhere in the room. Stan started the playback in reverse at enhanced speed and all six segments moved backwards in time.

"Four times speed works out well to spot comings and goings," Stan said. "I can speed it up if your eyes can keep up."

"Do it," I said.

My eyes moved across the screen. I put my finger in the air and rotated it.

"Eight times," he said.

The images flew by. I was amazed by the lack of real turnover in the room as everyone just sat and drank and clapped.

"Stop," I said.

Stan tapped a key and all six images froze. I moved forward more and pointed to a segment. Stan tapped another key and that segment expanded to full screen, and there she was. Ronnie Broussard, sitting there without Ashley Monreale. The time showed 02:33:15. I pointed to the screen.

"That's one," I said.

"Cute girl," Stan said. "Looks underage."

"She is," I said. "Got in using fake IDs."

Stan tapped a couple of keys and the screen went blank.

"Goddammit, William, are you sandbagging me on some underage drinking bullshit?"

I swiveled in the chair, gave him the 'are you kidding me?' look.

"I wouldn't do that to you, and you know it, Stan. Jesus. Now can we get back to the tapes?"

He tapped some keys and the screen came back.

We tracked the tapes back at eight times speed until we got to the time when Ashley left, then ran it backwards from that point and found the beginning point when the girls entered the room. We then tracked them through the entry hallway and out onto the street and tagged each point. The whole process took half an hour. Then we watched each segment at two times speed.

I made notes.

The girls had entered the club from St. Peters Street at 00:04:10, just after midnight. They had been pulled from the line by one of the bouncers. Stan jotted a note, for later followup on his bouncers recognizing underage girls, I imagined. They came in alone and were seated alone at an already overcrowded, front-row table at 00:09:44. They drank a number of Hurricanes, did several shots as well. Nobody approached them, and aside from Ronnie taking a bathroom break, they didn't leave the room for any reason until 02:12:55 when Ashley stood up. She was hugged by another woman seated at the table and shook a man's hand. She had touched Ronnie on the shoulder and left. Again, the cameras from the hallway and street showed her leaving alone. She walked toward the river, not back toward Bourbon. She turned right on Royal and we lost her.

A man approached Ronnie at 02:19:00, she was receptive and the man took Ashley's old seat, one of three available at the table. He and Ronnie left the bar arm-in-arm at 02:44:17. The guy worked fast. I was impressed. I looked at Stan. He was impressed too. When the man and Ronnie left, they got into a cab on St. Peters. Ronnie told me she spent the rest of the night with him at the Sheraton until she went back to Fairmont to find Ashley missing. Since she was fine, I saw no reason to track the guy down.

Stan agreed to put the clips onto DVDs for me, said he'd have them messengered to our office in the morning. As he walked me out, we talked about family stuff, and he congratulated me on the good news. I smiled, shook his hand at the curb, got into my car and started the engine. Then, I just sat there, my hands on the wheel and stick, the clutch depressed, ready for me to jog the shift lever into first gear. I mentally kicked myself for losing my touch and shut off the engine, jumped out of the car, nodded to the bouncer, and chased Stan down in the hallway.

"We need to look at the tape again," I said. "Just a segment."

"I told you I'd send it over in the morning, you can look at them all you want," Stan said. He spread out his hands in a pleading gesture. "It's my dinner time; I only get an hour. Gonna walk over to K-Paul's, man."

"Stan, seriously," I said. "It's important, and it will only take a minute or two."

He sighed. We returned to his office. I told him where to go on the tape. He took us there. The face came up on the full screen.

"Son of a bitch," I said, amazed I had missed it earlier.

I had him run the tape fast forward to when Ashley left the bar, then from there at normal speed. One minute, seven-seconds after Ashley had walked into the night, Dave Saunders left the bar. He had been sitting right next to Ashley and I hadn't seen it, but luckily my subconscious did. The girl, Cindy, left with him. We ran the other angles. Dave and Cindy walked to Royal Street and turned right.

"Can you print these two faces, Stan?" I said.

"You find what you're looking for?" he said as he tapped more keys and the printer behind his desk began humming.

"I don't know," I said. "I've got a great big coincidence, though, and you know how I hate coincidences."

I walked out again a couple of minutes later, wishing Stan a good dinner at K-Paul's, which, if you know chef Paul Prudhomme's restaurant, is not something you need to wish anyone. It's always epic. When I got into my car that time, I did drive away.

Dace concluded relating nearly every detail of his story to his father. When he had finished, he picked up the sweating glass from the side table, swirled the liquor and melted ice and drained the tumbler of the watered-down single-malt. It was like warm velvet going down, nothing at all like most of the cheap booze he had consumed over the past week. He watched the sunlight filter through the facets of the cut crystal with satisfied fascination. It was done.

The Senator observed his son. The words he had heard over the last hour were powerful and frightening, and he had to admit Dace had been right about at least one thing: the rules had changed. Part of him wanted to grab his son by the collar and throttle him, screaming, 'What have you done?' The pragmatic part of him appreciated, and even admired, the play. Dace's acts were as unconventional as they were brilliant; as dangerous as they were laden with potential - for him. The entirety was pure Dace, and could only be called amazing. The Senator had no thoughts whatsoever for the young girl.

If what his son had said was true, and there was no reason to disbelieve him, Dace now held the Lamoureux legacy by the throat, and he could crush the life out of over two-hundred years of family history with one loose word. Regardless of whether a word was loosed or not, Dace had discovered a path to the ultimate control over Destiny. The Senator may retain the title of kingmaker, but Dace now held the only key to the kingdom; and could use it to open the door to Heaven or to Hell solely at his whim. It was done. It could not be undone.

His son now controlled both the sword and the shield. The Senator's mind spun. He drained the remaining single malt and lit upon an idea. Even though the simple act of making inquiry could spell disaster, Senator Allard Lamoureux never went into battle unarmed.

I took the printouts from Pat O'Brien's to the Fairmont. The night doormen were scheduled to be on duty by then and I hoped it would be the same crew from the night before. I played the same parking game with the new valet and asked him if he had been on duty last night. He had been off. As it turns out, the kid I had met earlier had worked a double shift on Tuesday night and Wednesday and by then had gone home for a few days or vacation. His name was DeShawn, and he had been floating as the overnight valet and had worked the day shift on the Baronne Street entrance as well.

I showed the screenshots to the doorman on the Baronne Street side. He said he had been working Tuesday, but was manning the University Place entrance all night.   I showed him the photo of Ashley I had obtained from Ronnie. I described the outfit she had been wearing. He studied the photo and printouts but didn't remember her, then went on to explain how crazy things had been around there for the past two weeks.

Walking down the block-long hall to the University Place entrance, I considered the odds of the case of Ashley Monreale's attack and the Vacherie job being related.   Was there a rogue psycho loose in New Orleans from some powerful, political family?   That's not such a far-fetched scenario. I recalled there were rumors, and some evidence, in the unsolved Jack the Ripper cases in 19th century London which pointed to a rich, possibly royal assailant. Did the family know about this guy before the attack and that's why they had been so desperate to put their hands on an adult who had run away from home?   Or, was it all just coincidence? I'd have Sandy do a background check on this Saunders kid. I also had to track down DeShawn at home and ask him about the '86 Mustang GT Liftback being around the hotel. He should remember something like that.

The doorman at the University Place entrance watched me approach.  As I stopped at the podium, I noticed the small walkie-talkie lying there. He had been given a head's up. He nodded to me before I began speaking. He had indeed been working the Baronne Street door overnight, and after looking at the photo, he remembered Ashley.  She had come in around two-thirty, he said, walked into the lobby, then immediately left with a young guy. I asked what the man looked like. He said he was over six-feet tall, early twenties, but beyond that he couldn't remember. He had been paying more attention to the girl, whom he said was very attractive and suggestively dressed.   I said there had to be hundreds of attractive, suggestively dressed women who had been around on Mardi Gras. He just smiled, then described her outfit down to the last detail, and the girl down to the last curve.  I had to give him credit for being observant.

I showed him the printed black and white screenshot of Dave Saunders. He couldn't be certain, but said it could be the guy. I showed him the shots of Cindy and Ronnie, but he had no recollection of seeing either of them. He echoed his partner across the way in telling me how crazy things had been for the last couple of weeks. He also confirmed what the day doorman had told me, there was no camera coverage of the area the two had occupied before they had left together.   They hadn't gone far enough into the lobby area, he said.  Finally, I asked how the couple had arrived and departed the premises.

He thought about it a few moments.

"They walked up; but then they left in a car," the doorman said, his eyes looking up and to the left which meant he was accessing his memory. He nodded. "Yeah, that's right."

"Do you remember what type of car? Make, model, year, color? Anything?"

"It was white, an SUV, a big one," he said. "It looked fairly new. DeShawn should remember. I had to call him to bring it around. He retrieved the guy's car from the garage."

My eyes bored into him. This was huge.

"The guy was parked in your lot? He was a guest in the hotel?"

He confirmed the first answer as yes, assumed the second answer would be the same because it was hotel policy that garage parking during Mardi Gras season was reserved for guests of the Fairmont only. No exceptions.

He leaned in close and spoke confidentially.

"DeShawn can probably get you that information, if the price is right," he said and rubbed his first two fingers against his thumb.

"You got a number for DeShawn?" I asked.

The right price for that was fifty bucks, but I then had DeShawn's cell phone number. As I walked through the lobby back to the Baronne Street entrance where I had left my car, I hoped DeShawn was a bit less pricey when it came to information.

I nodded to the other doorman, used the revolving door, then went down the marble steps and across the sidewalk to my car. The valet was working it, and I gave him a five for opening my door. Pulling from the curb, I turned right at the corner and made my way to South Claiborne Avenue for the quickest way to the address on the fishermen's truck registration. I called Sandy and gave her some new research chores, then I dialed the number for DeShawn.

It sounded like I woke him up and I apologized. He remembered me: 'the dickhead with the 'Vette.' 'That's the guy,' I said. I told him I needed some information. I described the girl and synopsized the information the doorman had provided. He said he remembered the girl, not so much the guy, and that the vehicle was a Cadillac Escalade. 'Pearl white exterior, slate gray, leather interior, less than two thousand miles on the odometer,' he said. I asked the million dollar question. He hesitated, then with my agreement that I'd stop by the coming weekend and 'slide him a Benjamin', gave me the two-cent response.

I disconnected and called Sandy again. My dashboard clock reported the time as 8:38. The 'Vette glided along the arcing South Claiborne Avenue. I brought her up-to-date and could hear she was taking notes. The admission by DeShawn that he had risked his job by busting hotel policy for a lousy hundred dollar bribe from the guy with the Escalade I took as honest, but knew it would turn into a dual-edged sword.  The driver was not a guest at the hotel which meant there was no record of the license number in the valet log.  DeShawn told me the guy had stopped by in the early evening and slipped him a hundred to park the Escalade for a few hours.  He hadn't given the guy a valet ticket, which would have left a hole in the log, but had written a note on the back of one of his cards and gave him that.  The only thing DeShawn remembered was that the guy had been a 'young, white dude', adding with an ironic laugh: 'all you white folks look alike to me.'

Just after South Claiborne became the Jefferson Highway, I made a right into an industrial area.  The address for the fishermen's truck registration was beginning to look like a dead end.  There were no houses in that area.  I slowed to check numbers on the buildings, then found digits matching my note on a small, burnt-orange, metal building.  The sign read: 'Uptown Upholsterers' and featured a logo of a skinless gator up on its rear legs running away while using the front legs to cover its sensitive areas.  Cute, I thought.  I pulled into the small parking lot up front and shut off the motor.  The yard around the side and back of the building was enclosed with a cyclone fence topped by two rows of razor-wire.  I fished a Mag-Lite flashlight from behind the passenger seat and exited the vehicle.  I gripped the light behind the bulb end and held the body over my shoulder, in the cop-trained position to quickly use the heavy aluminum body as a defensive weapon should a hostile man or beast show up on the scene, and powered the beam.

I walked up to the front door of the building, peered in through the glass, shined the light through.  A sign with business hours hung in a prominent position and was supplanted by a handwritten paper underneath which advised they would be closed for Ash Wednesday.  I moved across the front of the building, looked through a window into a typical small business office; desks and file cabinets piled with papers.  It appeared this was a legitimate operation.  I approached the gate, saw a newer pickup truck parked outside a walk door toward the back of the building.  I shined my light onto the plate of the pickup, checked the number against my note.  No match.  I moved the light beam around the door, noticed it was slightly ajar.  A quick look at the lock on the sliding gate on the fence revealed the padlock was in place, but open.

Knowing this was Louisiana, and that far too many people carry far too many guns for far too few reasons, I weighed my options carefully.  Had every minute not counted in the case, I *may* have taken the safe route of just waiting in my car for whomever was back there to finish up and come out, but I didn't have the luxury of possibly hours of time.  So, I twisted the lock and removed it from the yoke and slid the gate enough to get my bulk through the opening.  I walked along the building, the flashlight over my shoulder.  At the door, I used the butt of the Mag-Lite to bang on the metal door, then moved to the other side of the pickup, laid the flashlight on the roof of the cab and waited. I fully expected what happened next.

The door popped open and the first thing to appear was the twin-barrel of a shotgun followed next by a squat Hispanic man with a dot of black ash in the center of his forehead. I called out, showed my empty hands over the top of the truck. He held the gun at me and told me to move into the open. I knew that was the dangerous part, but I did it anyway. It took several minutes of talking, but eventually the shop owner lowered his shotgun. He didn't put it away, he just lowered it. I explained I was a P.I. and who I was looking for and he became suspicious. I could tell he knew the men, and the truck, the question was how much of the story I'd have to divulge to get him to give me the answers I needed. The mark on his forehead and the fact that he'd close his business on a Church Holy Day helped me quickly decide to lay out the details exclusive of Ashley's identity. As I told the story, he relaxed even more and then set the shotgun down against the wall just inside the shop. I told him I was William, he said I could just call him Manny.

Five minutes later, I was back in my car and headed to a small hotel near Airline Highway. Manny had agreed to call ahead and to vouch for me with the two fishermen who I now knew were brothers, Jose and Javier Ruiz. They had worked for Manny for nearly a year and had bought the pickup from him when he got his new truck. He liked the pair, and had agreed to keep the title registered to the shop address. I promised him I had no interest in the legal status of his employees. We concluded a gentlemen's agreement sealed with a handshake following an introduction at the point of a gun. The best kind.

Manny's directions were excellent and I located the cheap hotel easily, even though the neon segments on the old, black and white sign out front were half burned out. A single, gravel drive led to a dead end at the bottom of a U-shaped, cinderblock, single-story building with a flat roof and peeling paint. I parked my Corvette amongst an assemblage of old pickups, vans, and vintage vehicles with plates from all over the south. I exited the car, stood alongside for several extended moments just to give anyone who was looking a chance to not make any mistakes about me, and then walked casually down to room 113. I knocked on the door and it opened immediately.

I was invited in by Javier, the younger of the two. I shook hands with both men. Jose offered me a can of Red Stripe beer which I accepted just to be friendly, and Javier directed me to the one chair in the room to sit. They sat on the foot of the two beds. Over the next minutes, they related their story and had I not had the past I had, it would have sent chills down my spine. Long ago, I had learned to survive being a cop - or a P.I. - you had to leave your emotions behind a wall or what you encountered would eat you up.  I could usually do that, unless someone came after me or mine.

When they were finished, I asked questions to fill in some holes. Lastly, as I rose to leave and placed the half-full beer on the chipped top of the old dresser, I told them there was a significant amount of money found in the girl's jacket pocket, along with her ID.  I wanted to see what they had to say about it.

"Four-hundred-twenty-seven dollars," Javier said with a proud smile.

I nodded.  They had given me the answer I wanted and I offered them something for their trouble.  They each adamantly refused, saying it would be a sin for them to accept money for doing a good deed.  Javier asked about the 'little girl' and I told them that the doctor said their quick action had most likely saved her life.

"We've been praying," Javier said.  "Jose and I lit candles for her at the feet of the Virgin Mother after Mass tonight."

I shook their hands and walked outside.  Something inside me felt just a little lighter as I retraced my steps to my car.  As much bad as there was in this world, I had stumbled upon an oasis of good.  It made me feel a bit better about my new child's future.

Sandy answered on the first ring when I phoned home.

When Dace left his father's office to go upstairs to shower and get some sleep, The Senator summoned Rudy and Travis inside.  He spoke to them for nearly half an hour, shading much of what Dace had told him, giving them only what he thought they'd need to accomplish the mission and then offered them the assignment for which he'd pay well, and for which he'd expect their eternal discretion.  Travis and Rudy exchanged glances, nodded, and accepted the job which meant they would be turning around within the hour to return to New Orleans.  The Senator told them to say nothing to Tom, that he personally would ensure their arrangements were made.  They would communicate only through landlines to the private phone number of his office in the McClean house.

When Travis asked what the limits of the mission were, The Senator's eyes grew hard and he simply said: 'Whatever it takes to discover the facts, and, if they are true, leave nothing to be discovered. Ever.'

Sandy had spoken to Tracey, who had taken up residence at the Broussard's home for the duration.  My wife, the lawyer, had some concerns and she expressed them; and, when she did, I had a few of my own which I kept to myself.

I listened carefully to Sandy as I navigated to the foot of South Carrollton.  When we she was finished, I told her that I would be home 'later' and clicked off, then cursed and slapped my hand against the steering wheel. When I arrived at the Ruiz's fishing spot, I parked the 'Vette just off Leake Street with a group of other cars and hiked across the pair of railroad tracks and up the side of levee. In my right hand, I carried the Mag-Lite. In the back pockets of my jeans I had tucked away a small, plastic garbage bag and a pair of blue nitrile gloves.

I could hear the sound of crickets and frogs on the other side of the huge, earthen berm as I climbed. They were the only known witnesses to what had occurred out there less than twenty-four hours ago, and sadly, they weren't talking. For an instant, I let something creep around my emotional wall and drew in a quick gasp of breath as the images of my three beautiful daughters floated into my head. I owed them another call. I made a mental note. Fortunately, they were all getting old enough to realize that sometimes when dad calls, it's because *he* needs to talk or to *he* needs to just hear their voices.

I crested the levee, moved carefully down the backside. Jose and Javier had described the thick fog they had encountered when they had come to fish that morning, how it had hugged the river and softly fell over the backside of the levee, but that evening everything was crystal clear. I studied the numerous vehicle tracks in the hard-packed gravel drive and quickly concluded - television cop show scenes of plaster casts of tire tracks leading to a perpetrator notwithstanding - there would be no evidence showing up there. I walked to the flat area where the brothers had parked their pickup truck and began a grid-style search which extended out in every direction.

As described by Jose and Javier, the level area between the levee and the river was indeed extensive, compared to other areas of the riverbank, and I deduced the Escalade must have been parked down here just as had the Ruiz's truck hours later. I had no way of knowing if the attack had entirely taken place there or if the area was merely used as the dumping spot until I got the chance to talk to Ashley, so I wasn't looking for microscopic-type items with only a flashlight in the dark night; finding that type of forensic evidence in an outdoor environment such as along the banks of the Mississippi River was mostly another fiction of television and movies.

I was more concerned with locating any clothing items the two fishermen had missed in their rush to get the injured girl home; and, anything else Ashley's attacker may have inadvertently left behind. I walked carefully, but progressed quickly. There was plenty of flotsam and jetsam scattered about, most of it showing the obvious age of weathering. What I was looking for would be new to the area, and fairly easy to spot since the brothers had described little attempt to hide the items they had spotted. The sheer arrogance of this animal was pissing me off even more.

Near the river, I found one of what I concluded to be Ashley's high heels. The shoe, being solid surfaced, held the chance for fingerprints, so I slipped on the nitrile gloves, picked it up by the tip of the heel and placed it into the bag. I knew there would be few clothing items to be found since the Ruiz boys had discovered much of the girl's outfit as confirmed by Ronnie. Finding the single shoe so near the water meant the other one might be underwater and gone forever. I swept the immediate area with my flashlight, knowing often things like that are hastily discarded in a group, like an angry wife throwing armfuls of her cheating husband's clothes out the bedroom window onto the front yard.

At the edge of the light beam, I noticed a reflective flash sticking up out of the mud right next to the water. I moved along the waterline carefully and reached down to check out the license plate. I pulled it free from the mud. There was no telling how long it had been there since these things were designed to hold up in the elements fairly well, but it looked fairly new. I turned it over, scanned the backside with the flashlight beam, saw no evidence of corrosion or waterline markings, then flipped it over. A sticker in the upper right corner indicated the plate was still valid in 1998. It was obviously a rear plate because most states had gone to using only one yearly sticker; that, and the lack of stone impact marks and bug remains confirmed the assumption. I shook my head slowly as I read the information. The bottom line in blue lettering read: 'The Spirit of America'; above that in red letters: 644 9MN, and above that on the upper left: 'SEP'; and lastly, at the top center, again in blue: 'Massachusetts'.

"Son of a bitch," I said.

I dropped the license plate into the bag and concluded the search about fifteen minutes later without finding anything else. I stood in the middle of the level area and looked around one last time. During my time with the CPD, I had never worked sex crimes, except for a couple peripheral encounters during my time riding a blue and white, and I was quickly discovering with this case that I didn't much have the stomach for it. The guys who did work that emotionally-charged side of crime had seemed to grow even more callous than most of us, and as I stood there considering everything, I could understand why. I turned my back on the river and climbed the levee. At the top, I took one last look.

Teddy would be the person I could turn to again for a bit of quick, discreet help, but first I had some processing to do back at the office. I knew if this eventually did turn into a full-blown police investigation, I'd be answering questions for a week, but I had to continue as things were currently configured. I drove the short distance to our office. It was 11:04 on the dashboard clock when I arrived.

I parked out front, unlocked the door and went upstairs to our office. In a room down the hall from my office and across from Sandy's which we had set up mainly for secure storage, I had a little work bench and a few tools of the trade. From the top shelf I pulled down a large, wooden toolbox. Inside, I had the powders, inks, papers, and miscellany needed to take and extract fingerprints. Not that I was an expert in the art, but any decent cop, or ex-cop, should be able to take a set of prints from someone and pull a few latents off of solid surfaces from time to time.

There are three basic types of fingerprints left behind. *Plastic* prints are easily discernible because physical ridges are left in a pliable material such as wax or soap. *Visible* prints are those which can be seen without the help of additional powders and are usually composed of some sort of liquid residual the person had touched just before making the print, such as blood, paint, or dye. *Latent* prints are those which are invisible to the naked eye, and require something such as black carbon powder be applied so it adheres to the residual oils and then shows up as a visible print.

I opened the container of carbon powder and removed a fine-haired brush from the case. I started with the license plate. Dipping the brush into the powder, I tapped off the excess and began lightly dusting the backside of the plate. Dusting is the application of the powder to the surface in an attempt to first locate any fingerprints, then the art of the craft shows when the technician carefully works what becomes visible so an acceptable print can be pulled by the application of clear adhesive tape which permanently locks the powder pattern. The tape is then adhered to a paper card. From there, I can scan, photograph, or photocopy the print and fax or, now email, it to anyone, anywhere in the world, in seconds. I also usually take a Polaroid of the print before I lift it, just in case I accidentally mess it up with the tape. With fingerprints, you don't get a second chance.

There were several good prints on the backside of the license, mostly along the edge where someone would have gripped the plate during installation or removal, however, most of those were partials, pieces of fingertips. I photographed them, then lifted each one individually. On the frontside, however, I hit pay dirt. It was as if someone had used all five fingers splayed across the center of the surface to hold the license plate against the frame while the fasteners were either installed or removed, because I got a full set of perfect prints.

Next, I tested the shoe and found nothing usable, just a couple of smudges. I placed the license plate and shoe into separate plastic bags, tagged each one and put them into a cardboard box. I repacked the fingerprint kit, collected the Polaroids and my digital camera and went to our outer office area where I made photocopies of the cards and blew them up, then took them to my desk to have a look-see. Not being a qualified expert, I took a long time going over each print and making comparisons front to back. From my perspective, the partial prints on the backside were not left by the same person as had given me the perfect set on the front, however, to confirm that assessment and find out if we could match them to a known individual, I needed someone else to run them all against known prints on file. That meant access to the FBI database.

I had heard scuttlebutt about the Bureau being in the process of assembling a fully automated system for cataloguing and searching what had grown to a collection of nearly seventy-million criminal sets and more than thirty-million civil prints which included military, security clearance holders, government employees, and other individuals, but hadn't heard it was fully operational yet. Teddy might have more updated information, so I called him, knowing he would have to make any request to the Fibbies anyway. I checked my cell phone. It was a couple of minutes to midnight. He'd either be awake or he'd be asleep, but either way I would have to endure some ball-busting over what time it was.

"This better be friggin' important," Teddy said.

"I hope I interrupted something," I said.

He laughed.

"Yeah, right, asshole. Just wait until you get to be my age," he said.

"You're only fifty," I said. "Just wait, I hear it's all downhill from there."

"Yeah, yeah, you just wait, pappy." He paused, I thought I heard him light a cigarette. "What do you need now? Please don't ask for bail, my Captain pay scale hasn't kicked in yet."

"I need some prints run," I told him. "How fast can you turn things these days with the FBI?"

There was a pause.

"Do you have any idea what time it is?"

"Midnight."

He informed me they'd been told the FBI's new system, which the Bureau had named the 'Integrated Automated Fingerprint Identification System or IAFIS in government acronym-speak, was about a year out, but they had been running tests. If it truly was important he could get a fairly quick turnaround, but if I was just jerking around, he said it was a favor I really shouldn't ask and he'd still do it for me, but go through slower channels.

I told him it was very important, but not the details, and that my clock was ticking, but not why.

I heard him exhale, and wait for more. The plea alone obviously wasn't good enough, so I gave Teddy the bare-bones rundown on what had been going on, including that the case involved the rape and beating of a young girl which I knew would piss him off as much as it did me. Nothing motivates either of us more than being pissed off about something.

"How fast a turnaround?" I asked.

"Fibbies tell us their target once the system is fully operational is under an hour for criminal inquiries, and that means we'll have the complete package which will include prints, mugs, physical description, full history, all back in that time by email or fax."

"Jesus," I said. "Things certainly are changing. That type of return used to take weeks."

"Yeah, Big Brother is coming for us, pal. It's fourteen years after Orwell predicted it, but there's no stopping it now. Just wait until they tell you that you can't have your movie popcorn and giant Coke, buddy."

"Like that could happen," I said.

"Ya never know. And next comes the computer chip up your kazoo." He laughed.

I know the joking was just to purge the mental images we both now carried, and I appreciated the effort. I truly did.

He gave me a fax number to send the prints off to; said he'd make the call ahead to run it through for his eyes only on the return, which he said to expect sometime in the morning. I thanked him profusely and he tossed it off by saying he'd add it to the ledger when he got the chance.

"Just nail the sombitch," he added. "That's all the thanks I need."

Travis and Rudy prepared to drive out of the New Orleans airport just after midnight for the second time in the past several days. Before leaving, they confirmed the Escalade was indeed where The Senator had told them it was parked. They looked inside since the doors had been left unlocked, located the keys on the visor. They found nothing unusual in the vehicle except for a small, gold cross on a chain in between the carpet and side trim in the cargo area which Travis dropped into his pocket.

They had been booked into the Sheraton downtown, and planned to talk to Dave Saunders as their first order of business in the morning. After grabbing a couple of po' boy sandwiches and fountain drinks on the drive in at a place recommended by the airport staff, they settled in to separate beds in adjoining rooms on the twelfth floor for a few hours of sleep.

After faxing the prints to Teddy, I drove home, which was nearly as fast as calling, and I decided to wake my bride with a kiss rather than an electronic chirp. When I walked in, I found Sandy curled up on the couch in the den. On the coffee table, she had her laptop and a scattering of papers. Scattering is really an overstatement, the papers were more appropriately described as being organized into about a dozen separate piles. I poured a couple of fingers of bourbon over ice at the bar, then walked over and bent and kissed her on the top of her head.

She opened her eyes and smiled.

"What time is it?" she said.

"Nearly one in the morning," I said.

"Are you hungry?"

"I could eat something."

I followed her into the kitchen and took a stool at the breakfast bar while Sandy made me a sandwich. We had some good pastrami and Swiss cheese on hand and Sandy had stopped at a favorite bakery and picked up a loaf of fresh, light rye bread. She packed the bread with meat and cheese, added Dijon mustard, cut the sandwich diagonally, then went to the refrigerator and extracted one of those big, home-canned, dill pickles I liked from a half-gallon jar her mother had sent along from Wisconsin.

"That must have been fun to carry through security," I said, pointing the pickle at the jar it had just come from.

"It wasn't too bad," she said. "I told them I was expecting, and having intermittent cravings."

We laughed.

"You want to talk about the case?" she said while she waited for the milk she had placed onto the stove to warm.

"I'd rather talk about how you're doing," I said.

She smiled, her blue eyes melting into mine. We talked about her, me, the baby, and us, while the milk heated and I wolfed down the sandwich. I nursed the bourbon between bites. Wisps of vapor rose from the small pot as the milk became perfectly ready. It reminded me of the descriptive of the fog on the river and I was jerked back to the case. I kept that connection to myself, knowing talking about it to Sandy would have her lose her taste for the warm milk, and watched her pour the liquid into a mug. Sandy put the pan into the sink, ran water into it, grabbed her mug, I grabbed the rest of the pickle and my glass of bourbon and we walked back to the den.

I sat next to her on the couch, we set our drinks on coasters on the end tables and I crunched my pickle. She leaned forward and began going through the information she had assembled for me.

She had already compiled a large dossier of public, background information on southern Louisiana's Don, Vincent Anthony Monreale, and had even called a friend in the U.S. Attorney's office at home to find out what they had which might be outside of the public records. The friend had been helpful, but said since almost everyone who runs afoul of Tony Gators tends to disappear, reputedly into the swamps outside of Thibodaux, there was currently no viable path toward any federal prosecution of the man. Mr. Monreale also had extensive legitimate assets and businesses, but the U.S. attorney said the man was first considered by his office to be the sole control of illegal activities from loan sharking, gambling, and prostitution to drugs and even trafficking in illegal alien workers.  Bottom line, he was every bit as bad an actor as I had already understood, but the feds just couldn't prove it.  Yet.

Sandy next went over the information she discovered on Dave Saunders of Groton, Connecticut.  He was twenty-two, an average student at Harvard, which I was certain was an above-average student almost anywhere else, was majoring in business and scheduled to graduate in the spring.  He was a football player for the Harvard Crimson, starting on the offensive line all four of his years and there was NFL scouting which had tracked him.  His parents were still together.  He had no siblings.

Without a last name for the Cindy I saw, Sandy had been unable to turn much on the woman.  I wasn't surprised, but I was curious as to exactly who she was and about her relationship to Dave.  From his reaction to my expressed assumption she was his wife, I deduced there had been, or still was, some sort of romantic connection between the two.

The vehicles were properly registered, she found, both in Connecticut.  Dave had owned the Mustang since he was eighteen, before that it had been registered to his dad for two years.  The Escalade was a new vehicle, leased from a dealership in Cambridge, the license and registration transferred the day of the lease to Connecticut.

"What?" I said, pushing the last of the pickle into my mouth.

I wiped my fingers together, then to Sandy's chagrin, dried them on my jeans.  She rolled her eyes.  I shrugged.

"I said the Escalade lease was created on Monday, February 16, 1998, in Cambridge, and originally registered in that state, but the registration was transferred later that day to Connecticut."

"Cambridge?" I said, sensing I knew the answer.

"Cambridge, Massachusetts," Sandy said.  "It's the Boston suburb where Harvard is located."

"Harvard is in Massachusetts?"

"Always has been," she said.

"When the Escalade left Massachusetts to go to Connecticut, it had Massachusetts license plates?" I said, knowing the answer.

"I would imagine," Sandy said.  "I think that's how it works."

"It is," I said.

"Do you have the Massachusetts license number anywhere in your research," I asked.

"I don't," Sandy said.  "Why do you ask?"

I told Sandy about the Massachusetts license plate I found at the river's edge, just down from what I was assuming was one of Ashley Monreale's shoes.  I told her I found fingerprints on the plate and had already sent them off to Teddy for an attempted ID.  She sat back, sipped warm milk from her mug, stared at the far wall.  I could see her wheels working, but waited to see if she would indeed come to the same conclusion I had reached.    While she correlated the information, I removed the photo of Ashley and the surveillance camera prints from Stan from my jacket pocket and laid them on the coffee table.    She looked down.

"Ashley Monreale," I said, pointing to the photograph, then indicated the pages of printed shots.    "These I got from Stan.    They're screenshots taken from security footage from Tuesday night at Pat O'Brien's piano lounge."    I pointed to the figures seated next to Ashley and Ronnie. "This is Dave Saunders, and this is Cindy."

"You think this is all tied together?" Sandy said.

"I am beginning to think so," I replied and finished the bourbon.    I considered another splash at the thought, but stayed put.    "The question is what is Ashley's father going to do with the information if it is."

"If Vincent Monreale gets wind of it all, I don't think it's going to matter much how it ties together, just who it leads him to," she said, sitting back, cupping her mug with her hands.

I rose and did add a touch more bourbon to my glass.    I took a drink, turned to face her from the bar.

"I think you can put book on that," I said.    "The kid struck me as a fairly decent sort, even given the trepidation, and the fact the girl was hiding something behind her back when I stopped by as John Portman, however, if he is the animal that did that to that young girl, he deserves everything he gets."    I took another drink.    "The problem is, Sandy, am I qualified to be judge, jury, and executioner on this kid should the rest of the evidence fall into line?    Because that's what this is leading to, you know, with no police involvement."

"It's not like you're going to hand the kid over to Tony Gators, Will. No matter what he may have done, you can't do that."

"I know, Sandy," I said.    "But even if it does go to the cops, this guy won't last a day in jail.    Tony may not get him, but somebody working for him will."

I was being torn.    Part of me wanted justice done to the animal who raped and beat Ashley Monreale, whoever that was; and the other part of me understood that if my current suspicions should get back to her father, Dave Saunders would come to a violent, and perhaps not-so-quick end in the swamp whether he was guilty or not.    Sandy could see the concerns playing on my face, and being Sandy, she had the simple answer.

"You know what you have to do," Sandy said.    "You have to go out to see the girl.    She'll tell you."    She watched my eyes and then stretched and yawned.    "Let's go to bed.    I'm sleeping for two, and you need some rest before you drive out to White Castle in the morning.    Maybe by then, you'll have some information back on the prints from Teddy."

Sandy could see the restlessness remaining in my eyes. She stood up and walked to me, hugged me close. I was surprised that our bodies were beginning to touch in a slightly different way. She was right. There wasn't anything more to do that night, and an emotional chore for me and Ashley awaited the coming dawn.

We turned off the lights and went up to bed.

# Chapter Twenty-eight

Travis and Rudy drove along I-10 heading west at the same time as did William and Sandy on Thursday morning, February 26, 1998. On the backside of a weak high pressure system, an enveloping haze consisting mainly of Gulf moisture and industrial pollution had built over the area overnight, and the heat and humidity had returned. The sun had shown itself as a giant, red-orange ball climbing out of an indistinct horizon at six-twenty-nine that morning, and of the four, only William had observed it.

I decided to ask Sandy to come along to White Castle that morning because she could act as a distraction to Tracey Walker and the Broussards while I attempted to speak to Ashley Monreale. It would also give Sandy a chance to get a little lawyer-to-lawyer time with Tracey. I told her there was a gazebo in the yard which seemed to bring out Tracey's more forthcoming side. She smiled.

Just before we pulled off the interstate onto highway 70 toward the bridge to cross the river, my phone vibrated in my jacket pocket. I removed it just as it began to chirp.

"Teddy," I said to Sandy and flipped open my phone. "Good morning, buddy, how are things in Chicago?"

"Cooler than it's going to be for you down there today, in many ways," he said.

I put the phone on speaker after I told him I would do that and that Sandy was in the car. After the two of them exchanged congratulations and things between friends, he gave me the information. Sandy took some notes as I drove the Corvette. The T-tops were on that morning, and so was the air conditioning.

As it turned out, Dave Saunders had a police record. He had been busted and booked for drunk driving, the charge later amended under a plea arrangement to underage drinking three years ago in Connecticut.

He had paid a two-hundred-ninety-one dollar fine and surrendered his driver's license for six months. The five splayed-finger prints on the front side of the license plate I had found were an indisputable match to the booking set for him. The other prints, the partials on the back side, came back without any hits, and Teddy had a tech do a comparative with the known Dave Saunders prints and she had ruled him out as being the source.

I thanked Teddy for the information, promised I'd keep him unofficially up-to-speed, which didn't exactly please Sandy, and clicked off. As I crossed the Mississippi, I dialed a number Sandy had tracked down in Cambridge, Massachusetts. The call was answered on the first ring by a friendly woman with a strong Bostonian accent. She listened to my request, forwarded me to the lease department manager.

"Les Frakes," the man said, pronouncing his last name to sound like 'freaks'.

I explained who I was, why I was calling, to a point, and what I needed to know. He balked, said I'd need to speak to their attorney, and since I wasn't real police, he doubted even that would do me much good. When I told him this was part of a felony investigation, and that if he'd prefer, the next call *would* come from a real cop, and if that didn't work he'd get a visit from another real cop who would invite him to spend the rest of his day downtown, he changed his tune. I hated being a dick, but sometimes that's what it took.

"What do you *really* need, Mr. Langdon?" he asked.

"The simplest of information, Mr. Frakes," I said. "What was the license number originally placed on this Escalade." I gave him the VIN number Sandy had pulled from the Connecticut record.

He begged off the line for a moment to check the files, then came back a few seconds later.

"That's a relatively new lease," he said. "Went out of here with a Massachusetts plate: 644 9MN. My records show the client immediately reregistered the vehicle in Connecticut and was to return the Massachusetts plates to the dealership. To date, I don't show they've been received."

"Thank you, Mr. Frakes," I said. "You have a nice day."

Before he could begin asking me questions, I clicked off.

"Wow," said Sandy. "This is looking like a slam dunk, Will. Your feeling about Saunders and this Cindy being squirrelly appears to be right on. Maybe this situation is just the tip of the iceberg. Why else would people freak out over an adult running away from home?"

I looked across at her. I had thought the same thing.

I wasn't convinced, though. Like making a puzzle all one color, every piece had to fit for me to consider a case complete. This one had pieces missing. I could feel it.

"How does this all tie to the initial hiring by the political guy?" I said. "That still makes no sense to me.   Everything I know so far says that Saunders and Ashley Monreale are totally unrelated.   Was it mere coincidence, Sandy?"

Sandy shrugged.

"Stranger things have happened, Will.   What if this kid had some political connection and they knew about him being some kind of whacko loose cannon?   Maybe they thought he could become some kind of embarrassment and needed him tracked down and the leash clamped on him.   From the way they moved to lock you out and bring in their own people right after you confirmed where Dave Saunders was, that makes sense.   Maybe we were just too late to find him, or, since McDaniel told you they were going to take over with their own people, maybe *they* got there too late.   Like I said, stranger things have happened."

"Yeah, but you checked all these guys out.   Dave Saunders is not politically connected.   His parents are teachers, for God's sake.   Yet, Tom McDaniel shows up everywhere you check as a political hack."

"A political hack with dozens of very powerful clients," she said.

I nodded.   She continued.

"Then there's the connection with Jack Stempler, international financier.   What's that all about?   The guy's a multibillionaire several times over, he owns the plantation property where this purportedly unconnected kid is staying.   How does he tie in?"

"Maybe Stempler *is* the link to the politics," Sandy said.   "He's certainly connected."

"Yeah, but you found no connection between him and the Saunders family, Sandy."

"I know, but that doesn't mean one doesn't exist, Will."

"It's a loose end, and you know I hate loose ends."

Sandy reached over and touched my hand which rested upon the stick shift.   I looked over as we pulled up the drive at the Broussard home.

"If Dave Saunders did this to that little girl up there," she said, pointing toward the house.   "Does any of the *why* really matter?"

Travis and Rudy made their way to the Vacherie plantation.   They had taken their time that morning, slept in, had breakfast in the hotel cafe while they reviewed the day's Times-Picayune for any stories mentioning a woman being found along the banks of the Mississippi; plus, they still had the GPS device in place on the Mustang so they knew Dave and Cindy hadn't gone anywhere.   There was no rush to get this particular mission accomplished.   What counted was security, not speed.

As they turned off the Great River Road and passed through the gap in the hedgerow, they saw what they expected to see: the Mustang parked in the turnaround by the house.   They made no surreptitious approach that day, simply drove in, parked behind the other vehicle, got out and strode up the cobbled walk, climbed the steps and rang the doorbell.

Dave Saunders opened the door a few moments later.

"Mr. Saunders," Travis said. "It's a pleasure to finally meet you face-to-face. May we speak to you and Ms. Spagliano, please?"

Cindy appeared coming from the parlor off to Dave's left. When she saw the men at the door, her eyes darted right and left and she moved behind Dave.

"Ah, there she is, too," Rudy said. "Thank you for the love note in your apartment, Ms. Spagliano." He smiled at her menacingly. "We still laugh about it."

"Don't worry," Travis said. "We're only here to talk, and we can accomplish that in either of two ways, but believe me, the first option is much easier on you."

Dave Saunders was a good-sized man, but these two were monsters in comparison. He'd faced guys that size on the other side of the line on the football field, but this obviously wasn't a game, and he had Cindy to think about. Even if he told her to run out the back to Auntie D's, would it make things better or worse? Would getting the old woman involved put her in jeopardy? In the next moments, he made a decision, and invited them in.

They moved into the hallway as Dave and Cindy took steps backward. The newcomers looked around, then suggested they sit in the parlor. Travis issued the invitation with a directional wave which surprised both Dave and Cindy, who suddenly realized the pair had obviously been in the house before. The foursome made their way into the front room and everyone but Rudy found seats. He paced between Dave and Cindy and the door.

"Dace Lamoureux is back home," Travis said perfunctorily. "Your Escalade is at the New Orleans airport, in the general aviation parking lot. The keys are inside, on the driver's visor. We checked it last evening, and it's just fine. I think Dace even may have had it washed for you."

Dave glanced at Cindy, then returned his attention to Travis.

"Okay," Dave said. "You came all this way to tell me this? A phone call would have worked just fine."

Rudy smirked at him.

"If it were only that simple, Dave," Rudy said.

Cindy suddenly looked panicked, but Travis put his hands out in a placating gesture before he spoke again.

"We just want you to tell us everything that happened since you and Dace left Providence ten days ago," Travis said. He removed a micro-recorder from the breast pocket of his suit coat and placed it onto the coffee table between them and switched it on. "I hope you don't mind, but my memory isn't all it used to be."

"Why?" Dave asked.

"It may be age, or it may just be my brain is already full," Travis said with a wave of his hand and a glance to Rudy, who smirked.

"No, why do you want to know?" Dave said.

"Because we asked you, Dave," Rudy snarled and leaned over placing his face inches from Dave's. "We're not going to ask you again."

Tracey Walker opened the door for us and Sandy and I walked into the foyer. Tracey wore a medium-grey, flannel business suit and matching suede pumps. She looked reasonably rested, and frankly, a bit cocksure. Dr. Broussard arrived downstairs and greeted me with another limp handshake and word that Ashley had rested well overnight, but was still under strong sedation for the pain.

"She truly was badly beaten," he said. "The evidence of more deep-tissue bruising showed late yesterday after you had left, Mr. Langdon, so I warn you now, if you're going to look in on her, she appears even worse this morning than yesterday, although I am still confident she's well on the mend."

I thanked the man for the update, and the words of warning, but reminded him of my background and that I'd seen it all before, and worse; the kind of things which would give the mousey G.P. nightmares. I introduced him to Sandy as my wife, partner, and an attorney. His eyebrows lifted and he smiled congenially and shook my wife's hand with vigor, then invited us into the parlor.

As we walked into the coldly antiseptic room, I asked if Ronnie could join us, told him that I had some questions, and Tracey excused herself to go upstairs to get the girl. As if on cue, Marcella appeared at the door to ask if we would like coffee. I deferred, and Sandy asked if she could have a glass of water, no ice. Marcella smiled and disappeared on the task.

"What about Mrs. Broussard?" I asked. "How is she doing today?"

The doctor's eyes rolled toward the ceiling. Whether that was an expression of his attitude toward the woman, or to merely indicate his wife was upstairs I had no way of knowing, but I had my suspicions it could be both.

"She's resting this morning," he said. There was a pause before he added: "She gets migraines."

I nodded. Sandy sat quietly, hands in her lap, making her observations to go with my opinions on the personalities involved which I had relayed to her over the past hours. My eyes moved over her discreetly as we waited. There was little I had to say to Dr. Broussard at the moment, so looking at my wife was a wonderful way to fill the wait for Ronnie. Sandy was perfectly attired in a professional, charcoal, pinstripe, silk pantsuit. The intersection of her pumps and cuff revealed an enticing bit of ankle and arch as she sat with her legs crossed in my direction. I had noticed last evening her breasts had begun to grow even more full, and her belly was just beginning to protrude.

"If it's not too indelicate to ask, Mrs. Langdon," the doctor said, "but when are you due?"

Sandy blushed slightly, then told him. He congratulated us both, and said it was such a joy for young parents. The man wasn't that much older than we were, perhaps six or seven years, and frankly, had he not been a doctor making that assumption simply by my wife's growing profile, the statement would have been, at the least, indelicate, and at the worst, risky.

Ronnie arrived with Tracey in trail. The girl was still dressed in the same T-shirt and sweatpants I had last seen her in, and her hair was tousled and eyes were sleepy as if Tracey had awoken the girl. I didn't need to check my cell phone for the time because I knew it was just before eleven in the morning.

Without making much eye contact with either Sandy or myself, the girl padded in bare feet across the carpet and curled herself into the corner of the couch opposite to her father. She rubbed her eyes, brushed her hand through her hair. Marcella appeared with Sandy's glass of water. Ronnie asked for a glass of orange juice and the woman again returned to the kitchen. Tracey stood near the fireplace, resting her arm dangerously close to a crystal jar on the mantle. I was certain she would not take such a dominant stance were the good doctor's wife in the room.

After Marcella had returned with a tall glass of orange juice for Ronnie and departed again, and we determined that the girl was 'okay' that morning, I removed the packet of surveillance prints from my jacket pocket. I unfolded them, began to rise to hand one to the girl when Tracey intercepted the document like a lawyer in court. She reviewed the printout, asked me to describe its origin and location and then finally walked to Ronnie and placed it in her hands.

"That's you and Ashley at Pat O'Brien's piano room on Tuesday night into Wednesday morning, isn't it?" I said.

The girl looked at the picture and nodded. Her father leaned over to see. His tightlipped grimace at his daughter which followed was to be expected, but it didn't appear to negatively affect the girl. I next peeled off a shot taken a bit later after Dave Saunders and Cindy had moved closer to the girls. Tracey did the same intercept and delivery.

"Do you recognize those two people?" I asked.

Ronnie nodded.

"Do you know their names?"

Ronnie nodded.

"Would you tell me their names?"

Ronnie's eyes rose from the page to meet mine with a touch of teenage defiance. Internally, I smiled, understanding daughter was much more like mother than father; externally, I returned a professionally neutral gaze.

"The woman is Cindy and the man is Dave," Ronnie said. "Before you ask, we didn't get last names."

"I have a last name for the man," I said. "I've met him, and Cindy."

"How?" Tracey asked, her eyes darting between myself and Sandy.

"Long story," I said. "For now, chalk it up to coincidence."

Lastly, I asked about the man who came to Ronnie's side after Ashley had left, to which I received back an emotional explosion and the girl stormed from the room telling everyone this was about Ashley, not about 'her personal life'. She ran up the stairs and we heard a door slam.

"Well, I guess that's it for my picture show," I said in an attempt to lighten the tension in the room as I collected the photos and returned them to my jacket pocket. I looked to the doctor and said: "What are the chances we can see Ashley and speak to her?"

Dr. Broussard's eyes went from me to Tracey and back again. He told me that he could rouse her, reminding me the sedation was now more for pain management than for sleep induction as it had been for the first twelve hours.

"We can wake the girl," he said. "The concern would be stamina, focus, and lucidity should you need to question her extensively. People on her current pharmacological cocktail often have a problem discerning reality from dream state when initially roused. It sometimes takes a while to fully establish themselves."

His eyes went to Tracey again.

"If it's medically advisable, Dr. Broussard," Tracey said. "How about I take some time with William and Sandy while you see to Ashley. If it's beneficial to the patient, we can then allow William to ask her a few questions."

"That sounds like the perfect way to go," Dr. Broussard said as he rose from the couch and headed for the door without further ceremony. Then over his shoulder to Tracey: "Just bring them upstairs whenever you're through down here."

Then he was gone.

I suggested the three of us take a walk outside to the gazebo; I did truly have some questions for Tracey. Not only would the walk allow for some fresh air, but the warm and muggy day would do wonders for making Tracey sweat in her flannel suit. There was nothing better for eliciting something from someone who doesn't want to tell you than making them physically uncomfortable. I led, the women trailed out of the house and across the lawn.

Seated in the gazebo, we had refuge from the haze-filtered sun, but the air was stagnant and I began to sweat before Tracey. I removed my jacket and she began to question me.

"Who is the man in the photo?" Tracey said.

"The one who left with Ronnie?" I said.

"No, the other one. Dave whomever."

She still wasn't sweating, but even without my jacket, I was. Dammit.

"His name is Dave Saunders - Dave, not David - twenty-two, and he's from Groton, Connecticut. He's a senior at Harvard, majoring in business. Mr. Saunders has a record of a DUI arrest three years ago."

Tracey looked stunned.

"How do you know this from a surveillance photograph in a bar that probably hosted tens of thousands of people over the last week?"

I grinned.

"It's my job, Tracey," I said.

"Will," Sandy said.

I looked at my wife, she was encouraging me to share, not warning me to clam up or be nice.

"Okay," I said. "Coincidence. I met the kid several days ago before this all happened to Ashley. It was on another case, kind of a locate and confirm job."

"Locate? Why?"

"Because someone hired me to," I said. "Simple as that."

"When you did find him?"

"I was fired," I said. "Again, simple as that."

Tracey looked at me, cocked her head to the side. She still wasn't sweating. I could feel a trickle of moisture run down my back.

"The girl?"

"All I know about her is that her name is Cindy. She's not married to Dave; according to him, 'just a friend'."

I needed to turn this around.

"What is the plan here, Tracey?" I said. "I mean this delicate situation between the Broussards and Mr. Monreale?"

"They've asked, I've advised them," Tracey said. "Beyond that, I can't say."

I looked to Sandy for help. She nodded discretely.

"I'm going up to see Ashley," I said and I exited the gazebo before Tracey could protest. I knew Sandy would do her best lawyer stuff to delay the younger attorney. "Come up when you're done, Sandy," I said over my shoulder, then I crossed the lawn to the house.

"So, you haven't seen Dace since returning from a night on the town, early Monday morning?" Travis said.

"That's right," Dave said. "We got back here in the early morning hours, he was as drunk as I've ever seen anyone. Not just him, but anyone. I helped him into the house and up to his bed. I forgot my keys in the Escalade. That's the night Cindy got here. We talked for a while on the front porch, then went to bed just before sunrise. When we got up later in the day, Dace was gone; and so was my Escalade."

"Didn't you get concerned?" Rudy asked. "I mean, the dude just takes off without saying a word, doesn't leave a note, doesn't call? I'd be a little pissed, but somehow you seem fairly calm about this whole thing, Dave. Kinda like some doormat, ain't ya, buddy?"

"You got a point, numb nuts?" Cindy interjected. "The *dude* is a selfish, inconsiderate, punk-ass bastard and Dave here is the kindest, most giving person I know on the face of the planet whose loyalty to a lifelong friend is unwavering. I don't understand it myself; if you want to get it, you do the math."

"This one's got quite to mouth on her, Dave," Rudy said with a smirk. "I hope she puts it to good use now and again."

Again, Travis had to intercede to avoid a physical confrontation. He could tell Dave was getting annoyed, and size differential or not, the kid was no coward. He had been cooperative for the main reason of protecting the girl from an unknown, that Travis understood. Unfortunately, Rudy wasn't quite as perceptive.

"Let's get back to it," Travis said. "Just a little review of the last several days and then we'll be out of here. Then, you two can go on to do whatever you wish, so long as you keep your mouths shut about this whole, ah, adventure, shall we call it?" He checked the digital recorder for remaining space. "Okay, Dave, from the morning you and Dace got back from New Orleans one more time."

Dave relayed everything again, without the story varying more than a word or two. It was what it was, and Travis could see that. Dace had obviously gone on his mission alone, and Dave knew nothing about it. He asked a few pointed questions, and Dave answered them honestly. Travis leaned forward in his seat and retrieved the recorder and slipped it back into his jacket pocket. He looked to Rudy.

"I think we're done here," Travis said, then stood. He brushed nothing off his trouser legs. "Rudy? Shall we leave these two good people to their day?"

Rudy smiled. He crossed over to where Dave sat, extended a hand. Dave looked at it a moment, then reluctantly accepted the gesture. What happened next took less than two-seconds. Travis moved closer to Dave and Cindy, but didn't offer a hand. He stood near the end of the couch occupied by the still-seated Dave. He watched out of the corner of his eye as Rudy twisted a heavy, onyx and diamond pinky ring on his finger. It was a nonthreatening gesture, as if the ring had been displaced by the handshake. Then he backhanded Cindy across the face as hard as he could, leaving an immediate red mark and dazing her. Dave jumped toward his feet in Rudy's direction. Travis caught the kid with one arm around the shoulders and pushed him roughly back onto the couch. Dave tried the move again, but was pushed back again.

"You son of a bitch," Dave said through gritted teeth. His eyes were filled with hate, his fists balled in white-knuckle rage.

Rudy smiled, repositioned his ring again, then stepped back from the couch.

"Why, Dave, that's the least pussified as I've seen you, buddy," Rudy said with a derisive laugh. "Keep that up and you just might get your balls to drop one day." To Cindy: "Don't cry, sweetheart; with your bad attitude, this ain't gonna be the last time some real man smacks you in that smart mouth of yours."

"It's over," Travis said, raising his hands and backing off. "Okay? No hard feelings, Dave. Before we leave, however, I have three pieces of advice and I'd suggest you think this through carefully and then accept each one of them." He ticked off the items on three fingers. "One, you keep your mouths shut about this all or we'll be back to see you. Two, you had better find a new best friend. Dace Lamoureux is off limits from here on. Stay away from him." He looked to each of them. Cindy was holding her face and Dave had moved over to comfort her. "Three," he said brushing his jacket back to reveal the holstered semiautomatic pistol in his belt. "This last one, I'd remember, kids. There will be no further warnings."

Dave and Cindy stared at the gun, then up into Travis' eyes and they each felt an icy chill run through their body.

The two large gentlemen turned to leave without another word. Dave went to the door to lock it when he heard it slam, then he returned to Cindy, walked her into the kitchen and applied an ice pack to her swelling cheek. He kissed the top of her head. He considered Travis' advice and swore he'd be paying Rudy a visit for what the bastard had done to Cindy, but, at the moment, had no thoughts about anything else.


Dr. Broussard was standing at Ashley's bedside when I arrived at the door. Ronnie and Mrs. Broussard were in their rooms, resting, he told me as I walked in and crossed to stand next to him.

"She's been on pain medication in her IV," he said.

I looked to see the partially deflated plastic bag hanging with the now disconnected tube draped over the wheeled stanchion.

"She'll rouse more readily now," he said. "Remember the cautions I mentioned earlier. She'll be in and out, growing more lucid as the medication dissipates in her system, however, as it does, the pain will return, and believe, me, this little girl is in severe pain."

The doc patted her hand gently.

"Ashley," he said. "Honey, it's Dr. Broussard. You're safe in my home, Ashley. We have a few questions for you. There's a man here, he's a friend, not a policeman. Can you open your eyes, Ashley?"

I saw her eyelids begin to flicker.

"That's it, honey," the doc said, rubbing her hand. "Just a few moments and we'll let you get back to resting. You're doing great, Ashley." To me: "Just a few moments, mind you, Mr. Langdon. We already understand *what* happened to this child. I'd suggest you stick to finding out *who* did it."

I nodded.

Ashley Monreale tried to open her eyes. Her left eye was still nearly swollen shut, but getting better. Her right eye looked about and I saw a brilliant, green iris in a bloodshot sclera beneath the bruised lid. Her mouth moved to clear the dryness, and the doc swabbed some water on her battered lips which she took in hungrily. He cautioned her on the water, dropped the swab into a garbage pail next to the bed.

I moved into a closer position where the girl could see me. In the background, I heard Sandy and Tracey arrive at the door. The doc put his hand up to stop them there. Ashley's gaze shifted momentarily to the two women, then returned to me.

"Ashley, my name is William Langdon, I'm working for you. I'm a private investigator and you're the boss here. No police have been involved, just as you asked the fishermen who found you. Do you understand?"

The girl licked her lips again, nodded. The slight movement caused her pain and she winced and drew in breath through her teeth. I took her hand in mine, the one the doc had been patting, and told her to just squeeze my hand once for yes, twice for no. I asked if she understood and she squeezed my hand limply one time.

"Good, honey. This won't take long. Do you remember the man who did this to you?"

One squeeze.

"I won't ask you to describe him because that will be a too much for you right now, Ashley, but do you know the man's name?"

One squeeze.

Her lips began to quiver, then move to form words. She spoke a name, or part of one. It was a hoarse whisper. I leaned closer and asked her to repeat it. What I heard fit with what I suspected and expected to hear.

"Da...," was all that came out.

I pulled away a bit. Whispered the name back to her.

One squeeze.

I reached into my jacket pocket, removed the best surveillance shot of Dave Saunders, held it for her. Her eyelids blinked and she focused her good eye as best she could. She moaned, twisted slightly in the bed, began to cry. The doc attempted to move between us. I held my ground for a moment longer.

"Do you recognize this man, Ashley?" I said.

One squeeze.

The doc moved in then.

"That's enough, Mr. Langdon," he said and reattached the IV.

I watched Ashley drift back to sleep.

I walked to the hallway. Tracey suggested the three of us talk in the parlor and we descended the stairs. Tracey slid the pair of pocket doors closed. I was pissed. I paced the room. Sandy sat on the love seat, Tracey sat next to her.

"She identified this Dave?" Sandy said. "Was that the name she said, Will?"

I nodded.

"She said 'Dave'," I said, my mind churning. "When I showed her the photo, she squeezed my hand."

The girl had confirmed what I expected, but there was something gnawing at my gut. In the moment, I took it as my anger.

"I'd like to know the whole story on this Dave," Tracey said.

"Sit down, Will," Sandy said.

I looked at the pair. Sandy's eyes were soft and worried. Tracey's showed something else, a glimmer of sorts. I sat.

"As I said earlier, kid's name is Dave Saunders, from Connecticut. A student at Harvard. Twenty-two."

The words came out with precision, but something was still gnawing at my gut, and I felt as if I were dragging the words loose and observing them coming out rather than speaking them. Again, I attributed it to anger. There's something about being the father of three daughters which makes me despise anyone hurting a little girl. I felt the bile rise in my stomach; felt as if I was going to throw up. Holding the hand of that little girl in that bed upstairs had breached my wall. I couldn't get the image of her broken body out of my head.

"I located him for a client on Monday, he's staying at a plantation home just outside of Vacherie," I said.

I leaned forward, placed my elbows on my knees. When I looked to my wife, the image of her was blurred, as if I was seeing her through a veil. I wiped my fingers across my eyes, sat back in the chair in agitation.

"The plantation home is owned by Jackson Stempler, just west of Oak Alley. I found the kid there, talked to him. He seemed a decent sort. Later that night, a couple of guys showed up in a rental car and took up surveillance when I was moving onto the property."

"You went onto the property? Was that before or after you were fired?" Tracey asked.

I looked at Tracey. My eyes had cleared.

"After. Why?"

Tracey shook her head.

"Doesn't matter," she said. "Go on."

"That's about it. I watched the guys who were watching, then they went into the house, came out a few minutes later. They talked as if there was a third person at the house, but I never saw anyone there besides Dave and this Cindy. They left. I left. I went out there again on Tuesday afternoon after breakfast at the IHOP in Metairie. There's a two-mile hedgerow fronting the property, and a small gap about in the middle of it which leads to the house. If you're driving on the Great River Road, you can't even see the house unless you know where to find the gap because of the way the road runs and the height of the hedges. Just as I was slowed to look up the drive, Dave and Cindy pulled out of the property in a 1986 Mustang GT. I tailed them into New Orleans, the French Quarter, then I let them go."

Something struck me.

"You know, there's an old black woman who lives in an apartment above this high-tech building disguised as a dilapidated barn out back. Maybe that's the third person they were talking about, but something tells me no."

I was beginning to ramble and I knew it. My mind refused to focus with Ashley's image in that bed alternately morphing into each of my girls. Little girls capture a father's heart the instant they are born and each of mine held tightly to mine; and that's just fine with me. Hell, even the ignominious bastard who was my father, had an obvious soft spot for my sister. I looked around the room for the bar. I needed a bourbon. As long as I had spilled so much of it, I might as well let Tracey have the rest, I thought. I knew if I was going too far, Sandy would reach out to save me. She didn't.

"Yesterday, when I left here, I went into the city to do some backtracking with the information Ronnie gave up. I went to the Fairmont, checked their room, found it just the way she described it. I went to see a buddy at Pat O'Brien's where the girls had last been together and obtained the security shots. Then, I went back to the Fairmont and talked to the doorman who remembered Ashley coming back with some guy between two and three in the morning. Nobody remembered the guy, but they certainly remembered Ashley. There are no security cameras in the area yet, so they went by memory. The pair immediately left the Fairmont in a Cadillac Escalade which had been parked in the garage."

Tracey paused me with a hand.

"An Escalade? I thought you said Dave and Cindy were driving a Mustang."

"They had both, from the information I had from my client. The Mustang and a brand new, pearl white, 1998 Cadillac Escalade."

"If you saw them leave in the Mustang and they took that to The Quarter, where would they have picked up the Escalade?"

"The Escalade had been parked at the Fairmont by bribing the valet, a kid named DeShawn." I looked at Sandy. "That reminds me, I still owe him a Benjamin. He said this big white guy drops the vehicle, isn't staying at the hotel, slips DeShawn a hundred bucks to park it in the garage for a while. DeShawn gets it for him between two and three in the morning, holds the door for Ashley and watches the two drive off, friendly as can be."

"Why do you still owe the kid a hundred dollars?" Sandy said.

"He wasn't there. I had met him and he parked the 'Vette the first time I was there, but I didn't know the connection until after I had seen Stan. So, when I got back and talked to the night doormen, I found out DeShawn was the valet on duty the night before and had worked a double. I called him on his cell."

Sandy and Tracey nodded in unison. I went on.

"After that, I tracked down the two fishermen who brought Ashley here yesterday morning."

"The fishermen? How?" Tracey asked.

"It's what I do," I said, keeping my promise to Marcella. "They're a couple of brothers, illegals. That's mainly why they didn't just call the cops, I think; plus Ashley had asked them to take her home and leave the police out of it. Most people would just call the cops, but they both said she had been adamant about just coming 'home' as she put it before she passed out. They brought her here because this is the address on Ashley's fake driver's license."

I shot Tracey a warning look.

"They're good people, Tracey, as evidenced by all of Ashley's money still being in her jacket pocket which they knew to the dollar and they're scared, so that's as much as I'm going to say about them. They directed me to the spot where they found the girl. I went there, searched the area, found a couple of items they had missed when they collected her clothes."

"What items?" Tracey asked.

"One shoe," I said. The pieces of the puzzle were all fitting together as I spoke the words, but something was still tugging at my gut. "That, and a Massachusetts license plate."

"Massachusetts? I thought you said the kid was from Connecticut."

"Harvard's in Cambridge, attached to Boston," I said. "I learned that last night."

Tracey rolled her eyes at me. Was I the only one who didn't know where Harvard was, for God's sake? I completed the story about the license plates still not turned in, the reregistration in Connecticut, the fingerprints identified as belonging to Dave Saunders on the Massachusetts plate at the scene."

"Jesus, William, you *are* good," Tracey said. "I never held any hope we'd catch a whiff of this monster, and you've got it all wrapped up and tied in a bow in twenty-four hours." To Sandy: "You're certainly right about your husband, Sandy. He's the best P.I. I've ever seen."

Sandy smiled and we both let the compliment drift to space.

"I need a drink," I finally said, standing up and beginning to pace the perimeter of the room, hoping the doc had a hidden bar like I did in the office since he obviously didn't have one out in the open.

"No, you don't," Sandy said. "You're driving."

My puppy dog look didn't seem to sway her.

Sandy stood, so did Tracey. We were done. I obviously wasn't going to get my drink.

Travis and Rudy were driving into Vacherie when Rudy told Travis to turn around and go back to the plantation home.

"What for?" Travis said. "We're done with them."

"I forgot something and I want it back. It's a loose end."

"What?"

"The GPS transmitter is still on the Mustang. Like I said, it's a loose end that somebody will eventually find and maybe track back to us."

Travis checked his mirrors and swung their SUV around and drove west on the Great River Road.

I drove east on highway 1 after leaving the Broussard home. I was quiet, Sandy was too. In Donaldsonville, I connected with highway 70 to the bridge. Just before we began the climb on the approach, I swerved the Corvette to the right and onto a parallel road.

"Where are you going?" Sandy said.

"Vacherie," I said. "Something's bugging me."

Sandy looked at me with trepidation.

"Will?"

"What?" I said as I rounded the corner and drove east on the Great River Road.

"It's not your fight anymore," Sandy said. "You're the best and you pulled off a miracle for that little girl. It's her decision going forward. Don't do something stupid."

"I'm going to see the Saunders kid," I said. "Talk to him. That's it."

I slapped the car into fourth gear and accelerated.

Rudy rolled out of the car and walked to the Mustang. He reached into the wheel well and pried the GPS locator free, then dropped it into his jacket pocket and returned to the Navigator.

"Good catch," Travis said as he drove out to the main road.

"I have my moments," Rudy said.

A black, Lincoln Navigator pulled from the break in the hedgerow as I rounded a ninety-degree turn in the road which mimicked the river. They turned east. One minute later, I turned into the gap they had just exited. I recognized the vehicle, and the two men seated inside. I said nothing to Sandy. They continued east.

"Did you see that?" Rudy said.

Travis was watching in the rearview mirror.

"Mm-hmm," he replied. "Pull the notes on that P.I. What kind of vehicles are registered to him?"

"He's got a red Corvette," Rudy said without looking.

"I thought so," Travis said and he wheeled the SUV into the Oak Alley parking lot.

I parked behind the Mustang, assured Sandy I'd be good. I left the car idling so she would be comfortable with the air conditioning going. Before I got out, I pulled a leather wallet from the center console. My wife, as the attorney, gave me a cross look.

"Do you know what you can get for impersonating a police officer down here?" Sandy said. "Five years, at least."

I shrugged, smiled, got out, and closed the door. I walked along the cobbled path, up the steps, across the veranda and knocked at the door. I also used the doorbell, then I moved to watch through the needlepoint-curtained sidelight. A face appeared from far down the hall, then disappeared. I rang the bell again, knocked, called out for Dave Saunders using my best cop voice.

The face reappeared, it was Dave Saunders. He looked to be having a conversation with someone in the room, Cindy, no doubt, and then he came up the hall. I made myself seen in the sidelight, took out the leather wallet, unfolded it and clapped the CPD badge against the glass. I saw Dave turn his head, say something I couldn't discern, then he came to the door. I heard it unlock, then it swung open just a bit.

"Mr. Portman?" he said.

Given the little girl lying in the bed over in White Castle, and the fact that everything pointed to this guy as being the assailant, I wasn't in the mood for games.

"My name is Langdon, Mr. Saunders, William Langdon."

I let him see the badge, but not too closely, before I slapped it closed and returned it to my breast jacket pocket.  I didn't have to look over my shoulder to know that Sandy was having a quiet fit in the car.

"I need to speak to you," I said.

"Certainly," he said with a strangely obvious level of relief, then opened the door wider and allowed me inside.

Another face appeared at the back room portal.

"You, too, Cindy," I called down the hall again flipping open my badge in her direction.  "If you don't mind."

She walked out into the hallway.  In her right hand, she carried a cold pack and as she got nearer, I could make out a small cut on her right cheek which had begun to swell.  Something lit my internal fuse.

"Are you all right, Cindy?" I asked protectively.

She laughed nervously.  I eyed Dave.

"Oh, this?" she said.  "I walked into an open cabinet door."

She lied.  I watched them both as she spoke, and Dave seemed as surprised by her explanation as was I.  The question I had was why do women protect their batterers?  My dad could put on a public face, too.  Everyone thought he was a righteous dude.  But they didn't have to live with the man, but karma did eventually catch up with him.  As to the guy standing two feet from me at the moment, I'd have to say Dave Saunders' karma clock was now ticking down, too, as far as I was concerned.

We stood in the hallway and I questioned them both about peripheral issues about which I knew the truth to establish a baseline, and apart from the lie about the cabinet door causing the injury to her cheek, each of them answered fully and honestly.  The girl's last name was Spagliano, she was from Minnesota, and a student at Harvard.  A junior.  Then I changed the subject to the attack on Ashley Monreale.  Their reactions of shock and horror at the mention of such a heinous crime appeared genuine, as if they were hearing about it for the first time.  I began at that moment to reconsider the conclusion I had earlier drawn.  The puzzle was indeed still missing pieces, I thought, somewhat confused.  They each swore they had returned together in the Mustang after leaving Pat O'Brien's Tuesday night, went to bed together, and awoke together.  I picked up no deception from either of them, and unless they *both* were sociopaths, one of them should have been detectable by me in a lie.

"Then who had the Escalade?" I asked.

"The Escalade?" Dave said, blinking before he spoke and then his gaze drifted to bare feet on old cypress planks.

Geeze, just when I was about ready to cut this kid some slack and he's gonna lie to me on a critical issue.

"Come on, Dave," I said.  "I know about the Escalade.  I know about the Massachusetts plates from the dealership in Cambridge.  I suspect there was someone else here with you.  I was beginning to believe you had nothing to do with the attack on that young girl, but I found one of the Massachusetts plates with your fingerprints on it at the scene of the attack. Don't bullshit me, kid, I don't need it today."

I watched their eyes seek out the other and then they clammed up. No more questions could get either of them to say anything further. They asked to see the badge again, and when I refused, they threatened to call the police. They asked me to leave, and Dave moved to open the door. I had to consider Ashley's wishes about police involvement as well as my own desire to not have some Bubba confiscate my CPD badge, which using the way I had earlier to gain entrance could cost me my P.I. license in the state of Louisiana as well as give me some time living in close quarters with some not so nice folks, so I walked out to the porch. I had my limits, and as Sandy has repeatedly reminded me over time, I wasn't a real cop anymore.

Before he closed the door, I asked one final question, mainly to leave a seed behind to assuage my gnawing gut. I could always come back tomorrow after the seed sprouted. Dave Saunders struck me as someone who may be protecting someone else, but not someone who would sleep well knowing what that someone had done to a sixteen-year-old girl he had met two nights ago.

"Are you right or left handed, Dave?" I asked.

"Left. Why?"

"Just wondering. The attacker was white, your age, and described as a big guy. Oh, and he was most likely a righty based on the injuries predominantly to the girl's left side of her face. Know anybody like that?"

His face flashed an emotion, then turned to stone and he said nothing. At that moment, I knew what I would be doing in twenty-four hours.

He closed the door. I heard the deadbolt lock engage.

Travis and Rudy watched as the red Corvette passed by on the Great River Road heading east. The people inside were involved in an animated conversation and did not appear to see them sitting behind a small, Blue Line tour bus in the Oak Alley parking lot. Five minutes later, Travis drove out of the lot and made the short jaunt to the plantation home. As they drove in, Rudy made an observation.

"I do hope poor Dave and Cindy don't feel put upon by all this attention today," Rudy said with mocked concern. He smiled. "Of course, I wouldn't mind giving that loudmouth wench another smack."

Travis again parked next to the Mustang.

"Chill, buddy," Travis said. "That's an order. If they are scared enough, they'll keep their mouths shut until long after you and I have cashed in, but if they're driven over the edge, they may just make problems; and I am not dropping the hammer on a woman for that piece of crap Dace Lamoureux *or* his old man."

"Tell that to Sarah Avidago," Rudy said, his tone a bit too flippant for his partner.

"That was an accident," Travis said, sticking his finger into Rudy's face, "and you fucking know it. How was I supposed to know that patch of ice was there? I was only trying to scare her."

Rudy put his hands up.

"I know, I know," Rudy said. "Now look who needs to chill."

Travis fought to retain his composure, his face red with anger. He slowly turned again to Rudy, his words considered in the moment and carefully chosen.

"I may have issues with dropping the hammer on a woman, old buddy," he said, "but, as you saw in Desert Storm, I have absolutely no compunction about dropping it on a man. Remember that."

Rudy glared into Travis' dead-eyed stare. He did remember.

"Let's get this over with," Rudy said as he again rolled out of the Navigator.

Rudy and Travis walked around the outside of the house to the back veranda, climbed the stairs and peeked in the kitchen window. Dave and Cindy were seated at the table, a bottle of beer in front of each of them. Cindy held a cold pack to her cheek. She jumped when she saw Rudy smirking at her through the glass.

Rudy tapped his pinky ring on the pane and waved.

"Dave, a couple more questions if you don't mind, buddy," Rudy said. "We'll even come in the back and promise to wipe our feet." He smiled broadly.

Dave slid his chair back, Cindy reached for his hand but it was gone before hers got to it. He walked out of the kitchen, opened the back door and screen, closed the solid door behind himself and walked out onto the porch. Cindy watched from the kitchen window, ready to move quickly if it became necessary.

"What now?" Dave said.

"Your visitor, Dave?" Travis said. "The P.I. in the Corvette. What did he want?"

"He's a P.I.?" Dave said, his eyebrows rising.

"His name is William Langdon, his wife is Sandy. Pretty lady from the pictures I've seen."

"I didn't meet her, just him," Dave said.

"So?" Rudy said, opening his hands in a well-understood gesture to go with the one-word question.

"He came to ask us some questions," Dave said. "About a rape and beating of a *sixteen-year-old girl* Tuesday night. Apparently, the *unknown assailant* used my Escalade and left a license plate on the scene. I have every belief that this Langdon thinks I did it."

Rudy looked at Travis and he did the same.

"My, my, Davie boy, you are an animal, aren't you?" Rudy said. "You know they give you the chair down here for that."

"I didn't do it, you dumb fuck," Dave said, even surprising himself at the use of the expletive. "We all know who did."

Rudy was shaking his head slowly and clicking his tongue derisively.

"A sixteen-year-old girl, Dave?" Travis said, feeling his anger rise inside, but not directed in the direction of Dave Saunders. "Did Langdon give her name?"

Dave thought a moment. Shook his head.

"Ashley," Dave said. "Langdon didn't tell me a last name."

Rudy looked through the glass toward Cindy who stared back. Her expression needed to be slapped off her face, Rudy thought, but that was for another time. He, too, felt repulsed by the thought of the *assault* being a *rape and beating* and the *woman* they had been told about by The Senator being, in reality, a sixteen-year-old *girl*.

"Maybe she knows," Travis said, tossing a thumb point in Cindy's direction.

"She wasn't part of the conversation," Dave lied. "She was nursing her cheek in the kitchen."

Travis nodded. Dave shot Rudy a threatening look.

"So, fill us in, Dave," Rudy said.

Dave told them much of what William Langdon had told him, some of the questions he had asked. He was very careful to use proper pronoun control so a 'we' or 'us' or 'she' didn't slip out and further endanger Cindy. Who knew what these two creeps were capable of and given they worked for The Senator, what they would do to protect the Lamoureux family. He thought about Dace. Was he really capable of raping and beating a young girl? Of course he was. From what that Langdon guy had said, it happened, and tied to his Escalade which Dace had. Who else could it have been? Is that what Auntie D and everyone else saw that he missed? Could he have somehow prevented this from happening if he had been faster or had he stood up to his best friend? He thought back to the words he had so apologetically written to Dace in the note he and Cindy had gone into New Orleans and was repulsed in the realization that he was, indeed, the last sucker.

That's a hard realization for a twenty-two year old.

After ten minutes out on the porch, Rudy patted Dave on the cheek and the large gentlemen left the way they had come. Cindy rushed to Dave when he came inside.

"Let's get out of here, Dave," she said. "Tonight. Sooner if possible."

Dave thought about it for a moment.

"And go where? For how long? Anywhere we go, they can find us, Cindy. If Dace did have something to do with what happened to that girl, then this isn't going away anytime soon. We met her for God's sake. We talked to her. My God, Auntie D was right. You were right. Everyone was right; and I missed it. What have I done?"

His head dropped and Cindy could see his eyes welling with tears.

"Dave?"

He said nothing. He didn't react. He simply walked slowly away from her and climbed the stairs like a prisoner going to the gallows. She stood there a moment, double-checked the locks on the downstairs doors and then went up to the bedroom to find him.

She had to snap Dave out of this and get them out of there. Somehow.


"Did you buy it?" Rudy said when they were back in the Navigator. "Dave's story?"

"Not all of it, but I do believe there is an underlying truth in there. You saw that punk, Dace, when we got to him yesterday. His shoes still had mud on them, his knuckles were scraped, the knees of his jeans abraded. It could very well be true."

Travis started the engine and put the SUV into gear. He started down the crushed shell drive as he thought things through. Rudy had more questions, wouldn't let it drop.

"You think Dave kept his mouth shut about Dace to Langdon? Cuz, I'll tell you, pal, I don't. I think that wimp dumped his guts to him. Now Langdon knows. I think Saunders lied to us, Travis."

Travis glanced across the cabin at his partner. He wanted to shift the conversation, but understood Rudy's unspoken point if Langdon did know about Dace Lamoureux. But Dave Saunders wasn't his prime focus at the moment, he was more concerned about The Senator.

"Then The Senator lied to us, too," Travis said. "Remember that."

"He's a politician. It's what they do." Rudy paused. "The question is what do *we* do?"

Travis thought of that as they drove back toward New Orleans. Rudy also drifted in his thoughts, even though he knew what he wanted to do to Dace Lamoureux. Hell, what he wanted to do to all of them. Clean up the world a bit, he thought. One cleansing act.

They rode in silence for a long time; then Travis spoke.

"I'd say we're off the mission plan right now, buddy, and we have to make it up as we go along here. The thing is, whatever the truth is, this could turn out to be a big payday for you and me."

"What about the girl?" Rudy said. "That changes things, doesn't it?"

Travis' eyes were locked on the road in the late afternoon light. His mind was churning.

"The girl?" Travis said. "Casualty of war. From what Dave said, she'll live."

Rudy mulled it over, nodded.

"Rog, I can live with that. What's the next move, then?"

"We go see the P.I., find out what he knows and shut him up. He's the last loose end as far as I can see."

"How?"

Travis gripped the wheel firmly.

"Whatever it takes, my man. Whatever it takes."


Vincent Anthony Monreale arrived in the driveway of Dr. and Mrs. Broussard's home with a convoy of three vehicles an hour before sunset. He had come to take his daughter home. The hired nurse and doctor, along with two paramedics rode in the ambulance which followed Tony Gators' onyx black, 1998 S-Class Mercedes-Benz. What Mr. Monreale had paid them all in advance, and for their silence, would put a kid through college. Of course, it was a sliding scale.

Two rotund associates who were Tony Gators' most trusted men, arrived in the tail of the convoy in the driver's Cadillac de Ville. As instructed, they all waited in their respective vehicles while Tracey Walker exited the home and tucked herself into the passenger seat of the mobster's Benz.

The call from Tracey had found Tony in the back room of one of his clubs in downtown Baton Rouge two hours earlier. She was frankly not surprised the man could assemble things so quickly, given his reputation for both connections and on-hand cash. He had remained remarkably calm when she had given him the news about Ashley, and when she played her ace-in-the-hole, he had gone silent, then thanked her and said he'd arrive within two hours. He was right on time.

"I want you to understand, Mr. Monreale, the Broussards knew nothing of the girls' plans for this past weekend. Ronnie had told them the same thing Ashley had told you. The girls had played both sides figuring neither side would check with the other. They are all devastated by what has happened to your daughter, and have taken every action to both protect her health and safety, as well as your family's privacy in this matter."

"What about the other thing?"

She handed over several sheets of paper which included a synopsis of William's report as well as some ancillary information she was able to dig up on her own in the interim. He scanned the pages, rapidly absorbed everything printed there. Tracey was impressed. She had heard the man was smarter than your average organized crime thug, and had made as much money outside of the rackets as he had inside. Of course, she thought, the boost of the reputation of a man like Tony Gators helped grease the skids along the way.

"This is everything?" he said.

Tracey nodded.

"All right," he said, folding the papers and slipping them into his jacket pocket. "Now, my daughter." He turned off the ignition and exited the car in one fluid motion.

The man caught and held the door for Tracey on the other side, he moved that quickly. Simultaneously, the doors of the trailing ambulance and Cadillac popped open and six people piled out to join them heading toward the Broussard's front door.

"You must tell the Broussards I hold no animus toward them or their daughter." He paused on the porch and held her with his eyes when he removed his sunglasses. "I appreciate what they did for Ashley, and completely understand the delay in contacting me." He smiled as they reached the door, then leaned close to whisper in her ear. "A man's reputation, earned or not, sometimes precedes him in polite society. Don't you agree, Ms. Walker?"

She nodded, her eyes wide.

Tracey opened the door for the group and they followed her inside and up the stairs. The paramedics carried their gurney and brought up the rear.

At the door to Ashley's room, Tracey paused before opening, and said to Mr. Monreale: "Perhaps your friends should wait in the hall."

Tony Gators stared right through her.

"Ms. Walker, these associates of mine I trust with my daughter's life. They have known Ashley since the day she was born. I believe they deserve to see what I would appreciate you now showing us. In addition, I believe my doctor will have some questions for Dr. Broussard. I hope he's going to join us."

"The entire family is inside, Mr. Monreale, should you have any questions for any of them."

Tracey opened the door and led them in.

The Broussards huddled in a far corner, away from the bed. Ever the courtroom choreographer, Tracey had suggested they not be in the field of vision of the first glimpse of Ashley by her father. The new doctor shook hands with Dr. Broussard, then the two moved toward the patient and a briefing ensued. Mr. Monreale moved to his daughter's side and took her hand in his. He whispered in her ear even though she was fast asleep. Nobody in the room made any attempt to eavesdrop on the moment. Tracey watched the two associates who took station in the corner opposite to where Mrs. Broussard and Ronnie remained. She saw the glances they exchanged and, even though she had played the role of

Judas, her heart ran cold when she thought of what they were going to do to Dave Saunders when they got their hands on him.

I drove at a leisurely pace. Something was nagging at me the entire drive back to the city. Sandy understood and left me to my thoughts; she knew if I needed to bounce an idea or two off her, I would, but she also had been around me long enough to just leave me alone while I chewed on a bone. Just past the canal where I-10 makes a sweeping, ninety-degree turn toward the south and becomes what the locals know as the Pontchartrain Expressway, I was ready to discuss it.

"I don't think he did it at all, Sandy," I said. "I think there was someone else involved. I just have that feeling."

"I didn't meet them, Will," she said, pivoting in her seat. "I don't know how to judge your interaction, but from a strictly legal perspective, it's a fairly tight circumstantial case. The Escalade, the license plate, the fingerprints, the description of the valet. Dave Saunders had the means and opportunity. The only thing lacking is the motive."

I ticked off the items and my growing problems with each of the pieces we did have. Sandy was savvy enough to know that things are often not as they initially appear, but she does hold tight to first impressions. I demonstrated how Dave Saunders may have had held the license plate with his one hand while he removed the screws with the other when he swapped out the plates by splaying my fingers against the dash. That's how his fingerprints could get there, I told her. What about the issue of the unidentified prints on the back edge of the plate? Her retort to that was perhaps they were made by the person at the dealership who initially installed the Massachusetts plates. I had to accept that as a possible answer since all the prints had been made recently and hadn't been out in the elements for very long before the plates were riding around in the back of Dave's Escalade. Finally, I told her, something didn't jibe with the ID.

"The valet never saw a photo of Dave, you know; there could have been another 'big, white guy'," I said.

"Well, what about Ashley's ID of him when you showed her the picture?" she said. "If anyone should know who did that to her, she should."

"Good point," I replied, "and that's where I'm stuck, Sandy. I just don't know why it's bugging me."

"You're the only one who can dig it out if it's stuck in your craw, Will," Sandy said, placing her hand in mine. "I still say I'd indict and prosecute with what we know."

"That's the problem, Sandy, if things get out before I can figure this out, the kid won't get the benefit of a trial. He'll disappear into the swamps."

I navigated from the highway to the surface streets and toward our office.  Sandy and I continued to debate the issues surrounding Dave Saunders.  She had come to the conclusion were she a prosecutor, she'd prosecute, and once Sandy sets her mind to something, she tenaciously holds to it.  I just wasn't certain anymore if I'd arrest if I had that power.  My problem was, I didn't know *why* I was stepping back from my original conclusion that Dave Saunders fit the bill.  Just as having a natural curiosity was necessary for being a good cop, so was having a 'gut', and I'm talking about an instinct, not the kind many of my brethren obtain from eating the free donuts.

I turned onto Magazine Street a few blocks from our building and then Sandy said something which hit me square in the chest.  I wheeled the Corvette to the curb and braked hard, removed my cell phone and found the stored number, then hit the SEND button.  My wife's eyes were wide with concern, but I didn't have time to explain it to her.

Tracey Walker headed toward New Orleans in her BMW with the stereo playing loudly and a big smile on her face.  The sun was warm on her back.  She felt proud that over the last two days she had been the bulwark for her clients, the Broussards.  It could mean a feather in her cap with the partner's in the firm, however, letting word out on exactly what happened and how it was resolved would have to be the realm of whispered legend rather than shouted fact.  She didn't want anything to risk her handshake agreement with the reputed Don of southern Louisiana.

Her cell phone began to vibrate.  She picked it off the passenger seat as it began to ring and checked the caller ID.  She tossed the phone back onto the seat and let it go to voicemail, then turned up the stereo.

"Dammit," I said.  "Voicemail."

Sandy's right hand was still braced on the dash and she stared wide-eyed across the car at me.

"Who?" she said.

"Tracey Walker," I said.

"What is it, Will?"

I pivoted as much as it was possible for a man my size to do so in a Corvette seat; it was more of a shoulder and head turn.

"You said it," I said, pointing at my wife.  "You said, 'her clients'."

"So?  The Broussards *are* Tracey's clients, that much is clear to anyone who understands legal ethics."  She spread her hands.  "That should have been fairly obvious without being stated, Will.  What, you didn't know that?  Why does it matter?"

"She used me, Sandy, that's why it matters," I said, the argument sounding whiny, even to me. "She told me what she was looking for, but not in so many words. Legalese shit you lawyers always pull."

"Don't lump us all together," Sandy said, her tone terse.

I pulled from the curb and drove to the office. I parked in the street out front, left the car idling. Again I pivoted.

"Yesterday, she said it and I was so focused on being the cop in the equation that I didn't even hear it."

"Hear what?"

"Trade," I said. "Yesterday Tracey told me that the Broussards had nothing to trade with Tony Gators."

"Trade? Trade for what?"

"For their safety, Sandy," I said in a condescending tone. "Don't play stupid."

Well, that was the wrong thing to say to a hormonal woman, but there was no taking it back. My eyes pleaded for mercy, however, Sandy was already moving to get out of the car.

"Don't you ever call me stupid, William Langdon," Sandy said from the sidewalk.

She slammed the door and stormed across the toward our building. I started to get out of my car when my cell phone rang in my hand. I watched Sandy unlock the front door then disappear up the stairs toward our offices as I settled back into my seat and answered the call.

"William," Tracey said, music blaring in the background. "I'm sorry I missed your call. What can I do for you?"

"It sounds like you're driving," I said.

"I am. Heading home. Job well done, and I have you to thank for that."

My heart sank.

"Please tell me you didn't do what I think you did, Tracey," I said.

"What are you talking about, William?"

Is every lawyer so intentionally obtuse, I wondered, but I didn't want to tick off another woman by implying she was being stupid. Even though Tracey Walker was and we both knew it.

Over the years, I have seen the attorneys playing at legal trickery and the revolving doors of our judicial system which far too often let the guilty walk free. Far be it from me to not understand there are other ways to obtain justice, but if what I suspected now was true...was I the pot calling the kettle black? I found I just couldn't bring myself to say the words, because doing so would make me even more complicit in what may be the ultimate injustice, even though I knew I already knew. So I skirted the issue.

"Tracey, where is Ashley?" I asked.

"Her father picked her up a half hour ago," she said perfunctorily.

Then she added with a bit too much self-satisfaction considering what may at that very moment be happening to Dave Saunders: "Everything is okay between him and the Broussards. They wanted me to thank you for all you did for them."

'Dammit, Tracey,' I thought.

"What was the trade?" I asked in a defeated voice as my hand massaged my forehead. "What did you do?"

"Oh, I traded Mr. Monreale the only thing we had, what *you* gave us, William," she said. "I gave him Dave Saunders."

I heard the line go dead.

"Friggin' lawyers," I hollered, looking at my disconnected cell.

I threw the phone across the car and disregarded the cracking sound I heard when it bounced off the door panel. I thought for an instant about going up and telling Sandy where I was headed, but instead just slammed the 'Vette into first and burned a U in Magazine Street. I figured she'd see it from our office windows and get the message.

Travis and Rudy pulled up and parked in the black SUV two blocks down Magazine Street. Travis left the engine running to power the air conditioning against the residual heat of the late afternoon. Rudy brushed French bread crumbs from his pants and drank from the super-size soft drink cup. During the drive in, they had decided to deliver a simple message to William Langdon, but he hadn't gone into the office with his wife. Instead, he had just headed in the opposite direction, leaving noise and black smoke behind.

Travis looked at his watch. It was five-fifty. Sunset would be in seven minutes, according to that morning's Times-Picayune.

"Well?" Rudy said, still chewing on the last of the fried shrimp po' boy sandwich. "Not that I'm getting all that eager to get out of here before we enjoy more of this Cajun cuisine, but my ass is going numb from spending so much time on it today."

"Keep eating like that, and you'll need more ass to support more you," Travis said with a snort.

"Funny," Rudy said. "Just remember I saw you in boxers and T-shirt the other morning, too. Not a pretty sight, my brother."

"Must be all this high living," he said, then flicked a fugitive crumb from Rudy's sandwich from his pants.

"All right, that's all well and good, but the initial question still begs an answer." He paused, looked across at Travis. "Well?"

"I'm thinking," Travis said, his thumb supporting his chin and index finger over his lips. "From the way she stormed away from the car, and the way he left, I sense some friction in paradise."

"So?"

"So, we could be waiting a long time for him to come back if they had a fight." His fingers moved from his face to accentuate his thought. "I'm thinking now, rather than tick off the ex-cop, we leave the message with the missus."

Rudy pondered the idea.

"Makes sense," he said. "Less margin for error."

Travis put the SUV into gear. He stopped across the street from the building with the sign 'William Langdon Investigations' in gold lettering on one of the second floor windows. The first floor store was dark, the painted lettering on each picture window in white script announcing it to be 'Nellie's Notions'. Through the glassed double front doors they could see the staircase which led to the second floor offices where several windows glowed with light.

He turned off the ignition. The sun set; long shadows of afternoon faded into twilight. The day had been stagnant, and the evening promised little relief as the two men in silk suits stepped into it from their rented Lincoln Navigator.

As instructed, they had waited until full darkness outside the hedgerow before driving onto the property with the headlights off.

The trunk of the white with blue racing stripes Mustang GT Liftback stood open when they arrived. The front door was open and three duffles lay just inside the house. The coach lights on either side of the door flickered, electric bulbs mimicking gaslights. The kids had been upstairs when they had walked inside.

They had surprised them.

The two men had no names, or at least they offered none. They stood in the front hallway of the plantation home peering into the darkness outside; their Cadillac de Ville waited in the drive next to the old Mustang. At their feet, lay the handcuffed Dave Saunders and Cindy Spagliano. The boy had fought them, and received a blackjack to the back of the head for his efforts. The girl had given them lip, and in return had received an Italian loafer to the face. She sobbed quietly as a trickle of blood ran down her cheek and onto her hair on the polished cypress planking. The boy didn't move.

The older of the two men walked outside onto the veranda and pointed a fob at the Caddy and the trunk popped open. The compartment was lined with two layers of heavy, black plastic sheeting.

He returned to the hallway.

# Chapter Twenty-nine

I pushed the Corvette to one-twenty on the interstate headed west. Moments ago, the sun had set as it had risen, as a red-orange ball in a hazy sky against an indistinct horizon. I tossed my sunglasses onto the empty passenger seat. My phone was screwed; a fact I discovered when I had retrieved it from the floorboard to call Sandy before I was out of the city. I cursed my temper.

As I slid into the right lane and sailed past some jerk in a canary yellow Camaro who thought he owned the left side of the highway, I prayed I wasn't too late. Men like Vincent Monreale don't waste time when they have someone in their sights, and this wasn't merely business as the movie cliché goes. This was personal. Someone had raped and beaten the man's sixteen-year-old daughter and then disposed of her like garbage on the banks of the Mississippi. Oh, yes, this was personal in the extreme; and because of me, Tony Gators thought the man responsible was a kid named Dave Saunders and because of Tracey Walker, Tony knew just where to find him.

I exited on highway 641 and raced south to the river, crossed the bridge, then picked up the Great River Road on the other side. Full darkness had replaced the twilight. As I passed Oak Alley, the last of the day's Blue Line tour busses rolled to a stop at the end of the parking lot's drive, waited for me as I flew past, then swung wide to the right and headed back to New Orleans. The car hugged the smaller S-turn and the bus's red tail lights were gone, sped past the tiny subdivision, then hugged the larger S-turn. There was no other traffic on the road and I slowed nearing the gap in the hedgerow, then turned up the drive.

"Son of a bitch," I said as I steered with my knees, leaned forward in the seat and reached behind my back. I chambered a round in Willie and thumbed the safety before replacing the SIG in my belt.

The Cadillac's trunk was open and I could see black plastic hanging from the inside of the lid, held in place with duct tape. The front door of the house was open. A nightlight was on in the hallway and I could make out movement inside. My heart pounded in my chest. Don't let anyone kid you, you're always scared going into a life and death situation, no matter how many times you've done it.

I pulled the 'Vette to the side of the narrow drive about fifty feet from the Caddy, left it idling, the headlights on. I exited my car, closed the door when two squat mountains appeared in the doorway. They separated, but remained on the veranda. From their girth alone, I could quickly tell neither one was Vincent Monreale. I put my arms out to my side.

"This don't concern you, mister," the one on the left said. "Why don't you just get in your car and be somewhere else?"

I stepped forward. I had my headlights making me a silhouette to their view, while each of them appeared to be attempting to inch toward the shadows beyond the range of the flickering bulbs of the dual coach lights. There was no way I could take both of them down before they got shots at me, and I had no cover other than diving for the Caddy and that was still forty feet away. I continued slowly forward, trying my best to be non-confrontational.

"You're making a mistake, boys," I said. "He's not guilty of what you think he is."

"Ain't my problem," said the one on the right who had made it out of the light's reach. "You don't want none of this." A pause. "Trust me on that one."

"Last chance, mister," the other one said.

I mentally ticked off my options. None of them were much use in the long term. Even if I could take out Tony's men and extricate Dave and Cindy from the jaws of death, he'd just send more, and the kids' lives would never be safe. Tracey had too much information on Dave Saunders for him to just disappear back into his world, and if she gave Tony enough to get his people here, she most likely gave him everything I had reported to her. Thankfully, I hadn't told her every detail, but anyone could figure out the rest, given enough time.

"Can't we talk about this?" I said, buying a bit more time to think.

"There ain't nothin' to talk about," the one of the right said. Then he snorted derisively. "Unless you want to give us a hand with the broad, that is. She's a chunky one and I don't think she's gonna walk out and hop into the trunk for us."

"My name is William Langdon," I said. "I'm the P.I. who tracked the trail this far, but I know now it doesn't end here."

"We know who you are, Mr. Langdon," the left one said. "That lady lawyer told Tony you might show up. My orders if you did show and wouldn't leave right away were to send you on your way with a message."

"What's the message?" I said.

I stepped wide of the Caddy to not give them the idea I was looking to take cover and escalate this thing to gunfire, but had moved close enough to see into the trunk. Dave Saunders lay crumpled and face down on the plastic. He was breathing, but wasn't otherwise moving.

"Congratulations," the left one said.

"What?" I said.

"On your upcoming blessed event," he clarified.

My blood ran cold at the implied threat to both my wife and unborn child and wondered if there were right now more people at my office where Sandy may still be all alone. I cursed Tracey Walker under my breath; appended the words 'burn in hell' to my standard imprecation.

"Get it, Langdon?" he said. "Or do you want me to spell it out?"

I was running out of options, and they were obviously becoming restless with the delay caused by the standoff.

"Two fingers," I said.

"What?" the right one said.

"I'm going to reach behind my back and come out holding with only two fingers," I explained. "Then, you take me to see Tony."

They exchanged glances. Obviously they hadn't planned for that eventuality.

"Deal?" I said.

"Okay," the one on the left said. "Turn around first."

I turned my back to them, reached behind my back, inside my jacket and lifted Willie free with two fingers, as promised. I held the gun out, then tossed it onto the grass about ten feet away. When I turned back toward them, they had moved back into the reach of the coach lights and were each tucking .38 snubs into tight belt lines.

"Come up here," the guy on the right instructed. "We gotta pat you down."

He waddled to the center of the porch and waited for me at the top of the steps. I walked the cobbled path, up the steps, raised my arms and let him pat me down. The guy was breathing hard from the effort, and grunted when he bent over, never going below my knees with his frisk.

"Wait here, and don't go doin' nothin' stupid," he instructed and accentuated the words with a pointed, chubby finger, then followed his partner back inside the hallway.

A moment later, they emerged with Cindy Spagliano. She was cuffed behind her back and each of them had an arm. Her toes dragged behind her. Her hair hung down and I could hear her crying softly.

"Shit, lady," the one who had patted me down said. "You could stand to lose a few pounds."

"Look who's talking, asshole," she said, then spit a bloody wad onto one of his expensive-looking loafers.

I smiled at her guts. Him, not so much.

They dragged her off the porch and tossed her roughly on top of Dave Saunders' limp body, then slammed the trunk. I remained in place, waited out the expected invitation.

"Get his piece," the left one said, "and his keys from the Corvette."

The other one did as he was told. The left one opened a front door on the Caddy and slid into the driver's seat. The right one returned with my keys and Willie. He opened the right front door and with his eyes barely over the top of the car, extended the invitation, of sorts.

"You comin' or not?"

I moved off the porch, took a seat behind the driver.

The passenger turned his head on a fat neck and looked me in the eye.

"Sorry, but we can't guarantee this will be a round trip, ya know?" he said, then laughed and faced forward.

Ten-seconds later, we were headed up the drive away from the plantation house. A minute after that, we turned left on the Great River Road. At 3218, we again made a left, then a mile later at 3127 a third left. We turned right onto 20. A couple of minutes later, we left behind the last of the lights of civilization and passed into bayou country and drove south toward Thibodaux.

Thibodaux was a storied place and an appropriate home for Vincent Anthony Monreale, a man reputed to be one of the most bloodthirsty criminal leaders in the history of the Louisiana Mafia.

Nicknamed the Queen City of Lafourche, Thibodaux was the Lafourche Parish seat - Louisiana doesn't have counties, it has parishes - and was the site of one of the bloodiest labor disputes in U.S. history during the sugar cane workers' strike of 1887. At least thirty-five black workers and their families were slaughtered and buried in shallow graves by white vigilantes allegedly organized by district court judge Taylor Beattie, himself a cane planter, ex-Confederate, ex-slaveholder, and former member of the Knights of the White Camelia, a group associated with the Ku Klux Klan.

Lying along a minor tributary of the Mississippi flowing south from the main river branch at Donaldsonville, which, since the construction of the modern levee system was maintained as a waterway by gates and mechanical pumps as a flood-control measure, Thibodaux was by then a relatively clean and modern city of fourteen-thousand people.

The Monreale home was on old plantation land several miles northeast of the city.

When our driver turned southeast onto 307, I suspected we weren't going anywhere near Thibodaux.

Travis and Rudy checked the outside doors and found the right one unlocked. They entered the building at the base of the stairs to the second floor. Off to the left was the locked entrance to the notions store. The door at the top of the stairs was ajar. Light came through the frosted glass pane which sported a smaller version of the company sign, about the same size as the 'William Langdon Investigations' with an arrow painted on the wall to their right at the base of the stairs.

Travis lead the way. The steps creaked in protest at the combined load. As they neared the top, they could hear someone speaking in the office. They listened at the door, soon concluded it was some sort of talk radio program with the host discussing the burgeoning Lewinsky affair and ranting about 'Bill Clinton's absolute lack of morals'. Rudy smirked. Travis nodded.

A moment later, Travis quietly pushed the door open. The public office included a small waiting area off to the right which contained a couch in mauve, gray, and white stripes and a pair of blue velvet wingback chairs. Off to the left, an expansive desk in yellow oak with matching file cabinets beyond and various office machines took up the space. A hallway traversed the far end of the area with bathrooms marked 'Ladies' and 'Gentlemen' in the center. Off to the left, they saw a closed door marked with a polished brass plaque etched with the name 'William Langdon'. Down the hallway to the right was the source of the radio.

Travis led the way along the carpeted hallway. At the end, there were two doors. The door to the left was slightly ajar and sported a similar plaque to William's proclaiming this as the office of 'Sandy Langdon'. The door to the right was unmarked. Rudy tried the knob and it was locked.

Travis tapped twice lightly on the oak door to the left and then walked in without waiting for an invitation.

Sandy Langdon sat behind her desk. When she heard the knock and then sensed the movement of the door, she looked up to see two large gentlemen striding into her office. She removed a pair of reading glasses and placed them on her blotter.

"May I help you, gentlemen?" she said.

Rudy stood near the door and grinned at her as Travis moved across the office and peered through plantation shutters onto the alley behind the building.

"You always leave your door unlocked, Mrs. Langdon?" Rudy said, then returned his gaze inside to the attractive woman behind the desk.

"My husband is coming up," she lied. "Perhaps it's him you were coming to see."

"No, Sandy, he's not," Travis said. "We watched him drive off about twenty minutes ago. Left in quite the rush, tires squealing and all."

Sandy had heard, and saw through their front office windows, as William executed the rubber-burning U-turn.

"We're really here to see you anyway, Mrs. Langdon," Rudy said, continuing to smirk. "I don't think your husband will be back for a while." He walked the couple of steps to the couch along the wall next to the door and sat. "Mind if I take a load off?"

Sandy felt the knot in her stomach tighten.

Senator Lamoureux and his son, Dace, strode through the lobby of the United Brotherhood of Carpenters building on Constitution Avenue, across from the Capitol, and entered Charlie Palmer Steak.

The maitre d immediately recognized The Senator and promptly excused himself from the young, anonymous man and woman standing at the podium. The couple turned to see who had superseded them in the D.C. hierarchy and immediately recognized the senior senator from Connecticut. The man, a staffer for the junior senator from Vermont, nodded a greeting. The Senator smiled, but had no idea who he was.

The Senator introduced the maitre d to his son.

"Remember this young man," The Senator said. "One day he's going to be even more important in this town than his father ever was. One day, Mitchell, my son Dace is going to be president."

Dace smiled, shook the man's offered hand. Mitchell personally escorted them to a private, yet highly visible table in a quiet corner of the dining room. Heads turned, some discretely nodded to The Senator.

"Daniel will be your waiter this evening, Senator," Mitchell said as he seated the duo.

"I already know what we want, Mitchell," The Senator said with a wave of his hand. "Please tell Daniel to send over two of my stock over the rocks, doubles, a couple of Porterhouse steaks, medium rare, baked potatoes, asparagus."

Mitchell nodded. He was used to this type of power play by his customers. It was part of the game. He turned to leave. The Senator caught his sleeve.

"Oh, and have Daniel send it all over with Beccah," he said, patting the man's arm, then dismissing him. "That's a good man."

We moved east as the roadway carved itself deeper into bayou country. A scattering of trailer homes dotted one section of the landscape, then we quickly passed again into the darkness. Behind me in the trunk I could hear talking, then there erupted kicking of the lid which I could feel in the back of the seat.

The passenger swung around, my gun in his hand. He pointed it toward the back seat.

"Scrunch over, Mr. Langdon," he said with an evil grin and aimed off my right elbow, his thumb releasing the safety.

I held my ground.

The driver pushed his partner's shoulder.

"You shoot my car and I'll feed *you* to the gators," he said, then swerved violently across both lanes, tossing me, and the kids in the trunk from side-to-side.

Cindy and Dave quieted down.

Several minutes later, we turned up a gravel lane barely wide enough for one car. Cane grass leaves slapped at the Caddy and I could tell the driver wasn't too happy about it. Several hundred yards in, he stopped and his partner exited, then lowered a heavy chain which had been strung between sturdy pipes on each side of the road. He rolled across the line, then waited for the passenger to reconnect the chain and get back into the car before we continued.

Eventually, we entered a small clearing. A rusted metal building appeared in the headlights. A black Mercedes sat near the single metal walk door. A single bulb hung in an old dome fixture and lit the area. In the grass just outside the door, lay two wooden pallets.

"Wait here," the driver said, then shut off the car, rolled out and waddled toward the building. He went inside and closed the door.

"Feel free to stretch your legs, but don't go wanderin' around out here," the passenger said with a wide grin. "Lotta bad things in them bushes and cane."

"I'm good," I said.

"Can't be shy if you gotta piss, either," he said. "Them gators seem attracted to the smell."

I stared at him. If he thought he could scare me, he was dead wrong. Most tough guys don't talk it, and those who do usually turn out to be the biggest pussies. He did have my gun, though, and that tends to even things up.

The door on the building opened and two men walked out. One was the driver, the other a man of small stature. They moved to the left side of the car and the driver opened my door. I stepped out onto a patch of grass and shook the offered hand of perhaps the most feared mobster in the country, Vincent Anthony Monreale.

"Mr. Langdon," he said. "A pleasure to have the opportunity to finally meet you. Ms. Walker was kind enough to inform me you may show up following your little conversation after she left the Broussard's home a bit earlier. It's why I had instructed my associates to not put a bullet between your eyes if you interrupted their retrieval work. Call it professional courtesy for what you did for my daughter, although this may not be the best place for us to have our first face-to-face. Frankly, I am a bit surprised you didn't take the warning. That's disappointing."

He released my hand and his unblinking eyes looked up at me. He was a small man, his rap sheet said five-feet-six, and he weighed in at one-hundred-forty-five pounds. His handshake had been strong, his hand diminutive, yet wiry. Even in the relative darkness, I could see his eyes were cold and black, and matched his hair. He extended his arm in the direction of the building.

"If you please," he said. "I am told you wish to speak to me, and we can do that inside the building much more comfortably than out here. My associates will be along shortly; they have some heavy lifting to do."

I hesitated. He smiled as warmly as any reptile can.

"Oh, please, Mr. Langdon, nothing will happen to these two until after you've had your time to speak in their defense. Of that, you have my word."

He turned and walked toward the building. I followed.

"In case you don't know, this is my private little retreat on Lac des Allemands," he said. "That means..."

"Lake of the Germans," I said, a bit surprised he would advertise it to me. "I know it. I've fished for catfish on it several times, but obviously never on this particular side."

"It's a large lake," he said absently, stepping onto the pallets and holding the door for me.

I walked into a brightly lit space, which was a warehouse containing commercial fishing equipment: nets, dozens of spools of rope and cable, hardware, propellers, and diesel engines. He guided me between the racks and stacks toward the far wall.

"Impressive, but aren't you a bit off the main drag out here for this kind of stuff?"

He ignored the smart-aleck comment.

"As I said, it's a large lake, about twelve-thousand acres, but not really that deep, only about ten feet at the maximum," he said.

He reached for a yellow, rectangular, control which hung from a heavy, black electrical cable running from the ceiling. I realized this was all theater for the man as I watched him press one of the rubber-covered buttons on the box and a pair of diamond plate steel doors opened on the floor. He never took his eyes off me. When fully opened, the pit was perhaps ten feet wide and twelve feet long.

He motioned me closer. More theatrics.

"That's why this may not be the best place for us to have had our first meeting," he said, pointing down into the pit.

I looked inside and saw what I expected, about a dozen very large alligators, each at least fourteen feet long in the shallow water of a caged pit much larger than the opening in the floor. They moved excitedly under the open hatch and hissed at the Pavlovian stimulus of the doors being opened. They were hungry.

He tossed several chunks of what looked like chicken into the pit from a nearby pail and the gators climbed over one another to get at them and swallowed them whole. Okay, no more theatrics; he had my attention.

"Few people have seen what you are witnessing tonight, Mr. Langdon," he said. "Fewer still have been here and walked out. Time will tell which group to which you will belong at the end of the night. Much of that is up to you." He laughed from the belly.

There was a commotion on the far side of the building as Tony's associates entered carrying Cindy Spagliano, then dropped her on her belly onto the concrete floor on the edge of the hole. Blood had dried on her face and matted her hair and several strips of duct tape had been applied over her mouth. She lifted her head and looked about the room, then she apparently heard the hissing and thrashing of the alligators and she looked down into the pit. Her eyes became frantic, then found mine. I don't know what she saw reflected in my eyes, but she looked away and began to sob.

Several minutes later, they dragged Dave Saunders in, his bare feet skidding along the concrete, his head lolling. As they moved him past me, I could see his eyes were glazed and barely focusing. There was no tape over his mouth. Instead of dropping him on the floor next to Cindy, they dragged him to the far edge of the pit and stood him upright.

"You promised me I'd get my say," I said to Tony.

His head snapped in my direction. His eyes were wild. He raised a finger, held it to his lips. I got it.

They inched Dave to the edge of the pit. The alligators hissed more loudly, leapt toward the floor. Dave stood there, his toes on the metal angle which formed the edge of the concrete, firmly in the grasp of our driver, and his eyes rapidly gained focus. The other associate retrieved a hook attached to a cable which I saw ran to a trolley on a beam along the ceiling. The beam ran directly over the center of the opening. He clipped the hook over the handcuffs on Dave's hands.

"This way, we get the cuffs back," the passenger said, a grin on his face as his eyes focused upon me.

I was feeling sick to my stomach. I had seen men die before, some at my hand, but never anything like this. The sadistic pleasure seemingly taken by these men turned the instinctual horror of the thought of being eaten alive into a living nightmare which must drive the victim to near insanity long before they were ever lowered into the pit.

Tony pressed another button on his control box and held it until a reel on the trolly had taken up the slack and centered directly above the kid. Dave's arms were pulled taught behind him, then Tony pressed the button in quick touches which reeled in more cable, bending Dave's arms back at an unnatural angle and forcing Dave onto the balls of his feet. He cried out in pain.

Beccah removed their dinner plates, dipping low over the table. The Senator smiled. Dace also enjoyed the show from his angle of view.

"How were the steaks this evening, Senator?" she asked, straightening up and returning a big, bright smile.

"Wonderful, my dear," The Senator said. "Isn't that right, son?"

"Delicious," Dace said, his gaze moving hungrily over her body, then connecting to her soft, brown eyes.

"I'll tell the chef," she said, then sauntered off toward the kitchen which was undetectable from that area of the restaurant.

The Senator and his son had enjoyed a long day of talking. They understood one another now perhaps better than they ever had. The night's outing was a bit of a celebration of a new cooperative pact.

"Dessert, boy?" The Senator said.

Dace stared after the girl who was long gone around the corner.

"Always, father," Dace said.

The sandwich was sitting well in Rudy's stomach, however, the super-sized cola had quickly worked its way through his system and his bladder was about to overflow. He shifted on the couch.

Sandy had paid very close attention to Travis' monologue over the last half hour. He had explained the situation to her and she had nodded at the appropriate times. The threats the man had made were specific, involved her family, and William's, and Sandy was as frightened as she had ever been.

When she had been a criminal lawyer, she was threatened on several occasions, and once or twice by people she knew could well carry through on the words. Despite her best legal efforts on behalf of her clients, the system had worked and they all eventually went away for a very long time. To date, none of them had made parole. Their words had long since evaporated, along with their memories of the free world. These two sitting in her office had not only the ability to carry things through, they were walking the streets and were obviously connected to powerful forces.

That's when Rudy excused himself to use the restroom.

He rose from the couch and left the office. Sandy heard the heavy door close behind him down the hall. That's when Sandy slipped out of her heels under her desk and made a break for the door. The move caught Travis off-guard and he reacted a moment too late. Sandy was through her office door by the time he got to his feet. She bounced off the locked workroom door across the hallway. Rudy heard the commotion and tried to squeeze off the flow. Travis reached for her, but she slipped just beyond his grasp and rabbited down the hall.

She heard the bathroom door open and out the corner of her eye saw Rudy pop out from around the corner just as she began to make the turn through the public office area.

"Grab that bitch, Rudy," Travis yelled.

The door was steps away.  Sandy prayed they hadn't turned the deadbolt, then felt relief when she saw the knob was in the open position. She pulled a small plant across the way behind her, heard Rudy swear as he stumbled over it.  Her hand was inches from the door when she felt a hand grab for her shoulder.  She screamed, then stumbled.

The next instants passed in slow motion as Sandy fell against the large, glass panel of the door, felt it give way and then she was moving through the opening, suspended in space along with hundreds of bits of glass which seemed to float with her.  Her momentum carried her across the small upper landing and she hit the staircase hard.  Her body tumbled onto the stairs, her head hit the railing several times as she fell. Sandy felt a sudden, searing pain shoot through her abdomen, then her head struck the second last stair and everything went black.

Tony let the control box dangle from the cord.  He crossed his arms and looked at me.

"Okay, Mr. Langdon," he said.  "Now you may speak."

I took several steps closer to him.

"Just be brief," he said, pointing toward Dave.  "Mr. Saunders over there appears to be in quite a bit of discomfort at the moment, and we must remember he has needs as well."

I made my plea for Dave's innocence, enumerating all the evidence which pointed away from him as being the man who attacked Ashley. Tony appeared unmoved.

"But, Ashley herself identified him," Tony said, "or have you forgotten, Mr. Langdon?  Isn't that what you told Tracey Walker"

"I didn't do anything to your daughter," Dave hollered.  "I was with Cindy every minute of that night."

Tony turned toward Dave.

"What night?" he said.

"Tuesday, the night I met your daughter and her friend at Pat O'Brien's," Dave said.

"She identified you, Mr. Saunders," Tony said.  "Are you trying to call my little girl a liar?  Have you seen the results of what you did to my baby?  She's going to carry physical and emotional scars for the rest of her life. You, Mr. Saunders, on the other hand, won't have that burden." He pointed to the alligators which were nearing a frenzy, snapping and hissing.  "Obviously."

"I didn't do anything to anyone," Dave said, his voice cracking.

"If not you, then who, Mr. Saunders?  Just give me a name."

I saw something in Dave's eyes. He shook his head, tears welled.

"I don't know a name," Dave said.

"Tony, listen to me, please," I said.

"Are we on a first name basis, Mr. Langdon?" he snapped.

"I'm sorry, Mr. Monreale. This kid didn't do it. There was someone else with him at the house. I'm certain of it. Give me time to prove it. Goddammit, you have to listen to me. Just give me time."

"I have been listening to you, Mr. Langdon," he said. "You haven't told me anything which lessens the impact of the evidence you collected *against* this young man. At least not in the eyes of this particular court." He pointed a finger at me and his black eyes held mine. "You swear again and I'll hold you in contempt. There are better ways to prove things, Mr. Langdon. Much quicker ways, and since we're all here, I say we do this my way. Whatcha say?"

His eyes moved past me and I was grabbed by each arm. I felt the barrel of a gun, possibly my own, in the small of my back. My God, I thought, the man must be insane.

"Stand her up," Tony said.

The associate who wasn't holding a gun to me released his grip and walked over and stood Cindy up. The girl stood on uncertain feet attached to rubbery legs. Tears marked her cheeks. She attempted to speak, but the effort fell impotent to the grip of the tape.

"Bring her to the edge," Tony said. "Let her look at her boyfriend."

The driver maneuvered the girl to the opposite edge of the opening. Her bare toes hung over the side. Dave struggled to lift his head. I will swear to the day I die that he mouthed the words 'I love you, say nothing'.

"Mr. Monreale," I said. "You don't have to do this. It's not justice. This man didn't hurt Ashley. Someone else did."

I felt the gun push into my back.

"It's the somebody else done it excuse, boss," the passenger said sarcastically around my arm.

"Shut up," Tony snapped. "Next person who says a word, goes into the pit. I'm done listening. There's only three words I want to hear, and those words are going to come out of Mr. Saunders' mouth."

His eyes stopped at each of us. Nobody spoke. Cindy's head hung down. Her eyes were closed. She began to totter on the edge.

"I'm through arguing, Mr. Saunders," Tony said, the control box in his hand again. "Nod if you understand. Remember there are only three words I want to hear from you, so please don't speak. Just nod."

Dave nodded.

Tony flicked a button on the control box. The boy was pulled forward slightly by the trolley; he rocked up onto his toes.

"Do you love this girl, Mr. Saunders? Remember, nod only."

Dave looked across the chasm at Cindy. Her head raised, her eyes opened and she looked at him. He nodded. She began to cry again.

This was sick. It was beyond anything I had ever witnessed. My mind reeled, floated back to Sandy and my kids: the three girls and my unborn child. I had to do something, but I also had to return to them. I owed it to them. I began to plan my move, watched for the opportunity, but I knew I was quickly running out of time; and more imperatively, so was Dave Saunders.

"Well, I love my daughter. More than anything in this world. Today, I had to see her beaten and bruised, her body used by you for your pleasure, then left like trash on the banks of the Mississippi. Ironically, do you know your soon-to-be executioners are known as Alligator Mississippiensis?"

Dave moaned.

"Sorry," Tony said. "I forgot you weren't feeling so well right now. I'll move this along." He paused. "Three words, Mr. Saunders, and all this ends. Do you know what those words are?"

Dave shook his head.

"I did it," Tony said. "That's all I want to hear. Can you say those words to me to make this all end, Mr. Saunders?"

Dave shook his head.

I shifted my feet. The guy with the gun pushed it against me. The driver was back behind me. They each held an arm firmly.

"Okay, I'll trade you something you want. How's that?"

Dave looked, neither nodded nor shook his head.

"Good, negotiations are open, then," Tony said, mocking the boy. "If you admit to this, I'll shoot the girl so she doesn't go in alive like you will. How's that?"

Dave's eyes grew wild, yet he held his tongue. He shook his head emphatically. Cindy's head was again down, her eyes closed.

"No? You want more? You're an excellent negotiator, Mr. Saunders." Tony paused, making a show of thinking about the process of bartering for the pair's lives. "Okay, how's this? If you will say those three little words, I'll let the girl go altogether. Unharmed. That offer expires in ten-seconds, however, and upon expiry she goes in first. Alive."

My eyes shot to seek out Dave's, but he was staring at Tony, who was making a show of looking at his watch.

"Starting." He paused. "Now."

Tony began counting.

"One Mississippi, two Mississippi, three Mississippi, four Mississippi."

I wondered for an instant if I could still get to Sam in my ankle holster with a bullet in the kidney. Possibly with a .38 slug, but a 10mm at close range would likely vaporize anything in its path and come out my gut. I felt the grip of the two men behind me tighten.

"Five, six," Tony said, looking up.

Dave still refused to look at me. Cindy began to shake, and I feared she was about to fall forward.

"Seven, eight."

Tony's hand moved onto Cindy's shoulder, the girl stiffened, urine ran down her legs and puddled onto the floor. It trickled over the edge.

"Nine."

"I did it."

Cindy's head popped up, her eyes wild, she shook her head, struggled against the tape. Tony removed his hand from the girl's shoulder.

"What was that, Mr. Saunders? I was counting. I didn't quite hear you."

Dave looked to Cindy, then defiantly through Tony. My heart sank.

"I did it."

What happened next only Dave Saunders didn't see coming.

I hollered for Tony to stop. He looked at me, smiled broadly, placed his hand in the center of Cindy's back and pushed. The girl tumbled into the pit and the alligators swarmed her. Dave's eyes went wild and he began thrashing against the cuffs and cable.

I twisted in the grasp of the two associates and heard Willie go off, felt something hot tear against my side. I put a shoulder into the driver on my right, sent him stumbling toward the pit. He reached out for the raised metal plate. I heard him go in, the screams seemed to go on and on. I dropped to my knee, pulled Sam from my ankle holster and fired one shot between the passenger's eyes. He went down on the floor like a sack of potatoes. I spun and aimed at Tony. Out the corner of my eye, I noticed Dave was now suspended over the pit. Somehow I understood his will had already left his body. Mine had not, however, and I pulled the hammer back while I aimed Sam across the short distance between my hand and Tony Gators' head. The earlier gunshot still rang in my ears, but everything else had gone deathly silent apart from the continued thrashing in the pit. There were no more screams.

"Looks like we have us a standoff, Mr. Langdon," Tony said with a smile, his thumb poised above a red button.

"Ashley's an orphan either way, Tony," I snarled. "You call it."

Tony Gators' smile morphed into a wild-eyed grin.

My finger twitched the same time as did Tony's thumb. Sam's trigger slid back, the hammer moved forward. Out of the corner of my eye, I saw Dave free fall. The percussion filled the room as the bullet left the short barrel and traversed the distance in microseconds, striking Tony in the forehead. Blood and brains exited the back of his skull along with the bullet and he slumped to the concrete. I came up off my knee and lunged across to the distance. I emptied my remaining four bullets into the pit as I grabbed the swinging controller with my free hand and pushed a green button. The motor of the trolley whirred overhead as the cable pulled and whipped.

Several moments later, all that came up was an empty pair of hand cuffs attached to a hook spattered with blood.

# Chapter Thirty

I knelt down on one knee and searched through the pockets of the fat lump lying on the floor and found my car keys. I put Sam back in my ankle holster and picked up Willie near the dead man's hand. A single spent 10mm casing lay several feet away. I touched my side where I had felt the hot flash moments earlier and found holes in both my jacket and shirt, but there was no blood. I was tender there, most likely burned by the muzzle flash; but while the bullet had passed through my clothing, it hadn't even grazed my flesh. I looked down at the hole in the fat lump's forehead, his wide-eyed look of surprise frozen in time.

Two shots had been fired between us.

I was lucky. He was dead.

I scanned the area as I stood. Vincent Anthony Monreale, the Don of southern Louisiana, lay crumpled in a small pile several feet from the open pit. I moved closer. I didn't want to look down into the alligator hold again, but I knew I had to. There was at least one dead alligator, and the others were tearing what was left of the two innocent kids from Harvard, and one fat lump of shit into pieces. They were all obviously dead. There was nothing I could do for any of them, but I emptied the last twelve bullets in Willie's clip into the mass of squirming gators, stopping four or five in the process. It was what some would call the ultimate impotent act of rage, and it didn't make me feel any better.

I stood there looking down, a spent and smoking Willie dangling at the end of my limp arm, and momentarily froze as the past rushed over me. Another warehouse. Another night of violence and death. Unlike the circumstances of this night, however, Eric had signed on to the risks. He was a cop. A good cop. That night his luck just ran out. Today I had served up two unwitting kids to Tony Gators on a silver platter, and I could already feel that weight chained to my burdened soul.

We Catholics are rumored to relish our 'precious guilt', but that was said by people who didn't understand how guilt worked for us, and how easily we could shed it every Saturday simply by telling our sins anonymously to a priest, who then, with a wave of his hand and recitation of a few prayers, administered God's absolution. It was a pact between us and The Big Guy upstairs. We relied on it. It worked well; but this particular guilt wasn't going to be waved away. Nobody was going to absolve me of what I had done and tell me to cleanse my soul with the recitation of a couple *Hail Mary* or *Our Father* prayers. The events of the past couple of days culminating in that night's murders were going to take time, and a quantity of bourbon, to ease the heaviness in my heart.

I went through Tony's pockets and neither he nor the fat lump had a cell phone on them. I searched the warehouse. There were no landline phones I could find. The local authorities needed to be brought in on this, so the only way to notify them was to get back to civilization and call from the nearest pay phone. I walked outside past Tony's Benz and across the grass to the Caddy, hoping the driver hadn't taken his keys with him into the pit. There was no way I was driving that sick fuck's Benz out of here; I'd walk to town first, and I think you all know I'm no huge fan of walking anywhere. I opened the driver's door on the Caddy and the interior light went on. I saw the keys hanging from the ignition. I climbed in part way, powered back the seat and slid in the rest of the way, started the engine and turned the vehicle around in the open area, then rolled down the narrow graveled drive cut through the cane grass. At the chain across the road, I got out, dropped it and left it down, then made my way out to the main highway.

I drove the fat lump's Caddy west on 307 then picked up highway 20 south into Thibodaux. While I had passed a number of trailers and houses on the way, the first public place I came across with a pay phone was a small diner along the river. I parked on the narrow strip of asphalt between building and road and went inside to call the Parish Sheriff's office. The non-emergency number was printed on a sticker on the phone. I told the dispatcher where I was and that I needed a squad car or two to come to me; she asked why, and I told her that some people were dead out at the lake, then I hung up.

While I waited for the deputies to arrive, I took a stool at the counter and ordered a fountain Coke from the high school girl in the pink uniform dress and white apron. She brought the drink moments later, served up in an old-style glass with the scripted 'Coca-Cola' in white enamel near the rim. A white plastic straw with the paper wrap still on the top half protruded from the crushed ice and cola. The imagery and that first sip took me back to how they'd serve it that very same way at Al & Al's Bar & Grill on Twelfth Street in Sheboygan when I was kid and my brother and I would be sent into the grill side for an order of French fries in a cardboard boat and a couple of Cokes while our father sat and drank himself into his version of happiness with tap beers on the bar side.

I carried the Coke back to the pay phone and tried home, then the office, then Sandy's cell phone. There was no answer at any of the numbers and I didn't leave a voicemail. She must really be pissed at me, I thought, then returned to my seat at the counter and began sorting through things and how I'd describe the night's events to the cops. I owed Ashley Monreale some discretion, I believed, as well as confidentiality to my client from up north. Of course, I needed to pay Tracey Walker a private visit when I could, but they didn't need to know about that either. I wondered if I should make a call to Tom McDaniel and fill him in or whether it would be cleaner for the story to filter its way up to Connecticut, or wherever, through the channels of officialdom. I decided I'd sleep on that decision, but knew, by the morning they'd most likely know anyway making my outreach unnecessary. Yeah, I was copping out.

About five minutes into my contemplation and Coke, a pair of deputies strode into the cafe and looked around. I waved to them, finished the last of the drink, tossed a few bucks onto the counter and then stood and walked over. I told them who I was, showed them my impressive P.I. credentials, then suggested we talk outside, away from the prying ears of the handful of locals who'd already taken a passing interest in this tall stranger. Once let out of the bag, the news of Tony Gators' demise and ensuing gossip would sweep the small town of Thibodaux fast enough.

They followed me into the night and under the neon of the diner's sign I relayed to them everything that had taken place during the evening beginning from the time I arrived at Jackson Stempler's plantation house west of Vacherie. They seemed to take it all in stride, or perhaps they were wondering if an extra long sleeved jacket and ride to the special hospital would be in my near future. Neither of them took notes during the first telling. When I finished the narrative, one of them asked what had precipitated the entire situation and I told the first lie of the night to the cops. It was a white lie, one designed mainly to maintain Ashley's privacy, but also to protect the reputation of Dave Saunders, who didn't deserve those types of headlines to follow him into the afterlife. The deputies shared glances, then excused themselves and huddled a few steps away, finally deciding I wasn't some kind of loon and concluding they needed the Sheriff himself brought in on this one. I thought the second conclusion was a good one, while admitting only to myself the first one may be debatable. I didn't push my luck by telling them either of my conclusions.

One of the deputies walked to his car and radioed in, made the call for the Sheriff come to the diner. I noticed he didn't give any details for the request or even use code numbers, all of which anyone with a scanner already knew. That either meant they weren't yet fully taking me seriously, or, if they were, just wanted this kept in the family for now. While we all waited, there was some discussion between the deputies whether the scene was even located within Lafourche Parish or if the potential problem fell in the lap of St. John the Baptist or St. Charles Parish authorities. Lac des Allemands touched all three parishes, they told me when I looked confused. My conclusion was they were hoping this mess, were it not just a figment of my imagination, would fall outside of their jurisdiction.

The Sheriff arrived in his shiny new squad a few minutes later, accompanied by - as announced by the deputies - the mayor of Thibodaux, of all people. Don't ask me why, I still don't know. The Sheriff was a large man, and when he rolled out of the driver's side door the squad seemed to exhale in relief; the mayor had the opposite build and when he hopped out of the passenger side the Crown Victoria barely noticed. They approached our little group preceded by the dangerous air of southern, small town authority; the visual, however, was a bit more cartoonish.

I introduced myself, produced my credentials again, then recited the details of the story for the second time, and while that was going on the people began to trickle out of the diner while others stopped in from the street and formed a loose circle around our little group to try to catch a bit of local gossip. I noticed one of the deputies took notes that time. When I finished, the Sheriff looked at the mayor, shrugged broad shoulders and suggested the easiest thing to do was go out to the scene to confirm my story. I was placed in the back of the Sheriff's squad and together with the pair of deputies, we formed a three-car convoy out to Tony's warehouse on the shores of Lac des Allemands.

Once we arrived on scene and entered the building and they confirmed at least the broad strokes of my story, the informal gathering smoothly transitioned into a professional crime scene investigation. Calls went out to a forensics team, detectives, the coroner, a pair of ambulances for the people, and a team from the state animal control division for the gators. Ballistics wouldn't be much of an issue since the only weapons in play belonged to me and I turned over both Willie and Sam. After some on-scene testing, collection of the spent shell casings from Sam and the floor of the warehouse for Willie's ejected cartridges, and transcription of the serial numbers, they were returned to me by the Sheriff as a professional accommodation.

Courtesy calls were put out to the sheriffs of the other two parishes which bordered the lake, and then some bright boy suggested that since the warehouse extended out over the lake, perhaps the crime scene fell under state jurisdiction. They'd sort that out soon enough, I knew, but at that point it appeared to me the scene was fully in the control of the hometown Lafourche authorities. Soon, the small cleared area outside the warehouse was packed and vehicles were being stacked up the small roadway. I related my story several times more to detectives and the coroner, and after a couple of hours I had obviously become more an object tripped over than useful, so I found the Lafourche Parish Sheriff and asked if I could go. Then I asked for a ride.

He looked me over one last time, told me to remain available and then instructed a pair of his deputies to take me back to Vacherie and check out the house. Since Mr. Stempler's place was in a whole new parish, while en route they radioed for the Sheriff of St. James to meet us there.

Half an hour later, we rolled into the drive at Vacherie to find four St. James Parish cruisers already there. One of the deputies was hovering over my 'Vette with a flashlight and peering through the windows and several more were scattered on the front porch. They watched us pull up. I was let out of the back and introduced to the new Sheriff. I showed my identification and credentials and related the redacted story one more time. The new Sheriff told me that a local named Samantha something managed the property while the owner was absent and that she had been called and was presently headed out from New Orleans. The St. James Sheriff then said it appeared as if the kids had been preparing to clear out when Tony's men had shown up. He walked me inside the house and indeed there was an assemblage of packed duffles downstairs, on the floor just inside the door. I looked them over. Three duffles.

By that time I had told everything I had intended to tell a dozen times over. The rest the various authorities would have to ferret out in their investigations, and knowing cops like I do, they may suspect I had held some things back, but I was sure they'd cut me some slack given the circumstances no matter what they suspected. It had been a long day and I still had a drive to make and a wife to apologize to, so, again I asked if I could go, and again I was asked to remain available in the coming days. I agreed. There was no need to play the ex-cop brotherhood card at that point, they'd have my full package by morning, if they didn't already.

I stepped back outside, paused a moment, then crossed the veranda, descended the three stairs, walked along the cobbled path and finally made my way down the drive to where I had left my car. I removed my keys from my jacket pocket as I approached. I knew by morning the news of the demise of Vincent Monreale would have swept the state. My name would leak out and our phones at home and the office would begin ringing off the hook. I also knew that in two homes up north, two families would get news about two kids who tonight had paid the ultimate price for simply being in the wrong place at the wrong time, and they'd rightfully blame the man who hadn't been fast enough to save them. As the adrenaline slowly burned off, the weight in my heart quickly grew.

There would be much sorting through to be done by many people over the next days and weeks. I'd play whatever required role as it came, help where I could. I always did. I opened the driver's door and took one last look toward the old plantation house. Years ago it had been in disrepair by the assault of time and the elements and had been brought back to life with time and some TLC. The walls around my emotions had likewise been breached by an assault and lay in a shambles and needed some rebuilding. I slid into the leather seat and promised myself next time I'd be more careful. I smirked at the thought. Yeah, right.

My phone lay on the passenger seat, dead as a doornail. Every time I had borrowed a cell over the last hours, I had been unable to get through to Sandy at any of our numbers. I hoped she was in bed sleeping, over being angry at my careless remark which really hadn't been directed at her anyway. I picked up my phone, turned it around in my hand to inspect it and then noticed that there was a slight gap between the casing and the battery. I squeezed the phone together and it powered on. Geeze. I shook my head and turned the ignition, then placed the phone into my breast jacket pocket and closed the car door. I put the Corvette into first and turned around on the drive.

After a few moments of registering with my cellular carrier's towers, the phone vibrated and beeped in my pocket. I removed it and flipped it open as I reached the gap in the hedgerow. There were eleven voicemails. When I checked the missed call log, all eleven calls had come from the cell phone of our downstairs tenant, Nell. I checked the time on the dash and it was just after one in the morning. Looking at the phone's display, I saw the last missed call had come in about fifteen minutes earlier.

Rather than going through eleven voicemails, I simply called Nell back, expecting to hear there was some problem at the office building. As the call connected, I hoped it wasn't a water leak or something else which would keep me up the rest of the night. The last thing I expected was what I heard in the next moments of conversation as I drove east on the Great River Road.

"Jesus, William," Nell said in hushed anxiety when she answered. "Where have you been?"

"My phone was broken, Nell, but it turned out to be the battery had just come loose," I said. "What's up?"

"It's Sandy," she said. "Oh, William, where are you?"

As Nell related what she had discovered when she had returned on an errand to her store around eight that evening, I accelerated. By the time I was on I-10, I was pushing the 'Vette for everything it had.

Travis phoned from the jet. The Senator listened to the man's report on the last day's activity in and around New Orleans. When Travis concluded his narrative, The Senator asked questions.

The father's eyes never left his son who sat across the desk. The younger man was fully relaxed, his legs crossed, hands clasped loosely in his lap. He continue to wear the same self-satisfied expression he had when he had come home the day before. The pair had come to The Senator's Russell Building office across from the Capitol following their dinner to await the call from Travis when The Senator had been informed the jet was in the air. He didn't want to wait to get home to McClean to hear what the men had dug up in Louisiana.

Dace returned The Senator's stare with continued defiance, but as the son suspected the father was indeed receiving confirmation, the expression morphed to include a new affect, something even more disturbing. The Senator's stomach roiled, the events threatening to ruin a very good dinner by what he saw as his son's total lack of concern about the possible ramifications which could come should a connection to the now-confirmed girl be made to Dace. The only consolation came from the fact that Dace had said the girl was dead, bouncing along the bottom of the Mississippi. Perhaps the river would simply swallow the sin and there would be nothing more of it.

At that moment, The Senator had no idea what else had transpired in Louisiana that night, and wouldn't for at least several more hours. Rudy also didn't tell his boss that the P.I.'s wife had been left by them unconscious and bleeding at the foot of the stairs to their office when they had departed. They'd have that conversation later, Travis had decided, when they talked money.

When Travis disconnected, he joined Rudy in a toast of Dom Pérignon. They had the ultimate Washington power chit in their pocket, and they intended to play it for all it was worth.

I exited the interstate at Causeway Boulevard in Metairie, headed south, then took a left on Jefferson Highway the remaining ten blocks to the modern brick and glass buildings of the Ochsner Medical Center campus. I located a spot in the drive to park the car and ran inside the main building near a sign with an arrow pointing toward 'Admissions'.

Ironically, Ochsner was the closest hospital to where Ashley had been found two mornings ago, and would have been where the two brothers probably would have taken the girl had she not insisted on being taken home. As I ran into the near vacant lobby in the wee hours of that Friday morning, I was there to locate my wife, who had been found nearly six hours earlier at the bottom of our stairs.

The security guard at the security desk took note of me, and I nodded in his direction and slowed to a brisk walk across the lobby. The pair of women at the information desk watched me approach and were amazingly perky and welcoming at that ungodly hour. After checking her computer and confirming my relationship, the one on the right told me Sandy Langdon could be found in a room on the fifth floor. She pointed toward the bank of elevators and directed me to check in with the floor nurse before I went to the room.

I rode the polished aluminum box to the fifth floor, then, as I had been instructed, followed at a jog the blue line on the tile floor to the nurse's station. On a bench across the hall from the brightly lit workspace, I found Nell sitting and reading a well-worn, two-year-old People magazine proclaiming on its cover that Denzel Washington was the sexiest man alive. I approached and she looked up at me, her eyes showing the concern of a friend. While I'm much harder to get to know, Sandy warms to everyone and everyone to her and the women had become fast friends ever since Nell had come in asking about leasing our first floor shortly after we bought the building. Nell was good people.

She stood up to hug me. It was then that I noticed dried blood smeared near the hem of her skirt. She saw the direction of my eyes and sat down again in an attempt to hide the mark, but I had already seen it. My heart pounded harder. Nell had told me on the phone the bare facts: that she had found Sandy, unconscious at the base of the stairs and that she had called an ambulance and was now at Ochsner. Apart from that, she had provided few details, and because she wasn't a blood relative the hospital wouldn't give her much of anything in the line of updates on Sandy's condition. All she knew medically, was that my wife had been treated in Emergency, admitted, and sent to the fifth floor.

I looked around the area, saw nobody at the nurse's station, then patted Nell's shoulder and left her sitting on the bench while I set off down yet another hallway in search of Sandy's room. I found the number on a wall plaque, pushed open the door and when I first saw my wife, my pounding heart nearly ripped itself from my chest. Sandy was in the room alone, lying in the bed, her head and part of the left side of her face bandaged in white gauze tinged along the edge with Betadine. She was covered with a light blanket up to her breasts, her arms on top. Her eyes were closed. An IV bottle providing a steady drip was connected to her left hand, her right upper arm had a blood pressure cuff which at that moment inflated, then released, updating the numbers on the monitor above her bed. Her BP was 118 / 77, heart rate 62.

There were four electrical leads which protruded from the neckline of a white-with-blue-dots hospital gown and connected to the same monitor. Her heartbeat tracing appeared normal, at least to my layman's eyes. As I moved closer, I spotted another set of leads which ran from under her bandaged head to a second monitor. Six rows of squiggly green lines worked their way endlessly across the screen. They were labeled from top to bottom as: D, T, A, B, G and M. It was obviously an electroencephalogram, but I had no understanding of what I was seeing, or why, although I thought all six lines showing motion was a good thing.

I reached down and took Sandy's right hand. It was cool and dry. I bent over and kissed her bandaged head gently and spoke to her. She made no reaction; not even the little green lines changed their rhythm. The door opened quietly behind me and a nurse of generous proportions sporting squeaky white shoes entered the room. She crossed to Sandy's bedside, checked the monitors and IV drip, then asked if I was 'the husband'. I nodded, my mind swirling a million questions. Before she said anything further, I watched as the woman lowered the blanket and sheet and changed a dressing over Sandy's private area. She obviously could see the confusion in my eyes and began a recitation of the standard professional monologue as she went about her other duties of checking, poking, and prodding my wife. Each profession has their own version of those monologues, the bullet points of emotionless reporting, often done in shorthand to colleagues but with a bit more explanation provided for the civilians.

"The patient arrived via ambulance at approximately eight-thirty this past evening. Initial reports from the scene were of a female in her mid to late thirties attended by a friend who found her at the foot of a flight of stairs amongst broken glass from a doorway above. The patient, identified by the friend as Sandy Langdon, exhibited stable vital signs on scene along with visible head trauma, minor cuts, contusions and abrasions to the back and lower extremities, some containing fragments of glass and wood splinters, and was experiencing a sustained LOC - loss of consciousness - event with an inability to be roused, and light vaginal bleeding. Evidence of additional, recent head trauma was discovered during initial examination by EMTs." She took a breath and eyed 'the husband'. "Did your wife suffer additional trauma recently, Mr. Langdon?"

Her look was wary, gauging, and skirting accusatory. I didn't like her assumption, but hadn't I made the same one with Cindy hours before?

"Um, yes, about ten days ago on South Padre Island in Texas," I said. "We got caught out in a storm and a stack of pilings shifted on the beach. I tossed her out of the way and she bumped her head on a rock in the sand. I took a hit as well on the pier." I raised my hairline to reveal my stitches. "Sandy was knocked out for several minutes then as well, but treated and released and was given a clean bill by the doctors." I squeezed my wife's hand but she didn't squeeze back.

Nurse squeaky shoes nodded, then continued.

"Mrs. Langdon was admitted through the ER and triage was completed there before sending her to radiology for a head CT. No intracranial bleed was detected at that point, however, the EEG monitor was ordered due to the continued LOC and potential for subarachnoid hemorrhage, especially given the suspected, recent head trauma. Her vaginal bleeding was considered light, and initially thought to be the result of menses, however, the blood work and a palpation exam revealed that Mrs. Langdon was indeed pregnant and since she was not exhibiting any indications of internal organ damage, the treating physician postponed any type of radiologic torso scan until more could be determined in the coming hours as to the health and viability of the fetus. Dr. Santhosh will be in to see her in the morning. Any questions?"

I had plenty, but even in my emotionally challenging state, I was able to comprehend most of the cold, hard, medical facts. As a lifelong Catholic, the word 'fetus' struck me as harsh, but I supposed it was medically appropriate; remaining emotionally disconnected, I suspected, was as necessary for health care workers as it was for cops, and P.Is. To me, the 'fetus' was my unborn son or daughter, and I was gravely concerned for both he or she and Sandy.

Squeaky shoes told me there was nothing I could do for now other than be there for my wife and assured me that Sandy was at one of the best hospitals in Louisiana. I was't certain that comparative made me feel better, although I knew everything possible was being done for her. Her head lacerations had been stitched and would not affect her 'external appearance', I was told, the other cuts had been superficial and were cleaned and dressed in the E.R. Those were the preliminary issues, she said, and the real concerns circled around her continued loss of consciousness and the health of the fetus. I asked her if we could refer to it as the baby when discussing it in the presence of my wife and her face softened and she nodded.

The nurse couldn't answer what had happened to Sandy to cause the fall, or obviously speak to anything else which had occurred before medical help had arrived. For that, I'd need to ask my wife when she awoke, and speak with Nell, since we had no security monitoring of the premises. I know not having security cameras seems odd for a private detective agency, but it was an oversight, and one I intended to remedy at the first opportunity. The nurse said I could stay in the room, and the recliner in the corner was pointed out for me. She retrieved a blanket and pillow from a nearby closet, then asked if I had any other questions. I shook my head and she told me to come out to the nurse's station if anything came to mind.

After that, she gave a final glance to the monitors, told me again not to worry and that Sandy would be just fine, then left the room, her squeaky shoes trailing off into the night as the door slowly closed behind her. I sat in the chair with the folded blanket on my lap and felt as if my world was crumbling from under my feet. I wanted to yell, to hit a wall. This may be the strangest life I've ever known to again steal a quote from

Jim Morrison, and I'm okay with that, but the events of the last few days were coming close to smothering my soul and I'm definitely not okay with that.

A few minutes later, I remembered poor Nell out on that bench for hours with no news and walked out to find her. A different nurse was seated at the desk tapping the keys of a computer terminal, and I heard squeaky shoes moving down another hallway. When I asked about Nell, the desk nurse said she had gone down the cafeteria for some coffee and something to eat. I glanced at the clock on the wall beyond the desk. The black hands were approaching three in the morning. I wanted to stay with Sandy, but I also felt guilty about Nell sticking it out there with nothing to do but feel like a third wheel on a bicycle, so I asked the nurse to have someone come get me should anything change with Sandy saying I'd be in the cafeteria trying to find out more details from our tenant and friend about what may have happened to my wife. She smiled and nodded, then started tapping the keys again.

Following the signage to the cafeteria, I walked in to find the place remarkably active for that time of morning. I spotted Nell's back across the room, then remembered I hadn't eaten since breakfast nearly twenty hours ago and thought how Sandy would admonish me for not taking care of myself, so I grabbed a banana off the line and a bottle of orange juice from the cooler. I payed the cashier then walked over to join Nell who had the remains of a croissant, a couple of open strawberry jam packets and cup of coffee in front of her.

"You want a refill, Nell?" I asked before sliding out an orange, formed, plastic chair on chromed legs to sit down.

She thanked me but declined.

"Do you want something else to eat?"

"No, William," she said. "I'm fine."

She folded a napkin around the crumbs and remaining end of the croissant.

"Did you speak to the nurse?" she asked.

I nodded. Then a thought struck me. Had Nell not come back to the store this evening, nobody would have found Sandy until I got back to town. The idea that my wife could have died there at the base of those stairs tonight was an emotional wave which nearly overwhelmed me. Our snippy misunderstanding could have been the last words we ever spoke to one another. I shuddered, then willed to shake off the thought. It was just one thing too much at the moment.

I related the broad outline of the nurse's report. Nell listened and nodded. She then told me more details of finding Sandy. She had closed the store at four p.m., two hours earlier than normal because one of her kids had a dance recital at five. I recalled seeing the store dark when Sandy and I had returned from the country. After the recital, she and the kids had gone out for dinner, then she had dropped them at home and returned to the store because she remembered that she had forgotten to take a package to FedEx, an errand she had promised an out-of-state customer she'd do. When she arrived, Nell found the front doors unlocked, all the lights off, and Sandy lying at the base of the stairs. The glass in the door to our upstairs office had been broken outward and it appeared to Nell as if Sandy had somehow fallen through the glass and then down the stairs.

It occurred to me that there was a considerable landing outside of that door on the second floor and for Sandy to have continued through the glass and down the stairs would have meant she had some healthy momentum remaining after breaking through the glass. Nell said she had checked the office before following the ambulance to the hospital. A planter with a fake tree had been toppled just inside the door, the office door was unlocked just like the downstairs door had been and all the lights were off. She did a quick survey of the rest of the upstairs and found nothing further disturbed. Sandy's cell phone was on her desk blotter and Nell pulled it from her purse and handed it across the table. I rotated it in my hand and looked at all the missed calls from me from a host of different numbers. Sandy had made no outgoing calls after she had left the car before I headed back to Vacherie. Nell concluded by saying she had locked the street side doors before leaving the building to follow the ambulance.

I wondered if the earlier head trauma could have caused another blacking out event, but Sandy had been just fine after the South Padre Island incident. She had traveled to her parents without issue, displayed no distress during our day together when we went out to the country. I'd have to ask the doctors in the morning about it, but since they already did another head CT and just had her monitored for now, I doubted they noticed anything abnormal going on in there.

Nell yawned and I told her she should get home to her kids. I thanked her for everything and for being a good friend to Sandy and myself. She said she'd be praying for Sandy and would be in the store later if I needed to speak to her. I told her I'd keep her up-to-date with any news and we walked out of the cafeteria together. She hugged me again and I watched her walk across the lobby toward the doors.

A thought came to me and I called her name and jogged to catch her.

"Did you touch anything at the office, or clean anything up?" I asked.

She shook her head, said she would sweep up the glass and clean up the blood when she went in to open the store. I asked if she'd leave it alone and told her I wanted to see it before it was more disturbed. Something just wasn't adding up in my head. She agreed and I watched her begin to walk across the lobby as I considered walking her to her car. She paused at the door, then turned and looked at me.

"Shoes," she said. "Sandy wasn't wearing shoes."

I closed the distance between us as the security guard watched.

"What did you say, Nell?"

She looked at me with confusion on her face.

"There were no shoes anywhere," she said. "Not on the stairs, not in the office. I just thought about it now."

"Sandy was wearing a pair of gray pumps which matched her business suit," I said.

"I don't know, William," Nell said while shaking her head. "There were no shoes."

She shrugged her shoulders and again offered a good-night, saying she'd look around again when she went in later in the day. I watched her go out into the night.

"Where was she going without shoes?" I asked rhetorically as I walked back across the lobby toward the bank of elevators.

Upstairs again in the room, I settled into the recliner after checking on Sandy and finding nothing had changed. I watched her breathe, tracked the little electronic lines as they jiggled across the screen, listened to the automatic blood pressure cuff inflate and register every fifteen minutes, observed the nurses comings and goings as they repeatedly checked the state of Sandy's bleeding under the sheet, and waited anxiously for the morning when the doctors would come in.

They arrived in force around seven o'clock. Ochsner was a teaching hospital, and Sandy was obviously one of the cases of interest that morning. I shook hands with Dr. Santhosh - good solid shake. An intern recited the facts of the case to the group while Dr. Santhosh reviewed the overnight chart entries then pried open Sandy's eyelids and flashed a light several times across her baby blues. When the crowd adjourned, Dr. Santhosh remained a few minutes and told me that neurologically my wife seemed fine, but he was bringing in a specialist later that morning after rounds for consult. I told him the story of the earlier head trauma Sandy had suffered and all he said was 'mm-hmm'. I asked him about the baby and he said that for now things were indeterminate, yet stable, but they'd also be addressing that later in the morning when Dr. Simmons, Sandy's gynecologist, came through. Before he left, he told me not to worry, that Sandy would be just fine.

Everything took a back seat to Sandy and the baby. I gave not one more thought to Dave Saunders or Cindy Spagliano, the mystery person, Ashley Monreale, Tony Gators, or Tracey Walker. My laser-like focus was my wife and unborn child. The shift of nurses changed, and a young, black R.N. stopped in around eight to check Sandy and asked me if she could have a breakfast tray sent up for me. I told her I wasn't hungry, that I'd had a banana around three. She took a 'don't give me that' pose and reminded me that I needed to keep up my strength and that Sandy would want me to eat. You women sure know how to guilt a husband. I smiled and shook my head. 'I'll eat when Sandy eats,' I told her before she left the room.

Around nine Dr. Simmons arrived. She introduced herself to me since we hadn't before met, expressed her condolences for the accident, told me not to worry, that Sandy would be just fine. A minute later, the nurse rolled in a small machine with a screen, told me it was an ultrasound. They were going to be checking the fetus, she said. Apparently, my little agreement with the night staff hadn't continued on the day shift. I observed from standing in the corner as Dr. Simmons uncovered Sandy to the knees, examined under a dressing applied to my wife's private area, then removed a small wand from the cart. The nurse informed me it was called a Doppler instrument used to listen for fetal heartbeat and she applied some gel to Sandy's barely protruding stomach and moved it about. I remember seeing them use the same device in the hospital in Texas, and how I had felt the first time I heard my unborn child's heartbeat. Dr. Simmons' eyes touched the nurse's, but not mine. Next, they powered up the ultrasound and after more gel, slid the transceiver over the same areas. Again, her eyes exchanged something with the nurse, but that time, they also touched mine and my aching heart shattered.

The procedure was known clinically as a D&C - dilation and curettage. It meant the worst. They took Sandy around noon after Dr. Simmons had her conclusions confirmed by another on-staff OB/GYN and after she had spoken to me in the hallway. Sandy had been in her early second trimester, Dr. Simmons said, which was a much more vulnerable time for the baby because the position of the uterus changes and enlarges as the baby grows. In the first trimester, she said, a fall like what Sandy had experienced would be very unlikely to harm the more protected baby, but her accident had caused a partial umbilical abruption, a simple disconnection of the child's lifeline from the uterine wall, and there was no way to repair that. Our baby had most likely passed shortly after the fall due to lack of oxygen supply. The abruption was why Sandy had been bleeding and they had to act to stop that.

They brought my wife back alone about an hour later.

The hospital chaplain, a very genteel gentleman of Baptist persuasion stopped by in the early afternoon. He spoke to me about how the Hand of God was protecting Sandy and told me the accident and death of our baby was God's Will and we must accept it. I heard little of it, but thanked him for coming by. He suggested I pray, and told me that Sandy would be just fine.

There were few times in this man's life when I felt more alone. I sat, stood, paced, asked questions of the doctors and nurses who came and went. I didn't know whom to call, or what I'd say to them when I did. Sandy's parents deserved to know what had happened to their daughter, but I wasn't yet ready to have that conversation. I called my mother. I gave her the news and she cried. I cried. My heart remained shattered in a billion little pieces and I couldn't even imagine having to break the news to Sandy when she awoke. If she awoke. Mom agreed to call Sandy's parents, my girls, and my brother and sister. It's what mom's do. Before she hung up, she told me not to worry, and that Sandy would be just fine.

Nell dropped by with flowers near sundown when visiting hours began. She had been into the offices again and found Sandy's shoes underneath her desk. It made no sense to me. Nothing made any sense to me anymore. I didn't care. Nothing mattered.

Nell held Sandy's hand and I could tell she was praying. I lowered my head and closed my eyes, adding a few words to the Big Guy of my own, not that He hadn't been hearing from me quite a bit over the last couple of days.

Before she left, I asked Nell to please clean up the mess at the office. I didn't need to see it anymore. It didn't matter. The only thing that mattered was that Sandy woke up.

At midnight, as I stood watching out the window at an approaching line of thunderstorms on the western horizon, she did.

# PART II

October 31, 2008 -
November 4, 2008

# Chapter Thirty-one

Sandy and I had been going through a tough year. Hell, we'd been having a roller coaster decade, if truth be told. It seemed I didn't know all the right things to say anymore, and Sandy had begun refusing to hear the things I did manage. It was probably working the same way in reverse, too. When someone you love stops listening to you, eventually, you stop trying. And then pride steps in, and as my mother is fond of saying: 'Pride goeth before the fall'. Somewhere along the way, we'd lost our compass, but still had enough between us to cling to true north in our hearts while we weathered the low points and waited for the next rise. It's hard to talk about our relationship problems to outsiders, so please just accept it as fact that each of us can be prideful and stubborn; and each of us loves the other dearly.

Our issues began developing shortly after Sandy awoke in the hospital after falling down the stairs at our office and losing our baby as a result in February 1998. Though Sandy turned out to be *just fine*, as everyone seemed eager to tell me at the time she would be, afterward she sank into a major depression; and I waded into a bottle of Jim Beam. Each of us nearly drowned before we dragged the other up for air on New Year's Eve going into the new millennium when we called a truce and recommitted ourselves to one another. Then the Vanessa Lafontaine situation occurred. It was a one time indiscretion with a client which I confessed immediately after. Don't ask my why I did it. I just did. That was in mid-2001 and, no matter what I did, resulted in Sandy divorcing me in early 2002, which was also when she started referring to me as 'Otto'. People still ask why she chose that particular epithet for me during that time, and though I've asked, she's refused to tell anyone.

Even though we hurt one another in those years, we never fell out of love, which is a paradox that many of you may not fully believe. Just as I asked you to just accept as fact my wife and I can be prideful and stubborn, I'm asking you take it on faith that we both know deep in our hearts we were made for each other. We also remained business partners through it all, which I think was our device to stay close to one another until one or both of us came to our senses. Through it all, I'd still tell her I loved her when she couldn't hear me. I think she did the same thing a time or two, but she's never admitted it.

Then, in 2003, Cassie Yeats, my first puppy love, sauntered back into my life decades after she had sauntered out of it one cold October morning nearly thirty years earlier, leaving me standing alone, hurt, and confused on the steps of our high school. She had gone on to marry Gregory Thomason, one of the country's richest men, and after a twenty-plus year marriage had looked me up to enlist my assistance in getting out. She beguiled me into coming to Maui, ostensibly to search for information she could use against her husband. For that, and my own reasons, which Sandy claimed to understand at the time, I went. During a week or so on the island, I unearthed the dark secrets which lurked within Cassie's marriage, some of which she had wanted me to find, and others I am certain she had hoped I would miss. In the end, let's just say the breakup really didn't work out well for either Cassandra or Gregory.

While I was on Maui, Sandy worked the mainland trails which had developed, and that eventually led her to Maui, too. What happened in the aftermath, you can choose to credit to the warm, tropical breezes, sunsets, swaying palm trees, or Mai Tai cocktails, but whatever it was, we were finally able to override our pride and overcome our mutual stubbornness as the case wrapped up.

Through the years, Sandy has referred to me as her own, personal bad penny - or lucky penny, depending on where we were on the roller coaster at the time - which I guess was okay by me, so long as I kept turning up in her life. For me, Sandy is my life. It was what made this all so hard.

Whatever it was with Maui, it worked. We rediscovered our passion and were able to express our love for one another *to* each other. Finally, we found we could say to each other the things we'd been reserving for mumbles out of earshot because neither of us wanted to risk showing our own vulnerability first. Stupid, huh? I don't know who braved the first step there on that rock in the middle of the Pacific, but does it really matter? We remarried shortly after on the same beach on Snipe Point out front of our house on Little Cayman where we had originally tied the knot back in 1996. Teddy and Valeria came down, along with other friends and family who had missed the first one. There was also a new pair of friends who flew from one island to another just to help us celebrate.

I had met a couple who lived in the condo upstairs from the one I rented on Maui; friendly folks from Wisconsin, like Sandy and me. Shelly was cute, generous, and pleasant; Steve was a decent sort once I got to know him a bit, although he wore the ugliest pair of shoes I've ever seen in my life and just didn't seem to care about how bad they looked. He called them his Bullwinkle shoes, and said they were comfortable so he wore them. I learned something from that expressed attitude. Sandy took a liking to Shelly and Steve as well when she arrived. They're about our age, Packer fans, even though Shelly proclaims a loyalty to the Minnesota Vikings, and seem to share a relationship which is familiar to us. Comfortable. Loving. Eager. Fun.

Later, Steve wrote a book around the stories I told him about the Cassandra Yeats-Thomason case over beers and some pizza one night. He titled the book *Cassandra's Crossing*, and used my name in the subtitle. He sent me an autographed copy. It was a good read, and even though it was claimed to be fiction, I was surprised how he got most of it right.

Fast forward to 2008. Sandy and I turned fifty earlier in the year. Whether it was age or hormones or the fact she had finally accepted what the doctors have been telling her for the past ten years about the inadvisability of her becoming pregnant again, lately Sandy had begun lobbying me to adopt a baby. That hasn't been good timing for me for many reasons, not the least of which was I had been thinking about my own mortality of late. My father drank and smoked himself to death when he was only three years older than I was then, and so had his father, only granddad had made it to fifty-six before a relatively sedentary lifestyle as an over-the-road trucker and a beer gut triggered the major heart attack which took the big bull down one night.

It's not that I was drinking that much anymore, have never smoked, and wasn't *that* out of shape, but I did share the Langdon genetics. Let's just say, by the time my birthday rolled around the past August, I had already convinced myself that longevity wasn't on my side and on top of everything else, I had begun wondering in those dark corners of the night whom Sandy may find to spend the rest of her life with after I was gone.

My girls were grown up and established in their lives and careers. All three had married good guys. My youngest was a newlywed and a doctor of physical therapy, the middle one an ICU nurse, and I'd even become a grandfather a year earlier by my oldest, who, along with her husband, worked at LSU just up the road in Baton Rouge. That part of my life as daddy having run, I felt I wasn't much use to anyone anymore. I was redundant equipment, they had their mother to take them the rest of the way. Outside of business, the only phone calls I received were from telemarketers hawking life insurance and Viagra, and with the ease of email and communication through MySpace, my girls had stopped calling except on special days when protocols dictated one reach out and touch someone. You can call it a pity party and have all those tiny violins playing for me, but that's what I thought, and it was how I felt.

Now Sandy wanted me to adopt a baby? Me? A petulant teenager in the body of a nearly dead old man whose life, in the final analysis, had amounted to relatively little in the world, and yet who had far too many chains locked to his soul to look forward to his coming great reward? By the day it all started again, I was too tired and angry and fed up to keep walking, and too frightened to lay down. In the final analysis, I wasn't certain I wanted to become responsible for another human being who wouldn't be graduating from college until I was in my early seventies. The ten years had passed and I had caught up to where Teddy had been when Sandy and I had been expecting and Valeria had beat the drum of her biological clock. I knew how Teddy felt; and being the butt of those jokes about my adopted son or daughter bringing great-granddad to the commencement ceremonies wasn't high on my bucket list.

Okay, so enough history and histrionics. We'll get on with it.

It was shortly after lunch on Friday, October 31, 2008, and I was in my office. Sandy had me going over some expense reports for some invoicing she wanted to get processed for the end of the month. I was doing that, sort of, and waiting for my lone afternoon appointment to arrive. I was pouting, and also licking the emotional wounds inflicted by some very stinging words spoken by my wife over lunch. Sandy was out front, probably doing the same over my stinging words spoken back to her.

I think we both realized we had arrived at the point where something had to change in our lives or we weren't going to survive as a married couple, or even as individuals, no matter how much love and synergism we shared. That much had become very clear to me; and I was very frightened at the prospect. I thought - and hoped - she felt the same way, but we'd stopped talking about those things in that particular valley, like I said. Before she dropped the file of expenses onto my desk and stormed out of my office a half hour earlier, Sandy had accused me of being a selfish child trapped in a man's body. I had stuck my tongue out at her. She used to find that cute and adorable; even when she was angry with me, it used to make her smile. That day, it hadn't.

I was in a sour mood, and something told me it wasn't going to get any better anytime soon.

My desk phone buzzed.

"Your appointment is here," Sandy said curtly over the intercom.

"Send her in," I said just as curtly and clicked off without even a 'thank you'. I dropped my feet off my desk and slid my MacBook Pro onto the blotter. I closed the computer, putting it to sleep and hiding my Solitaire game which had been running above my expense spreadsheets, pushed it off to the side, leaned forward, elbows on my desk, hands clasped on the blotter, and awaited the entry of my day's only appointment: Ms. Carol Huntley of Santa Barbara, California.

The door opened several moments later and the woman strode into my office dressed in a canary-yellow, obviously off-the-rack business suit with skirt and matching low-heeled shoes. She closed the door behind herself and boldly approached my desk, her eyes never leaving mine. The only jewelry she wore was a small silver crucifix on a simple silver chain around her neck and a thin silver band on the ring finger of her left hand. Her ears were bare. In her right hand, she held a medium-sized, yellow, leather clutch which roughly matched her suit and shoes. She wore no perfume, or at least none which preceded her. When she reached the other side of my desk, she stood there and waited. Neither she nor I extended a hand.

I stood.

"Ms. Huntley?" I asked.

Her eyes didn't waver. She said nothing.

"Frankly, I was expecting someone a bit older," I said. "Late fifties or so?"

"My aunt," she said, and then sat in one of the guest chairs in front of my desk, uninvited. "Carol Huntley."

"That's *who* I was expecting," I said, retaking my seat. "The *why* I was hoping she'd share when she arrived. According to Sandy, the caller had been a bit vague when making the appointment."

"My aunt passed away two and a half years ago, Mr. Langdon. Ovarian cancer. By the time the doctors discovered it, the disease had metastasized to her liver and brain. Stage four. No viable options for treatment. She was gone six weeks after the diagnosis."

"I'm sorry," I said. It's what one says out of reflex to be civilized, but in this case I meant it, even though I had never met Carol Huntley face-to-face.

"No need," she said, waving her hand. "You didn't know her, but thank you."

I studied my guest for a long moment. She allowed it, waited for me to speak when I was ready. Her hair was shorter, and perhaps a bit lighter than the last time I had seen her. She was older, and had clearly acquired the grace and elegance as an adult she had reputedly craved and merely affected as a teenager. The visible scars I had expected were not there, or perhaps they had been expertly treated by the abundance of plastic surgeons I've heard they had out there in Disneyland. Her eyes hadn't changed; they still held the same fire and strength I had spotted behind battered lids, and deeper, contained the same vulnerability.

"What can I do for you, Ashley?" I said.

"So you do remember, Mr. Langdon," she said. "I thought I may have slipped from your memory over the last ten years. After all, you only saw me briefly on two occasions from what I've been told, and I was frightfully messed up." Her head cocked as she studied me. "You knew me only through photographs and the words of others; and, frankly, I don't remember meeting you at all."

"There's not a chance in he...I mean, I could never forget you, Ashley," I said. "The memories of that time are far too numerous and deep within me to ever purge them from my soul. Believe me, I've tried. I can displace the worst of them for a time, but they always come back, mostly at night." I looked beyond her, toward the wall between Sandy and myself. "Some of them which I nurture keep me afloat these days, while others lurk in the shadows and threaten to drag me under." I took a deep breath, realizing in hearing my selfish, little rant that my pain was nothing compared to what the girl on the other side of my desk had suffered and the demons she must still face every day of her life. I was embarrassed, but unable to speak an apology. "I'm certain *my* life is not why you're here today."

She followed my gaze, then recaptured my eyes with hers. I thought I perceived a soft smile touch her lips, then quickly disappear.

"Your wife looks as good as I was told she did," Ashley said, sliding back in the chair and demurely crossing her ankles. Even seated, I noticed her skirt covered her knees. "She is a beautiful woman. At least I assume that woman out front is the Sandy to whom you were married back then." She paused and her eyes dropped to her lap for a moment. "I was genuinely sorry to hear of her accident and your own loss after I had recovered and the stories were told to me."

I saw she meant the words, but also detected a hint of shame in the admission.

"Thank you, Ashley," I said. "It's been a long time."

"But still the pain persists, doesn't it, Mr. Langdon?"

I nodded, even though I wasn't certain which particular pain to which she was referring. There was more than enough pain involved with so many aspects of the Ashley Monreale case to go around. I decided not to go down that road and rather returned to her earlier question.

"She's the one," I said with more than a hint of impatience in my tone. "What do you want, Ashley?"

"We'll get to that, Mr. Langdon," she said. "I've got some things to say, first. To clear the air, so to speak."

I smirked and sat back in my chair. Nothing is ever easy, is it?

In the aftermath of the events which had transpired when Fate entwined our lives a decade ago, I had lost track of Ashley after her aunt had come to take her back to Santa Barbara to live and recover. I had more than enough on my plate at the time, yet I had peeked in on the girl's life about five years ago. She was graduating from UCLA. It was during a high point in my life, when I felt strong enough to dredge up a bit of the past, shortly after Sandy and I had returned from our second honeymoon. It was the one time I had spoken to Carol Huntley. It has been a short conversation.

Ashley being here now was churning up way too much silt from the floor of my soul at a very bad time in my life. I wasn't happy about it. Besides, I was much too old to be playing coy little games with a twenty-seven year old woman. I was short-fused and irritable. I get that way sometimes.

"Look, Ashley," I said, "I really wasn't doing much this afternoon, so I agreed to see you, I mean your aunt, however, if it's games you're looking to play, I'd just as soon go back to Solitaire on my computer. At least I have a chance at winning that one."

"I thought I'd at least warrant a few minutes from the man who murdered my father," she said with a steady stare, but no more emotion than if she were announcing the time of day.

I found the content of her statement discordant with her tone, but gave little thought of it beyond that observation. I was far too steeped in my own mire to open that particular channel. Besides, if the girl was there to test my patience, she had chosen the wrong day.

"Murder is a harsh characterization for what I did to your father," I said, my annoyance barely restrained. "However, that's not a crime with which he was unfamiliar. He murdered those two kids from Harvard, and only God knows how many others over the course of his unsavory life. His thug tried to murder me, but I was quicker than he was that night. So if we're tossing around the epithet of murderer, let's more rightly append it to your father's name and not mine." My stare became hard across the distance between us. "I killed your father, Ashley. Shot him right between the eyes as I recall." I realized the instant the words spilled from my mouth that I had gone too far. This girl had been a victim of a horrific crime against her body and soul and had nothing at all to do with what her father was, or did in misguided retribution. My tongue had grown acidic, and my verbal filter, marginal in the best of times, had become nonexistent. I felt ashamed. "I'm sorry, Ashley. That was uncalled for."

She nodded, then I watched her gaze drop to her lap where they found her clasped hands resting upon her yellow clutch. She sat like that for several long moments before she looked up at me again.

"I'm sorry, too, Mr. Langdon," she said, straightening her posture in the chair again. "You are right about my father, and I was wrong to challenge you for something which everyone who reviewed the facts surrounding that night concluded your innocence. At least as to the death of my father." She paused, as if she were closing a book and replacing it on the shelf. She took a breath before continuing. "Over the last decade, I have come to grips with who and what my father was. I attend Mass every day and pray for the salvation of his immortal soul; just as I had for the first several years after he died when I prayed for the damnation of yours and everyone's who was ever close to you."

"I deserved that, Ashley," I said, ashamed. "I was wrong."

"You are wrong about many things, Mr. Langdon. I'm certain of it."

I felt the jab. She was right, but that assessment could be hung around the neck of nearly everyone who drew breaths. Yet, there was something else in her words. Her heart held a secret, I could see it behind the mask she affected. Our little jousting was only a preliminary testing of the proverbial waters for what she had truly come to see me for, and curiosity overtaking impatience, I sat back in my chair and waited for the unmasking.

"I'm listening," I said. "Go ahead, enlighten me."

"My father was a powerful man who did evil things, Mr. Langdon," she said. "However, he was not an evil man. There is a difference."

Perhaps if she had seen the maniacal eyes of her father that night and the pleasure the man took in torturing and then killing those kids, she'd reconsider that conclusion, I thought. There was nothing but pure evil living in the man; of course, had someone done something like that to one of my daughters as was done to his, who knows to what ends I'd have gone to obtain justice. I shuddered at the thought of what sometimes separates us in this human mire.

"I think philosophers may call it a distinction without a difference," I said, refusing to acknowledge my last thought. "I don't see it."

"I am his daughter, and no child should view their parents as evil. It's hard on the soul."

I nodded slowly, although I had hardened conclusions regarding the perniciousness of my own father. There existed no distinction without difference in my memories of him.

"There are some who would disagree with that assessment, Ashley," I said.

"With which part?" she asked. "The divergent conclusions concerning my father's actions versus his true nature, or the observation of how children should consider their parents?"

"Both, I guess," I said after a moment's ponder, then wondering if she had come all this way to have a philosophical conversation on parenthood and threw my hands up. "Neither, maybe. Does it truly matter?"

"Really?" she said, her eyes studying me, then nodded. "I think it does matter."

"I was raised Catholic, Ashley, just as you were, and in my generation of the Catechism, we were taught of the existence of both Good and Evil in the universe. All people are capable of doing good or perpetrating evil, that's true, and while some actions people take may be classified by society or the Church as either, the actions don't necessarily define their souls which are said to be known only to God."  In my case, I hoped it was true.   "However, in my personal worldview, I absolutely believe people can be truly good or truly evil outside of their actions.  It's why we have Heaven for the saints, and it's also why we have Hell for the purely evil.  In my time, we also had Purgatory for the in-betweens, like me, but we lost that option after Vatican II."

She smiled.  It was the smile of the knowing, and it was patient.

"Some believe that, Mr. Langdon, but what the Second Vatican Council actually did was not abolish Purgatory, but rather opened for discussion the concept of Limbo, which as you know, is different and was where the souls of unbaptized infants were said to reside.  Limbo was a 13th century theoretical construct in response to the Faithfuls' concerns over the Church's rather harsh teachings which created a paradox between the belief in an all-loving God and Christ's teaching that baptism was necessary for salvation.  That creation, if you will, of Limbo from whole cloth gave the Church of the time a palatable option to Hell for the innocents.  Since no foundation for it appears in the Scriptures, the Holy Father removed Limbo from Church doctrine just last year, although, since no human can know the mind of God, believers are free to still accept the concept.  Purgatory still exists in the Church's teachings as the place for the souls of the in-betweens, as you put it, go for spiritual perfection before ultimately being reunited with God.  You can breathe easily, Mr. Langdon."

I cocked my head and stared across at her, studying this young woman.  I was confused, off balance, then concluded she must want me that way for some reason.  Why, I didn't know, but I decided to let her peel some line from the reel although I was ready to tighten the drag if she didn't get to the real purpose of her coming here soon.

She studied me back, probably thinking I could peel some line before she tightened the drag and set the hook.

"You still carry the scars of your childhood, I take it," she said. "From *your* father, I mean; or was it your mother?"

I slid my chair abruptly from my desk, stood to her wide-eyed surprise and walked to my bookcases and opened them to reveal my bar. I poured a splash of Jim Beam bourbon into a cut crystal tumbler.  I held it up, the aromatic, brown liquid nearly touching my lips and teasing my nose, then I set the glass onto the counter.  I returned and stood above her and pointed a finger down toward her face.

"Is that why you came all the way from California?  To analyze me?  To torment me?  To philosophize with me? Because whatever the reason, my demons are my own, Ashley, and believe me, they are vicious and you don't want any part of them."

She shot me a wary look, clearly frightened by the difference of our sizes and my aggressive, angry posture. I lowered my hand, then stepped backward. My emotions were raw and jumbled, mainly because of the current and ongoing issues between Sandy and myself, but also now due to this woman reentering my life for some, yet, unknown reason. No, those aren't the reasons I was on edge. I can't lie to you. Those were the excuses. The reason was because the man in the mirror every morning had begun to look back, and effectuate judgement on a life marginally lived. So many mistakes over one's life can craft an unwieldy burden. My shoulders collapsed slightly, and I returned behind my desk, dropped into my chair. I breathed slowly, a technique I had learned when going to the doctor when the first blood pressure check raised one of his eyebrows.

"Please tell me you are here for another purpose, Ashley," I said, tired from running and just wanting the freedom of the hook.

"I'll leave you to your own demons, Mr. Langdon, and no, I haven't come to analyze or torment you, or to discuss the philosophy of the Church or the trials and tribulations of parent/child relationships." She glanced over her shoulder at the bar and the tumbler. "I have no reason to antagonize you today or any day. I am truly sorry if I have. I will pray for you in your battle with the demons you carry. Given what I know of your life, I am certain they are indeed a powerful lot." She paused to allow the air to clear. "I am here today to ask you to help me. Again."

"You have a strange way of going about requesting a favor, Ashley," I said, relaxing a bit and sliding back in my chair while wondering how long it had been that someone had told me I'd be in their prayers. Aside from my mother, I couldn't immediately recall.

"Favor?" she asked, her eyebrows rising and her head shaking. "You misunderstand, Mr. Langdon. I want to hire you."

"Hire me?" I asked, sliding forward in my chair again. "I don't want your father's money, Ashley." I paused, drew a breath and my eyes searched my blotter for nothing in particular. "Frankly, I'd rather consider anything I may agree to do for you as a favor."

"Be it as you wish, Mr. Langdon, however, the money is mine," she said. "It has no connection to my father's wealth, which I placed into a charitable blind trust several years ago. My father's money, as you call it, whether it came from legal or illegal activities is finally doing some good for many, many people."

I shrugged, said nothing, slid back in my chair again. I crossed my legs, crossed my arms to work out some remaining anxiety, and hoped there was a point in our near future.

"Are you familiar with the news story of the man who will most likely be elected the new junior senator from the state of Connecticut in six days?" she asked.

"I'm not really the political type, Ashley," I said, now more confused than ever. "That's more my wife's thing. I worked under the entrenched corruption of the Daley regime in Chicago and I live in Louisiana now. I'm more of a realist and a pragmatist than an ideologue, a complain-no-matter-who-gets-elected type because they're all the same."

She smiled demurely. I did too, I think - but not demurely - at the change of subject.

"Well, I'm not particularly political, either," Ashley said. "The subject in school always bored me and, well, following current events these days is...disheartening, at the very least. However, one cannot truly disconnect oneself from the world and become an island unto themselves, can one?"

I nodded once. I know I smiled at that one; Ashley had never seen me drink, although I don't think she had that type of disconnecting from the world in mind when she said that. Many a time, I've proven if one were truly motivated, one could indeed disconnect from the world, at least for a while. The problem was, you always came back to the same place, and usually the world was in worse condition than when you had checked out.

"Have you ever heard of the Lamoureux family, Mr. Langdon?" she said, studying my reaction.

Of course I had heard of the Lamoureux family. It was a surname as familiar to most Americans as Kennedy or Rockefeller; or Trump in the current days of pop culture icons. The Lamoureux family was a longstanding political dynasty and economic powerhouse, which in comparison, relegated the aforementioned Kennedy or Rockefeller - or Trump - families to a status as the 'poor relation'. I told her so.

"Well, I must lead a cloistered life, because I truly just heard the name about a week ago in a passing news story about the son running to serve in the United States Senate with his father. According to the report I overheard, should the son win election in six days, it will mark the first time in history that a father and son will serve simultaneously in the Senate from the same state." She paused. "In case you're curious, I looked it up and one other father and son team served together during the mid-19th century, but from different states - your Wisconsin and Iowa. In my vocation, being politically active is down the priority list a bit, so I really didn't pay much attention beyond the trivia aspect of the story, and had even set aside the Lamoureux name until I saw some video of the man three days ago."

"The son or the father," I asked, not seeing where the road was leading.

"Both." Her gaze held fast across the desk. "However, it was the son whom I recognized." Ashley's eyes misted, then teared. She absently swiped a finger under each eye. Her gaze returned to her lap, then up at me again. The tears had dried up. "Certainly, you remember the names Dave Saunders and Cindy Spagliano."

I felt as if hit in the chest with a sledgehammer, and slowly nodded. Those were two names I'd never forget, they were etched upon my soul. The father of the woman sitting across from me had murdered them both; the Saunders boy for the crimes of raping and beating his daughter, and Cindy Spagliano for being in the wrong place at the wrong time. I reminded her of those finer details. She backtracked.

"As I said earlier, my father wasn't an evil man, Mr. Langdon, but I know he did evil things. I cannot answer for him, nor do I have the power to forgive him for what he did to others; that is God's purview. My father did what he felt was right, as he saw it, armed with the information he had at the time. Information, which I have been told, came from *both* you and I."

I didn't respond, but felt as if she had put down the sledgehammer and just punched me in the abdomen. The evidence I had found initially pointed strongly to the Saunders kid. It was the Massachusetts license plate initially issued to his pearl white Cadillac Escalade I found near her shoe on the shore of the Mississippi. He had been down in the French Quarter on Fat Tuesday, as had Ashley and Ronnie; surveillance tapes from the piano lounge at Pat O'Brien's clearly showed him and Cindy seated at the table next to the girls. They had interacted, and Dave and Cindy had left Pat O'Brien's within minutes of Ashley's solo departure. They had followed the girl to Royal Street where they all had been lost to the surveillance footage I saw. The doorman and valet at the Fairmont had identified Ashley, and the valet had confirmed her leaving willingly with a 'young, white dude' in a pearl white Cadillac Escalade. I had heard, or thought I heard, Ashley herself say the name 'Dave' to me when I asked who had attacked her and the girl had squeezed my hand when I showed her the photo of Dave Saunders. I recited it all to her.

I didn't, however, tell her about the third person whom I never identified which had been staying at the house. I hadn't discovered the identity of that person before Dave and Cindy paid for the crimes I had unwittingly condemned him for; crimes I quickly realized Dave Saunders did not commit. With what Sandy and I had to confront after her accident and her ongoing medical and emotional issues she endured because of the two disparate injuries to her brain and the death of our child, I did not pursue that information afterward. That was another one of my demons; a big one.

"I had met Dave Saunders that night, that's true. I remembered his face. I don't remember you showing me his photograph, but I have been told I squeezed your hand when you asked if I knew him."

My stomach tumbled. That's what had stuck with me that night. The something wrong I couldn't identify. I sprang forward in my chair, she jumped.

"What did you say?" I said, my hands reaching across the desk as if for a lifeline, hoping not to be given an anchor tether.

"Which part?"

She appeared confused.

"The last."

"I don't remember you showing me Dave Saunders' photograph, but I have been told I squeezed your hand when you asked me if I knew him."

"Who told you this?" I asked.

"Tracey Walker," she said.

"She used those words? I asked you if you 'knew him'?"

Ashley nodded.

"Yes. Those exact words."

My God. I had asked the wrong question. I remembered now. I had meant to ask her further questions, to follow up, but Dr. Broussard had interceded, and I had allowed it. That single mistake had sealed Dave Saunders' fate, and that of Cindy Spagliano. Tracey Walker had seen it, heard it, passed it along. The retaliation against the two kids from Harvard was now even more my fault. I had made a rookie's error; I knew better than that. As Teddy had reminded me many times: 'Sometimes, it isn't what is said which has the greatest power to cloud justice, but what *isn't* said, or what isn't *asked* the right way.' I became immediately heartsick; the list of my demons just grew longer, their chains to my soul now fully forged.

Her face then telegraphed what was coming next. I braced to hear the words which would now temper the chains, words which would forever seal the fact the events of that night were totally my fault. For a decade, I had placed a Band-Aid on my conscience and the next words out of Ashley Monreale's mouth were going to rip it off and reopen a very infected wound. I had known in my gut Dave Saunders was innocent. I knew it within an hour of when my actions had unwittingly condemned him; but in ten years, no person other than I had the capacity to verbalize it, and I could drown my own accusations with alcohol early on, and hide them with the fog of time thereafter. Ashley Monreale was about to say the words only she could speak, she was poised to unleash the whirlwind to clear the fog and render alcohol impotent, and thus indelibly emblazon the mark upon my soul that I had not the courage to place myself.

I had caused it all. My hands were sweating, my heart was pounding so hard I feared the sound of its beating may obscure the next words from her mouth. I swallowed, wanted that glass of bourbon across the room on the bar, but could not will my body to move to retrieve it. No other person, living or dead, knew the whole story. Tracey Walker only had known what she had seen and heard, and what I had told her, and she and I hadn't spoken to one another since she hung up on me when it had dawned on me what she was going to do; what she *had* done with every bit of information I had provided her. I had acted too soon, and reacted too late.

Sandy had known more, but she had awoken in the Ochsner hospital the following midnight thinking she was still in the hospital in South Padre after we had just beat the surging Gulf off the pier. The doctors had called it 'multiple-trauma-induced, retrograde amnesia' and advised us the memories of the period between the two head injuries may come back in time. That had never occurred, the memories of that period had never reappeared, and the whole discussion of the time tended to upset Sandy, so I stopped speaking of those nine days lost to her after a while. My wife had no more knowledge or emotional connection to the events which had taken place in Vacherie than someone who had read the police reports. For perhaps the first time in my life, during the past ten years there had been no person who could help me shoulder the burden of my own actions but me.

Then, the only person on earth who could confirm my worst fears about that whole matter, did; in a voice that was soft, and controlled, and certain.

"Dave Saunders did not rape and beat me, Mr. Langdon." She opened the clasp and reached into her purse and removed a couple of folded sheets. "This man did."

She first handed a photograph of a young man, about thirty, which appeared to be clipped from a magazine across my desk. I looked at it; didn't recognize the person. She followed that with what appeared to be a printout of a yearbook photo of the same man, probably ten years younger.

"That's Dace Lamoureux," she said. "The son of the sitting senior United States Senator from the state of Connecticut. *He's* the person who raped me, beat me, and left me to die on the banks of the Mississippi in 1998, Mr. Langdon. Dace. That's the name I most likely attempted to say to you, not Dave. I swear it on my soul, and if you knew me better, you'd understand what that vow means to me."

I looked at both photos, intentionally lingered there, then slowly raised my gaze to her. Her eyes were locked on me, and I knew what she said was the truth.

That's the first time I could recall ever hearing the name Dace Lamoureux. I had never even heard the name Dace before in my life. Her word whispered to me from her bed had been incomplete, and I had just assumed she had said Dave. I had heard what I had expected to hear. It fit. My eyes moved from Ashley back to the two photographs and then back to Ashley. She handed across a third sheet which contained short bios of Dace Lamoureux and his father, Senator Allard Lamoureux. I read the page, then again looked across to her. Ashley's stare was hard and committed when she spoke the accusation, but her eyes became filled with profound sadness as she continued moments later. I was uncharacteristically speechless.

"Dave Saunders was an innocent man. He paid a horrible price for a crime he didn't commit. I realize that now, and I can see in your eyes that you long ago knew that truth as well. My father had been misinformed by Tracey Walker and had lashed out based on what he believed was the truth. That's not an excuse for him, it's the verbalization of a fact, something which obviously needed doing. Cindy Spagliano had been just a victim of circumstance. See, nobody had ever shown me a picture of Dave Saunders after you reportedly had, and I never recalled you doing so, probably due to the medication and induced dream state. My aunt also did everything she could to shield me from the memories of that time after she took me to her home. The entire situation was never discussed." Her eyes went distant. "I understand now I played a role in condemning Dave in my father's eyes, even though I had no idea I had at the time or for all these years." She paused, drew a deep breath, looked hard across the desk. "You had a hand in their tragic fate as well, Mr. Langdon. Of all of them, including my father and his associates. But, you already knew that, didn't you, Mr. Langdon?"

My mind reeled and my chest constricted. I felt sick to my stomach. An epiphany is rarely a shared experience, and though Ashley and I had come to conclusions about Dave Saunders' innocence a decade apart, we now each knew the full, unvarnished truth. We also understood that each of us carried the burden of a massive guilt, although in vastly different proportions.

My cop's brain moved to the possible next steps from this realization. There would be no way to prove ten-year-old allegations of rape and no Louisiana prosecutor or empaneled grand jury would be persuaded to issue an indictment against someone as politically powerful as the son of Senator Allard Lamoureux on pure say-so. Any physical evidence was long gone, I was certain of it. There had been no contemporaneous report of the crime made with the authorities, and I had lied to multiple sheriffs and their deputies and detectives to protect Ashley's privacy. That wouldn't bode well for my credibility. Hell, the police had never even been involved in the situation until I had called them to handle the aftermath of the events in the warehouse on Lac des Allemands.

What *did* we have? The decade-old memories of a woman brought to the fore by a passing newscast? Even though repressed memories had been given more judicial credibility in recent years, they had also been discredited time and again and were currently out of favor because of those who had tried to abuse the system. My gut? That wouldn't carry much weight against a person such as Dace Lamoureux. It would be career suicide for anyone in Louisiana officialdom to accuse a man who, from press accounts, would soon sit in the United States Senate solely on the spontaneity of Ashley's newfound memories. One doesn't strike against a king unless one is certain one can kill him. Even I knew that.

What did she want of me? To what end do I investigate further at this time, or did she expect justice be extracted outside the legal channels?

"You said you wanted to hire me earlier. What exactly do you want me to do for you, Ashley?" I asked.

She removed a letter from her purse and passed it across. I read it.

I looked at her.

Then, when she had me totally conditioned to the request, she told me what she wanted. The hook had been set.

I nodded.

With a simple handshake, Ashley Monreale became my client.

After escorting Ashley out of my office, through the empty public area and to our outer door at the top of the stairs, I walked down the hall to Sandy's office. Her door was ajar and Sandy had her back turned to it and was working at her credenza on her iMac. I tapped my knuckles on her door and moved inside a couple of steps and waited, then wondered when it was that I had stopped sneaking up behind her to nuzzle her neck to announce my arrival into her space. I wasn't exactly certain. I wanted to do it, I just...didn't.

Sandy turned in her chair, slipped her reading glasses from her nose. I took a seat fifteen feet from her on the couch.

"How did it go?" she said.

"I took the case," I said. "It will take up several days, perhaps a week, and there's going to be some travel involved."

"It pays the bills," she said, then slipped her glasses back onto her nose and swiveled her chair so she could again face her computer screen. "By the way, I need those expense reports as soon as you can have them done," she said without turning.

I stood up, considered saying something, but overrode the thought and returned to my office.

After I closed my door, I picked up the untouched tumbler of bourbon from my bar, downed it in one swallow, poured another and took the glass along to my desk. I sat, opened my laptop, closed the Solitaire program, then finished off the expense reports and emailed them to Sandy.

I then launched my browser and went onto the internet and began to do some background research on Dace Lamoureux and his family. Normally, that would have been Sandy's purview, but I knew the emotional wrestling match I'd have on my hands if I even mentioned the Monreale case. Sandy had obviously not recognized Ashley when she had come in. I briefly wondered how I'd feel if had I a nine-day hole in my memory, and understood her frustration with the whole subject. Like Carol Huntley with her niece, I just never talked much about those days with Sandy. What was to be gained?

As Google worked its nanosecond search magic and the results screen appeared and then blurred in my vision, I allowed my mind to drift back to midnight on Friday, February 27, 1998, when Sandy awoke. I was in her room, watching the light show of an approaching line of thunderstorms and making a series of silent entreaties to the Big Guy upstairs. Doctors had been in and out through the day; Sandy remained stable, but unconscious, and they all assured me she was going to be just fine, that it would simply be a matter of time. I had held her hand, stroked her cheek, talked to her, and even sang a few of my trademarked, goofy song parodies to her. I'm not good at being patient and I was nearing the end of the line when God decided to answer one of my prayers and Sandy said my name.

I at first thought I had imagined it, but then I turned to see her baby blues looking at me from her hospital bed. That was the most beautiful sight I could have imagined at that moment. I crossed to her side, and she reached for my hand and the next words from her lips were an apology for dragging me out on that pier on South Padre Island and asking how my head was. Deep inside myself, at that moment, I sensed something was wrong, but I had been so relieved that she had finally awoken that I didn't think twice about it until later.

The night nurse, the one with the squeaky shoes had come in response to my repeatedly pushing of the call button. She moved bedside and immediately began asking Sandy a series of questions. What year is it? '1998.' Who's the president of the United States? 'Clinton.' What is your husband's first name? 'William, but I call him Will.' What city are you in? 'South Padre Island, although, since this is obviously a hospital, I'd think Port Isabel.' What state are you in? 'Texas.' What's the last thing you remember? 'Walking on the beach with Will, going out on the pier, waves crashing, running to shore, pilings falling, Will pushing me, then waking up here.'

"Honey," I had said, reaching up to stroke her cheek. "That was nine days ago." My gaze jumped to nurse squeaky shoes for some answers, saw nothing to cling to. "You're in Ochsner Hospital in Kenner, Sandy. You fell down the stairs at our office two nights ago. Nell found you and called the ambulance."

She had looked at me like I had just stepped from a space ship from another planet, then she smiled and told me to quit goofing around. She looked to nurse squeaky shoes.

"He's always doing this," she said with a wry smile. "Sick sense of humor, my husband has, but I still love him."

We said nothing. Sandy's eyes darted between squeaky shoes and myself and then I saw the confusion filling her eyes as she fixed upon the nurse's ID badge with the words 'Ochsner Medical Center Campus' on it. Her eyes came back to me, went wide with fear and welled with tears.

"Will?"

"It's true, Sandy," I said, holding her hand tightly. "This is now moving into Saturday, February 28, and you're going to be just fine."

"I fell down the stairs at our office?" she asked, then panic swept across her face and she dropped my hand and both of hers moved to her abdomen. She lifted the covers, looked under. I don't ever again want to see the look Sandy then gave me. Her mouth fell open and was moving, but no words came out.

I sat on the edge of that bed, clasped both her hands in mine and looked into her eyes. My voice cracked and my eyes leaked onto my cheeks as I slowly nodded.

"We lost the baby, Sandy."

I tapped the keys on my laptop and pulled myself back to the present before I had to endure the unbearable memory of the keening cries which erupted from my wife that night and continued unabated for the days after as I held her close and tried to fill in the gaps for her. I took a deep breath, glanced at the glass of bourbon on my blotter and then used the sleeves of my shirt to wipe my eyes. That past was gone, its events long ago written in stone and despite my best efforts to wash away the etching with anger and bourbon, it remained affixed to history and earlier today it had been once again revealed by a girl who had stood in the center of that very past. I was being forced to look upon the writing on that stone for the first time in a very long time and I wasn't certain I was ready for the task. I did know, however, that Sandy's and my present was becoming nearly unbearable, and our future was locked behind a door of uncertainty. All I could hope for at that moment was the hope I held deep in my heart for the longest time: that Sandy and I could unlock that door in time, if only we found the key.

I shook my head to clear it, then dug into the Google search results. I decided to print some of the information I found, saved as digital pdf files more expansive items for later reading, and logged web pages to a new folder in my browser's header.

From Ashley's mini-bio on the man, I knew Dace Lamoureux hailed from New London, Connecticut, and had attended Harvard and Harvard Law, graduating near the top of both classes in 1998 and 2001, respectively, so I figured that would be the best place to begin if I wanted information from back then.

I navigated to the Harvard website and found a link to the yearbook pages. Never having gone to college, I was a bit surprised to discover they participated in such a pedestrian social convention as yearbooks at that level, especially in the Ivy League. Hell, as of 2008, I learned, Harvard still didn't even have a homecoming event like the proletariat rabble of most colleges; rather the upper-crusters celebrated for a weekend each fall since 1875 what they modestly referred to as 'The Game' when the Crimson of Harvard would battle the rival Bulldogs of Yale on the gridiron. In the fall of 1997, Dace's senior year, the Crimson had won, 17-7, on Yale's home field.

I searched the yearbook for Dace Lamoureux and found, among other things, he had been the starting quarterback for the Crimson his senior year and was a starting forward and co-captain of the basketball teams from his sophomore year on. The kid was an elite amongst the elite, it appeared, both academically successful and a campus sports icon.

Fortunately, the yearbook listed persons included in most of the photos in an index section and sped up my searching. Along with the sports teams' lineup and action photos, I found several snapped at various social events which showed Dace Lamoureux dancing and partying with a number of attractive, young women.

Dave Saunders also showed up in the photos of the sports teams, which confirmed what he had told my John Portman persona about his playing on the team and confirmed that he and Dace knew each other, at least in passing. It was when I clicked around outside of the indexed pages of photos where I stumbled across a shot included in the 1997 issue which provided possibly the biggest connection yet between the two men. 1997 would have been their junior year. It was a two-page, center spread of a colorful, candid photograph of anonymous students scattered on the green between ivy-covered, red brick walls like so many colorful leaves. The caption read: 'Enjoying a beautiful, late fall afternoon in 1996.'

I nearly missed it, but then zoomed in on three now familiar faces seated on a plaid blanket encircling a pair of wine bottles and plates containing an assortment of fruit and cheeses. I printed and digitally saved the photo, as well as a cropped blowup which better revealed the smiling faces of Dace Lamoureux, Dave Saunders, Cindy Spagliano, and the profile of an unidentified woman with long, black hair.

# Chapter Thirty-two

"I'm leaving, Will," Sandy said when she poked her head in my office, then began to withdraw. "Thanks for the expense reports, by the way."

I looked up from my MacBook Pro and nodded. I was neck deep into the background search and being alternately bored and intrigued; bored by the process and tedium, intrigued by the information I was uncovering. It normally would be Sandy's job to unearth the facts for me to run with; research was what she enjoyed most about our work, but not this time as I had already decided to pursue the case without consulting her in order to protect her from the dredging of unpleasant memories. I glanced at the upper right corner of my screen and noted the time was shortly after four.

"I've got a couple of stops to make before I'm done today, Sandy," I said back. "I don't know how you do all this background crap."

She took a step inside my office, her eyes perking up.

"Can I help?" she asked.

I shook my head, closed the lid on my computer. Her eyes moved to the open bar, the empty glass on my desk.

"I see," she said, and turned on the ball of her foot and left.

A few seconds later, I heard the door slam and the sound of her heels moving down the stairs.

According to some information Ashley provided, Ronnie Broussard had stayed local in the years after the attack, but moved to the big city after returning to and graduating from the countrified Catholic girls' high school. Even without the information provided by my new client, Ronnie would not have been difficult to track down, especially after relocating for her new day job to Baton Rouge, Louisiana's other big city.

Her night job, however, was a little more underground and I could have dug it up with a little time, but since the clock was again ticking on this case, I was thankful to Ashley for saving me both the effort and a trip to the state's capitol just to have a short conversation with the woman. In the office of her day job, Ronnie Broussard may have been a difficult interview, but in the seedy strip joint on Bourbon Street, I guessed I would have the upper hand.

Ronnie Broussard had used the stage name 'Lusty' for the past nine years. Since graduating summa cum laude in 2006 from Tulane University Law School, which was located a mere handful of blocks from our office, Lusty had cut back to only working Friday evenings at her sultry avocation. I had confirmed by calling a number Ashley had provided me that Ronnie, I mean, Lusty, would be working that night. I didn't ask how Ashley had obtained the information, or the number which had connected me directly to a surly gent, sitting, no doubt, in what I envisioned as a small, dark, smoke-filled office cluttered with booze boxes and the occasional swag surrounded by black-painted plaster walls that pulsed with the guttural beat of grinding jazz from the show room beyond. Perhaps I was just allowing my imagination to drift off to tried-and-true stereotypes because New Orleans, playfully known as The Big Easy, just lent itself to revealing them as being based in our own special reality.

During the normal workweek, and many weekends, Ronnie Broussard, Esquire, could be found hard at her day job, attired in a conservative business suit and modest coiffure in her associate's office at an old, prestigious law firm in downtown Baton Rouge, but every Friday evening Lusty could still be found sporting not much more than stripper glitter, wild hair, and her now trademark, tiny, gold and feathered Mardi Gras mask at a strip club on Bourbon Street. According to the gent on the phone, she would first appear at nine that night.

As I closed my computer down for the day at a bit before five, I calculated that I'd have plenty of time before Lusty took the stage to renew another old acquaintanceship downtown at One Shell Square. I had called the number I looked up in our office's database and spoken to a friendly woman in reception who had confirmed Tracey Walker would also be working that Friday evening.

I packed my computer and printouts in my soft-sided, leather case, rinsed and dried the tumbler and closed up the bar, locked the office and went outside into a cool, late afternoon. I paused on the stoop. When I was a kid back in Wisconsin, burnt-orange afternoons like this would be filled with the drifting smell of burning leaves, and since it was Halloween, the wide-eyed anticipation of candy and treats later that evening in a haul the size of which the world had never before witnessed. That night, as a grownup, I had a confrontation with someone I hadn't spoken to in a decade and an hour or so in a Bourbon Street strip club to look forward to before heading home to a wife who was less and less hoping it was me walking through the door.    Frankly, I'd take the childhood memories of burning leaves and trick-or-treating anytime.

As I rounded the back of our building, I noticed that Sandy had taken my car and left me her silver Saab, which meant it was probably low on gas.  I used the remote to unlock the doors and the damn thing chirped at me, then flashed its lights.  I hated that car; and as I turned the ignition after sliding back its ridiculously over-engineered seat, I found I was right: the gas gauge was wedged below the 'E'.    The damn needle didn't even move as I jounced across our potholed lot and down our drive to the street, rather it remained pegged to the bottom like the Titanic. The nearest gas station was six blocks away and I cursed under my breath as its oversize tires on ugly rims rolled out every foot of every block.    Momentary memories of childhood Halloweens aside, my sour mood hadn't sweetened as the day had gone on, and I had every belief it was only going to get worse before the night was through, even if I didn't run out of gas before making the station.

Six blocks from our office, I turned in front of a honking delivery van and pulled to the pump.   The engine stopped on its own.   I snorted derisively.

"Friggin' Swedes," I said under my breath, figuring it was better to slander an entire country than spew any more venom in Sandy's direction.

Somehow, I managed to pump twenty-one gallons into the twenty gallon tank, then tore the credit card receipt from the pump, returned to the uncomfortable seat and drove to the parking lot under New Orleans' tallest downtown skyscraper at the corner of Poydras and St. Charles streets: One Shell Square.  I pulled the ticket from the machine, parked, grabbed my computer bag off the equally uncomfortable passenger seat, made my way through the lot, took the escalator up a flight past the palm trees to the lobby and caught an elevator to Tracey's office near the top of the complex's tower building.  I passed the law firm's receptionist on her way out, confirmed that Tracey Walker was still there, then graciously declined her offer to announce me.  I told the woman I knew the way to Tracey's office, lied by saying Ms. Walker was expecting me, and wished the woman a wonderful weekend.   She smiled in that indecipherable southern manner and wished me the same before disappearing into another elevator cab headed down.

I pulled open one side and passed through the double, glass doors, and followed my memory to Tracey Walker's office.  When I arrived at the correct door, I found it slightly ajar and labeled with a different name. I knocked lightly and apologized to the too-skinny young man with rolled up shirt sleeves, askew tie, and unbuttoned collar behind a mountain of papers who looked up at me with tired eyes behind out-of-style glasses.

"Yes?" he said, stopping his pencil in mid-stroke.

"Tracey Walker?" I replied.

"Not guilty," he said, attempting lawyerly humor.

"I was told she was still here," I said, giving up a small smile. "This is where I always came to see her."

"Must have been a long time ago," he said. "She's been upstairs for as long as I've been here."

"Upstairs?" I asked.

He looked me over, probably wondering exactly how I managed to sneak past the receptionist, glanced at his watch and found his answer before speaking. He obviously found me acceptably professional in slacks and sport jacket, because he then mimed the directions for me as he spoke.

"Down the hall, left, right, up the circular staircase, southeast corner of the building."

Tracy had obviously moved up - professionally and literally - since I last had seen her. I thanked the galley slave and he returned his attention to his piles of paper before I had withdrawn from the doorway. As I moved through the quiet hallways, I wondered how anyone could be an attorney; stuck in a tiny office which more often than not at that level smelled of fast food, and sweat socks from the seldom used gym bag tossed in the corner, enduring the ungodly long hours and arrogant bosses who thought they were, in fact, God, and burdened by a looming mountain of student debt. I didn't go to college and even now made less than most attorneys with twenty-five-plus years on the job, but I had never had to put up with most of the garbage, plus I got to shoot the occasional asshole. Not a bad tradeoff, I thought. I smiled to myself as I negotiated the final turn and saw the foretold circular stairway of glass cutting between concrete and steel floors.

I climbed the steps to the hidden-away upper floor of the firm's offices and worked my way along richly appointed halls, past plush and much larger offices to the building's southeast corner. Even though it was after normal business hours, several legal assistants still labored at ample desks in open nooks along the hallway across from closed, heavy doors labeled with names most New Orleanians would recognize. None of the assistants looked up to watch me pass; they had been well trained. Finally, I arrived at the door labeled as belonging 'Tracey M. Walker, Esquire'. The assistant's desk across the hall was vacant and devoid of even one stray paperclip.

Tracey's door was closed. There was a sidelight, but it was frosted and all I could tell was that there was light inside. I tried the knob, then opened the door without knocking and strode in. After her initial surprise at my unannounced entry subsided an instant later, the indignation set in.

"Hi, Tracey," I said, walking to one of the windows to take in the view. "Long time, no see." I could almost feel the daggers her eyes were tossing at my back as I crossed the office and peered out at the city. "Wow, you can see for miles from up here."

"What the hell are you doing here?" she said. "How did you get past reception?"

I didn't respond, just kept my back turned to her and in the glass, I could see the reflection of her agitation growing. When I saw her image rising from the desk and picking up the phone, I turned to face her. The dark warning she saw reflected in my eyes froze her and gave me several moments to consider the next steps. Tracey still looked great, but after reading the letter earlier which she had written to Ashley's aunt years ago, I doubted she made it to this office and partner status on looks alone. Ferreting out Tony Gator's money and managing the pool of investments which totaled in the nine-digit range, first for the guardianship of Ashley Monreale and more recently as the charitable blind trust over the past decade had most likely helped her career trajectory too. Considering the classes of people: criminals and politicians - which in Louisiana have too often been the same folks - she had needed to deal with on some of the more lucrative underground investments, I was frankly surprised Tracey Walker wasn't long ago feeding catfish at the bottom of the Mississippi River nearly seven-hundred-feet below.

I padded across carpet which probably cost more per square yard than I charged in an hour and took a seat in one of the chairs across the desk from her. I placed my computer bag on the floor alongside the surprisingly comfortable antique and smiled up at her. I didn't offer to shake hands with her, recalling the old joke that if I did, I would be well advised to count the number of fingers I got back. The thought reminded me of how the late Tony Monreale had lost two of his fingers to one of his namesake reptiles, or so went the back room story.

"Got a bourbon for an old friend?" I asked, glancing toward several cut crystal decanters on a side table across the room, each containing a varying quantity of caramel-colored or clear spirits.

She remained standing and glared at me in silence, the phone still poised in her hand.

"You've got to be out of your mind," she said.

I pursed my lips and nodded with a sardonic smile on my face.

"There are days when I'd agree with that assessment, counselor."

I watched her punch several buttons on the phone, could hear ringing as she held the handset an inch from her ear.

"However, today isn't one of them," I said, then I shifted in the chair. "You know, this is a very comfortable piece of furniture, Tracey. Remind me to inquire with your decorator.

I heard a male voice answer with the single word 'Security'.

"Hang up the phone, counselor. You and I need to have a little chat."

She glared at me. Were I made of ice, I'd be puddled on the floor right about then.

"Ashley Monreale came to see me today," I said, meeting her heated stare with one of my own.

"Never mind," she said into the phone and replaced the handset.

She stood there, unmoving, but I could see that Ashley Monreale was the last possible eventuality in her mind for me turning up in her office that afternoon.

"Now, how about that bourbon?" I said, settling in and crossing my legs. "What do you say, in honor of the late Tony Gators, we make it three fingers?"

Realizing from our long-ago dealings that my ball-busting personality never carried quite the level of displayed arrogance it now did, Tracey obviously decided to play it safe until she discovered exactly what I knew and wanted before really pissing me off. She moved from behind her desk, removed the stoppers from two decanters and then brought over three fingers of bourbon for me and a similar quantity of one of the clear liquids for herself. As she walked away from me, I detected the odor of pine needles. God, I hated the smell of gin; it was an odor like someone had swished a car deodorizer through cheap vodka.

She retook her seat and I hoisted my glass in mock salute to her, then took a strong draw. It wasn't Jim Beam, but it wasn't bad.

"Maker's Mark?" I said.

She held her glass two inches above an expensive desk inlaid with leather and gold-leaf imprinting and intricate veneer banding and stared at me. I pointed to my tumbler.

"You know, I have this very set of cut crystal glassware in my office bar," I said.

She glared.

"Waterford?" I said.

"Baccarat," she said.

I inspected the glass; lifted it above my head and looked at the bottom.

"Hmm, can't tell the difference," I said.

"What the hell do you want, William," she said. "I'm far too busy to discuss the finer points of leaded crystal glassware or Kentucky bourbon with you?"

I shook my head and took another draw from my glass, then held the tumbler to the light. The caramel liquid and cut crystal played prismatic magic in the last of the afternoon light streaming in from the windows.

"I'm getting to it," I said, "but first you must tell me: Is this Maker's Mark or not?"

She slammed her glass onto the desk, gin splashed everywhere, which, in my not-so-humble opinion is the best thing one can do with gin. It's better than drinking it.

"Goddammit," she spat.

I grinned.

"Geeze, Tracey, I didn't come here to piss you off," I said, draining a little more from my glass and fighting back the formation of a more sarcastic version of the grin I wore. "Although, I have to admit, I'm finding that *is* a bit of an unexpected bonus."

I unfolded my legs and slid forward in my chair, set the Baccarat tumbler on the desk and locked her eyes to mine with my glare.

"I've got blood on my hands," I said. A pause. "And so do you. Of course, you already knew that, didn't you, counselor?"

"Are you drunk?" she said. "What are you talking about?"

"Don't try to kid a kidder, Tracey," I said slowly shaking my head mockingly and wagging a finger in her direction, then I picked up my glass again and slid back onto the chair. "You know exactly what I'm talking about, you knew why I'd come to see you after all these years the instant I mentioned Ashley Monreale's name a few minutes ago. Otherwise, I'd be standing with a security man on each of my arms rather than enjoying this private, little interlude with you." My eyes continued to challenge hers and she didn't back down an inch. She was good. "Ten years ago you sold out two innocent kids..." My hands indicated the room. "...for this."

"Bullshit. I protected my clients," she said defiantly and pointed a finger in my direction. "Don't try to put your screw up on my shoulders."

"I told you the kid didn't do it," I said. "I told you an hour before Tony's guys got to the plantation house and took him and Cindy away. You had time to call it off, and you didn't, because it suited your purposes; and then you lied to the Broussards. You even talked to Tony after I talked to you, so I know you had the chance to correct it all, give me a little more time to get to the right person. His guys knew to expect me. You sold me out, too. But you saw stars for yourself, so you didn't care who had to pay for it all, did you?"

"You're dreaming," she said, adding a dismissive snort and backhanded wave.

"No, I'm still in the middle of a decade-long nightmare," I said, momentarily thinking there was perhaps light at the end of that tunnel while hoping it wasn't coming from an oncoming locomotive.

"If you're not dreaming, then you're bluffing?" she said. "You can't prove a thing."

I didn't answer. This is the part of poker playing that I truly enjoyed: the reveal. I reached down into the back pocket of my computer bag and removed a copy of the letter Ashley brought me earlier. It was addressed to her aunt, Carol Huntley, hand scripted by the sender and dated the day Dr. Broussard had put a syringe containing potassium chloride into his vein and taken his own life in 2002. I unfolded it and handed it across the desk.

"You can keep that," I said. "It's a copy."

She snatched it from my fingers, held it up and read it. I watched her eyes move across each line, then return to the top and do it a second time. A good cop will always watch the subject's eyes, not the action, and that's what I did. I could tell before she had finished the first reading that she understood I had her by the short hairs, and knew she reread it merely to buy time. I could see all of it in her eyes, yet she still attempted a bluff. She paused a moment, then tossed the letter back toward me. It fluttered to the desk, soaked up several puddles of her splashed gin now mixed with dissolved mahogany wax, and the paper became spotted with the color of aged blood. Frankly, I got chills at the imagery. Tracey's face turned as white as the original paper, yet she continued with the feint.

"So?" she said and picked up the letter and tossed it out of sight under her desk. "Everyone knew the poor doctor had become a persecuted soul; some would perhaps say he was unbalanced at the end. Delusional. Besides, what difference could it possibly make a decade after the fact? Even were any of what he wrote six years ago true."

"Keep trying, counselor. You'll come up with something with which to make a legal argument should this ever come to that, but as I told you before, don't try to kid a kidder."

I stood up, drained the last of the bourbon, then replaced the glass on the edge of her desk. I picked up my computer bag by the strap and hung it from my left shoulder. I had reconsidered my initial plan of telling her where I was going with all this, decided it was best for my new client that the good counselor not know at that point. Besides, Tracey Walker was now on notice, and, she had, without saying a single word, already answered every question I had intended to ask her that evening. She had also managed to reignite my anger toward her, and, oddly discomfiting to me, my own disappointment in myself.

The infected wound from which Ashley had ripped the Band-Aid just hours ago, was beginning to open. Soon it would begin to seep. I walked out of Tracey's office without further dialogue and wove my way back to the bank of elevators. On the ride down, I was struck with a thought which caused my puffed bravado to shrink like a frightened turtle. I removed my cell phone from my jacket pocket and hit the autodial for Sandy's cell. It went directly to voicemail.

"Shit," I said, disconnecting.

It was clear to me by the time I stepped into the lobby and retraced my steps back to the garage level that I'd have some explaining to do when I got home; if what I think had just happened happened. Great, I thought, this case had only just begun and already I was headed for another messy entanglement with my wife, all because I wanted to do the right thing and protect Sandy. It had been one hell of a week.

Tracey Walker had always gotten along better with Sandy than with me; and apart from the personality conflict between Tracey and myself, it was partly because as attorneys they spoke the same language. I also think they truly had liked one another on a personal level. I cursed my arrogance and lack of foresight. I should have known that Tracey would go running to Sandy after I confronted her, but I had been too blinded by anger and revenge.

After Sandy and I left the Broussards that day ten years ago and I called Tracey to warn her off doing something stupid before rushing back to Vacherie when it was clear she had no intention of changing course, I hadn't, and, to the best of my knowledge, neither had my wife, spoken to or heard from Tracey Walker. Even after word of Sandy's accident spread in the city, we never heard a word from Tracey. Not a card, no flowers, no calls of condolence or to find out how Sandy was faring, not even the most impersonal of touches: an email. She simply dropped out of Sandy's life. And now I knew why.

I think the lack of outreach by Tracey had hurt Sandy deeply, and when a person hurts someone near and dear, they become dead to me, which was an easy enough transition with the woman I had just left for yours truly. Tracey Walker had simply ceased to exist in my world. However, I could tell there was a hole in Sandy's life over the disconnection, and what was worse, for a while she had begun doubting her own abilities of discernment. When someone you love comes to believe they can't trust their own instincts anymore, it's like helplessly watching an airplane spiral in, praying for chutes, but seeing none.

The entanglement I was anticipating when I got home would be much more than a simple remonstration from Sandy because Tracey tattled on my behavior today, it would open Sandy's wounds on this whole thing. The gap in her memory had never closed, and that had been one of those emotional grenades with the pin pulled which we balanced on a metaphorical, rickety shelf in a closet somewhere. Over the last ten years, I've accidentally bumped the shelf and sent the grenade rolling and there have been other instances when it just had begun moving seemingly on its own volition, but each time I had managed to catch it just before it blew up. Sandy and I process the end of interpersonal relationships differently. I am fine to walk away and never look back. Sandy not only finds it hard to walk away initially, but looking back invariably devastates her; and Sandy's emotions were the bottom line of what I intended to protect here.

I drove out of the parking garage, paid twenty bucks for the privilege and wondered briefly if Tracey would have validated for me. Probably not. Since I had time before Lusty would hit the stage, I decided to drop in on my old friend Stan at Pat O'Brien's. I called him with a head's up. He sounded happy to take some time for me, but I didn't tell him what I had wanted. He might not be so happy when I told him.

Apart from the professional need I had for him that afternoon, I also looked forward to seeing him on a personal level. Stan had undergone a gastric bypass operation about eighteen months earlier after suffering a mild heart attack and being told by the doctors that it was lose the weight or start cemetery plot shopping. The last time I saw him about three months ago, he had gone from being a beach ball to a deflated beach ball. I heard he had some surgery to take care of the extra skin about a month earlier and looked good now. I pulled the Saab onto St. Peters Street in The Quarter, then parked across the street from the bar.

Stan met me out front. He looked like a new man; his was a physical transition which would have shamed Al Roker. Stan instructed the bouncer out front to keep an eye on my ride, after he had a good laugh at my expense as I crossed the street.

"A Saab?" he said, laughing much too hard. "When are you moving to suburbia and having your balls put up in a jar on the mantle?"

"Funny," I said shaking his hand. When shaking hands with Stan, you'd sometimes find you had extra fingers when you pulled it back. That's just how he rolls, and it's one of the reasons, after Teddy, he'd be the man I'd trust with the lives of my family. "Sandy left me with the thing this afternoon."

"No gas in it, right?"

I nodded.

"Why do they do that?" I said.

We walked up the main hallway back to the stairs up to his office. The piano bar off to the right was already in full swing.

"I know. Pam used to do that. Pissed me off royally every time and I'd pitch a royal fit, but she didn't care. I guess that's one of the reasons she never calls me any more." A pause. "How is Sandy?"

I took a deep breath at the question.

"She was just fine the last time I saw her a few hours ago," I said. "That could all have changed by now."

I gave Stan the summary of my afternoon, omitting any mention of the nature of the help sought by Ashley Monreale because that's the way she had wanted it. Apart from me, Stan and Teddy were the only people who second-handedly knew all the details of what went down back in 1998, because I believe if you're going to trust someone with the lives of your family, you had to trust them with everything else. At least that's how I roll. Stan didn't ask me why I had decided to reopen this whole mess again. He trusted I had a good reason and invited me into his office while shaking his head as I talked. He understood what I was up against, and he offered me a finger or two of Jim Beam from a bottle in his desk, then poured it out into two, regular bar glasses, keeping mine short as I requested.

"To women," he said, clinking his glass to mine, then downing a swig. "Can't live with 'em..."

I drank without doing my guy job of completing the joke, and watched as Stan settled into his chair and typed and clicked around on his computer. A moment later, one of his storage drives on the shelf above the monitors began to whir, its lights flickering.

"I saved this for you that night you came to see me," he said. "I figured someday you'd be back."

"How?" I said.

"Call it a hunch," he said and he poured another finger of Beam into his glass. "I just didn't think you'd take this long."

"Have you looked at the rest of it?" I asked. "I've still got the pieces you gave me on discs at the office, stored with the shoe and license plate and the rest of the stuff I had put together."

Stan shook his head, pointed to the wall mounted monitor.

Just like ten years ago, we turned our attention to a big screen, segmented into six sets of video images, and again we watched Ashley and Ronnie come into the piano bar. Then Dave and Cindy were alive again, having a good time and interacting with the girls. Stan manipulated the computer and some of the images changed angles and we saw different areas of the room. The screen was higher resolution than I remember the old one to be, the faces clearer, more alive. More haunting.

Stan continued to sort through the video while I watched. At one point, Ronnie got up from the table and walked toward the back of the room. I assumed she was headed for the restroom. Stan followed her with the video, then there he was, for only an instant, standing in a shadow along the wall.

"Stop," I said. "Go back."

The playback stopped.

"What?" he said. "You see something?"

I told Stan to go back, and asked to see if he had more of the back wall area. He typed and clicked, the screen images all changed. We now had time-synched views concentrating along the back wall and Ronnie's face. As she passed through the portal, her eyes appeared to look directly into the face of Dace Lamoureux and his at her, for an instant. I told Stan to freeze it.

"The son of a bitch was there," I said, "hiding in the back of the room like some predator."

"Who?" Stan said.

There were several people in the screen shot. I stood up and walked to the screen and pointed to the face.

"Can you print me some images of that segment, Stan?"

I heard the printer start up and pages eject onto the top.

"Can you also burn me some of the video segments with date and time stamps?"

"Already doing it," he said.

"Can you forward it now to the time Ashley leaves? But keep a view on this guy?

Stan typed and clicked again, the images changed. Ashley was standing up and hugging Cindy. Dace Lamoureux remained in his place but appeared to come to a higher level of alert.

Now, if my hunch is right," I said, "he followed Ashley out before the Saunders kid and his girl left."

We watched Ashley walk out, and with the additional camera shots of the back wall on the screen, could see Dace's eyes move and watch her go. Then, he followed her out of the piano lounge, down the hallway and out onto the street. He turned right on St. Peter, just like she did. At Royal Street, he disappeared around the corner two-seconds after Ashley. It was several minutes later that Dave and Cindy walked the same route. Stan knew what to print, what to burn onto the DVD, and he handed over both the disc and the hardcopies.

I stood there, my insides churning. Had I only caught that ten years ago, things would have all been different. If I had taken the time and not jumped to conclusions at a simple coincidence, the whole world would be changed from the way it currently was stitched together. I would never have left Sandy alone at the office, she never would have taken that tumble, our son or daughter would be in the fifth grade by now. My heart ripped, for so many reasons, but mainly because it was *all* my fault. My arrogance had once again impacted the world in a negative way. I looked up to see Stan staring at me. He was a good friend and enough of a pro to know not to ask about any of it. He understood I'd tell him somewhere along the way when I was ready. I wondered how long I had been standing there lost in thought when my eyes met his.

"You want another finger?" was all he said, lifting the bottle.

I shook my head and turned to go. I wanted it, and more, but felt myself at an emotional tipping point. If I fell into the bottle again, I may never get out, or worse yet, decide to make my own offramp on the bridge over Lake Pontchartrain as had the real estate broker who had previously owned our office building. Wouldn't that be ironic? Although, it might add a whole new legend to city lore about an ominous curse attached to our building on Magazine Street. New Orleans does love its spooky tales.

Stan got up to walk me out. We retraced our steps out to the street without speaking.

Since the club Ronnie Broussard worked at was just a handful of blocks away, I asked if I could leave the Saab parked on St. Peter while I walked over.

"Maybe you'll get lucky and somebody will steal it," Stan said with a raucous laugh and the bouncer joined in. "You want me to have Max here walk you over, dearie?"

I declined with a one-finger salute, then shook his hand and thanked him for everything. *Everything.*

"Someday, we're going to be even, you know," he said. "Then what are you going to do?"

"I'll let you know when that happens, buddy," I said, then smiled before I turned to walk toward Bourbon Street. The crowd ahead appeared to be typical Friday evening size and makeup, although since it was Halloween, there may have been a few more ghosts and ghouls roaming the streets of The Quarter. I could feel them stirring in my soul.

"Hey, William," Stan called.

I turned around.

"Nail that son of a bitch," he said, "and watch your back."

I nodded and turned and continued toward the lights and music. I hadn't told Stan one thing about my meeting with Ashley Monreale that afternoon. He deserved to know, but I had given my word to my client. I wonder what Stan would say if he knew what I would be going up against. Someday, I decided then, we'd share that extra finger, or more, of Beam together and I'd fill him in. As I thought of Ashley's request of me, I hoped that someday would come.

The exotic dance club I was headed for was well known in New Orleans. It had been a fixture on Bourbon Street since before the days when Alderman Sidney Story had crafted the legislation which created Storyville, New Orleans' notorious red-light district just two blocks outside the French Quarter. It was a wrongheaded attempt to remove a bit of winked-at debauchery out of the area and Storyville had operated legally in an area locals knew simply as 'The District' for twenty years from 1897 to 1917. While many gentlemen and less-than-gentlemen moved their more prurient needs to the cheap 'cribs' along Iberville and Basin streets, some remained loyal to the class of ladies who plied their trade of sultry seduction on the main floor in the house I was headed for, then rewarded the most generous with more private interludes upstairs. Storyville had been closed and cleaned out by the United States Army in 1917 on the grounds of public health, but New Orleans' wink and nod policies and public demand had kept clubs like the one where Lusty danced going strong and probably always would.

I stopped at the glassed display out front and immediately picked out Ronnie Broussard from the array of R-rated photographs, mainly because of her trademark Mardi Gras mask she always wore now. She had begun wearing the mask when she graduated from Tulane Law School and went out in search of a daytime job. It certainly wouldn't do for a client, or worse, a partner at her old, conservative law firm to drop by and recognize her. Not that lawyers did that sort of thing, did they? I smiled at the thought.

I nodded to the bouncer, talked to him a bit, and then walked into the club. Two side stages had girls working their wares to fixed lights and competing beats. The tables and counter closest to them were fairly full, as was the area by the darkened main stage. As I took a seat at the bar toward the back of the room, the lights dimmed on the side stages and the main stage was hit with spotlights and a single new beat pulsed. A moment later, the speakers announced the arrival of one of 'New Orleans' favorite exotic entertainers, Lusty' and I watched over my shoulder as Ronnie Broussard strutted onto the stage in the costume of a Catholic school girl. I smiled. She had filled out over the years in all the areas where she had been previously lacking, I saw, then I turned my back and called over the bartender.

By negotiation, the bartender brought me the three drink minimum in one glass, then took my thirty dollars and dropped it onto the open till. She also took my fifty and pocketed that and the note I had given her for Lusty after she finished her first set. Half an hour later, and halfway through my glass of Coke, I sensed movement nearby and then felt a hand on my shoulder. My eyes went to the bartender who was nodding at the person behind me.

"Mr. Langdon," she said as she slid onto the adjacent stool.

The bar itself was fairly deserted as most of the patrons choose to sit closer to the girls, and most of the speakers were directed around the stages, so even though the return of the two competing beats was loud in the place, Lusty and I could hold a private conversation in reasonably normal tones of voice.

"Hello, Ronnie," I said, "or should I call you Lusty here?"

She smiled and the bartender set what appeared to be a club soda with wedge of lime in a tall glass in front of her. She drew from the straw.

"Doesn't matter," she said, then her eyes searched me. "Did you watch the show?"

"Just to see you walk in," I said. "The stereotypical school girl outfit was cute. Made me smile. The rest isn't my thing." I pointed to my wedding band. "Married man, you know."

Ronnie laughed.

"So are most of them, Mr. Langdon," she said, indicating the roomful of patrons with a bob of her head. "What brings you here tonight? Do I need to ask?" She formed a coquettish smile with playful eyes behind her Mardi Gras mask. "Would you like me to guess?"

"I was going to tell you whether you asked or not, Ronnie," I said. Referring to this woman as Lusty, even though she was clad in little more than a French bikini under a nearly transparent white robe, was a bit beyond me tonight. "You'd most likely never guess. I certainly wouldn't have been able to this morning, even though I had read the name in the appointment book." I paused. "Ashley came to see me today."

Thirty seconds later, I was being hustled down a darkened hallway and into an office much like I had envisioned earlier when I talked to the surly gent at this end of Ashley's provided phone number. Ronnie closed the door, took off her mask, and I filled her in as much as Ashley had directed. I removed from my jacket the photos of Dace Lamoureux supplied by Ashley and asked Ronnie if she could remember seeing him the night of the attack. She held the photos without looking at them for a long moment after I handed them across, perhaps waiting for me to provide the name of the perpetrator, but I had been sworn to silence by my client. I wondered what thoughts were rushing through Ronnie's mind. Finally, her eyes drifted down.

"Is this the motherfu...I mean, the prick who did that to Ash?" she said, staring through the paper held in tight grips. "My father told me just before he, um, died, that the boy who was murdered that night wasn't the person who raped and beat Ashley. We were never allowed to talk about any of that to anyone outside the family. Hell, we didn't talk about it hardly at all between ourselves after Mr. Monreale came to get Ashley from our house. My mother would have a fit if anyone even mentioned that day and, of course, I had been forbidden from reaching out to her." Her eyes went distant with memories, then welled with tears. "How is Ash?"

I knew at least as much as Ronnie did about regrets over this all, but gave her no reaction and merely repeated my question about her remembering the person in the photographs. I wasn't there as an intermediary to repair a lost friendship, I was there on behalf of a client to ferret out the facts and prove a case the way it should have been done a decade ago.

"Ronnie," I said, "the photographs? Do you recognize the man?"

She shook her head slowly, then returned her gaze to the photographs of Dace Lamoureux and continued to either search her memory or burn the images there. I next showed her one of the photos which contained both her and Dace making eye contact at the back of the room. I could almost see the memory coming into focus for her.

Then I showed her a full face of him against the back wall of the piano bar. The look he wore that night was not at all like either of the publicity shots from the magazine and yearbook which I had first showed her; it was primal, animalistic, haunting. She nodded slowly.

"I did see him, Mr. Langdon," she said, her eyes misting again. "I did. I remember now. He looked at me as I walked by on my way to the bathroom. We had been drinking that night, and I was fairly drunk, but I do remember. Is that him? Did he do that to Ash? Do we know that for certain now?"

Her questions went unanswered, as much as it pained me. There was nothing more I needed *from* Ronnie Broussard, and had been instructed to give her nothing beyond what little I had. I collected the images and replaced them in my jacket. I finished off my Coke and was about to stand to go when she stopped me.

"Mr. Langdon, if you see Ashley, please tell her I miss her. It wasn't my decision for us to drift apart. My parents and her aunt made that call." She shrugged. "After a while, life goes on, you understand?"

I nodded. I did understand the drifting apart and life going on parts. For some reason, she reached out and hugged me, then asked me for a favor. I looked into her eyes and with the image of that petulant and frightened sixteen going on seventeen-year-old girl in my mind, nodded.

I walked away then.

Nobody had stolen the Saab, and I stopped and talked to Max for a minute before I went home as an old Elton John tune floated outside from the piano bar. It was one of my favorites of his from the '70s.

As I talked and listened to the distorted acoustics of the song waxing and waning on a shifting breeze, I realized I didn't really need to stop and talk to Max, but I didn't really want to go home and face that particular music.

As I walked into the quiet house just before eleven, I found a note on the kitchen counter.

# Chapter Thirty-three

I awoke in my recliner in the den. The local Saturday morning news was on the television. What had been a new bottle of bourbon, now about half drained, was on the end table next to a fully drained tumbler. Under the glass was Sandy's note. I slid it free and read it again. It didn't get any better through bloodshot eyes.

*Will:*
*Something is wrong in our lives and I'm at a loss to figure it out. I've tried so very hard to make our marriages work, and realize you have as well. Yet we always seem to be out of synch. You've become secretive again and please don't say you are just trying to shelter me by handling whatever this is all by yourself. That pretty young woman who came in yesterday worries me; and whatever you do, please do not attempt to placate me about her. Frankly, I'd rather you just tell me the truth - however hurtful - than attempt to beguile, or how you put it: protect me.*
*As much as it pains me, my darling, I have to tell you that I've concluded we are not going to make it if things don't change...SOON.*
*I've gone to bed with a sleeping pill and have turned off my phone. There's a rack of ribs from what used to be our favorite BBQ place in the oven, if you are hungry. I stopped on the way home, not knowing when you'd be here, or if you would have eaten when you did get back.*
*If you were with that woman tonight, please tell me, okay? I just need to know where WE are going.*
*Love, Sandy*
*P.S. Sorry about the gas in the Saab. Call it me being passive aggressive. ;)*

The house was quiet. I padded out to the kitchen in stocking feet. I had slept in my clothes on the chair after I had looked in on Sandy upstairs last night. I rubbed the stubble on my face. I needed a change and a shower. I could still smell the smoke from the bars in my jacket I had draped on the kitchen chair when I had come in. I picked it up and noticed it was full of stripper glitter from the hug Ronnie had given me before we parted company and I agreed to pass a message to Ashley for her. I removed the items from the pockets and rolled up the jacket then took it out to the garage and dropped it into the trunk of my car. I went back inside, grabbed the room temperature ribs from the oven and ripped one off the rack. I gnawed the bone clean and pulled another free. I walked to the guest bathroom, found a spare razor and shaving cream and put them to work. In the mirror I could see the collar of my shirt had glitter on it and when I looked, so did my pants. What was more disturbing, was the collar was smeared with ruddy makeup.

I undressed, rolled up my shirt and pants and then went back out to my car in my underwear and dropped them into the trunk on top of the jacket. When I came in again, I avoided the remaining ribs and jumped into the shower. The house was still quiet when I emerged ten minutes later. I went to the laundry room and found a clean pair of jeans and a relatively wrinkle-free shirt hanging there. There was a load of clothes in the dryer and I extracted a pair of underwear and socks. I dressed in the bathroom, brushed my teeth with my finger and some Colgate from a travel-sized tube I found in one of the drawers.

I returned to the kitchen and left Sandy a note.

*My dearest Sandy,*
*I agree we've been on a roller coaster, but know that I have remained true to you. I do what I do because it's the best I can do. It's all I can do. I'm trying very hard. I'll be home later. I've got to run out to the country for this case. PLEASE do not worry, Sandy. We're going to be just fine. Hope you slept well.*
*Love, Will*
*P.S. It's okay about the gas. I filled your tank. Can we get a new car? I hate that Saab. :P*

After transferring my computer bag from the Saab, I rolled out of our driveway in my new fun car which had replaced my 1998 Corvette on my 50th birthday the past August. The red Corvette had been great fun through my forties, but my 2008 jet-black Lexus SC430, while still a two-door convertible, fit my new body much better; and it still had plenty of the sportiness and get-up-and-go.

On my way out of town, I stopped in at the office and pulled the box from storage that contained the shoe and license plate which I had found on the river bank and the cards with the fingerprints I pulled from the plate, as well as other information developed on both the Monreale and Tom McDaniel cases. The McDaniel case, of course, was what had me initially locating Dave Saunders. I then picked up a breakfast wrap and a VitaminWater at a local bodega. Sandy had finally persuaded me to avoid as much junk food as possible and I hadn't been through a McDonald's drive thru in months. As a result, I'd lost a little weight and had been feeling better. Sorry, Hamburgler, but that's the truth.

I drove west on I-10. I've driven that road countless times in the past decade, but that morning was the first time since 1998 that I'd taken highway 70 south across the bridge at Donaldsonville. I found the Broussard home without a wrong turn and drove up to the unchanged house. As I turned off the ignition, I noticed the gazebo still stood, although it was no longer white, but a hideous orangey, cedar color. I stepped out, stretched and brushed a few stray breakfast wrap crumbs from my jeans, then walked to the door and rang the bell. The door opened moments later.

"Hello, Marcella," I said. "How have you been."

"Just fine, sir," she said, her brow knitting in confusion.

"William Langdon," I said, refreshing her memory and bringing a smile of recognition to her face. "I'd like to see Mrs. Broussard, if she's available."

Marcella stepped aside and I stepped into a time machine. Nothing had changed over the last decade, not even the furniture in the parlor where Marcella led me to await the lady of the house. As I stretched my legs around the room, I did notice that one thing had changed. There were no photographs anywhere which showed Dr. Broussard.

"Mr. Langdon?" she said.

I turned to see Debbie Broussard standing in the doorway. She had aged ten hard years. Her face was sallow, her eyes bloodshot above puffy, purplish bags she had obviously long ago stopped trying to hide with makeup.

"Mrs. Broussard," I said. "Thank you for seeing me."

"I'm seeing you long enough to tell you that I will not see you," she said. "I'm on my way out."

"It would only take a bit of time, Mrs. Broussard. It's fairly important and has to do with Ashley Monreale. I spoke with Ronnie yesterday." I omitted the where and when. "I know how you feel about this whole matter, but was still hoping you'd be willing to help."

I had tossed in everything I could, but I could see immediately the woman would not be swayed. There were only a couple of things I needed from her, but if worse came to worst I probably could go on without them. Part of me understood how she felt. The Monreale situation had taken nearly as large a toll on this woman's husband and family as it had on me. The only difference being, I hadn't taken the easy way out from under the guilt and pain.

"I'm sorry, Mr. Langdon," she said, nervously shifting her feet.

She walked clear of the parlor portal in the direction of the front door, obviously assuming I would follow. I did. She opened the door for me and asked that I not come again. I nodded and stepped onto the step. As she began to close the door, I noticed Marcella down the hallway waving to me and pointing to her watch. She held up five fingers. I walked out to my car and drove off the property. Several minutes later, I watched from the roadway opposite the way I assumed she'd go as Mrs. Broussard's winter frost 2008 Jaguar came out and disappeared around the corner. I knew the line's colors because we had looked at Jags before I bought the Lexus. I smiled to myself at the thought of how the color fit her. I waited a minute or two, then drove back up the Broussard's drive. Marcella opened the door and came out to the car before I could get out.

"The Missus is a cold, hard woman, Mr. Langdon," Marcella said. "The doctor was a good man. A kind man. But a weak man, God rest him. The only time I saw him win an argument with his wife was the day those brothers brought Ashley to this house. Mrs. Broussard had wanted to turn her back on that poor girl."

"I don't want to cause you any problems, Marcella," I said. "I just need to know if Dr. Broussard had kept records or anything else from the time Ashley was here, before her father came for her. It's important or I wouldn't be here."

Marcella nodded and indicated for me to follow. She walked with me in trail to the garage in the back of the house. I watched her pull down a ladder and climb into the attic area. A minute later, she came down carrying as small box.

"Mrs. Broussard told me to burn these things when the doctor killed himself," she said. "It's everything that he had kept. I don't know why I saved it, but I did. Please take it and use whatever you find helpful. I know the doctor would want you to have it."

I carried the box out of the garage with Marcella in trail to my car and dropped it onto the passenger seat. It would be best for the woman if Debbie Broussard didn't come back for some reason and find me there.

"Thank you, Marcella. I appreciate your help."

She stood on the passenger side of my car as I walked around to the driver's side.

"You kept your word to me, Mr. Langdon," she said. "You tried to help those people." Her eyes moved toward the box on my seat. "I hope these things help. Whatever you're doing."

I drove back out to the road and wove my way to a park well away from the house. I pulled into a parking spot, got out and walked to a picnic table where I placed the box. With the top popped, my eyes went wide as I spied the items inside. One by one, I removed each piece of Ashley's clothing she had worn the night of her attack, each sealed in a plastic zip-top bag. At the bottom of the box, I found a manilla envelope.

I replaced the bags with the clothing items into the box and spilled the contents of the envelope onto the upturned cover.

It contained Ashley's phony driver's license, the cash which was still all there, medical notes regarding the girl's condition, examination, and treatment in remarkably legible handwriting which when I checked against the document in my computer bag matched the suicide note. Lastly, I picked up another letter-size envelope which had the doctor's Baton Rouge office address in the upper left corner. I unfolded the single piece of paper it contained and quickly scanned the document. It was what had been promised in the doctor's last writing. I smiled, refolded the paper and placed it back into the envelope.

A minute later, I was headed east out of White Castle, calling Teddy.

Over the nearly thirty years we have known each other, Teddy had never turned me down for a favor; although this time he sounded skeptical about the idea I was relaying.

"The Fibbies have become really paranoid since 9-11, Big Dog," he said. "It's not a free-for-all anymore, plus they track down every login to their CODIS and IAFIS sites. Everyone is tiptoeing around their databases these days because they don't want to get a visit from the guys with no sense of humor."

"DHS?"

"To mention just one group of humorless assholes," he said.

"This is important, Teddy," I said. "I've got a DNA report done on the rape kit taken by a medical doctor proximate to the Ashley Monreale attack in 1998. I just need to know if we've got this piece of shit locked down or not."

I brought Teddy fully up-to-date, telling him the girl had come to see me and why I was looking for what I was looking for, but held back Ashley's specific requests of me.

"You don't need to convince me, buddy," Teddy said. "I'm just thinking of a cover story for making a CODIS inquiry on one sitting and one soon-to-be-sitting United States senator without raising every set of federal eyebrows from Chicago to D.C."

CODIS was the acronym for the FBI's computerized 'Combined DNA Index System', which the Bureau first envisioned and proposed to Congress in the late 1980s when it hoped to do with the newly emerging science of DNA identification using a computerized database which they had done with digital fingerprint cataloguing in the early 1980s. For political purposes, CODIS was originally specified to maintain records only for convicted sex offenders. Nobody would go on record opposing that, and yet, like everything the government does, the scope of CODIS grew over time.

By 1989, DNA had made its way into the first courtrooms and had begun convicting perpetrators as well as exonerating suspects wrongfully charged.   The CODIS system was legislated into existence with the passage of the DNA Identification Act of 1994.  By the end of 2007, the system boasted the largest DNA database in the world, *officially* claiming over five million records in its files.  Many suspected the number was much higher, given nearly every state, as well as the federal government had passed subsequent laws allowing DNA sampling of many different classes of individuals, including in some cases, those merely arrested for misdemeanor offenses.   Sampling was done on arrest, not conviction, which drove the ACLU types nuts and they sued, but there was little they could do about it when the lower courts ruled repeatedly in favor of the laws and collection practices.   Along with criminal and arrestee DNA coding, records were stored on military personnel and many employees of the federal government, which rumored to include, although was not acknowledged publicly, elected federal officials.  The last category was the most highly classified segment of the database.

"Tell you what," Teddy said finally.  "Let me think about it a while, make a call or two to people I know I can trust, then I'll call you back."

"Sounds like a plan to me," I said.  "I'll be around.  I'm thinking a trip is on the horizon, but most likely tomorrow.  Monday at the latest."

"Election day is Tuesday," he said.   "You thinking of playing Superman again and making a difference before then?"

"Can't say, Teddy," I said.  "I love you like a brother and owe you more than I'll ever be able to repay, but I gave my word to the client on this one."

"Say no more," he said.  "I'll call you."

We disconnected and I was feeling a bit lighter.   Teddy always seemed to know just what to say, and what not to say to me.  I stopped and put the top down.  Around the next turn on the Great River Road, I spotted the long hedgerow fronting Jackson Stempler's plantation home. In searching the parish records online after Ashley had left my office the day before, I determined he still owned the property.  According to his local manager, who was listed as the preferred contact in the public records, he was currently staying there.  That morning, on the drive out to the Broussard's place in White Castle, I had received a return call from Samantha Mimieux advising the man agreed to see me.

My research revealed Jackson Stempler was a self-made man born of hardscrabble roots in 1927 in a small farmhouse on the plains of western Minnesota.  He had tried his hands at many things, according to articles I had read, before stumbling by shear coincidence into the world of international venture capital at the age of fifty-two when he lent a small amount of money to a burgeoning computer entrepreneur and taken a share of the company in lieu of repayment.   Two years later, he had become an instant multimillionaire when the entrepreneur's company went public and Jackson Stempler became what the press then labeled an 'overnight success story'.

The gap in the hedgerow was still there, only now it was bookended with two, substantial, red-bricked columns and a black, wrought iron gate.  I pulled off the road and inched close to the call box, pressed the button and waited.   When the man answered, I identified myself and informed him that Mr. Stempler was expecting me; he replied that he wasn't senile and remembered quite well he had agreed to see me.   The gate swung open and I drove in.

The plantation home and grounds looked nearly identical to the last time I was there, ten years ago, although there were no vehicles parked out front and the old Mustang had been certainly long gone.   As I approached the end of the drive, the front door opened and a man, easily recognized as Jackson Stempler, strode onto the porch.   He was in his early eighties and articles on the internet reported he was a 'vibrant octogenarian' and as charming, dashing, and debonair as he always had been.   The man was of average height, slender, wearing charcoal slacks, white shirt open at the collar and a blue blazer.   His hair was light brown touched with gray, cut conservatively, and thinning.   It was reported his eyes were black, penetrating, and unreadable, however, from the driveway, I couldn't tell.   His face was neutral as I pulled to a stop and shut off the ignition; and he smiled as I got out of the car.   He had come down off the porch and was looking at my Lexus as I came around and offered my hand.

"How do you like it?" he said as he accepted the handshake, his focus on the car and not yet the visitor.   "I've read some good things.   You may not know it, but I'm a bit of an automophile."

I had read the man was more than just a 'bit of an automophile' - a lover of cars - he was one of the world's preeminent collectors.

"It's good for an old man like me," I said.   "Fits me better than my Corvette did."

He laughed.

"Old man, my ass," he said, putting his hand on my shoulder.   "Just wait twenty years or so, then come talk to me about being an old man."

He extended his arm in invitation and I walked with him along the cobbled path to the house.   It was a beautiful day for the first of November in Louisiana and as we climbed the three steps onto the veranda, he suggested we use the oversized wicker rocking chairs to have a chat.   As we sat, he asked if I wanted something to drink, and suggested lemonade.   I accepted, and a minute later a tray with a pitcher of lemonade and glasses with ice was placed on the small table between the two of us by a young woman who returned to the house without a word, closing the door behind her.

My host poured, I sampled, and when he asked, I had to admit the lemonade was as good as I'd ever tasted. He told me the lemons were organically grown on his estate on the Amalfi coast in Italy and he always brought a supply with him. How he got the fruit into the United States and past customs wasn't a question one needed to ask of a man like Jackson Stempler, so I just enjoyed the drink and the late morning quiet for a moment before I began. Soon, however, the memories pushed into the fore and I became eager to begin.

I started by telling the man I appreciated his time, especially given that he may not know who I am or why I had asked to see him on such short notice. I had been a bit vague with Samantha.

He leaned forward, elbows on his knees, his glass of lemonade gripped tightly in a large, sinewy hand. He looked straight into me and I can attest the stories about the man's piercing, unflinching eyes are accurate.

"Mr. Langdon, I know exactly who you are and that's why I agreed to see you. I consider myself a gregarious host, but I treasure my private times, and this place is one of the retreats where I can just come and sit and rock." He sat back in the chair and rocked slightly. He sipped his lemonade. "And, drink lemonade. Now, I can suspect why you are here, and when you tell me, we'll both know, but we'll get to that shortly." His eyes focused on the distance. "First, let's just try to enjoy the moment, shall we?"

I tried. I really did. I took a deep breath and another drink of lemonade. I rocked. I listened to the quiet. It *was* peaceful out there, even with the memories the place carried; and quiet behind the hedge that far from the road's traffic which wasn't even heard and only seen as an occasional brief flash of color and chrome through the iron gate. It had been a long time since I'd sat like this. Too long. After several minutes, I did begin to relax a little, although my mind never truly stops churning. It's just how I'm wired.

There were many things which had not been made public back in 1998. The police never did figure out the connection between Tony and the two kids from Harvard, and me. Neither I, nor anyone else who knew about the abduction, rape, and beating of Ashley Monreale had ever said a word about it outside of our little secret circle, except for me confiding in Teddy and Stan, that is, so the local cops never had that link in the chain. Being an ex-member of the cop brotherhood, I know they never totally bought my story about being out there that night as mere happenstance, but I stuck to it and eventually their visits and questions ebbed, then stopped altogether; interest faded and manpower was needed on other things. The case files were closed, and southern Louisiana moved on, another juicy mystery appended to its long and colorful local lore.

Neither would the whole truth be divulged that day on this porch. From the articles I had read on the man seated across from me, sipping lemonade and rocking with his being seemingly detached from anything but the moment, I understood this was one of his more notable negotiating tactics, one he used quite successfully in business to lull people off their guard. However, no matter how much of his delicious lemonade I drank, or how much rocking and relaxing my guest led me to do, I knew I would only share with Jackson Stempler the information he needed to know, while I sought to obtain what I needed to forge yet another nail in what had become in my mind as Dace Lamoureux's metaphorical coffin. Jackson Stempler may be a wealthy, successful, internationally renowned businessman and rule the upper stratosphere in that world, but I'm William Langdon, an ex-cop and P.I., and this was cop stuff.

The key for me would be to tie the soon-to-be senator to this place, to the trip made by Dave Saunders and Cindy Spagliano, whom I now knew from the yearbook photos were all friends. Confirming that they were all here together would then make it all the more difficult for Dace Lamoureux, and his people up north, to lie to me. Not that I wasn't certain they'd try.

I finished my lemonade, set my glass back onto the tray, then declined a refill. Mr. Stempler set his glass down as well and we both understood it was time to get down to business. My host suggested we drop the formalities and use each other's first name. He told me to call him by the familiar Jack, and asked what I prefer to be called by friends. I told him that most people called me William, that only my wife called me Will - the Otto times aside - nobody got away with Willy with a 'y' anymore, Bill was totally out of the question, and one of my old partners called me Big Dog. The whole litany made him laugh. The man had an honest and easy laugh. I'd also read about that. I didn't mention that he needed more padding on the rockers because Willie, with an 'ie', was digging into my back at the moment, but that was a different matter.

"Well, how about we settle on William?" he said, still smiling. "Seems the least complicated of the batch."

"It's a deal, Jack," I said.

I realized if he knew who I was and suspected why I was there, he probably knew as much about me as I did about him and most likely more. So, I told him everything that could be found in the public record, then added how and why I had initially come to track down Dave Saunders. His eyebrows raised at that disclosure, although it had been provided to the various, local authorities several times and I was certain it was recorded in the investigative files, even though I had never mentioned who had hired me to any of the detectives or deputies, other than as an allusion to a client from up north. They had accepted that at face value. I wasn't certain my new friend, Jack, would.

I told him a redacted version of how I had first heard of Dave Saunders and how I had come to his house days before the night I met up with Tony Gators' men. I did not mention Dace Lamoureux or his growing connection to what had precipitated Tony's vendetta, nor did I mention Tom McDaniel by name or the other two large gentlemen who showed up on the scene several times. He watched me, nodded from time to time. In essence, I told him that I had been hired by a client from up north to track down and confirm the whereabouts of Dave Saunders. I told him there had been no mention of Cindy Spagliano, but that she had been there the first time I had met the boy. I didn't tell him about their apprehensive behavior, like they had expected someone who wasn't me, or about my short-lived suspicion they were caught up in some type of illicit activity at the place, perhaps involving drugs. He accepted what I told him at face value, or at least I thought he did.

"And the night they died?" he said when I paused.

I continued the lie which had started outside the diner in Thibodaux that night.

"I had come out one last time and walked in on the kidnapping," I said, which was truthful, semantically. "I played it the only way I could, given the totality of the circumstances."

He nodded. He knew my background, which meant Jack surely understood I had been a pro.

"Kidnapping?" he said, his eyebrows rising again. "Interesting word with sinister undertones. You consider there was some type of ransom situation in play? Perhaps that involved me? That this criminal was interested in holding them and extorting a ransom from me? That's an interesting twist I hadn't heard before. Not that I hadn't given it some thought myself over the years, though."

I shook my head. He clearly knew better than to ask, and I knew it was all a test. He didn't want me to lie to him any more than I wanted to do it.

"No," I said. "Mr. Monreale clearly had other motivations." I paused. "That much was quite clear from the way things went, and whatever those motivations were, they died with the man."

He leaned forward in his chair, stared deeply into me, then nodded again. He'd read the reports; he certainly had the means to obtain them, and from what I was about to learn, a deeper, personal connection to the girl.

Jack's impenetrable eyes misted, then gazed into the distance. He appeared to come to a conclusion, then began to speak.

"What I'm going to tell you, William, isn't known by anyone but myself. The investigator whom I had hired is long since dead, and my time is coming soon enough, so what does it matter now?" He paused. "I've been diagnosed with inoperable pancreatic cancer, and have perhaps six months to live. There are many people who could profit handsomely with that knowledge, including you, were you to sell it to any number of them. But, from what I know of you, and it's probably far more than you suspect, you're a man I don't even have to ask to keep the confidences I am about to relate to you, including what I already have regarding my health."

I nodded. He settled back into the rocker. I did the same.

"I had no connection to Dave Saunders, only knew him by name in passing through Cindy. Her given name was Lorelei, you may or may not know - Cynthia was her middle name, yet since leaving Minnesota for Harvard, she always went by Cindy. I first learned of her existence in 1987 when I hired a private detective to track down some overgrown trails of my past. I had turned sixty that year and if you've read the public information on me, you'll know I had lead a dichotic life. For fifty-four years, I rolled across the world like the tumbleweeds we'd see on the prairies when I was a boy. I was unanchored to anything or anyone. In 1981, I began a new life, merely by happenstance. I was an overnight success story, a fortune made by a lucky investment or with shrewd insight into the future, depending upon which media concoction you cared to believe. Frankly, I was just helping out the son of a friend and never expected a return of my investment."

He laughed.

"I left home when I was fifteen, 'hit the rails' as we used to call it. For a couple of years, I worked odd jobs wherever I could find them, which in those days of early World War II was fairly easy to do. I'd roll into a town, pick up a job for a few weeks or a month, and then light out again. I swept floors, hauled asbestos, painted, plumbed, and wired all sorts of buildings. You name any menial job in this world, and over the years, I probably tried my hand at it. I had only gone through eight years of schooling before my father had insisted that was all the learning which was necessary for any farmer and I obediently settled into that as my life's lot. I tried to honor my father's plan for me, but I was a curious, and precocious, and restless young man. So after two seasons of full-time plowing and planting, I set out to see the world.

"I was self educated after leaving the farm, and would read anything I could get my hands on. In 1944, I joined the Navy and shipped out on a submarine to the South Pacific. SS-245, the U.S.S. Cobia. We sailed her from Pearl Harbor in June of 1944 on her first war patrol. She was a new boat and when we returned to Hawaii in August, we joked the paint fumes came closer to killing us than any Japanese had on that first outing. It would be a much different story on the next outing, let me tell you."

He grinned, poured himself another glass of lemonade and took a sip.

"It was on that return to port from that first sail that I met a young girl in Honolulu. Her name was Kailani, which meant sea and sky. Unbeknownst to me when we again went out on patrol that September, I had left something of myself behind with the girl. She gave birth to my son in May of 1945, which is something I didn't know until long after he was gone."

Jack told me things that hadn't appeared in the articles which had described him as a lifelong bachelor without children. The son he had never known even existed had in-turn sired a son out of wedlock in 1960 in Oregon at the age of fifteen, but then had pulled his life together, attended the Citadel, came out and joined the Army as a second lieutenant, married the mother, left his new wife behind and seven-year-old son to go off to war in Viet Nam and was killed in 1968 during the Tet offensive. The grandson had carried on the growing Stempler tradition by fathering a child with a young girl at a Minneapolis Styx concert in 1976, then promptly disappeared and never resurfaced. I sat silently and watched him drift into memories.

"We Stempler men are a wild lot when we're young, I guess; I was, my son was, my grandson was. See, Cindy was my great-granddaughter, William, although she never knew it. She always called me Uncle Jack, and that's the role I played in her life. Not even her mother knew of the blood connection. Now, in all the world, I know, and you know."

I had seen nothing of any of that in the media articles. When he finished, I briefly wondered how he had managed to put it all aside and not look further into the events after the kids were murdered, but then I realized, who could he really blame beyond Tony, and he was already dead. I also fully understood his sense of helplessness in it all, and his desire to put it all behind him since there was little else to be done. It was a tragedy, and it was over. I had the same reaction after Sandy's accident and the loss of our unborn child. I had just wanted the whole nightmare to be tucked into the past because nothing could be undone, but unlike Jackson Stempler who had used the time and pain to redouble his global fortune and then put most of it to work in charitable trusts, I had used much of the time to try to drown the pain in Kentucky bourbon.

Like Jack, however - and this I merely assumed from his current state of melancholy - through the years, I had dreamed of it often. Only my dreams included not only the visions of seeing both Dave Saunders and Cindy Spagliano die horrible, violent deaths, but Ashely Monreale, who many times was replaced in that bed in White Castle by each of my own daughters in turn, battered and broken. I'd wake each time in a cold sweat, wondering what more I could have, or should have done.

I accepted a refill on the lemonade then, and Jack had another as well. It was how we closed that narrative.

After a moment passed, I told him that I had suspicions that another person had come down with Dave and Cindy. His eyes narrowed as he weighed the implications, but we had made enough of a connection that he didn't ask. Somehow, I felt he knew I'd tell him, in the right time.

"I can't say if anyone had been with Dave and Cindy here in 1998," he said. "I was in Singapore at the time. Cindy had called me out of the blue and said a friend needed to get away for a while and I agreed to let them use the place. She had asked me a year or so earlier if she and Dave, who were dating then, could use the house for a getaway, but they had had a falling out before that trip ever happened. I just assumed they had gotten back together when I heard it was Dave who was down here with her. I never suspected there was anyone else other than the two of them." He paused and sipped his lemonade and his eyes focused beyond the distant hedgerow. "Before or after."

"You know I was here, Jack, several times. I never saw anyone other than Dave and Cindy, although I did have reason to suspect there was a third person, another man." I remembered the old black woman. "Oh, and there was an old, black woman I saw out back who appeared a couple of times. She'd come and go from what I'd assume was an apartment in that old barn out back."

He smiled and his eyes went wide in realization, not in the remembrance of the old woman, but in what she may have seen a decade ago and how they had never spoken of it before. He set down his glass of lemonade on the tray and stood and invited me to walk along with him. I set down my glass as well and stood. We both stretched out a few kinks before we moved far from the chairs. He led the way around the veranda to the back.

"That would be Auntie D," he said with an affection. "She's the end of the line of folks who had been born on this land and I promised when I bought the place she could stay on for life. She's still back there, in an apartment I built for her above my garage; the old barn you mention is a very modern garage and workshop for some of my collectibles." He winked over his shoulder as he descended the steps and started across the lawn. "It fools most folks, and rightly so. I spent a great deal of money on the ruse. Auntie D turned ninety-seven this year, and is bedridden now. She used to be a helluva cook and remains a true treasure. I've hired full-time people to care for her. Her body is failing, but she remains sharp as a tack. Her daddy and late husband were share croppers here and her grandparents had been slaves on the plantation. You know, William, it's sobering to be this close to an institution as evil as slavery. I they told us they didn't have any kids and Chrissy was intimating to Sandy that they most likely would continue to hold off for a while longer. Good idea, I thought. Kids shouldn't be around that kind of thing. I could tell them stories.

About the time we all had finished our salads of beets, cucumbers, tomatoes, and goat cheese, the conversation slid to sports between John, myself, and the rest of the men at the table, while the women chatted about whatever women chat about. I wasn't listening. When Anita and Mr. Eugene brought out the heaping, steaming, oversize serving bowls filled with Anita's fresh Gulf seafood pasta all conversation stopped. There were four large bowls for the table and Anita assured us that there was plenty in the kitchen and invited us all to eat hearty. From the way people dug in, I'd consider the last part of that was unnecessary.

As I worked my way through a second helping of the main course my cell phone began to vibrate in my pocket. I pulled it out, checked the caller ID and silenced the ring tone which was coming next so I wouldn't disturb my fellow guests.

"The bad guys," I whispered in Sandy's ear.

She rolled her eyes.

"Don't let Anita take my plate," I whispered into her ear and then sliding my chair backward.

"I'm certain she has more plates, Will," she said.

"Well, I'm kind of fond of this one."

I excused myself from the table and answered the call in the front hall, moving outside onto the oversized porch before continuing the conversation.

"Mr. Langdon, I hate to disturb your evening," the woman said. "I'm in the process of doing some follow-up with many of those who returned our contracts for The August Project."

So, that's what they called spying on the attendees to the opposite party's convention: The August Project. She had pronounced the first word like the month the convention would be held in, but something told me the true believers used a pronunciation which turned 'August' from a month to 'august' meaning auspicious, grand, impressive. At least the woman on the other end of the phone didn't make the leap, and as a man with a wife on the opposite end of the political spectrum, I silently thanked her for not making me force a laugh at the word play.

"That's all right, Susan," I said. That was her name: Susan Delp, and we had spoken on the phone and faxed back and forth a couple of times. "Is there a problem with the contract I signed?"

"Oh, not at all, Mr. Langdon, this is an informal follow up." A pause. "It's something we don't normally put on paper, you see?"

"Okay," I said, wondering exactly what that could mean since I really didn't *see*.

"What I'm calling for is to ask if you'd be available at your established rates and terms for any special projects others in our organization may have. We prefer they remain with approved vendors, you see, and there are times when we get a request from outside our national offices."

Whatever that may mean, I thought. I still didn't *see*. I'd play along, though; it can't hurt to be on a list. I could always say no if they did call.

"So long as it's not illegal or in conflict with the interests of any other client, I would have to say we'd be happy to consider accepting referral cases at out established rates and terms."

I was really glad Sandy insisted I bump our standard rates by twenty-five percent for The August Project. Her expressed reasoning was they may be very slow to pay, however, I secretly suspect she just wanted to sock it to the party which held diametrically opposed political beliefs from her own. "Of course, we'd anticipate establishing a separate retainer for each outside project."

"Of course," she said. "That seems to be the position of most of the savvy among your competitors as well."

"Glad to hear we're in good company," I said.

"All right, I'll note the file and let you get back to your evening. Again, I'm sorry to intrude. Good night."

"Good night, Susan."

I flipped the phone closed, let the conversation slide into deep memory, and went back inside to continue enjoying Anita's fresh Gulf seafood pasta, and to further deconstruct John and Chrissy's relationship. Why do I continue to use the full name of Anita's signature dish? Well, it's just that wonderful and I feel using a shorthand version in these pages would do it, and her, an injustice. If you ever get the chance to sample it, you'll know exactly what I'm talking about.

Ashley and Ronnie locked themselves in their room and studied from right after their last class on Wednesday until the wee hours of Thursday to get a jump on projects and homework which would be due over the course of the next week. They skipped dinner in the cafeteria which was gummy cheese pizza on Wednesdays, and instead munched a couple of granola bars and drank Pepsi. They were on a mission to have nothing on their minds but partying and Mardi Gras once they left school on Saturday afternoon. Most of the other girls would be going home for the long weekend after Friday's classes and return for Ash Wednesday afternoon Mass, which was when Ashley and Ronnie planned to come back as well.

Classes were scheduled to resume in the morning on Thursday next, with assignments due beginning with the first morning class that day. Things were so much different at a Catholic boarding school than it was for their counterparts at public schools. There was accountability there, and no lying to the nuns about homework eaten by the family dog. After their brains were fried, their bodies remained too hopped up on caffeine and sugar to sleep, so they decided to take a walk around the grounds about three in the morning. The night was cool, and the grass dewy as they shuffled along in canvas sneakers, jeans and sweatshirts.

"Hey, Ash, I've got a question for you," Ronnie said.

"What's up?"

"Bobby's pressuring me again. You know, to go all the way." She looked around in the darkness to make certain they were away from any prying ears, and then in a low, conspiratorial tone: "Sex."

"I know what going all the way is, Ronnie. I'm not *that* innocent."

"What do you think, Ash?"

"That's your call, Ronnie," Ashley said, hoping the subject would resolve itself with that. Being not that innocent aside, she just wasn't comfortable talking about sex, even with Ronnie.

"I know," Ronnie said, flopping her arms nervously and taking huge, bouncing, sugar-fueled steps to pull ahead of Ashley. Ronnie turned and faced her. "I like him, and all, but I'm not sure I love him. Heck, Ash, I don't think I even know what love is yet." She tossed up her arms and again fell in step beside Ashley.

"Then don't do it." Ashley saw that as an opening to steer the conversation more toward love and away from sex, and she took it. "Now, if it's love you want to talk about, you've come to the right girl. I'm in love with the thought of being in love. Someday."

"You're a hopeless romantic, that's what you are," Ronnie said. "Do you *really* think you have to be in love to do it?"

"Geeze, Ronnie, do you want to be known as some kind of slut?"

"No, duh," Ronnie said and again began her nervous flopping and bouncing. "It's just that I like him and don't want to lose him over something as stupid as sex. I mean, it's just sex."

"Those are his words, aren't they. The 'it's just sex' thing."

Ashley had stopped walking. She crossed her arms and extended a foot. It was her 'don't mess with my girlfriend' stance.

"Yeah. That's what Bobby said, Ash." Ronnie hung her head. "I'm just confused."

Ashley felt an anger rising inside her. If Bobby was there right now, she'd probably twist his nuts off. That would fix him, she thought; but since Bobby was not there and his nuts were relatively safe, for now, she started walking again.

"You know, Ronnie, last summer I went to visit my aunt in California."

"I remember. My dad almost killed me when he saw the cell phone bill the next month."

"Well, my aunt is my mom's older sister. I think sometimes she feels the need to replace my mom, especially as I'm getting older. She says a young woman needs to talk to another woman about certain things. Things the young woman just cannot discuss with her dad. So, she sat me down and had what she called 'The Talk' one afternoon. Not the silly birds and bees metaphors, or the strict mechanics of the biology, or the right versus wrong that they preach about in church, but about the connection between sex and love, and the regrets she had about the choices she made way back in the 60s."

"The 60s? Geeze, how old is she?"

"She's a year older than my mom would have been now, so, like forty-seven. I think she was born in the 50s. Really old, I know, but what she said still made sense to me."

They had come to a small concrete bench along the back courtyard wall, so Ashley sat down and Ronnie joined her. They each crooked one leg across the bench, tossed their other leg over their ankle and sat facing each other. The only sounds back there that time of night were crickets chirping and frogs calling others for mating. Ashley momentarily tried to remember the formula for calculating the temperature by the number of cricket chirps per minute to erase the mental image of two fat frogs doing the nasty, but that was something she had learned way back in Brownies and so the image of frog on frog remained. Disgusting, she thought.

"Why didn't you talk to me about this before, Ash?"

"Because, you weren't going on and on about sex before."

Ronnie pursed her lips, hung her head again.

"My aunt says sex is a very personal thing. It's something that people talk about with other people and then often regret having said anything at all because it can be embarrassing later on..."

"I'm sorry, Ash," Ronnie interrupted. "You're the only person I can talk to about this stuff. I certainly can't talk to my mom about it. You see how cold she is to my dad most of the time. I don't ever want to be like that. You should see my dad's eyes sometimes when she gets that way. It really hurts him. Besides, I don't have any aunts."

"What?" Ashley asked. "Geeze, Ronnie, I don't mind talking to you about anything. I'm your best friend and I wasn't thinking you'd have regrets about bringing this up, but I wanted you to hear the high points of my aunt's advice."

"Oh," Ronnie said, a bit embarrassed. "Please go on, professor."

"So, anyway. She said back in the 60s, people were doing it whenever they wanted with whoever they wanted. Is it whoever or whomever?"

"Whomever, I think," Ronnie said. "The answer to the question of 'Who is she doing it with?' is 'him', not 'he'."

"What?"

travel the world and it always horrifies me that human beings still hold others in such brutal servitude even today."

He shook his head, pointed to a fire ant mound which we both avoided. Before we went up to see the old woman, Jack took me inside the workshop and gave me a tour. It was then that I told him I had inspected the building before from the outside, discovered its facade and had for a short while suspected some type of illicit activity such as drug manufacturing was going on. I left the story there and he laughed at the thought. After he relocked the garage, he took me upstairs to meet Auntie D.

The old woman studied me as I walked into her room with Jack. She was frail and thin, but well taken care of; she was sitting up in a hospital bed and her eyes were sharp and clear. Jack introduced me merely as a friend looking into the events of the time when Dave and Cindy had been here. Her eyes misted at the airing of the names.

"Ain't nobody asked me 'bout that in a long time," she said. "Not since them police come by." Her eyes hardened and moved to me. "Whatchu want rakin' up all that pain all over again, boy?"

Jack stepped aside, then left the room with the nurse, leaving me to sink or swim with the old woman on my own. I approached the bed, slid a chair over and sat down after I asked her if it was okay. As I moved the chair into place, I considered what I could and should say to her, selected a couple of easy questions, beginning with the most obvious.

"Auntie D," I began. "I'm sorry, may I call you that?"

"Ever'body does," she said. "If'n you're a friend of Uncle Jack, you can feel free, boy."

"I just have a couple of questions," I said. "I hope not to upset you."

She snorted and waved that away.

"Already been done, boy, I ain't lived my life in no posh parlors. I done lived on the hard side of this world, so I be used to pain. I seen all any woman ever had, and be the Good Lord willin', I gonna see a little bit more." She displayed a disarming, toothless grin. "But since neither of us know His timetable, don't you think you best get to it, boy?"

"Do you remember when Dave Saunders and Cindy Spagliano were here?"

"I sure do. He was a good boy, and she seemed a decent sort too."

"Was there anyone else with them?" I asked, taking her advice and cutting to the chase.

"That other one," she spat and her eyes narrowed.

"Do you remember who that was?"

"His name was Dace," she said. "Don't remember the last name, if I ever got it. He was no good, that one. Not like Dave. I could tell that the first time I met him, afore Cindy come."

"Didn't they all come together?" I asked, although thinking coming at two different times would make sense. I had seen only the Mustang, but from the recovered license plate and identifying of the vehicle by others, it could be considered a fact that Dave's Cadillac Escalade had been in Louisiana at the same time.

"Dave and the other one come first, three maybe four days afore Cindy come. Then, three days or so before they took 'em..."

Her voice caught and she began to cough. I gave her a glass of water from the nightstand, held it while Auntie D sipped. The coughing wore her down, and she rested a moment with her eyes closed before continuing.

"That Dace done up and disappeared one day. I seen and heard him light out early one mornin'. Didn't see him after that." She paused, appeared to be thinking. "No, I did see him again. Two days before, that would have been Fat Tuesday. I remember cuz Dave and Cindy went to Nawlins for the night. They was gonna stay here with me, but I kicked them in their butts and sent 'em to have some fun."

She smiled at the memory.

I wondered if she realized the chain of coincidences which began with that first link: a simple change of plans. Not that I'd ever tell her.

"So, Dace came back again after they left? What did he do?"

"He come back, look like he been sleepin' in the swamp. He sneaked into the house, then come out a bit later, all done up. Never seen him after that. Two nights later, them men come and took Dave and Cindy. But I never seen none of that."

I slipped an image from my pocket and unfolded the page. She took it, held it close and looked it over.

"That be him, that one," she said, then tossed the paper onto the thin blanket.

I could see the venom in her eyes as I retrieved the page.

"What he do?" she asked.

"I'm working on it, Auntie D," I said.

"You with the police, boy?"

"I used to be. In Chicago. Now I'm just trying to help someone."

"Chicago, huh?" she said. "What's your name, boy?

"William," I said. "William Langdon."

She nodded and patted my hand. I could see she was wearing down, but at the mention of my name she lifted a little, as if there was some recognition in the name.

"You a good man, William, tryin' to help them two like you done. They told me about you. The police." Her eyes narrowed. "Say you killed the man what done it to 'em."

I leaned forward and held her gaze.

"Shot him right between the eyes, Auntie D," I said.

"Good," she said, and then she closed her eyes.

I left the room when it sounded as if she had drifted off to sleep and Jack and I made our way back to the front porch. I had found what I had come looking for, but then a thought hit me and I asked Jack about the cars and the personal items left behind. He told me the Mustang had been picked up by someone after the police had released it to Samantha, and the duffles had also been taken by the police but never returned, to him anyway. He had no information about the Escalade.

I shook his hand and thanked him for everything. He made no final requests and asked no further questions. I was thankful I didn't have to lie to the man any more than I already had, mostly by omission. I left him sitting on the porch, a glass of lemonade in his hand and a distant look on his face. I started the car, gave a final wave and drove away. The gate swung open automatically as I approached. At the main road, I turned right and headed back to New Orleans.

My cell phone vibrated and rang as I drove along I-10; it was Teddy calling me back. He said he had been burning up the phone lines, pulling favors, and telling a few white lies. Teddy was now a deputy chief, and was only two years from retirement, but even his rank wouldn't sway the FBI contacts he had called. They had more to lose than he did if they got caught poking around in the high security areas of the CODIS database, they had all told him. What Teddy told me was there was just no way the Fibbies would release the DNA profile of a sitting United States senator to the Chicago P.D. Period. The best he could do was get a DNA expert with access agree to view my results and give him an off-the-record opinion with a blind search of CODIS.

I didn't deal with DNA evidence, and when I was on the force, the training we received was only enough to give a passing acquaintance with the burgeoning science. When I had left CPD in 1993, DNA was an emerging and promising technology in legal terms, but I was mainly working the narcotics end of things in those last years, and we didn't get much call for that kind of analysis.

Teddy asked if I could scan and email the report from Dr. Broussard and then he'd forward it to his contact at the FBI. He also suggested the sooner the better, before the woman had a chance to change her mind.

"If I can get some fresh DNA, can we get it tested?" I asked.

"Before Tuesday?" he said. "Not with the FBI lab. They have a thirty day backlog and I'm about out of favors with them."

In 1993, I did remember it would take weeks or more to get a sample worked up, and that was *after* you made it to the front of the backlog. They also needed a large enough sample to work with in those days, and from what I remembered of the training, that oftentimes meant replicating the DNA material repeatedly in the lab. By 2008, as I understood the news stories, DNA testing could be done nearly instantaneously with new technology, and the amount of the sample necessary was almost microscopic in contrast to those early days.

"What about an outside lab?" I said. "They do paternity testing all the time."

"Yeah, they're all over, and from what I've heard they can turn something around the same day if you really need it; and are willing to pay enough."

That sounded like something which could work when I could grab some of Dace's DNA. I had a handful of nails already forged and ready to hammer, but none of them would lock things down like a definitive DNA link between Dace Lamoureux and the rape test done and attested to by Dr. Broussard in his letter to Carol Huntley. Of course, any third year law student could drive a truck through the chain of evidence and create mountains of reasonable doubt for a jury to latch onto, facts which Teddy reminded me of, however, what Teddy didn't know was, if things worked out the way my client had asked, there wouldn't be a need for a courtroom in Dace Lamoureux's future.

Twenty minutes later, I arrived at our building. I parked out front on Magazine Street and went inside. In my office, I removed the printed items from Stan and the DNA test and rest of Dr. Broussard's documents and after firing up my laptop and connecting it to the scanner, sent the documents into digital storage. I attached just the DNA report to an email to Teddy, and fired it off.

While I waited, I combined the items from my evidence box with the items I had retrieved from Dr. Broussard's home. As I handled each of the sealed plastic bags containing Ashley's clothes, I could see the damage which had been done to the items in the attack. There were blood stains, torn seams and fabric, and organic debris stuck everywhere. Each bag was a treasure trove of forensic evidence, but it would never be processed. There would be no need.

I used the office phone to call the local number that Ashley had provided as a point of contact. It rang four times and then was answered with a simple 'yes'. I asked for Ashley, and was asked to hold. I heard the sounds of the handset being set down rather than the emptiness of an electronic hold, and then light footsteps on a hard surface floor.

"Mr. Langdon?" Ashley said several moments later. "Any progress?"

I filled her in on everything she needed to know about what I'd discovered since yesterday. She listened without interrupting, and when I concluded, she asked when I'd be going up to Connecticut.

"My thinking is tomorrow," I said.

"Good," she said. "I hope there won't be any problems tracking him down and then getting near him."

"I did some internet searches with the local newspaper sites. Dace is campaigning across the state and his schedule is fairly well publicized through election day."

"You don't know how much I appreciate you doing this for me, Mr. Langdon," she said. "All of it."

A single chime sounded on my laptop, indicating an incoming email message. I asked Ashley to hold on while I checked the program. The email was from Teddy. The subject line read: 'Sorry Buddy'. I clicked on the message. It was fairly short, but not at all sweet.

*Big Dog: I hope you're sitting down, pal, because you threw snake eyes. The DNA profile of the perp has NO match in CODIS - including the Classified area we discussed. According to my FBI analyst, there are two possible scenarios in play here: One, the suspect is not the rapist. Two, there is no genetic connection between father and son.*

*I know what else you've got, so you're probably on the right track with this slimeball. Her suggestion is you do anything you can to get firsthand DNA from him and get it tested at a private lab. For the right amount of grease they'll move you to the head of the line. Once they test your reference sample, my girl tells me anyone versed in the science will be able to give you an analysis from there.*

*These days, just about anything would work, even a can, bottle or glass that only he drank from contains enough DNA for testing, so you won't have to have him say 'ah' so you can swab his cheek.*

*Good luck, and good hunting.*

*Teddy*

I read the message twice then read it to Ashley. She said nothing.

"This doesn't mean we're wrong here, Ashley," I said. "It just means we have to take another step or two before we hammer the lid down on this guy."

"I understand, Mr. Langdon," she said, obviously disappointed. "Please call me when you have more information. I'm prepared to do my part when the time comes, you know."

"I know, Ashley. I'll be in touch."

I hung up the phone and reread Teddy's email. I called him on my cell phone and discussed things. I wanted to make certain I hadn't misread the possibilities, plus Teddy had the mind of an experienced cop and sometimes even the best of us need to be double-checked. You don't know how many times over the years I wished I had reached out to Teddy to talk things over before I spilled things to Tracey Walker. Like I said, though, you can't undo what's been done.

After I hung up, I shutdown my laptop and packed things up. I considered a bourbon before going home, but instead just locked up, dropped things into my car and drove home.

# Chapter Thirty-four

Her car had been moved from where I had left it last night, however, Sandy was home when I arrived. When I walked in, I found her seated at the kitchen table, staring at a glass of red wine in front of her. She looked up only after I was well inside the house, and that usually meant something bad.

"Hi," I said, testing the waters.

"What's going on, Will?" she said, looking at me hard.

I opened the refrigerator, putting the door between us and grabbed a beer to give me a moment before responding. I noticed the bottle of Merlot in there was over half gone. Sandy doesn't do well with red wine, especially Merlot. I closed the door and popped the top on the beer, took a drink. She kept watching me the whole time, looking like a tigress ready to pounce and I truly had no idea why.

"What are you talking about?" I said. "There's nothing going on." I walked around the island and sat down at the table across from her. "I'm working a case, you know that. Did you get my note?"

"I did," she said. "Thank you for the courtesy."

"Sandy, what's going on?" I said.

"I asked you first, Will."

She pushed the chair at the end of the table with her foot and it rolled clear. I looked and saw my rolled up clothes lying on the seat, stripper glitter all over. The collar of my shirt had been pulled free and the makeup there would be an ample accusation had there been a sordid tale to tell.

"I heard you get up this morning and looked out the window in time to see you hide these in your car. You didn't come upstairs, but rather showered and dressed downstairs. That means something, I assume. So, I'm going to give you one more chance to tell me the truth, and after that I'm done." She looked up with bloodshot blue-gray eyes. When Sandy was angry or ill, her baby blues faded to gray. "Do you understand what that means, Will? One more chance and then I'm done. We're done."

There have been any number of times in my previous life when I did have things to hide, but only once with Sandy, and every time I had paid dearly, whether I had been caught or not. This, however, was not one of them; I had done nothing wrong this time, but I had to admit, to a wife, circumstantially I looked guilty as hell.

"I had a stop last night, for the case," I said. "I swear it, Sandy, there's nothing going on."

I reached across the table to take her hands in mine. She pulled back, dropped her hands onto her lap.

"Tell me about the case then. Who is the client? That woman? Is that who you were out partying with last night? Like that time with Vanessa Lafontaine? Remember she was a client too, Will."

Don't women ever forget, I thought. Vanessa Lafontaine had been a huge one-time mistake and because I had been weak and stupid, it had cost me my marriage eight years ago. We recovered, but I could see we now stood on that very same precipice, and would soon tumble over the edge unless I could convince my angry and slightly intoxicated wife of my innocence. I considered my next words very carefully while she stared at me, then, like most men, said exactly the wrong thing.

"Can't you ever let that one little mistake, the only one I've made in the entirety of our marriages, by the way, slide into the past once and for all? Are you going to hold it over my head until the day I die and then etch it on my tombstone? Frankly, Sandy, I'm tired of having to defend myself repeatedly for one little slip."

Good job, Ace.

Her eyes welled with tears. She leaned forward, placed an elbow on the table and pointed her index finger in my direction.

"Me? No, you." Her finger bounced for emphasis. "You need to stop being so secretive. You need to include me in your life. You need to tell me the damned truth. You need to treat me like I deserve to be treated. Like a wife. I'm not a fool, Will. And I'm far from stupid."

I glared across at her. There was nothing I hated more than someone telling me what I need to do aside from being falsely accused, and my wife had just managed to combine both of those things into a handful of sentences in a tight little rant. I could feel my stomach start to churn and my anger to boil.

"I do include you in everything in my life, Sandy. What are you talking about?"

She sat back, removed the accusatory finger and picked up the glass of wine, drained it, then pushed from the table to go to the refrigerator and poured the rest of the bottle into the empty glass. She stood at the island and took another drink. I stood up and walked to face her. Her now fully gray eyes bored holes through me, although they looked glazed and unfocused.    My wife was drunk and angry.    Never a good combination for anyone.

"You always do this, Will.   You always shut me down, lock me out. You never treat me like the wife and partner the way I deserve to be treated.   You always have done this."

"That's not true, Sandy," I said.    "Nobody always or never does or doesn't do anything."

She looked momentarily confused, then her brow furrowed.

"Don't lecture me, William Langdon."

She took another drink and glared at me over the tipped wineglass.   I could see her eyes flicking from side to side.   She set the glass onto the island.   I understood my job was to defuse the situation; but, I'm a guy, a wrongfully accused guy, and I was pissed.

"I've always been there for you, Sandy," I said.    "I have never treated anyone better than I treat you."

"I thought nobody always or never does or doesn't do anything," she said in a mocking tone and a smirk on her face.

She reached for the wineglass and I grabbed it before she could.   I threw it toward the sink where it shattered and splashed Merlot everywhere.   Sandy cried out in pain an instant later and reached toward her eye where a drop of blood had appeared.   A small shard of glass lay on the island.   I reached for her.

"Sandy, are you all right?" I said.

"Don't touch me," she exclaimed as she dabbed at the tiny cut and inspected her fingertips for blood.

"I didn't mean to hurt you, Sandy," I said.    "It was an accident."

"Just go, Will, leave."

"Leave?"

"Yes, please leave this house.   Now."

I brushed past her and went upstairs.   She followed.

"What are you doing?" she said.

"Exactly what you told me to do.   I'm packing a bag and leaving."

I went into our closet and found a leather duffle, tossed it down onto the bed, then began throwing clothes into it.    Sandy went into the bathroom and brought back my shaving kit and tossed it on top of the clothes.   I stuffed everything inside and zipped it closed.

"I've always been there for you, Sandy," I said.    "When have you been there for me?"

I didn't wait for an answer, rather picked up the duffle and stormed out of the room.   She caught me at the stairs, grabbed my arm.

"What?" she said.    "What did you say?"

"You heard me," I said and I wrenched my arm free and started down the stairs.   "Even when you became so depressed after losing the baby, I was there for you. I nursed you out of it. I never deserted you, Sandy. I was always there, day in and day out; and those were some fairly bleak and dark days. I was there and I knew what you were going through." I should have left it at that, but I'm a guy, so I dropped the nuke. "I took better care of you than you did of our baby, Sandy."

I walked across the foyer, immediately regretting my last sentence and hoping she hadn't heard me and there wouldn't be any response. I didn't look up, but had I, I would have seen the tears tumbling down her cheeks. She stood at the rail on the balcony and took her final shot.

"How could you know? You fell into a bourbon bottle."

I could hear her crying echo through the house but I didn't turn back. I'm a guy.

I slammed the back door, walked to my car and drove off.

At first I was going to go sleep at the office. It wouldn't be the first time I had done that and it's got almost all the comforts of home. Instead, I called Continental and booked a flight to Newark. From there, I'd drive to Connecticut. Time was ticking on the case, and I had a job to get done. Sandy would cool off in a couple of days and she'd be there when I got back. I hoped.

I parked in the lot at the airport, grabbed my duffle and computer bag and a custom-made, locking briefcase in which I checked Willie and Sam when I flew. I unloaded the weapons and packed them and the ammunition away, locked the case and then walked across the roadway between the parking ramp and terminal to check in. The flight left in ninety minutes, so I'd have time to have a drink.

Going through security at an airport after 9-11 was a glorious experience. Millions of people taking off their shoes because some nitwit tried to light a sneaker one time can only make sense to bureaucrats. I can't wait until some idiot tries to set off a bomb in his underwear. That should be an interesting twist in the logic flow chart. Only in the good old, U.S. of A do we make everyone suffer because bureaucrats and functionaries failed in their jobs, yet still maintain them, or garner promotions.

I re-dressed after passing through all the detectors and scanners with my computer bag. To save some hassle en route and since I'd have to visit with baggage claim on the back end anyway, I checked the duffle along with the firearms case. Walking down the concourse to my gate, I was pleasantly surprised to find a little bar just across the hall from where we'd be boarding. Now, that's efficiency, I thought. If only TSA could learn from the people who designed airports.

I sat at the bar and set my computer bag on the stool next to me. A smiling young woman set a cocktail napkin in front of me and took my order: double Jim Beam bourbon on the rocks. She returned with a tumbler half-filled with the sparkling amber liquid poured over tiny cubes. I placed a twenty on the bar, she brought eleven dollars back, all in singles. Smart girl, I thought, she understood the game. I returned her smile and rolled the glass in my hands.

A bit over an hour later, they began boarding the flight. I was still rolling the glass in my hands, the tiny cubes had melted away and the bourbon it had cooled was again room temperature...and untouched. I set down the glass, left her five of the singles and walked across the hall to my flight. Although it was free in First Class, I also didn't have anything to drink on the airplane. Perhaps Sandy's final words had hit me harder than I had initially thought. So far that realization had only cost me fourteen dollars.

On the flight to Newark, I nursed a Coke over ice. The economy section of the airplane was packed, but I was alone in the eight seats up front. In the duffle I had packed at home, I had found a leather-bound notebook Sandy had bought for me on our anniversary a few years back which I tucked it into my computer bag before I checked in. I opened the notebook and read the inscribed note from her, dated three years earlier. It was the second anniversary of our second marriage.

> *Dearest Will,*
> *You are the love of my life. I love you with all that I am, and am so glad we have found each other in this world...again...and again...and again... Well, you get the idea. :)*
> *I want you to use this journal to record your feelings, your thoughts, your muses, anything at all that captures your attention. I will support you in whatever dreams you have for us. I'm your partner, your lover, your friend. Know I will always be there for you. No matter what!*
> *Yours, Sandy*

The pages within were blank; I had never used them for my feelings, my thoughts, or my muses. I didn't have any of them for it now either. There was nothing currently within me worthy of writing down. I'm normally not the type of person who wants to have his introspection turn up in print years after the feelings which brought the words have long since passed away. Perhaps my posterity - my girls - would like someday to come across a self-inscribed record of my years on this earth, but I'm just not wired that way. I knew people who would journal ever single day of their life, and I always found them to be pretentious and self-centered. Keep your comments to yourselves, please. Then a thought struck me. Or maybe it was a muse. It could have even been a feeling. Hell, maybe it was all three.

My world has degenerated into its own freaking Greek tragedy, and I am rapidly becoming the antihero of my own life's story. I opened the book to the first page and wrote those words across the top of the page.

*My world has degenerated into its own freaking Greek tragedy...*
*...and I am rapidly becoming the antihero of my own life's story.*

I reread the sentence. It wasn't Shakespeare, but it was okay for my first scribbled feeling, thought, or muse outside of a greeting card. It gave me some perspective. I closed the book, set it onto the empty seat next to me and slipped the pen back into my shirt pocket.

Out the windows on the left side of the aircraft, the sun was just setting and the streaks of orange light streaming into the cabin tinged everything with the color of a northern autumn. It brought comfortable feelings into all this life's chaos and I closed my eyes to enjoy just breathing for a few ticks of time. When I reopened them, the moment had slipped away and a purplish gray had settled upon the world. In contrast to the warmth of the orange, the new color was cold, the last transition of the day which would soon be followed by the full blackness of night. I turned on the reading lamp and picked up the book again. From my pocket I removed the pen and began to write.

I was still writing as we taxied to the gate in Newark. The entire coach section deplaned and as the pilots left the cockpit the flight attendant who had been my only companion up front asked if everything was okay. I smiled at up at her, closed the book and stowed the pen.

"Not everything," I said, rising from my seat, "but we're working on it."

I could have caught a small commuter flight to New London out of Newark, but the drive was only a little over two hours, so I rented a car and headed out on I-95 along the top of the Long Island Sound. I found a regional burger joint and bought a double bacon cheeseburger and chocolate malt. They threw in something they called oyster fries, which weren't too bad.

Before I left the airport, as I waited for my weapons to clear through security, I fired up the laptop and had found the website for a small hotel in Groton, across the river from New London, which had vacancies for a few nights. It promised to be anything but special, was within a stone's throw of I-95 and offered a rather industrial view of the Thames River, but I wasn't headed there to enjoy the amenities. From the photographs, it was a two-story, clapboarded building painted white with black trim. Frankly, the building had the look of one of those small, commercial fishing boats which would work Lake Michigan when I was a boy. I just hoped it didn't smell like one.

Two hours and five minutes after I left the airport, I arrived in New London, then drove across the bridge to Groton. I snaked my way through the surface streets and found the motel. The photographs posted on the web must have been taken on a good day years ago, because the place was quite a seedy affair. The people at the front desk were in not much better shape than their building, but they welcomed me with smiles, checked me in, and told me the room was on the second floor, accessed by an open stairs and hall. As I crossed the parking lot, the outside air wafted with the smell of ocean and fish, but fortunately, that stopped at the door to my room. The room smelled like Lysol, and the ceiling plaster seemed to shake loose a hint of dust with every semi passing by on the nearby interstate. I tossed my duffel, gun lockbox, and computer bag onto the bed and the leather-bound notebook spilled out of the back pocket. I tucked it away, because this room deserved neither recorded feeling, thought, nor muse.

Instead, I turned on the television to a local station and took a shower. The news would be on soon, and I wanted to see if there was any election coverage which might update me on Dace Lamoureux's next several days' wanderings around the state. I sat on the bed with an oversized hand towel pretending to be a bath towel mostly around my waist.

The senatorial election led the local coverage, with footage of the smiling and glad-handing father and son team attending an event in Hartford and several smaller towns upstate earlier in the day. They were reportedly headed back by way of Bridgeport and points in the southwest corner of the state on Sunday, and scheduled to arrive in the New London area on Monday afternoon for a planned rally, ironically, at Dace and Dave's old high school.

The presidential coverage came after, and it was the same boring fare we'd been getting in Louisiana over the last months. What was probably coming on Tuesday would not be news to anyone, especially the less-than-dynamic duo of John McCain and Sarah Palin. The local news story noted that Senator McCain had lived in New London as a child when his father worked at the naval submarine base with the sardonic notation that polling in the area did not bode well for the former favored son. Now there's some fodder for feelings, thoughts, and muses, just not mine.

I decided not to call Sandy before turning in, and there was nothing new to share with Ashley. Sandy would most likely be sleeping. It's how she handled the aftermath of red wine. She was either sleeping or throwing my clothes into the yard, and if she was engaged in the latter, I didn't want to know right at that moment. I could handle anything once I got home, but I had a job to do before I would be back there. So, I did a little local mapping and planned my stops and activities for the next day. Fortunately, there was a lab which could do DNA testing in the area, and advertised on their website that for a 'nominal additional fee', expedited, same-day results were available. There was an after-hours contact number listed on the site and I jotted it down for the morning. Lastly, before I turned off the lights, I unpacked Willie and Sam, loaded them and tucked them into the drawer of the nightstand.

On Sunday morning, I awoke with the rising sun. I rolled out of bed aided by groans to overcome aching bones and muscles. Turning fifty sucks, but the so-called mattress on that bed should have been fed to the horses years ago. I checked my cell phone and there were no calls or messages from Sandy. I frankly didn't expect any. After another shower and shave, I dressed in khakis, oxford shirt, and black cashmere blazer, tucked away Willie and Sam, then walked outside into a crisp fall morning and then across the parking lot to a small cafe I had spied when I arrived the previous evening. The aroma of bacon frying pumped through exhaust fans overpowered the fish and ocean smells and reminded me that I was starving.

I carried with me a copy of the local newspaper I bought from the rack near the lobby entrance and my leather-bound notebook. The restaurant was filled with the comfortable, heavy air of frying breakfast meats and eggs and potatoes, and I settled into an empty booth across from a counter lined with stools half filled by working class locals and military types. The place was doing a brisk business for so early on a Sunday morning, yet the waitress was tableside to pour me a cup of coffee before my butt came to a stop on the well-worn red vinyl. I nixed the pour because I don't drink coffee, asked for water and a glass of tomato juice and removed a slightly greasy, vinyl-covered menu from the condiment rack on the table. By the time she returned with the water and juice, I was ready to order. Her name tag read: 'Cheryl'.

"Bacon and eggs, over easy, country potatoes, wheat toast, please, Cheryl," I said, then pointed to the menu. "What are Johnnycakes?"

"Pan fried cornmeal flatbreads, a house specialty," she said with a smile. "They're addictive."

"You sold me, Cheryl," I said, replacing the menu and grabbing a napkin for my fingers. "Add an order of Johnnycakes."

She nodded and wrote it all down on one of those little pads then walked behind the counter and placed the slip under a spring on a stainless steel wheel and informed the cook he had an order up. I salted and peppered my tomato juice, then opened the newspaper.

I really didn't have much interest in the goings on of the greater New London County area, but I've learned over the years that a quick scan of the newspaper sometimes produced information that could prove useful during my investigations, especially when building a bridge with wary locals. The front page was filled with political news. A large photograph of George W. Bush walking that open hallway at the White House was below the fold. The current president had lost the prime real estate above to the contenders vying for his job. From the weary look on W's face in the photo, it was apparent to me that having the next guy take over the burdens of the office couldn't come too soon for him. I thought the man had done a fantastic job on many things, a reasonable job on some things, and a horrible job on the rest.

The race for the for the Connecticut senate seat had landed on page two. A color photograph of Dace Lamoureux behind a podium fronted with a red, white, and blue 'Lamoureux for Senate' placard, his arms raised with a double victory salute commanded the top spot on the page. His father was seated on the stage in background as part of the cheering section; from what I'd read in my earlier research, that was an uncomfortable role for the older man to assume. The tagline under the sign read: 'The Right Thing'. I was glad I hadn't eaten yet.

According to the story, the campaign had seized upon those three words and used them as their campaign theme in many variations: 'Doing The Right Thing', 'The Right Thing for Connecticut', 'Change - The Right Thing', to name a few.

"We'll see, hotshot," I said under my breath.

My breakfast arrived and I slid the paper off to the side while Cheryl set down the plates. It all smelled great, and it was hot off the griddle.

"I can't believe I went to high school with him," Cheryl said.

"Who?" I said, at first not making the age connection because the waitress looked at least half a dozen years older than thirty-one.

"Him," she said, pointing at the photo. "Dace Lamoureux. One day I just know he's going to be president. Everyone always said so."

I smiled.

"Well, then maybe he'll make the front page," I said, shooting for cute and witty rather than insulting; and, intentionally goading her a bit.

She took it well but didn't say anything.

"So, you went to high school with him? You look too young for that, what are you, twenty-three, twenty-four?"

She flushed, touched her hair.

"I wish," she said, but not telling me.

"So, what kind of guy is he?" I said.

She looked warily at me.

"You one of them reporters?" she asked, scrutinizing me with narrowed eyes.

I shook my head.

"Nope, can't stand reporters, all that prying into people's lives and sneaking around, poking through trash for any dirt they can dig up, peeking in windows." To distract her a bit, I cut a piece off one of the

Johnnycakes, pushed it to my mouth. The were good. "These are really good, Cheryl. Thank you for suggesting them. I just hope I don't get addicted before I go back to New Orleans in a few days."

Her eyes perked up.

"You're from New Orleans?" she said. "I've never been, but I heard it's a fun place."

"About as fun as anyplace," I said, shrugging my shoulders and taking another bite of the cornmeal delicacies. "You know, when you live someplace, it's no longer an exciting destination, it's home."

"I guess," she said.

"You gonna answer my question?"

"What question?" she said.

"About what kind of guy Dace Lamoureux is," I said, then raised my eyebrows and pointed a fork toward her. "I bet you don't even know him, just say that to the tourists." I smiled. "Never try to kid a kidder, Cheryl."

Well, that worked and for the next twenty minutes and while I finished my breakfast and Cheryl hopped to other customers, she popped back to my table and told me everything a local would know about the favored son from the other side of the river. Much of it was biographical stuff I already knew, but there were a few new tidbits she added. When she seemed near out of chatter, I asked her again.

"What *kind* of guy is he?"

Cheryl walked to the counter and retrieved the pitcher of ice water and returned to the table. She refilled my glass, even though I hadn't drained much. As she did set the glass back down, she leaned low.

"He's a snake," she said. "A user."

I nodded. She expounded.

"He has that flashy smile and all, but underneath he will do whatever he needs to get what he wants."

"Just right for politics, then, eh?" I said.

"Mister, this is Connecticut. We seen all kinds of politicians in this state, but those of us who have lived around him and his family know this guy isn't what he seems. It's why he may lose right here in New London County. We know him best, but we also know you don't talk bad about the Lamoureux family around here." She stood up and looked at me suspiciously and shook her head. "Geeze, I hope you aren't a reporter."

I watched her walk away. She didn't come back, except to drop my check on the table and thank me for coming in. The tab for the breakfast was eleven dollars and seventy-three cents. I left a twenty tucked under the corner of my plate and walked out.

When I went to drive out of the parking lot later, I saw Cheryl walking to her car. I pulled my rental up alongside her, she bent down and looked into the vehicle, smiled and waved. I rolled down the passenger window. She bent further and stuck her head near the opening.

"Thanks for the tip," she said. "I appreciate it."

"No thanks needed," I said. "The Jonnycakes recommendation alone was well worth the tip, plus I got to meet my first charming resident of the area."

Her eyes moved to the platinum band on my left ring finger.

"I don't date married men," she said. "No matter how good they tip or how cute they are." She began to stand up.

"No, Cheryl," I said. "I wasn't hitting on you. My goodness, I have a daughter your age. I was just being friendly."

She looked in the open window again, then smiled.

"Okay," she said. "Sorry I jumped to the conclusion, but believe it or not, it does happen. The hitting on me part. We have way too many horny sailors running around here."

I laughed.

"Isn't that unnecessarily redundant?" I said. "Horny sailor?" Like saying criminal attorney."

Her face morphed from puzzled to a smile as she got the joke.

"Say, Cheryl," I said. "Since you know I'm not a reporter, or a wayward husband on the prowl, can I ask you another question?"

"Sure," she said, "but do you mind if I sit? I've been on my feet for nine hours and it's only noon."

I reached for the passenger door handle and she slid into the seat.

"Shoot," she said.

"If you knew Dace Lamoureux in high school, did you also know Dave Saunders? Or did he go to another school?" I already knew the answer.

"Wait a minute," she said as she turned in the seat and pushed back into the corner like a threatened crawfish. "You said you're from New Orleans." She paused. "Louisiana."

I nodded.

"That's where Dave died," she said. "That accident with that girl." Her eyes narrowed again. "Who are you, Mister?"

"My name is William Langdon," I said. "I'm a private investigator. I used to be a cop in Chicago."

That didn't appear to make her feel any better because her eyes began to dart from side to side. Any moment she would bolt. I had one last chance. If the tact worked, it would fit perfectly into my evolving plan. If it didn't I could be blown out of the water before I even got close to fulfilling Ashley Monreale's request. It was worth the shot.

"I knew Dave Saunders," I exaggerated a bit. "The girl's name was Cindy Spagliano, and she was from a small town in Minnesota. Good people. Both of them."

She relaxed a bit. I could see daylight.

"Dave was good people," she said. "I didn't know the girl, Cindy; and yes, I did go to high school with Dave Saunders." She cocked her head. "But why do I think you already knew if I went to school with Dace that Dave was also there? And if you knew that, then you most likely knew they were best friends since grade school."

I nodded; I had made the friendship leap, but now Cheryl had confirmed it and added the 'best' modifier.

"Do you know where Dace was when Dave Saunders died?"

"Family said he was home, mourning the loss of his girlfriend."

"His girlfriend passed away?" I asked. There had been nothing I found in any research which had attached a situation such as that to Dace's bio.

"Yeah. She died going off the cliff just up the river toward Gales Ferry. Cops said she hit some ice in the road and lost control. She had been at a birthday party for Dace Lamoureux - the creep was born on Valentine's Day, can you believe that?"

"Was she a local girl?" I asked.

"No," Cheryl said. "I think they met at college."

Cheryl didn't remember the girl's name, but I knew it wouldn't be that hard to find something about a fatal accident like that in the news archives, especially since I had the date to work with. We chatted a bit more and I left her there in the parking lot a fifteen minutes later. I told her I was headed to Gales Ferry to try to catch Dave Saunders' parents, but first I wanted to do some research online so I stopped back in my room and fired up the laptop.

I learned Sarah Avidago had indeed died in the early morning hours of February 15, 1998. Her obituary said she had been from Providence, Rhode Island, a student at Harvard, slated to graduate in June of that year and headed for Stanford Medical. She left behind a grandmother and two brothers, but there was no mention of parents. The obit and the other articles I found online did not mention Dace Lamoureux or the fact the accident had happened after the girl had attended a birthday party at his home, but I knew that information wasn't too hard for the Lamoureux family to have manipulated.

The accident occurred near Gales Ferry and when I looked at the map it didn't take a genius to do the math. According to Cheryl, Sarah had attended Dace's birthday party at their home outside New London, that evening. Dave Saunders had been Dace's best friend and was probably there as well. For some reason, Sarah had driven Dave home, then slid off the road on her way back to the interstate to drive home to Providence, about an hour away.

All that was interesting, but it made no real difference to what Dace Lamoureux had done to Ashley Monreale in New Orleans, other than perhaps speak to the boy's mental state. With her obituary photograph, I was able to determine Sarah Avidago was the fourth in the 1997 yearbook photograph of the fall day in the quad taken in 1996, so the relationship with Dace had obviously been long-term. It also fit with Jack Stempler telling me Cindy had called and asked to use the plantation home for a while because a friend needed to get away. The friend who needed to get away was Dace Lamoureux, not Dave Saunders.

I again sat in my car in the motel parking lot after repacking the laptop and printed information into my computer bag in my room before I drove out to the Saunders home. It all was becoming much more clear now; like watching divers pull a car out of the lake. First you see the black shape at the end of the cable, then more definition, and finally a color and make. When the thing finally comes out of the water, you can see every detail; Dace Lamoureux's guilt and how I was going to play this all out to the end was beginning to become very clear to me.

I turned the key and put the car into reverse and slid out of the parking spot. I made my way out to the main road, checked the time on the dash, then made a left. While doing the research into Sarah Avidago's accident, I had received a return call from the after-hours number where I had left a message for the people at the DNA lab. That was the only stop I needed to make before I went out to Gales Ferry. It was a twenty minute drive, the woman had said. I was going to be late.

I arrived at the Genco Testing Laboratories office five minutes late. There was one car in the parking lot: a beige, late model Altima, which was empty when I pulled up and parked next to it. The building was a typical, nondescript metal shell in a mixed, light commercial and office park on the New London side of the Thames River. As I stepped out of my car, the building's front door opened and a slender woman in her mid-forties wearing a black pantsuit, cream colored top and indoor complexion stepped out and held the door. She had short, curly hair in an unnatural color somewhere between Lucille Ball and Carrot Top, and when I got closer, I could see the faded freckles of youth.

I reached out my hand and apologized for being late and she said it wasn't a problem. She introduced herself as Teri Genco, the daughter of the lab's founder, shook my hand firmly, locked the door when we were both inside and then led me through the reception area, around a windowed laboratory brightly lit with fluorescent fixtures in a drop ceiling and to the back right corner of the building where her small office was located.

She accepted my business card, gave me hers, then told me to sit while she explained the federal and Connecticut laws concerning warrantless DNA collection by private citizens. I explained I had been a Chicago cop in a previous life, so I understood the warrant process and she said that while she appreciated the association, with DNA, things had become a tad more complicated. She noted law enforcement actually had more rights to gather warrantless samples than did private citizens in many states, then added: "So, Mr. Langdon, we must be certain we comply with all the applicable laws or everyone could get sued, or tossed in jail."

"It's that serious?" I said.

"Well, it all depends from whom you obtain the sample and how you're going to use the results, Mr. Langdon, however, we do live in a very legally contentious society these days, don't we?" she said. "I just want you to understand our laboratory would be on the hook legally just as you would should we in any way assist you in breaking the law here. That's a risk my lab will not undertake, so we need you to understand the rules and sign a standard indemnity agreement."

"Well, there are no current legal issues surrounding my investigation, Ms. Genco," I said. "I really don't anticipate we will become embroiled in any, given the expressed wishes of my client."

She nodded, but that didn't derail her speech.

"There are two ways to protect yourself here, Mr. Langdon, and by extension, us." She reached into her desk drawer and removed several sheets, then handed them across the desk. "First, you get the donator to read and sign one of these. It's a standard voluntary disclosure form and liability waiver. As you can see, there are several use limitations there for them to acknowledge. They sign and date the form, then you have them vigorously swab the inside of their cheek with one of these." She handed across a cotton tipped stick which looked like longer, slightly larger and one-ended version of a Q-tip which protruded through a plastic container with snapping cap. Are you familiar with chain-of-custody forms?"

"I'm familiar with all these things, and the process," I said, accepting a copy of that too.

She nodded, and continued.

"Now as to surreptitious collection. Should that become necessary, I'd suggest you obtain something you have full assurance that only the subject has used, such as a cigarette butt, a coffee cup, soda can, water bottle, even a fork or spoon. Those items are placed into a plastic bag, sealed, and marked by you. Once the subject discards any of those items, it's considered legal abandonment, meaning the items are categorized as 'trash' and trash has no ownership attached, meaning the items are no longer considered a matter of personal privacy. Of course, I don't suggest you steal someone's silverware."

I thanked her for the information and left her office ten minutes later equipped with enough forms, swabs, and bags to get done what I needed to get done. To expedite things, Teri provided me with her personal cell phone number and assured me she would get the testing completed as needed and help me to interpret the results and make comparisons. I signed confidentiality, indemnity, and fee agreements. They would bill my agency, Ms. Genco assured me, but she took my credit card imprint on a pre-signed charge slip just in case. I headed to Gales Ferry.

The Saunders' lived in a modest, cookie-cutter home on a large lot in a 1970s vintage neighborhood. There were two newer model Hyundai SUVs in the drive when I pulled to the curb out front. Before getting out of my car, I placed a pair of release forms into my computer bag and slipped a couple of cheek swab kits into the breast pocket of my jacket. Just to be on the safe side, I tucked a couple plastic bags in my pocket.

During my time with Chicago PD, I'd met with the parents of several deceased kids, usually proximate to the time of death, but I couldn't recall ever calling on a mother and father who were ten years down the road from the devastation of losing a child. I wasn't certain how they would react to my showing up on their doorstep unannounced, or the questions they'd have for me, and I wasn't at liberty to tell them very much if they did ask. I prepared myself for the worst type of reaction as I walked up the drive and onto the porch. I rang the doorbell.

A minute later, a petite woman in her mid-fifties opened the inside door and looked at me through the glass of an aluminum storm door. She was dressed casually in a maroon, satin, two-piece sweatsuit and wore running shoes. Her hair was reddish-blonde with gray roots, thick, and coiffed in a low-maintenance, above-the-shoulders cut. She had dull green eyes behind brown-rimmed glasses. She unlatched the storm door and pushed it open about eight inches.

"Mrs. Saunders?" I said.

"Yes."

"My name is William Langdon."

Her eyes watched me carefully as I explained where I was from and that I had come to talk to them about Dave. At the mention of her son's name, she called inside for her husband and disappeared from the door. Mr. Saunders appeared a moment later.

He was a larger man, barrel chested, just under six feet tall and wore a blue satin sweatsuit and running shoes. His head was shaved, but his jowls carried a weekend worth of growth; his eyes were small, pale blue orbs closely set astride a prominent and veined nose. He stepped out onto the porch and closed the door behind himself. I reintroduced myself, told him I was a private investigator from Louisiana and that I wished to speak to him and his wife about something important having to do with Dave. He suggested we sit on the stoop. We did.

"Mr. Langdon," he said. "I don't know why you're here, but we settled this whole thing with the insurance company years ago. Not long after the accident, to be truthful."

I almost missed it, but that was the second time today that I had heard the word 'accident' used to describe the events surrounding the passing of Dave Saunders. Cheryl had used the same word. I decided before I said anything more, I'd better hear what the man had to say.

"We signed a confidentiality agreement when we settled with the insurance on Dave's accident. I don't know what you know about those type of things, but our attorney said we could run into some serious legal trouble if we were to talk about the situation to anyone."

My whole goal there that day was to obtain DNA samples from each parent so I could definitively rule out Dave Saunders as having any role in the rape and beating of Ashley. I had jumped to conclusions once in this case and I didn't want to make that mistake again, no matter how everything was pointing in Dace Lamoureux's direction currently. The next time when I acted, I wanted every 't' crossed and every 'i' dotted. If these parents thought their son had died as the result of an accident and not a murder, things just got much more difficult. I had to shift my plan to fit the new conditions, but before I said something which could possibly cause these people distress they didn't need or deserve, I had to know everything they believed.

The fact the CODIS search had come up empty on the rape test results was more than disconcerting to me at that point, especially if the expert's first possible conclusion was true, that the perpetrator was not Dace Lamoureux because there was no genetic link to anyone in the database; Senator Allard Lamoureux's DNA profile was certainly in that computer. The analyst's second conclusion of there existing no link between the senator and his presumed son was farfetched, but not unheard of.

If I was going to carry out my client's wishes to their fullest, I needed first to eliminate Dave's DNA from the equation. Regardless of what my client has told me about her newfound certainty as to the identity of the attacker, I had to view her revelation from a cop's perspective and that meant with skepticism, because it had been ten years in coming forward and she had suffered severe trauma. On the other hand, she hadn't exactly been fully questioned in 1998. As Mr. Saunders spoke, I was thinking the only way to eliminate Dave completely was to get parental samples and have the experts do the analysis against the rape kit.

"Mr. Saunders," I said. "I know I am asking something which may be painful to you, and believe me, if it wasn't critical to helping someone else I wouldn't even be here today, but can you tell me what you know about the circumstances of your son's death?"

He looked me over and remained silent for several moments. He struck me as a man given to rumination, so I used the time to allow my mind to sort through the possibilities because I had obviously stumbled upon something on that stoop which was outside of anything for which I could have planned or even foreseen. These people, for some reason, believed their son had not been murdered but rather had been killed in some kind of accident and that just didn't make sense. The parish authorities knew exactly what had happened in that warehouse. They had seen the evidence; they were familiar with Vincent Monreale's reputation. There was no way they could possibly classify what had taken place on the shores of Lac des Allemands as an accident, even for the sake of sparing the parents pain, and why would they? Even with the motivation lacking from the calculus meaning the cops couldn't complete the means, motive, opportunity equation, they certainly had enough to conclude the manner of death was homicide.

Everyone who knew the true motivation for Tony killing Dave Saunders had talked to me in the last couple of days. It was a small group: Ashley, Ronnie, Stan, and Teddy, and me. Except for Dace Lamoureux, that was, and I was not even certain that he knew his lifelong friend had paid for his crimes. As for Dave's parents, it would be one thing to be told that your son had been murdered by a Louisiana Mafioso and keep that fact within the family, but it was clear from the way Mr. Saunders acted when he talked of Dave's death as an accident that he truly believed it.

Of course, I thought, it was possible Louisiana had just swallowed yet another secret and these people hadn't been told the grizzly truth. Who had the kind of power and money it would take to make it all happen, including payment from a fictitious insurance company was the question. I shook my head slowly as it dawned upon me the Lamoureux fortune and influence made anything possible. I suddenly felt quite foolish. Here I had been running what I thought had been a clever shell game for a decade to keep all the connections secret according to the wishes of a young girl who was now my client, but it was becoming increasingly clear that once I had left Louisiana in pursuit of the truth, someone had long ago stolen my pea.

That someone had intercepted and changed the story somewhere between the Sheriff of Lafourche Parish and Dave's parents; it was the only thing that made sense right now. That meant setting the wheels in motion within days, or even hours of the rape and beating. Certainly within hours of the deaths of Dave and Cindy. And that meant Senator Lamoureux himself probably knew the entire story, most likely from the lips of his very own son. I suddenly felt as if an elephant was sitting on my chest. I wanted to end the bullshit and go directly to confront Dace Lamoureux and his old man, but I had to keep going along the path step-by-step or some very bad things could happen. The step right now involved the man sitting to my left and his wife.

"Mr. Saunders," I said when he didn't react after several moments of obvious contemplation. To sell it, I tried to look as uncomfortable as possible when I laid out the lie. It sucked I had to be dishonest with the man, but he didn't need the pain of the truth. What difference could it make to him and the reclusive Mrs. Saunders? "The problem is, sir, there's been another accident."

He jumped up and began to pace on the walk. He rubbed his stubbled chin and became more animated and visibly agitated with every turn. I had just handed the man a larger moral dilemma.

"That's Terrible," he said shaking his head. "Terrible."

I stood and squared myself with him on the walk. I looked him in his close set eyes. It was easy to lock my eyes to his when I spoke the next words, because they were one-hundred percent true and heartfelt.

"Mr. Saunders, I give you my word, whatever you tell me will go no further. Your information is safe with me and could help someone who's hurting. Someone who is devastated as badly as you and your wife were, and clearly still are. Someone who just wants to know why, and whose greatest wish is that something like what happened in Louisiana ten years ago never happens again. Please. You have my word, as a father myself."

He eyed me for several long moments, nodded slowly, then invited me inside. I followed him back onto the porch and into the modestly appointed house. We found Mrs. Saunders seated at the kitchen table, idly stirring a cup of hot tea. He told her my lie. She looked from her husband to me. Then he told her my truth. She nodded to him, but said nothing to it, then stood and asked if I would have a cup of tea, perhaps, a piece of cake with them. It was their Sunday afternoon reward after their walk, she said. I accepted on both the tea and cake and took the offered seat at the kitchen table. Mr. Saunders sat with me and began to speak while his wife prepared our cake and tea.

"Dave left home early on the morning of Tuesday, February 17, 1998, to attend a friend's funeral up in Providence. It was the last time we saw him; although, we did hear from him a couple of times after that, but just by phone. Dave had been withdrawn for several days after his best friend's birthday party the Saturday before. See, Dave liked his beer, just like I do." He applied a timid smile. "Well, Dave had apparently drank too much at the party to drive himself home safely, so his friend's fiancé agreed to drop him here since she was headed to Providence that night and this was sort of on the way. It really wasn't on her way, but that was Sarah. She was a wonderful girl."

I nodded.

"After dropping Dave out front, the girl was headed back to the interstate when she hit a patch of black ice on the road and her car tumbled down the bluff toward the river. It had been a warm day and the snow had melted then refroze when the temperatures had dropped that night. She was killed. Dave took it hard. I think he blamed himself, no matter what anyone would say to him. He'd sit where you're sitting right now and say that if it wasn't for him, Sarah would never have been on that road and would still be alive. He took it all upon himself, but that was our Dave."

Mrs. Saunders laid a plate with a piece of yellow cake with chocolate frosting in front of both of us, along with a cup of tea. She set another plate of cake at her place and sat down. She picked up the story.

"Dave was a very tender soul, in contrast to his exterior shell," she said. "He was our gentle giant. He left here the morning of Sarah's funeral, packed for going back to school after, yet instead he and Cindy went to Louisiana. When he spoke to me on the phone several days later, he said they just needed to get away. We had thought they had broken up over a year earlier, but apparently they had gotten back together; although he never told us about it for some reason." Her eyes went distant. "It was the last time we heard from our son."

"That's Cindy Spagliano?" I gently prodded, because I needed to hear them say the words. "The girl who died with him."

"Yes," she said with a nod. "She was quite the handful for Dave. Spirited and strong-willed. We really liked her. As you must know if you've made it this far in your investigation, she also went to Harvard and was raised in Minnesota."

I picked at the dessert; they each ate theirs in large bites like the reward they said it was. The cake was homemade and had been in the refrigerator so the chocolate frosting was solidly chilled, just the way my mom would do it when I was a kid. I wasn't much of a tea drinker, but it was fragrant and tasty without additives, and I sipped it with my hosts.

"What happened after the accident?" I asked Mrs. Saunders. "I mean, how were you first notified?"

"A sheriff's deputy came to our door. We learned later, when we received the Death Certificate, the notification had been two days after Dave and Cindy had died. I guess those things take time, given the distance, but two days?" Her eyes went unfocused again as she remembered. "It was ironic that the deputy who came to tell us about Dave was also the one who had found Sarah and came to follow up with us on that. He had been a schoolmate of our son, too, this Deputy Phil Neufeldt. He runs the town's police department now."

I nodded, ate more cake, sipped more tea. I let them talk. Mr. Saunders took over.

"The insurance company man came to see us a week later, shortly after we had Dave's funeral. It was a hard time for us, but the man was gentle and patient and understanding. Not at all what I would have expected from an insurance company. He said their insured wanted to avoid causing us any more pain and would like to just settle before lawyers got involved. We hadn't even have thought of that. It wasn't on our priority list at the time. We sat right here and talked it through with him. He suggested a figure and we agreed, then donated the funds in Dave's name to a charity which sends underprivileged kids to sports camps."

"It was what our Dave would have wanted," Mrs. Saunders added.

I left fifteen minutes later without asking them to either sign the release forms or to swab their own cheeks for DNA testing. As a final item, they had agreed to show me the Death Certificate, although they appeared confused by the request. They both went to find it. When they returned to the kitchen with the document, I studied it. It looked genuine, and had the manner of death marked as Accidental. The cause of death was as medically sterile as could be done for the family of someone torn apart by alligators. I stood and thanked them for their time and hospitality, and again apologized for my intrusion. They never once inquired about the other accident which I had used to initially gain entrance to their home. I imagine they didn't want that knowledge.

As I drove off, I removed my cell phone from the breast pocket of my jacket and dialed the number for Teri Genco from her card. She agreed to meet me at her office in half an hour. Though it would never be one of my proudest moments, yes, I had stolen their silverware. In my blazer's side pocket, I had, wrapped in a paper napkin, the cake forks used by Mr. and Mrs. Saunders.

# Chapter Thirty-five

Two hours later, I continued to cool my heels in Teri Genco's office, jotting down an expanding list of questions and thoughts I had about the Monreale case in the leather-bound notebook. I looked up as she returned wearing an open, long, white lab coat over a short skirt and billowy top into which she had changed from the androgynous pantsuit she wore on our first meeting earlier. She made certain I got the chance to take a good look, then sat behind her desk. I noticed she also wore a flirtatious smile and her professional demeanor had shifted. She had reading glasses perched on the end of her nose and she had two pieces of paper in her hand.

"We've got positive results, Mr. Langdon," she said, and then offered a coquettish smile. "Although you remember I had advised you not to go stealing people's silverware."

I shrugged. She didn't need to know.

"May I see the comparative sample?" she asked, holding our her hand.

I reached into my computer bag and removed a copy of the DNA results from the rape kit and handed it across to her. She studied the three sheets and a few minutes later looked up at me and shook her head.

"There is no genetic match possible here," she said, handing all threes sheets across. "The person indicated in your report could not have originated from these parents. I'm sorry."

I took the pages, smiled, and told her that was good news.

I dialed Ashley's contact number on the drive back to my hotel. I would not tell her about definitively eliminating Dave Saunders from having anything to do with her attack because that piece of the case was purely for my own edification. While I was lifted by the confirmation, it wasn't a reason for me to celebrate because having those three pieces of paper in my possession was the final link in my chain of self-condemnation. There could be no more gray area for me on what I had done, no more refuge for myself in the dark nights to come as there had been over the past decade.

Before the DNA proof had been generated, even after Ashley Monreale had come to my office with her allegations, I could salve my conscience with a degree of reasonable doubt on the matter. Dave had paid the ultimate price based on premature circumstantial evidence which I had cobbled together a decade ago; and he had paid that improper price, based solely on Ashley's word until I obtained comparative DNA from Dace Lamoureux, for the sins of his best friend, a man who had gone on with his life over the last ten years as if nothing had happened along that river in New Orleans, and who was poised to become the next United States Senator-elect from the state of Connecticut in the next forty-nine hours. That self-delusion was now a thing of the past. Not that I didn't already long know it, but as I said, there would be no more hiding.

The only redemption possible for me would be to finally prove the facts of the case, and then Ashley's justice would follow. Confirming Dace's guilt was the first part of my assignment; and what happened after was to come only when there was no doubt in my mind. At least that was the agreement; it was the one thing I had insisted upon. There had already been too much pain at my hands because of this matter. What Ashley had ultimately planned was all yet to unfold, however, as of that day, Dave Saunders had been cleared by science of the rape and beating of Ashely Monreale, and though I had anticipated those very results, hearing the analysis and seeing it in black-and-white did little to reduce my melancholy.

The phone rang four times before someone else answered it and moments later, Ashley came on the line.

"Hello, Mr. Langdon," she said.

"Just touching base, Ashley. I'll be making my first contact with Dace Lamoureux tomorrow afternoon when he's scheduled to return to New London," I told her. "My hope is to get the chance to speak to him alone, but my main goal in seeing him is to obtain his DNA to test it against the...um, previous sample and seal the case."

"Please remember our arrangement, Mr. Langdon," she said. "No matter what he says or how he may provoke you, this has to be done my way, as agreed. Are we one-hundred percent clear on that?"

I didn't like some parts of our arrangement, as she put it, but I had given my word to the woman. I hated to have my hands tied like this, yet I would fulfill my part of the bargain, and I told her so again.

"When I know more, I'll call," I said, and clicked off.

I parked in the same spot I had left that morning and stepped out of the car and scanned the area. Sandy calls that being paranoid, I say I'm just being careful.   The cafe across the way was doing a brisk dinner business, and I considered walking across for something to eat before going back to the room.   I also considered walking down the block to the liquor store I had seen the night I checked in.   Instead, I took a walk down to the river, leaving my computer bag along with Willie and Sam locked in the trunk.

The early evening was chilly, but not cold.   An offshore breeze was gently stirring the air, replacing the tinge of salt with the aromas of civilization.   I walked along Bridge Street to Thames Street, then south along the river.   The waters were black, and a crescent moon made its appearance in a sky saturated with ground light, even that far from New York City.   Only the heartiest of stars shone through.   Several blocks along, I detoured around the General Dynamics Electric Boat facility where submarines have been launched and taken to war or patrol in the world's oceans for over a hundred years.   I thought of Jack Stempler.

A cast bronze plaque near the front gate offered a glimpse into the facility's history and I paused to read it.   I hadn't known the USS Nautilus, the first U.S.-built nuclear submarine, was built on that location in 1954 and had been the first vessel to make submerged transit of the North Pole on the day I was born.   Of course, I was fairly young at the time to have noticed.

I continued along, all the way to Eastern Point Beach and found a driftwood log at the top of the sand on which to sit and watch the ocean. Across a narrow channel, perhaps three miles offshore, a small island rested, lights scattered across its hills from one end to the other.   A single-engine plane approached from over the Block Island Sound toward an airport on the island's western tip.   The airport's rotating green and white beacon cast its light into the sky and across the horizon to pilots and seafarers alike.   Further south, I could discern the eastern tip of Long Island, and the distant, overpowering glow of New York off to the west.

I don't know how long I sat there and thought.   At one point I prayed - for many people, and for myself - at another, I felt something come back from the petition and allowed a tear to well in my eye.   Normally, I didn't let that happen; usually I would short circuit what I had grown up thinking was a sign of male weakness with a strong, countervailing thought and a wiggle of my foot.   As a last option, there was the surreptitious swipe of a fingertip if I was too late.   Sandy always caught it when she'd see my foot begin to move during an emotional time or when we'd watch a movie with a touching scene, and she'd usually move in closer to me and nuzzle her head against my chest or slide her soft hand on my arm.   She was the only person to whom I had confided the true reason I have reacted that way since childhood: nobody in our little family unit should ever let my father see them cry.

I thought of Sandy. She hadn't been taking my calls since I left the house the day before. I could only guess at what she was thinking and how the words we had spoken and the acts we had undertaken would affect the two of us in the longterm. I retained my ultimate trust in her, and I hoped she still retained that level of faith in me, at least as much as she could, given a failing or two of mine along the way. I had the same hopes for...well, love, but time would tell about all that. I knew I loved her as much as I always had and more, all I could pray for was that she still felt the same. I snickered at the remembrance of a movie line I had once heard: 'We had all these wonderful hopes and aspirations for ourselves and each other, but then life got in the way.'

Eventually, I stood, stretched out the kinks brought on by the chilled night air and retraced my steps into the city lights. The offshore breeze had switched during my sit to an onshore type, and the temperature dropped while the humidity rose, and by the time I reached my motel, I felt damp and chilled. The cafe was closed by then, and when I looked at my cell phone and saw it was after midnight, I realized the liquor store would be as well. Not that I particularly had a desire for a drink, or food for that matter. I was weary in my body and my soul and I climbed the stairs and walked down the hall to my room. Once inside, I took a long, hot shower to banish the chill from my bones. Before settling in to get some sleep, I fired up my laptop and checked my email on the hopes Sandy would have sent something. There was nothing from my wife, although Teddy had sent me a few words of encouragement.

I smiled as I read his note, sent seven hours earlier. The man always knew what to say to me, even when he didn't know everything that was going on. If a man can love another man who's not a brother like a brother, then I loved Teddy like my brother. I fired off a quick response to him, then closed the computer and turned off the lights and stretched out on what the proprietors of the place passed off as a bed. The mattress hadn't gotten any better since I had rolled out of it twenty-one hours before, but I was drained by everything the day had wrought and the anticipation of what the next two days promised and soon drifted off to sleep.

I started awake on Monday morning to the sound of the phone ringing on the bedside table. My hand slapped around the surface of the nightstand and eventually I found the chittering device by the flashing red light which illuminated with each ring through slitted eyes and picked up the receiver.

"Hello?" I said in a raspy voice.

"Mr. Langdon?" came the man's voice in a sharply officious tone.

"Yes," I said recognizing the affect of another cop.

He introduced himself as Lieutenant Philip Neufeldt, the administrative head of the police department in the Town of Ledyard, which included Gales Ferry, where the Saunders family continued to live, and whose office now held jurisdiction over the location of Sarah Avidago's accident in 1998. I had learned by surfing the internet while I waited for the lab results yesterday, that since the year 2000, there no longer existed a Sheriff's office for New London County, with many of that agency's previous responsibilities having been delegated to the individual municipalities and the Connecticut State Marshal's office. The Ledyard Police Department was headed by a Resident State Trooper, a sergeant who was member of the Connecticut State Police, and was administratively overseen by the man on the other end of the phone; and I thought we had some screwy systems in Louisiana. I had left a message with Lieutenant Neufeldt's office yesterday afternoon after leaving the Saunders' house en route to Genco Labs.

"I received your message and do have some time about midmorning if you'd like to stop by my office," he said. "Do you need directions?"

"I can find it," I told him.

"How's ten-thirty?" he said.

"I'll see you then."

"You're ex-CPD, correct?" he said.

It truly was a small world now, I thought. There are no secrets which cannot be uncovered in milliseconds with a simple Google search.

"That's right," I said. "Though that was a lifetime ago."

I heard him chuckle.

"So much is, Mr. Langdon," he said. "I'll see you at ten-thirty."

The line went dead, and I hung up the phone while my slowly focusing eyes drifted to the radio alarm clock. It was five minutes after six in the morning. My body hadn't quite adjusted to the one-hour difference so it was still wanting to sleep on Central time. I rolled out of bed, again thinking a horse somewhere was missing out on a meal - not a good meal, but a meal nonetheless. It wasn't until I was in the middle of another shower that I smiled to myself and recalled I hadn't mentioned the motel name where I was staying in the message I had left for Lieutenant Neufeldt the day before.

I ate breakfast at the cafe again, but didn't see Cheryl, and concluded it must have been her day off. The food was just as tasty, the Johnnycakes as addictive as advertised, and the service just as friendly and quick, but I had hoped to have another conversation with the woman. When I paid my check at the register that time, I asked when Cheryl would be returning and was told she had called that morning and quit without explanation.

Not knowing Lieutenant Philip Neufeldt, but knowing how cops operate, I packed up all my printed information and research for the case into my computer bag and tucked my MacBook Pro in there as well. I planned to leave it all locked in the trunk of the car, along with Willie and Sam, when I went in empty handed to see him.

I used a little spare time after my unusually early breakfast and drove across the river to New London to scope out the location of the afternoon's rally for Dace Lamoureux and other lesser notables running for state and local offices, then took a leisurely drive out to the Lamoureux estate north of New London.

The house sat majestically on a large, wooded lot, set back from the main road which it fronted with its backside overlooking the river. The home was mansion in every sense of the word; large, made of red brick and of Georgian architecture, with oversized, twelve-over-twelve pane, double hung windows with shutters on two floors and a hip roof capped in slate and punctuated with expansive dormers which indicated a third living level, a large columned portico, and was reached by a single drive ending in a roundabout centered on a park-sized, carved marble fountain. The entry to the drive was guarded by brick and white granite capped columns and a closed, wrought iron gate topped with a similarly constructed arch lit by a single, gas coach lamp. A stub of a smaller drive routed around the one side of the house, probably running all the way to the river. In one of the windows on the third floor, a round-faced woman, who I estimated as being in her mid-thirties peered out toward where I was parked, then disappeared moments later.

I drove further along the road, turned around in someone's ungated drive and then passed by without stopping and worked my way back to the interstate. I crossed the Thames River and continued on I-95 east to exit on highway 117, where I traveled north toward the Town of Ledyard's Police Department headquarters. I arrived ten minutes early for my appointment.

The town's offices, which contained its police department, was housed in a modern, one-story, multifunction building and reminded me of so many rural township headquarters in Wisconsin. I parked in the lot, walked into the building and without fanfare or having to pass through any type of security, found Lieutenant Neufeldt's office. I knocked on the frame of the open door. He looked up from behind his desk, then removed his reading glasses, rose and came around to greet me. Phil Neufeldt was in his early thirties, a small man about five-foot-six, wiry, and had a full head of dark brown hair cut like we used to wear it when I was in grade school. His brown eyes were cop friendly as he shook my hand firmly. Before we got down to business, he spent ten minutes telling me how much he enjoyed New Orleans and hinting around the edges for an invitation to look me up when he next visited. To move things along, I provided one.

"I've come to see you for a couple of reasons today, Lieutenant Neufeldt," I said, taking the offered seat in front of his desk. "I want to thank you for taking the time for me."

"Please, call me Phil," he said from behind his desk again.

I told him to please call me William, then I explained the reason I was there while he listened intently. Since Mr. Saunders had mentioned the car accident which had claimed Sarah Avidago's life on Dace's twenty-first birthday, I made passing note to it just to see what I'd get in response.

"That's all ancient history, William," he said. "Ten years ago I was a deputy for New London County. Two years later, they closed us up and people scattered where they could. I came out here and landed on my feet, so to speak."

"I realize it was a long time ago," I said, "but I was thinking you might remember the incidents."

"Of course I remember them," he said.

His voice contained the hint of an assumed insult, one I never intended, but before I could speak on it, he moved on.

"I am the one who delivered the news to both families."

"Both families?"

"Yes, I gave the news to Senator Lamoureux himself on the Avidago accident, then to Mr. Saunders when word came up from Louisiana about Dave twelve or fourteen days later."

"How did you know to track Sarah Avidago back to the Lamoureux family?" I asked.

"Good police instincts," he said with an oddly out-of-place smile. "We called on the registration of the vehicle, found out from Rhode Island Troopers who followed up with the girl's grandmother who told them Sarah had been down in New London to attend Dace Lamoureux's birthday party and that the two had been dating for a while. From what they were told by the grandmother, Sarah anticipated an engagement in her future."

I nodded.

"Were you the investigating officer on the accident?" I asked.

He nodded.

"A family on their way to church in Groton noticed the skid marks and damaged guardrail and brush broken down toward the river. When I arrived on scene in response the call, it was easy to see what had happened and only took a minute or so to locate the vehicle, about two hundred feet down the bluff on a small ledge just short of the Thames."

"The girl was dead on the scene?" I asked.

"Long gone," he said.     "The coroner said she was most likely deceased before the car came to a stop.  We recovered the body and then later that day, the vehicle.   One of her brothers came down to the morgue and gave the positive ID as Sarah Avidago.  He also confirmed the reason she had been down here, as well as the longterm relationship with Dace.  We went to the Lamoureux place to try to speak to him, but his old man downplayed the relationship she and Dace had and just sent us over to see Dave Saunders.  Said the girl had driven Dave home the night before."

"You sound like you know them," I said.  "The Lamoureux family, I mean."

"William, everyone around here knows of the Lamoureux family," he said, "but I did go to school with Dace, so I also know him personally."

"Then you must have also known Dave Saunders from school," I said.

"I did."

"That must have been hard to take the news of his, ah, accident to his parents a couple of weeks later."

"Dave was a good guy.   It was one of the hardest things I've ever done in police work to take that news to his parents.  I liked Dave; hell, everyone liked Dave Saunders."

"Dace not so much?" I said, picking up on his changing tone and facial expressions.

He smirked and sat back in his chair.

"No, Dace not so much," he said.  "In school, I disliked him, if you want the God's honest truth.  He would tease me because my father had died when I was young and it was just me and mom at home."

"Teased you?" I said.  "Because of your father dying?"

"Yep," he said, his lips pursed.  "It was a different time, I guess, or something.   Whatever it was, Dace Lamoureux latched onto it and just wouldn't let go.  I came to the school partway through the third grade when mom moved us here from Pensacola after dad passed, to be closer to family, you know.  She had grown up here, and for a while we lived with grandma and grandpa, my mom's parents.  We moved back to Florida four years later, after seventh grade, when mom rediscovered why she originally had put a little distance between her and family.  When mom died shortly after I graduated from high school, my grandparents talked me into coming back.  Been here ever since."

"Sounds like you had a good reason to hate him," I said.

"Did I say I hated him?"

"Good police instincts," I said with a smile.

He pointed a finger at me and grinned at the turnabout.

"You got me."  He leaned forward, elbows on the desk.  "How is it you're here asking about these two issues, William?  I mean, it's been ten years, and both situations were accidents, the connection in time mere coincidence from every indication. Or was it?"

"Two cases," I said truthfully. "I had a client in 1998 which led me to meet Dave Saunders and his girlfriend, Cindy Spagliano."

He didn't react. Obviously the girl's name meant nothing to him.

"Now I have a client who asked me to look into a new twist which may have peripherally touched Dave when he was down in Louisiana. I'm just crossing t's and dotting i's, I guess you could say."

If he suspected I'd shaded the truth there, his face didn't show it.

"Did you ever speak to Dace Lamoureux about the Sarah Avidago accident?" I asked.

"No," he said.

"How about when Dave had his accident? Did you tell Dace?"

"Why would I?" he said, a quizzical look on his face.

"Because they were friends, perhaps?" I said, reaching a bit.

"No," he said and shook his head, "but, Dave had plenty of friends. Word spread around here fairly fast."

"But I heard they were best friends," I said.

He said nothing, just stared back at me with a frustrated look which indicated had this been court, his attorney would be on his feet screaming 'Asked and answered, your Honor.' I moved on.

"Did you get a copy of Dave's Death Certificate?" I said.

"No, just the notice from the sheriff down there. Why?"

"Just wondering. Did you happen to take any photographs of Sarah Avidago's car?"

"Of course we did," he said, a bit annoyed at the question. "Standard practice. You know that."

"Do you have them in your files?" I asked, knowing if that was county, he probably didn't.

"Yeah," he said. "I used my own camera, a new digital I had back then, and I saved copies."

"Could I see them?" I said.

"I don't see why not," he said. "Case is long since closed, but I do it on one condition."

"What's that?"

His eyes seized mine.

"You tell me what Dace Lamoureux did in Louisiana that has you coming all the way up here after him?"

I forced myself to keep any reaction from my face.

"What makes you think Dace Lamoureux is why I'm here?"

"Good police instincts," he said and then his face produced a large grin, "plus, I'm always hoping to see that sonofabitch get his comeuppance someday; and I thought perhaps today was my lucky day."

I spent the next ten minutes bent over next to him looking at dozens of digital photographs of the accident scene and Sarah Avidago's car and the accident scene on his computer monitor, including a number of the dead girl. I could envision what had happened, having been on that very road just yesterday. Toward the end of the photos, when the car had been recovered to the roadway, I saw something in a reflection in one shot of the rear of the vehicle and asked if he could blow it up. He did and I immediately recognized what had caught my eye. I'd seen those scuff marks before. I knew what they were.

"What is it, William?" he said, obviously not seeing it.

I pointed to the screen.

"Sonofabitch," he said.

I asked for a copy of the photo and he burned it to a CD for me and ran me printouts of it and a couple of others.

We shook hands again, and I told him to make certain he looked me up next time he got to New Orleans. I meant it that time. He seemed like a decent enough sort. He promised he would, then added that if I needed anything more, to just give him a call. I think he just wanted to see me nail his ex-classmate.

I strode back outside to my rental car. I may have walked into Phil Neufeldt's office empty handed, but I walked out with a CD and printouts of some interesting photographs and a lot more background information.

The problem was, I also had many more questions, and I think, so did Phil Neufeldt.

The rally for the Dace Lamoureux campaign was to be held on Monday afternoon at his former high school in New London, a homecoming of sorts. There were to be other speakers, but the headliner was the thirty-one year old Senate candidate. If Cheryl's assessment on the undercurrent of local sentiment was correct, New London might just be an uncomfortable place for the man to make his final push for votes. That afternoon, I was hoping to make it just a little more so for him.

I arrived early at the expansive facilities on the western outskirts of the city. The school was located in what could be considered a mixed area: bounded by woodlands, a couple of low-density subdivisions, and the St. Mary Catholic Cemetery. The campus was large, with every imaginable athletic field and ancillary structure, but the buildings themselves were monstrous examples of utilitarian 1960s architecture linked haphazardly with later, ad hoc additions designed to blend. The overall effect was as compelling as vanilla licorice wrapped in plain white paper. I parked in the street and made my way toward the gymnasium building where the rally was to be held. Streams of human traffic flowed slowly to come together at the main set of doors. I had anticipated a high level of security screening at the door and had left Willie and Sam locked in the trunk to avoid any possible issues. Before I left the car, from my computer bag I retrieved several printed photographs and several other small items and slipped them into my jacket pockets.

Once inside, I asked a few people and eventually was able to track down a professionally pleasant young woman who introduced herself as Anne Mobley, the candidate's Site Coordinator. She was of average height, cute, even with her slightly-too-big brown eyes and brown hair tinged with auburn cut in a sexless, low-maintenance bob. She wore a plum-colored blouse under a tired, charcoal gray, sharkskin business suit and skirt, sensible shoes, and the distressed look wrought of the combination of near exasperation and complete exhaustion. Her handshake was firm and curt and her eyes judged me with a quick once over. She obviously was harried at the end of a campaign, but gave me a show of welcoming courtesy which meant she understood any potential vote counted at that point and until I explained to her that I wasn't from Connecticut, I could have been one. Her demeanor changed when I mentioned being from Louisiana and her eyes began to search the faces beyond me the moment it dawned upon her I wasn't there to support Dace Lamoureux for Senate. She may have been done with me, but I wasn't finished with her.

When I came upon Anne Mobley, she was attended by a single assistant, a buzzing fly of an intern obviously far too eager for the promised, coming perks of senatorial staffdom. He eyed me with curiosity and suspicion which turned to thinly veiled annoyance when he heard me tell his boss I was from Louisiana. I eyed him with a bit of cop-like menace, which caused him to magically recall a task which needed doing someplace else. He squirted off through the growing hallway crowd, many of whom appeared to be students sent by teachers sympathetic to the cause to fill any empty seats for the media cameras or perhaps they were just seeking any excuse to get out of classes. I gently moved the woman to the side of the hallway.

"I am going to need a few minutes of Dace Lamoureux's time," I said. "Today."

"Out of the question, Mr. Langdon," she said, shaking her head even before my full statement had been mouthed. "Mr. Lamoureux is on a very tight schedule today." She glanced at her watch. "Perhaps in a few days, after the election. Here's my card, call my office later in the week. Now, if you'll excuse me, I'm very busy. Good day."

She turned to leave and I touched her elbow and then moved around her and blocked her path. Her eyes went in search of someone to intervene and I knew I had seconds to get my point across. I leaned down and whispered into her ear.

"I'd strongly suggest you deliver the following message verbatim and perhaps there still may be a 'later this week' for Mr. Lamoureux."

I gave her the simple message, then straightened up and observed her with a bit of contained mirth as a puzzled look moved across her face.

"It's your choice to dismiss me as some crank, Ms. Mobley, but do you really want to assume that responsibility?" I gave her my menacing cop smile. "I'll be in the gymnasium. As you can see, I'm not that hard to spot in a crowd."

I walked past her and joined the lineup at one of the interior doors, declined the offered button and flag from a young, female student who couldn't have been any older than Ashley Monreale had been when the son of a bitch people had come to see and cheer had stolen her innocence, then found a seat several rows up, along a side aisle of one of the sets of bleachers. I wanted to be able to get out easily if what I suspected would happen did.

As promised, several candidates seeking election and incumbents seeking reelection to local offices spoke for several minutes and each received the anticipated, sporadic and weak applause, but when the introduction of Senator Allard Lamoureux and Dace Lamoureux began about a half-hour in, red, white, and blue card stock campaign signs appeared out of nowhere and the crowd was urged to its feet by the beats of a familiar, high-energy rock song. The room's lights lowered and the center-court stage was spotlighted. The podium was hit by an additional light from below to eliminate double-chin shadows and aid the press section's cameras which surged to life.

Senator Lamoureux led the way out of the darkness and onto the stage, followed closely by his son. Each wore the uniform: dark blue suit, starched white shirt, red tie. The only variation between them being the candidate's tie contained tiny white dots. The father was a couple of inches shorter than the son, and heavier. His full head of white hair was brushed back, like the oft-described lion's mane. Dace Lamoureux was much leaner than his father and could have easily passed for a reincarnation of the young and vibrant JFK. Together, they strode with cocksureness to just off-center on the small stage and assumed the pose: both hands in the air, the inner set coupled, big grins. Ah, politics.

The music faded, yet the crowd continued the choreographed welcome. Dace waved, shook hands in a show of solidarity with the candidates for local offices and took a seat on a metal folding chair at the far right. Senator Lamoureux moved behind the podium. He eventually settled the crowd with several calming waves of his hands and well-practiced, feinted starts at speaking.

"I'm going to make this short and sweet since we've finally come home to New London," The Senator said.

The crowd stood and cheered, although I couldn't tell if it was for the speaker or the easy applause line mention of their home town.

"You've been the foundation of support for my family and my career for decades now, and if you come out with this level of enthusiasm and continue that support tomorrow at the polls for my son, you'll add the final reward to my fifty plus years of having the honor to be your servant in the United States Senate. You'll give me the joy of working my final two years in Washington with someone I know will be one hell of a fighter for the people of New London and this great state, my son, and the next senator from our beloved Connecticut, Dace Lamoureux."

The candidate stood. The music played. The crowd rose again and added the echos of stomping feet on expanded bleachers to the cacophony. I stood just to see. The bleachers vibrated. Dace moved to his father's side, accepted a handshake and pat on the shoulder as a gesture of the handoff of power. Dace took to the podium and his father retreated and left the stage and walked off into the darkness. I grinned, but it was more aimed at the theatrics than the theme, while my eyes bored holes into Dace Lamoureux less than a hundred feet away. Dace calmed the crowd as had the old man, and everyone eventually took to their seats again.

I was so engrossed in absorbing every detail of the man's persona that I didn't notice a pair of rather large gentlemen in custom-made silk suits moving in the semidarkness along the far wall. I did notice, however, when one of them remained at the base of the bleachers and the other climbed the risers in my direction. He bent down and spoke to me as Dace was settling the crowd to fading music. I rose and followed the man down the steps and out into the hallway. His partner followed close behind. Neither said anything as they escorted me through the passages around the gymnasium and adjacent pool and into the locker room.

"You guys sure are a couple of chatterboxes," I said as we stood staring at each other in silence in between two rows of lockers and changing benches anchored to the floor in a room awash in the long forgotten combination of smells from high school: sweat, dirty socks, chlorine, and mildew; the milieu of high school gymnasiums everywhere.

They each eyed me. At six-foot-six and two-hundred-sixty pounds, I'm a big man, but these two accomplished the unusual, they made me feel undersize.

"We heard you're a smart ass," the younger one who had climbed the bleachers said as he tried to stare me down.

I smiled. He heard right, but there was no reason to congratulate him on being able to articulate the thought.

"Does this one talk?" I said, nodding toward the older one, "or is his job just to look ominous?"

"Just reel it back in for now," the younger one said. "There will be other times for that." He grinned menacingly. "At least I hope so."

"Hmm," I said, and I walked to get drink at the water fountain. We called it a 'bubbler' when I was growing up in Wisconsin, but I know many of you aren't familiar with the term so I mainstreamed it.

Fifteen minutes later, the door opened and in strode Dace Lamoureux. The two mountains moved outside into the hallway.

"Mr. Langdon," he said with an affixed smile and extended his hand.

I coughed into my hand and dropped it to my side. He lowered his.

"I didn't come up here to make friends, Dace," I said. "I came on a mission sent by two mutual acquaintances. Want to guess who?"

He glared at me with piercing green eyes filled with arrogance. His politician's smile, which I was certain had won him much favor over the years as part of an overall mask, remained unflinching.

"I don't have a clue," he said and then drank from the can of diet Mountain Dew he carried in his left hand, "but I am certain you are going to tell me."

He brought up his left arm and checked his watch. I caught the name on the inconspicuous dial: Vacheron Constantin; and knew the man wore at least a quarter million dollars on his wrist.

I reached into the breast pocket of my jacket, removed my cell phone and glanced at the time, then replaced it and removed the papers I had stashed in there. I showed him the first one.

"Dave Saunders," he said. "He was my best friend until the day he died." He shook his head slowly. "Such a tragic, senseless accident. I miss him every day."

"He didn't look like this the last time I saw him," I said, "but that's another story. We'll get to that."

I slipped the second page from the group and held it up for him.

"Cindy Spagliano," he said. "Who's next?"

"She didn't look like this the last time I saw her, either." I locked my eyes on him. "Would you like to hear about the last images I hold of your best friend and his girlfriend?"

"It was a tragic accident," he said and his eyes sought something other than my face upon which to focus. "I can only imagine the horror."

"I doubt you can, Dace," I said. "How about this one?"

I held up the third sheet, one of the several I had obtained just today. He looked at it and then his eyes flared with anger.

"You sick son of a bitch," he spat. "What the hell is this?"

Inside I smiled as he took the bait and swallowed it whole. He felt the hook, yet he made no move to run. I had him by the short hairs and he knew it. He was my guy and I knew it now. There were only a couple more nails I needed in my paw before slamming the lid and beginning to drive them home. My process of escalating the presentation cracked his fragile, thin shell; this type always cracked when they were guilty. I tucked away the death photo of Sarah Avidago at the back of the stack and slipped free the next sheet and held it up for him to see.

"How about this one?" I said. "She wasn't smiling like this the last time you saw her, I would imagine."

His face ticked, then he slowly shook his head but his eyes would not rise to meet mine. He had recovered in the moments since I flashed a death shot of his old girlfriend, but his hands were sweating and he wiped them absently on the sides of his jacket.

"Sorry, can't help you with that one, Mr. Langdon," he said and then looked at his watch again which seemed to help him recover his poise. "Is this going to take much longer? It's been fun playing who's in this picture with you, but I'm on a tight schedule today, as I'm certain you can understand."

"Take another look, Dace," I said, my eyes boring through him. "Ashley Monreale? Ring any bells now? No? Her father was the Louisiana crime boss, Vincent Anthony 'Tony Gators' Monreale. The man liked to feed people who crossed or disappointed him to his alligators. No? Still nothing?"

"Never saw that girl before in my life and I'm certain that's a very colorful and fascinating part of her father's personality, however I have no idea what this has to do with me," he said and he looked at the sheaf of papers. "I see you have a couple more there, so why not get this over with so I can get on to something important?"

I slid free the second from last picture, one from Stan's security camera which showed Ashley and Ronnie interacting with Dave and Cindy in Pat O'Brien's piano lounge. It was the one I had printed a decade earlier.

"This was taken at a bar in New Orleans, a couple of days before Dave Saunders and Cindy died. You can tell by the date and time stamp on the lower right corner there. The other girl is Veronica Broussard. She goes by Ronnie, well, mostly."

"I heard Dave and Cindy had gone down to New Orleans to get away for a while," he said. "So, they made some friends."

"Have you ever been to New Orleans, Dace," I said.

He drank the rest of the soda before responding, wiped a bead of sweat from his forehead with the back of his hand and then set the empty can on top of the lockers.

"No, never," he said, "though I'm certain it's beautiful and historic, and one day I hope to get the chance to visit your little corner of this great nation."

"Maybe in eight years when you run for president?" I said with a sarcastic grin and mocked clapping.

"Perhaps," he said, the politician's smile back on his face.

I showed him the last photograph. It was another shot from Stan's video which I had obtained from him several days ago.

"How about this person," I said. "Recognize him?"

His eyes grew wide and then like the petulant child who had never been held to account for his wrongdoings, he threw a tantrum. I held the photo up and watched, and grinned. This was the time, were I still a cop, that I'd slap the cuffs on him and read him his rights. The problems were I wasn't still a cop and I had agreed to abide by my client's instructions. To the letter. So, all I could do was watch in amused satisfaction as a grown man snorted and cursed and stomped back and forth while I stood holding a screenshot of him standing against the wall at the back of the room in Pat O'Brien's piano lounge. It wasn't slapping the cuffs on the crumb, but it still felt good.

"As you can see, Dace, the time and date stamp matches the one on the previous photo," I said. "You were there, in New Orleans, at this very location at the same time as Ashley Monreale. Minutes later you followed her out of the bar, used that ebullient smile and massive charm of yours to lure her into Dave Saunders' Cadillac Escalade, which you had parked at the Fairmont Hotel after slipping the valet a hundred dollar bill. The valet's name was DeShawn, by the way. You drove her through the Garden District, down St. Charles Avenue on the promise of the two of you getting something to eat at the Camellia Grill, which turned out to be closed at that time of night. You then turned on South Carrollton Avenue, crossed Leake Avenue and some railroad tracks and drove over the levee to the shore of the Mississippi River where you raped, beat, and left Ashley Monreale for dead awash in muddy water at the river's edge."

I moved to block his frenetic pacing and looked down the four inch difference in our height.

"Then you ran home to daddy; and left Dave Saunders to pay for your crimes." I moved closer and glared down into his face. "Let me tell you one thing, you cowardly son of a bitch, he covered your bill with honor and courage, and from what I could tell, he did it in the end because of his love for you."

Bubbles of white spittle were gathered in the corners of his mouth. He was trapped, caught in the net and gasping for air like a big old catfish hauled out of the bayou.

"How do you know about Dave?" he said, taking a step back.

I closed the gap again.

"I was there," I said. "I saw it all. I'm the guy who shot Tony Gators in the middle of the forehead without even blinking. Now, I've got you by your tiny balls, Dace, and I'm gonna start squeezing."

He began trembling. A fucking coward at the core, I saw. I grinned.

"Travis, Rudy," he said, his voice tremulous. "Get in here."

The doors swung open and in walked the two mountains, now bearing the names of Travis and Rudy. They immediately pushed me backward and Dace's courage and bravado seemed to return with that one action.

"I'll bury you, Langdon," Dace said, straightening his jacket and tie and pointing his finger. "I'll fucking bury you."

Dace turned and pushed through the doors into the hallway.

I grinned up at Travis and Rudy. Only the younger one grinned back. I rolled my stack of papers and returned them to my jacket pocket. That's when the younger one sucker punched me in the gut. I doubled over and then the two of them pushed me backward over the bench and into the lockers. I stumbled and fell, hit the back of my head and my shoulder hard as I fell to the floor with my legs draped over the bench.

"Hey, Langdon, say hello to your wife for me," the younger man said.

The pair laughed and turned then followed their boss out of the room. Through the open double doors I could see Senator Lamoureux speaking with an agitated Dace while a bulky, fireplug of a man in his mid-sixties with his arms crossed over his chest stood silently with is back against the wall across the hallway. The fireplug glanced up and made eye contact with me and a moment later they all were gone from view as the doors swung closed.

I pulled myself up and brushed off my clothes. I was getting too old for this crap, I thought. I prepared to walk out of the locker room, but first, I used a towel which was laying across the bench I had fallen over to grab the empty diet Mountain Dew can from the top of the lockers and placed it into one of the plastic bags from my pocket.

I left the room smiling and whistled an old rock tune.

# Chapter Thirty-six

For the third time in two days, I arranged to meet Teri Genco at her office outside of work hours. She arrived after I did and turned up again wearing a short skirt, but had added a skintight top with a deeply scooped neck, hose, high heels, and full makeup and perfume to complete the outfit. When I got closer to her, I could see she had done some tanning since yesterday, or had one sprayed on, given how quickly the process had lightly bronzed her pale skin. I was beginning to feel a weird vibe from the woman, and while part of me felt flattered, most of me did not.

Once inside the building, I declined her invitation to accompany her to the lab to observe the process, so, with a pout, she deposited me in her office after logging in the plastic bag containing Dace Lamoureux's soda can. As I waited for her to complete the testing, I wandered around her office a bit, looking at the various plaques and diplomas and photographs on the walls, then took a seat in one of the guest chairs in front of her desk. I removed the leather-bound notebook from my computer bag and continued scribbling notes and questions into it. A few feelings, thoughts, and muses had also begun making their way onto the expanding number of filled pages.

I stopped writing when I detected the return of Teri's perfume an hour later and looked up as she walked into the office carrying a single sheet of paper. She didn't come in wearing a lab coat, and she eschewed her chair behind the desk and sat in the mate at the frontside, next to me. She positioned herself on the forward edge of the chair, crossed her legs purposefully, and then leaned deeply forward toward me and asked for the comparative. I reached into my computer bag on the floor, which was thankfully on the far side of my chair, and handed the page across. Her fingertips brushed my hand during the transfer and when I looked at her, she was watching me and I felt a bit weirded out.

"What do you think?" I said, attempting to get her to focus for the couple of minutes I needed to obtain the information I needed so I could book it out of there.

"I think today I'm glad I went into biochemistry," she said with a come hither smile added to innuendo.

"I mean, what do you think about the match?" I said, closing the notebook and tucking it into my bag.

I was making ready to bolt the instant she gave her opinion. She slid her butt to the back on the chair as she made an extended show to study the two pages. Her leg began to wag slightly, and the pump fell off her heel and dangled on her hosed toes. It was then I noticed the hose didn't go all the way up, rather ended high on the thigh just under the hem of her skirt. She seemed to be taking an inordinately long time and as I observed her, I could see was squinting slightly, so I reached onto her desk and grabbed her reading glasses off the blotter, then handed them across.

"Try these," I said.

"Oh, thank you, Mr. Langdon," she said, "or may I call you William?"

She reached for the glasses and her hand slid on mine.

"William works," I said.

She set the sheets on her thigh, placed the glasses on her nose and smiled at me. I wondered briefly if she'd call me with the results. Moments later, she removed the glasses, folded them and tossed them onto the desk. Something told me she already knew the answer before coming into the office and this all had been for some kind of show or purpose, but to quote an often dismissive friend, 'whatever'.

"It's a match, William," she said and handed both pages across.

"How certain?" I asked.

"Well, given the DNA comparative from the rape kit had been extracted from a mixed sample, that is, from two people, and represented an unknown subject, and without knowing as a matter of certainty that there is not a monozygotic twin running around out there who would genetically match this now known contributor, both samples matched all thirteen markers plus the AMEL so I'd say the statistical evaluation would yield a match probability in the range of one in nine billion or so."

"One in nine billion?" I said. "Aren't there only about seven billion people on the planet?"

She nodded, reached down and reseated her shoe on her foot.

"About," she said, handing both pages back. "It's as good as it gets, William. Of course, we could run a GenCodex, but that would take twenty-four hours. Since I'm assuming we do not have access to the original sample, it would really do nothing to bolster the statistical probability of the match. GenCodex would only provide a unique DNA identity code matching the person from whom you retrieved the sample on the soda can today. It would help for future matching to the known individual, however, and we can do that for you if you wish. As things stand now, though, were I called to testify under oath in court, William, I could state, unequivocally, the 1998 rape swab and today's drink can submissions came from a single individual."

That was good enough for me. I nodded and stood, slid the shoulder strap of my computer bag onto my left shoulder in the same motion, thanked her and extended my right hand. She seemed caught off-guard by my quick shifting, unfolded herself from the chair and accepted the handshake. Though she held the shake for a moment too long, I had already circled around and was closer to the door than I had been a moment earlier, and I was briskly walking out before she could make another move. In my car a minute later, I waved through the windshield to her standing at the building door looking a bit disappointed or perplexed, and backed out of the parking spot, then hightailed it in the direction of my hotel.

On the drive, I phoned Teddy's cell.

"How's it hanging, Big Dog?" he said after the second ring.

"The problem is that it *is* hanging these days, Teddy," I said.

"I told you it sucked getting older, buddy," he said with a full belly laugh. "Want me to hook you up with my little blue pill doc?"

"Not yet," I said, 'but, I'll keep your number." A pause. "I know you're gonna think I only call when I need something these days, but this time you'd be right. I do need another favor."

"I'm going to ask for a title of some sort in your company soon," he said. "How about 'Theodore H. Ballantine, Of Counsel'?"

"Isn't that just for attorneys?"

"Probably so," he said with feigned disappointment, "but I'm going to need something to do when I retire in a couple of years. I'll think on it and get back to you."

"I'll take you sailing," I joked, both of us knowing how I hated being out on the water now.

"Yeah, that worked out well last time," he said with a laugh. "I still limp when it rains."

"Then, I'm out of ideas, pal," I said. "You want to know what this favor is or do you want to dance around a bit more?"

"Well, we can dance, but only if I get to lead." He laughed. "You sound serious. I take it this favor is important, and gonna cost me."

"Kinda important," I said. "It's more for me than for the client, but it could be costly to you." A pause to let the fact I understood how risky it was for him and his Fibbie contact to sink in. "I need you to have your FBI contact do a *direct* comparison with the stored DNA profile of one, Allard Lamoureux, United States Senator, to the rape kit sample from

1998 I sent you before, which, by the way, I just found out matches exactly the DNA I recovered this afternoon from one, Dace Lamoureux, scumbag."

"Really?" he said. "You matched a candidate to the United States Senate to the attack of Tony Gators' daughter ten years ago?"

"Probability is one in nine billion," I said.

"That's the baby," Teddy said with a whistle. "Now what? And what does it matter if his DNA shows lineage to his old man or not?"

"I've got an idea, Teddy," I said. "I know what I'd like to do to the guy. I'd like to slap cuffs on him and put his privileged ass into a six-by-eight for the next couple of decades, but I'm limited by the agreement with my client how far I can go with him. What got me thinking was what your Fibbie said the other day as the two possibilities since we had no match in CODIS on the blind run with the rape kit results. See, I've researched this family and think I understand who and what they are. They're rich and powerful, and seem to cherish their legacy more than anything. So, I've got an idea, but before I move on it, I need to know for certain. It's not like I am going to be against the framework of my agreement with my client, but I am going to be skirting the perimeter."

Teddy didn't say anything.

"So, you gonna do that for me?" I asked. "Teddy?"

"I was thinking of a way to distract so you would forget it. By the way, buddy, have you ever heard the old axiom about the dangers of striking at a king?"

I had.

"It's important, Teddy, or I wouldn't have asked."

I heard him sigh.

"Call me in an hour," he said, clicking off.

My next call went to Ashley, but the woman who answered said she was out and I was told my client didn't carry a cell phone, which I thought was odd these days. I thanked the woman and said I'd call back. As I pulled into the motel parking lot, I pushed and held the number two on my phone. I heard the ring go through on speaker as I turned off the ignition and dropped the keys into my jacket pocket. It rang six, then seven, then eight times and I was about to hang up before the voicemail came on after the ninth ring when the call connected.

"Yes?"

"I wasn't sure you'd answer," I said.

"What do you need, Will?" Sandy said.

"Are you in the middle of something?"

There was a pause. An uncomfortable one.

"You could say that," she said.

"Wanna share?" I prodded gently.

"Not really," she said. "Since you don't see fit to include me in your life, I think it's time I start doing the same with mine."

"Jesus, Sandy," I said.

The line went dead.

I got out of the car and stood in the cool evening air and stewed for a moment, then walked across the lot to the cafe for dinner. A card on the table advertised Salisbury steak with mashed potatoes and peas as the dinner special and I ordered it. The waitress called it comfort food, and said it was guaranteed to stick to my ribs. I ordered it and it did. I was finishing the meal by sopping up the last of the gravy with a buttered roll when my phone rang.

"I thought you were going to call me in an hour," Teddy said.

I glanced across the cafe at the wall clock and realized it had indeed been over ninety minutes since Teddy had told me to call back in an hour.

"Sorry. I was eating, and I forgot," I said, blending truth with a white lie and kinda hoping he didn't ask. "Did you find something?"

"Just so you know, I used my last marker with this particular Fibbie," he said. "I had been saving it for me, just in case, you know? I want you to know that, for the ledger. The good news is, I do have a result."

"Well?"

"Well? That's all you have to say after I tell you how far out I went for you tonight? Geeze, buddy, please tell me you had Corn Flakes for dinner, because you are sure sounding like someone pissed in them."

I took a deep breath.

"I'm sorry, Teddy," I said. "Sandy and I have been sniping lately, and I left on this trip without filling her in about the case and she got some wrong ideas. You know how upset she gets when I mention this whole situation from 1998, plus, we didn't part on the most pleasant of terms." I paused. "Things were said."

There was a moment of silence. I know how Teddy loves each of us and while I would never put him in the middle, I had shone a spotlight across our troubled waters. Teddy always thought Sandy and I had the perfect marriage. Nobody on the outside knows everything that goes on inside. Not even best friends.

"It happens, Big Dog," he said. "Think it has always been peaches and cream with me and Valeria?'

That did make me laugh. I knew it hadn't been.

"Everybody has troubles in their marriage from time to time," I said, "I'm old enough to know that. It's just this situation with Sandy has become chronic, and, I'm really afraid it's turning toxic; for both of us."

"Can I do anything? Just don't tell me to take your side, because you know I won't ever do that against Sandy. I know you too well, old chum. I know how you can be."

"No," I said, "and, you know me better than that. I wouldn't put you in the middle. And what do you mean how *I* can be?"

"Just sayin'," he said, ignoring the question. "I love you and I love Sandy. All I can do is be there for you both. And you can be a real, um, pain sometimes, buddy."

"It'll work out or it won't, Teddy."

"So, now you're a fatalist?" he said.

"No, I'm a pragmatist. You know that."

"Then don't just sit on your ass and wait for it to either work out or not. Do something to fix it, you stubborn asshole."

"Moi? Stubborn?" I said, accepting by default the asshole part because even my mother had told me once, or twice, over the past fifty years that I could be the south end of a northbound horse sometimes.

I knew Teddy was right. He didn't need to tell me I would have to do something to fix this problem between Sandy and myself, and frankly, the cure wasn't all that difficult to figure out, but for a man like me, it was a medicine I found very hard to swallow. For someone who had solved the problems of others and lived with their mayhem twenty-four/seven for so many years, the last thing I wanted to do was rehash every detail of my world at the end of the day with Sandy. There were things a man needed to keep locked inside, not the least of which involved his self doubts and perceived failings. I had both, in quantity, and I truly believed allowing Sandy to see those blemishes of character would diminish me in her eyes. Stupid, I know, but that's me.

"We're chipped from the same rock, Big Dog," he said. "I fully understand you. As well as I understand me. And Sandy understands you, too, if you just give her the chance."

"Sandy and I probably understand each other better than we understand ourselves," I said. "It's not that I want to shut her out, I want to protect her."

"You need to be strong enough to allow yourself to be vulnerable in her eyes," he said, "and I know what you're going to say, old chum; we both share that fault, if it is a fault."

"Why is that so hard for them to understand, Teddy? To realize that we don't want to let them fully inside our world, I mean. Do they really want to know about the shit we see and do and feel after we're done seeing and doing and feeling it at the end of the day? I wouldn't. It's bad enough to live through it in the first place. The thought of dragging Sandy down into the mire where I have to work makes me sick."

"That's what women want," he said, his voice resigned. "Why, I'll never know. They expect us to listen to their incessant outpouring of every excruciating detail of their life, over and over again. At first we offer fixes, but later learn - hopefully - not from their lips, mind you, but from the magazines and talk shows they shove in front of us, they don't want us to fix it, they just want us to listen and say nothing. Which is what we do then, right? Of course, we usually are half listening while we think about something else and occasionally toss in a sympathetic nod or utter a simple 'Mm-hmm' just for effect. Right? Then, they expect us to do the reverse, to open up to them like they do to us; but, being men, we not only want to solve their problems and move on, we truly want to fix ours on our own. We really do, right? We don't need to talk about our stuff, except maybe to each other now and again when we can bust a few balls and gain some perspective. And why?"

"Because we're guys?" I said.

"Yeah, and being guys, we think they will see our opening up like we see their incessant whining: as weak and an annoyance. I dunno, maybe it all boils down to the fact things are truly different on their planet, buddy. Perhaps we just have to accept it all as the single-most universal truth."

While I know Sandy's interest in my life and problems is real, and her questions are not meant to put me under the bright interrogation lights, why can't she understand that's how it feels to me? Why won't she just accept as fact that I'd much rather use my time-honored, three-part problem solving process: identification, rumination, solution, than to sit down and talk it all out? Problem sharing is just not who I am, or who I will ever be.

"And if you solve that riddle, men all over the world will erect a statue in your honor," he said. "Just know I'm here, William."

Teddy rarely called me by my name.

"I know, Teddy. I appreciate it."

"Bottom line on that," he said.

"Case closed," I said and punctuated that fact with a short pause. I had forgotten why we were talking originally, then remembered. "Oh, yeah, what do you have for me from the Fibbie?"

"Well, what I have to tell you may not improve your overall mood," Teddy said. "On the other hand, it just might. Are you sitting down?"

"Actually, I am."

"Senator Allard Lamoureux could *not* be the father of Dace Lamoureux. Zero percent chance."

An hour after I got off the phone with Teddy, I was sitting on the bed in my motel room waiting for Monday Night Football to come on in a couple of minutes when my cell phone rang. I checked the caller ID and saw it was Ashley Monreale calling me back. I set down my pen and closed the notebook, put them aside and picked up the phone.

"Hi, Ashley," I said and used the remote to mute the television.

"Hello, Mr. Langdon," she said. "I hope you don't mind me returning your call instead of waiting for you to call back. Is this a good time?"

"Perfect time, Ashley."

"I would imagine you've discovered something?"

"Yes," I said. "You were correct. The man who attacked you was Dace Lamoureux. No doubt."

I expected to hear some emotional outburst, but there was nothing but silence coming from the other end of the line. It seemed all so matter-of-fact. Perhaps the woman had already done all the crying she could muster about the whole nightmare, I thought. I'd seen it happen before, when, distant from the actual crimes, we'd finally arrest someone and go to tell the victim and they'd have no real reaction. Sometimes, people handle difficult situations and move on with their lives in different ways.

"Thank you, Mr. Langdon," she said, her voice flat. "Now, as to the other part?"

That was a quick move on. At that moment, something told me that I was taking this all more to heart than the victim. That conclusion should have set off a warning horn in my head, but it didn't. I had been sitting there plotting how to make Dace Lamoureux pay for his crimes, and factoring in the overpayment already placed onto account for him by Dave Saunders and Cindy Spagliano, while my client, the initial victim, seemed to concern herself with nothing but the second half of our agreement.

"That part is going to be a bit more difficult," I said. "It took some fairly harsh tactics to conclude the identification. I'm not so certain the rest can be accomplished now as easily as you may think. He's on high alert. I am not certain I can even get close to him, let alone get him in a room by himself again. I've been sitting here thinking about it for the last hour."

"I will hold you to your word to do this for me, Mr. Langdon," she said. "I trust you'll do the necessary things and get it accomplished." A pause. "Good night, Mr. Langdon."

She clicked off without waiting to hear my response, not that I had anything worth hearing at that point. I sat with the phone in my hand and stared blankly into the television. The football game had begun and the Steelers had the ball. I really didn't care about the night's matchup with the Redskins since neither team was one of my favorites, but I thought it would be something mindless to have on in the background while I thought all this through. I shut off the television a few minutes later and found my shoes in the corner of the room and slipped them on. I grabbed my jacket off the chair on my way out the door, shaking my head all the way out to the car, and wishing I could talk to Sandy. This, I could talk to her about.

Five days ago, Ashley Monreale had goaded me into agreeing to something I should have never taken upon myself. It was a bad fit for me; but, I had been weakened by guilt and remorse and her words and she had taken advantage of me. No, that wasn't true. Not entirely anyway. I had wanted to obtain this justice for her for the past ten years. I'd dream about it night after night for long periods, then it would recede into my subconscious only to return again on another dark night. I was ready to conclude this, and the closer I had come to nailing Dace Lamoureux, the more I had become torn between three masters: my justice, true justice, and these seemingly unfathomable instructions from the victim which I had chained to me by my own pledge to her.

Twenty minutes later, I rolled to the gate of the Lamoureux estate. There were a handful of cars parked in the drive and the house was lit up. I still didn't understand *why* I was there, but Ashley had asked me to do it this way, sort of, so after hanging up the phone with her, I had decided there was no time like the present to make the first attempt. Besides, the Steelers were already beating up on the hapless Redskins, so watching the rest of the game would in no way be as much fun as what I envisioned happening out here tonight. I pushed the call button and waited.

"Hello?" came a woman's slightly sluggish voice on the intercom.

"William Langdon to see Senator Lamoureux," I said.

There was the expected pause.

"Is daddy expecting you?"

"Possibly," I said. "He saw me at the rally today. At least I think he did. See, he was outside in the hallway and I was on my back in the locker room after Dace and his thugs assaulted me. I saw him through the open doors. My name is William Langdon. I'm a private detective from New Orleans. I think he'll want to see me."

There was a long pause; long enough that I was expecting flashing lights to roll up behind me at any moment.

"I'm sorry, but The Senator isn't home right now," a different female voice said. This one more mature.

"Mrs. Lamoureux?" I said, taking a shot.

"Yes?"

"May I please have a a few minutes? I think you should hear what I have to say."

I sat there for several long moments after I heard the click of the circuit closing on the intercom. Then, the gates began to swing open and I drove onto the Lamoureux estate. All I could think as I circled the fountain at the end of the drive and parked was: 'Now what?'

I stepped out of the car and the front door opened and interior light silhouetted the two women who appeared in the portal.    As I approached, their features became clearer.    The woman in front was obviously Mrs. Lamoureux, eighty-one from her biographical information I had pulled from the internet, but still quite attractive and looking at least ten years younger.  She was short, about five-foot-four, her auburn hair maintained in a time-frozen, yet age appropriate coiffure identical to the photos I had seen online.  When I came into the light, her emerald green eyes looked me up and down.    Behind her was the daughter, Mary Rose, who was three years older than Dace, and afflicted with Down Syndrome.  There hadn't been much more about Mary Rose in the online biographical information, not that the family hid the woman, but neither did they thrust her into the limelight.

"Mister, uh, Langdon, is it?" Mrs. Lamoureux said as she extended a hand.  "I'm Elizabeth Lamoureux."

Strong willed woman, I thought and shook her hand.  Her grip was firm, yet still feminine, her hand cool, smooth, and sinewy.    Her eyes locked upon mine.

"Yes, Mrs. Lamoureux.  William Langdon.  You may call me William if you prefer."

"I'm Mary Rose, William," she said and thrust her hand forward, derailing the rest of the introductions.

I shook Mary Rose's hand.    There was something sticky on her fingers.    Normally, when I put my hands onto something tactilely off-putting - such as Sandy's left behind remnants of whatever she was baking on the refrigerator door pulls - it tends to annoy me to no end, but there was something warm, inviting, and innocent in the girl's face which made me simply smile.

"Very nice to meet you, Mary Rose," I said.

"Won't you come in, William?" Mrs. Lamoureux said.    "Please feel free to call me Libby.  Everyone does."

I nodded and stepped into the foyer, immediately detecting the warm and dry air and subtle aroma of an active fireplace.  There were voices in a room beyond, cheerful voices and the occasional lilt of laughter.  The interior of the home was warmly appointed, with deep ruddy woods everywhere and after we stepped from the firmness of the marble-floored foyer, rich, wool carpets underfoot.    Libby led the way in a different direction to the voices and then sent Mary Rose back to join the rest of the family, as she put it.  I assumed that meant the other sisters, husbands, and perhaps their children.

"Would you like something to drink, William?  Coffee?  Tea?  Soft drink?" Libby asked as she led the way into the breakfast nook.  "Would you prefer something harder, because, as you can imagine, we have that, too."  She smiled over her shoulder as she circled the table.

"Nothing, thank you," I said. "I truly don't want to take too much of your time, what with your family here."

She waved off the inconvenience in a manner suggesting my arrival had been less than an intrusion and offered me a seat at the table. I sat and peered out the windows to my left. The outside was lighted and revealed a well-kept patio with a large, bricked fire pit ringed with a similarly constructed seating area and a stone pathway out into the woods. A single, carved marble bench sat alone at the end of the path amongst the remains of orange and yellow daisies. I assumed the river was beyond in the darkness. She sat next to me at the foot of the table to my right.

"You certainly have a lovely home, Libby," I said.

She smiled.

"You didn't come here tonight to see my house, William," she said. "You came to see my husband for some purpose, and for various reasons of which you may not be aware, I'm an able surrogate for anything you may wish to say to him. By the way, I know who you are, and where you are from, William. I've been married for a long time, and unlike most women of my position, I'm very much in the loop when it comes to external situations which can affect my family."

I was beginning to get cold feet. Everything I had read about the woman had been positive. She was well-regarded in the local community and in Washington. She had been raised in privilege, the daughter of a former governor, yet Libby Lamoureux was said to be a warm and genuine personality. The writings on the woman in the published media were always glowing, almost fawning. As I looked into her eyes, I could see the strength and warmth within, yet I also detected something else, something deeper and darker and more dangerous. Perhaps discerning that was the difference between being a reporter and being a cop. I took a deep breath and began to say what I had come to discuss with her husband. After all, what would occur tonight was for my sense of justice. The business I had yet to conclude directly with this woman's son for Ashley I had determined would be handled tomorrow, on election day, preferably with no prying eyes or ears nearby. What will dawn for the candidate as a day of high hopes will certainly come to a close in an unanticipated and overwhelmingly negative manner.

"Libby, what I have to say may not be pleasant to hear," I began.

She sat back in her chair and her hands moved to her lap. Libby Lamoureux had obviously heard unpleasant news in the past, and she knew how to prepare herself for it.

I detailed for her the events which had taken place in Louisiana a decade ago. As I spoke, it became clear much of what I related was not a surprise to her, but other things were. Her eyes momentarily misted when I described in detail the brutality of the attack on Ashley Monreale, then cleared just as quickly. She had no reaction whatever when I described the deaths of Dave Saunders and Cindy Spagliano. She had heard that part before, and knew the local lore of an accident was a fabrication. That much was quite obvious. I held nothing back. There was no longer any need to obfuscate, and while I held no malice for this old woman and no desire to cause her pain, it was time this all came out, and she was the able surrogate for her husband, to use her own words. When her eyes questioned me, I told her we indeed had all the DNA evidence necessary for any court, be it of public opinion or of law. She took a deep breath and I could see her mind forming the pertinent question when it was clear I was coming to what she would view as the worst of the information I had come to share, and she interrupted me and asked it.

I merely nodded.

The tears welled in her eyes and she allowed them to roll down her cheeks. Several droplets collected on the break of her chin, then fell onto her lap. I felt bad for the woman on many levels, but then a realization struck me like a lightning bolt and I decided in that moment to give her the rest of it. Even though I understood if the woman reacted the wrong way to what I was about to announce that Teddy's Fibbie would be hunted down in the next hours, my gut told me that's not how this all would end. Three decades of observing people in all manner of stressful situations told me exactly how Libby Lamoureux would play it out, and that's how I arrived at the answer to my self-posed question at the gate: 'Now what?'

Until tonight's thinking and realization about the Lamoureux family's love of legacy, I had planned the final bit of information uncovered tonight would stay between nobody but Teddy and myself, because it previously really served no purpose other than to provide me with an answer to a question. Natural curiosity, right? When I left the motel, I had planned on using the information with The Senator, not his wife, but what I realized as Libby's tears fell had changed my mind.

The woman seated to my right wasn't shedding tears for the horrific injuries and lifetime of nightmares inflicted upon an innocent, sixteen-year-old girl, nor was she crying for the gruesome deaths of Dave and Cindy and the pain that had caused their families and friends. She wasn't even crying over the knowledge her only son had instigated the entire series of tragedies which devastated three families just to satisfy his own lustful and dark purposes, or wondering how he could have gone so wrong. She had no sadness that her son may have to pay the penalty for what he had done and how it may affect the rest of her family. No, Libby Lamoureux was crying for the most selfish of reasons: how the news I came bearing tonight was going to affect *her*.

I told her the last.

Then, I stood and excused myself, surprised I didn't feel the pity for this old woman as I had expected I would when I entered her home. Rather, for so many reasons, I felt angry and sick to my stomach and needed some fresh air. I walked alone and unescorted out of the house and into the night.

The liquor store was still open as I passed by. At the end of the road, I turned around and went back and bought a bottle of Jim Beam bourbon, a Snickers, and a newspaper and drove to the motel. Tomorrow, all this would end, and life, or some semblance of it would return and fill the voids that would remain. That much was now very clear. In the moment, however, I felt no reason to look forward with hope and jubilation. I just wanted to numb the pain.

Before I got too drunk, I located the card for Anne Mobley and called the cell phone listed on it. To my surprise, she answered the call. The background noise indicated she was in some type of boisterous gathering. My eyes searched out the clock on the nightstand and I concluded it was too late for another campaign event so this must be some kind of party to celebrate the wrapping up of what they must hope to be a successful effort. 'Next stop, the United States Senate. Whoop, whoop.' I drained the plastic cup at the thought, then again gave the woman an ominous message to pass along to Dace Lamoureux.

When I disconnected the call, I double-checked Willie and Sam, then I poured more bourbon.

# Chapter Thirty-seven

The Senator arrived home just before midnight to find the house darkened and the roaring fire in the family room fireplace he had left just hours before mere glowing embers. Memories. The rest of the family had already turned in for the night and as he passed through the kitchen for a bottle of water, he became annoyed to discover that everyone had neglected to turn off the exterior patio lights before going to bed. He walked to the bank of switches near the breakfast nook and it was then that he noticed Libby sitting alone on the bench out in the garden.

He hiked the collar on his wool overcoat and walked outside. The chilly evening had turned into a frosty night and he saw Libby had wrapped herself in one of her full-length fur coats. He could see her breath as he drew near.

"Libby?" he said. "What in God's name are you doing out here?"

"Sit down, Allard," she said without taking her eyes off the last of the fall daisies, each petal fringed in frost. "I've got some things I need to tell you."

An hour later, The Senator was locked in his office. He used the secure house phone to place a call. A sleepy voice answered on the fourth ring. The Senator spoke few words, and needed to repeat none. The message had been understood. Then, the eighty-five-year-old hung up the receiver and removed a pad of paper and pen from his desk drawer. A cut crystal tumbler containing several ice cubes and a healthy dose of single malt sat poised on the edge of the blotter. He reached across the desk and grabbed the drink and took just a taste. It would be a long night with no sleep, and an even longer day dawning in the morning, he knew, so he'd be careful with the alcohol. As the taste of the deep amber liquid flowed down his throat, it warmed his core and immediately calmed his shaking hands. He set down the tumbler, unscrewed the cap of his father's fountain pen and began to scratch it across the paper.

The knock on the door was more like a pounding. I don't know how long it had been going on at less than the current, vigorous level. I cracked open my eyes which refused to focus on the bedside clock, but the intensity of the light fighting for access to the room around the edges of the heavy curtains told me it was well into the morning. I fumbled around the bed and located Willie on the rumpled covers. I stuck the gun into the back of my waistband and mumbled profanities at the incessant knocking. At that moment, it was hard to tell which was pounding harder, my head or the asshole outside my door.

I shuffled across the carpet in stocking feet while making dry mouth entreaties for the pounding to cease. I found the door and forced on eye to look through the peep hole. Brown suede filled the view, but at least the pounding had stopped - the ones on the door anyway. I moved back, rubbed my eye, then looked again. Yep, a brown suede mountain. That's all I could see. I twisted the deadbolt open, then turned the knob, slowly opening the door a crack. The door crashed open, the security chain hanging impotently at the attachment of two small, brass screws in cheap mahogany trim. The force of the flying slab caught me off-guard and I tumbled backward. In the next moment and for the second time in two days, I was on my back, looking up at Travis and Rudy. The problem was, this time they weren't walking away, they were coming toward me with malevolent grins on their faces and matching stainless steel forty-five caliber semiautomatics in their hands.

The younger one - I had names, but still don't know who was who - smiled widely as he menacingly pulled back the hammer with his thumb. The older one closed the door, then matched the thumb maneuver albeit without the grin. I was planted firmly on Willie and there was no way I could grab it and twist away from two slugs, so I had no choice but to see how this played out. It was fairly clear that if they had wanted to kill me, I'd already be dead, and they wouldn't have made all the noise outside the door which had most likely alerted everyone in the place. These two were obviously too well trained to make many rookie mistakes.

"Someone would like to see you, Langdon," the younger one said.

I was really beginning to have a dislike for him.

"Fuck you, asshole," was what I managed in a raspy voice.

That brought the first smile I had seen to the older one's face, but merely my bravado appeared to only further irritate his partner who uncocked the .45 and tucked it into his belt, then reached down and picked me up like I was a rag doll. In a deft move, he reached around and pulled Willie from the back of my pants, thumbed the release and dropped the clip out the bottom of the grip, then ratcheted the chambered round onto the carpet and tossed my Sig onto the bed. He removed his gun again, aimed it at the center of my chest and slid the hammer back again.

"You always carry a backup," he said. "A blue-steel, thirty-eight snub nose revolver you call Sam in an ankle holster." He grinned. "Willie and Sam. Cute. Like the line from the 1960s hit by the Turtles."

"Herman's Hermits," I said, running my dry tongue across even drier teeth.

"What?"

I picked up the plastic cup and drained about a quarter inch of bourbon from the bottom. That helped.

"I said, 'Herman's Hermits'. They did *Henry the Eighth*. The Turtles are best known for their 1967 number one hit, *Happy Together*. Which, I can say, boys, you two and I will obviously never be."

"Funny. You're a real card." He dropped the aim of his .45 and pushed it up against my thigh. "Now, give up the backup piece nice and easy, Langdon, then you can go clean up a bit and we'll take you to your appointment. With any luck, you'll be back here in an hour and then you can go home to that pretty wife of yours in New Orleans. So be good, Langdon, because I don't want to have to carry your ass and one way or another, you're going to make this meeting."

My brain was slowly clearing, and my other senses were fighting to sharpen themselves, but Travis and Rudy clearly had the drop on me. I told them that Sam was in the nightstand along with the holster for Willie.

"Then go clean up and let's get going," the younger one said. "You got two minutes, Langdon. You don't need to be beautiful."

I crossed the room to the sink outside the small bathroom. I ran cold water and rubbed it onto my face, then ran my wet fingers through my hair and dried my face in a small towel as I pictured Dace Lamoureux's eyes bulging as I squeezed his neck between my hands. I slipped on my shoes and grabbed my jacket off the chair and followed the older one out the door with the younger one right behind me.

Neither of them had looked in the nightstand.

We walked out into a bright, sunny day. The air was cold and there wasn't a cloud in the sky. I reached into the jacket pocket and removed my sunglasses, a pair of well-worn Maui Jim's I had picked up five years earlier when I was on the namesake island. I slipped them onto my face and my eyes thanked me.

They loaded me into the back seat of a black Lincoln Town Car and the younger one got in alongside me while the older one got in behind the wheel. As he started the car, I saw the display on the radio announce the time as 9:17. We pulled out of the lot and drove the now familiar roads out to the Lamoureux estate. Approaching the closed gates, the driver touched a button on the remote on the overhead and the gates swung open. At the head of the drive, he parked, then they hustled me out and across the walkway to the front door. I noted there were no other cars parked out front as there had been the previous night.

This obviously wasn't going to turn out to be the private meeting with Dace Lamoureux I had envisioned when I spoke to Anne Mobley last night, but with Sam securely attached to my ankle, I still realized I had what I needed to take care of the second half of the agreement I had with Ashley without too much trouble when the time was right.

We walked inside unannounced. I heard no sound from any part of the house as we crossed the foyer, then climbed the wide, carpeted stairs to the second floor. Down the hallway paneled in rich wood we quickly approached the closed door at the end. The older one knocked, then without hearing an invitation, opened the door while his partner pushed me in the small of the back and I stepped into the darkened room.

I heard the door close behind me and then muffled footsteps as they walked away. I slowly moved my eyes around the room without seeing much detail in the low light, then my foggy brain remembered my sunglasses and I tipped them onto the top of my head. The windows were shuttered and even with unshaded eyes, the room still quite dark. I heard the voice come from behind me. It was strong, but I detected a slight slurring of the words.

"Good morning, Mr. Langdon," he said. "I'm sorry for the way you were brought here..."

I turned and my eyes focused on the man seated behind the massive, ornate, antique desk, its top littered with crumpled sheets of expensive writing paper with several more wads scattered across the oriental rug.

"...but if you will indulge me, I don't have much time this morning, and there are more pressing matters which I will have to deal with shortly. Please sit down, and we'll talk. You must forgive the lack of any social graces this morning, Mr. Langdon, but as I said, I've got many things on my plate today and you are but the first with which to be dealt."

"Senator Lamoureux," I said and moved to the offered guest chair across his desk.

There was an empty tumbler on his blotter. His eyes were tired and the desk lamp was the only light in the room. It shown across the litter of crumpled discards to a small stack of sheets containing orotund scripting and topped with an old fountain pen laid at rest.

"I understand you came looking for me last evening," he said, tired blue eyes staring from puffy sockets, "and that you spoke to my wife."

"I did," I said. "I'm frankly sorry I missed you. What I had to say was intended for your ears, but your wife was kind enough..."

He waved a hand to stop me. I stopped.

"My wife relayed everything you had to say," he said, settling back into his chair and rubbing his eyes. "Everything."

His hand dropped away and his eyes locked upon mine.

"Well, Senator," I said, "then you can understand that I had expected to meet with your son today to discuss certain things in private. There's really nothing left to be said between you and I. The only issues currently pending conclusion in this matter are frankly between Dace and myself."

"My son is dead, Mr. Langdon," he said with no real emotion in his voice.

Immediately, I thought he was speaking figuratively since he indicated his wife had told him everything I had said to her last night which I assumed included the fact that Dace was sired by someone other than the man sitting across the desk from me; but when his unblinking eyes continued to stare me down, I realized The Senator was being quite literal.

"I have been up all night writing the words which I will speak to the media in several hours when the news breaks."

"Dead? How? When?" I said, falling back into my police training to obtain the facts, just the facts.

"He was assassinated at a couple of minutes past five o'clock this morning," he said.

"Assassinated? By who? Where?"

"In his hotel suite in Hartford. An unknown assailant, most likely some angry gun nut from the opposing fringe. Two bullets to the chest as he slept. A .38 caliber weapon." He leaned forward in his chair, slid his elbows onto the desk blotter. His face became deadly serious. "Without my help, ballistics will match the recovered slugs to the weapon currently strapped to your left ankle, which you so humorously anthropomorphize as Sam, I believe. That's where I have your back, Mr. Langdon. In a few moments, you'll understand how you have mine."

I began to reach for my ankle holster. I knew Sam was there, I could feel the weight when I walked. I stopped in mid-reach and looked across at him. He smiled, displayed an open palm invitation to continue.

"Go ahead, look for yourself," he said, then again sat back in his chair. "The boys were to take it off you before they brought year here, make a show of it, but I'm glad you were able to pull one over on them, as it were. It makes the demonstration a little simpler, and much more complete."

I slipped Sam free, but I didn't really need to look once I did; I could smell the expended cordite the instant the weapon came clear of the holster. I put my foot down on the floor and held the revolver in my right hand and released the cylinder. Two shells had indeed been fired, the casings were still in the weapon. I looked up at The Senator unable to dig loose a single word of protest from my bourbon addled brain.

"You see, Mr. Langdon, I have known of my son's crimes committed in Louisiana for a decade now. He sat me down the day he came home with the boys who brought you to me this morning, mere hours after he raped and beat that girl along the river." He chuckled derisively. "I imagine he still had the essence of the little slut on his dick as he told me about it."

I watched as he reached for the empty tumbler on the blotter, rose and walked across the room, dropped a couple of ice cubes into the bottom and splashed Scotch over them. I wanted to empty Sam into the bastard's chest. He hefted the decanter in my direction.

"Hair of the dog, Mr. Langdon?" he said. "You look as if you could use it."

I shook my head. He crossed back to behind the desk and sat.

"Yes, I heard you imbibed rather heavily last night after you left here. Travis said you polished off a whole bottle of bourbon in a couple of hours. Of course, that did make retrieving your gun for the job all the easier. Perhaps I should thank you."

He drank, stared into the glass a moment before continuing. I sat in silence. There was little I could say or do until all the cards had been played.

"The situation with the girl's father and Dave Saunders and the girlfriend was unexpected by Dace, of course," he continued, "and that could have turned into a sticky wicket, but some quick maneuvering on my part and a few well-placed dollars took care of the worst of it. You know, it's amazing how cheaply your southern officials can still be bought these days, and how few of them it takes to get a job done. Seems like they're all chomping at the bit to show you their clout, and irredeemably greedy to keep it all to themselves. Once the accident story arrived in Connecticut and the quick insurance settlement was made with the Saunders', any potential inquiry ended before it was begun. And, of course, for tying up all the loose ends, we had you to thank. Mr. Tony Gators could have become quite problematic had you not killed him that night, don't you think?"

I flipped the cylinder closed on Sam and held the weapon on top of my thigh. The next pull of the trigger would fall upon a live round. He traced my eyes and then snorted.

"Oh, put that away; you're not going to shoot me, Mr. Langdon," he said with a wicked smile on his face. "That would be very stupid indeed, and the one thing I've learned about you is that you're not stupid. You're a pain in the ass, a meddler with his own overinflated sense of importance and an anachronistic sense of justice, a sometimes borderline drunkard, with yet another failing marriage, but you're not stupid.

Notice I said 'justice' and not 'right and wrong', because I know you see right and wrong in pure black and white terms, don't you? No shades of gray for you in right and wrong, are there? For you, justice, on the other hand, contains many shades between black and white. You and I are alike in that. I live in a world made up almost entirely of shades of gray. Where you and I differ from the rest of the world is in how we judge the administration of justice. In that, we are the same. You see, I know all about you and Chicago. So put the gun, Sam, is it? Please put Sam away, Mr. Langdon."

I didn't move. He smiled and spread his hands.

"Oh, all right, hold it if it makes you feel better. But understand, starting today, I'm your new best friend; and oddly, as part of necessity, you are mine. We each will have the other's back, you could say."

He slid his chair back and stood and walked to a window and opened the shutters. Light spilled into the room. He stood there, looking out into the day and his fist found the center of his lower back. I could see his knuckles white with exertion and a slight trembling in his hand.

"You had your own son murdered, Senator?" I said.

"He wasn't my son, Mr. Langdon. Of anyone, you should know that fact. I have no son. Never did, as you so cleverly proved, and then kindly shared the existence of the proof with my wife last night. As I said earlier, she told me everything you had to say, and she admitted the affair which resulted in Dace, and Mary Rose, for that matter."

He crossed back to the desk but didn't sit. He leaned forward, his palms splayed on the desk on either side of the blotter. His eyes bore into mine.

"See, that's where you have my back. We're making what they call in Washington, a 'back room deal', although, as you can clearly see, this really isn't a back room." The fountain pen skittered across the desk as he roughly picked up the sheaf of papers and waved them at me and his voice rose in anger. "This is the only story the world will hear about the life and death of Dace Lamoureux. Understand?" He returned the papers to the blotter and his voice settled. "I have my legacy, and you have your life and freedom, Mr. Langdon. You have my back and I have yours." He thrust his finger in my direction. "And don't you ever try to fuck me, because if you do, I'll bury you, Langdon. You can count on that."

Travis and Rudy drove me back to my motel. I packed my things with them in the room, then they told me they were to drive me to Newark for me to catch a flight back to New Orleans. When I protested, they assured me someone had already arranged to get the car back to the rental agency. The older one put my bags into the trunk of the Town Car while the younger one accompanied me in while I settled up with the front desk. When I came out, I got into the back seat and we rolled out of the lot.

As I watched the miles tick away out the window on I-95, I didn't know what to think about this deal I had been forced to make this morning with the devil, and worst of all, my brain was currently working at less than half power so there was little chance I'd come up with anything anytime soon.

I knew I was innocent, but from a cop's and prosecutor's perspective they would have everything necessary for a jury to convict pointing directly at me. Not only did I have motive, means, and opportunity, there was the ballistics evidence which would directly link me to the murder. My prints were on the gun, obviously. I had no alibi other than 'I was sleeping', and I've been around the block enough to have seen juries nearly laugh themselves out of their seats when people with far less against them than what had been set up against me claimed to be home alone in bed sleeping when the crime went down.

My gaze moved into the front seat where Travis and Rudy now rode together. They had obviously come into my room as I slept in a drunken stupor and taken Sam and then driven the sixty miles to Hartford where one of them had surely entered Dace's room and pulled the trigger to fire the bullets which had killed him. Then, they had returned the gun to my possession before they woke me this morning. An excellent scenario and most likely true in every aspect, but, apart from conspiracy theorists who wrapped their heads in foil to protect themselves from alien thought beams, who would buy it? As Tom Cruise's character says in *A Few Good Men*: "It doesn't matter what I believe, it's what I can prove."

Was I really going to put my life at risk in some misguided attempt at obtaining justice *for* Dace Lamoureux? He was a scumbag rapist and God only knows what else, and someone finally had made him pay for his crimes. Did that bother me? Not in the least. The Senator was correct in his black and white analogy of how I saw right and wrong. When I looked across the chessboard, this game appeared to be in balance. As for the shade of gray in this particular justice, was it really any of my concern?

The bluff came in his implied threat about Chicago. Nobody but yours truly knew the truth there, but did I really want to go into a battle with a United States Senator and take the risk he really was bluffing? Over, again, the late Dace Lamoureux, scumbag? The universe has a way of sorting itself out and the further I got from New London and the more the Jim Beam evaporated from my brain, the more it appeared to be nearly so. Ashley would not be happy when I gave her my final report, but there was little I could do about that. What was done, was done.

After two hours on the road, we drove into Newark's Liberty Airport and to the curb at Continental Airlines' departure area. I slid out of the car and moved around to the trunk. Physically, I was feeling better, but I was hungry and thirsty. Travis and Rudy got out with me, although the driver had popped the trunk while still sitting in his seat. I removed my duffle and gun case and slipped the computer bag over my shoulder. My guns were already packed away. They no longer believed I was a threat, if they ever had. The Senator had made that point quite clear in his office.

The younger one stopped me after I stepped onto the curb. He stood in my path.

"Your flight leaves in a little over an hour, Langdon," he said. "We've got you booked into First Class, so behave."

I glared at him and then started to walk toward the entrance doors. He moved out of my way.

"Hey, Langdon," he called after me. "I'd advise you not to come back to Connecticut anytime soon."

I kept walking and just before the rubber mat, I turned.

"Hey, which of you assholes is which?" I said, looking back at them.

"What does it matter?" the older one said.

I smiled.

"Because I have a feeling things are not over between us, and I want to know what to tell 'em to write on the toe tags when it is."

They grinned at me but said nothing and the younger one got into the car and closed the passenger door, then rolled down the window.

"Tell your wife Rudy says hello," the passenger said with an evil grin.

I nodded and winked at him and turned toward the doors.

"Hey, Langdon."

I turned.

"You got balls," the older one, now Travis said, his smile neutral. "And honor. I may be on the other side in this, but I do admire honor."

Something unspoken passed between us in that moment. It wasn't right or wrong; black or white, or even a shade of gray. It was...well, it was just *something*. I nodded.

Then he reached into his jacket pocket and tossed a flickering, fluttering object in my direction. I snatched it out of the air. He got into the car and I watched them drive off. When I opened my fist, a small, gold cross dangled from a simple chain tangled in my fingers.

I checked in for the flight, eager to get out of Connecticut while at the same time dreading going home to New Orleans. I considered finding a flight to the Caribbean, thinking it might just do me some good to spend some time at our place on Snipe Point on Little Cayman to clear my head and find some direction for a life which seemingly had been without a compass for far too long, but quickly dismissed the idea. I had to face my situation with Sandy, and I had less than four hours in which to come up with a way of resolving our problems. I thought about calling Ashley to bring her up to date, but decided that it would be better to go through things with her face-to-face when I got back. I had let her down in the most important part of why she had sent me here, and on top of everything else, I needed some time to come to grips with that too.

After passing through security screening, I found a restaurant in the concourse from where my flight would depart. I picked out a sandwich and fruit combination plate in a plastic container and a twenty ounce Coke then crossed over to the gate area to eat. A television tuned to the airport version of CNN hung from the ceiling. As I crunched an apple slice and washed it down with a slug from the plastic bottle, a Breaking News graphic flashed on the screen. The sound was down low, but they had the closed captioning on and I watched and read as they announced the murder of Dace Lamoureux in his hotel suite in Hartford, then went to location in New London where Senator Lamoureux stood alone at a small podium in front of his home and read his prepared text.

After a few minutes of watching I lost my appetite and stood and threw the rest of my lunch into a nearby trash can. I boarded the plane on the first announcement and spent the trip writing in the leather-bound notebook. Senator Lamoureux may have my back, and me his at the moment, but that wasn't right in a black and white sense, and if any kind of gray shaded justice was going to be meted out down the road when I figured this all out, I needed to put some things on paper while they were fresh in my mind.

Three hours later, I walked from the parking lot behind our building around to the front entrance so I could go up into my office. I needed to drop some things there and I wanted to call Ashley to set up a meeting for the morning. As it was after five, I assumed Sandy had already gone home, if she had been in at all. I had no idea what she had been doing since I left. All I knew for certain was her car wasn't in our lot, but that didn't necessarily mean anything because some days she would walk over from our house.

The sun had baked down on Magazine Street all day and as the afternoon faded, the air had begun to cool, but only slightly. The sidewalk remained parched and still radiated the day's heat into the soles of my loafers. It was early November, but the pilots reported to us on our approach that the day had been as hot and sunny in Louisiana as any August could generate. 'Global warming' I chuckled to myself when I heard the announcement. When I had stepped off the plane and felt that rush of warm, moist air, however, I realized I was home, and something felt very good about that in the moment. It was a moment which quickly passed, however, in the realization of what else was waiting for me at home in New Orleans.

I was home and should feel happy about it, yet, I was angry, sullen, frustrated, and sad. I was every negative word one could apply to a person's emotional state as I walked around the corner of our building. I hadn't spoken to Sandy since she hung up on me last night. She hadn't called me one time while I was gone and had ducked several calls from me. I was what my southern brethren called hangdog, and I was dreading walking up those stairs because I had no idea what I'd find waiting for me. Sandy and I had managed to sail through several rough seas during our marriages, and somehow we'd come out stronger each time; but I knew things had been so much different this time. The words we had spoken to one another before I left represented what I feared were just the tips of deeper emotional icebergs and, well, some of the things we said are hard to forgive, and so often impossible to forget.

I paused to peer into the big picture window of our tenant's store. Nell was waving a feathered wand over the items on her shelves, the last rays of the days sun lighting mote trails in the stirred up dust. The notions business hadn't been exactly booming lately and I had begun to wonder if Nell would soon be leaving us. I thought about stopping inside to chat with her before walking up those stairs, perhaps finding Sandy something as a peace offering, something to help say what for me are the hardest of words: 'I'm sorry'. The problem was, I quickly realized, remedying what was wrong between us at the moment wasn't something a notion had the power to do. So I merely waved at Nell when she looked up and then continued my walk past the windows and slowly climbed the three concrete steps to the common set of outside doors.

My hand rested on the old copper knob of our front door as my eyes studied my shoes. My heart was throbbing, not pounding like it would be if I were just nervous about what I would find; and it was heavy in my chest, tugged upon by the gravity of what I saw as a life lived poorly in so many ways over so many years. I was fifty, and so very tired of everything. My soul ached, along with a body which was growing older with every passing moment. Life was relentlessly ticking away and it was leaving me behind. Life was leaving *us* behind.

Someone once told me you never get those seconds back once they've ticked away, but so many of us just seem to think the mainspring will never fully wind down and forever leave us with more ticks ahead. I took from the metaphor that we need to live in the now, making the most of the only thing we have, the precious present. I think someone even wrote a book about that. You all know what I'm talking about. You also all know I'm just buying time here before I go inside to see what's next in my life.

I was lost in those thoughts when the knob moved in my hand and startled me back to reality. I stepped back and looked up through the glass and saw a woman waiting to come out. My immediate assumption was she had been Nell's last customer and I flushed as I wondered how long she had stood there waiting for me to turn the knob and open the door before simply giving up the wait and doing it herself. I then saw she carried nothing in her hands, so I assumed the notions business hadn't gotten any better for Nell with the woman's visit. That's too bad.

"I'm so sorry, ma'am," I said as I stepped off to one side as she began to move through the door which I now held open for her.

She wore a black cotton habit which rustled when she stepped outside onto the top step and stood there with me. My downcast eyes watched her simple black shoes as she moved, then disappear again as the habit quickly fell into place when she stopped. I wondered why she didn't keep going, descend the steps and walk away.

"Mr. Langdon," she said.

Her words held the intonation of a statement, not a question, and I wondered to myself how she knew me. I hadn't been to church in years, didn't feel God needed or wanted me there, or that I needed to go there when I felt the need to speak to Him. I willed my eyes to slowly rise to hers as she stood and patiently waited. A black bead rosary hung against her skirt from a coarsely woven belt at her waist, the silver links connecting it all to the crucifix which appeared to be the same as worn by the nuns of my youth. The same stiff, white coif was there too, as was a simple silver crucifix which hung just above her heart on a simple, silver chain. Her black veil was draped behind and over her shoulders. I hadn't seen a nun in a full-length, formal habit like this in decades, but I assumed it was the dress of her Order. My eyes moved over her face, an anonymous oval of humanity in a starched, white frame; then her green eyes caught mine.

"I knew you'd be back this afternoon after I heard on the television news what had happened, so I stopped in to see your wife, Mr. Langdon," she said. "I wanted to explain to her the nature of what I had asked you to do for me, knowing how hard this all has been for both of you." She glanced up the stairs. "Your wife was very understanding. She's a lovely woman with an enormous heart and a glorious soul. You're a lucky man. I hope you know that."

"Ashley?" I said. "Sister Ashley?"

"It's Sister Carol Angeline," she said. "In honor of my aunt and Saint Angeline of Marsciano. I assumed their names when I recited my final vows last year." She smiled. "Surprised?"

"Why didn't you tell me this when you first came to see me?" I asked.

"Would my vocation have made any difference to how you reacted to what I had asked you to do for me, Mr. Langdon?"

I thought about that for a moment.

"No, I guess it wouldn't have mattered, Sister," I said, "but the attitude, the bitter, challenging words you came at me with that day. Why?"

She smiled.

"Would you have been as motivated to conclude this for me had I come in and simply told you before you left that because of my Faith, I had long ago been shown by God just what a wondrous gift forgiveness is and that I had long ago forgiven Dace Lamoureux for what he did to me? Would you have learned anything from being sent forth like that?

"Learned? Me?"

She smiled and nodded.

"You came here because you wanted *me* to learn something from all this?"

She just waited for the lightbulb to go on, but I was dumbfounded and still a bit drink-addled in the furthest reaches of my brain. I just stood there and looked at her as if she were an apparition and wondering with part of me when I would awaken and the day would begin anew. It was all way too much for one day which had begun with a rude awakening and a very bad hangover.

"You know, Mr. Langdon, when you killed my father and his men that night in defense of Dave and Cindy, there were people loyal to my father who came to me seeking my permission to extract a vendetta against you, and your wife. That wouldn't have been justice, would it?"

"I only did what I had to do in that warehouse, Sister. I was responsible. My wife had nothing to do with it. While I was living those events in the country with your father and his men, Sandy was at the same time suffering her own version hell."

"I heard about Sandy's accident," she said. "I was, and remain very sorry for the loss of your unborn child and everything your wife has suffered since that time. And what you have endured."

"Thank you," I said, my mind whirling. "But, you said 'learned'; what was I to have learned? I don't know if I have learned anything through this whole freaking nightmare. Learned? It doesn't make sense, Ash...I mean, Sister."

Her eyes searched mine. She didn't respond to my question.

"Did you get done what I asked you to do?" she said. "Did you get the chance to speak to Dace Lamoureux for me?" Her eyes closed for a moment, then reopened. "Before he passed, I mean."

"I never was able to speak to him alone on your behalf, Sister," I said. "I know it wasn't something you wanted me to shout across a rope line in public, and I didn't get another chance after our initial encounter." In reality I had had the chance to do what Ashley had sent me for during that first meeting in the locker room, but I was too proud and too driven to get the final evidence before I carried out her wishes, so I let a white lie hang between me and a nun. "I tried. Believe me, I did. I'm sorry."

"It's all right, Mr. Langdon," she said. "Dace knows now; and God knows all. It's not the way I wanted this to end, but God had His Plan and we are merely his servants. I understand, submit, and am at peace."

I nodded. Being a Catholic, I occasionally understood, submitted sometimes, and prayed for being at peace when I thought about it. I didn't tell her that.

"What about Sandy?" I asked, my eyes moving inside and up the stairs. "You said she understands. Understands what?"

"She does." Her eyes also moved toward the stairs beyond the doors to our building. "I believe she is ready to forgive you."

I could feel the downward pull on my heart lighten just a bit. Were that only true, I thought.

"You're a good man, Mr. Langdon," she said, her right hand reaching out for mine. "No matter what you think."

"Ah, Sister, you're not seeing everything I've done in my life and all that weighs upon my soul," I said, my hand remaining at my side.

"You kept my confidence, Mr. Langdon, as I asked you to do. You put at risk your life, your marriage, everything you hold dear, to perform one simple task a near stranger asked of you. You did a charity for someone in need and sought nothing in return."

Her hand reached down and I raised mine to it. Her fingers were small and delicate, smooth and warm. She squeezed my hand just as she had done lying in that bed ten years ago, but at that moment on the stoop of our building, I felt not the weakened response of a young, injured girl, but that of a strong, faithful woman. For what seemed the longest time, she didn't let go.

"It's time to forgive, Mr. Langdon," she said, her eyes finding mine and holding them fast. "It's time to put down your burdens, you've carried them long enough." Her left hand moved to cover mine. "What you needed to learn is before you can forgive others, Mr. Langdon, you must first forgive yourself."

I felt a stinging come to my eyes. She was right. I had carried the guilt of so many hurts I'd inflicted, so much pain I'd caused, so many mistakes I had made, and had held it for so long, I didn't know how, or even *if* it all could be set aside so I could take that first step and forgive myself. I had no idea about how to even begin to do so. How can a man forgive himself for everything he knows he has done in his life which has so negatively affected so many others? Isn't it from those people where the forgiveness should come? And even if it was forthcoming, what about the things I could see in my own eyes when I looked there? There can be no hiding from the man in the mirror, as the old saying goes. I almost snickered at the thought, but didn't, because I still looked into her eyes. There was fire in there, a strength, a Faith, but no mirth. She meant every word she said, and she meant me to listen to her words.

"I'm sorry, Ashley," I said, my gaze falling. "I failed you."

She smiled.

"No, you didn't, Mr. Langdon. Haven't you been listening? I came here for you, not me. My peace had already been made by my faith in God and His only Son, Jesus Christ. I've had that letter from Dr. Broussard for over two years, since my aunt passed away, but it was only when I saw the news story that I knew how I could help you."

"Help me?" I said. "Why?"

Her green eyes pierced deep within me.

"Because you had tried to help me. You were the only one who had sacrificed everything to do what you did for me, regardless of what it could cost you."

I thought of Dave and Cindy, what it had cost them. I was still confused. What had it cost me? I couldn't find it within myself, so I asked the nun still holding my hands and my gaze.

"What did I sacrifice to help you, Ashley?" I said.

"Your soul, Mr. Langdon," she said. "You carried the chains and burdens for so many people all these years, when all your intentions were for the good, for the right. You made a mistake. You risked everything to rectify your mistake and when you fell short, you carried the burdens alone. Let God carry the burdens for a while, Mr. Langdon. He's far stronger and more capable than you or I."

She released the cupping of my hand and reached up to place her hand on my arm. It looked small there.

"It wasn't your fault, Mr. Langdon," she said. "It's time you forgive yourself."

She squeezed my hand one last time, then let it go. My gaze found her eyes again. I still wasn't fully understanding all of it, but the simple message to lay down the burden somehow seemed right. Perhaps it was...

"It's time, Mr. Langdon," she said again, and her eyes held mine for an instant longer before she released me and turned and descended the steps to the concrete walk.

She started along Magazine Street toward the corner around which I had just come. I watched her move and knew she was walking from my life for the last time. I reached into my jacket pocket, touched the small cross on the cheap chain.

"Ashley," I called.

She turned, made no steps to come back.

I slipped the item Travis had tossed me from my pocket, the chain tangled in my fingers again. The small gold cross dangled free and reflected the last rays of the afternoon sun. From the distance, I saw an instant of recognition in her eyes, then saw them mist as a smile formed on her angelic face.

"I've got plenty, Mr. Langdon," she said, touching her fingertips to the small, silver crucifix lying against her chest just under her starched, white coif. "You keep that one to remember me by. God go with you, Mr. Langdon."

Those were the last words Sister Carol Angeline spoke to me that day, or since. I watched her walk away. She turned the corner and didn't look back. I stood there, frozen by the power of her words and felt a sudden warmth from the little gold cross in my palm. I wrapped my fingers tightly around it, then slipped it back into my pocket as I finally realized how truly simple the whole concept she had been trying to explain was. I got it. Finally.

In the next moments, as the sun disappeared and the depleted day surrendered to the coming night, I felt something flow into me, an electricity like I would sometimes feel in church on Sunday when the Holy Spirit would flow into my body and I would be assured there was indeed a loving God out there somewhere who truly cared about this particular poor soul struggling day to day down here.

It flowed through me and I released the pain, surrendered the guilt.

I set down the burdens.

And, I forgave myself.


I walked into the building, closed the outer door and took a deep breath. I looked up at the frosted glass in the door at the top of the stairs, then climbed the steps with a sense of renewed purpose, wondering what I would say to Sandy, and what she would say to me, and if words and love and faith would be enough for us to finally forgive each other for so many little wounds which had been bleeding us to death.

At the top of the stairs, I paused outside our door and asked God for just a little more help, then I turned the knob and slowly pushed open the door to find Sandy sitting at her desk out front, her head bowed, her hands folded together. Her eyes were closed. At the sound of the door closing behind me, she opened her eyes, raised her head and looked in my direction.

"Hi," I said.

It was the best I could manage.

"I see you had a visitor," I added.

"I did," Sandy said. "Did you get a chance to speak to her?"

"I did," I said.

Our eyes looked deep into each other's soul.

"I'm sorry," I said. "I forgive you."

"I'm sorry," she said. "I forgive you."

I moved to her, and she to me. I don't know which of us moved first or which of us moved the greater distance, and it truly didn't matter because we met somewhere near the middle. I picked up my wife in my arms and swung her around. She tossed her arms around my neck and we kissed.

It wasn't the most sensual kiss we have ever shared, or even the best, but it was the one I'll always carry closest to this old heart of mine, because it was during that kiss that redemption reached into us and retied the knot between Sandy and myself while promising nothing more than that loving and understanding and sharing and forgiving would continue to be lifelong challenges, but ones would we would always face together.

In that moment, there was no need for any more words.

We had found each other again.

# Epilogue

The next day, Sandy and I drove out to see Jackson Stempler. We sat on the porch with him and over the next hour I told him the rest of the story. All of it; and Sandy listened to every word. I felt he deserved to know. Sandy was ready to hear it, as well. His eyes misted, then turned hard and unreadable and for a moment I thought I had misjudged the situation. When he shook my hand before I left, I knew the right thing had been done.

Seventy-seven days after the election in 2008, a staffer entered The Senator's office to rouse him for a vote late in the afternoon. It was the beginning days of the 111th Congress, and the country had a brand new President whose party also controlled both houses of the legislative branch. Momentous, historical change lay ahead for the nation and Senator Allard Lamoureux was positioned to play an instrumental role. When the staffer touched The Senator's shoulder, however, she knew he would never get the chance. Destiny had come calling, and that time it was the hand of Death. The Senator was gone.

Three days later, following a twenty-four-hour period of his body lying in state in the Capitol rotunda where the bronze casket had been placed atop the same catafalque which had held the coffin of JFK in 1963, a funeral Mass was held for Senator Allard Guillaume Lamoureux in the Cathedral of St. Matthew the Apostle in Washington, D.C. The Archbishop himself presided; four of the five living ex-presidents were in attendance. Five people eulogized the man, including one former and the current President of the United States.

Libby Lamoureux occupied the left front pew, along with her daughters. Mary Rose sat closest to her mother on her left. On Libby's right, Tom McDaniel sat and listened to people say words he could not bring himself to utter. He had refused to eulogize his longtime client and friend and told nobody who asked, why. At one point in the service, the cameras caught the images as Tom reached for, and received, Libby's hand in his.

The President referred to Senator Lamoureux as 'The Lion of the Senate' and proclaimed him as having been 'a great man who was that rare blend of vision, leadership, and selfless dedication to public service that we are unlikely to encounter more than once in our lifetime'.

I was about to reach for the remote when they cut back to the studio and Brett Baier of the Fox News Channel concluded the coverage with the observation: 'And, so, with the untimely passing last November of The Senator's son, Dace Lamoureux, who became Connecticut's Senator-elect on the same day he was assassinated by a crazed, lone gunmen still on the loose, these coming days will mark the first time in two-hundred-twelve consecutive years of American history when a male member of the Lamoureux family is not sitting in some state or federal elective office.'

"I think we'll find a way to survive, Brett," I said to myself as I turned off the television, mainly so I didn't have to hear any more.

Closing the leather bound notebook which was nearly filled by then, I set it upon the side table and picked up a bottle of water. I stood up and stretched, then rubbed my eyes. Sandy was making dinner, but before I went into the kitchen to help, I picked up my cell phone from the side table and called a number in Maui. My eyes went to the notebook. I finally had the answer I had hoped for when I boarded the plane in Newark to come home that day. I finally knew how a final gray-shaded justice could be meted out. I listened to the distant electronic chittering. The phone rang seven times before it was answered. After a few minutes of catching up with the man who had written *Cassandra's Crossing* about the serial killer case five years ago, I told him I had the outline of a new story needing to be told and asked if he might be interested in putting it on paper.

I told him I thought history needed a little push.

He thought it was a great idea.

In May of 2010, a rumor said to originate in the United States Attorney's office in New Orleans that Tracey Walker was under investigation for fraud and embezzlement of client accounts began circulating around the city.

She hasn't been heard from since.

The U.S. Attorney later denied knowledge of any investigation.

# Author's Note

This book is both a prequel and sequel to the previously released *Cassandra's Crossing*, the first of the William Langdon novels.

When I began *Fortunate Son*, I had an idea for a storyline, and a set of new characters who would act it out. The working title was Mardi Gras - a hopelessly unimaginative moniker which I knew would never pass final muster - and the story had a beginning, an endpoint which shifted some over the writing, and rough-sketch outline in my head; then, as with all of my creative writing, the characters themselves filled in the middle. Often, they colored outside the lines and a couple of times they suggested border changes from my original sketch. This was a collaborative effort.

*Fortunate Son* originated as a simple, straightforward story in which the privileged son of a powerful political family from the Northeast runs afoul of a Louisiana mob boss who demands retribution after his daughter is raped, beaten, and left for dead along the river during Mardi Gras in New Orleans. When it morphed into a look inside the dynamics of friendship, fatherhood, legacy, guilt, regret, forgiveness, God, and ultimate redemption, I was frankly surprised. The characters themselves pitched and ultimately drove the final story changes, and as a good writer (or so I consider myself), I followed their lead. After all, I may be the one writing about it, but they are the ones who are living it all. I believe I owe them the courtesy to tell their story as they best see fit.

For me, novel writing is an interesting process and the way I engage in it is unique to me. I've read the suggestions from the 'experts' on how to create characters and how to write fiction and blah, blah, blah. In my view, the true expert is the one who dares bare his soul to the world and in return for a faithful effort is rewarded with a finished product which both thrills and satisfies its readers. What's the second line of that old axiom? Those who can't, teach; so, if you're going to do this, I welcome you and advise you do whatever works for you.

My process is simple, much like making soup:   1) I 'get' an idea for a storyline; 2) I become excited about it; 3) I assemble a cast of characters, first in two-dimensions: name, age, physical description, occupation, etc., and then let them evolve on their own into that complete, third dimension which includes personality and motivations, then I set them upon one another in various conflicts; 4) when the soup begins to simmer, they often take me on wild rides of conscious and unconscious thought, enter my dreams, and suggest themselves all manner of twists and turns. Then, *suddenly*, it's soup.

I find writing William and Sandy to be fun and rewarding, but, also, a bit cathartic on many levels.  Readers tell me they love the Sandy character and I can understand why.   She's the level ground for William's foundation of irreverence, his insecurities and fears, and his lighthearted, devil-may-care approach to a world in which he finds curiosity while holding the firm belief that it's all just an irredeemable, dysfunctional mess.  What is remarkable, after so many fitful starts and stops in their relationship over the years, they finally got it right.  We hope.

The characters in all my fiction writing are composites of people I've known or observed, blended with bits of me.   In this writer's humble opinion, most people on their own are not so compelling that strangers would deign to read an entire book about them, so by combining the most intriguing portions of many people in order to create one, three-dimensional, fictional character, I not only keep the lawyers happy, but also am able to offer you some very colorful individuals to get to know, and love, or hate, as the case may be.   For those of you wondering, William Langdon is 75% me, 15% fantasy me, and 10% pure bullsh...

Please check back in late 2012 - hopefully - for the third William Langdon Novel, the working title of which is **Snipe Point**.  Whatever the final title winds up to be, the novel will be a prequel to both previous works, set while William and Sandy still live in the Cayman Islands. Together with Teddy and his then new wife, Valeria - a feisty Venezuelan with plenty of her own secrets, and fifteen years Teddy's junior - the newly married Langdons (first time) set sail on a two-month adventure across the Lesser Antilles, also known as the Caribbees, from Antigua to Trinidad and Tobago, and a few lesser-known places, when vengeance comes calling.  If you know William and Sandy, you know we can expect a thrilling ride.

Stephen Fredrick
Maui, August 3, 2012

## Acknowledgements

I'd like to thank my wife, Shelly, and my mother, Shirley Reinhardt for their limitless confidence in my ability to bring this story to life. Shelly puts up with all my twists and turns as things move from imagination to zeros and ones in the digital realm to paper. She's the one who has to cope with all my characters' manipulations of my sleep and she's the person who has to smile when I tell her for the tenth time about this or that as the process plays itself out. What can I say about my mom? She's been there for my best times and my worst times and has remained perhaps my biggest fan. Together, they drive me and give me hope that some day, I'll be a success at what I love doing.

The cover photograph for this book comes from the United States Senate, whose consideration I wish to acknowledge. Hopefully, they feel the same about my decades of tax payments which funds their efforts.

The work of writing and editing is a solitary endeavor, but I'd like to offer special and heartfelt thanks to my beta-reader, Helen Gunter Mudd for her continued support and willingness to read this novel before I foisted it upon the general public. Helen was one of the first to read Cassandra's Crossing before I had the gumption to think I may be kinda good at this, and volunteered her time again for Fortunate Son. Helen and her children, Julie Gunter and Chuck Mudd, are some very good people from Indiana whom I met when they came to the aid of families in the aftermath of the loss of American Eagle Flight 4184. They were dubbed the Mission Un-Impossible team, and along with others in their community, selflessly offered their hearts and labors to people they never knew before that fateful day in October 1994. They embody the best of this world, in my eyes, and for their friendship, I am eternally grateful.

# About the Author

Stephen Fredrick is married and lives on Maui with his wife, Shelly. He is a businessperson, realtor, author, former airline pilot, and internationally recognized aviation safety and air crash victims' rights advocate and speaker. His aviation safety analysis has appeared in print, on radio, and on television programs around the world, most recently with Russian National Television in 2012 when he was sought out for his technical expertise following the loss of a Russian airliner. He's also getting back to flying after a 17 year hiatus and is enjoying new horizons in what he often calls 'the strangest life I've ever known'.

In 1996, McGraw-Hill published his first book, the nonfiction Unheeded Warning - The Inside Story of American Eagle Flight 4184.

From 1997 through 1998, he served as president of the National Air Disaster Alliance (NADA), an organization consisting of survivors and families of victims of international aviation and airline crashes. NADA was founded in 1995 by the families of American Eagle Flight 4184, and was instrumental in the origination, passing through Congress, and ultimate signing into law by President Clinton the Assistance to Families of Aviation Disasters Act of 1996, which codified the rules for humane treatment, both by government and the airlines, of the victims and families of aviation accidents.

He founded and ran a business in Wisconsin for 27 years prior to embarking on writing, real estate, and a return to the cockpit.

His first fiction novel, Cassandra's Crossing was published in 2011. It was the premier William Langdon novel.

Stephen has three daughters, Rebecca, Rachel, and Stephanie and two grandchildren, Morgan and William. His mother remains his biggest fan, and though he claims to be an only child, his brother David, and sister Cheri, do, in fact, exist.